THE BEST OF
ROBICHEAUX

James Lee Burke

THE BEST OF
ROBICHEAUX
THE AUTHOR'S CHOICE

**IN THE ELECTRIC MIST
WITH CONFEDERATE DEAD**

CADILLAC JUKEBOX

SUNSET LIMITED

ORION

In the Electric Mist with Confederate Dead
copyright © 1993 by James Lee Burke
Cadillac Jukebox copyright © 1996 by James Lee Burke
Sunset Limited copyright © 1998 by James Lee Burke

This omnibus edition first published in Great Britain in 2000
by Orion, an imprint of the Orion Publishing Group Ltd.

A CIP catalogue record for this book
is available from the British Library.

Typeset at The Spartan Press Ltd,
Lymington, Hants

Set in Minion

Printed in Great Britain by Clays Ltd, St Ives plc.

The Orion Publishing Group Ltd
Orion House
5 Upper Saint Martin's Lane
London, WC2H 9EA

Contents

**IN THE ELECTRIC MIST
WITH CONFEDERATE DEAD 1**

CADILLAC JUKEBOX 277

SUNSET LIMITED 531

IN THE ELECTRIC MIST
WITH CONFEDERATE DEAD

For Frank and Tina Kastor
and
Jerry and Maureen Hoag

1

The sky had gone black at sunset, and the storm had churned inland from the Gulf and drenched New Iberia and littered East Main with leaves and tree branches from the long canopy of oaks that covered the street from the old brick post office to the drawbridge over Bayou Teche at the edge of town. The air was cool now, laced with light rain, heavy with the fecund smell of wet humus, night-blooming jasmine, roses, and new bamboo. I was about to stop my truck at Del's and pick up three crawfish dinners to go when a lavender Cadillac fishtailed out of a side street, caromed off a curb, bounced a hubcap up on a sidewalk, and left long serpentine lines of tire prints through the glazed pools of yellow light from the street lamps.

I was off duty, tired, used up after a day of searching for a nineteen-year-old girl in the woods, then finding her where she had been left in the bottom of a coulee, her mouth and wrists wrapped with electrician's tape. Already I had tried to stop thinking about the rest of it. The medical examiner was a kind man. He bagged the body before any news people or family members got there.

I don't like to bust drunk drivers. I don't like to listen to their explanations, watch their pitiful attempts to affect sobriety, or see the sheen of fear break out in their eyes when they realize they're headed for the drunk tank with little to look forward to in the morning except the appearance of their names in the newspaper. Or maybe in truth I just don't like to see myself when I look into their faces.

But I didn't believe this particular driver could make it another block without ripping the side off a parked car or plowing the Cadillac deep into someone's shrubbery. I plugged my portable bubble into the cigarette lighter, clamped the magnets on the truck's roof, and pulled him to the curb in front of the Shadows, a huge brick, white-columned antebellum home built on Bayou Teche in 1831.

I had my Iberia Parish Sheriff's Department badge opened in my palm when I walked up to his window.

'Can I see your driver's license, please?'

He had rugged good looks, a Roman profile, square shoulders, and broad hands. When he smiled I saw that his teeth were capped. The woman next to him wore her hair in blond ringlets and her body was as lithe, tanned, and supple-looking as an Olympic swimmer's. Her mouth looked as red and vulnerable as a rose. She also looked like she was seasick.

'You want driver's what?' he said, trying to focus evenly on my face. Inside the car I could smell a drowsy, warm odor, like the smell of smoke rising from a smoldering pile of wet leaves.

'Your driver's license,' I repeated. 'Please take it out of your billfold and hand it to me.'

'Oh, yeah, sure, wow,' he said. 'I was really careless back there. I'm sorry about that. I really am.'

He got his license out of his wallet, dropped it in his lap, found it again, then handed it to me, trying to keep his eyes from drifting off my face. His breath smelled like fermented fruit that had been corked up for a long time in a stone jug.

I looked at the license under the street lamp.

'You're Elrod T. Sykes?' I asked.

'Yes, sir, that's who I am.'

'Would you step out of the car, Mr Sykes?'

'Yes, sir, anything you say.'

He was perhaps forty, but in good shape. He wore a light-blue golf shirt, loafers, and gray slacks that hung loosely on his flat stomach and narrow hips. He swayed slightly and propped one hand on the door to steady himself.

'We have a problem here, Mr Sykes. I think you've been smoking marijuana in your automobile.'

'Marijuana . . . Boy, that'd be bad, wouldn't it?'

'I think your lady friend just ate the roach, too.'

'That wouldn't be good, no, sir, not at all.' He shook his head profoundly.

'Well, we're going to let the reefer business slide for now. But I'm afraid you're under arrest for driving while intoxicated.'

'That's very bad news. This definitely was not on my agenda this evening.' He widened his eyes and opened and closed his mouth as though he were trying to clear an obstruction in his ear canals. 'Say, do you recognize me? What I mean is, there's news people who'd really like to put my ham hocks in the frying pan. Believe me, sir, I don't need this. I cain't say that enough.'

'I'm going to drive you just down the street to the city jail, Mr Sykes. Then I'll send a car to take Ms Drummond to wherever she's staying. But your Cadillac will be towed to the pound.'

4

He let out his breath in a long sigh. I turned my face away.

'You go to the movies, huh?' he said.

'Yeah, I always enjoyed your films. Ms Drummond's, too. Take your car keys out of the ignition, please.'

'Yeah, sure,' he said, despondently.

He leaned into the window and pulled the keys out of the ignition.

'El, *do* something,' the woman said.

He straightened his back and looked at me.

'I feel real bad about this,' he said. 'Can I make a contribution to Mothers Against Drunk Driving, or something like that?'

In the lights from the city park, I could see the rain denting the surface of Bayou Teche.

'My Sykes, you're under arrest. You can remain silent if you wish, or if you wish to speak, anything you say can be used against you,' I said. 'As a long-time fan of your work, I recommend that you not say anything else. Particularly about contributions.'

'It doesn't look like you mess around. Were you ever a Texas ranger? They don't mess around, either. You talk back to those boys and they'll hit you upside the head.'

'Well, we don't do that here,' I said. I put my hand under his arm and led him to my truck. I opened the door for him and helped him inside. 'You're not going to get sick in my truck, are you?'

'No, sir, I'm just fine.'

'That's good. I'll be right with you.'

I walked back to the Cadillac and tapped on the glass of the passenger's door. The woman, whose name was Kelly Drummond, rolled down the window. Her face was turned up into mine. Her eyes were an intense, deep green. She wet her lips, and I saw a smear of lipstick on her teeth.

'You'll have to wait here about ten minutes, then someone will drive you home,' I said.

'Officer, I'm responsible for this,' she said. 'We were having an argument. Elrod's a good driver. I don't think he should be punished because I got him upset. Can I get out of the car? My neck hurts.'

'I suggest you lock your automobile and stay where you are, Ms Drummond. I also suggest you do some research into the laws governing the possession of narcotics in the state of Louisiana.'

'Wow, I mean, it's not like we hurt anybody. This is going to get Elrod in a lot of trouble with Mikey. Why don't you show a little compassion?'

'Mikey?'

'Our *director*, the guy who's bringing about ten million dollars into your little town. Can I get out of the car now? I really don't want a neck like Quasimodo.'

5

'You can go anywhere you want. There's a pay phone in the pool-room you can use to call a bondsman. If I were you, I wouldn't go down to the station to help Mr Sykes, not until you shampoo the Mexican laughing grass out of your hair.'

'Boy, talk about wearing your genitalia outside your pants. Where'd they come up with you?'

I walked back to my truck and got in.

'Look maybe I can be a friend of the court,' Elrod Sykes said.

'What?'

'Isn't that what they call it? There's nothing wrong with that, is there? Man, I can really do without this bust.'

'Few people standing before a judge ever expected to be there,' I said, and started the engine.

He was quiet while I made a U-turn and headed for the city police station. He seemed to be thinking hard about something. Then he said: 'Listen, I know where there's a body. I saw it. Nobody'd pay me any mind, but I saw the dadburn thing. That's a fact.'

'You saw what?'

'A colored, I mean a black person, it looked like. Just a big dry web of skin, with bones inside it. Like a big rat's nest.'

'Where was this?'

'Out in the Atchafalaya swamp, about four days ago. We were shooting some scenes by an Indian reservation or something. I wandered back in these willows to take a leak and saw it sticking out of a sandbar.'

'And you didn't bother to report it until now?'

'I told Mikey. He said it was probably bones that had washed out of an Indian burial mound or something. Mikey's kind of hard-nosed. He said the last thing we needed was trouble with either cops or university archaeologists.'

'We'll talk about it tomorrow, Mr Sykes.'

'You don't pay me much mind, either. But that's all right. I told you what I saw. Y'all can do what you want to with it.'

He looked straight ahead through the beads of water on the window. His handsome face was wan, tired, more sober now, resigned perhaps to a booking room, drunk-tank scenario he knew all too well. I remembered two or three wire-service stories about him over the last few years – a brawl with a couple of cops in Dallas or Fort Worth, a violent ejection from a yacht club in Los Angeles, and a plea on a cocaine-possession bust. I had heard that bean sprouts, mineral water, and the sober life had become fashionable in Hollywood. It looked like Elrod Sykes had arrived late at the depot.

'I'm sorry, I didn't get your name,' he said.

'Dave Robicheaux.'

'Well, you see, Mr Robicheaux, a lot of people don't believe me when I tell them I see things. But the truth is, I *see* things all the time, like shadows moving around behind a veil. In my family we call it "touched." When I was a little boy, my grandpa told me, "Son, the Lord done touched you. He give you a third eye to see things that other people cain't. But it's a gift from the Lord, and you mustn't never use it otherwise." I haven't ever misused the gift, either, Mr Robicheaux, even though I've done a lot of other things I'm not proud of. So I don't care if people think I lasered my head with too many recreational chemicals or not.'

'I see.'

He was quiet again. We were almost to the jail now. The wind blew raindrops out of the oak trees, and the moon edged the storm clouds with a metallic silver light. He rolled down his window halfway and breathed in the cool smell of the night.

'But if that was an Indian washed out of a burial mound instead of a colored man, I wonder what he was doing with a chain wrapped around him,' he said.

I slowed the truck and pulled it to the curb.

'Say that again,' I said.

'There was a rusted chain, I mean with links as big as my fist, crisscrossed around his rib cage.'

I studied his face. It was innocuous, devoid of intention, pale in the moonlight, already growing puffy with hangover.

'You want some slack on the DWI for your knowledge about this body, Mr Sykes?'

'No, sir, I just wanted to tell you what I saw. I shouldn't have been driving. Maybe you kept me from having an accident.'

'Some people might call that jailhouse humility. What do you think?'

'I think you might make a tough film director.'

'Can you find that sandbar again?'

'Yes, sir, I believe I can.'

'Where are you and Ms Drummond staying?'

'The studio rented us a house out on Spanish Lake.'

'I'm going to make a confession to you, Mr Sykes. DWIs are a pain in the butt. Also I'm on city turf and doing their work. If I take y'all home, can I have your word you'll remain there until tomorrow morning?'

'Yes, sir, you sure can.'

'But I want you in my office by nine A.M.'

'Nine A.M. You got it. Absolutely. I really appreciate this.'

The transformation in his face was immediate, as though liquified ambrosia had been infused in the veins of a starving man. Then as I turned the truck around in the middle of the street to pick up the actress whose name was Kelly Drummond, he said something that gave me pause about his level of sanity.

'Does anybody around here ever talk about Confederate soldiers out on that Lake?'

'I don't understand.'

'Just what I said. Does anybody ever talk about guys in gray or butternut-brown uniforms out there? A bunch of them, at night, out there in the mist.'

'Aren't y'all making a film about the War Between the States? Are you talking about actors?' I looked sideways at him. His eyes were straight forward, focused on some private thought right outside the windshield.

'No, these guys weren't actors,' he said. 'They'd been shot up real bad. They looked hungry, too. It happened right around here, didn't it?'

'What?'

'The battle.'

'I'm afraid I'm not following you, Mr Sykes.'

Up ahead I saw Kelly Drummond walking in her spiked heels and Levis toward Tee Neg's poolroom.

'Yeah, you do,' he said. 'You *believe* when most people don't, Mr Robicheaux. You surely do. And when I say you *believe*, you know exactly what I'm talking about.'

He looked confidently, serenely, into my face and winked with one blood-flecked eye.

2

My dreams took me many places: sometimes back to a windswept firebase on the top of an orange hill gouged with shell holes; a soft, mist-streaked morning with ducks rising against a pink sun while my father and I crouched in the blind and waited for that heart-beating moment when their shadows would race across the cattails and reeds toward us; a lighted American Legion baseball diamond, where at age seventeen I pitched a perfect game against a team from Abbeville and a beautiful woman I didn't know, perhaps ten years my senior, kissed me so hard on the mouth that my ears rang.

But tonight I was back in the summer of my freshman year in college, July of 1957, deep in the Atchafalaya marsh, right after Hurricane Audrey had swept through southern Louisiana and killed over five hundred people in Cameron Parish alone. I worked offshore seismograph then, and the portable drill barge had just slid its iron pilings into the floor of a long, flat yellow bay, and the jug-boat crew had dropped me off by a chain of willow islands to roll up a long spool of recording cable that was strung through the trees and across the sand spits and sloughs. The sun was white in the sky, and the humidity was like the steam that rises from a pot of boiled vegetables. Once I was inside the shade of the trees, the mosquitoes swarmed around my ears and eyes in a gray fog as dense as a helmet.

The spool and crank hung off my chest by canvas straps, and after I had wound up several feet of cable, I would have to stop and submerge myself in the water to get the mosquitoes off my skin or smear more mud on my face and shoulders. It was our fifth day out on a ten-day hitch, which meant that tonight the party chief would allow a crew boat to take a bunch of us to the levee at Charenton, and from there we'd drive to a movie in some little town down by Morgan City. As I slapped mosquitoes into a bloody paste on my arms and waded across sand bogs that sucked over my knees, I kept thinking about the cold shower that I was going to take back on the quarter-boat, the fried-chicken dinner

9

that I was going to eat in the dining room, the ride to town between the sugarcane fields in the cooling evening. Then I popped out of the woods on the edge of another bay, into the breeze, the sunlight, the hint of rain in the south.

I dropped the heavy spool into the sand, knelt in the shallows, and washed the mud off my skin. One hundred yards across the bay, I saw a boat with a cabin moored by the mouth of a narrow bayou. A Negro man stepped off the bow onto the bank, followed by two white men. Then I looked again and realized that something was terribly wrong. One of the white men had a pistol in his hand, and the black man's arms were pinioned at his sides with a thick chain that had been trussed around his upper torso.

I stared in disbelief as the black man started running along a short stretch of beach, his head twisting back over his shoulder, and the man with the pistol took aim and fired. The first round must have hit him in the leg, because it crumpled under him as though the bone had been snapped in two with a hammer. He half rose to his feet, stumbled into the water, and fell sideways. I saw the bullets popping the surface around him as his kinky head went under. The man with the pistol waded after him and kept shooting, now almost straight down into the water, while the other white man watched from the bank.

I didn't see the black man again.

Then the two white men looked across the flat expanse of bay and saw me. I looked back at them, numbly, almost embarrassed, like a person who had opened a bedroom door at the wrong moment. Then they walked calmly back to their boat, with no sign of apprehension or urgency, as though I were not even worthy of notice.

Later, I told the party chief, the sheriff's department, and finally anybody who would listen to me, about what I had seen. But their interest was short-lived; no body was ever found in that area, nor was any black man from around there ever reported as missing. As time passed, I tried to convince myself that the man in chains had eluded his tormentors, had held his breath for an impossibly long time, and had burst to the surface and a new day somewhere downstream. At age nineteen I did not want to accept the possibility that a man's murder could be treated with the social significance of a hangnail that had been snipped off someone's finger.

At nine sharp the morning after I had stopped Elrod T. Sykes for drunk driving, a lawyer, not Elrod Sykes, was in my office. He was tall and had silver hair, and he wore a gray suit with red stones in his cuff links. He told me his name but it wouldn't register. In fact, I wasn't interested in anything he had to say.

'Of course, Mr Sykes is at your disposal,' he said, 'and both he and I appreciate the courtesy which you extended to him last night. He feels very bad about what happened, of course. I don't know if he told you that he was taking a new prescription for his asthma, but evidently his system has a violent reaction to it. The studio also appreciates—'

'What is your name again, sir?'

'Oliver Montrose.'

I hadn't asked him to sit down yet. I picked up several paper clips from a small tin can on my desk and began dropping them one by one on my desk blotter.

'Where's Sykes right now, Mr Montrose?'

He looked at his watch.

'By this time they're out on location,' he said. When I didn't respond, he shifted his feet and added, 'Out by Spanish Lake.'

'On location at Spanish Lake?'

'Yes.'

'Let's see, that's about five miles out of town. It should take no longer than fifteen minutes to drive there from here. So thirty minutes should be enough time for you to find Mr Sykes and have him sitting in that chair right across from me.'

He looked at me a moment, then nodded.

'I'm sure that'll be no problem,' he said.

'Yeah, I bet. That's why he sent you instead of keeping his word. Tell him I said that, too.'

Ten minutes later the sheriff, with a file folder open in his hands, came into my office and sat down across from me. He had owned a dry-cleaning business and been president of the local Lions Club before running for sheriff. He wore rimless glasses, and he had soft cheeks that were flecked with blue and red veins. In his green uniform he always made me think of a nursery manager rather than a law officer, but he was an honest and decent man and humble enough to listen to those who had more experience than he had.

'I got the autopsy and the photographs on that LeBlanc girl,' he said. He took off his glasses and pinched the red mark on the bridge of his nose. 'You know, I've been doing this stuff five years now, but one like this—'

'When it doesn't bother you anymore, that's when you should start to worry, sheriff.'

'Well, anyway, the report says that most of it was probably done to her after she was dead, poor girl.'

'Could I see it?' I said, and reached out my hand for the folder.

I had to swallow when I looked at the photographs, even though I had seen the real thing only yesterday. The killer had not harmed her face. In fact, he had covered it with her blouse, either during the rape or perhaps before he stopped her young heart with an ice pick. But in the fourteen years that I had been with the New Orleans Police Department, or during the three years I had worked on and off for the Iberia Parish sheriff's office, I had seen few cases that involved this degree of violence or rage against a woman's body.

Then I read through the clinical prose describing the autopsy, the nature of the wounds, the sexual penetration of the vagina, the absence of any skin samples under the girl's fingernails, the medical examiner's speculation about the moment and immediate cause of death, and the type of instrument the killer probably used to mutilate the victim.

'Any way you look at it, I guess we're talking about a psychopath or somebody wired to the eyes on crack or acid,' the sheriff said.

'Yeah, maybe,' I said.

'You think somebody *else* would disembowel a nineteen-year-old girl with a scalpel or a barber's razor?'

'Maybe the guy wants us to think he's a meltdown. He was smart enough not to leave anything at the scene except the ice pick, and it was free of prints. There weren't any prints on the tape he used on her wrists or mouth, either. She went out the front door of the jukejoint, by herself, at one in the morning, when the place was still full of people, and somehow he abducted her, or got her to go with him, between the front door and her automobile, which was parked only a hundred feet away.'

His eyes were thoughtful.

'Go on,' he said.

'I think she knew the guy.'

The sheriff put his glasses back on and scratched at the corner of his mouth with one fingernail.

'She left her purse at the table,' I said. 'I think she went outside to get something from her car and ran into somebody she knew. Psychopaths don't try to strongarm women in front of bars filled with drunk coonasses and oil-field workers.'

'What do we know about the girl?'

I took my notebook out of the desk drawer and thumbed through it on top of the blotter.

'Her mother died when she was twelve. She quit school in the ninth grade and ran away from her father a couple of times in Mamou. She was arrested for prostitution in Lafayette when she was sixteen. For the last year or so she lived here with her grandparents, out at the end of West Main. Her last job was waitressing in a bar about three weeks ago in St Martinville. Few close friends, if any, no current or recent romantic involvement, at least according to the grandparents. She didn't have a chance for much of a life, did she?'

12

I could hear the sheriff rubbing his thumb along his jawbone.

'No, she didn't,' he said. His eyes went out the window then refocused on my face. 'Do you buy that about no romantic involvement?'

'No.'

'Neither do I. Do you have any other theories except that she probably knew her killer?'

'One.'

'What?'

'That I'm all wrong, that we *are* dealing with a psychopath or a serial killer.'

He stood up to leave. He was overweight, constantly on a diet, and his stomach protruded over his gunbelt, but his erect posture always gave him the appearance of a taller and trimmer man than he actually was.

'I'm glad we operate out of this office with such a sense of certainty, Dave,' he said. 'Look, I want you to use everything available to us on this one. I want to nail this sonofabitch right through the breastbone.'

I nodded, unsure of his intention in stating the obvious.

'That's why we're going to be working with the FBI on this one,' he said.

I kept my eyes flat, my hands open and motionless on the desk blotter.

'You called them?' I said.

'I did, and so did the mayor. It's a kidnapping as well as a rape and murder, Dave.'

'Yeah, that could be the case.'

'You don't like the idea of working with these guys?'

'You don't *work* with the feds, sheriff. You take orders from them. If you're lucky, they won't treat you like an insignificant local douche bag in front of a television camera. It's a great learning exercise in humility.'

'No one can ever accuse you of successfully hiding your feelings, Dave.'

Almost thirty minutes from the moment the attorney, Oliver Montrose, had left my office, I looked out my window and saw Elrod T. Sykes pull his lavender Cadillac into a no-parking zone, scrape his white-walls against the curb, and step out into the bright sunlight. He wore brown striped slacks, shades, and a lemon-yellow short-sleeve shirt. The attorney got out on the passenger's side, but Sykes gestured for him to stay where he was. They argued briefly, then Sykes walked into the building by himself.

He had his shades in his hand when he stepped inside my office door, his hair wet and freshly combed, an uneasy grin at the corner of his mouth.

'Sit down a minute, please,' I said.

The skin around his eyes was pale with hangover. He sat down and touched at his temple as though it were bruised.

'I'm sorry about sending the mercenary. It wasn't my idea,' he said.

'Whose was it?'

'Mikey figures he makes the decisions on anything that affects the picture.'

'How old are you, Mr Sykes?'

He widened his eyes and crimped his lips.

'Forty. Well, actually forty-three,' he said.

'Did you have to ask that man's permission to drive an automobile while you were drunk?'

He blinked as though I'd struck him, then made a wet noise in his throat and wiped his mouth with the backs of his fingers.

'I really don't know what to say to you,' he said. He had a peculiar, north Texas accent, husky, slightly nasal, like he had a dime-sized piece of melting ice in his cheek. 'I broke my word, I'm aware of that. But I'm letting other people down, too, Mr Robicheaux. It costs ten thousand dollars an hour when you have to keep a hundred people standing around while a guy like me gets out of trouble.'

'I hope y'all work it out.'

'I guess this is the wrong place to look for aspirin and sympathy, isn't it?'

'A sheriff's deputy from St Mary Parish is going to meet us with a boat at the Chitimacha Indian reservation, Mr Sykes. I think he's probably waiting on us right now.'

'Well, actually I'm looking forward to it. Did I tell you last night my grandpa was a Texas ranger?'

'No, you didn't.' I looked at my watch.

'Well, it's a fact, he was. He worked with Frank Hammer, the ranger who got Bonnie and Clyde right up there at Arcadia, Louisiana.' He smiled at me. 'You know what he used to tell me when I was a kid? "Son, you got two speeds – wide-open and fuck it." I swear he was a pistol. He—'

'I'd like to explain something to you. I don't want you to take offense at it, either.'

'Yes, sir?'

'Yesterday somebody raped and murdered a nineteen-year-old girl on the south side of the parish. He cut her breasts off, he pulled her entrails out of her stomach, he pushed twigs up her vagina. I don't like waiting in my office for you to show up when it's convenient, I'm not interested in your film company's production problems, and on this particular morning I'd appreciate it if you'd leave your stories about your family history to your publicity people.'

His eyes tried to hold on mine, then they watered and glanced away.

'I'd like to use your bathroom, please,' he said. 'I'm afraid I got up with a case of the purple butterflies.'

'I'll be out front. I'll see you there in two minutes, Mr Sykes.'

The sky was bright and hazy, the wind hot as a flame as we drove toward the Atchafalaya River. I had to stop the truck twice to let Elrod Sykes vomit by the side of the road.

It felt strange to go back into that part of the Atchafalaya Basin after so many years. In July of 1957, after the hurricane had passed through and the rains had finally stopped, the flooded woods and willow islands, the canals whose canopies were so thick that sunlight seldom struck the water, the stretches of beach along the bays had smelled of death for weeks. The odor, which was like the heavy, gray, salty stench from a decaying rat, hung in the heat all day, and at night it blew through the screen windows on the quarter-boat and awaited you in the morning when you walked through the galley into the dining room.

Many of the animals that did not drown starved to death. Coons used to climb up the mooring ropes and scratch on the galley screen for food, and often we'd take rabbits out of the tops of trees that barely extended above the current and carry them on the jugboat to the levee at Charenton. Sometimes at night huge trees with root systems as broad as barn roofs floated by in the dark and scraped the hull with their branches from the bow to the stern. One night when the moon was full and yellow and low over the willow islands, I heard something hit the side of the boat hard, like a big wood fist rolling its knuckles along the planks. I stood on my bunk and looked through the screen window and saw a houseboat, upside down, spinning in the current, a tangle of fishing nets strung out of one window like flotsam from an eye socket.

I thought about the hundreds of people who had either been crushed under a tidal wave or drowned in Cameron Parish, their bodies washed deep into the marshes along the Calcasieu River, and again I smelled that thick, fetid odor on the wind. I could not sleep again until the sun rose like a red molten ball through the mists across the bay.

It didn't take us long to find the willow island where Elrod Sykes said he had seen the skeletal remains of either an Indian or a black person. We crossed the wide sweep of the Atchafalaya in a sheriff's department boat with two outboard engines mounted on the stern, took a channel between a row of sandbars whose sun-dried crests looked like the backs of dolphin jumping in a school, crossed a long bay, and slid the boat onto a narrow strip of beach that bled back into a thick stand of willow trees and chains of flooded sinkholes and sand bogs.

Elrod Sykes stepped off the bow onto the sand and stared into the trees. He had taken off his shirt and he used it to wipe the sweat off his tanned chest and shoulders.

'It's back in yonder,' he said, and pointed. 'You can see my footprints where I went in to take a whiz.'

The St Mary Parish deputy fitted a cloth cap on his head and sprayed his face, neck, and arms with mosquito dope, then handed the can to me.

'If I was you, I'd put my shirt on, Mr Sykes,' he said. 'We used to have a lot of bats down here. Till the mosquitoes ate them all.'

Sykes smiled good-naturedly and waited for his turn to use the can of repellent.

'I bet you won't believe this,' the deputy said, 'but it's been so dry here on occasion that I seen a catfish walking down the levee carrying his own canteen.'

Sykes's eyes crinkled at the corners, then he walked ahead of us into the gloom, his loafers sinking deep into the wet sand.

'That boy's a long way from his Hollywood poontang, ain't he?' the deputy said behind me.

'How about putting the cork in the humor for a while?' I said.

'What?'

'The man grew up down South. You're patronizing him.'

'I'm wha—'

I walked ahead of him and caught up with Sykes just as he stepped out of the willows into a shallow, water-filled depression between the woods and a sandbar. The water was stagnant and hot and smelled of dead garfish.

'There,' he said. 'Right under the roots of that dead tree. I told y'all.'

A barkless, sun-bleached cypress tree lay crossways in a sandbar, the water-smooth trunk eaten by worms, and gathered inside the root system, as though held by a gnarled hand, was a skeleton crimped in an embryonic position, wrapped in a web of dried algae and river trash.

The exposed bone was polished and weathered almost black, but sections of the skin had dried to the color and texture of desiccated leather. Just as Sykes had said, a thick chain encased with rust was wrapped around the arms and rib cage. The end links were fastened with a padlock as wide as my hand.

I tore a willow branch off a tree, shucked off the leaves with my Puma knife, and knelt down in front of the skeleton.

'How do you reckon it got up under those roots?' Sykes said.

'A bad hurricane came through here in '57,' I said. 'Trees like this were torn out of the ground like carrots. My bet is this man's body got caught under some floating trees and was covered up later in this sandbar.'

Sykes knelt beside me.

'I don't understand,' he said. 'How do you know it happened in '57? Hurricanes tear up this part of the country all the time, don't they?'

'Good question, podna,' I said, and I used the willow branch to peel away the dried web of algae from around one shinbone, then the other.

'That left one's clipped in half,' Sykes said.

'Yep. That's where he was shot when he tried to run away from two white men.'

'You clairvoyant or something?' Sykes said.

'No, I saw it happen. About a mile from here.'

'You saw it happen?' Sykes said.

'Yep.'

'What's going on here?' the deputy said behind us. 'You saying some white people lynched somebody or something?'

'Yeah, that's exactly what I'm saying. When we get back we'll need to talk to your sheriff and get your medical examiner out here.'

'I don't know about y'all over in Iberia Parish, but nobody around here's going to be real interested in nigger trouble that's thirty-five years old,' the deputy said.

I worked the willow branch around the base of the bones and peeled back a skein of algae over the legs, the pelvic bones, and the crown of the skull, which still had a section of grizzled black hair attached to the pate. I poked at the corrugated, blackened work boots and the strips of rag that hung off the pelvis.

I put down the branch and chewed on the corner of my thumb-nail.

'What are you looking for, Mr Robicheaux?' Sykes said.

'It's not what's there, it's what isn't,' I said. 'He wasn't wearing a belt on his trousers, and his boots have no laces.'

'Sonofabitch probably did his shopping at the Goodwill. Big fucking deal,' the deputy said, slapped a mosquito on his neck, and looked at the red and black paste on his palm.

Later that afternoon I went back to work on the case of the murdered girl, whose full name was Cherry LeBlanc. No one knew the whereabouts of her father, who had disappeared from Mamou after he was accused of molesting a black child in his neighborhood, but I interviewed her grandparents again, the owner of the bar in St Martinville where she had last worked, the girls she had been with in the clapboard jukejoint the night she died, and a police captain in Lafayette who had recommended probation for her after she had been busted on the prostitution charge. I learned little about her except that she seemed to have been an uneducated, unskilled, hapless, and fatally beautiful girl who thought she could be a viable player in a crap game where the dice for her kind were always shaved.

I learned that about her and the fact that she had loved zydeco music and had gone to the jukejoint to hear Sam 'Hogman' Patin play his harmonica and bottleneck blues twelve-string guitar.

My desk was covered with scribbled notes from my note pad, morgue and crime-scene photos, interview cassettes, and Xeroxes from the LeBlanc family's welfare case history when the sheriff walked into my office. The sky outside was lavender and pink now, and the fronds on the palm trees out by the sidewalk were limp in the heat and silhouetted darkly against the late sun.

'The sheriff over in St Mary Parish just called,' he said.

'Yes?'

'He said thanks a lot. They really appreciate the extra work.' He sat on the corner of my desk.

'Tell him to find another line of work.'

'He said you're welcome to come over on your days off and run the investigation.'

'What's he doing with it?'

'Their coroner's got the bones now. But I'll tell you the truth, Dave, I don't think it's going anywhere.'

I leaned back in my swivel chair and drummed my fingers on my desk. My eyes burned and my back hurt.

'It seems to me you've been vindicated,' the sheriff said. 'Let it go for now.'

'We'll see.'

'Look, I know you've got a big workload piled on you right now, but I've got a problem I need you to look into when you have a chance. Like maybe first thing tomorrow morning.'

I looked back at him without speaking.

'Baby Feet Balboni,' he said.

'What about him?'

'He's in New Iberia. At the Holiday Inn, with about six of his fellow greaseballs and their whores. The manager called me from a phone booth down the street he was so afraid one of them would hear him.'

'I don't know what I can do about it,' I said.

'We need to know what he's doing in town.'

'He grew up here.'

'Look, Dave, they can't even handle this guy in New Orleans. He cannibalized half the Giacano and Cardo families to get where he is. He's not coming back here. That's not going to happen.'

18

I rubbed my face. My whiskers felt stiff against my palm.

'You want me to send somebody else?' the sheriff asked.

'No, that's all right.'

'Y'all were friends in high school for a while, weren't you?'

'We played ball together, that's all.'

I gazed out the window at the lengthening shadows. He studied my face.

'What's the matter, Dave?'

'It's nothing.'

'You bothered because we want to bounce a baseball buddy out of town?'

'No, not really.'

'Did you ever hear that story about what he did to Didi Giacano's cousin? Supposedly he hung him from his colon by a meat hook.'

'I've heard that same story about a half-dozen wiseguys in Orleans and Jefferson parishes. It's an old NOPD heirloom.'

'Probably just bad press, huh?'

'I always tried to think of Julie as nine-tenths thespian,' I said.

'Yeah, and gorilla shit tastes like chocolate ice cream. Dave, you're a laugh a minute.'

3

Julie Balboni looked just like his father, who had owned most of the slot and racehorse machines in Iberia Parish during the 1940s and, with an Assyrian family, had run the gambling and prostitution in the Underpass area of Lafayette. Julie was already huge, six and a half feet tall, when he was in the eleventh grade, thick across the hips and tapered at both ends like a fat banana, with tiny ankles and size-seven feet and a head as big as a buffalo's. A year later he filled out in serious proportions. That was also the year he was arrested for burglarizing a liquor store. His father walked him out into the woods at gunpoint and whipped the skin off his back with the nozzle end of a garden hose.

His hair grew on his head like black snakes, and because a physician had injured a nerve in his face when he was delivered, the corner of his mouth would sometimes droop involuntarily and give him a lewd or leering expression that repelled most girls. He farted in class, belched during the pledge of allegiance, combed his dandruff out on top of the desk, and addressed anyone he didn't like by gathering up his scrotum and telling them to bite. We walked around him in the halls and the locker room. His teachers were secretly relieved when his mother and father did not show up on parents' night.

His other nickname was Julie the Bone, although it wasn't used to his face, because he went regularly to Mabel White's Negro brothel in Crowley and the Negro cribs on Hopkins Avenue in New Iberia.

But Julie had two uncontested talents. He was both a great kick boxer and a great baseball catcher. His ankles twisted too easily for him to play football; he was too fat to run track; but with one flick of a thick thigh he could leave a kick-box opponent heaving blood, and behind the plate he could steal the ball out of the batter's swing or vacuum a wild pitch out of the dust and zip the ball to third base like a BB.

In my last time out as a high school pitcher, I was going into the bottom of the ninth against Abbeville with a shut-out almost in my pocket. It was a soft, pink evening, with the smell of flowers and freshly cut grass in the air. Graduation was only three weeks away, and we all felt that we were painted with magic and that the spring season had been created as a song especially for us. Innocence, a lock on the future, the surge of victory in the loins, the confirmation of a girl's kiss among the dusky oak trees, like a strawberry bursting against the roof of the mouth, were all most assuredly our due.

We even felt an acceptance and camaraderie toward Baby Feet. Imminent graduation and the laurels of a winning season seemed to have melted away the differences in our backgrounds and experience.

Then their pitcher, a beanballer who used his elbows, knees, and spikes in a slide, hit a double and stole third base. Baby Feet called time and jogged out to the mound, sweat leaking out of his inverted cap. He rubbed up a new ball for me.

'Put it in the dirt. I'm gonna let that cocksucker have his chance,' he said.

'I don't know if that's smart, Feet,' I said.

'I've called a shutout for you so far, haven't I? Do what I tell you.'

On the next pitch I glanced at the runner, then fired low and outside, into the dirt. Baby Feet vacuumed it up, then spun around, throwing dust in the air like an elephant, and raced toward the backstop as though the ball had gotten past him.

The runner charged from third. Suddenly Baby Feet reappeared at the plate, the ball never having left his hand, his mask still on his face. The runner realized that he had stepped into it and he tried to bust up Baby Feet in the slide by throwing one spiked shoe up in Feet's face. Baby Feet caught the runner's spikes in his mask, tagged him across the head with the ball, then, when it was completely unnecessary at that point, razored his own spikes into the boy's ankles and twisted.

The players on the field, the coaches, the people in the stands, stared numbly at home plate. Baby Feet calmly scraped his spikes clean in the sand, then knelt and tightened the strap on a shin guard, his face cool and detached as he squinted up at the flag snapping on a metal pole behind the backstop.

It wasn't hard to find him at the Holiday Inn. He and his entourage were the only people in and around the swimming pool. Their tanned bodies glistened as though they had rubbed them with melted butter. They wore wraparound sunglasses that were as black as a blind man's, reclined luxuriously on deck chairs, their genitalia sculpted against the bikinis, or floated on rubber mattresses, tropical drinks in holders at their sides, a glaze of suntan oil emananting from the points of their fingers and toes.

A woman came out the sliding door of a room with her two children,

walked them to the wading pool, then obviously realized the nature of the company she was keeping; she looked around distractedly, as though she heard invisible birds cawing at her, and returned quickly to her room with her children's hands firmly in hers.

Julie the Bone hadn't changed a great deal since I had last seen him seven years ago in New Orleans. His eyes, which were like black marbles, were set a little more deeply in his face; his wild tangle of hair was flecked in places with gray; but his barrel chest and his washtub of a stomach still seemed to have the tone and texture of whale hide. When you looked at the ridges of scar tissue under the hair on his shoulders and back where his father had beaten him, at the nests of tendons and veins in his neck, and the white protrusion of knuckles in his huge hands, you had the feeling that nothing short of a wrecking ball, swung by a cable from a great height, could adequately deal with this man if he should choose to destroy everything in his immediate environment.

He raised himself on one elbow from his reclining chair, pushed his sunglasses up on his hair, and squinted through the haze at me as I approached him. Two of his men sat next to him at a glass table under an umbrella, playing cards with a woman with bleached hair and skin that was so tanned it looked like folds of soft leather. Both men put down their cards and got to their feet, and one of them, who looked as though he were hammered together from boilerplate, stepped directly into my path. His hair was orange and gray, flattened in damp curls on his head, and there were pachuco crosses tattooed on the backs of his hands. I opened my seersucker coat so he could see the badge clipped to my belt. But recognition was already working in his face.

'What's happening, Cholo?' I said.

'Hey, lieutenant, how you doin'?' he said, then turned to Baby Feet. 'Hey, Julie, it's Lieutenant Robicheaux. From the First District in New Orleans. You remember him when—'

'Yeah, I know who it is, Cholo,' Baby Feet said, smiling and nodding at me. 'What you up to, Dave? Somebody knock a pop fly over the swimming-pool wall?'

'I was just in the neighborhood. I heard you were back in town for a short visit.'

'No kidding.'

'That's a fact.'

'You were probably in the barbershop and somebody said, "The Bone's in town," and you thought, "Boy, that's great news. I'll just go say hello to ole Feet."'

'You're a famous man, Julie. Word gets around.'

'And I'm just here for a short visit, right?'

'Yeah, that's the word.'

22

His eyes moved up and down my body. He smiled to himself and took a sip from a tall glass wrapped in a napkin, with shaved ice, fruit, and a tiny paper umbrella in it.

'You're a sheriff's detective now, I hear.'

'On and off.'

He pushed a chair at me with his foot, then picked it up and set it in a shady area across from him. I took off my seersucker coat, folded it on my arm, and sat down.

'Y'all worried about me, Dave?'

'Some people in New Iberia think you're a hard act to follow. How many guys would burn down their own father's nightclub?'

He laughed.

'Yeah, the old man lost his interest in garden hoses after that,' he said.

'Everybody likes to come back to his hometown once in a while. That's a perfectly natural thing to do. No one's worried about that, Julie.' I looked at his eyes. Under his sweaty brows, they were as shiny and full of light as obsidian.

He took a cigarette out of a package on the cement and lit it. He blew smoke out into the sunlight and looked around the swimming-pool area.

'Except I've only got a visa, right?' he said. 'I'm supposed to spread a little money around, stay on the back streets, tell my crew not to spit on the sidewalks or blow their noses on their napkins in the restaurants. Does that kind of cover it for you, Dave?'

'It's a small town with small-town problems.'

'Fuck.' He took a deep breath, then twisted his neck as though there were a crick in it. 'Margot—' he said to the woman playing cards under the umbrella. She got up from her chair and stood behind him, her narrow face expressionless behind her sunglasses, and began kneading his neck with her fingers. He filled his mouth with ice, orange slices, and cherries from his glass and studied my face while he chewed.

'I get a little upset at these kind of attitudes, Dave. You got to forgive me,' he said, and pointed into his breastbone with his fingertips. 'But it don't seem to matter sometimes what a guy does *now*. It's always *yesterday* that's in people's minds. Like Cholo here. He made a mistake fifteen years ago and we're still hearing about it. What the fuck is that? You think that's fair?'

'He threw his brother-in-law off the roof of the Jax's brewery on top of a Mardi Gras float. That was a first even for New Orleans.'

'Hey, lieutenant, there was a lot of other things involved there. The guy beat up my sister. He was a fucking animal.'

'Look, Dave, you been gone from New Orleans for a long time,' Baby Feet said. 'The city ain't anything like it used to be. Black kids with shit for brains are provoking everybody in the fucking town. People get killed in Audubon Park, for God's sake. You try to get on the St Charles streetcar and there's either niggers or Japs hanging out the doors and windows. We used to have understandings with the city. Everybody knew the rules, nobody got hurt. Take a walk past the Desire or St Thomas project and see what happens.'

'What's the point, Julie?'

'The point is who the fuck needs it? I own a recording studio, the same place Jimmy Clanton cut his first record. I'm in the entertainment business. I talk on the phone every day to people in California you read about in *People* magazine. I come home to this shithole, they ought to have "Welcome Back Balboni Day." Instead, I get told maybe I'm like a bad smell in the air. You understand what I'm saying, that hurts me.'

I rubbed one palm against the other.

'I'm just a messenger,' I said.

'That laundry man you work for send you?'

'He has his concerns.'

He waved the woman away and sat up in his chair.

'Give me five minutes to get dressed. Then I want you to drive me somewhere,' he said.

'I'm a little tied up on time right now.'

'I'm asking fifteen minutes of you, max. You think you can give me that much of your day, Dave?' He got up and started past me to his room. There were tufts of black hair like pig bristles on his love handles. He cocked his index finger at me. 'Be here when I get back. You won't regret it.'

The woman with the bleached hair sat back down at the table. She took off her glasses, parted her legs a moment, and looked into my face, her eyes neither flirtatious nor hostile, simply dead. Cholo invited me to play gin rummy with them.

'Thanks. I never took it up,' I said.

'You sure took it up with horses, lieutenant,' he said.

'Yep, horses and Beam. They always made an interesting combination at the Fairgrounds.'

'Hey, you remember that time you lent me twenty bucks to get home from Jefferson Downs? I always remembered that, Loot. That was all right.'

Cholo Manelli had been born of a Mexican washerwoman, who probably wished she had given birth to a bowling ball instead, and fathered by a brain-damaged Sicilian numbers runner, whose head had been caved in by a cop's baton in the Irish Channel. He was raised in the Iberville welfare project across from the old St Louis cemeteries, and at age eleven was busted with his brothers for rolling and beating the winos who slept in the empty crypts. Their weapons of choice had been sand-filled socks.

He had the coarse, square hands of a bricklayer, the facial depth of a pie plate. I always suspected that if he was lobotomized you wouldn't know the difference. The psychiatrists at Mandeville diagnosed him as a sociopath and shot his head full of electricity. Evidently the treatment had as much effect as charging a car battery with three dead cells. On his first jolt at Angola he was put in with the big stripes, the violent and the incorrigible, back in the days when the state used trusty guards, mounted on horses and armed with double-barrel twelve-gauge shot-guns, who had to serve the time of any inmate who escaped while under their supervision. Cholo went to the bushes and didn't come back fast enough for the trusty gunbull. The gunbull put four pieces of buckshot in Cholo's back. Two weeks later a Mason jar of prune-o was found in the gunbull's cell. A month after that, when he was back in the main population, somebody dropped the loaded bed of a dump truck on his head.

'Julie told me about the time that boon almost popped you with a .38,' he said.

'What time was that?'

'When you were a patrolman. In the Quarter. Julie said he saved your life.'

'He did, huh?'

Cholo shrugged his shoulders.

'That's what the man said, lieutenant. What do I know?'

'Take the hint, Cholo. Our detective isn't a conversationalist,' the woman said, without removing her eyes from her cards. She clacked her lacquered nails on the glass tabletop, and her lips made a dry, sucking sound when she puffed on her cigarette.

'You working on that murder case? The one about that girl?' he said.

'How'd you know about that?'

His eyes clicked sideways.

'It was in the newspaper,' he said. 'Julie and me was talking about it this morning. Something like that's disgusting. You got a fucking maniac on the loose around here. Somebody ought to take him to a hospital and kill him.'

Baby Feet emerged resplendent from the sliding glass door of his room. He wore a white suit with gray pin stripes, a purple shirt scrolled with gray flowers, a half-dozen gold chains and medallions around his talcumed neck, tasseled loafers that seemed as small on his feet as ballet slippers.

'You look beautiful, Julie,' Cholo said.

25

'Fucking A,' Baby Feet said, lighting the cigarette in the corner of his mouth with a tiny gold lighter.

'Can I go with y'all?' Cholo asked.

'Keep an eye on things here for me.'

'Hey, you told me last night I could go.'

'I need you to take my calls.'

'Margot don't know how to pick up a phone anymore?' Cholo said.

'My meter's running, Julie,' I said.

'We're going out to dinner tonight with some interesting people,' Baby Feet said to Cholo. 'You'll enjoy it. Be patient.'

'They're quite excited about the possibility of meeting you. They called and said that, Cholo,' the woman said.

'Margot, why is it you got calluses on your back? Somebody been putting starch in your sheets or something?' Cholo said.

I started walking toward my truck. The sunlight off the cement by the poolside was blinding. Baby Feet caught up with me. One of his other women dove off the board and splashed water and the smell of chlorine and suntan oil across my back.

'Hey, I live in a fucking menagerie,' Baby Feet said as we went out onto the street. 'Don't go walking off from me with your nose bent out of joint. Did I ever treat you with a lack of respect?'

I got in the truck.

'Where we going, Feet?' I said.

'Out by Spanish Lake. Look, I want you to take a message back to the man you work for. I'm not the source of any problems you got around here. The coke you got in this parish has been stepped on so many times it's baby powder. If it was coming from some people I've been associated with in New Orleans, and I'm talking about past associations, you understand, it'd go from your nose to your brain like liquid Drano.'

I headed out toward the old two-lane highway that led to the little settlement of Burke and the lake where Spanish colonists had tried to establish plantations in the eighteenth century and had given Iberia Parish its name.

'I don't work narcotics, Julie, and I'm not good at passing on bullshit, either. My main concern right now is the girl we found south of town.'

'Oh, yeah? What girl's that?'

'The murdered girl, Cherry LeBlanc.'

'I don't guess I heard about it.'

I turned and looked at him. He gazed idly out the window at the passing oak trees on the edge of town and a roadside watermelon and strawberry stand.

'You don't read the local papers?' I said.

'I been busy. You saying I talk bullshit, Dave?'

'Put it this way, Feet. If you've got something to tell the sheriff, do it yourself.'

He pinched his nose, then blew air through it.

'We used to be friends, Dave. I even maybe did you a little favor once. So I'm going to line it out for you and any of the locals who want to clean the wax out of their ears. The oil business is still in the toilet and your town's flat-ass broke. Frankly, in my opinion, it deserves anything that happens to it. But me and all those people you see back on that lake—' He pointed out the window. Through a pecan orchard, silhouetted against the light winking off the water, I could see cameras mounted on booms and actors in Confederate uniforms toiling through the shallows in retreat from imaginary federal troops. 'We're going to leave around ten million dollars in Lafayette and Iberia Parish. They don't like the name Balboni around here, tell them we can move the whole fucking operation over to Mississippi. See how that floats with some of those coonass jackoffs in the Chamber of Commerce.'

'You're telling me you're in the movie business?'

'Coproducer with Michael Goldman. What do you think of that?'

I turned into the dirt road that led through the pecan trees to the lake.

'I'm sure everyone wishes you success, Julie.'

'I'm going to make a baseball movie next. You want a part in it?' He smiled at me.

'I don't think I'd be up to it.'

'Hey, Dave, don't get me wrong.' He was grinning broadly now. 'But my main actor sees dead people out in the mist, his punch is usually ripped by nine A.M. on weed or whites, and Mikey's got peptic ulcers and some kind of obsession with the Holocaust. Dave, I ain't shitting you, I mean this sincerely, with no offense, with your record, you could fit right in.'

I stopped the truck by a small wood-frame security office. A wiry man in a khaki uniform and a bill cap, with a white scar like a chicken's foot on his throat, approached my window.

'We'll see you, Feet,' I said.

'You don't want to look around?'

'Adios, partner,' I said, waited for him to close the door, then turned around in the weeds and drove back through the pecan trees to the highway, the sun's reflection bouncing on my hood like a yellow balloon.

It happened my second year on the New Orleans police force, when I was a patrolman in the French Quarter and somebody called in a prowler report at an address on Dumaine. The lock on the iron gate was rusted and had been bent out of the jamb with a bar and sprung back on the hinges. Down the narrow brick walkway I could see bits of broken glass, like tiny rat's teeth, where someone had broken out the overhead light bulb. But the courtyard ahead was lighted, filled with the waving shadows of banana trees and palm fronds, and I could hear a baseball game playing on a radio or television set.

I slipped my revolver out of its holster and moved along the coolness of the bricks, through a ticking pool of water, to the entrance of the courtyard, where a second scrolled-iron gate yawned back on its hinges. I could smell the damp earth in the flower beds, spearmint growing against a stucco wall, the thick clumps of purple wisteria that hung from a tile roof.

Then I smelled *him*, even before I saw him, an odor that was at once like snuff, synthetic wine, rotting teeth, and stomach bile. He was a huge black man, dressed in a Donald Duck T-shirt, filthy tennis shoes, and a pair of purple slacks that were bursting on his thighs. In his left hand was a drawstring bag filled with goods from the apartment he'd just creeped. He swung the gate with all his weight into my hand, snapped something in it like a Popsicle stick breaking, and sent my revolver skidding across the flagstones.

I tried to get my baton loose, but it was his show now. He came out of his back pocket with a worn one-inch .38, the grips wrapped with black electrician's tape, and screwed the barrel into my ear. There was a dark clot of blood in his right eye, and his breath slid across the side of my face like an unwashed hand.

'Get back in the walkway, motherfucker,' he whispered.

We stumbled backward into the gloom. I could hear revelers out on the street, a beer can tinkling along the cement.

'Don't be a dumb guy,' I said.

'Shut up,' he said. Then, almost as as angry afterthought, he drove my head into the bricks. I fell to my knees in the water, my baton twisted uselessly in my belt.

His eyes were dilated, his hair haloed with sweat, his pulse leaping in his neck. He was a cop's worst possible adversary in that situation – strung-out, frightened, and stupid enough to carry a weapon on a simple B & E.

'Why'd you have to come along, man? Why'd you have to do that?' he said.

His thumb curled around the spur of the pistol's hammer and I heard the cylinder rotate and the chamber lock into place.

'There's cops on both ends of the street,' I said. 'You won't get out of the Quarter.'

'Don't say no more, man. It won't do no good. You messed everything up.'

He wiped the sweat out of his eyes, blew out his breath, and pointed the pistol downward at my chest.

Baby Feet had on only a bathrobe, his jockey underwear, and a pair of loafers without socks when he appeared in the brick walkway behind the black man.

'What the fuck do you think you're doing here?' he said.

The black man stepped back, the revolver drifting to his thigh.

'Mr Julie?' he said.

'Yeah. What the fuck you doing? You creeping an apartment in my building?'

'I didn't know you was living here, Mr Julie.'

Baby Feet took the revolver out of the black man's hand and eased down the hammer.

'Walter, if I want to, I can make you piss blood for six months,' he said.

'Yes, suh, I knows that.'

'I'm glad you've taken that attitude. Now, you get your sorry ass out of here.' He pushed the black man toward the entrance. 'Go on.' He kept nudging the black man along the bricks, then he kicked him hard, as fast as a snake striking, between the buttocks. 'I said go on, now.' He kicked him again, his small pointed shoe biting deep into the man's crotch. Tears welled up in the man's eyes as he looked back over his shoulder. 'Move it, Walter, unless you want balls the size of coconuts.'

The black man limped down Dumaine. Baby Feet stood in front of the sprung gate, dumped the shells from the .38 on the sidewalk, and flung the .38 into the darkness after the black man.

'Come on upstairs and I'll put your hand in some ice,' he said.

I had found my hat and revolver.

'I'm going after that guy,' I said.

'Pick him up in the morning. He shines shoes in a barbershop on Calliope and St Charles. You sure you want to stay in this line of work, Dave?'

He laughed, lit a purple-and-gold cigarette, and put his round, thick arm over my shoulders.

The sheriff was right: Baby Feet might be a movie producer, but he could never be dismissed as a thespian.

4

My brief visit with Julie Balboni should have been a forgettable and minor interlude in my morning. Instead, my conversation with him in the truck had added a disturbing question mark in the murder of Cherry LeBlanc. He said he had heard nothing about it, nor had he read about it in the local newspaper. This was ten minutes after Cholo Manelli had told me that he and Baby Feet had been talking about the girl's death earlier.

Was Baby Feet lying or was he simply not interested in talking about something that wasn't connected with his well-being? Or had the electroshock therapists in Mandeville overheated Cholo's brain pan?

My experience with members of the Mafia and sociopaths in general had been that they lie as a matter of course. They are convincing because they often lie when there is no need to. To apply some form of forensic psychology in attempting to understand how they think is as productive as placing your head inside a microwave oven in order to study the nature of electricity.

I spent the rest of the day retracing the geography of Cherry LeBlanc's last hours and trying to recreate the marginal world in which she had lived. At three that afternoon I parked my truck in the shade by the old wood-frame church in St Martinville and looked at a color photograph of her that had been given to me by the grandparents. Her hair was black, with a mahogany tint in it, her mouth bright red with too much lipstick, her face soft, slightly plump with baby fat; her dark eyes were bright and masked no hidden thought; she was smiling.

Busted at sixteen for prostitution, dead at nineteen, I thought. And that's what we knew about. God only knew what else had befallen her in her life. But she wasn't born a prostitute or the kind of girl who would be passed from hand to hand until someone opened a car door for her and drove her deep into a woods, where he revealed to her the instruments of her denouement, perhaps even convinced her that this moment was one she had elected for herself.

Others had helped her get there. My first vote would be for the father, the child molester, in Mamou. But our legal system looks at nouns, seldom at adverbs.

I gazed at the spreading oaks in the church's graveyard, where Evangeline and her lover Gabriel were buried. The tombstones were stained with lichen and looked cool and gray in the shade. Beyond the trees, the sun reflected off Bayou Teche like a yellow flame.

Where was the boyfriend in this? I thought. A girl that pretty either has a beau or there is somebody in her life who would like to be one. She hadn't gone far in school, but necessity must have given her a survivor's instinct about people, about men in particular, certainly about the variety who drifted in and out of a south Louisiana jukejoint.

She had to know her killer. I was convinced of that.

I walked to the bar, a ramshackle nineteenth-century wooden building with scaling paint and a sagging upstairs gallery. The inside was dark and cool and almost deserted. A fat black woman was scrubbing the front windows with a brush and a bucket of soap and water. I walked the length of the bar to the small office in back where I had found the owner before. Along the counter in front of the bar's mirror were rows upon rows of bottles – dark green and slender, stoppered with wet corks: obsidian black with arterial-red wax seals; frosted-white, like ice sawed out of a lake; whiskey-brown, singing with heat and light.

The smell of the green sawdust on the floor, the wood-handled beer taps dripping through an aluminum grate, the Collins mix and the bowls of cherries and sliced limes and oranges, they were only the stuff of memory, I told myself, swallowing. They belong to your Higher Power now. Just like an old girlfriend who winks at you on the street one day, I thought. You already gave her up. You just walk on by. It's that easy.

But you don't think about it, you don't think about it, you don't think about it.

The owner was a preoccupied man who combed his black hair straight back on his narrow head and kept his comb clipped inside his shirt pocket. The receipts and whiskey invoices on his desk were a magnet for his eyes. My questions couldn't compete. He kept running his tongue behind his teeth while I talked.

'So you didn't know anything about her friends?' I said.

'No, sir. She was here three weeks. They come and they go. That's the way it is. I don't know what else to tell you.'

'Do you know anything about your bartenders?'

His eyes focused on a spot inside his cigarette smoke.

'I'm not understanding you,' he said.

31

'Do you hire a bartender who hangs around with ex-cons or who's in a lot of debt? I suspect you probably don't. Those are the kind of guys who set up their friends with free doubles or make change out of an open drawer without ringing up the sale, aren't they?'

'What's your point?'

'Did you know she had been arrested for prostitution?'

'I didn't know that.'

'You hired her because you thought she was an honor student at USL?'

The corner of his mouth wrinkled slightly with the beginnings of a smile. He stirred the ashes in the ashtray with the tip of his cigarette.

'I'll leave you my card and a thought, Mr Trajan. One way or another we're going to nail the guy who killed her. In the meantime, if he kills somebody else and I find out that you held back information on me, I'll be back with a warrant for your arrest.'

'I don't care for the way you're talking to me.'

I left his office without replying and walked back down the length of the bar. The black woman was now outside, washing the front window. She put down her scrub brush, flung the whole bucket of soapy water on the glass, then began rinising it off with a hose. Her skin was the color of burnt brick, her eyes turquoise, her breasts sagging like water-filled balloons inside her cotton-print dress. I opened my badge in my palm.

'Did you know the white girl Cherry LeBlanc?' I asked.

'She worked here, ain't she?' She squinted her eyes against the water spray bouncing off the glass.

'Do you know if she had a boyfriend, *tante*?'

'If that's what you want to call it.'

'What do you mean?' I asked, already knowing the answer that I didn't want to hear.

'She in the bidness.'

'Full time, in a serious way?'

'What you all sellin' out of your pants?'

'Was Mr Trajan involved?'

'Ax him.'

'I don't think he was, otherwise you wouldn't be telling me these things, *tante*.' I smiled at her.

She began refilling the bucket with clear water. She suddenly looked tired.

'She a sad girl,' she said. She wiped the perspiration off her round face with her palm and looked at it. 'I tole her they ain't no amount of money gonna he'p her when some man make her sick, no. I tole her a pretty white girl like her can have anything she want – school, car, a husband wit' a job on them oil rig. When that girl dress up, she look like a movie star. She say, "Jennifer, some people is suppose to have only what people let them have." Lord God, her age and white and believing somet'ing like that.'

'Who was her pimp, Jennifer?'

'They come here for her.'

'Who?'

'The mens. When they want her. They come here and take her home.'

'Do you know who they were, their names?'

'Them kind ain't got no names. They just drive their car up when she get off work and that po' girl get in.'

'I see. All right, Jennifer, this is my card with my telephone number on it. Would you call me if you remember anything else that might help me?'

'I don't be knowin' anything else, me. She wasn't goin' to give the name of some rich white man to an old nigger.'

'What white man?'

'That's what I tellin' you. I don't know, me.'

'I'm sorry, I don't understand what you're saying.'

'You don't understand English, you? Where you from? She say they a rich white man maybe gonna get her out of sellin' jellyroll. She say that the last time I seen her, right befo' somebody do them awful t'ings to that young girl. Mister, when they in the bidness, every man got a sweet word in his mouth, every man got a special way to keep jellyroll in his bed and the dollar in his pocket.'

She threw the bucket of clear water on the glass, splashing both of us, then walked heavily with her brushes, cleaning rags, and empty bucket down the alley next to the bar.

The rain fell through the canopy of oaks as I drove down the dirt road along the bayou toward my house. During the summer it rains almost every afternoon in southern Louisiana. From my gallery, around three o'clock, you could watch the clouds build as high and dark as mountains out on the Gulf, then within minutes the barometer would drop, the air would suddenly turn cool and smell like ozone and gun metal and fish spawning, the wind would begin to blow out of the south and straighten the moss on the dead cypress trees in the marsh, bend the cattails in the bayou, and swell and ruffle the pecan trees in my front yard; then a sheet of gray rain would move out of the marsh, across the floating islands of purple hyacinths in the bayou, my bait shop and the canvas awning over my boat-rental dock, and ring as loud on my gallery as marbles bouncing on corrugated tin.

I parked the truck under the pecan trees and ran up the incline to the front steps. My father, a trapper and oil-field roughneck who worked high up on the derrick, on what they called the monkey board, built the house of cypress and oak back in the Depression. The planks in the walls and floors were notched and joined with wooden pegs. You couldn't shove a playing card in a seam. With age the wood had weathered almost black. I think rifle balls would have bounced off it.

My wife's car was gone, but through the screen door I could smell shrimp on the stove. I looked for Alafair, my adopted daughter, but didn't see her either. Then I saw that the horse lot and shed were empty and Alafair's three-legged coon, Tripod, was not in his cage on top of the rabbit hutches or on the chain that allowed him to run along a clothesline between two tree trunks.

I started to go inside, then I heard her horse paw the leaves around the side of the house.

'Alafair?'

Nothing.

'Alf, I've got a feeling somebody is doing something she isn't supposed to.'

'What's that, Dave?' she said.

'Would you please come out here and bring your friends with you?'

She rode her Appaloosa out from under the eave. Her tennis shoes, pink shorts, and T-shirt were sopping, and her tanned skin glistened with water. She grinned under her straw hat.

'Alf, what happened the last time you took Tripod for a ride?'

She looked off reflectively at the rain falling in the trees. Tripod squirmed in her hands. He was a beautiful coon, silver-tipped, with a black mask and black rings on his thick tail.

'I told him not to do that no more, Dave.'

'It's "anymore." '

'Anymore. He ain't gonna do it anymore, Dave.'

She was grinning again. Tex, her Appaloosa, was steel gray, with white stockings and a spray of black and white spots on his rump. Last week Tripod had spiked his claws into Tex's rump, and Alafair had been thrown end over end into the tomato plants.

'Where's Bootsie?'

'At the store in town.'

'How about putting Tex in the shed and coming in for some ice cream? You think you can handle that, little guy?'

'Yeah, that's a pretty good idea, Dave,' she said, as though both of us had just thought our way through a problem. She continued to look at me, her dark eyes full of light. 'What about Tripod?'

'I think Tripod probably needs some ice cream, too.'

Her face beamed. She set Tripod on top of the hutches, then slid down off her horse into a mud puddle. I watched her hook Tripod to his chain and lead Tex back to the lot. She was eleven years old now. Her body was round and hard and full of energy, her Indian-black hair as shiny as a raven's wing; when she smiled, her eyes squinted almost completely shut. Six years ago I had pulled her from a wobbling envelope of air inside the submerged wreckage of a twin-engine plane out on the salt.

She hooked Tripod's chain on the back porch and went into her bedroom to change clothes. I put a small amount of ice cream in two bowls and set them on the table. Above the counter a telephone number was written on the small blackboard we used for messages. Alafair came back into the kitchen, rubbing her head with a towel. She wore her slippers, her elastic-waisted blue jeans, and an oversized University of Southwestern Louisiana T-shirt. She kept blowing her bangs out of her eyes.

'You promise you're going to eat your supper?' I said.

'Of course. What difference does it make if you eat ice cream before supper instead of after? You're silly sometimes, Dave.'

'Oh, I see.'

'You have funny ideas sometimes.'

'You're growing up on me.'

'What?'

'Never mind.'

She brought Tripod's pan in from the porch and put a scoop of ice cream in it. The rain had slackened, and I could see the late sun breaking through the mist, like a pink wafer, above the sugarcane at the back of my property.

'Oh, I forgot, a man called,' she said. 'That's his number.'

'Who was it?'

'He said he was a friend of yours. I couldn't hear because it was real noisy.'

'Next time have the person spell his name and write it on the blackboard with his number, Alf.'

'He said he wanted to talk with you about some man with one arm and one leg.'

'What?'

'He said a soldier. He was mixing up his words. I couldn't understand him.'

'What kind of soldier? That doesn't make too much sense, Alf.'

'He kept burping while he talked. He said his grandfather was a Texas ranger. What's a Texas ranger?'

Oh, boy, I thought.

'How about Elrod T. Sykes?' I said.

'Yeah, that's it.'

Time for an unlisted number, I thought.

'What was he talking about, Dave?'

'He was probably drunk. Don't pay attention to what drunk people say. If he calls again like that when Bootsie and I aren't here, tell him I'll call him and then hang up.'

'Don't you like him?'

'When a person is drunk, he's sick, Alafair. If you talk to that person while he's drunk, in a funny way you become like him. Don't worry, I'll have a talk with him later.'

'He didn't say anything bad, Dave.'

'But he shouldn't be calling here and bothering little people,' I said, and winked at her. I watched the concern in her face. The corners of her mouth were turned down, and her eyes looked into an empty space above her ice-cream dish. 'You're right, little guy. We shouldn't be mad at people. I think Elrod Sykes is probably an all-right guy. He probably just opens too many bottles in one day sometimes.'

She was smiling again. She had big, wide-set white teeth, and there was a smear of ice cream on her tan cheek. I hugged her shoulders and kissed her on the top of her head.

'I'm going to run now. Watch the shrimp, okay?' I said. 'And no more horseback rides for Tripod. Got it, Alf?'

'Got it, big guy.'

I put on my tennis shoes and running shorts and started down the dirt road toward the drawbridge over the bayou. The rain looked like flecks of spun glass in the air now, and the reflection of the dying sun was blood-red in the water. After a mile I was sweating heavily in the damp air, but I could feel the day's fatigue rise from my body, and I sprang across the puddles and hit it hard all the way to the bridge.

I did leg stretches against the rusted girders and watched the fireflies lighting in the trees and alligator gars turning in the shadows of a flooded canebrake. The sound of the tree frogs and cicadas in the marsh was almost deafening now.

At this time of day, particularly in summer, I always felt a sense of mortality that I could never adequately describe to another person. Sometimes it was like the late sun was about to burn itself into a dead cinder on the earth's rim, never to rise again. It made sweat run down my sides like snakes. Maybe it was because I wanted to believe that summer was an eternal song, that living in your fifty-third year was of no more significance than entering the sixth inning when your sidearm was still like a resilient whip and the prospect of your fork-ball made a batter swallow and step back from the plate.

And if it all ended tomorrow, I should have no complaint, I thought. I could have caught the bus any number of times years ago. To be reminded of that fact I only had to touch the punji-stick scar, coiled like a flattened, gray worm, on my stomach; the shiny, arrow-shaped welts from a bouncing Betty on my thigh; the puckered indentation below my collarbone where a .38 round had cored through my shoulder.

They were not wounds received in a heroic fashion, either. In each case I got them because I did something that was careless or impetuous. I also had tried to destroy myself in increments, a jigger at a time.

Get outside your thoughts, partner, I told myself. I waved to the bridge tender in his tiny house at the far end of the bridge and headed for home.

I poured it on the last half mile, then stopped at the dock and did fifty pushups and stomach crunches on the wood planks that still glowed with the day's heat and smelled of dried fish scales.

I walked up the incline through the trees and the layer of moldy leaves and pecan husks toward the lighted gallery of my house. Then I heard a car behind me on the dirt road and I turned and saw a taxicab stop by my mailbox. A man and woman got out, then the man paid the driver and sent him back toward town.

I rubbed the salt out of my eyes with my forearm and stared through the gloom. The man drained the foam out of a long-necked beer bottle and set the empty behind a tree trunk. Then the woman touched him on the shoulder and pointed toward me.

'Hey, there you are,' Elrod Sykes said. 'How you doin', Mr Robicheaux? You don't mind us coming out, do you? Wow, you've got a great place.'

He swayed slightly. The woman, Kelly Drummond, caught him by the arm. I walked back down the slope.

'I'm afraid I was just going in to take a shower and eat supper,' I said.

'We want to take y'all to dinner,' he said. 'There's this place called Mulate's in Breaux Bridge. They make gumbo you could start a new religion with.'

'Thanks, anyway. My wife's already fixed supper.'

'Bad time of day to knock on doors, El,' Kelly Drummond said, but she looked at me when she said it, her eyes fixed directly on mine. She wore tan slacks, flats, and a yellow blouse with a button open that exposed her bra. When she raised her hand to move a blond ringlet off her forehead, you could see a half-moon sweat stain under her arm.

'We didn't mean to cause a problem,' Elrod said. 'I'm afraid a drunk-front blew through the area this afternoon. Hey, we're all right, though. We took a cab. Did you notice that? How about that? Look, I tell you what, we'll just get us some liquids to go down at that bait shop yonder and call us a cab.'

'Tell him why you came out, El,' Kelly Drummond said.

'That's all right. We stumbled in at a bad time. I'm real sorry, Mr Robicheaux.'

'Call me Dave. Would you mind waiting for me at the bait shop a few minutes, then I'll shower and drive y'all home.'

'You sure know how to avoid the stereotypes, don't you?' the woman said.

'I beg your pardon?' I said.

'Nobody can ever beat up on you for showing off your southern hospitality,' she said.

'Hey, it's okay,' Elrod said, turning her by the arm toward the bait shop.

I had gone only a short distance up the slope when I heard the woman's footsteps behind me.

'Just hold on a minute, Dick Tracy,' she said.

Behind her I could see Elrod walking down the dock to the shop, where Batist, the black man who worked for me, was drawing back the canvas awning over the tables for the night.

'Look, Ms Drummond—'

'You don't have to invite us into your house, you don't have to believe the stuff he says about what he sees and hears, but you ought to know that it took guts for him to come out here. He fucks up with Mikey, he fucks up with this film, maybe he blows it for good this time.'

'You'll have to excuse me, but I'm not sure what that has to do with the Iberia Parish Sheriff's Department.'

She carried a doeskin drawstring bag in her hand. She propped her hand on her hip. She looked up at me and ran her tongue over her bottom lip.

'Are you that dumb?' she asked.

'You're telling me a mob guy, maybe Baby Feet Balboni, is involved with your movie?'

'A mob guy? That's good. I bet y'all really send a lot of them up the road.'

'Where are you from, Ms Drummond?'

'East Kentucky.'

'Have you thought about making your next movie there?'

I started toward the house again.

'Wait a minute, Mr Smart Ass,' she said. 'Elrod respects you. Did you ever hear of the Chicken Ranch in LaGrange, Texas?'

'Yes.'

'Do you know what it was?'

'It was a hot-pillow joint.'

'His mother was a prostitute there. That's why he never talks about anyone in his family except his gran'daddy, the Texas ranger. That's why he likes you, and you'd damn well better be aware of it.'

She turned on her heel, her doeskin bag hitting her rump, and walked erectly down the slope toward the bait shop, where I could see Elrod opening a beer with his pocket knife under the light bulb above the screen door.

Well, you could do a lot worse than have one like her on your side, Elrod, I thought.

I took a shower, dried off, and was buttoning on a fresh shirt in the kitchen when the telephone rang on the counter. Bootsie put down a pan on the stove and answered it.

'It's Batist,' she said, and handed it to me.

'*Qui t'as pr'est faire?*' I said into the receiver.

'Some drunk white man down here done fell in the bayou,' he said.

'What's he doing now?'

'Sittin' in the middle of the shop, drippin' water on my flo'.'

'I'll be there in a minute,' I said.

'Dave, a lady wit' him was smokin' a cigarette out on the dock didn't smell like no tobacco, no.'

'All right, podna. Thanks,' I said, and hung up the phone.

Bootsie was looking at me with a question mark in the middle of her face. Her auburn hair, which she had pinned up in swirls on her head, was full of tiny lights.

'A man fell in the bayou. I have to drive him and his girlfriend home,' I said.

'Where's their car?'

'They came out in a cab.'

'A cab? Who comes fishing in a cab?'

'He's a weird guy.'

'*Dave—*' she said, drawing my name out in exasperation.

'He's one of those actors working out at Spanish Lake. I guess he came out here to tell me about something.'

'Which actor?'

'Elrod Sykes.'

'*Elrod Sykes* is out at the bait shop?'

'Yep.'

'Who's the woman with him?'

'Kelly Drummond.'

'Dave, I don't believe it. You left Kelly Drummond and Elrod Sykes in the bait shop? You didn't invite them in?'

'He's bombed, Boots.'

39

'I don't care. They came out to see you and you left them in the shop while you took a shower?'

'Bootsie, this guy's head glows in the dark, even when he's not on chemicals.'

She went out the front door and down the slope to the bayou. In the mauve twilight I could see her touching at her hair before she entered the bait shop. Five minutes later Kelly Drummond was sitting at our kitchen table, a cup of coffee balanced in her fingers, a reefer-induced wistfulness on her face, while Elrod Sykes changed into dry clothes in our bedroom. He walked into the kitchen in a pair of my sandals, khaki trousers, and the Ragin' Cajuns T-shirt, with my name ironed on the back, that Alafair had given me for Father's Day.

His face was flushed with gin roses, and his gaze drifted automatically to the icebox.

'Would you like a beer?' Bootsie said.

'Yes, if you wouldn't mind,' he said.

'Boots, I think we're out,' I said.

'Oh, that's all right. I really don't need one,' he said.

Bootsie's eyes were bright with embarrassment. Then I saw her face set.

'I'm sure there's one back in here somewhere,' she said, then slid a long-necked Dixie out of the bottom shelf and opened it for him.

Elrod looked casually out the back door while he sipped from the bottle.

'I have to feed the rabbits. You want to take a walk with me, Elrod?' I said.

'The rice will be ready in a minute,' Bootsie said.

'That's all it'll take,' I said.

Outside, under the pecan trees that were now black-green in the fading light, I could feel Elrod watching the side of my face.

'Boy, I don't know quite what to say, Mr Robicheaux, I mean Dave.'

'Don't worry about it. Just tell me what it is you had on your mind all day.'

'It's these guys out yonder on that lake. I told you before.'

'Which guys? What are you talking about?'

'Confederate infantry. One guy in particular, with gold epaulets on his coat. He's got a bad arm and he's missing a leg. I think maybe he's a general.'

'I'll be straight with you. I think maybe you're delusional.'

'A lot of people do. I just didn't think I'd get the same kind of bullshit from you.'

'I'd appreciate it if you didn't use profanity around my home.'

40

'I apologize. But that Confederate officer was saying something. It didn't make sense to me, but I thought it might to you.'

I filled one of the rabbit bowls with alfalfa pellets and latched the screen door on the hutch. I looked at Elrod Sykes. His face was absolutely devoid of guile or any apparent attempt at manipulation; in fact, it reminded me of someone who might have just been struck in the head by a bolt of lightning.

'Look, Elrod, years ago, when I was on the grog, I believed dead people called me up on the telephone. Sometimes my dead wife or members of my platoon would talk to me out of the rain. I was convinced that their voices were real and that maybe I was supposed to join them. It wasn't a good way to be.'

He poured the foam out of his bottle, then flicked the remaining drops reflectively at the bark of a pecan tree.

'I wasn't drunk,' he said. 'This guy with the bad arm and one leg, he said to me, "You and your friend, the police officer in town, must repel them." He was standing by the water, in the fog, on a crutch. He looked right in my face when he said it.'

'I see.'

'What do you think he meant?'

'I'm afraid I wouldn't know, partner.'

'I got the notion he thought you would.'

'I don't want to hurt your feelings, but I think you're imagining all this and I'm not going to pursue it any further. Instead, how about your clarifying something Ms Drummond said earlier?'

'What's that?'

'Why is it a problem to your director, this fellow Mikey, if you come out to my place?'

'She told you that?'

'That's what the lady said.'

'Well, the way he put it was, "Stay out of that cop's face, El. Don't give him reason to be out here causing us trouble. We need to remember that a lot of things happened in this part of the country that are none of our business."'

'He's worried about the dead black man you found?' I said. 'That doesn't make too much sense.'

'You got another one of these?' he said, and held up his empty bottle.

'Why is he worried about the black man?'

'When Mikey worries, it's about money, Mr Robicheaux. Or actually about the money he needs to make the kind of pictures he wants. He did a mini-series for television on the Holocaust. It lost ten million dollars for the network. Nobody's lining up to throw money at Mikey's projects right now.'

41

'Julie Balboni is.'

'You ever heard of a college turning down money from a defense company because it makes napalm?'

He opened and closed his mouth as though he were experiencing cabin pressure in an airplane. The moon was up now, and in the glow of light through the tree branches the skin of his face looked pale and grained, stretched tight against the bone. 'Mr Robicheaux . . . Dave . . . I'm being honest with you, I need a drink.'

'We'd better go inside and get you one, then. I'll make you a deal, though. Maybe you might want to think about going to a meeting with me. I don't necessarily mean that you belong there. But some people think it beats waking up like a chainsaw every morning.'

He looked away at a lighted boat on the bayou.

'It's just a thought. I didn't mean to be intrusive,' I said. 'Let's go inside.'

'You ever see lights out in the cypress trees at night?'

'It's swamp gas. It ignites and rolls across the water's surface like ball lightning.'

'No, sir, that's not what it is,' he said. 'They had lanterns hanging on some of their ambulances. The horses got mired in the bogs. A lot of those soldiers had maggots in their wounds. That's the only reason they lived. The maggots ate out the infection.'

I wasn't going to talk any more about the strange psychological terrain that evidently he had created as a petting zoo for all the protean shapes that lived in his unconscious.

I put the bag of alfalfa pellets on top of the hutches and turned to go back to the house.

'That general said something else,' Elrod said behind me.

I waved my hand negatively and kept walking.

'Well, I cain't blame you for not listening,' he said. 'Maybe I *was* drunk this time. How could your father have his adjutant's pistol?'

I stopped.

'What?' I said.

'The general said, "Your friend's father took the revolver of my adjutant, Major Moss." . . . Hey, Mr Robicheaux, I didn't mean to say the wrong thing, now.'

I chewed on the corner of my lip and waited before I spoke again.

'Elrod, I've got the feeling that maybe I'm dealing with some kind of self-manufactured mojo-drama here,' I said. 'Maybe it's related to the promotion of your film, or it might have something to do with a guy floating his brain in alcohol too long. But no matter how you cut it, I don't want anyone, and I mean *anyone*, to try to use a member of my family to jerk me around.'

42

He turned his palms up and his long eyelashes fluttered.

'I don't know what to say. I apologize to you, sir,' he said. Then his eyes focused on nothing and he pinched his mouth in his hand as though he were squeezing a dry lemon.

At eleven that night I undressed and lay down on the bed next to Bootsie. The window fan billowed the curtains and drew the breeze across the streets, and I could smell watermelons and night-blooming jasmine out in the moonlight. The closet door was open, and I stared at the wooden footlocker that was set back under my hangered shirts and trousers. Bootsie turned her head on the pillow and brushed her fingers along the side of my face.

'Are you mad at me?' she asked.

'No, of course not.'

'They seem to be truly nice people. It would have been wrong not to invite them in.'

'Yeah, they're not bad.'

'But when you came back inside with Elrod, you looked bothered about something. Did something happen?'

'He says he talks with dead people. Maybe he's crazy. I don't know, Boots, I—'

'What is it, Dave?' She raised herself on her elbow and looked into my face.

'He said this dead Confederate general told him that my father took his adjutant's revolver.'

'He had too much to drink, that's all.'

I continued to stare at the closet. She smiled at me and pressed her body against me.

'You had a long day. You're tired,' she said. 'He didn't mean any harm. He probably won't remember what he said tomorrow.'

'You don't understand, Boots,' I said, and sat up on the edge of the bed.

'Understand what?' She put her hand on my bare back. 'Dave, your muscles are tight as iron. What's the matter?'

'Just a minute.'

I didn't want to fall prey to superstition or my own imaginings or Elrod Sykes's manipulations. But I did. I clicked on the table lamp and pulled my old footlocker out of the closet. Inside a half-dozen shoe boxes at the bottom were the memorabilia of my childhood years with my father back in the 1940s: my collections of baseball cards, Indian banner stones and quartz arrow points, and the minié balls that we used to find in a freshly plowed sugarcane field right after the first rain.

I took out a crushed shoe box that was tied with kite twine and sat back down on the bed with it. I slipped off the twine, removed the top of the box, and set it on the nightstand.

'This was the best gift my father ever gave me,' I said. 'On my brother's and my birthday he'd always fix *cush-cush* and sausage for our breakfast, and we'd always find an unusual present waiting for us by our plate. On my twelfth birthday I got this.'

I lifted the heavy revolver out of the box and unwrapped the blackened oil rag from it.

'He had been laid off in the oil field and he took a job tearing down some old slave quarters on a sugar plantation about ten miles down the bayou. There was one cabin separate from the others, with a brick foundation, and he figured it must have belonged to the overseer. Anyway, when he started tearing the boards out of the walls he found some flattened minié balls in the wood, and he knew there had probably been a skirmish between some federals and Confederates around there. Then he tore out what was left of the floor, and in a crawl space, stuck back in the bricks, was this Remington .44 revolver.'

It had been painted with rust and cobweb when my father had found it, the cylinder and hammer frozen against the frame, the wood grips eaten away by mold and insects, but I had soaked it for a week in gasoline and rubbed the steel smooth with emery paper and rags until it had the dull sheen of an old nickel.

'It's just an antique pistol your father gave you, Dave,' she said. 'Maybe you said something about it to Elrod. Then he got drunk and mixed it up with some kind of fantasy he has.'

'No, he said the officer's name.' I opened the nightstand drawer and took out a small magnifying glass. 'He said it had belonged to a Major Moss.'

'So what?'

'Boots, there's a name cut into the trigger guard. I haven't thought about it in years. I couldn't have mentioned it to him.'

I rested the revolver across my thighs and looked through the magnifying glass at the soft glow of light off the brass housing around the trigger. The steel felt cold and slick with oil against my thighs.

'Take a look,' I said, and handed her the glass and the revolver.

She folded her legs under her and squinted one eye through the glass. 'It says "CSA," ' she said.

'Wrong place. Right at the back of the guard.'

She held the pistol closer to the glass. Then she looked up at me and there were white spots in her cheeks.

'J. Moss.' Her voice was dry when she said it. Then she said the name again. 'It says J. Moss.'

'It sure does.'

She wrapped the blackened oil cloth around the pistol and replaced it in the shoe box. She put her hand in mine and squeezed it.

'Dave?'

'Yes?'

'I think Elrod Sykes is a nice man, but we mustn't have him here again.'

She turned out the light, lay back on the pillow, and looked out at the moonlight in the pecan trees, her face caught with a private, troubled thought like the silent beating of a bird's wings inside a cage.

5

Early the next morning the sheriff stopped me in the corridor as I was on my way to my office.

'Special Agent Gomez is here,' he said. A smile worked at the corner of his mouth.

'Where?'

'In your office.'

'So?'

'I think it's a break the FBI's working with us on this one.'

'You told me that before.'

'Yeah, I did, didn't I?' His eyes grew brighter, then he looked away and laughed out loud.

'What's the big joke?' I asked.

'Nothing.' He rubbed his lips with his knuckle, and his eyes kept crinkling at the corners.

'Let me ask you something between insider jokes,' I said. 'Why is the FBI coming in on this one so early? They don't have enough work to do with the resident wiseguys in New Orleans?'

'That's a good question, Dave. Ask Agent Gomez about that and give me feedback later.' He walked off smiling to himself. Uniformed deputies in the corridor were smiling back at him.

I picked up my mail, walked through my office door, and stared at the woman who was sitting in my chair and talking on my telephone. She was looking out the window at a mockingbird on a tree limb while she talked. She turned her head long enough to point to a chair where I could sit down if I wished.

She was short and dark-skinned, and her thick, black hair was chopped stiffly along her neck. Her white suit coat hung on the back of my chair. There was a huge silk bow on her blouse of the sort that Bugs Bunny might wear.

Her eyes flicked back at me again, and she took the telephone receiver away from her ear and slipped her hand over the mouthpiece.

'Have a seat. I'll be right with you,' she said.

'Thank you,' I said.

I sat down, looked idly through my mail, and a moment later heard her put down the phone receiver.

'Can I help you with something?' she asked.

'Maybe. My name's Dave Robicheaux. This is my office.'

Her face colored.

'I'm sorry,' she said. 'A call came in for me on your extension, and I automatically sat behind your desk.'

'It's all right.'

She stood up and straightened her shoulders. Her breasts looked unnaturally large and heavy for a woman her height. She picked up her purse and walked around the desk.

'I'm Special Agent Rosa Gomez,' she said. Then she stuck her hand out, as though her motor control was out of sync with her words.

'It's nice to know you,' I said.

'I think they're putting a desk in here for me.'

'Oh?'

'Do you mind?'

'No, not at all. It's very nice to have you here.'

She remained standing, both of her hands on her purse, her shoulders as rigid as a coat hanger.

'Why don't you sit down, Ms . . . Agent Gomez?'

'Call me Rosie. Everyone calls me Rosie.'

I sat down behind my desk, then noticed that she was looking at the side of my head. Involuntarily I touched my hair.

'You've been with the Bureau a long time?' I said.

'Not really.'

'So you're fairly new?'

'Well, just to this kind of assignment. I mean, out in the field, that sort of thing.' Her hands looked small on top of her big purse. I think it took everything in her to prevent them from clenching with anxiety. Then her eyes focused again on the side of my head.

'I have a white patch in my hair,' I said.

She closed then opened her eyes with embarrassment.

'Someone once told me I have skunk blood in me,' I said.

'I think I'm doing a lot of wrong things this morning,' she said.

'No, you're not.'

But somebody at Fart, Barf, and Itch is, I thought.

Then she sat erect in her chair and concentrated her vision on something outside the window until her face became composed again.

'The sheriff said you don't believe we're dealing with a serial killer or a random killing,' she said.

47

'That's not quite how I put it. I told him, I think she knew the killer.'

'Why?'

'Her father appears to have been a child molester. She was streetwise herself. She had one prostitution beef when she was sixteen. Yesterday I found out she was still hooking – out of a club in St Martinville. A girl like that doesn't usually get forced into cars in front of crowded jukejoints.'

'Maybe she went off with a john.'

'Not without her purse. She left it at her table. In it we found some—'

'Rubbers,' she said.

'That's right. So I don't think it was a john. In her car we found a carton of cigarettes, a brand-new hairbrush, and a half-dozen joints in a Baggy in the trunk. I think she went outside to get some cigarettes, a joint, or the hairbrush, she saw somebody she knew, got in his car, and never came back.'

'Maybe it was an old customer, somebody she trusted. Maybe he told her he just wanted to get something up for later.'

'It doesn't fit. A john doesn't pay one time, then come back the next time with a razor blade or scalpel.'

She put her thumbnail between her teeth. Her eyes were brown and had small lights in them.

'Then you think the killer is from this area, she knew him, and she trusted him enough to get in the car with him?'

'I think it's something like that.'

'We think he's a psychopath, possibly a serial killer.'

'*We?*'

'Well, actually *I*. I had a behavioral profile run on him. Everything he did indicates a personality that seeks control and dominance. During the abduction, the rape, the killing itself, he was absolutely in control. He becomes sexually aroused by power, by instilling fear and loathing in a woman, by being able to smother her with his body. In all probability he has ice water in his veins.'

I nodded and moved some paper clips around on my desk blotter.

'You don't seem impressed,' she said.

'What do you make of the fact that he covered her face with her blouse?' I said.

'Blindfolding humiliates the victim and inspires even greater terror in her.'

'Yeah, I guess it does.'

'But you don't buy the profile.'

'I'm not too keen on psychoanalysis. I belong to a twelve-step fellowship that subscribes to the notion that most bad or evil behavior is generated by what we call a self-centered fear. I think our man was afraid of Cherry LeBlanc. I don't think he could look into her eyes while he raped her.'

She reached for a folder she had left on the corner of my desk.

'Do you know how many similar unsolved murders of women have been committed in the state of Louisiana in the last twenty-five years?'

'I sent in an information-search request to Baton Rouge yesterday.'

'We have an unfair advantage on you in terms of resources,' she said. She leafed through the printouts that were clipped together at the top of the folder. Behind her, I saw two uniformed deputies grinning at me through the glass in my office partition.

'Excuse me,' I said, got up, closed the door, and sat back down again.

'Is this place full of comedians?' she said. 'I seem to make a lot of people smile.'

'Some of them don't get a lot of exposure to the outside world.'

'Anyway, narrowing it down to the last ten years, there are at least seventeen unsolved homicides involving females that share some similarity with the murder of Cherry LeBlanc. You want to take a look?' she said, and handed me the folder. 'I have to go down to the sheriff's office and get my building keys. I'll be right back.'

It was grim material to read. There was nothing abstruse about the prose. It was unimaginative, flat, brutally casual in its depiction of the bestial potential among the human family, like a banal rendering of our worst nightmares: slasher cases, usually involving prostitutes; the garroting of housewives who had been abducted in broad daylight in supermarket and bowling-alley parking lots; the roadside murders of women whose cars had broken down at night; prostitutes who had probably been set on fire by their pimps; the drowning of two black women who had been wrapped to an automobile engine block with barbed wire.

In almost all the cases rape, sodomy, or torture of some kind was involved. And what bothered me most was the fact that the perpetrators were probably still out there, unless they were doing time for other crimes; few of them had known their victims, and consequently few of them would ever be caught.

Then I noticed that Rosie Gomez had made check marks in the margins by six cases that shared more common denominators with the death of Cherry LeBlanc than the others: three runaways who had been found buried off highways in a woods; a high school girl who had been raped, tied to a tree in a fish camp at Lake Chicot, and shot at point-blank range; two waitresses who had gone off from their jobs without explanation and a few hours later had been thrown, bludgeoned to death, into irrigation ditches.

Their bodies had all showed marks, in one way or another, of having been bound. They all had been young, working class, and perhaps unsuspecting when a degenerate had come violently and irrevocably into their lives and had departed without leaving a sign of his identity.

My respect for Rosie Gomez's ability was appreciating.

She walked back through the door, clipping two keys onto a ring.

'You want to talk while we take a ride out to Spanish Lake?' I said.

'What's at Spanish Lake?'

'A movie director I'd like to meet.'

'What's that have to do with our case?'

'Probably nothing. But it beats staying indoors.'

'Sure. I have to make a call to the Bureau, then I'll be right with you.'

'Let me ask you an unrelated question,' I said.

'Sure.'

'If you found the remains of a black man, and he had on no belt and there were no laces in his boots, what speculation might you make about him?'

She looked at me with a quizzical smile.

'He was poor?' she said.

'Could be. In fact, someone else told me about the same thing in a less charitable way.'

'No,' she said. She looked thoughtfully into space, puffed out one jaw, then the other, like a chipmunk might. 'No, I'd bet he'd been in jail, in a parish or a city holding unit of some kind, where they were afraid he'd do harm to himself.'

'That's not bad,' I said. Not at all, I thought. 'Well, let's take a ride.'

I waited for her outside in the shade of the building. I was sweating inside my shirt, and the sunlight off the cement parking lot made my eyes film. Two of the uniformed deputies who had been grinning through my glass earlier came out the door with clipboards in their hands, then stopped when they saw me. The taller one, a man named Rufus Arceneaux, took a matchstick out of his mouth and smiled at me from behind his shades.

'Hey, Dave,' he said, 'does that gal wear a Bureau buzzer on each of her boobs or is she just a little top-heavy?'

They were both grinning now. I could hear bottleflies buzzing above an iron grate in the shade of the building.

'You guys can take this for what it's worth,' I said. 'I don't want you to hold it against me, either, just because I outrank you or something like that. Okay?'

'You gotta make plainclothes before you get any federal snatch?' Arceneaux said, and put the matchstick back in the corner of his mouth.

I put on my sunglasses, folded my seersucker coat over my arm, and looked across the street at a black man selling rattlesnake watermelons off the tailgate of a pickup truck.

'If y'all want to act like public clowns, that's your business,' I said. 'But you'd better wipe that stupid expression off your faces when you're around my partner. Also, if I hear you making remarks about her, either to me or somebody else, we're going to take it up in a serious way. You get my drift?'

Arceneaux rotated his head on his neck, then pulled the front of his shirt loose from his damp skin with his fingers.

'Boy, it's hot, ain't it?' he said. 'I think I'm gonna come in this afternoon and take a cold shower. You ought to try it too, Dave. A cold shower might get the wrong thing off your mind.'

They walked into the shimmering haze, their leather holsters and cartridge belts creaking on their hips, the backs of their shirts peppered with sweat.

Rosie Gomez and I turned off the highway in my pickup truck and drove down the dirt lane through the pecan orchard toward Spanish Lake, where we could see elevated camera platforms and camera booms silhouetted against the sun's reflection on the water. A chain was hung across the road between a post and the side of the wood-frame security building. The security guard, the wiry man with the white scar embossed on his throat like a chicken's foot, approached my window. His face looked pinched and heated in the shadow of his bill cap.

I showed him my badge.

'Yeah, y'all go on in,' he said. 'You remember me, Detective Robicheaux?'

His hair was gray, cut close to the scalp, and his skin was browned and as coarse as a lizard's from the sun. His blue eyes seemed to have an optical defect of some kind, a nervous shudder like marbles clicking on a plate.

'It's Doucet, isn't it?' I said.

'Yes, sir, Murphy Doucet. You got a good memory. I used to be with the Jefferson Parish Sheriff's Department when you were with NOPD.'

His stomach was as flat as a shingle. He wore a .357 chromeplated revolver, and also a clip-on radio, a can of Mace, and a rubber baton on his belt.

'It looks like you're in the movie business now,' I said.

'Just for a while. I own half of a security service now and I'm a steward for the Teamsters out of Lafayette, too. So I'm kind of on board both ways here.'

'This is Special Agent Gomez from the FBI. We'd like to talk to Mr Goldman a few minutes if he's not too busy.'

'Is there been some kind of trouble?'

'Is Mr Goldman here?'

'Yes, sir, that's him right up yonder in the trees. I'll tell him y'all on your way.' He started to take his radio off his belt.

'That's all right. We'll find him.'

'Yes, sir, anything you say.'

He dropped the chain and waited for us to pass. In the rearview mirror I saw him hook it to the post again. Rosie Gomez was looking at the side of my face.

'What is it?' she said.

'The Teamsters. Why does a Hollywood production company want to come into a depressed rural area and contract for services from the Teamsters? They can hire labor around here for minimum wage.'

'Maybe they do business with unions as a matter of course.'

'Nope, they usually try to leave their unions back in California. I've got a feeling this has something to do with Julie Balboni being on board the ark.'

I watched her expression. She looked straight ahead.

'You know who Baby Feet Balboni is, don't you?' I said.

'Yes, Mr Balboni is well known to us.'

'You know he's in New Iberia, too, don't you?'

She waited before she spoke again. Her small hands were clenched on her purse.

'What's your implication?' she said.

'I think the Bureau has more than one reason for being in town.'

'You think the girl's murder has secondary importance to me?'

'No, not to you.'

'But probably to the people I work under?'

'You'd know that better than I.'

'You don't think well of us, do you?'

'My experience with the Bureau was never too good. But maybe the problem was mine. As the Bible says, I used to look through a glass darkly. Primarily because there was Jim Beam in it most of the time.'

'The Bureau's changed.'

'Yeah, I guess it has.'

Yes, I thought, they hired racial minorities and women at gunpoint, and they stopped wire-tapping civil-rights leaders and smearing innocent people's reputations after their years of illegal surveillance and character assassination were finally exposed.

I parked the truck in the shade of a moss-hung live-oak tree, and we walked toward the shore of the lake, where a dozen people listened attentively to a man in a canvas chair who waved his arms while he talked, jabbed his finger in the air to make a point, and shrugged his powerful shoulders as though he were desperate in his desire to be understood. His voice, his manner, made me think of a hurricane stuffed inside a pair of white tennis shorts and a dark-blue polo shirt.

'—the best fucking story editor in that fucking town,' he was saying. 'I don't care what those assholes say, they couldn't carry my fucking jock strap. When we come out of the cutting room with that, it's going to be solid fucking gold. Has everybody got that? This is a great picture. Believe it, they're going to spot their pants big time on this one.'

His strained face looked like a white balloon that was about to burst. But even while his histrionics grew to awesome levels and inspired mute reverence in his listeners, his eyes drifted to me and Rosie, and I had a feeling that Murphy Doucet, the security guard, had used his radio after all.

When we introduced ourselves and showed him our identification, he said, 'Do you have telephones where you work?'

'I beg your pardon?' I said.

'Do you have telephones where you work? Do you have people there who know how to make appointments for you?'

'Maybe you don't understand, Mr Goldman. During a criminal investigation we don't make appointments to talk to people.'

His face flexed as though it were made of white rubber.

'You saying you're out here investigating some crime? What crime we talking about here?' he said. 'You see a crime around here?' He swiveled his head around. 'I don't see one.'

'We can talk down at the sheriff's office if you wish,' Rosie said.

He stared at her as though she had stepped through a hole in the dimension.

'Do you have any idea of what it costs to keep one hundred and fifty people standing around while I'm playing pocket pool with somebody's *criminal* investigation?' he said.

'You heard what she said. What's it going to be, partner?' I asked.

'*Partner?*' he said, looking out at the lake with a kind of melancholy disbelief on his face. 'I think I screwed up in an earlier incarnation. I probably had something to do with the sinking of the *Titanic* or the assassination of the Archduke Ferdinand. That's gotta be it.'

Then he rose and faced me with the flat glare of a boxer waiting for the referee to finish with the ring instructions.

'You want to take a walk or go in my trailer?' he said. 'The air conditioner in my trailer is broken. You could fry eggs on the toilet seat. What d'you want to do?'

'This is fine,' I said.

'Fine, huh?' he said, as though he were addressing some cynical store of private knowledge within himself. 'What is it you want to say, Mr Robicheaux?'

He walked along the bank of the lake, his hair curling out of his polo shirt like bronze wire. His white tennis shorts seemed about to rip at the seams on his muscular buttocks and thighs.

'I understand that you've cautioned some of your people to stay away from me. Is that correct?' I said.

'What people? What are you talking about?'

'I believe you know what I'm talking about.'

'Elrod and his voices out in the fog? Elrod and skeletons buried in a sandbar? You think I care about stuff like that? You think that's what's on my mind when I'm making a picture?' He stopped and jabbed a thick finger at me. 'Hey, try to understand something here. I live with my balls in a skillet. It's a way of life. I got no interest, I got no involvement, in people's problems in a certain locale. Is that supposed to be bad? Is it all right for me to tell my actors what I think? Are we all still working on a First Amendment basis here?'

A group of actors in sweat-streaked gray and blue uniforms, eating hamburgers out of foam containers, walked past us. I turned and suddenly realized that Rosie was no longer with us.

'She probably stepped in a hole,' Goldman said.

'I think you *are* worried about something, Mr Goldman. I think we both know what it is, too.'

He took a deep breath. The sunlight shone through the oak branches over his head and made shifting patterns of shadow on his face.

'Let me try to explain something to you,' he said. 'Most everything in the film world is an illusion. An actor is somebody who never liked what he was. So he makes up a person and that's what he becomes. You think John Wayne came out of the womb John Wayne? He and a screenwriter created a character that was a cross between Captain Bly and Saint Francis of Assisi, and the Duke played it till he dropped.

'Elrod's convinced himself he has magic powers. Why? Because he melted his head five years ago and he has days when he can't tie his shoestrings without a diagram. So instead of admitting that maybe he's got baked mush between his ears, he's a mystic, a persecuted clairvoyant.'

'Let's cut the dog shit, Mr Goldman. You're in business with Baby Feet Balboni. *That's* your problem, not Elrod Sykes.'

'Wrong.'

'You know what a "fall partner" is?'

'No.'

'A guy who goes down on the same bust with you.'

'So?'

54

'Julie doesn't have fall partners. His hookers do parish time for him, his dealers do it for him in Angola, his accountants do it in Atlanta and Lewisburg. I don't think Julie has ever spent a whole day in the bag.'

'Neither have I. Because I don't break the law.'

'I think he'll cannibalize you.'

He looked away from me, and I saw his hands clench and unclench and the veins pulse in his neck.

'You look here,' he said. 'I worked nine years on a mini-series about the murder of six million people. I went to Auschwitz and set up cameras on the same spots the SS used to photograph the people being pulled out of the boxcars and herded with dogs to the ovens. I've had survivors tell me I'm the only person who ever described on film what they actually went through. I don't give a fuck what any critic says, that series will last a thousand years. You get something straight, Mr Robicheaux. People might fuck me over as an individual, but they'll never fuck me over as a director. You can take that to the bank.'

His pale eyes protruded from his head like marbles.

I looked back at him silently.

'There's something else?' he said.

'No, not really.'

'So why the stare? What's going on?'

'Nothing. I think you're probably a sincere man. But as someone once told me, hubris is a character defect better left to the writers of tragedy.'

He pressed his fingers on his chest.

'I got a problem with pride, you're saying?'

'I think Jimmy Hoffa was probably the toughest guy the labor movement ever produced,' I said. 'Then evidently he decided that he and the mob could have a fling at the dirty boogie together. I used to know a button man in New Orleans who told me they cut Hoffa into hundreds of pieces and used him for fish chum. I believe what he said, too.'

'Sounds like your friend ought to take it to a grand jury.'

'He can't. Three years ago one of Julie's hired lowlifes put a crack in his skull with a cold chisel. Just for kicks. He sells snowballs out of a cart in front of the K & B drugstore on St Charles now. We'll see you around, Mr Goldman.'

I walked away through the dead leaves and over a series of rubber-coated power cables that looked like a tangle of black snakes. When I looked back at Mikey Goldman, his eyes were staring disjointedly into space.

6

Rosie was waiting for me by the side of the pickup truck under the live-oak tree. The young sugarcane in the fields was green and bending in the wind. She fanned herself with a manila folder she had picked up off the truck seat.

'Where did you go?' I asked.

'To talk to Hogman Patin.'

'Where is he?'

'Over there, with those other black people, under the trees. He's playing a street musician in the film.'

'How'd you know to talk to him?'

'You put his name in the case file, and I recognized him from his picture on one of his albums.'

'You're quite a cop, Rosie.'

'Oh, I see. You didn't expect that from an agent who's short, Chicana, and a woman?'

'It was meant as a compliment. How about saving that stuff for the right people? What did Hogman have to say?'

Her eyes blinked at the abruptness of my tone.

'I'm sorry,' I said. 'I didn't mean to sound like that. I still have my mind on Goldman. I think he's hiding some serious problems, and I think they're with Julie Balboni. I also think there might be a tie-in between Julie and Cherry LeBlanc.'

She looked off at the group of black people under the trees.

'You didn't bother to tell me that earlier,' she said.

'I wasn't sure about it. I'm still not.'

'Dave, I'll be frank with you. Before I came here I read some of your history. You seem to have a way of doing things on your own. Maybe you've been in situations where you had no other choice. But I can't have a partner who holds out information on me.'

'It's a speculation, Rosie, and I just told you about it.'

'Where do you think there might be a tie-in?' she said, and her face became clear again.

'I'm not sure. But one of his hoods, a character named Cholo Manelli, told me that he and Julie had been talking about the girl's death. Then ten minutes later Julie told me he hadn't heard or read anything about it. So one of them is lying, and I think it's Julie.'

'Why not the hood, what's his name, Cholo?'

'When a guy like Cholo lies or tries to jerk somebody around, he doesn't involve his boss's name. He has no doubt about how dangerous that can be. Anyway, what did you get from Hogman?'

'Not much. He just pointed at you and said, "Tell that other one yonder ain't every person innocent, ain't every person listen when they ought to, either." What do you make of that?'

'Hogman likes to be an enigma.'

'Those scars on his arms—'

'He had a bunch of knife beefs in Angola. Back in the 1940s he murdered a white burial-insurance collector who was sleeping with his wife. Hogman's a piece of work, believe me. The hacks didn't know how to deal with him. They put him in the sweat box on Camp A for eighteen days one time.'

'How'd he kill the white man?'

'With a cane knife on the white man's front gallery. In broad daylight. People around here talked about that one for a long time.'

I could see a thought working in her eyes.

'He's not a viable suspect, Rosie,' I said.

'Why not?'

'Hogman's not a bad guy. He doesn't trust white people much, and he's a little prideful, but he wouldn't hurt a nineteen-year-old girl.'

'That's it? *He's not a bad guy*? Although he seems to have a lifetime history of violence with knives? Good God.'

'Also the nightclub owner says Hogman never left the club that night.'

She got in the truck and closed the door. Her shoulders were almost below the level of the window. I got in on the driver's side and started the engine.

'Well, that clears all that up, then,' she said. 'I guess the owner kept his eyes on our man all night. You all certainly have an interesting way of conducting an investigation.'

'I'll make you a deal. I'll talk with Hogman again if you'll check out this fellow Murphy Doucet.'

'Because he's with the Teamsters?'

'That's right. Let's find out how these guys developed an interest in the War Between the States.'

'You know what "transfer" is in psychology?'

'What's the point?'

'Earlier you suggested that maybe I had a private agenda about Julie Balboni. Do you think that perhaps it's you who's taking the investigation into a secondary area?'

'Could be. But you can't ever tell what'll fly out of the tree until you throw a rock into it.'

It was a flippant thing to say. But at the time it seemed innocent and of little more consequence than the warm breeze blowing across the cane and the plum-colored thunderclouds that were building out over the Gulf.

Sam 'Hogman' Patin lived on the bayou south of town in a paintless wood-frame house overgrown with banana trees and with leaf-clogged rain gutters and screens that were orange with rust. The roof was patched with R. C. Cola signs, the yard a tangle of weeds, automobile and washing-machine parts, morning-glory vines, and pig bones; the gallery and one corner of the house sagged to one side like a broken smile.

I had waited until later in the day to talk to him at his house. I knew that he wouldn't have talked to me in front of other people at the movie set, and actually I wasn't even sure that he would tell me anything of importance now. He had served seventeen years in Angola, the first four of which he had spent on the Red Hat gang. These were the murderers, the psychotics, and the uncontrollable. They wore black-and-white stripes and straw hats that had been dipped in red paint, always ran double-time under the mounted gunbulls, and were punished on anthills, in cast-iron sweatboxes, or with the Black Betty, a leather whip that could flay a man's back to marmalade.

Hogman would probably still be in there, except he got religion and a Baptist preacher in Baton Rouge worked a pardon for him through the state legislature. His backyard was dirt, deep in shadow from the live-oak trees, and sloped away to the bayou, where a rotted-out pirogue webbed with green algae lay half-submerged in the shallows. He sat in a straight-backed wood chair under a tree that was strung with blue Milk of Magnesia bottles and crucifixes fashioned out of sticks and aluminum foil. When the breeze lifted out of the south, the whole tree sang with silver and blue light.

Hogman tightened the key on a new string he had just strung on his guitar. His skin was so black it had a purple sheen to it; and his hair was grizzled, the curls ironed flat against his head. His shoulders were an ax handle wide, the muscles in his upper arms the size of grapefruit. There wasn't a tablespoon of fat on his body. I wondered what it must have been like to face down Hogman Patin back in the days when he carried a barber's razor on a leather cord around his neck.

58

'What did you want to tell me, Sam?' I asked.

'One or two t'ings that been botherin' me. Get a chair off the po'ch. You want some tea?'

'No, that's fine, thank you.'

I lifted a wicker chair off the back porch and walked back to the oak tree with it. He had slipped three metal picks onto his fingers and was running a blues progression up the neck of the guitar. He mashed the strings into the frets so that the sound continued to reverberate through the dark wood after he had struck the notes with his steel picks. Then he tightened the key again and rested the big curved belly of the twelve-string on his thigh.

'I don't like to have no truck with folks' bidness,' he said. 'But it bother me, what somebody done to that girl. It been botherin' me a whole lot.'

He picked up from the dirt a jelly glass filled with iced tea and drank out of it.

'She was messin' in somet'ing bad, wouldn't listen to me or pay me no mind about it, neither. When they that age, they know what they wanta do.'

'Messing in what?'

'I talked to her maybe two hours befo' she left the juke. I been knowing that girl a long time. She love zydeco and blues music. She tell me, "Hogman, in the next life me and you is gonna get married." That's what she say. I tole her, "Darlin', don't let them mens use you for no chicken."

'She say, "I ain't no chicken, Hogman. I going to New Orleans. I gonna have my own coop. Them others gonna be the chickens. I gonna have me a townhouse on Lake Pontchartrain." '

'Wait a minute, Sam. She told you she was going to have other girls working for her?'

'That's what I just tole you, ain't I?'

'Yes, you did.'

'I say, "Don't be talkin' like that. You get away from them pimps, Cherry. Them white trash ain't gonna give you no townhouse. They'll use you up, t'row you away, then find some other girl just like you, I mean in five minutes, that quick."

'She say, "No, they ain't, 'cause I got the mojo on the Man, Hogman. He know it, too."

'You know, when she say that, she smile up at me and her face look heart shape, like she just a little girl doin' some innocent t'ing 'stead of about to get herself killed.'

'What man did she mean?'

'Probably some pimp tole her she special, she pretty, she just like a

59

daughter to him. I seen the same t'ing in Angola. It ain't no different. A bunch take a young boy down on the flo', then when they get finish with him, he ready, he glad to put on a dress, make-up, be the punk for some wolf gonna take care of him, tell him he ain't just somebody's poke chops in the shower stall.'

'Why'd you wait to tell me this?'

''Cause ain't nothin' like this ever happen 'round here befo'. I don't like it, me. No, suh.'

'I see.'

He splayed his long fingers on the belly of the guitar. The nails were pink against his black skin. His eyes looked off reflectively at the bayou, where fireflies were lighting in the gloom above the flooded cattails.

Finally he said, 'I need to tell you somet'ing else.'

'Go ahead, Sam.'

'You mixed up with that skeleton they found over in the Atchafalaya, ain't you?'

'How'd you know about that?'

'When somebody find a dead black man, black people know about it. That man didn't have on no belt, didn't have no strings in his boots, did he?'

'That wasn't in the newspaper, podna.'

'The preacher they call up to do the burial is my first cousin. He brought a suit of clothes to the mo'tuary to dress the bones in. They was a black man workin' there, and my cousin say, "That fella was lynched, wasn't he?" The black man say, "Yeah, they probably drug him out of bed to do it, too. Didn't even have time to put strings in his boots or run a belt through his britches."'

'What are you telling me, Sam?'

'I remember somet'ing, a long time ago, maybe thirty, thirty-five years back.' He patted one hand on top of the other and his eyes became muddy.

'Just say it, Sam.'

'A bluejay don't set on a mockin'bird's nest. I ain't got no use for that stuff in people, neither. The Lord made people a different color for a reason.'

He shook his head back and forth, as though he were dispelling a troubling thought.

'You're not talking about a rape, are you?'

'White folk call it rape when it fit what they want,' he said. 'They see what they need to see. Black folk cain't be choicy. They see what they gots to see. They was a black man, no, that ain't right, this is a nigger I'm talkin' about, and he was carryin' on with a white woman whose husband he worked for. Black folk knowed it, too. They tole him he better stop what he doin' befo' the cars start comin' down in the quarters and some innocent black man end up on a tree. I t'ink them was the bones you drug up in that sandbar.'

'What was his name?'

'Who care what his name? Maybe he got what he ax for. But them people who done that still out there. I say past is past. I say don't be messin' in it.'

'Are you cautioning me?'

'When I was in the pen, yo' daddy, Mr Aldous, brought my mother food. He care for her when she sick, he pay for her medicine up at the sto'. I ain't forgot that, me.'

'Sam, if you have information about a murder, the law requires that you come forward with it.'

'Whose law? The law that run that pen up there? You want to find bodies, go dig in that levee for some of them boys the gunbulls shot down just for pure meanness. I seen it.' He touched the corner of his eye with one long finger. 'The hack get drunk on corn liquor, single out some boy on the wheelbarrow, hollor out, "Yow! You! Nigger! Run!" Then he'd pop him with his .45, just like bustin' a clay duck.'

'What was the white woman's name?'

'I got to be startin' my supper now.'

'Was the dead man in a jail?'

'Ain't nobody interested back then, ain't nobody interested now. You give it a few mo' years, we all gonna be dead. You ain't goin' change nothin' for a nigger been in the river thirty years. You want to do some good, catch the pimp tore up that young girl. 'Cause sho' as God made little green apples, he gonna do it again.'

He squinted one eye in a shaft of sunlight that fell through the tree branches and lighted one half of his face like an ebony stage mask that was sewn together from mismatched parts.

It was almost dusk when I got home that evening, but the sky was still as blue as a robin's egg in the west and the glow of the late sun looked like pools of pink fire in the clouds. After I ate supper, I walked down to the bait shop to help Batist close up. I was pulling back the canvas awning on the guy wires over the spool tables when I saw the sheriff's car drive down the dirt road and park under the trees.

He walked down the dock toward me. His face looked flushed from the heat, puffy with fatigue.

'I guarantee you, it's been one scorcher of a day,' he said, went inside the shop, and came back with a sweating bottle of orange pop in his hand. He sat down at a table and wiped the sweat off his neck with his handkerchief. Grains of ice slid down the neck of the pop bottle.

'What's up, sheriff?' I said.

'Have you seen Rosie this afternoon?' He took a drink out of the bottle.

I sat down across from him. Waves from a passing boat slapped against the pilings under the dock.

'We went out to the movie location, then she went to Lafayette to check out a couple of things,' I said.

'Yeah, that's why I'm here.'

'What do you mean?'

'I've gotten about a half-dozen phone calls this afternoon. I'm not sure what you guys are doing, Dave.'

'Conducting a murder investigation.'

'Oh, yeah? What does the director of a motion picture have to do with the death of Cherry LeBlanc?'

'Goldman got in your face?'

'*He* didn't. But you seem to have upset a few other people around here. Let's see, I received calls from two members of the Chamber of Commerce; Goldman's lawyer, who says you seem to be taking an undue interest in our visiting film community; and the mayor, who'd like to know what the hell my people think they're doing. If that wasn't enough, I also got a call from a Teamster official in Lafayette and a guy named Twinky Hebert Lemoyne who runs a bottling plant over there. Are you two working on some kind of negative outreach program? What was she doing over in Lafayette Parish?'

'Ask her.'

'I have a feeling she was sent over there.'

'She was checking out the Teamsters' involvement with Goldman and Julie Balboni.'

'What does that have to do with our investigation?'

'I'm not sure. Maybe nothing. What did this guy Twinky Lemoyne call about?'

'He owns half of a security service with a guy named Murphy Doucet. Lemoyne said Rosie came out to his bottling plant, asked him questions that were none of her business, and told him that he should give second thought to doing business with the mob. Do you know who Twinky Lemoyne is?'

'Not really.'

'He's a wealthy and respected man in Lafayette. In fact, he's a decent guy. What are y'all trying to do, Dave?'

'You sent me to invite Julie Balboni out of town. But now we find that Julie has made himself a big part of the local economy. I think that's the problem, sheriff, not me and Rosie.'

He rubbed his whiskers with the backs of his fingers.

'Maybe it is,' he said finally, 'but there's more than one way to do things.'

'What would you suggest that we do differently?'

His eyes studied a turkey buzzard that floated on the hot-air currents above the marsh.

'Concentrate on nailing this psychopath. For the time being forget about Balboni,' he said. His eyes didn't come back to meet mine when he spoke.

'Maybe Julie's involved.'

'He's not. Julie doesn't do anything unless it's for money.'

'I'm getting the strong feeling that the Spanish Lake area is becoming off limits.'

'No, I didn't say that. It's a matter of priorities. That brings up another subject, too – the remains of that black man you found out in the Atchafalaya Basin.'

'Yes?'

'That's St Mary Parish's jurisdiction. Let them work the case. We've got enough on our own plate.'

'They're not going to work it.'

'Then that's their choice.'

I didn't speak for a moment. The twilight was almost gone. The air was heavy and moist and full of insects, and out in the cypress I could hear wood ducks fluttering across the surface of the water.

'Would you like another cold drink?' I asked.

'No, this is fine,' he answered.

'I'd better help Batist lock up, then. We'll see you, sheriff,' I said, and went inside the bait shop. I didn't come back out until I heard his car start and head down the dirt road.

Sam 'Hogman' Patin was wrong. Cherry LeBlanc's killer would not merely find another victim in the future. He already had.

7

I got the call at eleven o'clock that night. A fisherman running a trotline by the levee, way down in the bottom of Vermilion Parish, almost to the salt water, had seen a lidless oil drum half submerged on its side in the cattails. He would have paid little attention to it, except for the fact that he saw the backs of alligator gars arching out of the water in the moonlight as they tore at something inside the barrel.

I drove down the narrow dirt track on top of the levee through the miles of flooded sawgrass that eventually bled into the Gulf. Strips of black cloud floated across the moon, and up ahead I could see an ambulance and a collection of sheriff's cars parked on the levee in a white and red glow of floodlamps, burning flares, and revolving emergency lights.

The girl was already in a body bag inside the ambulance. The coroner was a tired, overweight Jewish man with emphysema and a terrible cigarette odor whom I had known for years. There were deep circles under his eyes, and he kept rubbing mosquito repellent onto his face and fat arms.

Down the bank a Vermilion Parish plainclothes was interviewing the fisherman, whose unshaven face looked bloodless and gray in the glare of the floodlamps.

'You want to see her, Dave?' the coroner asked.

'Should I?'

'Probably.'

We climbed into the back of the ambulance. Even with the air conditioner running, it was hot and stale-smelling inside.

'I figure she was in the water only a couple of days, but she's probably been dead several weeks,' he said. 'The barrel was probably on the side of the levee, then it rolled into the water. Otherwise, the crabs and the gars would have torn her up a lot worse.'

He pulled the zipper from the girl's head all the way down to her ankles.

I took a breath and swallowed.

'I'd say she was in her early twenties, but I'm guessing,' he said. 'And you can see, we won't get much in the way of prints. I don't think an artist will be able to recreate what her face looked like, either. Cause of death doesn't appear to be a mystery – asphyxiation with a plastic bag taped around her neck. The same electrician's tape he used to bind her hands and ankles. Rape, sodomy, sexual degradation, that kind of stuff. When their clothes are gone, you can put it in the bank.'

'No rings, bracelets, tattoos?'

He shook his head.

'Have they found anything out there?'

'Nothing.'

'Tire tracks?'

'Not after all the rain we've had.'

'Do y'all have any missing-persons reports that coincide with—'

'Nope.'

A long strand of her blond hair hung outside the bag. For some reason it bothered me. I picked it up and placed it on her forehead. The coroner looked at me strangely.

'Why would he stuff her in a barrel?' I said.

'Dave, the day you can put yourself inside the head of a cocksucker like that, that's the day you eat your gun.'

I stepped back outside into the humid brilliance of the floodlamps, then walked along the slope of the levee and down by the water's edge. The darkness throbbled with the croaking of frogs, and fireflies were lighting in the tops of the sawgrass. The weeds along the levee had been trampled by cops' feet; fresh cigarette butts floated in the water; a sheriff's deputy was telling two others a racial joke.

The Vermilion Parish plainclothes finished interviewing the fisher-man, put his notebook in his shirt pocket, and walked up the slope to his car. The fisherman continued to stand by his pirogue, scratching at the mosquito bites on his arms, evidently unsure of what he was supposed to do next. Sweat leaked out of the band of his cloth cap and glistened on his jawbones. When I introduced myself, his handshake, like most Cajun men's, was effeminate.

'I ain't never seen nothing like that, me,' he said. 'I don't want to never see nothing like that again, neither.'

The bottom of his pirogue was piled with mudcat. They quivered on top of each other, their whiskers pasted back against their yellow sides and bloated white bellies. On the seat of his pirogue was a headlamp with an elastic strap on it.

'When'd you first see that metal barrel?' I said.

'Tonight.'

'Do you come down here often?' I asked.

'Not too often, no, suh.'

'You've got a nice bunch of fish there.'

'Yeah, they feed good when the moon's up.'

I gazed into the bottom of his pirogue, at the wet shine of moonlight on the fish's sides, the tangles of trotlines and corks, and a long object wrapped in a canvas tarp under the seat.

I caught the pirogue by the gunwale and slid it partly up on the mudbank.

'Do you mind if I look at this?' I said, and flipped back the folds of the canvas tarp.

He didn't answer. I took a pen flashlight out of my shirt pocket and shone it on the lever-action .30-.30 rifle. The bluing was worn off and the stock was wrapped with copper wire.

'Walk down here a little ways with me,' I said.

He followed me out to the edge of the lighted area, out of earshot of the Vermilion Parish deputies.

'We want to catch the guy who did this,' I said. 'I think you'd like to help us do that, wouldn't you?'

'Yes, suh, I sho' would.'

'But there's a problem here, isn't there? Something that's preventing you from telling me everying you want to?'

'I ain't real sho' what you—'

'Are you selling fish to restaurants?'

'No, suh, that ain't true.'

'Did you bring that .30-.30 along to shoot frogs?'

He grinned and shook his head. I grinned back at him.

'But you might just poach a 'gator or two?' I said.

'No, suh, I ain't got no 'gator. You can look.'

I let my expression go flat.

'That's right. So you don't have to be afraid,' I said. 'I just want you to tell me the truth. Nobody's going to bother you about that gun, or your headlamp, or what you might be doing with your fish. Do we have a deal?'

'Yes, suh.'

'When'd you first notice that barrel?'

'Maybe t'ree, fo' weeks ago. It was setting up on dry ground. I didn't have no reason to pay it no mind, no, but then I started to smell somet'ing. I t'ought it was a dead nutria, or maybe a big gar rotting up on the bank. It was real strong one night, then t'ree nights later you couldn't smell it 'less the wind blow it right across the water. Then it rained and the next night they wasn't no smell at all. I just never t'ought they might be a dead girl up there.'

66

'Did you see anyone up there?'

'Maybe about a mont' ago, at evening, I seen a car. I 'member t'inking it was new and why would anybody bring his new car down that dirt road full of holes.'

'What kind of car?'

'I don't remember, suh.'

'You remember the color?'

'No, suh, I'm sorry.'

His face looked fatigued and empty. 'I just wish I ain't been the one to find her,' he said. 'I ain't never gonna forget looking inside that barrel.'

I put my business card in his shirt pocket.

'Call me if you think of anything else. You did just fine, podna,' I said, and patted him on the arm.

I turned my truck around in the middle of the levee and headed back toward New Iberia. Up ahead the glow of the red and blue emergency lights on the ambulance sped across the tops of the sawgrass, cattails, and bleached sandpits where the husks of dead gars boiled with fire ants.

What had I learned from it all?'

Not much.

But maybe in his cynical way my friend the sleepless coroner had cut right to the heart of the problem: How do you go inside the head of a homicidal sadist who prowls the countryside like a tiger turned loose in a schoolyard?

I've seen films that portray detectives who try to absorb the moral insanity of their adversaries in order to trap them inside their own maniacal design. It makes an interesting story. Maybe it's even possible.

But four years ago I had to go to Huntsville, Texas, to interview a man on death row who had confessed to almost three hundred murders throughout the United States. Suddenly, from all over the country, cops with unsolved homicide cases flocked to Huntsville like flies on pig flop. We were no exception. A black woman in New Iberia had been abducted out of her house, strangled to death, and thrown in the Vermilion River. We had no suspects, and the man in Huntsville, Jack Hatfield, had been through Louisiana many times in his red tracings across the map.

He turned out to be neither shrewd nor cunning; there was no malevolent light in his eyes, nothing hostile or driven about his behavior. His accent was peckerwood, his demeanor finally that of a simpleton. He told me about his religious conversion and glowing presences that appeared to him in his cell; it was quickly apparent that he wanted me to like him, that he would tell me anything I wanted to hear. All I had to do was provide him the details of a murder, and he would make the crime his own.

(Later, an unemployed oil-field roughneck would confess to murdering the black woman after being given title to a ten-year-old car by her husband.)

I asked Jack Hatfield if he was trying to trade off his cooperation for a commutation of his sentence. He answered, 'Naw, I got no kick comin' about that, long as it's legal.'

With a benign expression on his face, he chronicled his long list of roadside murders from Maine to southern California. He could have been talking about a set of embossed ceramic plates that he had collected from each state that he had visited. If he had indeed done what he told me, he was completely without remorse.

'My victims didn't suffer none,' he said.

Then he began to talk about his mother and an incredible transformation took place in him. Tears streaked down his homely face, he trembled all over, his fingers left white marks on his arms. Evidently she had been not only a prostitute but perverse as well. When he was a little boy she had made him stand by the bed and watch her copulate with her johns. When he had tried to hide in the woods, she beat him with a quirt, brought him back to the house, and made him watch some more.

He spent fifteen years in the Wisconsin penitentiary for her murder.

Then he paused in his story, wiped his face with his hand, pulled his T-shirt out from his chest with his finger, and smelled himself.

'I killed three more people the day I come out of prison. I told them I was gonna do it, and I done it,' he said, and began cleaning his fingernails with a toothpick as though I were not there.

When I walked back out into the autumn sunshine that afternoon, back into the smell of east Texas piney woods and white-uniformed convicts burning piles of tree stumps on the edge of a cottonfield, I was convinced that Jack Hatfield's story about his mother was true but that almost everything else he had told me would remain as demonstrably elusive as a psychotic dream. Perhaps the answer to Jack Hatfield lay with others, I thought. Perhaps we should ask those who would eventually strap him to the gurney in the execution room, poke the IV needle into the vein, tape it lovingly to the skin, and watch him through the viewing glass as the injection dulled his eyes then hit his heart like a hammer. Would his life, his secret and dark knowledge, be passed on to them?

I'd had little sleep when I set out for the office the next morning. The sun had come up red and hot over the trees, and because I had left the windows down the night before, the inside of my truck was full of mosquitoes and dripping with humidity. I stopped at a traffic light on the east side of town and saw a purple Cadillac limousine, with tinted black windows, pull into a yellow zone by a restaurant and park squarely in front of the fire plug.

Cholo Manelli stepped out of the driver's door, stretched, rotated a crick out of his neck, looked up and down the street a couple of times, then walked around to the other side of the limo and opened the back door for Julie Balboni. Then the rest of Julie's entourage – three men and the woman named Margot – stepped out onto the sidewalk, their faces dour in the heat, their eyes sullen with the morning's early hour.

Cholo went up the sidewalk first, point man and good soldier that he was, his head turning slightly from side to side, his simian shoulders rolling under his flowered shirt. He opened the front door of the restaurant, and Julie walked inside, with the others in single file behind him.

I didn't plan any of the events that followed.

I drove through the light and went almost two blocks before I made a U-turn, drove back to the restaurant, and parked under a live-oak tree across the street from the limo. The early sun's heat was already rising from the cement, and I could smell dead water beetles in the curb gutters.

My eyes burned from lack of sleep, and though I had just shaved, I could feel stubble, like grit, along the edge of my jaw. I got out of the truck, put my seersucker coat over my arm, and walked across the street to the limo. The waxed purple surface had the soft glow of hard candy; the tinted black windows swam with the mirrored images of oak trees and azalea bushes moving in the breeze.

I unfolded the blade of my Puma knife, walked from fender to fender, and sawed the air stems off all four tires. The limo went down on the rims like it had been dropped from a chain. A black kid who had been putting circulars on doors stopped and watched me as he would a fascinating creature inside a zoo cage.

I walked to the filling station on the corner, called the dispatcher, and told him to have a wrecker tow the limo into the pound.

Then I went inside the restaurant, which gleamed with chrome and silverware and Formica surfaces, and walked past the long table where two waitresses were in the process of serving Julie and his group their breakfast. Cholo saw me first and started to speak, but I looked straight ahead and continued on into the men's room as though they were not there.

I washed my face with cold water, dried it with paper towels, and combed my hair in the mirror. There were flecks of white in my mustache now, and lines around my eyes that I hadn't noticed only a week before. I turned on the cold water and washed my face again, as though somehow I could rinse time and age out of my skin. Then I crumpled up the damp paper towel in my hand, flung it into the trash can, fixed my tie, put on my coat and sunglasses, and walked back into the restaurant.

Showtime, Julie, I thought.

Even sitting down, he towered above the others at the head of the table, in a pink short-sleeve shirt, suspenders, and gray striped slacks, his tangled black hair ruffling on his brow in the breeze from the fan, his mouth full of food while he told the waitress to bring more coffee and to reheat Margot's breakfast steak. Cholo kept trying to smile at me, his false teeth as stiff as whale bone in his mouth. Julie's other hoods looked up at me, then at Julie; when they read nothing in his face, they resumed eating.

'Hey, lieutenant, I thought that was you. You here for breakfast?' Cholo said.

'I was just passing by,' I said.

'What's going on, Dave?' Julie said, his mouth chewing, his eyes fixed on the flower vase in front of him.

'I had a long night last night,' I said.

'Yeah?' he said.

'We found a girl in a barrel down in south Vermilion Parish.'

He continued to chew, then he took a drink of water. He touched his mouth with his napkin.

'You want to sit down, or are you on your way out?' he said.

Just then I heard the steel hook of the wrecker clang somewhere on the limo's frame and the hydraulic cables start to tighten on the winch. Cholo craned his head to look beyond the angle of the front window that gave onto the street.

'I always thought you were standup, Feet,' I said.

'I appreciate the compliment, but that's a term they use in a place I've never been.'

'That's all right, I changed my mind. I don't think you're standup anymore, Feet.'

He blew up both his cheeks.

'What are you trying to say, Dave?'

'The man I work for got a bunch of phone calls yesterday. It looks like somebody dropped the dime on me with the Kiwanis Club.'

'It ain't a bunch I got a lot of influence with. Talk with Mikey Goldman if you got that kind of problem.'

'You use what works, Julie.'

'Hey, get real, Dave. When I want to send a message to somebody, it don't come through Dagwood Bumstead.'

Outside, the driver of the wrecker gunned his engine, pulled away from the curb, and dragged the limo past the front window. The limo's two front tires, which were totally deflated and still on the asphalt, were sliced into ribbons by the wheel rims.

Cholo's mouth was wide with unchewed scrambled eggs.

'Hey, a guy's got our car! A guy's driving off with the fucking limo, Julie!' he said.

Julie watched the wrecker and his limo disappear up the street. He pushed his plate away an inch with his thumb. One corner of his mouth dropped, and he pressed against it with his napkin.

'Sit down,' he said.

Everyone had stopped eating now. A waitress came to the table with a pitcher of ice water and started to refill the glasses, then hesitated and walked back behind the counter. I pulled out a chair and sat at the corner of the table, a foot from Julie's elbow.

'You're pissed off about something and you have my fucking car towed in?' he said.

'Don't park in front of fire plugs.'

'Fire plugs?'

'Right.'

'I'm getting this kind of dog shit because of a fucking fire plug?'

'No, what I'm wondering, Julie, is why you and Cholo have to hit on a small-town teenage hooker. Don't y'all have enough chippies back in New Orleans?'

'What?'

'Cherry LeBlanc,' I said.

'Who the fuck is Cherry LeBlanc?'

'Give it a break and stop acting like you just popped out of your mama's womb.'

He folded his napkin, placed it carefully by the side of his plate, pulled a carnation out of the flower vase, and pinched off the stem.

'You calling me a pimp?' he said. 'You trying to embarrass me in public. That's what this is about?'

'You didn't listen to what I said. We just found another murdered girl. Cholo knew about the murder of the LeBlanc girl, and he said you did, too. Except you lied about it when I mentioned her to you.'

His eyes drifted lazing to Cholo's face. Cholo squeezed his hands on his wrists.

'I'm all lost here. I'm—' he began.

'You know what the real trouble is, Dave?' Julie said. He flipped the carnation onto the tablecloth. 'You never understood how this town worked. You remember anybody complaining about the cathouses on Railroad and Hopkins? Or the slot machines that were in every bar and restaurant in town? Nobody complained 'cause my old man delivered an envelope to certain people at the end of every month. But those same people treated our family like we were spit on the sidewalk.

'So you and that FBI broad went around town stirring up the Bumstead crowd, shoving a broomstick up their ringus, and your boss man called you in to explain the facts of life. But it's no fun finding out that the guys you work for don't want to scare a few million dollars out of town. So you fuck my car and get in my face in a public place. I think maybe you should go back to work in New Orleans. I think maybe this shithole is starting to rub off on you.'

The manager had come from behind the glass cashier's counter and was now standing three feet from me and Julie, his clip-on bow tie askew, his tongue wetting his lips.

'Sir, could you gentlemen lower your, I mean, could you not use that language in—' he began.

Julie's eyes, which were filled with a black light, flipped up into the manager's face.

'Get the fuck away from my table,' he said.

'Sir—' the manager said.

'It's all right, Mr Meaux. I'm leaving in just a second,' I said.

'Oh, sad to hear it,' the woman, Margot, said. Except Cholo, the other hoods at the table smiled at her humor. She wore a sundress, and her hair, which was bleached the color of ash, was pulled back tightly on her head. She smoked a cigarette and the backs of her arms were covered with freckles.

'You want to come down to the office and look at some morgue pictures? I think that'd be a good idea,' I said. 'Bring your girlfriend along if you like.'

'I'm going to say this just once. I don't know none of these girls, I don't have nothing to do with your problems, you understand what I'm saying? You said some ugly things to me, Dave, but we're old friends and I'm going to let it slide. I'll call a couple of cabs, I'll pay the fine on my car, I'll buy new tires, and I'll forget everything you been saying to me. But don't you never try to get in my face in a public place again.'

One of his hoods was getting up, scraping back his chair, to use the restroom.

I folded my sunglasses, slipped them into my shirt pocket, and rubbed the burning sensation in my eyes with my thumb and forefinger.

'Feet, you're full of more shit than a broken pay toilet,' I said quietly.

The hood rested his hand on my shoulder. He was perhaps twenty-eight or thirty, lithe and olive-skinned, his dark hair boxed on his neck. A long pink scar, as thick as a soda straw, ran down the inside of one arm.

'Everybody's been pretty polite here,' he said.

I looked at his hand and at his feet. I could smell the faint hint of his sweat through his deodorant, the nicotine on the backs of his fingers.

'But you keep offending people,' he said. He raised his palm slightly, then set it on my shoulder again.

'Don't let your day get complicated,' I said.

'It's time to let people alone, Mr Robicheaux,' he said. Then he began to knead my shoulder as a fellow ballplayer might out on the pitcher's mound.

I felt a balloon of red-black color rise out of my chest into my head, heard a sound behind my eyes like wet newspaper tearing, and for some reason saw a kaleidoscopic image of the blond girl in the black body bag, a long strand of algae-streaked hair glued to the gray flesh of her forehead.

I hit him so hard in the stomach that my fist buried itself up to the wrist right under his sternum and spittle flew from his mouth onto the tabletop. Then I came up out of the chair and hooked him in the eye, saw the skin break against the bone and well with blood. He tried to regain his balance and swing a sugar shaker at my face, but I spun him sideways, caught him in the kidney, and drove him to his knees between two counter stools. I didn't remember hitting him in the mouth, but his bottom lip was drooling blood onto his shirt front.

I didn't want to stop. I heard the roar of wind in sea shells, the wheels of rusted engines clanging cog against cog. Then I saw Cholo in front of me, his big square hands raised in placation, his mouth small with sound.

'What?' I said.

'It ain't your style, Loot,' he was whispering hoarsely. 'Ease off, the guy's new, he don't know the rules, Loot. Come on, this ain't good for nobody.'

My knuckles were skinned, my palms ringing. I heard glass crunch under the sole of my shoe in the stunned silence, and looked down numbly at my broken sunglasses on the floor like a man emerging from a blackout.

Julie Balboni scraped back his chair, took his gold money clip from his slacks, and began counting out a series of ten-dollar bills on the table.

He didn't even look up at me when he spoke. But everybody in the restaurant heard what he said. 'I think you're losing it, Dave. Stop being a hired dildo for the local dipshits or get yourself some better tranqs.'

8

It was ten A.M. Batist had gone after a boat with a fouled engine down the bayou, and the bait shop and dock were empty. The tin roof was expanding in the heat, buckling and pinging against the bolts and wood joists. I pulled a can of Dr Pepper out of the crushed ice in the cooler and sat outside in the hot shade by myself and drank it. Green dragonflies hung suspended over the cattails along the bayou's banks; a needle-nose gar that had probably been wounded by a boat propeller turned in circles in the dead current, while a school of minnows fed off a red gash behind its gills; a smell like dead snakes, sour mud, and rotted hyacinth vines blew out of the marsh on the hot wind.

I didn't want to even think about the events of this morning. The scene in the restaurant was like a moment snipped out of a drunk dream, in which I was always out of control, publicly indecent or lewd in the eyes of others.

The soda can grew warm in my palm. The sky in the south had a bright sheen to it like blue silk. I hoped that it would storm that afternoon, that rain would thunder down on the marsh and bayou, roar like grapeshot on the roof of my house, pour in gullies through the dirt and dead leaves under the pecan trees in my yard.

I heard Bootsie behind me. She sat down in a canvas chair by a spool table and crossed her legs. She wore white shorts, sandals, and a denim shirt with the sleeves cut off. There were sweat rings under her arms, and the down on top of her thighs had been burned gold by the sun.

We met at a dance on Spanish Lake during the summer of 1957, and a short time later we lost our virginity together in my father's boathouse, while the rain fell out of the sunlight and dripped off the eaves and the willow trees into the lake and the inside of the boathouse trembled with a wet green-yellow light.

But even at that age I had already started my long commitment to sour mash straight up with a sweating jax on the side. Bootsie and I would go separate ways, far from Bayou Teche and the provincial Cajun world in which we had grown up. I would make the journey to Vietnam as one of our new colonials and return with a junkyard in my hip and thigh and nocturnal memories that neither whiskey nor army hospital dope could kill. She would marry an oil-field pilot who would later tip a guy wire on an offshore rig and crash his helicopter right on top of the quarter-boat; then she would discover that her second husband, an accounting graduate from Tulane, was a bookkeeper for the Mafia, although his career with them became short-lived when they shot-gunned him and his mistress to death in the parking lot of the Hialeah racetrack.

She had lupus disease that we had knocked into remission with medication, but it still lived in her blood like a sleeping parasite that waited for its moment to attack her kidneys and sever her connective tissue. She was supposed to avoid hard sunlight, but again and again I came home from work and found her working in the yard in shorts and a halter, her hot skin filmed with sweat and grains of dirt.

'Did something happen at work?' she said.

'I had some trouble at Del's.'

'What?'

'I busted up one of Baby Feet Balboni's lowlifes.'

'In the restaurant?'

'Yeah, that's where I did it.'

'What did he do?'

'He put his hand on me.' I set down my soda can and propped my forearms on my thighs. I looked out at the sun's reflection in the brown water.

'Have you been back to the office?' she said.

'Not yet. I'll probably go in later.'

She was quiet a moment.

'Have you talked to the sheriff?' she asked.

'There's not really much to talk about. The guy could make a beef but he won't. They don't like to get messed up in legal action against cops.'

She uncrossed her legs and brushed idly at her knee with her fingertips.

'Dave, is something else going on, something you're not telling me about?'

'The guy put his hand on my shoulder and I wanted to tear him apart. Maybe I would have done it if this guy named Manelli hadn't stepped in front of me.'

I saw her breasts rise and fall under her shirt. Far down the bayou Batist was towing a second boat behind his outboard and the waves were slapping the floating hyacinths against the banks. She got up from

75

her chair and stood behind me. She worked her fingers into my shoulders. I could feel her thigh touch my back.

'New Iberia is never going to be the same place we grew up in. That's just the way things are,' she said.

'It doesn't mean I have to like it.'

'The Balboni family was here a long time. We survived, didn't we? They'll make their movie and go away.'

'There're too many people willing to sell it down the drain.'

'Sell what?'

'Whatever makes a dollar for them. Redfish and *sac-a-lait* to restaurants, alligators to the Japanese. They let oil companies pollute the oyster beds and cut canals through the marsh so salt water can eat up thousands of square miles of wetlands. They take it on their knees from anybody who's got a checkbook.'

'Let it go, Dave.'

'I think a three-day open season on people would solve a lot of our problems.'

'Tell the sheriff what happened. Don't let it just hang there.'

'He's worried about some guys at the Chamber of Commerce, Bootsie. He's a good guy most of the time, but these are the people he's spent most of his life around.'

'I think you should talk to him.'

'All right, I'm going to take a shower, then I'll call him.'

'You're not going to the office?'

'I'm not sure. Maybe later.'

Batist cut the engine on his boat and floated on the swell into the dock and bumped against the strips of rubber tire we had nailed to the pilings. His shirt was piled on the board seat beside him, and his black shoulders and chest were beaded with sweat. His head looked like a cannonball. He grinned with an unlit cigar in the corner of his mouth.

I was glad for the distraction.

'I was up at the fo'-corners,' he said. 'A man there said you mopped up the restaurant flo' with one of them dagos.'

Thanks, Batist, I thought.

I showered in water that was so cold it left me breathless, changed clothes, and drove to the bottling works down by the Vermilion River in Lafayette. The two-story building was an old one, made of yellow brick, and surrounded by huge live-oak trees. In back was a parking lot, which was filled with delivery trucks, and a loading dock, where a dozen black men were rattling crates of soda pop out of the building's dark interior and stacking them inside the waiting trucks. Their physical strength was incredible. Some of them would pick up a half-dozen full cases at a time and lift them easily to eye level. Their muscles looked like water-streaked black stone.

I asked one of them where I could find Twinky Hebert Lemoyne.

'Mr Twinky in yonder, in the office. Better catch him quick, though. He fixin' to go out on the route,' he said.

'He goes out on the route?'

'Mr Twinky do everyt'ing, suh.'

I walked inside the warehouse to a cluttered, windowed office whose door was already open. The walls and cork boards were papered with invoices, old church calendars, unframed photographs of employees and fishermen with thick-bellied large-mouth bass draped across their hands. Lemoyne's face was pink and well-shaped, his eyebrows sandy, his gray hair still streaked in places with gold. He sat erect in his chair, his eyes behind his rimless glasses concentrated on the papers in his hands. He wore a short-sleeved shirt and a loose burnt-orange tie (a seersucker coat hung on the back of the chair) and a plastic pen holder in his pocket; his brown shoes were shined; his fingernails were trimmed and clean. But he had the large shoulders and hands of a working man, and he radiated the kind of quiet, hard-earned physical power that in some men neither age nor extra weight seems to diminish.

There was no air conditioning in his office, and he had weighted all the papers on his desk to keep them from blowing away in the breeze from the oscillating fan.

After I had introduced myself, he gazed out at the loading dock a moment, then lifted his hands from the desk blotter and put them down again as though somehow we had already reached a point in our conversation where there was nothing left to be said.

'Can I sit down?' I said.

'Go ahead. But I think you're wasting your time here.'

'It's been a slow day.' I smiled at him.

'Mr Robicheaux, I don't have any idea in the world why either you or that Mexican woman is interested in me. Could you be a little bit more forthcoming?'

'Actually, until yesterday I don't believe I ever heard your name.'

'What should I make of that?'

'The problem is you and a few others tried to stick a couple of thumbtacks in my boss's head.' I smiled again.

'Listen, that woman came into my office yesterday and accused me of working with the Mafia.'

'Why would she do that?'

'You tell me, please.'

'You own half of a security service with Murphy Doucet?'

'That's right, I surely do. Can you tell me what y'all are looking for, why y'all are in my place of business?'

'When you do business with a man like Julie Balboni, you create a certain degree of curiosity about yourself.'

'I don't do business with this man, and I don't know anything about him. I bought stock in this motion picture they're making. A lot of business people around here have. I've never met Julie Balboni and I don't plan to. Are we clear on this, sir?'

'My boss says you're a respected man. It looks like you have a good business, too. I'd be careful who I messed with, Mr Lemoyne.'

'I'm not interested in pursuing the subject.' He fixed his glasses, squared his shoulders slightly, and picked up several sheets of paper in his hands.

I drummed my fingers on the arms of my chair. Outside I could hear truck doors slamming and gears grinding.

'I guess I didn't explain myself very well,' I said.

'You don't need to,' he said, and looked up at the clock on the wall.

'You're a solid businessman. There's nothing wrong with buying stock in a movie company. There's nothing wrong with providing a security service for it, either. But a lady who's not much taller than a fireplug asks you a couple of questions and you try to drop the dime on her. That doesn't seem to fit, Mr Lemoyne.'

'There're people out there committing rapes, armed robberies, selling crack to children, God only knows what else, but you and that woman have the nerve to come in here and question me because I have a vague business relationship with a movie production. You don't think that's reason to make someone angry? What's wrong with you people?'

'Are your employees union?'

'No, they're not.'

'But your partner in your security service is a Teamster steward. I think you're involved in some strange contradictions, Mr Lemoyne.'

He rose from his chair and lifted a set of keys out of his desk drawer.

'I'm taking a new boy on his route today. I have to lock up now. Do you want to stay around and talk to somebody else?' he said.

'No, I'll be on my way. Here's my business card in case you might like to contact me later.'

He ignored it when I extended it to him. I placed it on his desk.

'Thank you for your time, sir,' I said, and walked back out onto the loading dock, into the heated liquid air, the blinding glare of light, the chalky smell of crushed oyster shells in the unsurfaced parking lot.

When I was walking out to my pickup truck, I recognized an elderly black man who used to work in the old icehouse in New Iberia years ago. He was picking up litter out by the street with a stick that had a nail in the end of it. He had a rag tied around his forehead to keep the sweat out of his eyes, and the rotted wet undershirt he wore looked like strips of cheesecloth on his body.

'How do you like working here, Dallas?' I said.

'I like it pretty good.'

'How does Mr Twinky treat y'all?'

His eyes glanced back toward the building, then he grinned.

'He know how to make the eagle scream, you know what I mean?'

'He's tight with a dollar?'

'Mr Twinky so tight he got to eat a whole box of Ex-Lax so he don't squeak when he walk.'

'He's that bad?'

He tapped some dried leaves off the nail of his stick against the trunk of an oak tree.

'That's just my little joke,' he said. 'Mr Twinky pay what he say he gonna pay, and he always pay it on time. He good to black folks, Mr Dave. They ain't no way 'round that.'

When I got back to New Iberia I didn't go to the office. Instead, I called from the house. The sheriff wasn't in.

'Where is he?' I said.

'He's probably out looking for you,' the dispatcher said. 'What's going on, Dave?'

'Nothing much.'

'Tell that to the greaseball you bounced off the furniture this morning.'

'Did he file a complaint?'

'No, but I heard the restaurant owner dug the guy's tooth out of the counter with a screwdriver. You sure know how to do it, Dave.'

'Tell the sheriff I'm going to check out some stuff in New Orleans. I'll call him this evening or I'll see him in the office early in the morning.'

'I got the impression it might be good if you came by this afternoon.'

'Is Agent Gomez there?'

'Yeah, hang on.'

A few seconds later Rosie picked up the extension.

'Dave?'

'How you doing?'

'*I'm* doing fine. How are you doing?'

'Everything's copacetic. I just talked with your man Twinky Lemoyne.'

'Oh?'

'It looks like you put your finger in his eye.'

'Why'd you go over there?'

'You never let them think they can make you flinch.'

'Hang on a minute. I want to close the door.' Then a moment later she scraped the receiver back up and said, 'Dave, what happens around here won't affect my job or career to any appreciable degree. But maybe you ought to start thinking about covering your butt for a change.'

'I had a bad night last night and I acted foolishly this morning. It's just one of those things,' I said.

'That's not what I'm talking about, and I think you know it. When you chase money out of a community, people discover new depths in themselves.'

'Have you gotten any feedback on the asphyxiated girl down in Vermilion Parish?'

'I just got back from the coroner's office. She's still Jane Doe.'

'You think we're dealing with the same guy?'

'Bondage, humiliation of the victim, a prolonged death, probable sexual violation, it's the same creep, you'd better believe it.' I could hear an edge in her voice, like a sliver of glass.

'I've got a couple of theories, too,' she said. 'He's left his last two victims where we could find them. Maybe he's becoming more compulsive, more desperate, less in control of his technique. Most psychopaths eventually reach a point where they're like sharks in feeding frenzy. They never satisfy the obsession.'

'Or he wants to stick it in our faces?'

'You got it.'

'Everything you say may be true, Rosie, but I think prostitution is connected with this stuff somewhere. You want to take a ride to New Orleans with me this afternoon?'

'A Vermilion Parish sheriff's detective is taking me out on the levee where you all found the girl last night. Do all these people spit Red Man?'

'A few of the women deputies don't.'

I heard her laugh into the telephone.

'Watch out for yourself, slick,' she said.

'You, too, Rosie.'

Neither Bootsie nor Alafair was home. I left them a note, packed a change of clothes in a canvas bag in case I had to stay overnight, and headed for I-10 and New Orleans as the temperature climbed to one hundred degrees and the willows along the bayou drooped motionlessly in the heat as though all the juices had been baked out of their leaves.

I drove down the elevated interstate and crossed the Atchafalaya Basin and its wind-ruffled bays dotted with the oil platforms and dead cypress, networks of canals and bayous, sand bogs, willow islands, stilt houses, flooded woods, and stretches of dry land where the mosquitoes swarmed in gray clouds out of the tangles of brush and intertwined trees. Then I crossed the wide, yellow sweep of the Mississippi at Baton Rouge, and forty-five minutes later I was rolling through Jefferson Parish, along the shores of Lake Pontchartrain, into New Orleans. The lake was slate green and capping, the sky almost white in the heat, and the fronds on the palm trees were lifting and rattling dryly in the hot breeze. The air smelled of salt and stagnant water and dead vegetation among the sand bogs on the west side of the highway; the asphalt looked like it could fry the palm of your hand.

But there were no rain clouds on the horizon, no hint of relief from the scorching white orb in the sky or the humidity that crawled and ran on the skin like angry insects.

I was on the New Orleans police force for fourteen years, first as a beat cop and finally as a lieutenant in Homicide. I never worked Vice, but there are a few areas in New Orleans law enforcement that don't eventually lead you back into it. Without its pagan and decadent ambiance, its strip shows, hookers, burlesque spielers, taxi pimps, and brain-damaged street dopers, the city would be as attractive to most tourists as an agrarian theme park in western Nebraska.

The French Quarter has two populations, almost two sensory climates. Early in the morning black children in uniforms line up to enter the Catholic elementary school by the park; parishioners from St Louis Cathedral have coffee *au lait* and *beignets* and read the newspaper at the outdoor tables in the Café du Monde; the streets are still cool, the tile roofs and pastel stucco walls of the buildings streaked with moisture, the scrolled ironwork on the balconies bursting with flowers; families have their pictures sketched by the artists who set up their easels along the piked fence in Jackson Square; in the background the breeze off the river blows through the azalea and hibiscus bushes, the magnolia blossoms that are as big as fists, and the clumps of banana trees under the equestrian statue of Andy Jackson; and as soon as you head deeper into the Quarter, under the iron, green-painted colonnades, you can smell the cold, clean odor of fresh fish laid out on ice, of boxed strawberries and plums and rattlesnake watermelons beaded with water from a spray hose.

But by late afternoon another crowd moves into the Quarter. Most of them are innocuous – college kids, service personnel, Midwestern families trying to see past the spielers into the interiors of the strip houses, blue-suited Japanese businessmen hung with cameras, rednecks from dry counties in Mississippi. But there's another kind, too – grifters, Murphy artists, dips and stalls, coke and skag dealers, stables of hookers who work the hotel trade only, and strippers who hook out of taxicabs after 2 A.M.

They have the franchise on the worm's-eye view of the world. They're usually joyless, indifferent to speculations about mortality, bored with almost all forms of experience. Almost all of them either free-base, mainline, do coke, or smoke crack. Often they straighten out the kinks with black speed.

They view ordinary people as carnival workers do rubes; they look upon their victims with contempt, sometimes with loathing. Most of them cannot think their way out of a paper bag; but the accuracy of their knowledge about various bondsmen, the hierarchy of the local mob, the law as it applies to themselves, and cops and judges on a pad, is awesome.

As the streets began to cool and turn purple with shadow, I went from one low-rent club to the next amid the din of Dixieland and rockabilly bands, black kids with clip-on taps dancing on the sidewalk for the tourists, spielers in straw boaters and candy-striped vests hollering at college boys, 'No cover, no minimum, you studs, come on in and get your battery charged.'

Jimmie Ryan's red mustache and florid, good-humored face made you think of a nineteenth-century bartender. But he was also known as Jimmie the Dime, because with a phone call he could connect you, in one way or another, with any form of illegal activity in New Orleans.

Inside the crook of both his arms his veins were laced with scar tissue, like flattened gray garden snakes.

He tilted his straw boater back on his head and drank from his beer. Above him, a topless girl in a sequined G-string danced barefoot on a runway, her hips moving like water to the music from the jukebox, her skin rippled with neon light, her mouth open in feigned ecstasy.

'How you been, Streak?' he said.

'Pretty good, Jimmie. How's the life?' I said.

'I ain't exactly in it anymore. Since I got off the super-fluid, I more or less went to reg'lar employment, you know what I mean? Being a human doorbell for geeks and dipshits has got some serious negative drawbacks, I'm talking about self-esteem here, this town's full of sick people, Streak, who needs it is what I'm trying to say.'

'I see. Look, Jimmie, do you know anybody who might be trying to recruit girls out of the parishes?'

He leaned his elbows back on the bar. His soft stomach swelled out of his striped vest like a water-filled bottom-heavy balloon.

'You mean somebody putting together his own stable?' he asked.

'Maybe.'

'A guy who goes out looking for the country girls, the ones who's waiting for a big sugar daddy or is about to get run out of town, anyway?'

'Possibly.'

'It don't sound right.'

'Why?'

'New Orleans is full of them. Why bring in more and drive the prices down?'

'Maybe this guy does more than jump pimp, Jimmie. Maybe he likes to hurt them. You know a guy like that?'

'We're talking about another type of guy now, somebody who operates way down on the bottom of the food chain. When I was in the business of dimeing for somebody, making various kinds of social arrangements around the city, I made it a point not to know no guys like that, in fact, maybe I'm a little bit taken aback here you think I associate with them kind of people.'

'I respect your knowledge and your judgment, Jimmie. That's why I came to you instead of someone else. My problem is two dead girls in Vermilion and Iberia parishes. The same guy may have killed others.'

He removed something from the back of his teeth with his little finger.

'The city ain't like it used to be,' he said. 'It's turning to shit.'

'Okay—'

'Years ago there were certain understandings with New Orleans cops. A guy got caught doing the wrong stuff, I'm talking about sick stuff, molesting a child, robbing and beating up old people, something like that, it didn't go to the jailhouse. They stomped the shit out of the guy right there, I mean they left him with his brains running out of his nose.

'Today, what'd you got? Try to take a stroll by the projects and see what happens. Look, Streak, I don't know what you're looking for, but there's one special kind of cocksucker that comes to mind here, a new kind of guy in the city, why somebody don't walk him outside, maybe punch his ticket real hard, maybe permanent, you know what I'm saying, I don't know the answer to that one, but when you go down to the bus depot, you might think about it, I mean you're from out of town, right, and there ain't nobody, I mean nobody, gonna be upset if this kind of guy maybe gets ripped from his liver to his lights.'

'The bus depot?'

'You got it. There's three or four of them. One of them stands out like shit in an ice-cream factory. Nothing against colored people.'

I had forgotten what a linguistic experience a conversation with Jimmie the Dime could be.

He suppressed a beer belch and stared up at the girl on the runway.

'Could Baby Feet Balboni be involved in this?' I asked.

He rolled a matchstick on his tongue, looked upward at an oblique angle to a spot on the ceiling.

'Take a walk with me, breathe the night air, this place is like the inside of an ashtray. Some nights I think somebody poured battery acid in my lungs,' he said.

I walked outside with him. The sidewalks were filled with tourists and revelers drinking beer out of deep paper cups. Jimmie looked up and down the street, blew air out his nose, smoothed his mustache with one knuckle.

'You're using the names of local personalities now,' he said.

'It stays with me, Jimmie. Nobody'll know where it came from.'

'Anything I might know about this certain man is already public knowledge, so it probably won't do no good for me to be commenting on the issue here.'

'There's no action around here that doesn't get pieced off to Julie one way or another. Why should procuring be any different?'

'Wrong. There's fifteen-year-old kids in the projects dealing rock, girls, guns, Mexican brown, crank, you name it, the Italians won't fool with it, it's too uncontrollable. You looking for a guy who kills hookers? It ain't Feet, lieutenant. The guy's got sub-zero feelings about people. I saw him wipe up a barroom in Algiers with three guys from the Giacano family who thought they could come on like wise-asses in front of their broads. He didn't even break a sweat. He even stopped stomping on one guy just so he could blow a long fart.'

'Thanks for your time, Jimmie. Get in touch if you hear anything, all right?'

'What do I know? We're living in sick times. You want my opinion? Open up some prison colonies at the North Pole, where those penguins live. Get rid of the dirt bags, bring back some decency, before the whole city becomes a toilet.' He rocked on the balls of his feet. His lips looked purple in the neo glow from the bar, his face an electric red, as though it were flaming from sunburn.

I gave him my business card. When I was down the block, under the marquee of a pornographic theater, and looked back at him, he was picking his teeth with it.

I hit two biker bars across the river in Algiers, where a few of the mamas hooked so their old men would have the money they needed to deal guns or dope. Why they allowed themselves to be used on that level was anybody's guess. But with some regularity they were chain-whipped, gang-raped, nailed through their hands to trees, and they usually came back for more until sometimes they were murdered and dumped in a swamp. One form of their sad, ongoing victimization probably makes about as much sense as another.

The ones who would talk to me all had the same odor, like sweaty leather, the warm female scent of unwashed hair, reefer smoke and nicotine, and engine grease rubbed into denim. But they had little knowledge or interest about anything outside of their tribal and atavistic world.

I found a mulatto pimp off Magazine who also ran a shooting gallery that specialized in black-tar heroin, which was selling at twenty-five dollars a hit and was back in fashion with adult addicts who didn't want to join the army of psychotic meltdowns produced by crack in the projects.

His name was Camel; he had one dead eye, like a colorless marble, and he wore a diamond clipped in one nostril and his hair shaved in ridges and dagger points. He peeled back the shell on a hard-boiled egg with his thumb at the sandwich counter of an old dilapidated grocery and package store with wood-bladed fans on the ceiling. His skin had the bright copper shine of a newly minted penny.

After he had listened to me for a while, he set his egg on a paper napkin and folded his long fingers reflectively.

'This is my neighborhood, place where all my friends live, and don't nobody here hurt my ladies,' he said.

'I didn't say they did, Camel. I just want you to tell me if you've heard about anybody who might be recruiting out in the parishes. Maybe a guy who's seriously out of control.'

'I don't get out of the neighborhood much no mo'. Age creeping up on me, I guess.'

'It's been a hot day, partner. My tolerance for bullshit is way down. You're dealing Mexican skag for Julie Balboni, and you know everything that's going on in this town.'

'What's that name again?'

I looked into his face for a long moment. He scraped at a bit of crust on the corner of his dead eye with his fingernail.

'You're a smart man, Camel. Tell me honestly, do you think you're going to jerk me around and I'm just going to disappear?'

He unscrewed the cap on a Tabasco bottle and began dotting drops of hot sauce on his egg.

'I hears stories about a white guy, they say a strange guy reg'lar peoples in the bidness don't like to fool with,' he said.

'All right—'

'You're looking in the wrong place.'

'What do you mean?'

'The guy don't live around here. He sets the girls up on the Airline

Highway, in Jefferson Parish, puts one in charge, then comes back to town once in a while to check everything out.'

'I see, a new kind of honor system. What are you trying to feed me, Camel?'

'You're not hearing me. The reg'lar peoples stay away from him for a reason. His chippies try to short him, they disappear. The word there is *disappear*, gone from the crib, blipped off the screen. Am I getting this acrost to you all right?'

'What's his name?'

'Don't know, don't want to know. Ax yourself something. Why y'all always come to a nigger to solve your problem? We ain't got nothing like that in a black neighborhood.'

'We'll see you around, Camel. Thanks for your help. Say, what's the name of the black guy working the bus depot?'

'I travel by plane, my man. That's what everybody do today,' he said, and licked the top of the peeled egg before he put it in his mouth.

For years the Airline had been the main highway between Baton Rouge and New Orleans. When I-10 was built, the Airline became a secondary road and was absorbed back into that quasi-rural slum culture that has always characterized the peckerwood South: ramshackle nightclubs with oyster-shell parking lots; roach-infested motels that feature water beds and pornographic movies and rent rooms by the day or week; truck stops with banks of rubber machines in the restrooms; all-night glaringly lit cafés where the smell of fried food permeates the counters and stools as tangibly as a film of grease.

I went to three clubs and got nowhere. Each time I walked through the door the bartender's eyes glanced up to meet me as they would somebody who had been expected all evening. As soon as I sat at the bar the girls went to the women's room or out the back door. The electronic noise of the country bands was deafening, the amplified squelch in the microphones like metal raking on a blackboard. When I tried to talk to someone, the person would nod politely in the din as though a man without vocal cords were speaking to him, then go back to his drink or stare in the opposite direction through the layers of cigarette smoke.

I gave up and walked back to my truck, which was parked between the clapboard side of a nightclub and a squat six-room motel with a small yellow lawn and a dead palm tree by the drive-in registration window. The air smelled of creosote and burnt diesel fuel from the railway tracks by the river, dust from the shell parking lot, liquor and beer from a trash barrel filled with empty bottles. The sky out over the Gulf trembled with dry lightning.

I didn't hear her behind me.

'Everyone on the strip knew you were coming two hours ago, cutie,' she said.

I turned and squinted my eyes at her. She drank out of her beer bottle, then puffed off her cigarette. Her face was porcine, her lipstick on crooked, her dyed red hair lacquered like tangled wire on her head. She put one hand on her hip and waited for me to recognize her.

'Charlotte?'

'What a memory. Have I tubbed up on you?'

'No, not really. You're looking good.'

She laughed to herself and blew her cigarette smoke at an upward angle into the dark.

Thirty years ago she had been a stripper and hooker on Bourbon Street, then the mistress of a loanshark who blew his brains out, the wife of an alcoholic ex-police sergeant who ended up in Angola for doping horses at the Fairgrounds, and the last I heard the operator of a massage parlor in Algiers.

'What are you doing out here on the Airline?' I said.

'I run the dump next door,' she said, and nodded toward the motel. 'Hey, I got to sit down. I really got crocked tonight.' She shook a wooden chair loose from the trash pile by the side of the nightclub and sat down in it with her knees splayed and took another drink from her beer bottle. An exhaust fan from a restroom was pinging above her head. 'I already heard what you're looking for, Streak. A guy bringing the chickens in from the country, right?'

'Do you know who he is?'

'They come and they go. I'm too old to keep track of it anymore.'

'I'd sure like to talk to this guy, Charlotte.'

'Yeah, somebody ought to run an iron hook through his balls, all right, but it's probably not going to happen.'

'Why not?'

'You got the right juice, the play pen stays open.'

'He's connected?'

'What do you think?'

'With the Balboni family?'

'Maybe. Maybe he's got juice with the cops or politicians. There's lots of ways to stay in business.'

'But one way or another, most of them go down. Right?'

She raised her beer bottle to her mouth and drank.

'I don't think anybody is going to be talking about this guy a whole lot,' she said. 'You hear stories, you know what I mean? That this guy you're looking for is somebody you don't want mad at you, that he can be real hard on his chippies.'

'Is it true?'

She set her empty bottle down on the shells and placed her hands loosely in her lap. For a moment the alcoholic shine left her eyes and her expression became strangely introverted, as though she were focusing on some forgotten image deep inside herself.

'When you're in the life, you hear a lot of bad stories, cutie. That's because there aren't many good ones,' she said.

'The man I'm looking for may be a serial killer, Charlotte.'

'That kind of guy is a john, not a pimp, Streak.' She leaned on her forearms, puffing on her cigarette, staring at the hundreds of bottle caps pressed into the dirt at her feet. Her lacquered hair was wreathed in smoke. 'Go on back home. You won't change anything here. Everybody out on this road signed up for it one way or another.'

'Nobody signed up to be dead.'

She didn't reply. She scratched a mosquito bite on her kneecap and looked at a car approaching the motel registration window.

'Who's the main man working the bus depot these days?' I said.

'That's Downtown Bobby Brown. He went up on a short-eyes once. Now he's a pro, a real piece of shit. Go back to your family, Streak, before you start to like your work.'

She flipped her cigarette away backhandedly, got to her feet, straightened her dress on her elephantine hips, winked at me as though she might be leaving a burlesque stage, and walked delicately across the oyster shells toward her motel and the couple who waited impatiently for her in the heat and the dust and the snapping of an electric bug killer over the registration window.

You can find the predators at the bus depot almost any time during the twenty-four-hour period. But they operate best during the late hours. That's usually when the adventurers from Vidalia or De Ridder or Wiggins, Mississippi, have run out of money, energy, and hope of finding a place to sleep besides an empty building or an official shelter where they'll be reported as runaways. It's not hard to spot the adventurers, either. The corners of their mouths are downturned, their hair is limp and lies like moist string on their necks; often their hands and thin arms are flecked with home-grown tattoos; they wash under their arms with paper towels and brush their teeth in the depot restroom.

I watched him walk across the waiting room, a leather satchel slung on a strap over his shoulder, his eyes bright, a rain hat at an angle on his head, his tropical white shirt hanging outside his khakis. A gold cross was painted on the side of his satchel.

The two girls were white, both blonde, dressed in shapeless jeans, tennis shoes without socks, blouses that looked salt-faded and stiff with dried perspiration. When he talked with them, his happy face made me think of a mythical goat-footed balloonman whistling far and wee to children in springtime. Then from his satchel he produced candy bars and ham sandwiches, a thermos of coffee, plums and red apples that would dwarf a child's hand.

The girls both bent into their sandwiches, then he was sitting next to them, talking without stop, the smile as wide as an ax blade, the eyes bright as an elf's, the gold cross on his satchel winking with light under his black arm.

I was tired, used up after the long day, wired with too many voices, too many people on the hustle, too many who bought and sold others or ruined themselves for money that you could make with a Fuller-brush route. There was grit in my clothes; my mouth tasted bad; I could smell my own odor. The inside of the depot reeked of cigar butts and the diesel exhaust that blew through the doors to the boarding foyer.

I took the receiver off a pay phone by the men's room and let it hang by its cord.

A minute later the ticket salesman stared down at my badge that I had slid across the counter.

'You want me to do what?' he said.

'Announce that there's a call at the pay phone for Mr Bob Brown.'

'We usually don't do that.'

'Consider it an emergency.'

'Yes, sir.'

'Wait at least one minute before you do it. Okay, podna?'

'Yes, sir.'

I bought a soft drink from a vending machine and looked casually out the glass doors while a bus marked 'Miami' was being loaded underneath with luggage. The ticket salesman picked up his microphone, and Bob Brown's name echoed and resonated off the depot walls.

Downtown Bobby Brown's face became quizzical, impish, in front of the girls, then momentarily apologetic as he explained that he'd be right back, that somebody at his shelter probably needed advice about a situation.

I dropped my soda can into a trash bin and followed him to the pay phone. Downtown Bobby was streetwise, and he turned around and looked into my face. But my eyes never registered his glance, and I passed him and stopped in front of the *USA Today* machine.

He picked up the telephone receiver, leaning on one arm against the wall, and said, 'This is Bobby. What's happenin'?'

'The end of your career,' I said, and clenched the back of his neck, driving his face into the restroom door. Then I pushed him through the door and flung him inside the room. Blood drained from his nose over his lip; his eyes were wide, yellow-white – like a peeled egg – with shock.

A man at the urinal stood dumbfounded with his fly opened. I held up my badge in front of him.

'This room's in use,' I said.

He zipped his trousers and went quickly out the door. I shot the bolt into the jamb.

'What you want? Why you comin' down on me for? You cain't run a shake on somebody, run somebody's face into a do' just because you—'

I pulled my .45 out of the back of my belt and aimed it into the center of his face.

He lifted his hands in front of him, as though he were holding back an invisible presence, and shook his head from side to side, his eyes averted, his mouth twisted like a broken plum.

'Don't do that, man,' he said. 'I ain't no threat to you. Look, I ain't got a gun. You want to bust me, do it. Come on, I swear it, they ain't no need for that piece, I ain't no trouble.'

He was breathing heavily now. Sweat glistened like oil on his temples. He blotted drops of blood off his nose with the backs of his fingers.

I walked closer to him, staring into his eyes, and cocked the hammer. He backed away from me into a stall, his breath rife with a smell like sardines.

'I want the name of the guy you're delivering the girls to,' I said.

'Nobody. I ain't bringing nobody to nobody.'

I fitted the opening in the barrel to the point of his chin.

'Oh, God,' he said, and fell backward onto the commode. The seat was up, and his butt plummeted deep into the bowl.

'You know the guy I'm talking about. He's just like you. He hunts on the game reserve,' I said.

His chest was bent forward toward his knees. He looked like a round clothespin that had been screwed into a hole.

'Don't do this to me, man,' he said. 'I just had an operation. Take me in. I'll he'p y'all out any way I can. I got a good record wit' y'all.'

'You've been up the road for child molesting, Bobby. Even cons don't like a short-eyes. Did you have to stay in lockdown with the snitches?'

'It was a statutory. I went down for nonconsent. Check it out, man. No shit, don't point that at me no more. I still got stitches inside my groin. They're gonna tear loose.'

'Who's the guy, Bobby?'

He shut his eyes and put his hand over his mouth.

'Just give me his name, and it all ends right here,' I said.

He opened his eyes and looked up at me.

'I messed my pants,' he said.

'This guy hurts people. Give me his name, Bobby.'

'There's a white guy sells dirty pictures or something. He carries a gun. Nobody fucks wit' him. Is that the guy you're talking about?'

'You tell me.'

'That's all I know. Look, I don't have nothin' to do wit' dangerous people. I don't hurt nobody. Why you doin' this to me, man?'

I stepped back from him and eased down the hammer on the .45. He put the heels of his hands on the rim of the commode and pushed himself slowly to his feet. Toilet water dripped off the seat of his khakis. I wadded up a handful of paper towels, soaked them under a faucet, and handed them to him.

'Wipe your face,' I said.

He kept sniffing, as though he had a cold.

'I cain't go back out there.'

'That's right.'

'I went to the bathroom in my pants. That's what you done, man.'

'You're never coming back here, Bobby. You're going to treat this bus depot like it's the center of a nuclear test zone.'

'I got a crib . . . a place . . . two blocks from here, man. What you—'

'Do you know who —— is?' I used the name of a notorious right-wing racist beat cop from the Irish Channel.

His hand stopped mopping at his nose with the towels.

'I got no beef wit' that peckerwood,' he said.

'He broke a pimp's trachea with his baton once. That's right, Bobby. The guy strangled to death in his own spit.'

'What you talkin' 'bout, man? I ain't said nothing 'bout ——. I know what you're doin', man, you're—'

'If I catch you in the depot again, if I hear you're scamming runaways and young girls again, I'm going to tell —— you've been working his neighborhood, maybe hanging around school grounds in the Channel.'

'Who the fuck are you, man? Why you makin' me miserable? I ain't done nothing to you.'

I unlocked the bolt on the door.

'Did you ever read the passage in the Bible about what happens to people who corrupt children?' I said.

He looked at me with a stupefied expression on his face.

'Start thinking about millstones or get into another line of work,' I said.

I had seventeen dollars in my billfold. I gave twelve to the two runaway girls and the address of an AA street priest who ran a shelter and wouldn't report them.

Outside, the air tasted like pennies and felt like it had been super-heated in an electric oven. Even the wind blew off the pavement like heat rising from a wood stove. I started my truck, unbuttoned my shirt to my waist, and headed toward I-10 and home.

When I passed Lake Pontchartrain, the moon was up and small waves were breaking against the rim of gray sandy beach by the highway. I wanted to stop the truck, strip to my skivvies, wade out to the drop-off, then dive down through the descending layers of temperature until I struck a cold, dark current at the bottom that would wash the last five hours out of my pores.

But Lake Pontchartrain, like the city of New Orleans, was deceptive. Under its slate-green, capping waves, its moon-glazed surfaces, its twenty-four-mile causeway glowing with electric light, waste of every kind lay trapped in the dark sediment, and the level of toxicity was so high that it was now against the law to swim in the lake.

I kept the truck wide open, the plastic ball on the floor stick shaking under my palm, all the way to the Mississippi bridge at Baton Rouge. Then I rolled down the elevated causeway through the Atchafalaya marsh and the warm night air that smelled of sour mud and hyacinths blooming back in the trees. Out over the pewter-colored bays, the dead cypress trunks were silhouetted against burning gas flares and the vast black-green expanse of sawgrass and flooded willow islands. Huge thunderclouds tumbled one upon another like curds of black smoke from an old fire, and networks of lightning were bursting silently all over the southern sky. I thought I could smell raindrops on the wind, as cool and clean and bright as the taste of white alcohol on the tip of the tongue.

9

Outside our bedroom window the pecan trees were motionless and gray, soaked with humidity, in the false dawn. Then the early red sun broke above the treeline in the marsh like a Lucifer match being scratched against the sky.

Bootsie slept on her side in her nightgown, the sheet molded against her thigh, her face cool, her auburn hair ruffled on the pillow by the window fan. In the early morning her skin always had a glow to it, like the pale pink light inside a rose. I moved her body against mine and kissed her mouth lightly. Without opening her eyes she smiled sleepily, slipped her arms around my back, widened her thighs, and pressed her stomach against me.

Out on the bayou, I thought I heard a bass leap from the water in a wet arc and then reenter the surface, slapping his tail, as he slid deep into the roots of the floating hyacinths.

Bootsie put her legs in mine, her breath warm against my cheek, one hand in the small of my back, her soft rump rolling against the bed; then I felt that heart-twisting moment begin to grow inside me, past any point of control, like a log dam in a canyon resisting a flooded streambed, then cracking and bursting loose in a rush of white water and uprooted boulders.

I lay beside her and held one of her hands and kissed the thin film of perspiration on her shoulders.

She felt my face with her fingers and touched the white patch in my hair as though she were exploring a physical curiosity in me for the first time.

'Ole Streak,' she said, and smiled.

'Cops get worse names.'

She was quiet a moment, then she said my name with a question mark beside it the way she always did when she was about to broach a difficult subject.

'Yes?' I said.

'Elrod Sykes called while you were in New Orleans. He wanted to apologize for coming to our house drunk.'

'Okay.'

'He wants to go to an AA meeting with you.'

'All right, I'll talk to him about it.'

She looked at the revolving shadows the window fan made on the wall.

'He's rented a big boat,' she said. 'He wants to go fishing out on the salt.'

'When?'

'Day after tomorrow.'

'What'd you tell him?'

'That I'd have to check with you.'

'You don't think we should go?'

'He troubles me, Dave.'

'Maybe the guy *is* psychic. That doesn't mean he's bad news.'

'I have a strange feeling about him. Like he's going to do something to us.'

'He's a practicing alcoholic, Boots. He's a sick man. How's he going to harm us?'

'I don't know. It's just the way I feel. I can't explain it.'

'Do you think he's trying to manipulate me?'

'How do you mean?'

I raised up on one elbow and looked into her face. I tried to smile.

'I have an obligation to help other alcoholics,' I said. 'Maybe it looks like Elrod's trying to pull some strings on me, that maybe instead of helping him I'll end up back on the dirty-boogie again.'

'Let him find his own help, Dave.'

'I think he's harmless.'

'I should have listened to you. I shouldn't have invited them into the house.'

'It's not good to do this, Boots. You're worrying about a problem that doesn't exist.'

'He's too interested in you. There's a reason for it. I know it.'

'I'll invite him to go to a meeting. We'll forget about the fishing trip.'

'Promise me that, Dave.'

'I do.'

'You mean it, no going back on it?'

'You've got my word.'

She cupped my fingers in her hand and put her head under my chin. In the shadowy light I could see her heart tripping against her breast.

I parked in the lot behind the office and walked toward the back door. Two uniformed deputies had just taken a black man in handcuffs into the building, and four others were drinking coffee out of foam cups and smoking cigarettes in the shade against the wall. I heard one of them use my name, then a couple of them laugh when I walked by.

I stopped and walked back to them.

'How y'all doing today?' I said.

'What's going on, Dave?' Rufus Arceneaux said. He had been a tech sergeant in the Marine Corps and he still wore his sunbleached hair in a military crewcut. He took off his shades and rubbed the bridge of his nose.

'I'd better get back on it,' one deputy said, flipped away his cigarette, and walked toward his cruiser.

'What's the joke about, Rufus?' I said.

'It's nothing I said, Dave. I was just quoting the boss man,' Rufus said. His green eyes were full of humor as he looked at the other deputies.

'What did the sheriff have to say?'

'Hey, Dave, fair is fair. Don't lay this off on me,' he said.

'Do you want to take the mashed potatoes out of your mouth and tell me what you're talking about?'

'Hey, come on, man,' he said, chuckling.

'What the fuck, it's no big deal. Tell him,' the deputy next to him said.

'The sheriff said if the governor of Lou'sana invited the whole department to dinner, Dave would be the one guy who'd manage to spit in the punch bowl.'

Then the three of them were silent, suppressing their grins, their eyes roving around the parking lot.

'Drop by my office sometime today, Rufus,' I said. 'Anytime before five o'clock. You think you can work it in?'

'It's just a joke, Dave. I'm not the guy who said it, either.'

'That's right. So it's nothing personal. I'd just like to go through your jacket with you.'

'What for?'

'You've been here eight or nine years, haven't you?'

'That's right.'

'Why is it that I always have the feeling you'd like to be an NCO again, that maybe you have some ambitions you're not quite telling us about?'

His lips became a tight, stitched line, and I saw a slit of yellow light in his eye.

'Think about it and I'll talk to you later, Rufus,' I said, and went inside the building, into the air-conditioned odor of cigar butts and tobacco spittle, and closed the door behind me.

Ten minutes later the sheriff walked into my office and sat down in front of my desk with his arms propped stiffly on his thighs. In his red-faced concentration he reminded me of a football coach sitting on the edge of a bench.

'Where do you think we should begin?' he said.

'You got me.'

'From what I hear about that scene in the restaurant, you tried to tear that fellow apart.'

'Those guys think they're in the provinces and they can do what they want. Sometimes you have to turn them around.'

'It looks like you got your message across. Balboni had to take the guy to the hospital. You broke his tooth off inside his gums.'

'It was a bad morning. I let things get out of control. It won't happen again.'

He didn't answer. I could hear him breathing through his nose.

'You want some coffee?' I said.

'No.'

I got up and filled my cup from my coffee maker in the corner.

'I've had two phone calls already about your trip to New Orleans last night,' he said.

'What about it?'

He took a folded-back notebook out of his shirt pocket and looked at the first page.

'Did you ever hear of a black guy named Robert Brown?' he asked.

'Yep, that's Downtown Bobby Brown.'

'He's trying to file charges against you. He says you smashed his face into a men's-room door at the bus depot.'

'I see.'

'What the hell are you doing, Dave?'

'He's a pimp and a convicted child molester. When I found him, he was scamming two girls who couldn't have been over sixteen years old. I wonder if he passed on that information when he filed his complaint.'

'I don't give a damn what this guy did. I'm worried about a member of my department who might have confused himself with Wyatt Earp.'

'This guy's charges aren't going anywhere and you know it.'

'I wish I had your confidence. It looks like you got some people's attention over in Jefferson Parish, too.'

'I don't understand.'

'The Jefferson Parish Sheriff's Department seems to think we may have a loose cannon crashing around on our deck.'

'What's their problem?'

'You didn't check in with them, you didn't coordinate with anybody, you simply went up and down the Airline Highway on your own, questioning hookers and bartenders about a pimp with no name.'

'So?'

He rubbed the cleft in his round chin, then dropped the flat of his hand on his thigh.

'They say you screwed up a surveillance, that you blew a sting operation of some kind,' he said.

'How?'

'I don't know.'

'It sounds like bullshit to me, sheriff. It sounds like cops on a pad who don't want outsiders walking around on their turf.'

'Maybe that's true, Dave, but I'm worried about you. I think you're overextending yourself and you're not hearing me when I talk to you about it.'

'Did Twinky Lemoyne call?'

'No. Why should he?'

'I went over to Lafayette and questioned him yesterday afternoon.'

He removed his rimless glasses, wiped them with a Kleenex, and put them back on. His eyes came back to meet mine.

'This was after I talked to you about involving people in the investigation who seem to have no central bearing in it?' he asked.

'I'm convinced that somehow Baby Feet was mixed up with Cherry LeBlanc, sheriff. Twinky Lemoyne has business ties to Feet. The way I read it, that makes him fair game.'

'I'm really sorry to hear this, Dave.'

'An investigation clears as well as implicates people. His black employees seem to think well of him. He didn't call in a complaint about my talking to him, either. Maybe he's an all-right guy.'

'You disregarded my instructions, Dave.'

'I saw the bodies of both those girls, sheriff.'

'And?'

'Frankly I'm not real concerned about whose toes I step on.'

He rose from his chair and tucked his shirt tightly into his gunbelt with his thumbs while his eyes seemed to study an unspoken thought in midair.

'I guess at this point I have to tell you something of a personal nature,' he said. 'I don't care for your tone, sir. I don't care for it in the least.'

I picked up my coffee cup and sipped off it and looked at nothing as he walked out of the room.

Rosie Gomez was down in Vermilion Parish almost all day. When she came back into the office late that afternoon her face was flushed from the heat and her dark hair stuck damply to her skin. She dropped her purse on top of her desk and propped her arms on the side of the air-conditioning unit so the windstream blew inside her sleeveless blouse.

'I thought Texas was the hottest place on earth. How did anyone ever live here before air conditioning?' she said.

'How'd you make out today?'

'Wait a minute and I'll tell you. Damn, it was hot out there. What happened to the rain?'

'I don't know. It's unusual.'

'Unusual? I felt like I was being cooked alive inside wet cabbage leaves. I'm going to ask for my next assignment in the Aleutians.'

'I'm afraid you'll never make the state Chamber of Commerce, Rosie.'

She walked back to her desk, blowing her breath up into her face, and opened her purse.

'What'd you do today?' she asked.

'I tried to run down some of those old cases, but they're pretty cold now – people have quit or retired or don't remember, files misplaced, that sort of thing. But there's one interesting thing here—' I spread a dozen National Crime Information Center fax sheets over the top of my desk. 'If one guy committed several of these unsolved murders, it doesn't look like he ever operated outside the state. In other words, there don't seem to be any unsolved female homicides that took place during the same time period in an adjoining area in Texas, Arkansas, or Mississippi.

'So this guy may not only be homegrown but for one reason or another he's confined his murders to the state of Louisiana.'

'That'd be a new one,' she said. 'Serial killers usually travel, unless they prey off a particular local community, like gays or street-walkers. Anyway, look at what jumped up out of the weeds today.'

She held up a plastic Ziploc bag with a wood-handled, brass-tipped pocket knife inside. The single blade was opened and streaked with rust.

'Where'd you find it?'

'A half mile back down the levee from where the girl was found in the barrel. It was about three feet down from the crest.'

'You covered all that ground by yourself?'

'More or less.'

I looked at her a moment before I spoke again. 'Rosie, you're kind of new to the area, but that levee is used by fishermen and hunters all the time. Sometimes they drop stuff.'

'All my work for nothing, huh?' She smiled and lifted a strand of hair off her eyebrow.

'I didn't say that—'

'I didn't tell you something else. I ran into an elderly black man down there who sells catfish and frogs legs off the back of his pickup truck. He said that about a month ago, late at night, he saw a white man in a new blue or black car looking for something on the levee with a flashlight. Just like that alligator poacher you questioned, he wondered why anybody would be down there at night with a new automobile. He said the man with the light wasn't towing a boat trailer and he didn't have a woman with him, either. Evidently he thinks those are the only two reasonable explanations for anyone ever going down there.'

'Could he give you a description of the white man?'

'No, he said he was busy stringing a trotline between some duck blinds. What's a trotline, anyway?'

'You stretch a long piece of twine above the water and tie it to a couple of stumps or flooded trees. Then intermittently you hang twelve-inch pieces of weighted line with baited hooks into the water. Catfish feed by the moon, and when they hook themselves, they usually work the hook all the way through their heads and they're still on the trotline when the fisherman picks it up in the morning.'

I sat on the corner of her desk and picked up the plastic bag and looked at the knife. It was the kind that was made in Pakistan or Taiwan and could be purchased for two dollars on the counter of almost any convenience store.

'If that was our man, what do you think happened?' I said.

'Maybe that's where he bound her with the electrician's tape. He used the knife to slice the tape, then dropped it. He either searched for it that night or came back another night when he discovered it was missing.'

'I don't want to mess up your day, Rosie, but our man doesn't seem to leave fingerprints. At least there were none on the electrician's tape in the two murders that we think he committed. Why should he worry about losing the knife?'

'He needs to orchestrate, to be in control. He can't abide accidents.'

'He left the ice pick in Cherry LeBlanc.'

'Because he meant to. He gave us the murder weapon; it'll never be found on him. But he didn't plan to give us his pocket knife. That bothers him.'

'That's not a bad theory. Our man is all about power, isn't he?'

She stood her purse up straight and started to snap it shut. It clunked on the desk when she moved it. She reached inside and lifted out her .357 magnum revolver, which looked huge in her small hand, and replaced it on top of her billfold. She snapped the catch on the purse.

'I said the obsession is about power, isn't it?'

'Always, always, always,' she said.

The concentration seemed to go out of her eyes, as though the day's fatigue had just caught up with her.

'Rosie?'

'What is it?'

'You feel okay?'

'I probably got dehydrated out there.'

'Drop the knife off with our fingerprint man and I'll buy you a Dr Pepper.'

'Another time. I want to see what's on the knife.'

'This time of day our fingerprint man is usually backed up. He probably won't get to it until tomorrow.'

'Then he's about to put in for some overtime.'

She straightened her shoulders, slung her purse on her shoulder, and walked out the door into the corridor. A deputy with a girth like a hogshead nodded to her deferentially and stepped aside to let her pass.

When I was helping Batist clean up the shop that evening I remembered that I hadn't called Elrod Sykes about his invitation to go fishing out on the salt. Or maybe I had deliberately pushed it out of my mind. I knew that Bootsie was probably right about Elrod. He was one of the walking wounded, the kind for whom you always felt sympathy, but you knew eventually he'd rake a whole dustpan of broken glass into your head.

I called up to the house and got the telephone number that he had left with Bootsie. While Elrod's phone was ringing, I gazed out the screen window at Alafair and a little black girl playing with Tripod by the edge of a corn garden down the road. Tripod was on his back, rolling in the baked dirt, digging his claws into a deflated football. Even though there was still moisture in the root systems, the corn looked sere and red against the late sun, and when the breeze lifted in the dust the leaves crackled dryly around the scarecrow that was tilted at an angle above the children's heads.

Kelly Drummond answered the phone, then put Elrod on.

'You cain't go?' he said.

'No, I'm afraid not.'

'Tomorrow's Saturday. Why don't you take some time off?'

'Saturday's a big day for us at the dock.'

'Mr Robicheaux . . . Dave . . . is there some other problem here? I guess I was pretty fried when I was at your house.'

'We were glad to have you all. How about I talk with you later? Maybe we'll go to a meeting, if you like.'

'Sure,' he said, his voice flat. 'That sounds okay.'

'I appreciate the invitation. I really do.'

'Sure. Don't mention it. Another time.'

'Yes, that might be fine.'

'So long, Mr Robicheaux.'

The line went dead, and I was left with the peculiar sensation that I had managed both to be dishonest and to injure the feelings of someone I liked.

Batist and I cleaned the ashes out of the barbecue pit, on which we cooked sausage links and split chickens with a *sauce piquante* and sold them at noon to fishermen for three-ninety-five a plate; then we seined the dead shiners out of the bait tanks, wiped down the counters, swept the grained floors clean, refilled the beer and soda-pop coolers, poured fresh crushed ice over the bottles, loaded the candy and cigarette machines, put the fried pies, hard-boiled eggs, and pickled hogs' feet in the icebox in case Tripod got into the shop again, folded up the beach umbrellas on the spool tables, slid back the canvas awning that stretched on wires over the dock, emptied water out of all our rental boats, ran a security chain through a welded ring on the housing of all the outboard engines, and finally latched the board flaps over the windows and turned keys in all the locks.

I walked across the road and stopped by the corn garden where Alafair and the black girl were playing. A pickup truck banged over the ruts in the road and dust drifted across the cornstalks. Out in the marsh, a solitary frog croaked, then the entire vault of sky seemed to ache with the reverberation of thousands of other frogs.

'What's Tripod been into today?' I said.

'Tripod's been good. He hasn't been into anything, Dave,' Alafair said. She picked Tripod up and thumped him down on his back in her lap. His paws pumped wildly at the air.

'What you got there, Poteet?' I said to the little black girl. Her pigtails were wrapped with rubber bands and her elbows and knees were gray with dust.

'Found it right here in the row,' she said, and opened her hand. 'What that is, Mr Dave?'

'I told you. It's a minié ball,' Alafair said.

'It don't look like no ball to me,' Poteet said.

I picked it out of her hand. It was smooth and cool in my palm, oxidized an off-white, cone-shaped at one end, grooved with three rings, and hollowed at the base. The French contribution to the science of killing people at long distances. It looked almost phallic.

'These were the bullets that were used during the War Between the States, Poteet,' I said, and handed it back to her. 'Confederate and federal soldiers fought all up and down this bayou.'

'That's the war Alafair say you was in, Mr Dave?'

'Do I look that old to you guys?'

'How much it worth?' Poteet said.

'You can buy them for a dollar at a store in New Orleans.'

'You give me a dollar for it?' Poteet said.

'Why don't you keep it instead Po'?' I said, and rubbed the top of her head.

'I don't want no nasty minié ball. It probably gone in somebody,' she said, and flung it into the cornstalks.

'Don't do that. You can use it in a slingshot or something,' Alafair said. She crawled on hands and knees up the row and put the minié ball in the pocket of her jeans. Then she came back and lifted Tripod up in her arms.

'Dave, who was that old man?' she said.

'What old man?'

'He got a stump,' Poteet said.

'A stump?'

'That's right, got a stump for a leg, got an arm look like a shriveled-up bird's claw,' Poteet said.

'What are y'all talking about?' I said.

'He was on a crutch, Dave. Standing there in the leaves,' Alafair said. I knelt down beside them.

'You guys aren't making a lot of sense,' I said.

'He was right up there in the corn leaves. Talking in the wind,' Poteet said. 'His mouth just a big hole in the wind without no sound coming out.'

'I bet y'all saw the scarecrow.'

'If scarecrows got BO', Poteet said.

'Where'd this old man go?' I said.

'He didn't go anywhere,' Alafair said. 'The wind started blowing real hard in the stalks and he just disappeared.'

'Disappeared? I said.

'That's right,' Poteet said. 'Him and his BO.'

'Did he have a black coat on, like that scarecrow there?' I tried to smile, but my heart had started clicking in my chest.

'No, suh, he didn't have no black coat on,' Poteet said.

'It was gray, Dave,' Alafair said. 'Just like your shirt.'

'Gray?' I said woodenly.

'Except it had some gold on the shoulders,' she said.

She smiled at me as though she had given me a detail that somehow would remove the expression she saw on my face.

My knees popped when I stood up.

'You'd better come home for supper now, Alf,' I said.

'You mad, Dave? We done something wrong?' Alafair said.

'Don't say "we done," little guy. No, of course, I'm not mad. It's just been a long day. We'll see you later, Poteet.'

Alafair swung on my hand as she held on to Tripod's leash, and we walked up the slope through the pecan trees toward the lighted gallery of our house. The thick layer of humus and leaves and moldy pecan husks cracked under our shoes. Behind the house the western horizon was still as blue as a robin's egg and streaked with low-lying pink clouds.

'You're real tired, huh?' she said.

'A little bit.'

'Take a nap.'

'Okay, little guy.'

'Then we can go to Vezey's for ice cream,' she said. She grinned up at me.

'Were they epaulets?' I said.

'What?'

'The gold you saw on his shoulders. Sometimes soldiers wear what they call epaulets on the shoulders of their coats.'

'How could he be a soldier? He was on a crutch. You say funny things sometimes, Dave.'

'I get it from a certain little fellow I know.'

'That man doesn't hurt children, does he?'

'No, I'm sure he's harmless. Let's don't worry about it anymore.'

'Okay, big guy.'

'I'll feed Tripod. Why don't you go inside and wash your hands for supper?'

The screen door slammed after her, and I looked back down the slope under the overhang of the trees at the corn garden in the fading twilight. The wind dented and bent the stalks and straightened the leaves and swirled a column of dust around the blank cheesecloth visage of the scarecrow. The dirt road was empty, the bait shop dark, the gray clouds of insects hovering over the far side of the bayou almost like a metamorphic and tangible shape in the damp heat and failing light. I stared at the cornstalks and the hot sky filled with angry birds, then pinched the moisture and salt out of my eyes and went inside the house.

A tropical storm that had been expected to hit the Alabama coast changed direction and made landfall at Grand Isle, Louisiana. At false dawn the sky had been bone white, then a red glow spread across the eastern horizon as though a distant fire were burning out of control. The barometer dropped; the air became suddenly cooler; the bream began popping the bayou's darkening surface; and in less than an hour a line of roiling, lightning-forked clouds moved out of the south and covered the wetlands from horizon to horizon like an enormous black lid. The rain thundered like hammers on the wood dock and the bait shop's tin roof, filled our unrented boats with water, clattered on the islands of lily pads in the bayou, and dissolved the marsh into a gray and shapeless mist.

Then I saw a sleek white cabin cruiser approaching the dock, its windows beaten with rain, riding in on its own wake as the pilot cut back the throttle. Batist and I were under the awning, carrying the barbecue pit into the lee of the shop. Batist had two inches of a dead cigar in the corner of his mouth; he squinted through the rain at the boat as it bumped against the strips of rubber tire nailed to the dock pilings.

'Who that is?' he said.

'I hate to think.'

'He wavin' at you, Dave. Hey, it's that drunk man done fell in the bayou the ot'er night. That man must surely love water.'

We set the barbecue pit under the eave of the building and got back inside. The rain was whipping off the roof like frothy ropes. Through the screen window I could see Elrod and Kelly Drummond moving around inside the boat's cabin.

'Oh, oh, he trying to get out on the dock, Dave. I ain't goin' out there to pull him out of the bayou this time, me. Somebody ought to give that man swimmin' lessons or a big rock, one, give people some relief.'

Our awning extended on wires all the way to the lip of the dock, and Elrod was trying to climb over the cruiser's gunwale into the protected area under the canvas. He was bare-chested, his white golf slacks soaked and pasted against his skin, his rubber-soled boat shoes sopping with water. His hand slipped off the piling, and he fell backward onto the deck, raked a fishing rod down with him and snapped it in half so that it looked like a broken coat hanger.

I put on my rain hat and went outside.

Elrod shielded his eyes with his hands and looked up at me in the rain. A purple and green rose was tattooed on his upper left chest.

'I guess I haven't got my sea legs yet,' he said.

'Get back inside,' I said, and jumped down into the boat.

'We're going after speckled trout. They always hit in the rain. At least they do on the Texas coast.'

The rain was cold and stung like BBs. From two feet away I could smell the heavy surge of beer on his breath.

'I'm going inside,' I said, and pulled open the cabin door.

'Sure. That's what I was trying to do. Invite you down for a sandwich or a Dr Pepper or a tonic or something,' he said, and closed the cabin door behind us.

Kelly Drummond wore leather sandals, a pair of jeans, and the Ragin' Cajuns T-shirt with my name ironed on the back that Alafair had given to Elrod after he had fallen into the bayou. She picked up a towel and began rubbing Elrod's hair with it. Her green eyes were clear, her face fresh, as though she had recently awakened from a deep sleep.

'You want to go fishing with us?' she said.

'I wouldn't advise going out on the salt today. You'll probably get knocked around pretty hard out there.'

She looked at Elrod.

'The wind'll die pretty soon', he said.

'I wouldn't count on that,' I said.

'The guy who rented us the boat said it can take pretty heavy seas. The weather's not that big a deal, is it?' he said.

On the floor was an open cooler filled with cracked ice, long-necked bottles of Dixie, soda pop, and tonic water.

'I can outfit you with some fly rods and popping bugs,' I said. 'Why not wait until the rain quits and then try for some bass and goggle-eye perch?'

'When's the last time you caught fresh-water fish right after a rain?' He smiled crookedly at me.

'Suit yourself. But I think what you're doing is a bad idea,' I said. I looked at Kelly.

'El, we don't have to go today,' she said. 'Why don't we just drive down to New Orleans and mess around in the French Quarter?'

'I planned this all week.'

'Come on, El. Give it up. It looks like Noah's flood out there.'

'Sorry, we've got to do it. You can understand that, cain't you, Mr Robicheaux?'

'Not really. Anyway, watch the bend in the channel about three miles south. The water's been low and there's some snags on the left.'

'Three miles south? Yeah, I'll watch it,' he said, his eyes refocusing on nothing. His suntanned, taut chest was beaded with water. His feet were wide spread to keep his balance, even though the boat was not moving. 'You sure you don't want a tonic?'

'Thanks, anyway. Good luck to you all,' I said.

Before I went out the cabin door, Kelly made her eyes jump at me, but I closed the door behind me and stepped up on the gunwale and onto the dock.

I began pushing huge balloons of water out of the awning with a broom handle and didn't hear her come up behind me.

'He'll listen to you. Tell him not to go out there,' she said. There was a pinched indentation high up on her right cheek.

'I think you should tell him that yourself.'

'You don't understand. He had a big fight with Mikey yesterday about the script and walked off the set. Then this morning he put the boat on Mikey's credit card. Maybe if we take the boat back now, the man'll tear up the credit slip. You think he might do that?'

'I don't know.'

'El's going to get fired, Mr Robicheaux.'

'Tell Elrod you're staying here. That's about all I can suggest.'

'He'll go anyway.'

'I wish I could help you.'

'That's it? *Au revoir*, fuck you, boat people?'

'In the last two days Elrod told both me and my wife he'd like to go to an AA meeting with me. Now it's ten in the morning and he's already ripped. What do you think the real problem is – the boat, your director, the rain, me, or maybe something else?'

She turned around as though to leave, then turned back and faced me again. There was a bright, painful light in her green eyes, the kind that comes right before tears.

'What do I do?' she said.

'Go inside the shop. I'll try again,' I said.

I climbed back down into the boat and went into the cabin. He had his elbows propped on the instrument panel, while he ate a po'-boy sandwich and stared at the rain dancing in a yellow spray on the bayou.

His face had become wan and indolent, either from fatigue or alcoholic stupor, passive to all insult or intimidation. The more I talked, the more he yawned.

'She's a good lady, El,' I said. 'A lot of men would cut off their fingers with tin snips to have one like her.'

'You got that right.'

'Then why don't you quit this bullshit, at least for one day, and let her have a little serenity?'

Then his eyes focused on the cooler, on an amber, sweating bottle of Dixie nestled in the ice.

'All right,' he said casually. 'Let me borrow your fly rods, Mr Robicheaux. I'll take good care of them.'

'You're not going out on the salt?'

'No, I get seasick anyway.'

'You want to leave the beer box with me?'

'It came with the boat. That fellow might get mad if I left it somewhere. Thanks for your thoughtfulness, though.'

'Yeah, you bet.'

After they were gone, I resolved that Elrod Sykes was on his own with his problems.

'Hey, Dave, that man really a big movie actor?' Batist said.

'He's big stuff out in Hollywood, Batist. Or at least he used to be.'

'He rich?'

'Yeah, I guess he is.'

'That's his reg'lar woman, too, huh?'

'Yep.'

'How come he's so unhappy?'

'I don't know, Batist. Probably because he's a drunk.'

'Then why don't he stop gettin' drunk?'

'I don't know, partner.'

'You mad 'cause I ax a question?'

'Not in the least, Batist,' I said, and headed for the back of the shop and began stacking crates of canned soda pop in the storeroom.

'You got some funny moods, you.' I heard him say behind me.

A half hour later the phone rang.

'Hello,' I said.

'We got a problem down here,' a voice said.

There was static on the line and rain was throbbing on the shop's tin roof.

'Elrod?'

'Yeah. We hit some logs or a sandbar or something.'

'Where are you?'

'At a pay phone in a little store. I waded ashore.'

'Where's the boat?'

'I told you, it's messed up.'

'Wait until the water rises, then you'll probably float free.'

'There's a bunch of junk in the propeller.'

'What are you asking me, Elrod?'

'Can you come down here?'

Batist was eating some chicken and dirty rice at the counter. He looked at my face and laughed to himself.

'How far down the bayou is the boat?' I said.

'About three miles. That bend you were talking about.'

'The bend I was talking about, huh?'

'Yeah, you were right. There's some dead trees or logs in the water there. We ran right into them.'

'We?'

'Yeah.'

'I'll come after you, but I'm also going to give you a bill for my time.'

'Sure thing, absolutely, Dave. This is really good of you. If I can—'

I put the receiver back on the hook.

'Tell Bootsie I'll be back in about an hour,' I said.

Batist had finished his lunch and was peeling the cellophane off a fresh cigar. The humor had gone out of his face.

'Dave, I ain't one to tell you what to do, no,' he said. 'But there's people that's always gonna be axin' for somet'ing. When you deal with them kind, it don't matter how much you give, it ain't never gonna be enough.'

He lit his cigar and fixed his eyes on me as he puffed on the smoke.

I put on my raincoat and hat, hitched a boat and trailer to my truck, and headed down the dirt road under the canopy of oak trees toward the general store where Elrod had made his call. The trailer was bouncing hard in the flooded chuckholes, and through the rearview mirror I could see the outboard engine on the boat's stern wobbling against the engine mounts. I shifted down to second gear, pulled to a wide spot on the road, and let a car behind me pass. The driver, a man wearing a shapeless fedora, looked in the opposite direction of me, out toward the bayou, as he passed.

Elrod was not at the general store, and I drove a quarter mile farther south to the bend where he had managed to put the cabin cruiser right through the limbs of a submerged tree and simultaneously scrape the bow up on a sandbar. The bayou was running high and yellow now, and gray nests of dead morning-glory vines had stuck to the bow and fanned back and forth in the current.

I backed my trailer into the shallows, then unwinched my boat into the water, started the engine, and opened it up in a shuddering whine against the steady clatter of the rain on the bayou's surface.

I came astern of the cabin cruiser and looped the painter on a cleat atop the gunwale so that my boat swung back in the lee of the cruiser. The current was swirling with mud and I couldn't see the propeller, but obviously it was fouled. From under the keel floated a streamer of torn hyacinth vines and lily pads, baited trotline, a divot ripped out of a conical fish net, and even the Clorox marker bottle that went with it.

Elrod came out of the cabin with a newspaper over his head.

'How does it look?' he said.

'I'll cut some of this trash loose, then we'll try to back her into deeper water. How'd you hit a fish net? Didn't you see the Clorox bottle?'

'Is that how they mark those things?'

I opened my Puma knife, reached as deep below the surface as I could, and began pulling and sawing away the flotsam from the propeller.

'I 'spect the truth is I don't have any business out here,' he said.

I flung a handful of twisted hyacinths and tangled fish line toward the bank and looked up into his face. The alcoholic shine had gone out of his eyes. Now they simply looked empty, on the edge of regret.

'You want me to get down in the water and do that?' he asked. Then he glanced away at something on the far bank.

'No, that's all right,' I said. I stepped up on the bow of my boat and over the rail of the cabin cruiser. 'Let's see what happens. If I can't shake

108

her loose, I'll tie my outboard onto the bow and try to pull her sideways into the current.'

We went inside the dryness of the cabin and closed the door. Kelly was sleeping on some cushions, her face nestled into one arm. When she woke, she looked around sleepily, her cheek wrinkled with the imprint of her arm; then she realized that little had changed in her and Elrod's dreary morning and she said, 'Oh,' almost like a child to whom awakenings are not good moments.

I started the engine, put it in reverse, and gave it the gas. The hull vibrated against the sandbar, and through the back windows I could see mud and dead vegetation boiling to the bayou's surface behind the stern. But we didn't move off the sandbar. I tried to go forward and rock it loose, then I finally cut the engine.

'It's set pretty hard, but it might come off if you push against the bow, Elrod,' I said. 'You want to do that?'

'Yeah, sure.'

'It's not deep there. Just stay on the sandbar, close to the hull.'

'Put on a life jacket, El,' Kelly said.

'I swam across the Trinity River once at flood stage when houses were floating down it,' he said.

She took a life jacket out of a top compartment, picked up his wrist, and slipped his arm through one of the loops. He grinned at me. Then his eyes looked out the glass at the far bank.

'What's that guy doing?' he said.

'Which guy?' I said.

'The guy knocking around in the brush out there.'

'How about we get your boat loose and worry about other people later?' I said.

'You got it,' he said, tied one lace on his jacket, and went out into the rain.

He held on to the rail on the cabin roof and worked his way forward toward the bow. Kelly watched him through the glass, biting down on the corner of his lip.

'He waded ashore before,' I said, and smiled at her. 'He's not in any danger there.'

'El has accidents. Always.'

'A psychologist might say there's a reason for that.'

She turned away from the glass, and her green eyes moved over my face.

'You don't know him, Mr Robicheaux. Not the gentle person who gives himself no credit for anything. You're too hard on him.'

'I don't mean to be.'

'You are. You judge him.'

'I'd like to see him get help. But he won't as long as he's on the juice or using.'

'I wish I had those kinds of easy answers.'

'They're not easy. Not at all.'

Elrod eased himself over the gunwale, sinking to his chest, then felt his way through the silt toward the slope on the sandbar.

'Can you stand in the stern? For the weight,' I said to Kelly.

'Where?'

'In the back of the boat.'

'Sure.'

'Take my raincoat.'

'I'm already sopped.'

I restarted the engine.

'Just a minute,' I said, and put my rain hat on her head. Her wet blond curls were flattened against her brow. 'I don't mean to be personal, but I think you're a special lady, Ms Drummond, a real soldier.'

She used both her hands to pull the hat's floppy brim down tightly on her hair. She didn't answer, but for the first time since I had met her, she looked directly into my eyes with no defensiveness or anger or fear and in fact with a measure of respect that I felt in all probability was not easily won.

I waved at Elrod through the front glass, kicked the engine into reverse, and opened the throttle. The exhaust pipes throbbed and blew spray high into the air at the waterline, the windows shook, the boards under my feet hummed with the vibrations from the engine compartment. I looked over my shoulder through the back glass and saw Kelly bent across the gunwale, pushing at the bottom of the bayou with a tarpon gaff; then suddenly the hull scraped backward in the sand, sliding out of a trench in a yellow and brown gush of silt and dead reeds, and popped free in the current.

Elrod was standing up on the sandbar, his balled fists raised over his head in victory.

I cut the gas and started out the cabin door to get the anchor.

Just as the rain struck my bare head and stung my eyes, just as I looked across the bayou and saw the man in the shapeless fedora kneeling hard against an oak tree, his shadowed face aimed along the sights of a bolt-action rifle, the leather sling twisted military style around the forearm, I knew that I was caught in one of those moments that will always remain forever too late, knew this even before I could yell, wave my arms, tell him that the person in the rain hat and Ragin' Cajuns T-shirt with my name on the back was not me. Then the rifle's muzzle flashed in the rain, the report echoing across the water and into the willow islands. The bullet cut a hole like a rose petal in the back of Kelly's shirt and left an exit wound in her throat that made me think of wolves with red mouths running through trees.

10

It was a strange week, for me as well as the town. Kelly's death brought journalists from all over the country to New Iberia. They filled all the motels, rented every available automobile in Lafayette, and dwarfed in both numbers and technical sophistication our small area news services.

Many of them were simply trying to do their jobs. But another kind came among us, too, those who have a voyeuristic glint in their eyes, whose real motivations and potential for callousness are unknown even to themselves.

I got an unlisted phone number for the house.

I began to be bothered by an odor, both in my sleep and during the late afternoon when the sun baked down on the collapsed barn at the back of our property. I noticed it the second day after Kelly's death, the day that Elrod escorted her body back to Kentucky for the burial. It smelled like dead rats. I scattered a bag of lime among the weeds and rotted boards and the smell went away. Then the next afternoon it was back, stronger than before, as invasive as a stranger's soiled palm held to your face.

I put our bedroom fan in the side window so it would draw air from the front of the house, but I would dream of turkey buzzards circling over a corrugated rice field, of sand-flecked winds blowing across the formless and decomposing shape of a large animal, of a woman's hair and fingernails wedging against the sides of a metal box.

On the seventh morning I woke early, walked past the duck pond in the soft blue light, soaked the pile of boards and strips of rusted tin with gasoline, and set it afire. The flames snapped upward in an enormous red-black handkerchief, and a cottonmouth moccasin, with a body as thick as my wrist, slithered out of the boards into the weeds, the hindquarters of an undigested rat protruding from its mouth.

The shooter left nothing behind, no ejected brass, no recoverable prints from the tree trunk where he had fired. The pocket knife Rosie had found on the levee turned out to be free of prints. Almost all of our work had proved worthless. We had no suspects; our theories about motivation were as potentially myriad as the time we were willing to invest in thinking about them. But one heart-sinking and unalterable conclusion remained in front of my eyes all day long, in my conversations with Rosie, the sheriff, and even the deuputies who went out of their way to say good morning through my office door – Kelly Drummond was dead, and she was dead because she had been mistaken for me.

I didn't even see Mikey Goldman walk into my office. I looked up and he was standing there, flexing the balls of his feet, his protruding, pale eyes roving about the room, a piece of cartilage working in his jaw like an angry dime.

'Can I sit down?' he said.

'Go ahead.'

'How you doing?'

'I'm fine, thanks. How are you?'

'I'm all right.' His eyes went all over me, as though I were an object he was seeing for the first time.

'Can I help you with something?' I said.

'Who's the fucking guy who did this?'

'When we know that, he'll be in custody.'

'In custody? How about blowing his head off instead?'

'What's up, Mr Goldman?'

'How you handling it?'

'I beg your pardon?'

'How you handling it? I'm talking about you. I've been there, my friend. First Marine Division, Chosin Reservoir. Don't try to bullshit me.'

I put down my fountain pen on the desk blotter, folded my hands, and stared at him.

'I'm afriad we're operating on two different wavelengths here,' I said.

'Yeah? The guy next to you takes a round, and then maybe you start wondering if you aren't secretly glad it was him instead of you. Am I wrong?'

'What do you want?'

He rubbed the curly locks of salt-and-pepper hair on his neck and rolled his eyes around the room. The skin around his mouth was taut, his chin and jaw hooked in a peculiar martial way like a drill instructor's.

'Elrod's going to go crazy on me. I know it, I've seen him there before. He's a good kid, but he traded off some of his frontal lobes for magic mushrooms a long time ago. He likes you, he'll listen to you. Are you following me?'

'No.'

'You keep him at your place, you stay out at his place, I don't care how you do it. I'm going to finish this picture.'

'You're an incredible man, Mr Goldman.'

'What?' He began curling his fingers backward, as though he wanted to pull words from his chest. 'You heard I got no feelings, I don't care about my actors, movie people are callous dipshits?'

'I never heard your name before you came to New Iberia. It seems to me, though, you have only one thing on your mind – getting what you want. Anyway, I'm not interested in taking care of Elrod Sykes.'

'If I get my hands on the fuckhead who shot Kelly, you're going to have to wipe him off the wallpaper.'

'Eventually we're going to get this guy, Mr Goldman. But in the meantime, the vigilante histrionics don't float too well in a sheriff's department. Frankly, they're not too convincing, either.'

'What?'

'Ask yourself a question: How many professional killers, and the guy who did this is a professional killer, could a rural parish like this have? Next question: Who comprises the one well-known group of professional criminals currently with us in New Iberia? Answer: Julie Balboni and his entourage of hired cretins. Next question: Who's in a movie partnership with these characters?'

He leaned back in his chair, bouncing his wrists lightly on the chair's arms, glancing about the room, his eyes mercurial, one moment almost amused, then suddenly focused on some festering inner concern.

'Mr Goldman?' I said.

'Yeah? You got something else to say?'

'No, sir, not a thing.'

'Good. That's good. You're not a bad guy. You've just got your head up your hole with your own problems. It's just human.'

'I see. I'm going down the hall for a cup of coffee now,' I said. 'I suspect you'll be gone when I get back.'

He rose to his feet and flexed a kink out of his back. He unwrapped a short length of peppermint candy and stuck it in his jaw.

'You want one?' he said.

'No, thanks.'

'Don't pretend to be a Rotary man. I checked out your background before I asked you to babysit Elrod. You're as crazy as any of us. You're always just one step away from blowing up somebody's shit.'

He cocked his finger, pointed it at me, and made a hollow popping sound with his mouth.

That night I dreamed that I was trying to save a woman from drowning way out on the Gulf of Mexico. We were sliding down a deep trough, the froth whipping across her blond curls and bloodless face, her eyes sealed against the cobalt sky. Our heads protruded from the water as though they had been severed and placed on a plate. Then her body turned to stone, heavier than a marble statue, and there was no way I could keep her afloat. She sank from my arms, plummeting downward into a vortex of spinning green light, down into a canyon hundreds of feet below, a gush of air bubbles rising from a pale wound in her throat.

Rosie came through the door, clunked her purse loudly on her desk, and began rummaging through the file cabinet. She had to stand on her toes to see down into the top drawer.

'You want to have lunch today?' she asked.

'What?'

'Lunch . . . do you want to have lunch? Come in, Earth.'

'Thanks, I'll probably go home.' Then as an afterthought I said, 'You're welcome to join us.'

'That's all right. Another time.' She sat down behind her desk and began shifting papers around in a couple of file folders. But her eyes kept glancing up into my face.

'Have you got something on your mind?' I asked.

'Yeah, you.'

'You must be having an uneventful day.'

'I worked late last night. The dispatcher and I had a cup of coffee together. He asked me how I was getting along here, and I told him real good, no complaints. Then he asked me if I'd experienced any more smart-aleck behavior from some of the resident clowns in the department. I told him they'd been perfect gentlemen. I bet you can't guess what he said next.'

'You got me.'

She imitated a Cajun accent. ' "Them guys give you any mo' trouble, you just tell Dave, Miz Rosie. He done tole 'em what's gonna happen the next time they bother you." '

'He was probably exaggerating a little bit.'

'You didn't need to do that for me, Dave.'

'I apologize.'

'Don't be a wise-ass, either.'

'Boy, you're a pistol.'

'How should I take that?'

'I don't know. How about easing up?'

She rested one small hand on top of the other. She had the same solid posture behind her desk that I remembered in the nuns at the elementary school I attended.

'You look tired,' she said.

'I have bouts of insomnia.'

'You want to talk about what happened out on the bayou?'

'No.'

'Do you feel guilty about it?'

'What do you think I feel? I feel angry about it.'

'Why?'

'What kind of question is that?'

'Do you feel angry because you couldn't control what happened? Do you think somehow you're to blame for her death?'

'What if I said "yes to all the above"? What difference would it make? She's dead.'

'I think beating up on yourself has about as much merit as masturbation.'

'You're a friend, Rosie, but let it go.'

I busied myself with my paperwork and did not look back up for almost a minute. When I did, her eyes were still fixed on me.

'I just got some interesting information from the Bureau about Julie Balboni,' she said. She waited, then said, 'Are you listening?'

'Yes.'

'This year NOPD Vice has closed up a half-dozen of his dirty movie theaters and two of his escort services. His fishing fleet just went into bankruptcy, too.' When I didn't respond, she continued. 'That's where he laundered a lot of his drug money. He'd declare all kinds of legitimate profits to the IRS that never existed.'

'That's how all the wiseguys do it, Rosie. In every city in the United States.'

'Except the auditors at the IRS say he just made a big mistake. He came up with millions of dollars for this Civil War movie and he's going to have a hard time explaining where he got it.'

'Don't count on it.'

'The IRS nails their butts to the wall when nobody else can.'

I sharpened a pencil over the wastebasket with my pocket knife.

'I have a feeling I'm boring you,' she said.

'No, you're just reviving some of my earlier misgivings.'

'What?'

'I think your agency wants Julie's ass in a sling. I think these murders have secondary status.'

'That's what you think, is it?'

'That's the way it looks from here.'

She rose from her chair, closed the office door, then stood by my desk. She wore a white silk blouse with a necklace of black wooden beads. Her fingers were hooked in front of her stomach like an opera singer's.

'Julie's been a longtime embarrassment to the feds,' I continued. 'He's connected to half the crime in New Orleans and so far he's never spent one day in the bag.'

'When I was sixteen something happened to me I thought I'd never get over.' There was a flush of color in her throat. 'Not just because of what two drunken crew leaders did to me in the back of a migrant farmworkers' bus, either. It was the way the cops treated it. In some ways that was even worse. Have I got your attention, sir?'

'You don't need to do this, Rosie.'

'Like hell I don't. The next day I was sitting with my father in the waiting room outside the sheriff's office. I heard two deputies laughing about it. They not only thought it was funny, one of them said something about pepper-belly poontang. I'll never forget that moment. Not as long as I live.'

I folded up my pocket knife and stared at the tops of my fingers. I brushed the pencil shavings off my fingers into the wastebasket.

'I'm sorry,' I said.

'When I went to work for the Bureau, I swore I'd never see a woman treated the way I was. So I take severe exception to your remarks, Dave. I'd like to bust Julie Balboni, but that has nothing to do with the way I feel about the man who raped and murdered these women.'

'Where'd this happen?'

'In a migrant camp outside of Bakersfield. It's not an unusual story. Ask any woman who's ever been on a crew bus.'

'I think you're a solid cop, Rosie. I think you'll nail any perp you put in your sights.'

'Then change your goddamn attitude.'

'All right.'

She was waiting for me to say something else, but I didn't.

Her shoulders sagged and she started back toward her desk. Then she turned around. Her eyes were wet.

'That's all you've got to say?' she asked.

'No, it's not.'

'What, then?'

'I'm proud to be working with you. I think you're a standup lady.'

She started to take a Kleenex out of her purse, then she snapped the purse shut again and took a breath.

'I'm going down the hall a minute,' she said.

'All right.'

'Are we both clear about the priority in this investigation, Dave?'

'Yeah, I think we are.'

'Good. Because I don't want to have this kind of discussion again.'

'Let me mention just one thing before you go. Several years ago my second wife was murdered by some drug dealers. You know that, don't you?'

'Yes.'

'One way or another, the guys and the woman who killed her went down for it. But sometimes I wake up in the middle of the night and the old anger comes back. Even though these people took a heavy fall, for a couple of them the whole trip, sometimes it still doesn't seem enough. You know the feeling I'm talking about, don't you?'

'Yes.'

'Fair enough.' Then I said, 'You're sure you don't want to come home and have lunch with us today?'

'This isn't the day for it, Dave. Thanks, anyway,' she said, and went out the door with her purse clutched under her arm, her face set as impassively as a soldier's.

Elrod Sykes called the office just after I had returned from lunch. His voice was deep, his accent more pronounced.

'You know where there's some ruins of an old plantation house south of your boat dock?' he asked.

'What about it?'

'Can you meet me there in a half hour?'

'What for?'

'I want to talk to you, that's what for.'

'Talk to me now, Elrod, or come into the office.'

'I get nervous down there. For some reason police uniforms always make me think of a breathalyzer machine. I don't know why that might be.'

'You sound like your boat might have caught the early tide.'

'Who cares? I want to show you something. Can you be there or not?'

'I don't think so.'

'What the fuck is with you? I've got some information about Kelly's death. You want it or not?'

'Maybe you ought to give some thought as to how you talk to people.'

'I left my etiquette in Kelly's family plot up in Kentucky. I'll meet you in thirty minutes. If you're not interested, fuck you, Mr Robicheaux.'

He hung up the phone. I had the feeling I was beginning to see the side of Elrod's personality that had earned him the attention of the tabloids.

Twenty minutes later I drove my pickup truck down a dirt lane through a canebrake to the ruins of a sugar planter's home that had been built on the bayou in the 1830s. In 1863 General Banks's federal troops had dragged the piano outside and smashed it apart in the coulee, then as an afterthought had torched the slave quarters and the second story of the planter's home. The roof and cypress timbers had collapsed inside the brick shell, the cisterns and outbuildings had decayed into humus, the smithy's forge was an orange smear in the damp earth, and vandals had knocked down most of the stone markers in the family cemetery and, looking for gold and silver coins, had pried up the flagstones in the fireplaces.

Why spend time with a rude drunk, particularly on the drunk's terms?

Beause it's difficult to be hard-nosed or righteous toward a man who, for the rest of his life, will probably wake sweating in the middle of the night with a recurring nightmare or whose series of gray dawns will offer no promise of light except that first shuddering razor-edged rush that comes out of a whiskey glass.

I leaned against the fender of my truck and watched Elrod's lavender Cadillac come down the dirt lane and into the shade of the oak trees that grew in front of the ruined house. The security guard from the set, Murphy Doucet, was behind the wheel, and Elrod sat in the passenger's seat, his tanned arm balanced on the window ledge, a can of Coca-Cola in his hand.

'How you doing today, Detective Robicheaux?' Doucet said.

'Fine. How are you?'

'Like they say, we all chop cotton for the white man one way or another, you know what I mean?' he said, and winked.

He rubbed the white scar that was embossed like a chicken's foot on his throat and opened a newspaper on the steering wheel. Elrod came around the side of the Cadillac in blue swimming shorts, a beige polo shirt, and brand-new Nike running shoes.

He drank from his Coca-Cola can, set it on the hood of the car, then put a breath mint in his mouth. His eyes wandered around the clearing, then focused wanly on the sunlight winking off the bayou beyond the willow trees.

'Would you like to continue our conversation?' I said.

'You think I was out of line or something?'

'What did you want to tell me, Elrod?'

'Take a walk with me out yonder in those trees and I'll show you something.'

'The old cemetery?'

'That isn't it. Something you probably don't know about.'

We walked through a thicket of stunted oaks and hackberry trees, briars and dead morning-glory vines, to a small cemetery with a rusted and sagging piked iron fence around it. Pines with deep-green needles grew out of the graves. A solitary brick crypt had long ago collapsed in upon itself and become overgrown with wild roses and showers of four o'clocks.

Elrod stood beside me, and I could smell the scent of bourbon and spearmint on his breath. He looked out into the dazzling sunlight but his eyes didn't squint. They had a peculiar look in them, what we used to call in Vietnam the thousand-yard stare.

'There,' he said, 'in the shade, right on the edge of those hackberry trees. You see those depressions?'

'No.'

He squeezed my arm hard and pointed.

'Right where the ground slopes down to the bayou,' he said, and walked ahead of me toward the rear of the property. He pointed down at the ground. 'There's four of them. You stick a shovel in here and you'll bring up bone.'

In a damp area, where rainwater drained off the incline into a narrow coulee, there were a series of indentations that were covered with mushrooms.

'What's the point of all this?' I said.

'They were cooking mush in an iron pot and an artillery shell got all four of them. The general put wood crosses on their graves, but they rotted away a long time ago. He was a hell of an officer, Mr Robicheaux.'

'I'll be going now,' I said. 'I'd like to help you, Elrod, but I think you've marked your own course.'

'I've been with these guys. I know what they went through. They had courage, by God. They made soup out of their shoes and rifle balls out of melted nails and wagon-wheel rims. There was no way in hell they were going to quit.'

I turned and began walking back to my truck. Through the shade I could see the security guard urinating by the open door of the Cadillac. Elrod caught up with me. His hand clenched on my arm again.

'You want to write me off as a wet-brain, that's your business,' he said. 'You don't care about what these guys went through, that's your business, too. I didn't bring you out here for this, anyway.'

'Then why am I here?'

He turned me toward him with his hand.

'Because I don't like somebody carrying my oil can,' he said.

'What?'

'That's a Texas expression. It means I don't want somebody else toting my load. You've convinced yourself the guy who killed Kelly thought he had you in his sights. That's right, isn't it?'

'Maybe.'

'What makes you so goddamn important?'

I continued to walk toward my truck. He caught up with me again.

'You listen to me,' he said. 'Before she was killed I had a blowout with

Mikey. I told him the script stinks, the screenwriters he's hired couldn't get jobs writing tampon ads, he's nickel-and-dimeing the whole project to death, and I'm walking off the set unless he gets his head on straight. The greaseballs heard me.'

'Which greaseballs?'

'Balboni's people. They're all over the set. They killed Kelly to keep me in line.'

His facial skin high up on one cheek crinkled and seemed almost to vibrate.

'Take it easy, El.'

'They made her an object lesson, Mr Robicheaux.'

I touched his arm with my hand.

'Maybe Julie's involved, maybe not,' I said. 'But if he is, it's not because of you. You've got to trust me on this one.'

He turned his face away and pushed at one eye with the heel of his hand.

'When Julie and his kind create object lessons, they go right to the source of their problem,' I said. 'They don't select out innocuous people. It causes them too many problems.'

I heard his breath in his throat.

'I made them keep the casket closed,' he said. 'I told the funeral director in Kentucky, if he let her parents see her like that, I'd be back, I'd—'

I put my arm over his shoulder and walked back through the cemetery with him.

'Let's go back to town and have something to eat,' I said. 'Like somebody said to me this morning, it's no good to kick ourselves around the block, is it? What do you think?'

'She's dead. I cain't see her, either. It's not right.'

'I beg your pardon?'

'I see those soldiers but I cain't see her. Why's that? It doesn't make any sense.'

'I'll be honest with you, partner. I think you're floating on the edge of delirium tremens. Put the cork in the jug before you get there, El. Believe me, you don't have to die to go to hell.'

'You figure me for plumb down the road and around the bend, don't you? I don't blame you. I got my doubts about what I see myself.'

'Maybe that's not a bad sign.'

'When we were driving through that canebrake, I said to Murph, the security guy, "Who's that standing behind Mr Robicheaux?" Then I looked again and I knew who it was. Except I've never seen him in daylight before. When I looked again, he was gone. Which isn't the way he does things.'

'I'm going to an AA meeting tonight. You want to come?'

'Yeah, why not? It cain't be worse than having dinner with Mikey and the greaseballs.'

'You might be a little careful about your vocabulary when you're around those guys.'

'Boy, I wonder what my grandpa would say if he saw me working with the likes of that bunch. I told you he was a Texas ranger, didn't I?'

'You surely did.'

'You know what he once told me about Bonnie Parker and Clyde Barrow? He said—'

'I have to get back to the office. How about I pick you up at your place at seven-thirty?'

'Sure. Thanks for coming out, Mr Robicheaux. I'm sorry about my bad manners on the phone. I'm not given to using profanity like that. I don't know what got into me.' He picked up his soda can off the hood of his Cadillac and started to drink out of it. 'It's just Coca-Cola. That's a fact.'

'You'd better drink it then.'

He smiled at me.

'It rots your teeth,' he said, and emptied the can into the dirt.

That night I sat alone in the bait shop, a glass of iced coffee in my hand, and tried to figure the connection between Kelly's death and the pursuit of a serial killer who might also be involved with prostitution. Nothing in the investigation seemed to fit. Was the serial killer also a pimp? Why did his crimes seem to be completely contained within the state of Louisiana? If he had indeed mistaken Kelly for me, what had I discovered in the investigation that would drive him to attempt the murder of a police officer? And what was Baby Feet Balboni's stake in all this?

Equally troubling was the possibility that Kelly's death had nothing to do with our hunt for a serial killer. Maybe the rifleman in the fedora had had another motivation, one that was connected with a rat's nest of bones, strips of dried skin, rotted clothing, and a patch of kinky hair attached to a skull plate. Did someone out there believe that somehow that gaping mouth, impacted with sand, strung with green algae, could whisper the names of two killers who thought they had buried their dark deed in water thirty-five years ago?

We live today in what people elect to call the New South. But racial fear, and certainly white guilt over racial injustice, die hard. Hogman Patin, who probably feared very little in this world, had cautioned me because of my discovery of the lynched black man out in the Atchafalaya. He had also suggested that the dead man had been involved with a white woman. To Hogman, those events of years ago were still alive, still emblematic of an unforgiven and collective shame, to be spoken about as obliquely as possible, in all probability because some of the participants were still alive, too.

Maybe it was time to have another talk with Hogman, I thought.

When I drove out to his house on the bayou, the interior was dark and the white curtains in his open windows were puffing outward in the breeze. In the back I could hear the tinkling of the Milk of Magnesia bottles and the silver crosses that he had hung all over the branches of a live oak.

Where are you, Hogman? I thought. I wedged my business card in the corner of his screen door.

The moon was yellow through the trees. I could smell the unmistakable odor of chitterlings that had been burned in a pot. Out on the blacktop I heard a car engine. The headlights bounced off the tree trunks along the roadside, then the driver slowed and I thought he was about to turn into the grove of trees at the front of Hogman's property. I thought the car was probably Hogman's, and I started to walk toward the blacktop. Then the driver accelerated and his headlights swept past me.

I would have given no more notice to the driver and his vehicle, except that just as I started to turn back toward my truck and leave, he cut his lights and really gave it the gas.

If his purpose had been to conceal his license number, he was successful. But two other details stuck in my mind: the car looked new and it was dark blue, the same characteristics as the automobile that two witnesses had seen on the levee in Vermilion Parish where the asphyxiated girl had been stuffed nude into a metal barrel.

Or maybe the car had simply contained a couple of teenage neckers looking for a little nocturnal privacy. I was too tired to think about it anymore. I started my truck and headed home.

The night was clear, the constellations bursting against the black dome of sky overhead. There was no hint of rain, no sudden drop or variation in temperature to cause fog to roll off the water. But two hundred yards down from Hogman's house the road was suddenly white with mist, so thick my headlights couldn't penetrate it. At first I thought a fire was burning in a field and the wind had blown the smoke across the road. But the air smelled sweet and cool, like freshly turned earth, and was almost wet to the touch. The mist rolled in clouds off the bayou, covered the tree trunks, closed about my truck like a white glove, drifted in wisps through my windows. I don't know whether I deliberately stopped the truck or my engine killed. But for at least thirty seconds my headlights flickered on and off, my starter refused to crank, and my radio screamed with static that was like fingernails on a blackboard.

Then as suddenly as it had come, the mist evaporated from the road and the tree trunks and the bayou's placid surface as though someone had held an invisible flame to it, and the night air was again as empty and pristine as wind trapped under a glass bell.

In the morning I made do with mechanical answers in the sunlight and cleaned the terminals on my truck battery with baking soda, water, and an old toothbrush.

Hogman called the next afternoon from the movie set out on Spanish Lake.

'What you want out at my house?' he said.

'I need to talk with you about the lynched black man.'

'I done already tole you what I know. That nigger went messin' in the wrong place.'

'That's not enough.'

'Is for me.'

'You said my father helped your mother when you were in prison. So now I'm asking you to help me.'

'I already have. You just ain't listen.'

'Are you afraid of somebody, Sam? Maybe some white people?'

'I fear God. Why you talkin' to me like this?'

'What time will you be home today?'

'When I get there. You got your truck?'

'Yes.'

'My car hit a tree last night. It ain't runnin' no mo'. Come out to the set this evenin' and give me a ride home. 'Bout eight or nine o'clock.'

'We'll see you then, partner,' I said, and hung up.

The sun was red and half below the horizon, the cicadas droning in the trees, when I drove down the lane through the pecan orchard to the movie set on Spanish Lake. But I soon discovered that I was not going to easily trap Hogman Patin alone. It was Mikey Goldman's birthday and the cast and crew were throwing him a party. A linen-covered buffet table was piled with catered food, a huge pink cake, and a bowl of champagne punch in the center. The tree trunks along the lake's edge were wrapped with paper bunting, and Goldman's director's chair must have had two dozen floating balloons tied to it.

It was a happy crowd. They sipped punch out of clear plastic glasses and ate boiled shrimp and thin slices of *boudin* off paper plates. Mikey Goldman's face seemed to almost shine in the ambiance of goodwill and affection that surrounded him.

In the crowd I saw Julie Balboni and his entourage, Elrod Sykes, the mayor of New Iberia, the president of the Chamber of Commerce, a couple of Teamster officials, a state legislator, and Twinky Hebert Lemoyne from Lafayette. In the middle of it all sat Hogman Patin on an up-ended crate, his twelve-string guitar resting on his crossed thighs. He was dressed like a nineteenth-century Negro street musician, except he also wore a white straw cowboy hat slanted across his eyes. The silver picks on his right hand rang across the strings as he sang,

> Soon as day break in the mornin'
> I gone take the dirt road home.
> 'Cause these blue Monday blues
> Is goin' kill me sure as you're born.

'You ought to get yourself a plate.'

It was Murphy Doucet, the security guard. He was talking to me but his eyes were looking at a blond girl in shorts and a halter by the punch bowl. He ate a slice of *boudin* off a toothpick, then slipped the toothpick into the corner of his mouth and sucked on it.

'It doesn't look like everybody's broken up about Kelly Drummond's death, does it?' I said.

'I guess they figure life goes on.'

'You're in business with Mr Lemoyne over there, Murph?'

'We own a security service together, if that's what you mean. For me it's a pretty good deal, but for him it's nothing. If there's a business around here making money, Twinky's probably got a piece of it. Lord God, that man knows how to make money.'

Lemoyne sat by the lake in a canvas chair, a julep glass filled with bourbon, shaved ice, and mint leaves in his hand. He looked relaxed and cool in the breeze off the water, his rimless glasses pink with the sun's afterglow. His eyes fixed for a moment on my face, then he took a sip from his glass and watched some kids waterskiing out on the lake.

'Get something to eat, Dave. It's free. Hell, I'm going to take some home,' Murphy Doucet said.

'Thanks, I've already eaten,' I said, and walked over to where Hogman sat next to two local black women who had been hired as extras.

'You want a ride?' I said.

'I ain't ready yet. They's people want me to play.'

'It was your idea for me to come out here, Sam.'

'I'll be comin' directly. That's clear, ain't it? Mr Goldman fixin' to cut his cake.'

Then he began singing,

> I ax my bossman, Bossman, tell me what's right.
> He whupped my left, said, Boy, now you know what's right.

I tole my bossman, Bossman, just give me my time.
He say, Damn yo' time, boy,
Boy, you time behind.

I waited another half hour as the twilight faded, the party grew louder, and someone turned on a bank of floodlamps that lit the whole area with the bright unnatural radiance of a phosphorus flare. The punch bowl was now empty and had been supplanted by washtubs filled with cracked ice and canned beer, a portable bar, and two white-jacketed black bartenders who were making mint juleps and Martinis as fast as they could.

'I've got to head for the barn, Hogman,' I said.

'This lady axin' me somet'ing. Give me ten minutes,' he said.

A waiter came by with a tray and handed Hogman and the black woman with him paper cups streaming with draft beer. Then he handed me a frosted julep glass packed with shaved ice, mint leaves, orange slices, and candied cherries.

'I didn't order this,' I said.

'Gentlemen over yonder say that's what you drink. Say bring it to you. It's a Dr Pepper, suh.'

'Which gentleman?'

'I don't rightly remember, suh.'

I took the cup off the tray and drank from it. The ice was so cold it made my throat ache.

The lake was black now, and out in the darkness, above the noise of the revelers, I could hear somebody trying to crank an outboard engine.

I finished my drink and set the empty glass on the buffet table.

'That's it for me, Sam,' I said. 'You coming or not?'

'This lady gonna carry me home,' he said. His eyes were red from drinking. They looked out at nothing from under the brim of his straw cowboy hat.

'Hogman—' I said.

'This lady live down the road from my house. Some trashy niggers been givin' her trouble. She don't want to go home by herself. That's the way it is. I be up to yo' office tomorrow mornin'.'

I tried to look into his face, but he occupied himself with twisting the tuning pegs on his guitar. I turned and walked back through the shadows to my pickup truck. When I looked back at the party through my windshield, the blonde girl in shorts and a halter was putting a spoonful of cake into Mikey Goldman's mouth while everyone applauded.

It rained hard as I approached the drawbridge over the bayou south of town. I could see the bridge tender in his lighted window, the wet sheen and streaks of rust on the steel girders, the green and red running lights of a passing boat in the mist. I was only a few minutes from home. I simply had to cross the bridge and follow the dirt road down to my dock.

But that was not what I did or what happened.

A bolt of lightning exploded in a white ball by the side of the road and blew the heart of a tree trunk, black and smoking, out into my headlights. I swallowed to clear my ears, and for just a second, in the back of my throat, I thought I could taste black cherries, bruised mint leaves, and orange rind. Then I felt a spasm go through me just as if someone had scratched a kitchen match inside my skull.

The truck veered off the shoulder, across a collapsed barbed-wire cattle gate, onto the levee that dissected the marsh. I remember the wild buttercups sweeping toward me out of the headlights, the rocks and mud whipping under the fenders, then the fog rolling out of the dead cypress trees and willow islands, encircling the truck, smothering the windows. I could hear thunder crashing deep in the marsh, echoing out of the bays, like distant artillery.

I knew that I was going off the levee, but I couldn't unlock my hands from the steering wheel or move my right foot onto the brake pedal. I felt myself trembling, my insides constricting, my back teeth grinding, as though all my nerve endings had been severed and painted with iodine. Then I heard lightning pop the levee and blow a spray of muddy water across my windshield.

Get out, I thought. *Knock the door handle down with your elbow and jump.*

But I couldn't move.

The mist was as pink and thick as cotton candy and seemed to snap with electric currents, like a kaleidoscopic flickering of snakes' tongues. I felt the front wheels of the truck dip over the side of the levee, gain momentum with the weight in the rear end, then suddenly I was rumbling down an incline through weeds and broken cane, willow saplings and cattails, until the front wheels were embedded up to the axle in water and sand.

I don't know how long I sat there. I felt a wave of color pass through me, like nausea or the violent shudder that cheap bourbon gives you when you're on the edge of delirium tremens; then it was gone and I could see the reflection of stars on the water, the tips of the dead cypress silhouetted against the moon, and a campfire, where there should have been no fire, burning in a misty grove of trees on high ground thirty yards out from the levee.

And I knew that was where I was supposed to go.

As I waded through the lily pads toward the trees, I could see the shadows of men moving about in the firelight and hear their cracker accents and the muted sound of spoons scraping on tin plates.

I walked up out of the shallows into the edge of the clearing, dripping water, hyacinth vines stringing from my legs. The men around the fire paid me little notice, as though, perhaps, I had been expected. They were cooking tripe in an iron pot, and they had hung their haversacks and wooden canteens in the trees and stacked their rifle-muskets in pyramids of fives. Their gray and butternut-brown uniforms were sun-bleached and stiff with dried salt, and their unshaved faces had the lean and hungry look of a rifle company that had been in the field a long time.

Then from the far side of the fire a bearded man with fierce eyes stared out at me from under a gray hat with gold cord around the crown. His left arm was pinned up in a black sling, and his right trouser leg flopped loosely around a shaved wooden peg.

He moved toward me on a single crutch. I could smell tobacco smoke and sweat in his clothes. Then he smiled stiffly, the skin of his face seeming almost to crack with the effort. His teeth were as yellow as corn.

'*I'm General John Bell Hood. Originally from Kentucky. How you do, suh?*' he said, and extended his hand.

11

'*Do you object to shaking hands?*' he said.

'*No. Not at all. Excuse me.*'

The heel of his hand was half-mooned with calluses, his voice as thick as wet sand. A holstered cap-and-ball revolver hung on his thigh.

'*You look puzzled,*' he said.

'*Is this how it comes? Death, I mean.*'

'*Ask them.*'

Some of his men were marked with open, bloodless wounds I could put my fist in. Beyond the stacked rifles, at the edge of the firelight, was an ambulance wagon. Someone had raked a tangle of crusted bandages off the tailgate onto the ground.

'*Am I dead?*' I said.

'*You don't look it to me.*'

'*You said you're John Bell Hood.*'

'*That's correct.*'

His face was narrow, his cheeks hollow, his skin grained with soot.

'*I've read a great deal about you.*'

'*I hope it met your approval.*'

'*You were at Gettysburg and Atlanta. You commanded the Texas Brigade. They could never make you quit.*'

'*My political enemies among President Davis's cabinet sometimes made note of that fact.*'

'*What's the date?*' I asked.

'*It's April 21, 1865.*'

'*I don't understand.*'

'*Understand what?*'

'*Lee has already surrendered. The war's over. What are you doing here?*'

'*It's never over. I would think you'd know that. You were a lieutenant in the United States Army, weren't you?*'

'*Yes, but I gave my war back to the people who started it. I did that a long time ago.*'

'*No, you didn't. It goes on and on.*'

He eased himself down on an oak stump, his narrow eyes lighting with pain. He straightened his artificial leg in front of him. The hand that hung out of his sling had wasted to the size of a monkey's paw. A corporal threw a log into the campfire, and sparks rose into the tree branches overhead.

'*It's us against them, my friend,*' he said. '*There's insidious men abroad in the land.*' He swept his crutch at the marsh. '*My God, man, use your eyes.*'

'*The federals?*'

'*Are your eyes and ears stopped with dirt?*'

'*I think this conversation is not real. I think all of this will be gone with daylight.*'

'*You're not a fool, Mr Robicheaux. Don't pretend to be one.*'

'*I've seen your grave in New Orleans. No, it's in Metairie. You died of the yellowjack.*'

'*That's not correct. I died when they struck the colors, suh.*' He lifted his crutch and pointed it at me as he would a weapon. The firelight shone on his yellow teeth. '*They'll try your soul, son. But don't give up your cause. Occupy the high ground and make them take it foot by bloody foot.*'

'*I don't know what we're talking about.*'

'*For God's sakes, what's wrong with you? Venal and evil men are destroying the world you were born in. Can't you understand that? Why do I see fear in your face?*'

'*I think maybe I'm drunk again. I used to have psychotic episodes when I went on benders. I thought dead men from my platoon were telephoning me in the rain.*'

'*You're not psychotic, lieutenant. No more than Sykes is.*'

'*Elrod is a wet-brain, general.*'

'*The boy has heart. He's not afraid to be an object of ridicule for his beliefs. You mustn't be either. I'm depending on you.*'

'*I have no understanding of your words.*'

'*Our bones are in this place. Do you think we'll surrender it to criminals, to those who would use our teeth and marrow for landfill?*'

'*I'm going now, general.*'

'*Ah, you'll simply turn your back on madness, will you? The quixotic vision is not for you, is it?*'

'*Something's pulling me back. I can feel it.*'

'*They put poison in your system, son. But you'll get through it. You've survived worse. The mine you stepped on, that sort of thing.*'

'*Poison?*'

He shrugged and put a cigar in his mouth. A corporal lit it with a burning stick from the fire. In the shadows a sergeant was putting together a patrol that was about to move out. Their faces were white and wrinkled like prunes with exhaustion and the tropical heat.

'*Come again,*' he said.

'*I don't think so.*'

'*Then goodnight to you, suh.*'

'*Goodnight to you, general. Goodnight to your men, too.*'

He nodded and puffed on his cigar. There were small round hollows in his cheeks.

'*General?*'

'*Yes, suh?*'

'*It's going to be bad, isn't it?*'

'*What?*'

'*What you were talking about, something that's waiting for me down the road.*'

'*I don't know. For one reason or another I seem to have more insight into the past than the future.*' He laughed to himself. Then his face sobered and he wiped a strand of tobacco off his lip. '*Try to keep this in mind. It's just like when they load with horseshoes and chain. You think the barrage will last forever, then suddenly there's a silence that's almost louder than their cannon. Please don't be alarmed by the severity of my comparison. Goodnight lieutenant.*'

'*Goodnight, general.*'

I waded through the shallows, into deeper water, back toward the levee. The mist hung on the water in wisps that were as dense as thick-bodied snakes. I saw ball lightning roll through the flooded trees and snap apart against a willow island; it was as bright and yellow as molten metal dipped from a forge. Then rain began twisting out of the sky, glistening like spun glass, and the firelight behind me became a red smudge inside a fog bank that billowed out of the marsh, slid across the water, and once again closed around my truck.

The air was so heavy with ozone I could almost taste it on my tongue; I could hear a downed power line sparking and popping in a pool of water and smell a scorched electrical odor in the air like the metallic, burnt odor the St Charles streetcar makes in the rain. I could hear a nutria crying in the marsh for its mate, a high-pitched shriek like the scream of a hysterical woman. I remember all these things. I remember the mud inside my shoes, the hyacinth vines binding around my knees, the gray-green film of algae that clung to my khaki trousers like cobweb.

When a sheriff's deputy and two paramedics lifted me out of the truck cab in the morning, the sun was as white as an arc welder's flame, the morning as muggy and ordinary as the previous day, and my clothes as dry as if I had recently taken them from my closet. The only physical change the supervising paramedic noted in me was an incised lump the

131

size of a darning sock over my right eye. That and one other cautious, almost humorous observation.

'Dave, you didn't fall off the wagon on your head last night, did you?' he asked. Then, 'Sorry. I was just kidding. Forget I said that.'

Our family physician, Dr Landry, sat on the side of my bed at Iberia General and looked into the corner of my eye with a small flashlight. It was late afternoon now, Bootsie and Alafair had gone home, and the rain was falling in the trees outside the window.

'Does the light hurt your eyes?' he asked.

'A little. Why?'

'Because your pupils are dilated when they shouldn't be. Tell me again what you felt just before you went off the road.'

'I could taste cherries and mint leaves and oranges. Then I felt like I'd bitten into an electric wire with my teeth.'

He put the small flashlight in his shirt pocket, adjusted his glasses, and looked at my face thoughtfully. He was an overweight, balding, deeply tanned golf player, with rings of blond hair on his forearms.

'How do you feel now?' he said.

'Like something's torn in my head. The way wet cardboard feels when you tear it with your hands.'

'Did you eat anything?'

'I threw it up.'

'You want the good news? The tests don't show any booze in your system.'

'How could there be? I didn't drink any alcohol.'

'People have their speculations sometimes, warranted or not.'

'I can't help that.'

'The bad news is I don't know what did this to you. But according to the medics you said some strange things, Dave.'

I looked away from his face.

'You said there were soldiers out there in the marsh. You kept insisting they were hurt.'

The wind began gusting, and rain and green leaves blew against the window.

'The medics thought maybe somebody had been with you. They looked all over the levee,' he said. 'They even sent a boat out into those willow islands.'

'I'm sorry I created so much trouble for them.'

'Dave, they say you were talking about Confederate soldiers.'

'It was an unusual night.'

He took a breath, then made a sucking sound with his lips.

'Well, you weren't drunk and you're not crazy, so I've got a theory,' he said. 'When I was an intern at Charity Hospital in New Orleans back in the sixties, I treated kids who acted like somebody had roasted their brains with a blowtorch. I'm talking about LSD, Dave. You think one of those Hollywood characters might have freshened up your Dr Pepper out there in Spanish Lake?'

'I don't know. Maybe.'

'It didn't show up in the tests, but that's not unusual. To really do a tox screen for LSD, you need a gas chromatograph. Not many hospitals have one. We sure don't, anyway. Has anything like this ever happened to you before?'

'When my wife was killed, I got drunk again and became delusional for a while.'

'Why don't we keep that to ourselves?'

'Is something being said about me, doc?'

He closed his black bag and stood up to go.

'When did you start worrying about what people say?' he said. 'Look, I want you to stay in here a couple of days.'

'Why?'

'Because you didn't feel any gradual effects, it hit you all at once. That indicates to me a troubling possibility. Maybe somebody really loaded you up. I'm a little worried about the possibility of residual consequences, Dave, something like delayed stress syndrome.'

'I need to get back to work.'

'No, you don't.'

'I'll talk with the sheriff. Actually I'm surprised he hasn't been up yet.'

Dr Landry rubbed the thick hair on his forearm and looked at the water pitcher and glass on my nightstand.

'What is it?' I said.

'I saw him a short while ago. He said he talked with you for a half hour this morning.'

I stared out the window at the gray sky and the rain falling in the trees. Thunder boomed and echoed out of the south, shaking the glass in the window, and for some reason in my mind's eye I saw rain-soaked enlisted men slipping in the mud around a cannon emplacement, swabbing out the smoking barrel, ramming home coils of chain and handfuls of twisted horseshoes.

I couldn't sleep that night, and in the morning I checked myself out of the hospital and went home. The doctor had asked me how I felt. My answer had not been quite accurate. I felt empty, washed-out inside, my skin rubbery and dead to the touch, my eyes jittering with refracted light that seemed to have no source. I felt as if I had been drinking sour mash for three days and had suddenly become disconnected from all the internal fires that I had nourished and fanned and depended upon with the religious love of an acolyte. There was no pain, no broken razor blades were twisting inside the conscience; there was just numbness, as though wind and fleecy clouds and rain showers marching across the canefields were a part of a curious summer phenomenon that I observed in a soundless place behind a glass wall.

I drank salt water to make myself throw up, ate handfuls of vitamins, made milkshakes filled with strawberries and bananas, did dozens of pushups and stomach crunches in the back yard, and ran wind sprints in the twilight until my chest was heaving for breath and my gym shorts were pasted to my skin with sweat.

I showered with hot water until there was none left in the tank, then kept my head under the cold water for another five minutes. Then I put on a fresh pair of khakis and a denim shirt and walked outside into the gathering dusk under the pecan trees. The marsh across the road was purple with haze, sparkling with fireflies. A black kid in a pirogue was cane fishing along the edge of the lily pads in the bayou. His dark skin seemed to glow with the sun's vanishing red light. His body and pole were absolutely still, his gaze riveted on his cork bobber. The evening was so quiet and languid, the boy so transfixed in his concentration, that I could have been looking at a painting.

Then I realized, with a twist of the heart, that something was wrong – there was no sound. A car passed on the dirt road, the boy scraped his paddle along the side of the pirogue to move to a different spot. But there was no sound except the dry resonance of my own breathing.

I went into the house, where Bootsie was reading under a lamp in the living room. I was about to speak, with the trepidation a person might have if he were violating the silence of a church, just to see if I could hear the sound of my own voice, when I heard the screen door slam behind me like a slap across the ear. Then suddenly I heard the television, the cicadas in the trees, my neighbor's sprinkler whirling against his myrtle bushes, Batist cranking an outboard down at the dock.

'What is it, Dave?' Bootsie said.

'Nothing.'

'Dave?'

'It's nothing. I guess I got some water in my ears.' I opened and closed my jaws.

'Your dinner is on the table. Do you want it?'

'Yeah, sure,' I said.

Her eyes studied mine.

'Let me heat it up for you,' she said.

'That'd be fine.'

When she walked past me she glanced into my face again.

'What's the deal, Boots? Do I look like I just emerged from a hole in the dimension?' I said, following her into the kitchen.

'You look tired, that's all.'

She kept her back to me while she wrapped my dinner in plastic to put in the microwave.

'What's wrong?' I said.

'Nothing, really. The sheriff called. He wants you to take a week off.'

'Why didn't he tell *me* that?'

'I don't know, Dave.'

'I think you're keeping something from me.'

She put my plate in the microwave and turned around. She wore a gold cross on a chain, and the cross hung at an angle outside her pink blouse. Her fingers came up and touched my cheek and the swelling over my right eye.

'You didn't shave today,' she said.

'What did the sheriff say, Boots?'

'It's what some other people are saying. In the mayor's office. In the department.'

'What?'

'That maybe you're having a breakdown.'

'Do you believe I am?'

'No.'

'Then who cares?'

'The sheriff does.'

'That's his problem.'

'A couple of deputies went out to the movie location and questioned some of the people who were at Mr Goldman's birthday party.'

'What for?'

'They asked people about your behavior, things like that.'

'Was one of those deputies Rufus Arceneaux?'

'Yes, I think so.'

'Boots, this is a guy who would sell his mother to a puppy farm to advance one grade in rank.'

'That's not the point. Some of those actors said you were walking around all evening with a drink in your hand. People believe what they want to hear.'

'I had blood and urine tests the next morning. There was no alcohol in my system. It's a matter of record at the hospital.'

'You beat up one of Julie Balboni's hoods in a public place, Dave. You keep sending local businessmen signals that you just might drive a lot of big money out of town. You tell the paramedics that there're wounded Confederate soldiers in the marsh. What do you think people are going to say about you?'

135

I sat down at the kitchen table and looked out the back screen at the deepening shadows on the lawn. My eyes burned, as though there were sand under my eyelids.

'I can't control what people say,' I said.

She stood behind me and rested her palms on my shoulders.

'Let's agree on one thing,' she said. 'We just can't allow ourselves to do anything that will help them hurt us. Okay, Dave?'

I put my right hand on top of hers.

'I won't,' I said.

'Don't try to explain what you think you heard or saw in the marsh. Don't talk about the accident. Don't defend yourself. You remember what you used to say? "Just grin and walk through the cannon smoke. It drives them crazy." '

'All right, Boots.'

'You promise?'

'I promise.'

She folded her arms across my chest and rested her chin on the top of my head. Then she said, 'What kind of person would try to do this to us, Dave?'

'Somebody who made a major mistake,' I said.

But it was a grandiose remark. The truth was that I had taken the drink at the party incautiously and that I had walked right into the script someone else had written for me.

Later that night, in bed, I stared at the ceiling and tried to recreate the scene under the oak trees at Spanish Lake. I wanted to believe that I could reach down into my unconscious and retrieve a photographic plate on which my eye had engraved an image of someone passing his hand over the glass of Dr Pepper, black cherries, orange slices, and bruised mint that a waiter was about to serve me.

But the only images in my mind were those of a levee extending out into gray water and an electrically charged fog bank rolling out of the cypress trees.

Bootsie turned on her side and put her arm across my chest. Then she moved her hand down my stomach and touched me.

I stared up into the darkness. The trees were motionless outside the window. I heard a 'gator flop in the marsh.

Then her hand went away from me and I felt her weight turn on the mattress toward the opposite wall.

An hour later I dressed in the darkness of the living room, slipped my pickup truck into neutral, rolled it silently down the dirt lane to the dock, and hooked my boat and trailer to the bumper hitch.

I put my boat into the water at the same place I had driven my truck off the levee. I used the paddle to push out into the deeper water, past the cattails and lily pads that grew along the bank's edge, then I lowered the engine and jerked it alive with the starter rope.

The wake off the stern looked like a long V-shaped trench roiling with yellow mud, bobbing with dead logs. Then the moon broke through the clouds, gilding the moss in the cypress with a silver light, and I could see cottonmouths coiled on the lower limbs of willow trees, the gnarled brown-green head of a 'gator in a floating island of leaves and sticks, the stiffened, partly eaten body of a coon on a sandbar, and a half-dozen wood ducks that skittered across the water in front of the high ground and the grove of trees where I had met the general.

I cut the throttle and let the boat ride on its wake until the bow slid up on the sand. Then I walked into the trees with a six-battery flashlight and a GI entrenching tool.

The ground was soft, oozing with moisture, matted with layers of dead leaves and debris left by receding water. Tangles of abandoned trotlines were strung about the tree trunks; Clorox marker bottles from fish traps lay half-buried in the sand.

In the center of the clearing I found the remains of a campfire.

A dozen blackened beer cans lay among the charred wood. Crushed into the grass at the edge of the fire was a used rubber.

I kicked the wood, ashes, and cans across the ground, propped my flashlight in the weeds, folded the E-tool into the shape of a hoe, screwed down and locked the socket at the base of the blade, and started chopping into the earth.

Eighteen inches down I hit what archaeologists call a 'fireline,' a layer of pure black charcoal sediment from a very old fire. I sifted it off the blade's tip a shovelful at a time. In it was a scorched brass button and the bottom of a hand-blown bottle, one that had tiny air bubbles inside the glass's green thickness.

But what did that prove? I asked myself.

Answer: That perhaps nineteenth-century trappers, cypress loggers, or even army surveyors had built a campfire there.

Then I thought about the scene the other night: the stacked rifle muskets, the haversacks suspended in the trees, the exhaustion in the men who were about to move out on patrol, the dry, bloodless wounds that looked like they had been eaten clean by maggots, the ambulance wagon and the crusted field dressings that had been raked out onto the ground.

The ambulance wagon.

I picked up my flashlight and moved to the far side of the clearing. The water was black under the canopy of flooded trees out in the marsh. I knelt and started digging out a two-by-four-foot trench. The clearing sloped here, and the ground was softer and wetter, wrinkled with small eroded gullies. I scraped the dirt into piles at each end of the hole; a foot down, water began to run from under the shovel blade.

I stopped to reset the blade and begin digging back toward the top of the incline. Then I saw the streaks of rust and bits of metal, like small red teeth, in the wet piles of dirt at each end of the hole. I shined the flashlight into the hole, and protruding from one wall, like a twisted snake, was a rusted metal band that might have been the rim of a wagon wheel.

Five minutes later I hit something hard, and I set the E-tool on the edge of the hole and used my fingers to pry up the hub of a wagon wheel with broken spokes the length of my hand radiating from it. I placed it on the slope, and in the next half hour I created next to it a pile of square nails, rotted wood as light as balsa, metal hinges, links of chain, a rusted wisp of a drinking cup, and a saw. The wood handle and the teeth had been almost totally eaten away by groundwater, but there was no mistaking the stubby, square, almost brutal shape; it was a surgeon's saw.

I carried everything that I had found back to the boat. My clothes were streaked with mud; I stunk of sweat and mosquito repellent. My palms rang with popped water blisters. I wanted to wake up Bootsie, call Elrod or perhaps even the sheriff, to tell anybody who would listen about what I had found.

But then I had to confront the foolishness of my thinking. How sane was any man, at least in the view of others, who would dig for Civil War artifacts in a swamp in the middle of the night in order to prove his sanity?

In fact, that kind of behavior was probably not unlike a self-professed extraterrestrial traveler showing you his validated seat reservations on a UFO as evidence of his rationality.

When I got back home I covered my boat with a tarp, took a shower, ate a ham-and-onion sandwich in the kitchen while night birds called to each other under the full moon, and decided that the general and I would not share our secrets with those whose lives and vision were defined by daylight and a rational point of view.

12

I slept late the next morning, and when I awoke, I found a note from Bootshie on the icebox saying that she had taken Alafair shopping in town. I fixed chicory coffee and hot milk, Grape-Nuts, and strawberries on a tray and carried it out to the redwood table under the mimosa tree in the backyard. The morning was not hot yet, and blue jays flew in and out of the dappled shade and my neighbor's sprinkler drifted in an iridescent haze across my grass.

Then I saw Rosie Gomez's motor-pool government car slow by our mailbox and turn into our drive. Her face was pointed at an upward angle so she could see adequately over the steering wheel. I got up from the table and waved her around back.

She wore a white blouse and white skirt with black pumps, a wide black belt, and black purse.

'How you feeling?' she asked.

'Pretty good. In fact, great.'

'Yeah?'

'Sure.'

'You look okay.'

'I am okay, Rosie. Here, I'll get you some coffee.'

When I came back outside with the pot and another cup and saucer, she was sitting on the redwood bench, looking out over my duck pond and my neighbor's sugarcane fields. Her face looked cool and composed.

'It's beautiful out here,' she said.

'I'm sorry Bootsie and Alafair aren't here. I'd like you to meet them.'

'Next time. I'm sorry I didn't come see you in the hospital. I'd left for New Orleans early that morning. I just got back.'

'What's up?'

'About three weeks ago an old hooker in the Quarter called the Bureau and said she wanted to seriously mess up Julie Balboni for us. Except she was drunk or stoned and the agent who took the call didn't give it a lot of credence.'

'What'd she have to offer?'

'Nothing, really. She just kept saying, "He's hurting these girls. Somebody ought to fix that rotten dago. He's got to stop hurting these girls."'

'So what happened?'

'Three days ago there was a power failure at the woman's apartment building on Ursulines. With the air conditioning off it didn't take long for the smell to leak through the windows to the courtyard. The ME says it was suicide.'

I watched her face. 'You don't think it was?' I said.

'How many women shoot themselves through the head with a .38 special?'

'Maybe she was drunk and didn't care how she bought it.'

'Her refrigerator and cupboards were full of food. The apartment was neat, all her dishes were washed. There was a sack of delicatessen items on the table she hadn't put away yet. Does that suggest the behavior of a despondent person to you?'

'What do they say at NOPD?'

'They don't. They yawn. They've got a murder rate as high as Washington, DC's. You think they want to turn the suicide of a hooker into another open homicide case?'

'What are you going to do?'

'I don't know. I think you've been right about a tie with Balboni. The most common denominator that keeps surfacing in this case is prostitution in and around New Orleans. There isn't a pimp or chippy working in Jefferson or Orleans parishes who don't piece off their action to Julie Balboni.'

'That doesn't mean Julie's involved with killing anyone, Rosie.'

'Be honest with me. Do I continue to underwhelm you as a representative of Fart, Barf, and Itch?'

'I'm not quite sure I—'

'Yeah, I bet. What do pimps call the girls in the life? "Cash on the hoof," right?'

'That's right.'

'Do you think anybody kills one of Balboni's hookers and gets away with it without his knowledge and consent?'

'Except there's a bump in the road here. The man who murdered Kelly Drummond probably thought he was shooting at me. The mob doesn't kill cops. Not intentionally, anyway.'

'Maybe he's a cowboy, out of control. We've got rogue cops. The wiseguys have rogue shitheads.'

I laughed. 'You're something else,' I said.

'Cut the patronizing attitude, Dave.'

'Sorry,' I said, still smiling.

Her eyes looked into mine and darkened.

'I'm worried about you. You don't know how to keep your butt down,' she said.

'Everything's copacetic. Believe me.'

'Sure it is.'

'You know something I don't?'

'Yes, human beings and money make a very bad combination,' she said.

'I'd appreciate it if you could stop speaking to me in hieroglyphics.'

'Few people care about the origins of money, Dave. All they see is a president's picture on a bill, not Julie Balboni's.'

'Let's spell it out, okay?'

'A few of the locals have talked to the sheriff about your taking an extended leave. At least that's what I've heard.'

'He's not a professional cop, but he's a decent man. He won't give in to them.'

'He's an elected official. He's president of the Lions Club. He eats lunch once a week with the Chamber of Commerce.'

'He knows I wasn't drinking. The people in my AA group know it, too. So do the personnel at the hospital. Dr Landry thinks somebody zapped me with LSD. What else can I say?'

Her face became melancholy, and she looked out at the sunlight on the field with a distant, unfocused expression in her eyes.

'What's the trouble?' I asked.

'You don't hear what you're saying. Your reputation, maybe your job, are hanging in the balance now, and you think it's acceptable to tell people that somebody loaded your head with acid.'

'I never made strong claims on mental health, anyway.'

I tried to smile when I said it. But the skin around my mouth felt stiff and misshaped.

'It isn't funny,' she said. She stood up to go, and the bottom of her purse, with the .357 magnum inside, sagged against her hip. 'I'm not going to let them do this to you, Dave.'

'Wait a minute, Rosie. I don't send other people out on the firing line.'

She began walking through the sideyard toward her car, her back as square and straight as a small door.

'Rosie, did you hear me?' I said. 'Rosie? Come back here and let's talk. I appreciate what you're trying to—'

She got into her automobile, gave me the thumbs-up sign over the steering wheel, and backed out onto the dirt road by the bayou. She dropped the transmission into low and drove down the long tunnel of oaks without glancing back.

*

Regardless of Rosie's intentions about my welfare, I still had not resolved the possibility that the racial murder I had witnessed in 1957 and the sack of skin and polished bones Elrod Sykes had discovered in the Atchafalaya Basin were not somehow involved in this case.

However, where do you start in investigating a thirty-five-year-old homicide that was never even reported as such?

Although southern Louisiana, which is largely French Catholic, has a long and depressing record of racial prejudice and injustice, it never compared in intensity and violence to the treatment of black people in the northern portion of the state or in Mississippi, where even the murder of a child, Emmett Till, by two Klansmen in 1955 not only went unpunished but was collectively endorsed after the fact by the town in which it took place. There was no doubt that financial exploitation of black people in general, and sexual exploitation of black women in particular, were historically commonplace in our area, but lynching was rare, and neither I nor anyone I spoke to remembered a violent incident, other than the one I witnessed, or a singularly bad racial situation from the summer of 1957.

The largest newspapers in Louisiana are the Baton Rouge *Morning Advocate* and the New Orleans *Times-Picayune*. They also have the best libraries, or 'morgues,' of old newspapers and cross-referenced clippings. However, I started my strange odyssey into the past on the microfilm in the morgue of the *Daily Iberian*.

Actually I had little hope of finding any information that would be helpful. During that era little was published in Louisiana newspapers about people of color, except in the police report or perhaps on a separate page that was designated for news about black marriages.

But in my mind's eye I kept seeing the dead man's stringless boots and the rotted strips of rag about his pelvis instead of a belt. Had he been in custody? Was he being transported by a couple of cops who had decided to execute him? If that was the case, why wasn't he in handcuffs? Maybe they had locked the chain on him to sink his body, I thought. No, that couldn't be right. If the victim was being transported by cops, they would have kept him in cuffs until they had murdered him, *then* they would have removed the cuffs and weighted down the body. Also, why would cops want to sink the body in the Atchafalaya, anyway? They could have claimed that they stopped the car to let him relieve himself, he had taken off for the woods, and they had been forced to shoot him. That particular explanation about a prisoner's death was one that was seldom challenged.

Then I found it, on the area news page dated July 27, 1957. A twenty-eight-year-old Negro man by the name of DeWitt Prejean had been arrested in St Landry Parish, north of Lafayette, for breaking into the home of a white family and threatening the wife with a butcher knife. There was no mention of motivation or intent. In fact, the story was not about his arrest but about his escape. He had been in custody only eleven hours, had not even been formally charged, when two armed men wearing gloves and Halloween masks entered the parish prison at four in the morning, locked the night jailer in the restroom, and took DeWitt Prejean out of a downstairs holding cell.

The story was no more than four column inches.

I rolled the microfilm through the viewer, looking for a follow-up story. If it was there, I didn't find it, and I went through every issue of the *Daily Iberian* to February 1958.

Every good cop who spends time in a newspaper morgue, particularly in the rural South, knows how certain kinds of news stories were reported or were not reported in the pre-civil-rights era. 'The suspect was subdued' usually meant that somebody had had his light switch clicked off with a baton or blackjack. Cases involving incest and child molestation were usually not treated at all. Stories about prisoners dying in custody were little more than obituaries, with a tag line to the effect that an autopsy was pending.

The rape or attempted rape of a white woman by a black man was a more complicated issue, however. The victim's identity was always protected by cops and prosecutors, even to the extent that sometimes the rapist was charged with another crime, one that the judge, if at all possible, would punish as severely as he would rape. But the level of white fear and injury was so collectively intense, the outrage so great, that the local paper would be compelled to report the story in such a way that no one would doubt what really happened, or what the fate of the rapist would be.

Also, the 1957 story in the *Iberian* had mentioned that DeWitt Prejean had been taken from a holding cell eleven hours after his arrest.

People didn't stay in holding cells eleven hours, particularly in a rural jail where a suspect could be processed into lock-down in twenty minutes.

I left Bootsie a note, then drove to Lafayette and continued on north for another twenty miles into St Landry Parish and the old jailhouse in Opelousas.

The town had once been the home of James Bowie before he became a wealthy cotton merchant and slave trader in New Orleans. But during the 1950s it acquired another kind of notoriety, namely for its political corruption, an infamous bordello named Margaret's that had operated since the War Between the States, and its gambling halls, which were owned or controlled by the sheriff and which were sometimes raided by the state police when a legislative faction in Baton Rouge wanted to force a change in the parish representatives' vote.

I parked my truck at the back of the courthouse square, right next to the brick shell of the old jail, whose roof had caved in on top of the cast-iron tank, perforated with small square holes, that had served as the lock-down area. As I walked under the live oaks toward the courthouse entrance, I looked through the jail's glassless windows at the mounds of soft, crumbled brick on the floor, the litter of moldy paper, and wondered where the two gloved men in Halloween masks had burst inside and what dark design they had planned for the Negro prisoner DeWitt Prejean.

I got nowhere at the courthouse. The man who had been sheriff during the fifties was dead, and no one now in the sheriff's department remembered the case or the escape; in fact, I couldn't even find a record of DeWitt Prejean's arrest.

'It *happened*. I didn't make it up,' I said to the sheriff, who was in his late thirties. 'I found the account in a 1957 issue of the *Daily Iberian*.'

'That might be,' he answered. He wore his hair in a military crewcut and his jaws were freshly shaved. He was trying to be polite, but the light of interest kept fading from his eyes. 'But they didn't always keep good records back then. Maybe some things happened that people don't want to remember, too, you know what I mean?'

'No.'

He twirled a pencil around on his desk blotter.

'Go talk to Mr Ben. That is, if you want to,' he said. 'That's Mr Ben Hebert. He was the jailer here for thirty years.'

'Was he the jailer in 1957?'

'Yeah, he probably was.'

'You don't sound enthusiastic.'

He rubbed the calluses on his hands without looking up at me.

'Put it this way,' he said. 'His only son ended up in Angola, his wife refused to see him on her deathbed, and there's still some black people who cross the street when they see him coming. Does that help form a picture for you?'

I left the courthouse and went to the local newspaper to look for a follow-up story on the jailbreak. There was none. Twenty minutes later I found the old jailer on the gallery of his weathered wood-frame home across from a Popeye's fast-food restaurant. His yard was almost black with shade, carpeted with a wet mat of rotted leaves, his sidewalks inset with tethering rings, cracked and pyramided from the oak roots that twisted under them. The straw chair he sat in seemed about to burst from his huge bulk.

144

I had to introduce myself twice before he responded. Then he simply said, 'What you want?'

'May I sit down, sir?'

His lips were purple with age, his skin covered with brown spots the size of dimes. He breathed loudly, as though he had emphysema.

'I ax you what you want,' he said.

'I wondered if you remembered a black man by the name of DeWitt Prejean.'

He looked at me carefully. His eyes were clear-blue, liquid, elongated, red along the rims.

'A nigger, you say?' he asked.

'That's right.'

'Yeah, I remember that sonofabitch. What about him?'

'Is it all right if I sit down, Mr Hebert?'

'Why should I give a shit?'

I sat down in the swing. He put a cigarette in his mouth and searched in his pocket for a match while his eyes went up and down my body. Gray hair grew out of his nose and on the back of his thick neck.

'Were you on duty the night somebody broke him out of jail?' I said.

'I was the jailer. A jailer don't work nights. You hire a man for that.'

'Do you remember what that fellow was charged with?'

'He wasn't charged with nothing. It never got to that.'

'I wonder why he was still in a holding cell eleven hours after he was arrested.'

'They busted him out of the tank.'

'Not according to the newspaper.'

'That's why a lot of people use newspaper to wipe their ass with.'

'He went into a white woman's home with a butcher knife, did he?'

'Find the nigger and ax him.'

'That's what puzzles me. Nobody seems to know what happened to this fellow, and nobody seems to care. Does that make sense to you?'

He puffed on his cigarette. It was wet and splayed when he took it out of his mouth. I waited for him to speak but he didn't.

'Did y'all just close the books on a jailbreak, Mr Hebert?' I asked.

'I don't remember what they done.'

'Was DeWitt Prejean a rapist?'

'He didn't know how to keep his prick in his pants, if that's what you mean.'

'You think her husband broke him out?'

'He might have.'

I looked into his face and waited.

'That is, if he could,' he said. 'He was a cripple-man. He got shot up in the war.'

'Could I talk to him?'

He tipped his cigarette into an ashtray and looked out toward the bright glare of sunlight on the edge of his yard. Across the street black people were going in and out of the Popeye's restaurant.

'Talk to him all you want. He's in the cemetery, out by the tracks east of town,' he said.

'What about the woman?'

'She moved away. Up North somewhere. What's your interest in nigger trouble that's thirty-five years old?'

'I think I saw him killed. Where's the man who was on duty the night of the jailbreak?'

'Got drunk, got hisself run over by a train. Wait a minute, what did you say? You saw what?'

'Sometimes rivers give up their dead, Mr Hebert. In this instance it took quite a while. Y'all took his boot strings and his belt, didn't you?'

'You do that with every prisoner.'

'You do it when they're booked and going into the tank. This guy was never booked. He was left in a holding cell for two armed men to find him. You didn't even leave him a way to take his own life.'

He stared at me, his face like a lopsided white cake.

'I think one of the men who killed Prejean tried to kill me,' I said. 'But he murdered a young woman instead. A film actress. Maybe you read about it.'

He stood up and dropped his cigarette over the gallery railing into a dead scrub. He smelled like Vick's VapoRub, nicotine, and an old man's stale sweat. His breath rasped as though his lungs were filled with tiny pinholes.

'You get the fuck off my gallery,' he said, and walked heavily on a cane into the darkness of his house, and let the screen slam behind him.

I stopped at Popeye's on Pinhook Road in Lafayette and ate an order of fried chicken and dirty rice, then I drove down Pinhook through the long corridor of oak trees, which had been planted by slaves, down toward the Vermilion River bridge and old Highway 90, which led through the little sugar town of Broussard to New Iberia.

Just before the river I passed a Victorian home set back in a grove of pecan trees. Between the road and the wide, columned porch a group of workmen were trenching a water or sewer line of some kind. The freshly piled black dirt ran in an even line past a decorative nineteenth-century flatbed wagon that was hung with baskets of blooming impatiens. The bodies and work clothes of the men looked gray and indistinct in the leafy shade, then a hard gust of wind blew off the river through the trees, the dappled light shifted back and forth across the ground like a bright yellow net, and when I looked back at the workmen I saw them dropping their tools, straightening their backs, fitting on their military caps that were embroidered with gold acorns, picking up their stacked muskets, and forming into ranks for muster.

The general sat in the spring seat of the wagon, his artificial leg propped stiffly on the iron rim of a wheel, a cigar in his mouth, the brim of his campaign hat set at a rakish angle over one eye.

He screwed his body around in the wagon seat and raised his hat high over his head in salute to me.

Gravel exploded like a fusillade of lead shot under my right fender. I cut the wheel back off the shoulder onto the pavement, then looked back at the wide sweep of leafy lawn under the pecan trees. A group of workmen were lowering a long strip of flexible plastic pipe into the ground like a white worm.

Back in New Iberia I parked behind the sheriff's department and started inside the building. Two deputies were on their way out.

'Hey, Dave, you're supposed to be in sick bay,' one of them said.

'I'm out.'

'Right. You look good.'

'Is the skipper in?'

'Yeah. Sure. Hey, you look great. I mean it.'

He gave me the thumbs-up sign.

His words were obviously well intended, but I remembered how I was treated after I stepped on a bouncing Betty in Vietnam – with a deference and kindness that not only separated me from those who had a lock on life but constantly reminded me that the cone of flame that had illuminated my bones had also given me a permanent nocturnal membership in a club to which I did not want to belong.

The dispatcher stopped me on my way to the sheriff's office. He weighed over three hundred pounds and had a round red face and a heart condition. His left-hand shirt pocket was bursting with cellophane-wrapped cigars. He had just finished writing out a message on a pink memo slip. He folded it and handed it to me.

'Here's another one,' he said. He had lowered his voice, and his eyes were hazy with meaning.

'Another what?'

'Call from this same party that keeps bugging me.'

'Which party?'

His eyebrows went up in half-moons.

'The Spanish broad. Or Mexican. Or whatever she is.'

I opened the memo and looked at it. It read, *Dave, why don't you return my calls? I'm still waiting at the same place. Have I done wrong in some way?* It was signed 'Amber.'

'*Amber?*' I said.

'You got eight or nine of them in your mailbox,' he said. 'Her last name sounded Spanish.'

'Who is she?'

'How should I know? You're the guy she's calling.'

'All right, thanks, Wally,' I said.

I took all my mail out of my box, then shuffled through the pink memo slips one at a time.

The ones from 'Amber' were truly an enigma. A few examples:

I've done what you asked. Please call.

Dave, leave a message on my answering machine.

It's me again. Am I supposed to drop dead?

You're starting to piss me off. If you don't want me to bother you again, say so. I'm getting tired of this shit.

I'm sorry, Dave. I was hurt when I said those things. But don't close doors on me.

I walked back to the dispatcher's cage.

'There's no telephone number on any of these,' I said.

'She didn't leave one.'

'Did you ask her for one?'

'No, I got the impression y'all were buddies or something. Hey, don't look at me like that. What is she, a snitch or something?'

'I don't have any idea.'

'She sounds like she's ready to bump uglies, though.'

'Why don't you give some thought to your language, Wally?'

'Sorry.'

'If she calls again, get her telephone number. If she doesn't want to give it to you, tell her to stop calling here.'

'Whatever you say.'

I wadded up the memo slips, dropped them into a tobacco-streaked brass cuspidor, and walked into the sheriff's office.

A manila folder was open on his desk. He was reading from it, with both his elbows propped on the desk blotter and his fingertips resting lightly on his temples. His mouth looked small and down-turned at the corners. On his wall was a framed and autographed picture of President Bush.

'How you doing?' I said.

'Oh, hello, Dave,' he said, looking up at me over his glasses. 'It's good to see you. How do you feel today?'

'Just fine, sheriff.'

'You didn't need to come in. I wanted you to take a week or so off. Didn't Bootsie tell you?'

'I went up to Opelousas this morning. I think I found out who those bones out in the Atchafalaya might belong to.'

'What?'

'A couple of armed men broke a black prisoner named DeWitt Prejean out of the St Landry Parish jail in 1957. The guy was in for threatening a white woman with a butcher knife. But it sounds like an attempted rape. Or maybe there's a possibility that something was going on with consent. The old jailer said something about Prejean not being able to keep his equipment in his pants. Maybe the woman and Prejean just got caught and Prejean got busted on a phony charge and set up for a lynching.'

The sheriff's eyes blinked steadily and he worked his teeth along his bottom lip.

'I don't understand you,' he said.

'Excuse me?'

'I've told you repeatedly that case belongs to St Mary Parish. Why is it that you seem to shut your ears to whatever I say?'

'Kelly Drummond's death doesn't belong to St Mary Parish, sheriff. I think the man who killed her was after me because of that lynched black man.'

'You don't know that. You don't know that at all.'

'Maybe not. But what's the harm?'

He rubbed his round cleft chin with his thumb. I could hear his whiskers scraping against the skin.

'An investigation puts the right people in jail,' he said. 'You don't throw a rope around half the people in two or three parishes. And that's what you and that woman are doing.'

'That's the problem, is it?'

'You're damn right it is. Thirty minutes ago Agent Gomez marched into my office with all her findings.' He touched the edge of the manila folder with his finger. 'According to Agent Gomez, New Iberia has somehow managed to become the new Evil Empire.'

I nodded.

'The New Orleans mob is laundering its drug money through Bal-Gold Productions,' he said. 'Julie Balboni is running a statewide prostitution operation from Spanish Lake, he's also having prostitutes killed, and maybe he laced your Dr Pepper with LSD when he wasn't cutting illegal deals with the Teamsters. Did you know we had all those problems right here in our town, Dave?'

'Julie's a walking shit storm. Who knows what his potential is?'

'She also called some of our local business people moral weenies and chicken-hearted buttheads.'

'She has some eloquent moments.'

'Before she left my office she said she wanted me to know that she liked me personally but in all honesty she had to confess that she thought I was full of shit.'

'I see,' I said, and fixed my eyes on a palm tree outside the window.

The room was quiet. I could hear a jail trusty mowing the grass outside. The sheriff turned his Southwestern class ring on his finger.

'I want you to understand something, Dave,' he said. '*I* was the one who wanted that fat sonofabitch Balboni out of town. *You* were the one who thought he was a source of humor. But now we're stuck with him, and that's the way it is.'

'Why?'

'Because he had legitimate business interests here. He's committed no crime here. In fact, there's no outstanding warrant on this man anywhere. He's never spent one day in jail.'

'I think that's the same shuck his lawyers try to sell.'

He exhaled his breath through his nose.

'Go home. You've got the week off,' he said.

'I heard my leave might even be longer.'

He chewed on a fingernail.

'Who told you that?' he said.

'Is it true or not?'

'You want the truth? The truth is your eyes don't look right. They bother me. There's a strange light in them. Go home, Dave.'

'People used to tell me that in bars. It doesn't sound too good to hear it where I work, sheriff.'

'What can I say?' he said, and held his hands up and turned his face into a rhetorical question mark.

When I walked back down the corridor toward the exit, I stuffed my mail back into my mailbox, unopened, and continued on past my own office without even glancing inside.

My clothes were damp with sweat when I got home. I took off my shirt, threw it into the dirty-clothes hamper, put on a fresh T-shirt, and took a glass of iced tea into the backyard where Bootsie was working chemical fertilizer into the roots of the tomato plants by the coulee. She was in the row, on her hands and knees, and the rump of her pink shorts was covered with dirt.

She raised up on her knees and smiled.

'Did you eat yet?' she asked.

'I stopped in Lafayette.'

'What were you doing over there?'

'I went to Opelousas to run down a lead on that '57 lynching.'

'I thought the sheriff had said—'

'He did. He didn't take well to my pursuing it.'

I sat down at the redwood picnic table under the mimosa tree. On the table were a pad of lined notebook paper and three city library books on Texas and southern history.

'What's this?' I said.

'Some books I checked out. I found out some interesting things.'

She got up from the row of tomato plants, brushing her hands, and sat down across from me. Her hair was damp on her forehead and flecked with grains of dirt. She picked up the note pad and began thumbing back pages. Then she set it down and looked at me uncertainly.

'You know how dreams work?' she said. 'I mean, how dates and people and places shift in and out of a mental picture that you wake up with in the morning? The picture seems to have no origin in your experience, but at the same time you're almost sure you lived it, you know what I mean?'

'Yeah, I guess.'

'I looked up some of the things that, well, maybe you believe you saw out there in the mist.'

I drank out of my iced tea and looked down the sloping lawn at the duck pond and the bright, humid haze on my neighbor's sugarcane.

'You see, Dave, according to these books, John Bell Hood never had a command in Louisiana,' she said. 'He fought at Gettysburg and in Tennessee and Georgia.'

'He was all through this country, Boots.'

'He lived here but he didn't fight here. You see, what's interesting, Dave, is that part of your information is correct but the rest you created from associations. Look here—'

She turned the notebook around so I could see the notes she had taken. 'You're right, he commanded the Texas Brigade,' she said. 'It was a famous cavalry outfit. But look here at this date. When you asked the general what the date was, he told you it was April 21, 1865, right?'

'Right.'

'April 21 is Texas Independence Day, the day the battle of San Jacinto was fought between the Mexican army and the Texans in 1836. Don't you see, your mind mixed up two historical periods. Nothing happened out in that mist, Dave.'

'Maybe not,' I said. 'Wait here a minute, will you?'

I walked to the front of the house, where my boat trailer was still parked, pulled back the tarp, which was dented with pools of rainwater, reached down inside the bow of the boat, and returned to the backyard.

'What is it?'

'Nothing.'

'Why'd you go out front?'

'I was going to show you some junk I found out in the marsh.'

'What junk?'

'Probably some stuff left by an old lumber crew. It's not important.'

Her face was puzzled, then her eyes cleared and she put her hand on top of mine.

'You want to go inside?' she said.

'Where's Alf?'

'Playing over at Poteet's house.'

'Sure, let's go inside.'

'I'm kind of dirty.'

She waited for me to say something but I didn't. I stared at my iced-tea glass.

'What is it, babe?' she said.

'Maybe it's time to start letting go of the department.'

'Let go how?'

'Hang it up.'

'Is that what you want?'

'Not really.'

'Then why not wait awhile? Don't make decisions when you're feeling down, *cher*.'

'I think I've already been cut loose, Boots. They look at me like I have lobotomy stitches across my forehead.'

'Maybe you read it wrong, Dave. Maybe they want to help but they just don't know how.'

I didn't answer. Later, after we had made love in the warm afternoon gloom of our bedroom, I rose from the softness of her body and sat listlessly on the side of the bed. A moment later I felt her nails tick lightly on my back.

'Ask the sheriff if he wants your resignation,' she said.

'It won't solve the problem.'

'Why won't it? Let them see how well they'll do without you.'

'You don't understand. I'm convinced Kelly Drummond's killer was after me. It's got something to do with that dead black man. That's the only thing that makes sense.'

'Why?'

'We've gotten virtually nowhere in trying to find this serial killer or psychopath or whatever he is. So why would *he* want to come after me? But the lynched black man is another matter. I'm the only one making noise about it. That's the connection. Why doesn't the sheriff see that?'

I felt her nails trace my vertebrae.

'You want to believe that all people are good, Dave,' she said. 'When your friends don't act the way they should, you feel all this anger and then it turns inward on you.'

'I'm going to take down that guy, Boots. Even if I have to do it outside the department.'

It was quiet for a long time. Then I felt her weight shift on the mattress and I thought she was getting up to get dressed. Instead, she rose to her knees, pressed her body hard against my back, and pulled my head against her breasts.

'I'll always love you, Dave,' she said. 'I don't care if you're a cop or a commercial fisherman or if you hunt down this bastard and kill him, I'll always love you for the man you are.'

How do you respond to a statement like that?

The phone call came at 9:30 that night. I answered it in the kitchen.

'You're a hard man to catch,' she said.

'Who's this?'

'The lady who's been trying to catch you, sugar.'

'How about giving me a name?'

'It's Amber. Who else, darlin'?' Her voice sounded sleepy, indolent, in slow motion.

'Ah, the lady of the mysterious phone messages.'

'You don't remember me? Don't hurt my feelings.'

'No, I'm sorry, I don't recall who you are. What can I do for you?'

'It's me that's going to do you a big favor, darlin'. It's because I like you. It's because I remember you from New Orleans a long time ago.'

'I appreciate all this, but how about we cut to it?'

'I'm gonna give you the guy you want, sweetheart.'

'Which guy are we talking about?'

'He's a nasty ole pimp and he's been doin' some nasty things to his little girls.'

Through the back window I could see my neighbor burning filed stumps in the dark. The sparks spun upward against the black sky.

'What's his name, Amber?'

'I've got a temporary problem, though. I want to go back to Florida for a little while, you know what I mean?'

'What do you need?'

'Just the air ticket and a little pin money. Three or four hundred dollars. That's not a lot to ask, is it?'

'We might be able to arrange that. Would you like to come into my office?'

'Oh, I don't know if I should do that. All those handsome men make me self-conscious. Do you know where Red's Bar is in Lafayette?'

'On the north side?'

'You got it, sugar. How about in an hour? I'll be at the bar, right by the door.'

'You wouldn't try to take me over the hurdles, would you, Amber?'

'Tell me you don't recognize me and break my heart. Ooou, ooou,' she said, and hung up.

Who was she? The rhetoric, the flippant cynicism, the pout in the voice, the feigned little-girlishness, all spelled hooker. And the messages she had left at my office were obviously meant to indicate to others that there was a personal relationship between us. It sounded like the beginning of a good scam. But she had also sounded stoned. Or maybe she was simply crazy, I thought. Or maybe she was both stoned and crazy and simply running a hustle. Why not?

There are always lots of possibilities when you deal with that vast army of psychological mutants for whom police and correctional and parole officers are supposed to be lifetime stewards. I once knew a young psychiatrist from Tulane who wanted to do volunteer counseling in the women's prison at St Gabriel. He lasted a month. The inkblot tests he gave his first subjects not only drove him into clinical depression but eventually caused him to drop his membership in the ACLU and join the National Rifle Association.

I made a call to the home of an AA friend named Lou Girard who was a detective sergeant in Vice at the Lafayette Police Department. He was one of those who drifted in and out of AA and never quite let go of the old way of life, but he was still a good cop and he would have made lieutenant had he not punched out an obnoxious local politician at Democratic headquarters.

'What's her name again?' he said.

I told him.

'Yeah, there's one broad around calls herself Amber, but she's a Mexican,' he said. 'You said this one sounds like she's from around here?'

'Yep.'

'Look, Dave, these broads got about two dozen names they trade around – Ginger, Consuela, Candy, Pepper, there's even a mulatto dancer named Brown Sugar. Anyway, there're three or four hookers that float in and out of Red's. They're low-rent, though. Their johns are oil-field workers and college boys, mostly.'

'I'm going to drive over there in a few minutes. Can you give me some backup?'

'To check out a snitch?'

'What about your own guys?'

'I'm supposed to be on sick leave right now.'

'Is something wrong over there, Dave?'

'Things could be better.'

'All right, I'll meet you behind the bar. I'll stay in my car, though. For some reason my face tends to empty out a place. Or maybe I need a better mouthwash.'

'Thanks for doing this.'

'It beats sitting at home listening to my liver rot.'

Red's Bar was located in a dilapidated, racially mixed neighborhood of unsurfaced streets, stagnant rain ditches coated with mosquitoes, and vacant lots strewn with lawn trash and automobile parts. Railway tracks intersected people's dirt yards at crazy angles, and Southern Pacific freight cars often lumbered by a few feet from clotheslines and privies and bedroom windows.

I parked my truck in the shadows behind the bar. The shell parking lot was covered with hundreds of flattened beer cans, and the bushes that bordered the neighbor's property stank from all the people who urinated into them nightly. The owner of Red's had built his bar by knocking out the front wall of a frame house and attaching a neon-lit house trailer to it perpendicularly. Originally he had probably intended it to be the place it looked like – a low-bottom bar where you didn't have to make comparisons or where you could get laid and not worry about your own inadequacies.

But the bar became a success in ways that the owner didn't anticipate. He hired black musicians because they were cheap, and through no fault of his own he ended up with one of the best new *zydeco* bands in southwestern Louisiana. And on Saturday nights he french-fried potatoes in chicken fat and served them free on newspaper to enormous crowds that spilled out into the parking lots.

But tonight wasn't Saturday, there was no band; little sound except the jukebox's came from the bar, and the dust from my truck tires floated in a cloud across the bushes that were sour with urinated beer.

Lou Girard got out of his car and walked over to my window. He was a huge man, his head as big as a basketball, who wore cowboy boots with his suits and a chrome-plated .357 magnum in a hand-tooled belt holster. He also carried a braided slapjack in his back pocket and handcuffs that he slipped through the back of his belt.

'It's good to see you, Streak,' he said.

'You too, Lou. How's everything at home?'

'My wife finally took off with her beautician. A woman, I'm talking about. I guess I finally figured out why she seemed a little remote in the sack. What are we doing tonight?'

'I'll go inside and look around. I'd like you to be out here to cover my back. It's not a big deal.'

He looked at the clapboard back of the bar, at the broken windows and the overflow of the garbage cans, and hooked his thumb in his belt.

'When'd you start needing backup for bullshit like this?'

'Maybe I'm getting over the hill for it.'

'Be serious, my friend.'

'You know about Kelly Drummond being killed?'

'That actress? Yeah, sure.'

'I think maybe the shooter was after me. I don't want to walk into a setup.'

'This is a weird fucking place for a setup, Dave. Why would a guy want to bring a cop to a public place in Lafayette for a whack?'

'Why do these guys do anything?'

'You have any idea who the shooter might be?'

'Maybe a guy who was in on a lynching thirty-five years ago.'

He nodded and his eyes became veiled.

'That doesn't sound plausible to you?' I asked.

'What's plausible? I try to get off the booze and my liver swells up like a football, my wife turns out to be a dyke, and for kicks I'm standing by a bunch of bushes that stink like somebody with a kidney disease pissed on them.'

I pulled my tropical shirt out of my khakis, stuck my .45 inside the back of my belt, and walked through the rear entrance of the building.

The inside smelled like refrigerated bathroom disinfectant and tobacco smoke. The wood floors were warped and covered with cigarette burns that looked like black insects. Some college boys were playing the jukebox and drinking pitcher beer at the bar, and two or three couples were dancing in the adjacent room. A lone biker, with a lion's mane of blond hair and arms wrapped with jailhouse art, hit the cue ball so hard on the pool table that it caromed off the side of the jukebox. But it was a dead night at Red's, and the only female at the bar was an elderly woman who was telling a long tale of grief and discontent to a yawning bartender.

'What'll you have?' he said to me.

'Has Amber been in?'

He shook his head to indicate either that she had not or he had no idea whom I was talking about.

'She hasn't been here?' I said.

'What do you want to drink?'

'A 7 Up.'

He opened it and poured it into a glass full of ice. But he didn't serve it to me. He walked to the rear of the long bar, which was empty, set it down, and waited for me. When he leaned on the bar, the biceps of his brown arms ridged with muscles like rocks. I walked down the length of the bar and sat on the stool in front of him.

'Which Amber you looking for?' he asked.

'I only know one.'

'She don't come in here reg'lar. But I could call somebody who probably knows where she's at. I mean if we're talking bout the same broad.'

'A Mexican?'

'Yeah, that's right.'

'She talks like a Mexican?'

'Yeah. What's a Mexican supposed to talk like?'

'That's not the one I'm looking for, then.'

'Enjoy your 7 Up,' he said, and walked away from me.

I waited a half hour. The biker went out and I heard him kick-start his motorcycle and peel down the dirt street in a roar of diminishing thunder. Then the college boys left and the bar was almost deserted. The bartender brought me another 7 Up. I reached for my billfold.

'It's on the house,' he said.

'It's my birthday?' I said.

'You're a cop.'

'I'm a cop.'

'It don't matter to me. I like having cops in. It keeps the riffraff out.'

'Why do you think I'm a cop, partner?'

'Because I just went out back for a breath of air and Lou Girard was taking a leak on our banana trees. Tell Lou thanks a lot for me.'

So I gave it up and walked back outside into the humid night, the drift of dust off the dirt road, and the heat lightning that flickered silently over the Gulf.

'I'm afraid it's a dud,' I said to Lou through his car window. 'I'm sorry to get you out for nothing.'

'Forget it. You want to get something to eat?'

'No, I'd better head home.'

'This hooker, Amber, her full name is Amber Martinez. I heard she was getting out of the life. But I can pick her up for you.'

'No, I think somebody was just jerking me around.'

'Let me know if I can do anything, then.'

'All right. Thanks again. Goodnight, Lou.'

'Goodnight, Dave.'

I watched him drive around the side of the building and out onto the dirt street. Raindrops began to ping on the top of my truck.

But maybe I was leaving too early, I thought. If the bartender had made Lou Girard, maybe the woman had, too.

I went back inside. All the bar stools were empty. The bartender was rinsing beer mugs in a tin sink. He looked up at me.

'She still ain't here. I don't know what else to tell you, buddy,' he said.

I put a quarter in the jukebox and played an old Clifton Chenier record, 'Hey 'Tite Fille', then I walked out onto the front steps. The rain was slanting across the neon glow of the Dixie beer sign and pattering in the ditches and on the shell parking lot. Across the street were two small frame houses, and next to them was a vacant lot with a vegetable garden and three dark oaks in it and an old white Buick parked in front. Then somebody turned on a light inside the house next to the lot, and I saw the silhouette of somebody in the passenger seat of the Buick. I saw the silhouette as clearly as if it had been snipped out of tin, and then I saw the light glint on a chrome or nickel-plated surface as brightly as a heliograph.

The shots were muffled in the rain – *pop, pop,* like Chinese firecrackers under a tin can – but I saw the sparks fly out from the pistol barrel through the interior darkness of the Buick. The shooter had fired at an odd angle, across the seat and through the back window, but I didn't wait to wonder why he had chosen an awkward position to take a shot at me.

I pulled the .45 from under my shirt, dropped to my knees behind the bumper of a pickup truck, and began firing with both hands extended in front of me. I let off all eight rounds as fast as I could pull the trigger. The roar was deafening, like someone had slapped both his palms violently against my eardrums. The hollow-points exploded the glass out of the Buick's windows, cored holes like a cold chisel through the doors, *whanged* off the steering wheel and dashboard, and blew the horn button like a tiddly-wink onto the hood.

The slide locked open on the empty magazine, and the last spent casing tinkled on the flattened beer cans at my feet. I stood erect, still in the lee of the pickup truck, slipped the empty magazine out of the .45's butt, inserted a fresh one, and eased a round into the chamber. The street was quiet except for the pattering of the rain in the ditches. Then I heard a siren in the distance and the bar door opening behind me.

'What the fuck's going on?' the bartender said, his whole body framed in the light. 'You fucking crazy or something?'

'Get back inside,' I said.

'We never had trouble here. Where the fuck are you from? People lose licenses because of bullshit like this.'

'Do you want to get shot?'

He slammed the door shut, locked it, and pulled the blinds.

I started across the street just as an electrical short in the Buick caused the horn to begin blowing non-stop. I kept the .45 pointed with both hands at the Buick's windows and moved in a circle around the front of the car. No one was visible above the level of the windows nor was there any movement inside. The hollow-points had cut exit holes the size of half-dollars in the passenger door.

A Lafayette city police car came hard around the corner, its emergency lights whirling in the rain. The police car stopped twenty yards from the Buick and both front doors sprang open. I could see the cop in the passenger's seat pulling his pump shotgun out of its vertical mount on the dashboard. I got my badge holder out of my back pocket and held it high over my head.

'Lay your weapon on the ground and step back from the car,' the driver said, aiming his revolver at me between the door and the jamb.

I held my right arm at a ninety-degree angle, the barrel of the .45 pointing into the sky.

'I'm Detective Dave Robicheaux, Iberia Parish Sheriff's Department,' I said. 'I'm complying with your request.'

I crouched in the beam of their headlights, laid my .45 by the front tire of the Buick, and raised back up again.

'Step away from it,' the driver said.

'You got it,' I said, and almost lost my balance in the rain ditch.

'Walk this way. Now,' the driver said.

People were standing in their front porches and the rain was coming down harder in big drops that stung my eyes. I kept my badge turned outward toward the two Lafayette city cops.

'I've identified myself. Now how about jacking it down a couple of notches?' I said.

The cop with the shotgun pulled my badge holder out of my hand and looked at it. Then he flexed the tension out of his shoulders, made a snuffing sound in his nose, and handed me back my badge.

'What the hell's going on?' he said.

'Somebody took two shots at me. In that Buick. I think maybe he's still inside.'

They both looked at each other.

'You're saying the guy's still in there?' the driver said.

'I didn't see him go anywhere.'

'Fuck, why didn't you say so?'

I didn't get a chance to answer. Just then, Lou Girard pulled abreast of the police car and got out in the rain.

'Damn, Dave, I thought you'd gone home. What happened?'

'Somebody opened up on me,' I said.

'You know this guy?' the cop with the shotgun said.

'Hell, yes, I do. Put your guns away. What's wrong with you guys?' Lou said.

'Lou, the shooter fired at me twice,' I said. 'I put eight rounds into the Buick. I think he's still in there.'

'What?' he said, and ripped his .357 from his belt holster. Then he said to the two uniformed cops. 'What have you fucking guys been doin' out here?'

'Hey, Lou, come on. We didn't know who this—'

'Shut up,' he said, walked up to the Buick, looked inside, then jerked open the passenger door. The interior light went on.

'What is it?' the cop with the shotgun said.

Lou didn't answer. He replaced his revolver in his holster and reached down with his right hand and felt something on the floor of the automobile.

I walked toward him. 'Lou?' I said.

His hands felt around on the seat of the car, then he stepped back and studied the ground and the weeds around his feet as though he were looking for something.

'Lou?'

'She's dead, Dave. It looks like she caught one right through the mouth.'

'*She*?' I said. I felt the blood drain from my heart.

'You popped Amber Martinez,' he said.

I started forward and he caught my arm. The headlights of the city police car were blinding in the rain. He pulled me past the open passenger door, and I saw a diminutive woman in an embryonic position, a white thigh through a slit in a cocktail dress, a mat of brown hair that stuck wetly to the floor carpet.

Our faces were turned in the opposite direction from the city cops'. Lou's mouth was an inch from my ear. I could smell cigarettes, bourbon, and mints on his breath.

'Dave, there's no fucking gun,' he whispered hoarsely.

'I saw the muzzle flashes. I heard the reports.'

'It's not there. I got a throw-down in my glove compartment. Tell me to do it.'

I stared woodenly at the two uniformed cops, who stood in hulking silhouette against their headlights like gargoyles awaiting the breath of life.

13

The sheriff called me personally at 5 A.M. the next morning so there would be no mistake about my status with the department: I was suspended without pay. Indefinitely.

It was 7 A.M. and already hot and muggy when Rosie Gomez and I pulled up in front of Red's Bar in her automobile. The white Buick was still parked across the street. The bar was locked, the blinds closed, the silver sides of the house-trailer entrance creaking with heat.

We walked back and forth in front of the building, feeling dents in the tin, scanning the improvised rain gutters, even studying the woodwork inside the door jamb.

'Could the bullets have struck a car or the pickup truck you took cover behind?' she said.

'Maybe. But I didn't hear them.'

She put her hands on her hips and let her eyes rove over the front of the bar again. Then she lifted her hair off the back of her neck. There was a sheen of sweat above the collar of her blouse.

'Well, let's take a look at the Buick before they tow it out of here,' she said.

'I really appreciate your doing this, Rosie.'

'You'd do the same for me, wouldn't you?'

'Who knows?'

'Yeah, you would.' She punched me on the arm with her little fist.

We walked across the dirt street to the Buick. On the other side of the vacant lot I could hear freight cars knocking together. I opened all four doors of the Buick and began throwing out the floor mats, tearing up the carpet, raking trash out from under the seats while Rosie hunted in the grass along the rain ditch.

Nothing.

I sat on the edge of the backseat and wiped the sweat out of my eyes. I felt tired all over and my hands were stiff and hard to open and close. In fact, I felt just like I had a hangover. I couldn't keep my thoughts straight, and torn pieces of color kept floating behind my eyes.

'Dave, listen to me,' she said. 'What you say happened is what happened. Otherwise you would have taken up your friend on his offer.'

'Maybe I should have.'

'You're not that kind of cop. You never will be, either.'

I didn't answer.

'What'd your friend call it?' she asked.

'A "throw-down." Sometimes cops calls it a "drop." It's usually a .22 or some other piece of junk with the registration numbers filed off.' I got up off the seat and popped the trunk. Inside, I found a jack handle. I drove the tapered end into the inside panel of the back door on the driver's side.

'What are you doing?' Rosie said.

I ripped the paneling away to expose the sliding frame and mechanism on which the window glass had been mounted.

'Let me show you something,' I said, and did the same to the inside panel on the driver's door. 'See, both windows on this side of the car were rolled partially up. That's why my first rounds blew glass all over the place.'

'Yes?'

'Why would the shooter try to fire through a partially opened window?'

'Good question.'

I walked around to the passenger side of the Buick. The carpet had a dried brown stain in it, and a roach as long and thick as my thumb was crawling across the stiffened fibers.

'But *this* window is all the way down,' I said. 'That doesn't make any sense. It had already started to rain. Why would this woman sit by an open window in the rain, particularly in the passenger seat of her own car?'

'It's registered to Amber Martinez?'

'That's right. According to Lou Girard, she was a hooker trying to get out of the life. She also did speedballs and was ninety pounds soaking wet. Does that sound like a hit artist to you?'

'Then why was she in the car? What was she doing here?'

'I don't know.'

'What did the homicide investigator have to say last night?'

'He said, "A .45 sure does leave a hole, don't it?" '

'What else?'

'He said, "Did you have to come over to Lafayette to fall in the shithouse?" '

162

'Look at me,' she said.

'What?'

'How much sleep did you get last night?'

'Two or three hours.'

I threw the tire iron on the front seat of the Buick.

'What do you feel now?' she said.

'What do you mean?' I was surprised at the level of irritation in my voice.

'You *know* what I mean.'

My eyes burned and filmed in the haze. I saw the three oaks in the vacant lot go out of focus, as though I were looking at them inside a drop of water.

'Everyone thinks I killed an unarmed woman. What do you think I feel?' I said. I had to swallow when I said it.

'It was a setup, Dave. We both know it.'

'If it was, what happened to the gun? Why aren't there any holes in the bar?'

'Because the guy behind this is one smart perp. He got a woman, probably a chippy, to make calls to your dispatcher to give the impression your fly was open, then he got you out of your jurisdiction and involved you in another hooker's death. I think this guy's probably a master at control.'

'Somehow that doesn't make me feel a lot better, Rosie.'

I looked at the stain on the Buick's carpet. The heat was rising from the ground now and I thought I could smell a salty odor like dead fish. I closed the passenger door.

'I really walked into it, didn't I?' I said.

'Don't worry, we're going to bust the guy behind this and lose the key on him.' Her eyes smiled, then she winked at me.

I had brought a garden rake from home. I took it out of Rosie's car and combed a pile of mud and soggy weeds from the bottom of the ditch next to the Buick. Then Rosie said, 'Dave, come over here and look at this.'

She stood next to the vegetable patch that was located on the edge of the vacant lot. She pointed at the ground.

'Look at the footprints,' she said. 'Somebody ran through the garden. He broke down the tomato stakes.'

The footprints were deep and wide-spaced in the soft earth. The person had been moving away from the street toward the three oak trees in the center of the lot. Some of the tomato and eggplant bushes were crushed down flat in the rows.

A wrecker came around the corner with two men in it and stopped behind the Buick. The driver got out and began hooking up the rear end of the Buick. A middle-aged plainclothes detective in short sleeves with his badge on his belt got out with him. His name was Doobie Patout, a wizened and xenophobic man, with faded blue tattoos on his forearms; some people believed he'd once been the official executioner at Angola.

He didn't speak. He simply stared through the heat at me and Rosie.

'What's happening, Doobie?' I said.

'What y'all doin' out here?' he said.

'Looking for a murder weapon,' I said.

'I heard you were suspended.'

'Word gets around.'

'You're not supposed to be messin' 'round the crime scene.'

'I'm really just an observer.'

'Who's she?' He raised one finger in Rosie's direction.

'Special Agent Gomez,' Rosie said. 'This is part of an FBI investigation. Do you have a problem with that?'

'You got to coordinate with the city,' he said.

'No, I don't,' she said.

The driver of the wrecker began winching the Buick's weight off its back wheels.

'I wouldn't hang around here if I was you,' Doobie said to me.

'Why not?' Rosie said.

'Because he don't have legal authority here. Because he made a mistake and nobody here'll probably hold it against him. Why piss people off, Robicheaux?'

'What are you saying, Doobie?'

'So you got to go up against Internal Affairs in your own department. That don't mean you're gonna get indicted in Lafayette Parish. Why put dog shit on a stick and hold it under somebody's nose?'

Behind us, an elderly fat mulatto woman in a print dress came out on her porch and began gesturing at us. Doobie Patout glanced at her, then opened the passenger door to the wrecker and paused before getting in.

'Y'all can rake spinach out of that ditch all you want,' he said. 'I ran a metal detector over it last night. There's no gun in it. So don't go back to New Iberia and be tellin' people you got a bad shake over here.'

'Y'all gonna do somet'ing 'bout my garden, you?' the woman shouted off the porch.

The wrecker drove off with the Buick wobbling on the winch cable behind it. At the corner the wrecker turned and a hubcap popped off the Buick and bounced on its own course down the empty dirt road.

'My, what a nasty little man,' Rosie said.

I looked back at the footprints in the vegetable patch. They exited in the Johnson grass and disappeared completely. We walked into the shade of the oaks and looked back at the road, the bits of broken glass that glinted in the dirt, the brilliant glare of sunlight on the white shell parking lot. I felt a weariness that I couldn't find words for.

'Let's talk to some of the neighbors, then pack it in,' I said.

We didn't have to go far. The elderly woman whom we had been ignoring labored down her porch steps with a cane and came toward us like a determined crab. Her legs were bowed and popping with varicose veins, her body ringed with fat, her skin gold and hairless, her turquoise eyes alive with indignation.

'Where that other one gone?' she said.

'Which one?' I said.

'That po-liceman you was talkin' to.'

'He went back to his office.'

'Who gonna pay for my li'l garden?' she asked. 'What I gone do wit' them smush tomato? What I gone do wit' them smush eggplant, me?'

'Did you see something last night, auntie?' I said.

'You ax me what I seen? Go look my li'l garden. You got eyes, you?'

'No, I mean did you see the shooting last night?'

'I was in the bat'room, me.'

'You didn't see anything?' Rosie said.

The woman jabbed at a ruined eggplant with her cane.

'I seen *that*. That look like a duck egg to you? They don't talk English where y'all come from?'

'Did you see a woman in a white car outside your house?' I said.

'I seen her. They put her in an ambulance. She was dead.'

'I see,' I said.

'What you gone do 'bout my garden?'

'I'm afraid I can't do anything,' I said.

'He can put his big feet all over my plants and I cain't do nothin' 'bout it?'

'Who?' I said.

'The man that run past my bat'room. I just tole you. You hard of hearin' just like you hard of seein'? I got up to go to the bat'room.'

My head was swimming.

'Listen, auntie, this is very important,' I said. 'You're telling me you saw a man run past your window?'

'That's right. I seen him smush my li'l plants, break down my tomato pole, keep on runnin' right out yonder t'ro them tree, right on 'cross the tracks till he was gone. I seen the light on that li'l gun in his hand, too.'

Rosie and I looked at each other.

'Can you describe this fellow, auntie?' I said.

'Yeah, he's a white man who don't care where he put his big muddy feet.'

'Did the gun look like this one?' Rosie said, opened her purse, and lifted out her .357 magnum.'

'No, it mo' li'l than that.'

'Why didn't you tell this to the police last night?' I asked.

'I tole them. I be talkin' and they be carryin' on with each other like I ain't here, like I some old woman just in they way. It ain't changed, no.'

'What hasn't?' I said.

'When the last time white people 'round here ax us what we t'ink about anyt'ing? Ain't nobody ax me if I want that juke 'cross from my li'l house, no. Ain't nobody worried 'bout my li'l garden. Black folk still black folk, livin' out here without no pave, with dust blowin' off the road t'rough my screens. Don't be pretendin' like it ain't so.'

'You've helped us a great deal, auntie,' I said.

She leaned over on her cane, wrapped a tangle of destroyed tomato vines around her hand, and flung them out into the grass. Then she began walking back toward her porch, the folds of skin in her neck and shoulders creasing like soft tallow.

'Would you mind if we came to see you again?' I asked.

'Waste mo' of my day, play like you care what happen down here on the dirt road? Why you ax me? You comin' when you want, anyway, ain't you?'

Her buttocks swelled like an elephant's against her dress when she worked her way up the steps. On the way out of town we stopped at a nursery and I paid cash to have a dozen tomato plants delivered to her address.

'Not smart giving anything to a potential witness, Slick,' Rosie said when we were back on the highway.

'You're used to operating in the normal world, Rosie. Did you hear what Doobie Patout said? Lafayette Homicide has given that girl's death the priority of a hangnail. Welcome to the New South.'

When I got back home I turned on the window fan in the bedroom, undressed, and lay down on top of the sheets with my arm across my eyes. The curtains, which were printed with small pink flowers, lifted and fell in the warm breeze, and I could hear Tripod running back and forth on his chain in the dead leaves under the pecan trees.

In my sleep I thought I could feel the .45 jumping in my palm, the slide slamming down on a fresh cartridge, the recoil climbing up my forearm like the reverberation from a jackhammer. Then, as though in slow motion, I saw a woman's face bursting apart; a small black hole appeared right below the mouth, then the fragile bone structure caved in upon itself, like a rubber mask collapsing, and the back of her head suddenly erupted in a bloody mist.

I wanted to wake from my dream, force myself even inside my sleep to realize that it was indeed only a dream, but instead the images changed and I heard the ragged popping of small-arms and saw the border of a hardwood forest in autumn, the leaves painted with fire, and a contingent of Confederate infantry retreating into it.

No, I didn't simply see them; I was in their midst, under fire with them, my throat burning with the same thirst, my hands trembling as I tried to reload my weapon, my skin twitching as though someone were about to peel it away in strips. I heard a toppling round *throp* close to my ear and whine away deep in the woods, saw the long scarlet streaks in the leaves where the wounded had been dragged behind tree trunks, and was secretly glad that someone else, not me, had crumpled to his knees, had cried out for his mother, had tried futilely to press his blue nest of entrails back inside his stomach.

The enemy advanced across an open field out of their own cannon smoke, their bayonets fixed, their artillery arching over their heads and exploding behind us in columns of dirt and flame. The light was as soft and golden as the season, but the air inside the woods was shifting, filled with dust and particles of leaves, the smell of cordite and bandages black with gangrene, the raw odor of blood.

Then I knew, even in sleep, what the dream meant. I could see the faces of the enemy now, hear the rattle of their equipment, their officers yelling, 'Form up, boys, form up!' They were young, frightened, unknowledgeable of politics or economics, trembling as much as I was, their mouths too dry now even to pray, their sweaty palms locked on the stocks of their rifles. But I didn't care about their innocence, their beardless faces, the crimson flowers that burst from their young breasts. I just wanted to live. I wanted every round we fired to find a target, to buckle bone, to shatter lungs and explode the heart; I wanted their ranks to dissolve into a cacophony of sorrow.

My head jerked erect on the pillow. The room was hot and close and motes of dust spun in the columns of weak light that shone through the curtains. My breath rasped in my throat, and my chest and stomach were slick with perspiration.

The general sat in a straight-backed chair by the foot of my bed, with his campaign hat resting on one knee. His beard was trimmed and he wore a brushed gray coat with a high gold collar. He was gazing out the window at the shifting patterns of light made by the pecan and oak trees.

'*You!*' I said.

'*I hope you don't mind my being here.*'

'*No, I – you simply surprised me.*'

'*You shouldn't have remorse about the kinds of feelings you just* experienced, Mr Robicheaux. A desire to live doesn't mean you lack humanity.'

'I opened up on the Buick too soon. I let off the whole magazine without seeing what I was shooting at.'

'You thought your life was at risk, suh. What were you supposed to do?'

'They say I killed an unarmed woman, general.'

'Yes, I think that would probably trouble me, too.' He turned his hat in a circle on his knee. 'I have the impression that you were very fond of your father, the trapper.'

'Excuse me?'

'Didn't he once tell you that if everyone agrees on something, it's probably wrong?'

'Those were his words.'

'Then why not give them some thought?'

'General, somebody has done a serious mind fuck on me. I can't trust what I see or hear anymore.'

'I'm sorry. Someone has done what?'

'It's the same kind of feeling I had once in Golden Gloves. A guy hooked me after the bell, hard, right behind the ear. For two or three days I felt like something was torn loose from the bone, like my brain was floating in a jar.'

'Be brave.'

'I see that woman, the back of her head . . . Her hair was glued to the carpet with her own blood.'

'Think about what you just said.'

'What?'

'You're a good police officer, an intelligent man. What does your eye tell you?'

'I need some help, general.'

'You belong to the quick, you wake in the morning to the smell of flowers, a woman responds to the touch of your fingers, and you ask help of the dead, suh?'

He lifted himself to his feet with his crutch.

'I didn't mean to offend you,' I said.

'In your dream you saw us retreating into a woods and you saw the long blue line advancing out of the smoke in the field, didn't you?'

'Yes.'

'Were you afraid?'

'Yes.'

'Because you thought time had run out for you, didn't you?'

'Yes, I knew it had.'

'We should have died there but we held them. Our thirst was terrible. We drank rainwater from the hoof prints of livestock. Then that night we

168

tied sticks in the mouths of our wounded so they wouldn't cry out while we
slipped out of the woods and joined the rest of our boys.'

The wind began blowing hard in the trees outside the window. Last fall's leaves swirled off the ground and blew against the house.

'I sense resentment in you,' he said.

'I already paid my dues. I don't want—'

'You don't want what?' He pared a piece of dirt from under his fingernail.

'To be the only man under a flag.'

'Ah, we never quit paying dues, my friend. I must be going now. The wind's out of the south. There'll be thunder by this afternoon. I always have a hard time distinguishing it from Yankee cannon.'

He made a clucking sound with his tongue, fitted his campaign hat on his head, took up his crutch, and walked through the blades of the window fan into a spinning vortex of gold and scarlet leaves.

When I finally woke from my sleep in midafternoon, like rising from the warm stickiness of an opium dream, I saw Alafair watching me through the partly opened bedroom door. Her lips were parted silently, her round, tan face wan with incomprehension. The sheets were moist and tangled around my legs. I tried to smile.

'You okay, Dave?'

'Yeah, I'm fine.'

'You were having a dream. You were making all kinds of sounds.'

'It's probably not too good to sleep in the daytime, little guy.'

'You got malaria again?'

'No, it doesn't bother me much anymore.'

She walked into the room and placed one hand on the bedstead. She looked at the floor.

'What's the matter, Alf?' I said.

'I went to the grocery down at the four-corners with Bootsie. A man had the newspaper open on the counter and was reading something out loud. A lady saw us and touched the man on the arm. Then both of them just stared at us. Bootsie gave them a real mean look.'

'What was the man saying?'

'A lady got shot.' Her palm was cupped tightly on the knob of the bedstead. She stared at the floor, and there was small white discolorations in her cheeks like slivers of ice. 'He said you shot the lady. You shot the lady, Dave.'

I sat up on the edge of the bed.

'I had some trouble last night, Alafair. Somebody fired a pistol at me and I shot back. I'm not sure who fired at me or what this lady was doing there. But the situation is a lot more complex than maybe some people think. The truth can be real hard to discover sometimes, little guy.'

'Did you do what they say, Dave?' I could see the shine of fear in her brown eyes.

'I don't know. But I never shot at anybody who didn't try to hurt me first. You have to believe me on that, Alf. I'm not sure what happened last night, but sooner or later I probably will. In the meantime, guys like you and me and Bootsie have to be standup and believe in each other.'

I brushed her bangs away from her eyes. She looked for a long time at the whirling blades of the window fan and the shadows they made on the bed.

'They don't have any right,' she said.

'Who?'

'Those people. They don't have the right to talk about you like that.'

'They have the right to read what's in the newspaper, don't they?'

'The lady at the counter was saying something just before we walked in. I heard her through the screen. She said, "If he's gone back to drinking, it don't surprise me he done that, no." That's when the man started reading out loud from the newspaper.'

I picked her up by the waist and sat her on the bed. Her muscular body felt as compact as a small log.

'Look, little guy,' I said, 'drinking isn't part of my life anymore. I gave it to my Higher Power.'

I stroked her hair and saw a smile begin to grow at the edge of her mouth and eyes.

'Dave?'

'What?'

'What's it mean when you say somebody's got to be standup?'

'No matter what the other side does to you, you grin and walk through the cannon smoke. It drives them crazy.'

She was grinning broadly now, her wide-set teeth white in the shadows of the room.

'Where's Bootsie?' I asked.

'Fixing supper.'

'What are we having?'

'*Sac-a-lait* and dirty rice.'

'Did you know they run freight trains on that in Louisiana?'

She started bouncing on the edge of the bed, then my words sank in. 'What? Freight . . . what?' she said.

'Let me get dressed, little guy, then we'll check out the food situation.'

My explanation to Alafair was the best I could offer, but the truth was I needed to get to an AA meeting. Since the night I had seen the general and his soldiers in the mist, I had talked once over the phone to my AA sponsor but had not attended a meeting, which was the place I needed to be most. What might be considered irrational, abnormal, aberrant, ludicrous, illogical, bizarre, schizoid, or schizophrenic to earth people (which is what AAs call nonalcoholics) is usually considered fairly normal by AA members.

The popular notion exists that Catholic priests become privy to the darkest corners of man's soul in the confessional. The truth is otherwise. Any candid Catholic minister will tell you that most people's confessions cause eye-crossing boredom in the confessor, and the average weekly penitent usually owns up to a level of moral failure on par with unpaid parking violations and overdue library books.

But at AA meetings I've heard it all at one time or another: extortion, theft, forgery, armed robbery, child molestation, sodomy with animals, arson, prostitution, vehicular homicide, and the murder of prisoners and civilians in Vietnam.

I went to an afternoon meeting on the second floor of an Episcopalian church. I knew almost everyone there: a few housewives, a black man who ran a tree nursery, a Catholic nun, an ex-con bartender named Tee Neg who was also my sponsor, a woman who used to hook in the Column Hotel Bar in Lafayette, a psychologist, a bakery owner, a freight conductor on the Southern Pacific, and a man who was once a famous aerialist with Ringling Brothers.

I told them the whole story about my psycho-historical encounters and left nothing out. I told them about the electricity that snapped and flickered like serpents' tongues in the mist, my conversations with the general, even the unwashed odor that rose from his clothes, the wounds in his men that maggots had eaten as slick as spoons.

As is usual with one's dramatic or surreal revelations at an AA meeting, the response was somewhat humbling. They listened attentively, their eyes sympathetic and good-natured, but a number of the people there at one time or another had ripped out their own wiring, thought they had gone to hell without dying, tried to kill themselves, or been one step away from frontal lobotomies.

When I had finished, the leader of the meeting, a pipeline welder, said, 'Damn, Dave, that's the best endorsement of Dr Pepper I ever heard. You ought to call up them sonsofbitches and get that one on TV.'

Then everyone laughed and the world didn't seem so bad after all.

When I left the meeting I bought a spearmint snowball in the city park at Bayou Teche and used the outdoor pay phone by the recreation building. Through the moss-hung oak trees I could see kids diving into the public pool, their tan bodies glistening with water in the hot sunlight.

It took a couple of minutes to get the Lafayette coroner on the line. He was a hard-nosed choleric pathologist named Sollie Rothberg, whom cops quickly learned to treat diplomatically.

'I wondered what you had on the Amber Martinez shooting,' I said.

I could hear the long-distance wires humming in the receiver.

'Robicheaux?' he said.

'That's right.'

'Why are you calling me?'

'I just told you.'

'It's my understanding you're suspended.'

'So what? Your medical findings are a matter of public record, aren't they?'

'When they become public they are. Right now they aren't public.'

'Come on, Sollie. Somebody's trying to deep-fry my *cojones* in a skillet.'

In my mind's eye I could see him idly throwing paper clips at his wastebasket.

'What's the big mystery I can clear up for you?' he said.

'What caliber weapon killed her?'

'From the size of the wound and the impact of the round, I'd say a .45.'

'What do you mean "size"?'

'Just what I said.'

'What about the round?'

'It passed through her. There wasn't much to recover. It was a clean exit wound.'

'It was a copper-jacketed round?'

'That's my opinion. In fact, I know it was. The exit hole wasn't much larger in diameter than the entry.'

I closed and opened my eyes. I could feel my heart beating in my chest.

'You there?' he said.

'Yes.'

'What's wrong?'

'Nothing, Sollie. I use hollow-points.'

I could hear birds singing in the trees, and the surface of the swimming pool seemed to be dancing with turquoise light.

'Anything else?' he asked.

'Yeah, time of death.'

'You're crowding me.'

'Sollie, I keep seeing the back of her head. Her hair stuck to the carpet. The blood had already dried, hadn't it?'

'I can't tell you about that because I wasn't there.'

'Come on, you know what I'm asking you.'

'Did she die earlier, you want to know?'

'Look partner, you're my lifeline. Don't be jerking me around.'

'How about I go you one better? Did she die in that car, you want to ask me?'

I had learned long ago not to interfere with or challenge Sollie's moods, intentions, or syntax.

'It's gravity,' he said. 'The earth's always pulling on us, trying to suck us into the ground.'

'What?'

'It's what the shooter didn't think about,' he said. 'Blood's just like anything else. It goes straight down. You stop the heart, in this case the brain and then the heart, and the blood takes the shortest course to the ground. You with me?'

'Not quite.'

'The blood settles out in the lowest areas of where the body is lying. The pictures show the woman curled up on her side on the floor of the Buick. Her head was higher than her knees. But the autopsy indicates that she was lying full length on her back at the time of death. She also had high levels of alcohol and cocaine in her blood. I suspect she may have been passed out when she died.'

'She was shot somewhere else and moved?'

'Unless the dead are walking around on their own these days.'

'You've really been a friend, Sollie.'

'Do you ever carry anything but a .45? A nine-millimeter or a .357 sometimes?'

'No, I've always carried the same Colt .45 auto I brought back from Vietnam.'

'How many people know that?'

'Not many. Mostly cops, I guess.'

'That thought would trouble me. So long, Robicheaux.'

But the moment was not one for brooding. I walked back to the hot-dog stand and bought snowballs for a half-dozen kids. When a baseball bounced my way from the diamond, I scooped it up in my palms, rubbed the roughness of the horse hide, fitted my fingers on the stitches, and whipped a side-arm slider into the catcher's glove like I was nineteen years old and could blow a hole through the backstop.

That night I called Lou Girard at his home in Lafayette, told him about my conversations with the coroner and the mulatto woman across from the bar, and asked him if anyone had vacuumed the inside of the Buick.

'Dave, I'm afraid this case isn't the first thing on everybody's mind around here,' he said.

'Why's that?'

'The detective assigned to it thinks you're a pain in the ass and you should have stayed in your own territory.'

'When's the last time anyone saw Amber Martinez?'

'Three or four days ago. She was a bender drinker and user. She was supposed to be getting out of the life, but I think she'd work up a real bad Jones and find a candy man to pick up her tab until she ended up in a tank or a detox center somewhere.'

'Who was her pimp?'

'Her husband. But he's been in jail the last three weeks on a check-writing charge. Whoever killed her probably got her out of a bar someplace.'

'Yeah, but he knew her before. He used another woman to keep leaving Amber's name on messages at my office.'

'If I can get the Buick vacuumed, what are we looking for?'

'I know I saw gun flashes inside the car. But there weren't any holes in the front of the bar. See what you come up with.'

'Like what?'

'I don't know.'

'Why don't you forget the forensic bullshit and concentrate on what your nose tells you?'

'What's that?'

'This isn't the work of some lone fuckhead running around. It has the smell of the greaseballs all over it. One smart greaseball in particular.'

'You think this is Julie's style?'

'I worked two years on a task force that tried to get an indictment on the Bone. When he gets rid of a personal enemy, he puts a meat hook up the guy's rectum. If he wants a cop or a judge or a labor official out of the way, he does it long distance, with a whole collection of lowlifes between him and the target.'

'That sounds like our man, all right.'

'Can I give you some advice?'

'Go ahead.'

'If Balboni is behind this, don't waste your time trying to make a case against him. It doesn't work. The guy's been oiling jurors and judges and scaring the shit out of witnesses for twenty years. You wait for the right moment, the right situation, and you smoke him.'

'I'll see you, Lou. Thanks for your help.'

'All right, excuse me. Who wants to talk about popping a cap on a guy like Balboni? Amber Martinez probably did herself. Take it easy, Dave.'

At six the next morning I took a cup of coffee and the newspaper out on the gallery and sat down on the steps. The air was cool and blue with shadow under the trees and the air smelled of blooming four o'clocks and the pecan husks that had moldered into the damp earth.

While I read the paper I could hear boats leaving my dock and fishermen's voices out on the water. Then I heard someone walking up the incline through the leaves, and I lowered the newspaper and saw Mikey Goldman striding toward me like a man in pursuit of an argument.

He wore shined black loafers with tassels on them, a pink polo shirt that hung out of his gray slacks, and a thick gold watch that gleamed like soft butter on his wrist. His mouth was a tight seam, down-turned at the corners, his jaw hooked forward, his strange, pale, bulging eyes flicking back and forth across the front of my house.

'I want a word with you,' he said.

'How are you today, Mr Goldman?' I said.

'It's 6 A.M., I'm at your house instead of at work; I got four hours sleep last night. Guess.'

'Do I have something to do with your problem?'

'Yeah, you do. You keep showing up in the middle of my problem. Why is that, Mr Robicheaux?'

'I don't have any idea.'

'I do. It's because Elrod has got some kind of hard-on for you and it's about to fuck my picture in a major way.'

'I'd appreciate it if you didn't use that kind of language around my home.'

'You got a problem with language? That's the kind of stuff that's on your mind? What's wrong with you people down here? The mosquitoes pass around clap of the brain or something?'

'What is it you want, sir?'

'He asks me what *I* want?' he said, looking around in the shadows as though there were other listeners there. 'Elrod doesn't like to see you get taken over the hurdles. Frankly I don't either. Maybe for other reasons. Namely nobody carries my load, nobody takes heat for me, you understand what I'm saying?'

'No.'

He cleared something from a nostril with his thumb and forefinger.

'What is it with you, you put your head in a bucket of wet cement every morning?' he asked.

'Can I be frank, too, Mr Goldman?'

'Be my guest.'

'A conversation with you is a head-numbing experience. I don't think any ordinary person is ready for it.'

'Let me try to put it in simple words that you can understand,' he said. 'You may not know it, but I try to be a fair man. That means I don't like somebody else getting a board kicked up his ass on my account. I'm talking about you. Your own people are dumping on you because they think you're going to chase some big money out of town. I leave places or I stay in places because I want to. Somebody gets in my face, I deal with it, personal. You ask anybody in the industry. I don't rat-fuck people behind their back.'

I set down my coffee cup, folded the newspaper on the step, and walked out into the trees toward his parked automobile. I waited for him to follow me.

'Is there anything else you wanted to tell me?' I said.

'No, of course not. I'm just out here to give you my personal profile. Listen to me, I'm going to finish this picture, then I'm never coming back to this state. In fact, I'm not even going to fly over it. But in the meantime no more of my people are going to the hospital.'

'What?'

'Good, the flashbulb went off.'

'What happened?' I said.

'Last night we'd wrapped it up and everybody had headed home. Except Elrod and this kid who does some stunt work got loaded and Elrod decides he's going to 'front Julie Balboni. He picks up a Coke bottle and starts banging on Julie's trailer with it. Julie opens the door in his jockey undershorts, and there's a twenty-year-old local broad trying to put on her clothes behind him. So Elrod calls him a coward and a dago bucket of shit and tells him he can fix him up in LA with Charlie Manson's chippies, like they got hair under their arms and none on their heads and they're more Julie's speed. Then El tells him that Julie had better not cause his buddy Robicheaux any more grief or El's going to punch his ticket for him, and if he finds out Julie murdered Kelly he's going to do it anyway, big time, with a shotgun right up Balboni's cheeks.

'I don't know what Balboni was doing with the broad, but he had some handcuffs. He walked outside, clamped one on El's wrist, the other on a light pole, and said, "You're a lucky man, Elrod. You're a valuable piece of fruit. But your friend there, he don't have any luck at all." Then he stomped the shit out of the stunt kid. "Stomped" is the word, Mr Robicheaux, I mean with his feet. He busted that kid's nose, stove in his ribs, and ripped his ear loose from his head.'

'Why didn't you stop it?'

'I wasn't there. I got all this from the kid at the hospital. That's why I didn't get any sleep last night.'

'Is the kid pressing charges?'

'Get real. He was on a flight back to Los Angeles this morning with enough dope in him to tranquilize a rhinoceros.'

'What do you want with me?'

'I want you to take care of Elrod. I don't want him hurt.'

'Tell me the truth. Do you have any concerns at all except making your pictures?'

'Yeah, human beings. If you don't accept that, I say fuck you.'

His tense, protruding eyes reminded me of hard-boiled eggs. I looked away from him, felt my palm close and unclose against my trousers. The sunlight on the bayou was like a yellow flare burning under the water.

'I'm not in the baby-sitting business, Mr Goldman,' I said. 'My advice is that you tell all this to the sheriff's department. Right now I'm still suspended. I'm going back to finish my coffee now. We'll see you around.'

'It's Dog Patch. I'm in a cartoon. I talk, nobody hears me.' He tapped himself on the cheek. 'Maybe I'm dead and this is hell.'

'What else do you want to say?' I heard the heat rising in my own voice.

'You accuse me of not having any humanity. Then I tell you Elrod's striking matches on Balboni's balls on your account and you blow me off. You want Balboni to put his foot through El's face?'

'He's your business partner. You brought him here. You didn't worry about the origins of his money till you—'

'That's all true. The question is what do we do now?'

'We?'

'Right. I'm getting through. Everybody around here doesn't have meatloaf for brains after all.'

'There's no *we* in this. I'll talk to Elrod, I'll take him to AA meetings, but he's not my charge.'

'Good. Tell him that. I'm on my way to work. Dump him in a cab.'

'What?'

'He's down there in your bait shop. Drunk. I think you have a serious hearing problem. Get some help.'

He stuck a peppermint candy cane in the corner of his mouth and walked back down the slope to his automobile, his shoulders rolling under his polo shirt, his jaws cracking the candy between his teeth, his profile turned into the freshening breeze like a gladiator's.

14

'You did what?' Bootsie said. She stared at me open-mouthed across the kitchen table.

I told her again.

'You *threw* him in the bayou? I don't believe it,' she said.

'He's used to it. Don't worry about him.'

'Mr Sykes started fighting with Dave on the dock, Bootsie,' Alafair said. 'He was drunk and making a lot of noise in front of the customers. He wouldn't come up to the house like Dave told him.'

Way to go, Alf, I thought.

'Where is he now?' Bootsie said, wiping her mouth with her napkin and starting to rise from her chair.

'Throwing up on the rose bushes the last I saw him.'

'Dave, that's disgusting,' she said, and sat back down.

'Tell Elrod.'

'Batist said he drank five beers without paying for them,' Alafair said.

'What are you going to do about him?' Bootsie said. Then she turned her head and looked out the back screen. 'Dave, he just went across the backyard.'

'I think El has pulled his suction cups loose for a while, Boots.'

'Suction cups?' Alafair said, her cereal spoon poised in front of her mouth.

'He's crawling around on his hands and knees. Do something,' Bootsie said.

'That brings up a question I was going to ask you.'

I saw the recognition grow in her eyes.

'The guy went up against Julie Balboni because of me,' I said. 'Or at least partly because of me.'

'You want him to stay *here*? Dave, this is our home,' she said.

'The guy's in bad shape.'

'It's still our home. We can't open it up to every person who has a problem.'

'The guy needs an AA friend or he's not going to make it. Look at him. He's pitiful. Should I take him down to the jail?'

Bootsie rested her fingers on her temples and stared at the sugar container.

'I'll make him a deal,' I said. 'The first time he takes a drink, he gets eighty-sixed back to Spanish Lake. He pays his share of the food, he doesn't tie up the telephone, he doesn't come in late.'

'Why's he squirting the hose in his mouth?' Alafair said.

'All right, we can try it for a couple of days,' Bootsie said. 'But, Dave, I don't want this man talking anymore about his visions or whatever it is he thinks he sees out on the lake.'

'You think that's where I got it from, huh?' I smiled.

'In a word, yes.'

'He's a pretty good guy when he's not wired. He just sees the world a little differently than some.'

'Oh, wonderful.'

Alafair got up from her chair and peered at an angle through the screen into the backyard.

'Oooops,' she said, and put her hand over her mouth.

'What is it?' Bootsie said.

'Mr Sykes just did the rainbow yawn.'

'What?' I said.

'He vomited on the picnic table,' Alafair said.

I waited until Bootsie and Alafair had driven off to the grocery store in town, then I went out into the backyard. Elrod's slacks and shirt were pasted to his skin with water from the bayou and grimed with mud and grass stains. He had washed down the top of the picnic table with the garden hose, and he now sat slack-jawed on the bench with his knees splayed, his shoulders stooped, his hands hanging between his thighs. His unshaved face had the gray colour of spoiled pork.

I handed him a cup of coffee.

'Thanks,' he said.

I winced at his breath.

'If you stay on at our house, do you think you can keep the cork in the jug?' I said.

'I cain't promise it. No, sir, I surely cain't promise it.'

'Can you try?'

He lifted his eyes up to mine. The iris of his right eye had a clot of blood in it as big as my fingernail.

'Nothing I ever tried did any good,' he said. 'Antabuse, psychiatrists, a dry-out at the navy hospital, two weeks hoeing vegetables on a county P-farm. Sooner or later I always went back to it, Mr Robicheaux.'

'Well, here's the house rules, partner,' I said, and I went through

179

them one at a time with him. He kept rubbing his whiskers with the flat of his hand and spitting between his knees.

'I guess I look downright pathetic to you, don't I?' he said.

'Forget what other people think. Don't drink, don't think, and go to meetings. If you do that, and you do it for yourself, you'll get out of all this bullshit.'

'I got that kid beat up real bad. It was awful. Balboni kept jumping up in the air, spinning around, and cracking the sole of his foot across the kid's head. You could hear the skin split against the bone.'

He placed his palms over his ears, then removed them.

'You stay away from Balboni,' I said. 'He's not your problem. Let the law deal with him.'

'Are you kidding? The guy does whatever he wants. He's even getting his porno dirt bag into the film.'

'What porno dirt bag?'

'He brought up some guy of his from New Orleans, some character who thinks he's the new Johnny Wadd. He's worked the guy into a half-dozen scenes in the picture. Look, Mr Robicheaux, I'm getting the shakes. How about cutting me a little slack? Two raw eggs in a beer with a shot on the side. That's all I'll need. Then I won't touch it.'

'I'm afraid not, partner.'

'Oh man, I'm really sick. I've never been this sick. I'm going into the DTs.'

I put my hand on his shoulder. His muscles were as tight and hard as cable wire and quivering with anxiety. Then he covered his eyes and began weeping, his wet hair matted with dirt, his body trembling like that of a man whose soul was being consumed by its own special flame.

I drove out to Spanish Lake to find Julie Balboni. No one was in the security building by the dirt road that led into the movie location, and I dropped the chain into the dirt and parked in the shade, close by the lake, next to a catering truck. The sky was darkening with rain clouds, and the wind off the water blew leaves across the ground under the oak trees. I walked through a group of actors dressed as Confederate infantry. They were smoking cigarettes and lounging around a freshly dug rifle pit and ramparts made out of huge stick-woven baskets filled with dirt. Close by, a wheeled cannon faced out at the empty lake. I could smell the drowsy, warm odor of reefer on the breeze.

'Could y'all tell me where to find Julie Balboni?' I said.

None of them answered. Their faces had turned dour. I asked again.

'We're just the hired help,' a man with sergeant's stripes said.

180

'If you see him, would you tell him Dave Robicheaux is looking for him?'

'You'd better tell him yourself,' another actor said.

'Do you know where Mr Goldman is?'

'He went into town with some lawyers. He'll be back in a few minutes,' the sergeant said.

'Thank you,' I said.

I walked back to my truck and had just opened the door when I heard someone's feet in the leaves behind me.

'I need a moment of your time, please,' Twinky Lemoyne said. He had been walking fast, holding his ballpoint pens in his shirt pocket with one hand; a strand of hair hung over his rimless glasses and his face was flushed.

'What can I do for you?'

'I'd like to know what your investigation has found out.'

'You would?'

'Yes. What have you learned about these murders?'

I shouldn't have been surprised at the presumption and intrusiveness of his question. Successful businessmen in any small town usually think of policemen as extensions of their mercantile fraternity, dedicated in some ill-defined way to the financial good of the community. But previously he had stonewalled me, had even been self-righteous, and it was hard to accept him now as an innocuous Rotarian.

'Maybe you should call the sheriff's office or the FBI, Mr Lemoyne. I'm suspended from the department right now.'

'Is this man Balboni connected with the deaths of these women?'

'Did someone tell you he was?'

'I'm asking you an honest question, sir.'

'And I'm asking you one, Mr Lemoyne, and I advise you to take it quite seriously. Do you have some personal knowledge about Balboni's involvement with a murder?'

'No, I don't.'

'You don't?'

'No, of course not. How could I?'

'Then why your sense of urgency, sir?'

'You wouldn't keep coming out here unless you suspected him. Isn't that right?'

'What difference should it make to you?'

The skin of his face was grained and red, and his eyelashes fluttered with his frustration.

'Mr Robicheaux, I think . . . I feel . . .'

'What?'

'I believe you've been treated unfairly.'

'Oh?'

'I believe I've contributed to it, too. I've complained to others about both you and the FBI woman.'

'I think there's another problem here, Mr Lemoyne. Maybe it has to do with the price of dealing with a man like Julie Balboni.'

'I've tried to be honest with you.'

'That's fine. Get away from Balboni. Divest yourself of your stock or whatever it takes.'

'Then maybe he *was* involved with those dead girls?' His eyes were bright and riveted on mine.

'You tell me, Mr Lemoyne. Would you like Julie for your next-door neighbor? Would you like your daughter around him? Would you, sir?'

'I find your remark very offensive.'

'*Offensive* is when a stunt man gets his nose and ribs broken and an ear torn loose from his head as an object lesson.'

I could see the insult and injury in his eyes. His lips parted and then closed.

'Why are you out here, Mr Lemoyne?'

'To see Mr Goldman. To find out what I can.'

'I think your concern is late in coming.'

'I have nothing else to say to you. Good day to you, sir.'

He walked to his automobile and got in. As I watched him turn onto the dirt road and head back toward the security building, I had to wonder at the self-serving naïveté that was characteristic of him and his kind. It was as much a part of their personae as the rows of credit and membership cards they carried in their billfolds, and when the proper occasion arose they used it with a collective disingenuousness worthy of a theatrical award.

At least that was what I thought – perhaps in my own naïveté – about Twinky Hebert Lemoyne at the time.

When I reached the security building Murphy Doucet, the guard, was back inside, and the chain was down in the road. He was bent over a table, working on something. He waved to me through the open window, then went back to his work. I parked my truck on the grass and walked inside.

It was hot and close inside the building and smelled of airplane glue. Murphy Doucet looked up from a huge balsa-wood model of a B-17 Flying Fortress that he was sanding. His blue eyes jittered back and forth behind a pair of thick bifocals.

'How you doing, Dave?' he said.

'Pretty good, Murph. I was looking for Julie Balboni.'

'He's playing ball.'

'Ball?'

'Yeah, sometimes he takes two or three guys into town with him for a pepper game.'

'Where?'

'I think at his old high school. Say, did you get Twinky steamed up about something.'

'Why's that?'

'I saw you talking to him, then he went barreling-ass down the road like his noise was out of joint.'

'Maybe he was late for lunch.'

'Yeah, probably. It don't take too much to get Twinky's nose out of joint, anyway. I've always suspected he could do with a little more pussy in his life.'

'He's not married?'

'He used to be till his wife run off on him. Right after she emptied his bank account and all the money in his safe. I didn't think Twinky was going to survive that one. That was a long time ago, though.'

He used an Exacto knife to trim away a tiny piece of dried glue from one of the motors on his model airplane. He blew sawdust off the wings and held the plane aloft.

'What do you think of it?' he asked.

'It looks good.'

'I've got a whole collection of them. All the planes from World War II. I showed Mikey Goldman my B-17 and he said maybe he could use my collection in one of his films.'

'That sounds all right, Murph.'

'You kidding? He meant I should donate them. I figured out why that stingy Jew has such a big nose. The air's free.'

'He seems like an upfront guy to me,' I said.

'Try working for one of them.'

I looked at him. 'You say Julie's at his old high school?' I said.

'Yeah, him and some actor and that guy named Cholo.'

He set his bifocals on the work table and rubbed his hands on the smooth blond surface of his plane. His skin was wrinkled and brown as a cured tobacco leaf.

'Thanks for your time,' I said.

'Stop by more often and have coffee. It's lonely sitting out here in this shack.'

'By the way, do you know why Goldman might be with a bunch of attorneys?'

'Who knows why these Hollywood sonsofbitches do anything? You're lucky, Dave. I wish I was still a real cop. I do miss it.'

He brushed with the backs of his fingers at the starch-white scar on his throat.

*

A half hour later, as rain clouds churned thick and black overhead, like curds of smoke from an oil fire, I parked my truck by the baseball diamond of my old high school, now deserted for the summer, where Baby Feet and I had played ball as boys. He stood at home plate, wearing only a pair of spikes and purple gym shorts, the black hair on his enormous body glistening with sweat, his muscles rippling each time he belted a ball deep into the outfield with a shiny blue aluminum bat.

I walked past the oak trees that were carved with the names of high school lovers, past the sagging, paintless bleachers, across the worn infield grass toward the chicken-wire backstop and the powerful swing of his bat, which arched balls like tiny white dots high over the heads of Cholo and a handsome shirtless man whose rhythmic movements and smooth body tone reminded me of undulating water. A canvas bag filled with baseballs spilled out at Julie's feet. There were drops of moisture in his thick brows, and I could see the concentrated, hot lights in his eyes. He bent over effortlessly, in spite of his great weight, picked up a ball with his fingers, and tossed it in the air; then I saw his eyes flick at me, his left foot step forward in the batter's box, just as he swung the aluminum bat and ripped a grounder like a rocket past my ankles.

I watched it bounce between the oak trees and roll into the street.

'Pretty good shot for a foul ball,' I said.

'It looked right down the line to me.'

'You were never big on rules and boundaries, Feet.'

'What counts is the final score, my man.'

Another ball rang off his metal bat and arched high into the outfield. Cholo wandered around in a circle, trying to get under it, his reddish-gray curls glued to his head, his glove outstretched like an amphibian's flipper. The ball dropped two feet behind him.

'I hear you've been busy out at the movie set,' I said.

'How's that?'

'Tearing up a young guy who didn't do anything to you.'

'There's two sides to every story.'

'This kid hurt you in some way, Julie?'

'Maybe he keeps bad company.'

'Oh, I see. Elrod Sykes gave you a bad time? He's the bad company? You're bothered by a guy who's either drunk or hungover twenty-four hours a day?'

'Read it like you want.' He flipped a ball into the air and lined it over second base. 'What's your stake in it, Dave?'

'It seems Elrod felt he had to come to my defense with you. I wish he hadn't done that.'

'So everybody's sorry.'

'Except it bothers me that you seriously hurt a man, maybe because of me.'

'Maybe you flatter yourself.' He balanced himself on one foot and began tapping the dirt out of his spikes with his bat.

'I don't think so. You've got a big problem with pride, Julie. You always did.'

'Because of you? If my memory hasn't failed me, some years ago a colored shoe-shine man was about to pull real hard on your light chain. I don't remember you minding when I pulled your butt out of the fire that night.'

'Yesterday's box score, Feet.'

'So don't take everything so serious. There's another glove in the bag.'

'The stunt man left town. He's not going to file charges. I guess you already know that.'

He rubbed his palm up and down the tapered shank of the bat.

'It was a chicken-shit thing to do,' I said.

'Maybe it was. Maybe I got my point of view, too. Maybe like I was with a broad when this fucking wild man starts beating on the side of my trailer.'

'He's staying at my house now, Julie. I want you to leave him alone. I don't care if he gets in your face or not.'

He flipped another ball in the air and *whanged* it to the shirtless man deep in left field. Then he took a hard breath through his nostrils.

'All right, I got no plans to bother the guy,' he said. 'But not because you're out here, Dave. Why would I want to have trouble with the guy who's the star of my picture? You think I like headaches with these people, you think I like losing money? . . . We clear on this now? . . . Why you keep staring at me?'

'A cop over in Lafayette thinks you set me up.'

'You mean that shooting in front of Red's Bar? Get serious, will you?' He splintered a shot all the way to the street, then leaned over and picked up another ball, his stomach creasing like elephant hide.

'It's not your style, huh?' I said.

'No, it's not.'

'Come on, Julie, fair and square – look back over your own record. Even when we were kids, you always had to get even, you could never let an insult or an injury pass. Remember the time you came down on that kid's ankle with your spikes?'

'Yeah, I remember it. I remember him trying to take my eyes out with *his*.'

The sky had turned almost black now, and the wind was blowing dust across the diamond.

'You're a powerful and wealthy man. Why don't you give it up?'

'Give what up? What the fuck are you talking about?'

'Carrying around all that anger, trying to prove you're big shit, fighting with your old man, whatever it is that drives you.'

'Where do you think you get off talking to me like this?'

'Come on, Julie. We grew up together. Save the hand job for somebody else.'

'That's right. That's why maybe I overlook things from you that I don't take from nobody else.'

'What's to take? Your father used to beat you with a garden hose. I didn't make that up. You burned down his nightclub.'

'It's starting to rain. I think it's time for you to go.' He picked up another ball and bounced it in his palm.

'I tried, partner.'

'Oh, yeah? What's that mean?'

'Nothing.'

'No, you mean you came out here and gave me a warning.'

'Why do you think every pitch is a slider, Julie?'

He looked away at the outfield, then back at me.

'You've made remarks about my family. I don't like that,' he said. 'I'm proud to be Italian. I was even proud of my old man. The people who ran this town back then weren't worth the sweat off his balls. In New Iberia we were always "wops," "dagos," and "guineas" because you coonasses were too fucking stupid to know what the Roman Empire was. So you get your nose out of the air when you talk about my family, or about my problems, or anything about my life, you understand what I'm saying, Dave?'

'Somebody made you become a dope dealer? That's what you're telling me?'

'I'm telling you to stay the fuck away from me.'

'You don't make a convincing victim, Julie. I'll see you around. Tell your man out there not to spit on the ball.'

'What?'

'Isn't that your porno star? I'd be careful. I think AIDS is a lot more easily transmitted than people think.'

I saw the rain pattering in the dust as I walked away from him toward the bleachers behind first base. Then I heard a ball ring off the aluminum bat and crash through the tree limbs overhead. I turned around in time to see Julie toss another ball into the air and swing again, his legs wide spread, his torso twisting, his wrists snapping as the bat bit into the ball and laced it in a straight white line toward my face.

When I opened my eyes I could see a thick layer of black clouds stretched across the sky from the southern horizon to a silken stretch of blue in the north. The rain had the warm amber color of whiskey, but it made no sound and it struck against my skin as dryly as flower petals in a windstorm.

The general sat on the bottom bench in the bleachers, coatless, the wind flowing through his shirt, a holstered cap-and-ball revolver hanging loosely from his right shoulder. The polished brass letters CSA gleamed softly on the crown of his gray hat. I could smell horses and hear teamsters shouting and wagons creaking in the street. Two enlisted men separated themselves from a group in the oak trees, lifted me to my feet, and sat me down on the wood plank next to the general.

He pointed toward first base with his crutch. My body lay on its side in the dirt, my eyes partially rolled. Cholo and the pornographic actor were running toward home plate from the outfield while Julie was fitting the aluminum bat back in the canvas ball bag. But they were all moving in slow motion, like creatures that were trying to burst free from an invisible gelatinous presence that encased their bodies.

The general took a gold watch as thick as a buttermilk biscuit from his pants pocket, snapped open the cover, glanced at the time, then twisted around in his seat and looked at the soldiers forming into ranks in the street. They were screwing their bayonets on the ends of their rifles, sliding their pouches of paper cartridges and minié balls to the centers of their belts, tying their haversacks and rolled blankets across their backs so their arms would be unencumbered. I saw a man put rolls of socks inside his coat and over his heart. I saw another man put a Bible in the same place. A boy, not over sixteen, his cap crimped tightly on his small head, unfurled the Stars and Bars from its wooden staff and lifted it popping into the wind.

Then in the north, where the sky was still blue and not sealed by storm clouds, I saw bursts of black smoke, like birds with ragged wings, and I heard thunder echoing in the trees and between the wooden buildings across the street.

'What's that?' I asked him.

'You've never heard that sound, the electric snap, before?'

'They're air bursts, aren't they?'

'It's General Banks's artillery firing from down the Teche. He's targetted the wrong area, though. There's a community of darkies under those shells. Did you see things like that in your war?'

'Yes, up the Mekong. Some villagers tried to run away from a barrage. They got caught out in the rice field. When we buried them, their faces all looked like they had been inside a terrible wind.'

'Then you know it's the innocent about whom we need to be most concerned?'

Before I could answer I saw Cholo and the man without a shirt staring down at my body, their faces beaded with rain. Julie pulled the drawstring tight on the ball bag and heaved it over his shoulder.

'Get in the Caddy, you guys,' he said.

'What happened, Julie?' Cholo said. He wore tennis shoes without socks, a tie-dyed undershirt, and a urine-yellow bikini knotted up tightly around his scrotum. Hair grew around the edges of his bikini like tiny pieces of copper wire.

'He got in the way of the ball,' Julie said.

'The guy's got a real goose egg in his hair,' the shirtless man said. 'Maybe we ought to take him to a hospital or something.'

'Leave him alone,' Julie said.

'We just gonna leave him here?' Cholo said.

'Unless you want to sit around out here in the rain,' Julie said.

'Hey come on, Feet,' Cholo said.

'What's the problem?' Julie said.

'He's not a bad guy for a cop. Y'all go back, right?'

'He's got diarrhea of the mouth. Maybe he learned a lesson this time,' Julie said.

'Yeah, but that don't mean we can't drop the guy off at the hospital. I mean, it ain't right to leave him in the fucking rain, Julie.'

'You want to start signing your own paychecks? Is that what you're telling me, Cholo?'

'No, I didn't say that. I was just trying to act reasonable. Ain't that what you're always saying? Why piss off the locals?'

'We're not pissing off anybody. Even his own department thinks he's a drunk and a pain in the ass. He got what he deserved. Are you guys coming or not?' Julie said.

He opened the trunk of the purple Cadillac limousine and threw the ball bag clattering inside. The porn actor followed him, wiping his chest and handsome face with his balled-up shirt. Cholo hesitated, stared after them, then pulled the first-base pad loose from its anchor pins and rested it across the side of my face to protect it from the rain. Then he ran after the others.

The blue strip of sky in the north was now filled with torn pieces of smoke. I could hear a loud *snap* each time a shell burst over the distant line of trees.

'What were you going to tell me?' I said to the general.

'That it's the innocent we need to worry about. And when it comes to their protection, we shouldn't hesitate to do it under a black flag.'

'I don't understand.'

'I feel perhaps I've deceived you.'

'How?'

188

'Perhaps I gave you the indication that you had been chosen as part of some chivalric cause.'

'I didn't think that, general.'

His face was troubled, as though his vocabulary was inadequate to explain what he was thinking. Then he looked out into the rain and his eyes became melancholy.

'My real loss wasn't in the war,' he said. 'It came later.'

He turned slowly and looked into my face. 'Yellowjack took not only my life but also the lives of my wife and daughter, Mr Robicheaux.'

He waited. The rain felt like confetti blowing against my skin. I searched his eyes, and my heart began to beat against my ribs.

'My family?' I said.

'If you're brave and honorable and your enemies can't destroy you personally, they'll seek to destroy what you love.'

He gestured with his crutch to a sergeant, who led a saddled white gelding around the side of the bleachers.

'Wait a minute, general. That's not good enough,' I said.

'It's all I have,' he answered, now seated in the saddle, his back erect, the reins wrapped around his gloved fist.

'Who would try to hurt them? What would they have to gain?'

'I don't know. Keep the Sykes boy with you, though. He's a good one. You remember what Robert Lee once said? "Texans move them every time." Good day to you, lieutenant. It's time we go give Bonnie Nate Banks his welcome to southwestern Louisiana.' Then he cut the spur on his left boot into his horse's flank, galloped to the head of his infantry, and hollered out brightly, 'Hideeho, boys! It's a fine day for it! Let's make religious fellows of them all!'

Sometime later, I sat up on the ground in the rain, my clothes soaked, the base pad in my lap, a knot as hard and round as a half-dollar throbbing three inches behind my ear. An elderly black yardman bent over me, his face filled with concern. Down the street I could see an ambulance coming toward me through the rain.

'You okay, mister?' the black man said.

'Yes, I think so.'

'I seen you there and I t'ought you was drunk. But it look like somebody done gone upside yo' head.'

'Would you help me up, please?'

'Sho. You all right?'

'Why, yes, I'm sure I am. Did you see a man on horseback?'

'The Popsicle man gone by. His li'l cart got a horse. That's what you talkin' about?'

The black man eased me down on the bottom plank of the bleachers.

It was starting to rain hard now, but right next to me, where the general had been sitting, was a pale, dry area in the wood that was as warm to the touch as living tissue.

15

The sky was clear when I woke in the morning, and I could hear gray squirrels racing across the bark of the trees outside the window. The icebag I had put on the lump behind my ear fell to the floor when I got out of bed to answer the phone.

'I called your office and found out you're still suspended,' Lou Girard said. 'What's going on over there?'

'Just that. I'm still suspended.'

'It sounds like somebody's got a serious bone on for you, Dave. Anyway, I talked to this FBI agent, what's her name, Gomez, as well as your boss. We vacuumed the Buick. Guess what we found?'

'I don't know.'

'Paper wadding. The kind that's used to seal blank cartridges. It looks like somebody fired a starter's gun at you. He probably leaned down through the passenger window, let off a couple of rounds, then bagged out.'

'What'd the sheriff have to say when you told him?'

'Not much. I got the feeling that maybe he was a little uncomfortable. He doesn't look too good, right, when one of his own men has to be cleared by a cop and a pathologist in another parish? I thought I could hear a little Pontius Pilate tap water running in the background.'

'He's always been an okay guy. He just got too close to a couple of the oil cans in the Chamber of Commerce.'

'Your friends don't stand around playing pocket pool while civilians kick a two-by-four up your butt, either.'

'Anyway, that's real good news, Lou. I owe you a redfishing trip out to Pecan Island.'

'Wait a minute, I'm not finished. That Gomez woman has some interesting theories about serial killers. She said these guys want control and power over people. So I got to thinking about the LeBlanc girl. If your FBI friend is right and the guy who killed her is from around here, what kind of work would he be in?'

'He may be just a pimp, Lou.'

'Yeah, but she got nailed on a prostitution charge when she was sixteen, right? That means the court gave somebody a lot of control over her life. What if a probation or parole officer had her selling out of her pants?'

'I saw the body. I think the guy who mutilated her has a furnace instead of a brain. I think he'd have a hard time hiding inside a white-collar environment.'

'It was the pencil pushers who gave the world Auschwitz, Dave. Anyway, her prostitution bust was in Lafayette. I'll find out if her PO or social worker is still around.'

'Okay, but I still believe we're after a pimp of some kind.'

'Dave, if this guy's just a pimp, particularly if he's mobbed-up, he would have been in custody a long time ago. These are dumb guys. That's why they do what they do. Most of them couldn't get jobs cleaning gum off movie seats.'

'So maybe Balboni's got a smart pimp working for him.'

'No, this guy knows how things work from the inside. He sucked us both in on that deal at Red's Bar.'

Lou had never gotten along with white-collar authority, in fact, was almost obsessed about it, and I wasn't going to argue with him.

'Let me know what you come up with,' I said.

But he wasn't going to let it drop that easily.

'I've been in law enforcement for thirty-seven years,' he said. 'I've lost count of the lowlifes I've helped send up the road. Is Louisiana any better for it? You know the answer to that one. Face it. The real sonsofbitches are the ones we don't get to touch.'

'Don't be too down, Lou.' I told him about Julie line-driving a ball off the side of my head. Then I told him the rest of it. 'I asked the paramedics who called in the report. They said it was anonymous. So I went down later and listened to the 911 tapes. It was a guy named Cholo Manelli. He's a—'

'Yeah, I know who he is. Cholo did that?'

'There's no mistaking that broken-nose Irish Channel accent.'

'He owes you or something?'

'Not really. But he's an old-time mob soldier. He knows you don't antagonize cops unnecessarily. Maybe Julie's starting to lose control of his people.'

'It's a thought. But stay away from Balboni till you get your shield back. Stay off baseball diamonds, too. For a sober guy you sure have a way of spitting in the lion's mouth.'

After I hung up the phone I showered, dressed in a pair of seersucker slacks, brown loafers, a charcoal shirt with a gray and red striped tie, and got a haircut and a shoe shine in town. My scalp twitched when the barber's scissors clipped across the lump behind my ear. Through the front window I saw Julie Balboni's purple limo drive down Main Street. The barber stopped clipping. The shop was empty except for the shoe-shine man.

'Dave, how come that man's still around here?' the barber said. His round stomach touched lightly against my elbow.

'He hasn't made the right people mad at him.'

'He ain't no good, that one. He don't have no bidness here.'

'I think you're right, Sid.'

He started clipping again. Then, almost as a casual afterthought, he said, 'Y'all gonna get him out of town?'

'There're some business people making a lot of money off of Julie. I think they'd like to keep him around awhile.'

His hands paused again, and he stepped around the side of the chair so I could see his face.

'That ain't the rest of us, no,' he said. 'We don't like having that man in New Iberia. We don't like his dope, we don't like his criminals he bring up here from New Orleans. You tell that man you work for we gonna 'member him when we vote, too.'

'Could I buy you a cup of coffee and a doughnut this morning, Sid?'

A little later, with my hair still wet and combed, I walked out of the heat into the air-conditioned coolness of the sheriff's department and headed toward the sheriff's office. I glanced inside my office door as I passed it. Rosie was not inside but Rufus Arceneaux was, out of uniform now, dressed in a blue suit and tie and a silk shirt that had the bright sheen of tin. He was sitting behind my desk.

I leaned against the door jamb.

'The pencil sharpener doesn't work very well, but there's a penknife in my drawer that you can use,' I said.

'I wasn't bucking for plainclothes. The old man gave it to me,' he said.

'I'm glad to see you're moving on up, Rufe.'

'Look, Dave, I'm not the one who went out and got fucked up at that movie set.'

'I hear you were out there, though. Looking into things. Probably trying to clear me of any suspicion that I got loaded.'

'I got a GED in the corps. You're a college graduate. You were a homicide lieutenant in New Orleans. You want to blame me for your troubles?'

'Where's Rosie?'

'Down in Vermilion Parish.'

'What for?'

'How would I know?'

'Did she say anything about Balboni having legal troubles with Mikey Goldman?'

'What legal—' His eyes clouded, like silt being disturbed in dark water.

'When you see her, would you ask her to call me?'

'Leave a message in her box,' he said, positioned his forearms on my desk blotter, straightened his back, and looked out the window as though I were not there.

When I walked into the sheriff's office he was pouring a chalky liquid from a brown prescription bottle into a water glass. A dozen sheets of paper were spread around on his desk. The 'hold' light was flashing on his telephone. He didn't speak. He drank from the glass, then refilled it from the water cooler and drank again, his throat working as though he were washing out an unwanted presence from his metabolism.

'How you doin', podna?' he said.

'Pretty good now. I had a talk with Lou Girard this morning.'

'So did I. Sit down,' he said, then picked up the phone and spoke to whoever was on hold. 'I'm not sure *what* happened. When I am, I'll call you. In the meantime, Rufus is going to be suspended. Just hope we don't have to pass a sales tax to pay the bills on this one.'

He hung up the phone and pressed the flat of his hand against his stomach. He made a face like a small flame was rising up his windpipe.

'Did you ever have ulcers?' he asked.

'Nope.'

'I've got one. If this medicine I'm drinking doesn't get rid of it, they may have to cut it out.'

'I'm sorry to hear that.'

'That was the prosecutor's office I was talking to. We're being sued.'

'Over what?'

'A seventy-six-year-old black woman shot her old man to death last night, then killed both her dogs and shot herself through the stomach. Rufus in there handcuffed her to the gurney, then came back to the office. He didn't bother to give the paramedics a key to the cuffs, either. She died outside the emergency room.'

I didn't say anything.

'You think we got what we deserved, huh?' he said.

'Maybe he would have done it even if he hadn't been kicked up to plainclothes, sheriff.'

'No, he wouldn't have been the supervising officer. He wouldn't have had the opportunity.'

'What's my status this morning?'

He brushed at a nostril with one knuckle.

'I don't know how to say this,' he said. 'We messed up. No *I* messed up.'

I waited.

'I did wrong by you, Dave,' he said.

'People make mistakes. Maybe you made the best decision you could at the time.'

He held out his hands, palms front.

'Nope, none of that,' he said. 'I learned in Korea a good officer takes care of his men. I didn't get this ulcer over Rufus Arceneaux's stupidity. I got it because I was listening to some local guys I should have told to butt out of sheriff's department business.'

'Nobody's supposed to bat a thousand, sheriff.'

'I want you back at work today. I'll talk to Rufus about his new status. That old black woman is part my responsibility. I don't know why I made that guy plainclothes. You don't send a warthog to a beauty contest.'

I shook hands with him, walked across the street to a barbecue stand in a grove of live oaks, ate a plate filled with dirty rice, pork ribs, and red beans, then strolled back to the office, sipping an ice-cold can of Dr Pepper. Rufus Arceneaux was gone. I clipped my badge on my belt, sat in the swivel chair behind my desk, turned the air-conditioner vents into my face, and opened my mail.

Rosie was beaming when she came through the office door an hour later.

'What's that I see?' she said. 'With a haircut and a shoe shine, too.'

'How's my favorite Fed?'

'Dave, you look wonderful!'

'Thanks, Rosie.'

'I can't tell you how fine it is to have you back.'

Her face was genuinely happy, to such an extent that I felt vaguely ill at ease.

'I owe you and Lou Girard a lot on this one,' I said.

'Have you had lunch yet?'

'Yeah, I did.'

'Too bad. Tomorrow I'm taking you out, though. Okay?'

'Yeah, that'd be swell.'

She sat down behind her desk. Her neck was flushed and her breasts rose against her blouse when she breathed. 'I got a call this morning from an old Frenchman who runs a general store on Highway 35 down in Vermilion Parish. You know what he said? "Hey, y'all catch the man put dat young girl in dat barrel?"'

I filled a water glass for her and put it on her desk.

'He knows something?' I said.

'Better than that. I think he saw the guy who did it. He said he remembers a month or so ago a blonde girl coming in his store at night in the rain. He said he became worried about her because of the way a man in the store was watching her.' She opened her notebook pad and looked at it. 'These are the old fellow's words: "You didn't need but look at that man's face to know he had a dirty mind." He said the girl had a convas backpack and she went back out in the rain to the highway with it. The man followed her, then he came back in a few minutes and asked the old fellow if he had any red balloons for sale.'

'Balloons?'

'If you think that sounds weird, how about this? When the old fellow said no, the man found an old box of Valentine candy on the back shelf and said he wanted that instead.'

'I'm not making connections here,' I said.

'The store owner watched the man with the candy box through the window. He said just before he pulled out of the parking lot he threw the candy box in the ditch. In the morning the old fellow went out and found it in the weeds. The cellophone wrapping was gone.' She watched my face. 'What are you thinking?'

'Did he see the man pick up the girl?'

'He's not sure. He remembers the man was in a dark-blue car and he remembers the brake lights going on in the rain.' She continued to watch my face. 'Here's the rest of it. I looked around on the back shelves of the store and found another candy box that the owner says is like the one the man in the blue car bought. Guess what tint the cellophane was.'

'Red or purple.'

'You got it, slick,' she said, and leaned back in her chair.

'He wrapped it around a spotlight, didn't he?'

'That'd be my bet.'

'Could the store owner describe this guy?'

'That's the problem.' She tapped a ballpoint pen on her desk blotter. 'All the old fellow remembers is that the man had a rain hood.'

'Too bad. Why didn't he contact us sooner?'

'He said he told all this to somebody, he doesn't know who, in the Vermilion Parish Sheriff's Department. He said when he called again yesterday, they gave him my number. Is your interagency cooperation always this good?'

'Always. Does he still have the candy box?'

'He said he gave the candy to his dog, then threw the box in the trash.'

'So maybe we've got a guy impersonating a cop?' I said.

'It might explain a lot of things.'

Unconsciously I fingered the lump behind my ear.

'What's the matter?' she said.

'Nothing. Maybe our man is simply a serial killer and psychopath after all. Maybe he doesn't have anything to do with Julie Balboni.'

'Would that make you feel good or bad?'

'I honestly can't say, Rosie.'

'Yeah, you can,' she said. 'You're always hoping that even the worst of them has something of good in him. Don't do that with Balboni. Deep down inside all that whale fat is a real piece of shit, Dave.'

Outside, a jail trusty cutting the grass broke the brass head off a sprinkler with the lawnmower. A violent jet of water showered the wall and ran down the windows. In the clatter of noise, in the time it takes the mind's eye to be distracted by shards of wet light, I thought of horses fording a stream, of sun-browned men in uniform looking back over their shoulders at the safety of a crimson and gold hardwood forest, while ahead of them dirty puffs of rifle fire exploded from a distant treeline that swarmed with the shapes of the enemy.

It's the innocent we need to worry about, he had said. And when it comes to their protection we shouldn't hesitate to do it under a black flag.

'Are you all right?' she said.

'Yeah, it's a fine day. Let's go across the street and I'll buy you a Dr Pepper.'

That evening, at sunset, I was sprinkling the grass and the flower beds in the backyard while Elrod and Alafair were playing with Tripod on top of the picnic table. The air was cool in the fading light and smelled of hydrangeas and water from the hose and the fertilizer I had just spaded into the roots of my rosebushes.

The phone rang inside, and a moment later Bootsie brought it and the extension cord to the back screen. I sat down on the step and put the receiver to my ear.

'Hello,' I said.

I could hear someone breathing on the other end.

'Hello?'

'I want to talk to you tonight.'

'Sam?'

'That's right. I'm playing up at the black juke in St Martinville. You know where that's at?'

'The last time I had an appointment with you, things didn't work out too well.'

'That was last time. I was drinkin' then. Then them womens was hangin' around, made me forget what I was supposed to do.'

'I think you let me down, partner.'

He was quiet except for the sound of his breathing.

'Is something wrong?' I said.

'I got to tell you somet'ing, somet'ing I ain't tole no white man.'

'Say it.'

'You come up to the juke.'

'I'll meet you at my office tomorrow morning.'

'What I got to say can put me back on the farm. I sure ain't gonna do it down there.'

Elrod picked Tripod up horizontally in his arms, then bounced him up and down by tugging on his tail.

'I'll be there in an hour or so,' I said. 'Don't jerk me around again, Sam.'

'You might be a po-liceman, you might even be different from most white folks, but you still white and you ain't got no idea 'bout the world y'all give people of color to live in. That's a fact, suh. It surely is,' he said, and hung up.

I should have known that Hogman would not be outdone in eloquence.

'Don't pull his tail,' Alafair was saying.

'He likes it. It gets his blood moving,' Elrod said.

She sighed as though Elrod were unteachable, then took Tripod out of his arms and carried him around the side of the house to the hutch.

'Can you take yourself to the meeting tonight?' I asked Elrod.

'You cain't go?'

'No.'

'How about I just wait till we can go together?' He rubbed the top of the table with his fingers and didn't look up.

'What if I drop you off and then come back before the meeting's over?'

'Look, this is a, what do you call it, a step meeting?'

'That's right.'

'You said it's about amends, about atoning to people for what you did wrong?'

'Something like that.'

'How do I atone for Kelly? How do I make up for that one, Dave?' He stared out at the late red sun over the canefield so I couldn't see his eyes.

'You get those thoughts out of your head. Kelly's dead because we have a psychopath in our midst. Her death doesn't have anything to do with you.'

'You can say that all you want, but I know better.'

198

'Oh, yeah?'

'Yeah.'

I could see the clean, tight line of his jaw and a wet gleaming in the corner of his eye.

'Tell me, did you respect Kelly?' I asked.

He swiveled around on the picnic bench. 'What kind of question is that?'

'I'm going to be a little hard on you, El. I think you're using her death to feel sorry for yourself.'

'What?' His face was incredulous.

'When I lost my wife I found out that self-pity and guilt could be a real rush, particularly when I didn't have Brother Jim Beam to do the job.'

'That's a lousy fucking thing to say.'

'I was talking about myself. Maybe you're different from me.'

'What the hell's the matter with you? You don't think its natural to feel loss, to feel grief, when somebody dies? I tried to close the hole in her throat with my hands, her blood was running through my fingers. She was still alive and looking straight into my eyes. Like she was drowning and neither one of us could do anything about it.' He pressed his forehead against his fist; his flexed thigh trembled against his slacks.

'I got four of my men killed on a trail in Vietnam. Then I got drunk over it. I used them, I didn't respect them for the brave men they were. That's the way alcoholism works, El.'

'I'd appreciate it if you'd leave me be for a while.'

'Will you go to the meeting?'

He didn't answer. There was a pained light in his eyes like someone had twisted barbed wire around his forehead.

'You don't have to talk, just listen to what these guys have to say about their own experience,' I said.

'I'd rather pass tonight.'

'Suit yourself,' I said.

I told Bootsie where I was going and walked out to the truck. The cicadas droned from horizon to horizon under the vault of plum-colored sky. Then I heard Elrod walking through the leaves and pecan husks behind me.

'If I sit around here, I'll end up in the beer joint,' he said, and opened the passenger door to the truck. Then he raised his finger at me. 'But I'm going to ask you one thing, Dave. Don't ever accuse me of using Kelly again. If you do, I'm going to knock your teeth down your goddamn throat.'

There were probably a number of things I could have said in reply;

but you don't deny a momentary mental opiate to somebody who has made an appointment in the garden of Gethsemane.

The black jukejoint in St Martinville was set back in a grove of trees off a yellow dirt road not far from Bayou Teche. It was one of those places that could be dropped by a tornado in the middle of an Iowa cornfield and you would instantly know that its origins were in the Deep South. The plank walls and taped windows vibrated with noise from Friday afternoon until late Sunday night. Strings of Christmas-tree lights rimmed the doors and windows year round; somebody was barbecuing ribs on top of a tin barrel, only a few feet from a pair of dilapidated privies that were caked under the eaves with yellow-jacket and mud-dauber nests; people copulated back in the woods against tree trunks and fought in the parking lot with knives, bottles, and razors. Inside, the air was always thick with the smell of muscatel, smoke, cracklings, draft beer and busthead whiskey, expectorated snuff, pickled hogs' feet, perfume, body powder, sweat, and home-grown reefer.

Sam Patin sat on a small stage with a canopy over it hung with red tassels and miniature whiskey bottles that clinked in the backdraft from a huge ventilator fan. His white suit gleamed with an electric purple glow from the floor lamps, and the waxed black surfaces of his twelve-string guitar winked with tiny lights. The floor in front of him was packed with dancers. When he blew into the harmonica attached to a wire brace on his neck and began rolling the steel picks on his fingers across an E-major blues run, the crowd moaned in unison. They yelled at the stage as though they were confirming a Biblical statement he had made at a revival, pressed their loins together with no consciousness of other people around them, and roared with laughter even though Hogman sang of a man who had sold his soul for an ox-blood Stetson hat he had just lost in a crap game:

> Stagolee went runnin'
> In the red-hot boilin' sun,
> Say look in my chiffro drawer, woman,
> Get me my smokeless .41.
> Stagolee tole Miz Billy,
> You don't believe your man is dead,
> Come down to the barroom,
> See the .41 hole in his head.
> That li'l judge found Stagolee guilty
> And that li'l clerk wrote it down,
> On a cold winter morning,
> Stagolee was Angola bound.

Forty-dollar coffin,
Eighty-dollar hack,
Carried that po' man to the burying ground,
Ain't never comin' back.

Two feet away from me the bartender filled a tray with draft beers without ever looking at me. He was bald and had thick gray muttonchop sideburns that looked like they were pasted on his cheeks. Then he wiped his hands on his apron and lit a cigar.

'You sho' you in the right place?' he said.

'I'm a friend of Hogman's,' I said.

'So this is where you come to see him?'

'Why not?'

'What you havin', chief?'

'A 7 Up.'

He opened a bottle, placed it in front of me without a glass, and walked away. The sides of the bottle were warm and filmed with dust. Twenty minutes later Hogman had not taken a break and was still playing.

'You want another one?' the bartender said.

'Yeah, I would. How about some ice or a cold one this time?' I said.

'The gentleman wants a cold one,' he said to no one in particular. Then he filled a tall glass with cracked ice and set it on the bar with another dusty bottle of 7 Up. 'Why cain't y'all leave him alone? He done his time, ain't he?'

'I look like the heat?' I said.

'You *are* the heat, chief. You and that other one out yonder.'

'What other one? What are you talking about, partner?'

'The white man that was out yonder in that blue Mercury.'

I got off the stool and looked into the parking lot through the Venetian blinds and the scrolled neon tubing of a Dixie beer sign.

'I don't see any blue Merc,' I said.

''Cause he gone now, chief. Like it's a black people's club, like he figured that out, you understand what I'm sayin'?'

'What'd this guy look like?' I said.

'White. He look white. That he'p you out?' he said. He tossed a towel into the tin sink, and walked down the duckboards toward the far end of the bar.

Finally Hogman slipped his harmonica brace and guitar strap off his neck, looked directly at me, and went through a curtained door into a back storage room. I followed him inside. He sat on a wood chair, among stacks of beer cases, and had already started eating a dinner of pork chops, greens, and cornbread from a tin plate that rested on another chair.

201

'I ain't had a chance to eat today. This movie-star life is gettin' rough on my time. You want some?' he said.

'No, thanks.' I leaned against a stack of beer cartons.

'The lady fix me these chops don't know how to season, but they ain't too bad.'

'You want to get to it, Sam?'

'You t'ink I just messin' with you, huh? All right, this is how it play. A long time ago up at Angola I got into trouble over a punk. Not my punk, you understand, I didn't do none of that unnatural kind of stuff, a punk that belong to a guy name Big Melon. Big Melon was growin' and sellin' dope for a couple of the hacks. Him and his punk had a whole truck patch of it behind the cornfield.'

'Hogman, I'm afraid this sounds a little remote.'

'You always *know*, you always got somet'ing smart to say. That's why you runnin' around in circles, that's why them men laughin' at you.'

'Which men?'

'The ones who killed that nigger you dug up in the Atchafalaya. You gonna be patient now, or you want to go back to doin' it your way?'

'I'm looking forward to hearing your story, Hogman.'

'See, these two hacks had them a good bidness. Big Melon and the punk growed the dope, cured it, bagged it all up, and the hacks sold it in Lafayette. They carried it down there themselves sometimes, or the executioner and another cop picked it up for them. They didn't let nobody get back there by that cornfield. But I was half-trusty then, livin' in Camp I, and I used to cut across the field to get to the hog lot. That's how come I found out they was growin' dope back there. So Big Melon tole the hack I knowed what they was doin', that I was gonna snitch them off, and then the punk planted a jar of julep under my bunk so I'd lose my trusty job and my good-time.

'I tole the hack it ain't right, I earn my job. He say, "Hogman, you fuck with the wrong people in here, you goin' in the box and you goin' stay in there till you come out a white man." That's what the bossman say. I tole him it don't matter how long they keep me in there, it still ain't right. They wrote me up for sassin' and put me to pickin' cotton. When I get down in a thin patch and come up short, they make me stand up all night on an oil barrel, dirty and smellin' bad and without no supper.

'I went to the bossman in the field, say I don't care what Big Melon do, what them hacks do, it ain't my bidness, I just want my job back on the hog lot. He say, "You better keep shut, boy, you better fill that bag, you better not put no dirt clods in it when you weigh in, neither, like you tried to do yesterday." I say, "Boss, what's I gonna do? I ain't put no dirt clods in my bag, I ain't give nobody trouble, I don't be carin' Big

Melon want to grow dope for the hacks." He knock me down with a horse quirt and put me in the sweatbox on Camp A for three days, in August, with the sun boilin' off them iron sides, with a bucket between my knees to go to the bat'room in.'

He had stopped eating now and his face looked solitary and bemused, as though his own experience had become strange and unfamiliar in his recounting of it.

'You were a standup guy, Hogman. I always admired your courage,' I said.

'No, I was scared of them people, 'cause when I come out of the box I knowed the gunbulls was gonna kill me. I seen them do it befo', up on the levee, where they work them Red Hat boys double-time from cain't-see to cain't-see. They shot and buried them po' boys without never missin' a beat, just the way somebody run over a dog with a truck and keep right on goin'.

'I had me a big Stella twelve-string guitar, bought it off a Mexican on Congress Street in Houston. I used to keep it in the count-man's cage so nobody wouldn't be foolin' with it while I was workin' or sleepin'. When I come out of the box and taken a shower and eat a big plate of rice and beans, I ax the count-man first thing for my guitar. He say, "I'm sorry, Sam, but the bossman let Big Melon take it while you was in the box."

'I waited till that night and went to Big Melon's "hunk," that's what we call the place where a wolf stay with his punk. There's that big fat nigger sittin' naked on his mattress, like a big pile of black inner tubes, while the punk is playin' my guitar on the floor, lipstick and rouge all over his face and pink panties on his li'l ass.

'I say, "Melon, you or your punk fuck wit' my guitar again and I gone cut that black dick off. It don't matter if I go to the electric chair for it or not. I'm gonna joog you in the shower, in the chow line, or while you pumpin' your poke chops here. They's gonna be one fat nigger they gonna have to haul in a piano crate down to the graveyard."

'Melon smile at me and say, "We just borrowed it, Hogman. We was gonna give it back. Here, you want Pookie to rub your back for you?"

'But I knowed they was comin'. Two nights later, right befo' lockup, I was goin' to the toilet and I turn around and his punk is standin' in the do'. I say, "What you want, Pookie?" He say, "I'm sorry I was playin' your guitar, Hogman. I wanta be yo' friend, maybe come stay up at your hunk some nights."

'When I reached down to pull up my britches, he come outta his back pocket with a dirk and aim it right at my heart. I catched him around the neck and bent him backwards, then I kept bendin' him backwards and squeezin' acrost his windpipe, and he was floppin' real hard, shakin' all over, he shit in his pants, 'cause I could smell it, then it went *snap*, just like you bust a real dry piece of firewood acrost your knee.

'I look up and there's one of the hacks who's selling the dope. He say, "Hogman, we ain't gonna let this be a problem. We'll just stuff this li'l bitch out yonder in the levee with them others. Won't nobody care, won't make no difference to nobody, not even to Big Melon. It'll just be our secret."

'All that time they'd been smarter than me. They sent Pookie to joog me, but they didn't care if he killed me or if I killed him. It worked out for them just fine. They knew I'd never cause them no trouble. They was right, too. I didn't sass, I done what they tole me, I even he'ped hoe them dope plants a couple of times.'

'I don't understand, Sam. You're telling me that the lynched black man was killed by one of these guards?'

'I ain't said that. I said they was a bunch of them sellin' that dope. They was takin' it out of the pen in a police car. What was the name of that nigger you dug out of the sandbar?'

'DeWitt Prejean.'

'I'll tell you this. He was fuckin' a white man's wife. Start axin' what he done for a livin', you'll find the people been causin' you all this grief.'

'Who's the guy I'm looking for?'

'I said all I can say.'

'Look, Sam, don't be afraid of these gunbulls or cops from years ago. They can't harm you now.'

He put a toothpick in the corner of his mouth, then took a pint bottle of rum from his coat pocket and unscrewed the cap with his thumb. He held the bottle below his mouth. His long fingers were glistening with grease from the pork chops he had eaten.

'This still the state of Lou'sana, or are we livin' somewhere else these days?' he said.

I couldn't sleep that night. I poured a glass of milk and walked down by the duck pond in the starlight. A pair of mudhens spooked out of the flooded reeds and skittered across the water's surface toward the far bank. The pieces of the case wouldn't come together. Were we looking for a serial killer who had operated all over the state, a local psychopath, a pimp, or perhaps even a hit man from the mob? Were cops involved? Hogman thought so, and even believed there was someone out there with the power to send him back to prison. But his perspective was colored by his own experience as a career recidivist. And what about the lynched black man, DeWitt Prejean? Would the solution to his murder in 1957 lead us to the deviate who had mutilated Cherry LeBlanc?

No, the case was not as simple as Hogman had wanted me to think, even though he was obviously sincere and his fears about retribution were real. But I had no answers, either.

Unfortunately, they would come in a way that I never anticipated. I saw Elrod come out of the lighted kitchen and walk down the slope toward the pond. He was shirtless and barefoot and his slacks were unbuttoned over his skivvies. He clutched a sheet of lined notebook paper in his right hand. He looked at me uncertainly, and his lips started to form words that obviously he didn't want to speak.

'What's wrong?' I said.

'The phone rang while I was in the kitchen. I answered it so y'all wouldn't get woke up.'

'Who was it? What's that in your hand?'

'The sheriff . . .' He straightened the piece of paper in his fingers and read the words to himself, then looked up into my face. 'It's a friend of yours, Lou Girard, Dave. The sheriff says maybe you should go over to Lafayette. He says, I'm sorry, man, he says your friend got drunk and killed himself.'

Elrod held the sheet of paper out toward me, his eyes looking askance at the duck pond. The moonlight was white on his hand.

16

He did it with a dogleg twenty-gauge in his little garage apartment, whose windows were overgrown with bamboo and banana trees. Or at least that's what the investigative officer, Doobie Patout, was telling me when I got there at 4 A.M., just as the photographer was finishing and the paramedics were about to lift Lou's body out of a wide pool of blood and zipper it inside a black bag.

'There's a half-empty bottle of Wild Turkey on the drainboard and a spilled bottle of Valium on the coffee table,' Doobie said. 'I think maybe Lou just got real down and decided to do it.'

The single-shot twenty-gauge lay at the foot of a beige-colored stuffed chair. The top of the chair, the wall behind it, and the ceiling were streaked with blood. One side of Lou's face looked perfectly normal, the eye staring straight ahead like a blue marble pressed into dough. The opposite side of his face, where the jawbone should have been, had sunk into the rug like a broken pomegranate. Lou's right arm was pointed straight out onto the wood floor. At the end of his fingers, painted in red, were the letters *SI*.

'You guys are writing it off as suicide?' I said.

'That's the way it looks to me,' Doobie said. The tops of his jug ears were scaled with sunburn. 'He was in bad shape. The mattress is covered with piss stains, the sink's full of raw garbage. Go in the bedroom and take a whiff.'

'Why would a suicide try to write a note in his own blood?'

'I think they change their minds when they know it's too late. Then they want to hold on any way they can. They're not any different from anybody else. It was probably for his ex-wife. Her name's Silvia.'

'Where's his piece?'

'On his dresser in the bedroom.'

'If Lou wanted to buy it, why wouldn't he use his .357?' I said. I scratched at a lead BB that had scoured upward along the wallpaper. 'Why would he do it with twenty-gauge birdshot, then botch it?'

'Because he was drunk on his ass. It wasn't an unusual condition for him.'

'He was helping me on a case, Doobie.'

'And?'

'Maybe he found out something that somebody didn't want him to pass along.'

The paramedics lifted Lou's body off the rug, then lowered it inside the plastic bag, straightened his arms by his sides, and zipped the bag over his face.

'Look, his career was on third base,' Doobie said, as the medics worked the gurney past him. 'His wife dumped him for another dyke, he was getting freebies from a couple of whores down at the Underpass, he was trembling and eating pills in front of the whole department every morning. You might believe otherwise, but there's no big mystery to what happened here tonight.'

'Lou had trouble with booze, but I think you're lying about his being on a pad with hookers. He was a good cop.'

'Think whatever you want. He was a drunk. That fact's not going to go away. I'm going to seal the place now. You want to look at anything else?'

'Is it true you were an executioner up at Angola?'

'None of your goddamn business what I was.'

'I'm going to look around a little more. In the meantime I want to ask you a favor, Doobie. I'd appreciate your waiting outside. In fact, I'd really appreciate your staying as far away from me as possible.'

'You'd appreciate it—'

'Yes. Thanks very much.'

His breath was stale, his eyes liquid and resentful. Then the interest went out of them and he glanced outside at the pale glow of the sun on the eastern horizon. He stuck a cigarette in the corner of his mouth, walked out onto the porch, and watched the paramedics load Lou's body into the back of the ambulance, not out of fear of me or even personal humiliation; he was simply one of those law officers for whom insensitivity, cynicism, cruelty, and indifference toward principle eventually become normal and interchangeable attitudes, one having no more value or significance than another.

In the sink, on top of a layer of unwashed dishes, was a pile of garbage – coffee grounds, banana peels, burned oatmeal, crushed beer cans, cigarette butts, wadded newspapers. The trash can by the icebox was empty, except for a line of wet coffee grinds that ran from the lip of the can to the bottom, where a solitary banana peel rested.

In the bedroom one drawer was open in the dresser. On top of the dresser were a roll of white socks, a framed photograph of Lou and his wife at a Las Vegas wedding chapel, Lou's holstered revolver, and the small notebook with a pencil attachment that he always carried in his shirt pocket. The first eight pages were filled with notes about an accidental drowning and a stabbing in a black nightclub. The next few pages had been torn out. Tiny bits of paper clung to the wire spirals, and the first blank page had no pencil impressions on it from the previous one.

In his sock drawer I found a bottle of vodka and his 'throw-down,' an old .32 revolver with worn bluing, taped wooden grips, and serial numbers that had been eaten and disfigured with acid. I flipped open the cylinder. Five of the chambers were loaded, and the sixth had been left empty for the hammer to rest on.

I started to replace the revolver in the drawer; instead, I pushed the drawer shut and dropped the revolver into my pants pocket.

On the way out of the apartment I looked again at Lou's blood on the floor. Doobie Patout's shoes had tracked through the edge of it and printed the logo of his rubber heel brightly on the wood.

What a way to exit thirty-seven years of law enforcement, I thought. You died face down in a rented garage apartment that wouldn't meet the standards of public housing; then your colleagues write you off as a drunk and step in your blood.

I looked at the smudged letters *SI* again. What were you trying to tell us, Lou?

Doobie Patout locked the door behind me when I walked outside. A red glow was spreading from the eastern horizon upward into the sky.

'This is what I think happened, Doobie. You can do with it what you want,' I said. 'Somebody found Lou passed out and tossed the place. After he ripped some pages out of Lou's notebook, he put Lou's twenty-gauge under his chin.'

'If he tossed the place first, he would have found Lou's .357, right? Why wouldn't he use it? That's the first thing you jumped on, Robicheaux.'

'Because he would have had to put it in Lou's hand. He didn't want to wake him up. It was easier to do it with the shotgun.'

His eyes fixed on mine; then they became murky and veiled as they studied a place in the air about six inches to the right of my face. A dead palm tree in the small yard clattered in the warm morning breeze.

It was Saturday, and I didn't have to go to the office, but I called Rosie at the motel where she was living and told her about Lou's death.

At noon of the same day Cholo Manelli drove a battered fire-engine-red Cadillac convertible down the dirt road by the bayou and parked by the dock just as I was headed up to the house for lunch. The left front fender had been cut away with an acetylene torch and looked like an empty eye socket. The top was down, and the back seat and the partly opened trunk were filled with wrought-iron patio furniture, including a glass-topped table and a furled beach umbrella.

He wore white shorts and a green Hawaiian shirt with pink flamingoes printed on it. He squinted up at me from under his white golf cap, which was slanted over one eye. When he grinned I saw that an incisor tooth was broken off in his lower mouth and there was still blood in the empty space above his gum.

'I wanted to say good-bye,' he said. 'Give you something, too.'

'Where you going, Cholo?'

'I thought I might go to Florida for a while, take it easy, maybe open up a business like you got. Do some marlin fishing, stuff like that. Look, can we talk someplace a minute?'

'Sure. Come on inside the shop.'

'No, you got customers around and I got a bad problem with language. It don't matter what I say, it comes out sounding like a toilet flushing. Take a ride with me, lieutenant.'

I got into the passenger's seat, and we drove down to the old grocery store with the wide gallery at the four-corners. The white-painted iron patio furniture vibrated and rattled in the back seat. On the leg of one chair was the green trademark of Holiday Inn. Cholo parked in the shade of the huge oak tree that stretched over the store's gallery.

'What's with the furniture?' I said.

'The owner wanted me to take it when I checked out. He said he's been needing some new stuff, it's a write-off, anyway, and I'm kind of doing him a favor. They got po'-boys in here? It's on me.'

Before I could answer he went inside the store and came back with two shrimp-and-fried-oyster sandwiches dripping with mayonnaise, lettuce, and sliced tomatoes. He unwrapped the wax paper on his and chewed carefully on one side of his mouth.

'What's going on, Cholo?' I said.

'Just like I said, it's time to hang it up.'

'You had some problems with Baby Feet?'

'Maybe.'

'Because you called an ambulance for me?'

He stopped chewing, removed a piece of lettuce from his teeth, and flicked it out onto the shell parking lot.

'Margot told him. She heard me on the phone,' he said. 'So last night we was all having dinner at this class place out on the highway, with some movie people there, people who still think Julie's shit don't stink, and Julie says, "Did y'all know Cholo thinks he's Florence Nightingale?

That it's his job to take care of people who get hurt on ball fields, even though that means betraying his old friends?"

'I say, "What are you talking, Julie? Who's fucking Florence Nightingale or whatever?"

'He don't even look at me. He says to all the others, "So, we're gonna get Cholo another job 'cause he don't like what he's doing now. He's gonna start work in one of my restaurants, down the street from the Iberville project. Bus dishes for a little while, get the feel of things, make sure the toilets are clean, 'cause a lot of middle-class niggers eat in there and they don't like dirty toilets. What d'you say, Cholo?"

'Everybody at the table's grinning and I go, "I ain't done anything wrong, Julie. I made a fucking phone call. What if the guy'd died out there?"

'Julie goes, "There you go again, Cholo. Always opening your face when you ain't supposed to. Maybe you ought to leave the table. You got wax in your ears, you talk shit, you rat-fuck your friends. I don't want you around no more."

'When I walked out, everybody in the restaurant was looking at me, like I was a bug, like I was somebody didn't have no business around regular people. Nobody ever done anything like that to me.'

His face was bright with perspiration in the warm shade. He rubbed his nose on the back of his wrist.

'What happened to your tooth, Cholo?' I asked.

'I went down to Julie's room last night. I told him that he was a douche bag. I wouldn't work for him again if he begged me, that just like Cherry LeBlanc told him, he's a needle-dick and the only reason a broad like Margot stays with him is because what she's got is so wore out it's like the Grand Canyon down there and it don't matter if he's a needle-dick or not. That's when he come across my mouth with this big glass ashtray, the sonofabitch.

'Here, you want to see what he's into, lieutenant,' he said, pulled a video cassette out of the glove box, and put it in my hand. 'Go to the movies.'

'Wait a minute. What's this about Cherry LeBlanc?'

'If he tells you he never knew her, ask him about this. Julie forgot he told me to take some souvenir pictures when we drove over to Biloxi once. Is that her or not?'

He slipped a black-and-white photograph from his shirt pocket and placed it in my hand. In it, Julie and Cherry LeBlanc sat at an outdoor table under an umbrella. They wore swimsuits and held napkin-wrapped drinks in their hands; both were smiling. The background was hazy with sunshine and out of focus. An indistinct man at another table read a newspaper; his eyes looked like diamonds embedded in his flesh.

'I want you to be straight with me, Cholo. Did Feet kill her?' I said.

'I don't know. I'll tell you what happened the night she got killed, though. They had a big blowup in the motel room. I could hear it coming through the walls. She said she wasn't nobody's chicken, she wanted her own action, her own girls, a place out on Lake Pontchartrain, maybe a spot in a movie. So he goes. "There's broads who'd do an awful lot just to be in the same room with me, Cherry. Maybe you ought to count your blessings." That's when she started to make fun of him. She said he looked like a whale with hair on it, and besides that, he had a putz like a Vienna sausage.'

'The next thing I know she's roaring out of the place and Julie's yelling into the phone at somebody, I don't know who, all I heard him say was Cherry is a fucking nightmare who's snorting up six hundred dollars' worth of his coke a day and he don't need any more nightmares in his life, particularly a teenage moron who thinks she can go apeshit any time she feels like it.'

'Who killed her, Cholo?'

He tossed his unfinished po'-boy sandwich at a rusted trash barrel. He missed, and the bread, shrimp, and oysters broke apart on the ground.

'Come on, lieutenant, You know how it works. A guy like Julie don't do hits. He says something to somebody, then he forgets it. If it's a special kind of job, maybe somebody calls up a geek, a guy with real sick thoughts in his head.

'Look, you remember a street dip in New Orleans named Tommy Figorelli, people used to call him Tommy Fig, Tommy Fingers, Tommy Five? Used to be a part-time meat cutter in a butcher shop on Louisiana Avenue? He got into trouble for something besides picking pockets, he molested a couple of little girls, and one of them turned out to be related to the Giacano family. So the word went out that Tommy Fig was anybody's fuck, but it wasn't supposed to be no ordinary hit, not for what he done. Did I ever tell you I worked in the kitchen up at Angola? That's right. So when Tommy got taken out, three guys done it, and when that butcher shop opened on Monday morning, it was the day before Christmas, see, Tommy was hung in parts, freeze-dried and clean, all over the shop like tree ornaments.

'That sounds sick, don't it, but the people who ran the shop didn't have no use for a child molester, either, and to show how they felt, they called up some guys from the Giacano family and they had a party with eggnog and fruitcake and music and Tommy Fig twirling around in pieces on the blades of the ceiling fan.

'What I'm saying, lieutenant, is I ain't gonna get locked up as a material witness and I ain't going before no grand jury, I been that route before, eight months in the New Orleans city prison, with a half-dozen guys trying to whack me out, even though I was standup and was gonna take the fall for a couple of guys I wouldn't piss on if they was burning to death.'

'You're sure Julie didn't catch up with Cherry LeBlanc later that same night?'

'It ain't his style. But then—' He poked his tongue into the space where his incisor tooth was broken off— 'who knows what goes on in Julie's head? He had the hots for the LeBlanc broad real bad, and she knew how to kick a Coke bottle up his ass. Go to the movies, lieutenant, make up your own mind. Hey, but remember something, okay? I didn't have nothing to do with this movie shit. You seen my rap sheet. When maybe I done something to somebody, I ain't saying I did, the guy had it coming. The big word there is the *guy*, lieutenant, you understand what I'm saying?'

I clicked my nails on the plastic cassette that rested on my thigh.

'A Lafayette detective named Lou Girard was killed last night. Did you hear anything about it?' I said.

'Who?' he said.

I said Lou's name again and watched Cholo's face.

'I never heard of him. Was he a friend of yours or something?'

'Yes, he was.'

He yawned and watched two black children sailing a Frisbee on the gallery of the grocery store. Then the light of recognition worked its way into his eyes and he looked back at my face.

'Hey, Loot, old-time lesson from your days at the First District,' he said. 'Nobody, and I mean *nobody*, from the New Orleans families does a cop. The guy who pulls something like that ends up a lot worse than Tommy Fig. His parts come off while he's still living.'

He nodded like a sage delivering a universal truth, then hawked, sucked the saliva out of his mouth, and spat a bloody clot out onto the shell.

A half hour later I closed the blinds in the sheriff's empty office and used his VCR to watch the cassette that Cholo had given me. Then I clicked it off, went to the men's room, rinsed my face in the lavatory, and dried it with paper towels.

'Something wrong, Dave?' a uniformed deputy standing at the urinal said.

'No, not really,' I said. 'I look like something's wrong?'

'There's some kind of stomach flu going around. I thought you might have a touch of it, that's all.'

'No, I'm feeling fine, Harry.'

212

'That's good,' he said, and glanced away from my face.

I went back inside the sheriff's office, opened the blinds, and watched the traffic on the street, the wind bending the tops of some myrtle trees, a black kid riding his bike down the sidewalk with a fishing rod propped across his handlebars.

I thought of the liberals I knew who spoke in such a cavalier fashion about pornography, who dismissed it as inconsequential or who somehow associated its existence with the survival of the First Amendment. I wondered what they would have to say about the film I had just watched. I wondered how they would like a theater that showed it to be located in their neighborhoods; I wondered how they would like the patrons of that theater to be around their children.

Finally I called Rosie at her motel. I told her where I was.

'Cholo Manelli gave me a pornographic film that you need to know about,' I said. 'Evidently Julie has branched out into some dark stuff.'

'What is it, what do you mean?'

'It's pretty sadistic, Rosie. It looks like the real thing, too.'

'Can we connect it to Balboni?'

'I doubt if Cholo would ever testify, but maybe we can find some of the people who made the film.'

'I'll be over in a few minutes.'

'Rosie, I—'

'You don't think I'm up to looking at it?'

'I don't know that it'll serve any purpose.'

'If you don't want to hang around, Dave, just stick the tape in my mailbox.'

Twenty minutes later she came through the door in a pair of blue jeans, tennis shoes, and a short-sleeve denim shirt with purple and white flowers sewn on it. I closed the blinds again and started the film, except this time I used the fast-forward device to isolate the violent scenes and to get through it as quickly as possible.

When the screen went blank I pulled the blinds and filled the room with sunlight. Rosie sat very still and erect, her hands in her lap. Her nostrils were pinched when she breathed. Then she stood and looked out the window a moment.

'The beating of those girls . . . I've never seen anything like that,' she said.

I heard her take a breath and let it out, then she turned back toward me.

'They weren't acting, were they?' she said.

'I don't think so. It's too convincing for a low-rent bunch like this.'

'Dave, we've got to get these guys.'

'We will, one way or another.'

213

She took a Kleenex out of her purse and blew her nose. She blinked, and her eyes were shiny.

'Excuse me, I have hay fever today,' she said.

'It's that kind of weather.'

Then she had to turn and look out the window again. When she faced me again, her eyes had become impassive.

'What's the profit margin on a film like this?' she said.

'I've heard they make an ordinary porno movie for about five grand and get a six-figure return. I don't know about one like this.'

'I'd like to lock up Cholo Manelli as a material witness.'

'Even if we could do it, Rosie, it'd be a waste of time. Cholo's got the thinking powers of a cantaloupe but he doesn't roll over or cop pleas.'

'You seem to say that almost with admiration.'

'There're worse guys around.'

'I have difficulty sharing your sympathies sometimes, Dave.'

'Look, the film was made around New Orleans somewhere. Those were the docks in Algiers in the background. I'd like to make a copy and send it to NOPD Vice. They might recognize some of the players. This kind of stuff is their bailiwick, anyway.'

'All right, let's get a print for the Bureau, too. Maybe Balboni's going across state lines with it.' Then she picked up her purse and I saw a dark concern come into her face again.

'I'll buy you a drink,' I said.

'Of what?'

'Whatever you like.'

'I'm all right, Dave. We don't need to go to any bars.'

'That's up to you. How about a Dr Pepper across the street or a spearmint snowball in the park?'

'That sounds nice.'

We drove in my truck to the park. The sky was filling with afternoon rain clouds that had the bright sheen of steam. She tried to pretend that she was listening to my conversation, but her eyes seemed locked on a distant spot just above the horizon, as though perhaps she were staring through an inverted telescope at an old atrocity that was always a-borning at the wrong moment in her mind.

I had tried several times that day to pursue Hogman's peculiar implication about the type of work done by DeWitt Prejean, the chained black man I had seen shot down in the Atchafalaya marsh in 1957. But neither the Opelousas chief of police nor the St Landry Parish sheriff knew anything that was helpful about DeWitt Prejean, and when I finally reached the old jailer at his house he hung up the phone on me as soon as he recognized my voice.

Late that afternoon the sleeplessness of the previous night finally caught up with me, and I lay down in the hammock that I had stretched between two shade trees on the edge of the coulee in the backyard. I closed my eyes and tried to listen to the sound of the water coursing over the rocks and to forget the images from Lou's apartment that seemed to live behind my eyelids like red paint slung from a brush. I could smell the ferns in the coulee, the networks of roots that trailed in the current, the cool odor of wet stone, the periwinkles that ruffled in the grass.

I had never thought of my coulee as a place where members of the Confederate Signal Corps would gather for a drink on a hot day. But out of the rain clouds and the smell of sulfur and the lightning that had already begun to flicker in the south, I watched the general descend, along with two junior officers, in the wicker basket of an observation balloon, one that looked sewn together from silk cuttings of a half-dozen colors. Five enlisted men moored the basket and balloon to the earth with ropes and helped the general down and handed him a crutch. By the mooring place were a table and chair and telegraph key with a long wire that was attached to the balloon's basket. The balloon tugged upward against its ropes and bobbled and shook in the wind that blew across my neighbor's sugarcane field.

One of the general's aides helped him to a canvas lawn chair by my hammock and then went away.

'Magnificent, isn't it?' he said.

'It surely is,' I said.

'Ladies from all over Louisiana donated their silk dresses for the balloon. The wicker basket was made by an Italian pickle merchant in New Orleans. The view's extraordinary. In the next life I'm coming back as a bird. Would you like to take a ride up?'

'Not right now, thanks.'

'A bad day for it?'

'Another time, general.'

'You grieve for your friend?'

'Yes.'

'You plan revenge, don't you?'

'The Lafayette cops are putting it down as a suicide.'

'I want you to listen to me very carefully, lieutenant. No matter what occurs in your life, no matter how bad the circumstances seem to be, you must never consider a dishonorable act as a viable alternative.'

'The times you lived in were different, general. This afternoon I watched a film that showed young women being beaten and tortured, perhaps even killed, by sadists and degenerates. This stuff is sold in stores and shown in public theaters. The sonsofbitches who make it are seldom arrested unless they get nailed in a mail sting.'

215

'I'm not quite sure I follow all your allusions, but let me tell you of an experience we had three days ago. My standard-bearer was a boy of sixteen. He got caught in their crossfire in a fallow cornfield. There was no place for him to hide. He tried to surrender by waving his shirt over his head. They killed him anyway, whether intentionally or by accident, I don't know.

'By evening we retook the ground and recovered his body. It was torn by miniés as though wild dogs had chewed it. He was so thin you could count his bones with your fingers. In his haversack was his day's ration – a handful of black beans, some roasted acorns, and a dried sweet potato. That's the only food I could provide this boy who followed me unto the death. What do you think I felt toward those who killed him?'

'Maybe you were justified in your feelings.'

'Yes, that's what I told myself throughout the night or when I remembered the bloodless glow that his skin gave off when we wrapped him for burial. Then an opportunity presented itself. From aloft in our balloon I looked down upon a copse of hackberry trees. Hard by a surgeon's tent a dozen federals were squatting along a latrine with their breeches down to their ankles. Two hundred yards up the bayou, unseen by any of them, was one of our boats with a twelve-pounder on its bow. I simply had to tap the order on the telegrapher's key and our gunners would have loaded with grape and raked those poor devils through their own excrement. But that's not our way, is it?'

'Speak for yourself.'

'Your pretense as cynic is unconvincing.'

'Let me ask you a question, general. The women who donated their dresses and petticoats for your balloon . . . what if they were raped, sodomized, and methodically beaten and you got your hands on the men who did it to them?'

'They'd be arrested by my provost, tried in a provisional court, and hanged.'

'You wouldn't find that the case today.'

His long, narrow face was perplexed.

'Why not?' he said.

'I don't know. Maybe we have so much collective guilt as a society that we fear to punish our individual members.'

He put his hat on the back of his head, crossed his good leg across his cork knee, and wet the end of a cheroot. Several of his enlisted men were kneeling by my coulee, filling their canteens. Their faces were dusty, their lips blackened with gunpowder from biting through cartridge papers. The patchwork silk balloon shuddered in the wind and shimmered with the silvery light of the coming rainstorm.

'I won't presume to be your conscience,' the general said. 'But as your *friend who wishes to see you do no harm to yourself, I advise you to give serious thought about keeping your dead friend's weapon.'*

'I have.'

'I think you're making a serious mistake, suh. You disappoint me, too.'

He waved his hand impatiently at his aides, and they helped him to his feet.

'I'm sorry you feel that way,' I said.

But the general was not one given to debate. He stumped along on his crutch and cork leg toward the balloon's basket, his cigar clenched at an upward angle in his teeth, his eyes flicking about at the wind-torn clouds and the lightning that trembled whitely like heated wires out on the Gulf.

The incoming storm blew clouds of dust out of my neighbor's canefield just as the general's balloon lifted him and his aides aloft, their telegraph wire flopping from the wicker basket like an umbilical cord.

When I woke from my dream, the gray skies were filled with a dozen silken hot-air balloons, painted in the outrageous colors of circus wagons, their dim shadows streaking across barn roofs, dirt roads, clapboard houses, general stores, clumps of cows, winding bayous, until the balloons themselves were only distant specks above the summer-green horizon outside Lafayette.

17

On Monday morning I went to Lou Girard's funeral in Lafayette. It was a boiling green-gold day. At the cemetery a layer of heat seemed to rise off the spongy grass and grow in intensity as the white sun climbed toward the top of the sky. During the graveside service someone was running a power mower behind the brick wall that separated the crypts from a subdivision. The mower coughed and backfired and echoed off the bricks like someone firing rounds from a small-caliber revolver. The eyes of the cops who stood at attention in full uniform kept watering from the heat and the smell of weed killer. When the police chief and a captain removed the flag from Lou's casket and folded it into a military square, there was no family member there to receive it. The casket remained closed during the ceremony. Before the casket was lowered into the ground, the department chaplin removed a framed picture of Lou in uniform from the top and set it on a folding table under the funeral canopy. Accidentally he tipped it with the back of his hand so that it fell face down on the linen.

I drove back home for lunch before heading for the office. It was cool under the ceiling fan in the kitchen, and the breeze swayed the baskets of impatiens that hung on hooks from the eave of the back porch. Bootsie set a glass of iced tea with mint leaves and a plate of ham-and-onion sandwiches and deviled eggs in front of me.

'Where's Alafair?' I said.

'Elrod took her and Tripod out to Spanish Lake,' she said from the sink.

'To the movie location?'

'Yes, I think so.'

When I didn't speak, she turned around and looked at me.

'Did I do something wrong?' she asked.

'Julie Balboni's out there, Boots.'

'He lives here now, Dave. He's lots of places. I don't think we should start choosing where we go and don't go because of a man like that.'

'I don't want Alafair around him.'

'I'm sorry. I didn't know you'd object.'

'Boots, there's something I didn't tell you about. Saturday a hood named Cholo Manelli gave me a pornographic video that evidently Balboni and his people made. It's as dark as dark gets. There's one scene where it looks like a woman is actually beaten to death.'

Her eyes blinked, then she said, 'I'll go out to Spanish Lake and bring her home. Why don't you finish eating?'

'Don't worry about it. There's no harm done. I'll go get her before I go to the office.'

'Can't somebody do something about him?'

'When people make a contract with the devil and give him an air-conditioned office to work in, he doesn't go back home easily.'

'Where did you get that piece of Puritan theology?'

'It's not funny. The morons on the Chamber of Commerce who brought this guy here would screw up the recipe for ice water.'

I heard her laugh and walk round behind me. Then I felt her hands on my shoulders and her mouth kiss the top of my head.

'Dave, you're just too much,' she said, and hugged me across the chest.

I listened to the news on the radio as I drove out to Spanish Lake. A tropical storm off Cuba was gaining hurricane status and was expected to turn northwest toward the gulf coast. I glanced to the south, but the sky was brassy and hot and virtually free of clouds. Then as I passed the little watermelon and fruit stand at the end of West Main and headed out into the parish, my radio filled with static and my engine began to misfire.

The truck jerked and sputtered all the way to the entrance of the movie location at the lake. I pulled off the dirt road onto the grass by the security building where Murphy Doucet worked and opened the hood. He stepped out the door in his gray uniform and bifocals.

'What's wrong, Dave?' he asked. His glasses had half-moons of light in them. His blue eyes jittered back and forth when he looked at me.

'It looks like a loose wire on the voltage regulator.' I felt at my pants pocket. 'Do you have a knife I could use?'

'Yeah, I ought to have something.'

I followed him inside his office. His work table was covered with the balsa-wood parts of an amphibian airplane. In the middle of the blueprints was a utility knife with a detachable blade inset in the aluminum handle. But his hand passed over it and opened a drawer and removed a black-handled switchblade knife. He pushed the release button and the blade leaped open in his hand.

'This should do it,' he said. 'A Mexican pulled this on me in Lake Charles.'

'I didn't know you were a cop in Lake Charles.'

'I wasn't. I was out on the highway with the State Police. That's what I retired from last year.'

'Thanks for the loan of the knife.'

I trimmed the insulation away from the end of the loose wire and reattached it to the voltage regulator, then returned the knife to Murphy Doucet and drove into the grove of oak trees by the lake. When I looked in the rearview mirror Doucet was watching me with an unlit cigarette in his mouth.

The cast and crew were just finishing lunch by the water's edge at picnic tables that were spread with checkered cloths and buckets of fried chicken, potato salad, dirty rice, cole slaw, and sweating plastic pitchers of iced tea and lemonade. Alafair sat on a wood bench in the shade, next to Elrod, the lake shimmering behind her. She was dressed like a nineteenth-century street urchin.

'What happened to your clothes?' I said.

'I'm in the movie, Dave!' she said. 'In this scene with Hogman and Elrod. We're walking down the road with a plantation burning behind us and the Yankees are about to take over the town.'

'I'm not kidding you, Dave,' Elrod said. He wore a collarless gray shirt, officer's striped trousers, and black suspenders. 'She's a natural. Mikey said the same thing. She looks good from any camera angle. We worked her right into the scene.'

'What about Tripod?' I said.

'He's in it, too,' Alafair said.

'You're kidding?'

'We're getting him a membership in the Screen Actors Guild,' Elrod said.

Elrod poured a paper cup of iced tea for me. The wind blew leaves out of the trees and flapped the corners of the checkered table covers. For the first time that day I could smell salt in the air.

'This looks like the good life,' I said.

'Don't be too quick to judge,' Elrod said. 'A healthy lifestyle in southern California means running three miles on the beach in the morning, eating bean sprouts all day, and shoving five hundred bucks' worth of coke up your nose at night.'

The other actors began drifting away from the table to return to work. Tripod was on his chain, eating a drumstick by the trunk of a tree. On the grass next to him was a model of a German Messerschmitt, its wooden fuselage bright with silver paint, its red-edged iron crosses and Nazi swastikas as darkly beguiling as the light in a serpent's eye.

'I gave her that. I hope you didn't mind,' Elrod said.

'Where'd you get it?'

'From Murph, up there at the security building. I'm afraid he thinks I can get him on making props for Mikey or something. I think he's kind of a lonely guy, isn't he?'

'I don't know much about him.'

'Alafair, can you go find Hogman and tell him we need to do that scene again in about fifteen minutes?' Elrod said.

'Sure, El,' she said, swung her legs over the bench, scooped Tripod over her shoulder, and ran off through the trees.

'Look, El, I appreciate your working Alafair into your movie, but frankly I don't want her out here as long as Julie Balboni's around.'

'I thought you heard.'

'What?'

'Mikey's filing Chapter Eleven bankruptcy. He's eighty-sixing the greaseballs out of the corporation. The last thing those guys want is the court examining their finances. He told off Balboni this morning in front of the whole crew.'

'What do you mean he told him off?'

'He said Balboni was never going to put a hand on one of Mikey's people again. He told him to take his porno actor and his hoods and his bimbos and haul his ass back to New Orleans. I was really proud of Mikey . . . What's the matter?'

'What did Julie have to say?'

'He cleaned his fingernails with a toothpick, then walked out to the lake and started talking to somebody on his cellular phone and skipping rocks across the water at the ducks.'

'Where is he now?'

'He drove off with his whole crew in his limo.'

'I'd like to talk with Mr Goldman.'

'He's on the other side of the lake.'

'Ask him to call me, will you? If he doesn't catch me at the office, he can call me at home tonight.'

'He'll be back in a few minutes to shoot the scene with me and Hogman and Alafair.'

'We're not going to be here for it.'

'You won't let her be in the film?'

'Nobody humiliates Julie Balboni in front of other people, El. I don't know what he's going to do, but I don't want Alafair here when he does it.'

The wind had turned out of the south and was blowing hotly through the trees when we walked back toward my truck. The air smelled like fish spawning, and clouds with the dark convolutions of newly opened purple roses were massing in a long, low humped line on the southern horizon.

Later, after I had taken Alafair home and checked in at the office, I drove to Opelousas to talk once again with the old jailer Ben Hebert. A black man raking leaves in Hebert's yard told me where I could find him on a bayou just outside of town.

He sat on top of an inverted plastic bucket under a tree, his cane pole extended out into the sunlight, his red bobber drifting on the edge of the reeds. He wore a crushed straw hat on the side of his head and smoked a hand-rolled saliva-soaked cigarette without removing it from the corner of his mouth. The layers of white fat on his hips and stomach protruded between his shirt and khakis like lard curling over the edges of a washtub.

Ten feet down from him a middle-aged mulatto woman with a small round head, a perforated dime tied on her ankle, was also fishing as she sat on top of an inverted bucket. The ground around her was strewn with empty beer cans. She spit snuff to one side and jigged her line up and down through a torn hole in a lily pad.

Ben Hebert pitched his cigarette out onto the current, where it hissed and turned in a brown eddy.

'Why you keep bothering me?' he said. There was beer on his breath and an eye-watering smell in his clothes that was like both dried sweat and urine.

'I need to know what kind of work DeWitt Prejean did,' I said.

'You what?' His lips were as purple as though they had been painted, his teeth small and yellow as pieces of corn.

'Just what I said.'

'You leave me the hell alone.'

I sat down on the grass by the edge of the slope.

'It's not my intention to bother you, Mr Hebert,' I said. 'But you're refusing to cooperate with a police investigation and you're creating problems for both of us.'

'He done . . . I don't know what he done. What difference does it make?' His eyes glanced sideways at the mulatto woman.

'You seem to have a good memory for detail. Why not about DeWitt Prejean?'

The woman rose from her seat on the bucket and walked farther down the bank, trailing her cork bobber in the water.

'He done nigger work,' Hebert said. 'He cut lawns, cleaned out grease traps, got dead rats out from under people's houses. What the fuck you think he did?'

'That doesn't sound right to me. I think he did some other kind of work, too.'

His nostrils were dilated, as though a bad odor were rising from his own lap.

'He was in bed with a white woman here. Is that what you want to know?'

'Which woman?'

'I done tole you. The wife of a cripple-man got shot up in the war.'

'He raped her?'

'Who gives a shit?'

'But the crippled man didn't break Prejean out of jail, Mr Hebert.'

'It wasn't the first time that nigger got in trouble over white women. There's more than one man wanted to see him put over a fire.'

'Who broke him out?'

'I don't know and I don't care.'

Mr LeBlanc, you're probably a good judge of people. Do I look like I'm just going to go away?'

The skin of his chest was sickly white, and under it were nests of green veins.

'It was better back then,' he said. 'You know it was.'

'What kind of work did he do, Ben?'

'Drove a truck.'

'For whom?'

'It was down in Lafayette. He worked for a white man there till he come up here. Don't know nothing about the white man. You saying I do, then you're a goddamn liar.' He leaned over to look past me at the mulatto woman, who was fishing among a group of willows now. Then his face snapped back at me. 'I brung her out here 'cause she works for me. 'Cause I can't get in and out of the car good by myself.'

'What kind of truck did he drive?' I asked.

'Beer truck. No, that wasn't it. Soda pop. Sonofabitch had a soda-pop truck route when white people was making four dollars a day in the rice field.' He set down his cane pole and began rolling a cigarette. His fingernails looked as thick and horned as tortoise-shell against the thin white square of paper into which he poured tobacco. His fingers trembled almost uncontrollably with anger and defeat.

I drove to Twinky Lemoyne's bottling works in Lafayette, but it was closed for the day. Twenty minutes later I found Lemoyne working in his yard at home. The sky was the pink of salmon eggs, and the wind thrashed the banana and lime trees along the side of his house. He had stopped pruning the roses on his trellis and had dropped his shears in the baggy back pocket of his faded denim work pants.

'A lot of bad things happened back in that era between the races. But we're not the same people we used to be, are we?' he said.

'I think we are.'

'You seem unable to let the past rest, sir.'

'My experience has been that you let go of the past by addressing it, Mr Lemoyne.'

'For some reason I have the feeling that you want me to confirm what so far are only speculations on your part.' There were tiny pieces of grit in his combed sandy hair and a film of perspiration and rose dust on his glasses.

'Read it like you want. But somehow my investigation keeps winding its way back to your front door.'

He began snipping roses again and placing them stem down in a milk bottle full of green water. His two-story peaked white house in an old residential neighborhood off St Mary Boulevard in Lafayette was surrounded by spectacular moss-hung oak trees and walls of bamboo and soft pink brick.

'Should I call my lawyer? Is that what you're suggesting?'

'You can if you want to. I don't think it'll solve your problem, though.'

'I beg your pardon.' His shears hung motionlessly over a rose.

'I think you committed a murder back in 1957, but in all probability you don't have the psychology of a killer. That means that you probably live with an awful guilt, Mr Lemoyne. You go to bed with it and you wake with it. You drag it around all day long like a clanking chain.'

'Why is it that you seem to have this fixation about me? At first you accused me of being involved with a New Orleans gangster. Now this business about the murdered Negro.'

'I saw you do it.'

His egg-shaped face was absolutely still. Blood pooled in his cheeks like pink flowers.

'I was only nineteen,' I said. 'I watched y'all from across the bay. The black man tried to run, and one of you shot him in the leg, then continued shooting him in the water. You didn't even think me worthy of notice, did you? You were right, too. No one ever paid much attention to my story. That was a hard lesson for a nineteen-year-old.'

He closed the shears, locked the clasp on the handles, and set them down on a glass-topped patio table. He poured two inches of whiskey into a glass with no ice and squeezed a lemon into it. He seemed as solitary as a man might who had lived alone all his life.

'Would you care for one?' he said.

'No, thank you.'

'I have high blood pressure and shouldn't drink, but I put lemon in it and convince myself that I'm drinking something healthy along with the alcohol. It's my little joke with myself.' He took a deep breath.

'You want to tell me about it?'

'I don't think so. Am I under arrest?'

'Not right now. But I think that's the least of your problems.'

'You bewilder me, sir.'

'You're partners in a security service with Murphy Doucet. A fellow like that doesn't fit in the same shoe box with you.'

'He's an ex-police officer. He has the background that I don't.'

'He's a resentful and angry man. He's also anti-Semitic. One of your black employees told me you're good to people of color. Why would a man such as yourself go into business with a bigot?'

'He's uneducated. That doesn't mean he's a bad person.'

'I believe he's been blackmailing you, Mr Lemoyne. I believe he was the other white man I saw across the bay with DeWitt Prejean.'

'You can believe whatever you wish.'

'We still haven't gotten to what's really troubling you, though, have we? It's those young women, isn't it?'

His eyes closed and opened, and then he looked away at the south where lightning was forking into the Gulf and the sky looked like it was covered with the yellow-black smoke from a chemical fire.

'I don't . . . I don't . . .' he began, then finished his whiskey and set his glass down. He wiped at the wet ring with the flat of his hand as though he wanted to scrub it out of the tabletop.

'That day you stopped me out under the trees at the lake,' I said, 'you wanted assurance that it was somebody else, somebody you don't know, who mutilated and killed those girls, didn't you? You didn't want that sin on your conscience as well as Prejean's murder.'

'My God, man, give some thought to what you're saying. You're telling me I'm responsible for a fiend being loose in our midst.'

'Call your attorney and come into the office and make a statement. End it now, Mr Lemoyne. You'll probably get off with minimum time on Prejean's death. You've got a good reputation and a lot of friends. You might even walk.'

'Please leave.'

'It won't change anything.'

He turned away from me and gazed at the approaching storm. Leaves exploded out of the trees that towered above his garden walls.

'Go do what you have to do, but right now please respect my privacy,' he said.

'You strayed out of the gentleman's world a long time ago.'

'Don't you have any sense of mercy?'

'Maybe you should come down to my office and look at the morgue photographs of Cherry LeBlanc and a girl we pried out of an oil barrel down in Vermilion Parish.'

He didn't answer. As I let myself out his grden gate I glanced back at him. His cheeks were red and streaked with moisture as though his face had been glazed by freezing winds.

That evening the weatherman said the hurricane had become stationary one hundred miles due south of Mobile. As I fell asleep later with the window open on a lightning-charged sky, I thought surely the electricity would bring the general back in my dreams.

Instead, it was Lou Girard who stood under the wind-tormented pecan trees at three in the morning, his jaw shot away at the hinge, a sliver of white bone protruding from a flap of skin by his ear.

He tried to speak, and spittle gurgled on his exposed teeth and tongue and dripped off the point of his chin.

'What is it, Lou?'

The wind whipped and molded his shapeless brown suit against his body. He picked up a long stick that had been blown out of the tree above him and began scratching lines in the layers of dead leaves and pecan husks at his feet. He made an S, and then drew a straight line like an I and then put a half bubble on it and turned it into a P.

He dropped the stick to the ground and stared at me, his deformed face filled with expectation.

18

The connection had been there all along. I just hadn't looked in the right place. As soon as I went into the office at 8 A.M. the next morning I called the probation and parole office in Lafayette and asked the supervising PO to pull the file on Cherry LeBlanc.

'Who busted her on the prostitution charge?' I said.

I heard him leafing back and forth through the pages in the file.

'It wasn't one officer. There was a state-police raid on a bar and some trailers out on the Breaux Bridge highway.'

SP. Yes, the state police. Thanks, Lou, old friend.

'Who signed the arrest report?' I asked.

'Let's see. It's pretty hard to read. Somebody set a coffee cup down on the signature.'

'It's real important, partner.'

'It could be Doucet. Wasn't there a state policeman around here by that name? Yeah, I'd say initial M., then Doucet.'

'Can you make copies of her file and lock them in separate places?'

'What's going on?'

'It may become evidence.'

'No, I mean Lou Girard was looking at her file last week. What's the deal?'

'Do this for me, will you? If anybody else tries to get his hands on that file, you call me, okay?'

'There's an implication here that I think you should clarify.'

Outside, the skies were gray, and dust and pieces of paper were blowing in the street.

'Maybe we have a fireman setting fires,' I said.

He was quiet a moment, then he said, 'I'll lock up the file for you, detective, and I'll keep your call confidential. But since this may involve a reflection on our office, I expect a little more in the way of detailed information from you in the next few days.'

After I hung up, I opened my desk drawer and took out the black-

and-white photograph that Cholo Manelli had given me of Cherry LeBlanc and Julie Balboni at the beach in Biloxi. I looked again at the man who was reading a newspaper at another table. His face was beyond the field of focus in the picture, but the light had struck his glasses in such a way that it looked as if there were chips of crystal where his eyes should have been, and my guess was that he was wearing bifocals.

As with most police investigations, the problem had now become one of the time lag between the approaching conclusion of an investigation and the actual arrest of a suspect. It's a peculiar two-way street that both cops and criminals live on. As a cop grows in certainty about the guilt of a suspect and begins to put enough evidence together to make his case, the suspect usually becomes equally aware of the impending denouement and concludes that midsummer isn't a bad time to visit Phoenix after all.

The supervising PO in Lafayette now knew my suspicions about Doucet, so did Twinky Hebert Lemoyne, and it wouldn't be long before Doucet did, too.

The other problem was that so far all the evidence was circumstantial.

When Rosie came in I told her everything I had.

'Do you think Lemoyne will make a confession?' she said.

'He might eventually. It's obvious he's a tormented man.'

'Because I don't think you'll ever get an indictment on the lynching unless he does.'

'I want to get a search warrant and toss everything Doucet owns, starting with the security building out at Spanish Lake.'

'Okay, Dave, but let me be honest with you. So far I think what we've got is pretty thin.'

'I didn't tell you something else. I already checked Doucet's name through motor vehicle registration in Baton Rouge. He owns a blue 1989 Mercury. I'll bet that's the car that's been showing up through the whole investigation.'

'We still don't have enough to start talking to a prosecutor, though, do we?'

'That's what a search warrant is for.'

'What I'm trying to say is we don't have witnesses, Dave. We're going to need some hard forensic evidence, a murder weapon, clothing from one of the victims, something that will leave no doubt in a jury's mind that this guy is a creature out of their worst nightmares. I just hope Doucet hasn't already talked to Lemoyne and gotten rid of everything we could use against him, provided there is anything.'

'We'll soon find out.'

She measured me carefully with her eyes.

'You seem a little more confident than you should be,' she said.

228

'It all fits, Rosie. A black pimp in the New Orleans bus depot told me about a white man selling dirty pictures. I thought he was talking about photographs or postcards. Don't you see it? Doucet's probably been delivering girls to Balboni's pornographic film operation.'

'The only direct tie that we have is the fact that Doucet arrested Cherry LeBlanc.'

'Right. And even though he knew I was investigating her murder, he never mentioned it, did he? He wasn't even curious about how the investigation was going. Does that seem reasonable to you?'

'Well, let's get the warrant and see what Mr Doucet has to say to us this morning.'

We had it in thirty minutes and were on our way out of the office when my extension rang. It was Bootsie. She said she was going to town to buy candles and tape for the windows in case the hurricane turned in to the coast and I would find lunch for me and Alafair in the oven.

Then she said, 'Dave, did you leave the house last night?'

'Just a second,' I said, and took the receiver away from my ear. 'Rosie, I'll be along in just a minute.'

Rosie went out the door and bent over the water cooler.

'I'm sorry, what did you say?'

'I thought I heard your truck start up in the middle of the night. Then I thought I just dreamed it. Did I just dream it?'

'I had to take care of something. I left a note on the lamp for you in case you woke up, but you were sound asleep when I came back.'

'What are you doing, Dave?'

'Nothing. I'll tell you about it later.'

'Is it those apparitions in the marsh again?'

'No, of course not.'

'Dave?'

'It's nothing to worry about. Believe me.'

'I *am* worried if you have to conceal something from me.'

'Let's go out to eat tonight.'

'I think we'd better have a talk first.'

'A very bad guy is about to go off the board. That's what it amounts to. I'll explain it later.'

'Does the sheriff know what you're doing?'

'He didn't ask. Come on, Boots. Let's don't be this way.'

'Whatever you say. I'm sorry I asked. Everybody's husband goes in and out of the house in the middle of the night. I'll see you this afternoon.'

She hung up before I could speak again; but in truth I didn't know how to explain to her the feelings I had that morning. If Murphy Doucet was our serial killer, and I believed he was, then with a little luck we were about to throw a steel net over one of those pathological and malformed individuals who ferret their way among us, occasionally for a lifetime, and leave behind a trail of suffering whose severity can only be appreciated by the survivors who futilely seek explanations for their loss the rest of their lives.

I lost my wife Annie to two such men. A therapist told me that I would never have any peace until I learned to forgive not only myself for her death but the human race as well for producing the men who killed her. I didn't know what he meant until several months later when I remembered an event that occurred on a winter afternoon when I was seven years old and I had returned home early, unexpectedly, from school.

My mother was not at work at the Tabasco bottling plant, where she should have been. Instead, I looked from the hallway through the bedroom door and saw a man's candy-striped shirt, suspenders, and sharkskin zoot slacks and panama hat hung on the bedpost, his socks sticking out of his two-tone shoes on the floor. My mother was naked, on all fours, on top of the bedspread, and the man, whose name was Mack, was about to mount her. A cypress plank creaked under my foot, and Mack twisted his head and looked at me, his pencil mustache like a bird's wings above his lip. Then he entered my mother.

For months I had dreams about a white wolf who lived in a skeletal black tree on an infinite white landscape. At the base of the tree was a nest of pups. In the dream the wolf would drop to the ground, her teats sagging with milk, and eat her young one by one.

I would deliberately miss the school bus in the afternoon and hang around the playground until the last kids took their footballs or kites and walked off through the dusk and dead leaves toward lighted houses and the sound of *Jack Armstrong* or *Terry and the Pirates* through a screen door. When my father returned home from trapping on Marsh Island, I never told him what I had seen take place in their bedroom. When they fought at night, I sat on the back steps and watched the sugarcane stubble burning in the fields. The fires looked like thousands of red handkerchiefs twisting in the smoke.

I knew the wolf waited for me in my dreams.

Then one afternoon, when I started walking home late from school, I passed an open door in the back of the convent. It was the music room, and it had a piano in it, a record player, and a polished oak floor. But the two young nuns who were supposed to be waxing the floor had set aside their mops and rags, turned on a radio, and were jitterbugging with each other in their bare feet, their veils flying, their wooden rosary beads swirling on their waists.

They didn't see me, and I must have watched them for almost five minutes, fascinated with their flushed faces inside their wimples and the laughter that they tried to hide behind their hands when it got too loud.

I could not explain it to myself, but I knew each night thereafter that if I thought of the dancing nuns before I fell asleep, I would not dream about the white wolf in the tree.

I wondered what kind of dreams Murphy Doucet had. Maybe at one time they were the same as mine. Or maybe it was better not to know.

I had no doubt, though, that he was ready for us when we arrived at the security building at Spanish Lake. He stood with his legs slightly spread, as though at parade rest, in front of the door, his hands propped on his gunbelt, his stomach flat as a plank, his eyes glinting with a cynical light.

I unfolded the search warrant in front of him.

'You want to look it over?' I said.

'What for? I don't give a good fuck what y'all do here,' he replied.

'I'd appreciate it if you'd watch your language,' I said.

'She can't handle it?' he said.

'Stand over by my truck until we're finished,' I said.

'What do you think y'all gonna find?' he said.

'You never know, Murph. You were a cop. People get careless sometimes, mess up in a serious way, maybe even forget they had their picture taken with one of their victims.'

Tiny webs of brown lines spread from the corners of his eyes.

'What are you talking about?'

'If I'd been you, I wouldn't have let Cholo take my picture with Baby Feet and Cherry LeBlanc over in Biloxi.'

His blue eyes shuttered back and forth; the pupils looked like black pinheads. The point of his tongue licked across his bottom lip.

'I don't want *her* in my stuff,' he said.

'Would you like to prevent me from getting in your "stuff," Mr Doucet?' Rosie said. 'Would you like to be charged this morning with interfering with a federal officer in the performance of her duty?'

Without ever removing his eyes from her face, he lifted a Lucky Strike with two fingers from the pack in his shirt pocket and put it in the corner of his mouth. Then he leaned back against my truck, shook open his Zippo lighter, cupped the flame in his hands, sucked in on the smoke, and looked away at the pecan trees bending and straightening in the wind and an apple basket bouncing crazily across a field.

On his work table were a set of Exacto knives, tubes of glue, small bottles of paint, tiny brushes, pieces of used sandpaper, and the delicate balsa-wood wing struts of a model airplane pinned to a blueprint. Outside, Doucet smoked his cigarette and watched us through the door and showed no expression or interest when I dropped his Exacto knives into a Ziploc bag.

His desk drawers contained *Playboy* magazines, candy wrappers, a carton of Lucky Strikes, a thermos of split pea soup, two ham sandwiches, paper clips, eraser filings, a brochure advertising a Teamster convention in Atlantic City, a package of condoms.

I opened the drawer of his work table. In it were more sheets of sandpaper, an unopened model airplane kit, and the black-handled switchblade knife he had lent me to trim back the insulation on an electrical wire in my truck. I put it in another Ziploc bag.

Doucet yawned.

'Rosie, would you kick over that trash basket behind his desk, please?' I said.

'There's nothing in it,' she said, leaning over the corner of the desk.

My back was turned to both her and Doucet when I closed the drawer to the work table and turned around with an aluminum-handled utility knife in my fingers. I dropped it into a third plastic bag.

'Well, I guess this covers it,' I said.

Through the door I saw his hand with the cigarette stop in midair and his eyes lock on the utility knife.

He stepped toward us as we came out of the building.

'What do you think you're doing?' he said.

'You have a problem with something that happened here?' I said.

'You planted that,' he said, pointing at the bag with the utility knife in it. 'You sonofabitch, you planted it, you know you did.'

'How could I plant something that belongs to you?' I said. 'This is one of the tools you use on your airplane models, isn't it?'

Rosie was looking at me strangely.

'This woman's a witness,' he said. 'You're salting the shaft. That knife wasn't there.'

'I say it was. I say your fingerprints are all over it, too. It's probably going to be hard to prove it's not yours, Murph.'

'This pepper-belly bitch is in on it, isn't she?' he said.

I tapped him on the cheek with the flat of my hand. 'You say anything else, your day is going to deteriorate in a serious way,' I said.

Mistake.

He leaped into my face, his left hand like a claw in my eyes, his right fist flailing at my head, his knees jerking at my groin. I lost my balance, tried to turn away from him and raise my arm in front of my face; his fists rained down on the crown of my skull.

Rosie pulled her .357 from her purse, extended it straight out with both hands, and pointed the barrel into his ear.

'Down on the ground, you understand me?' she shouted. 'Do it!

Now! Don't look at me! Get your face on the ground! Did you hear me? Don't look at me! Put your hands behind your head!'

He went to his knees, then lay prone with the side of his face in the grass, his lined, deeply tanned neck oozing sweat, his eyes filled with the mindless light that an animal's might have if it were pinned under an automobile tire.

I slipped my handcuffs from the back of my belt and snipped them onto his wrists. I pulled his revolver and can of Mace from his gunbelt, then raised him to his feet. His arm felt like bone in my hand.

'You're under arrest for assaulting an officer of the law, Murph,' I said.

He turned toward me. The top button of his shirt was torn and I could see white lumps of scar tissue on his chest like fingers on a broken hand.

'It won't stick. You've got a bum warrant,' he said.

'That knife is the one you used on Cherry LeBlanc, isn't it?' I said.

Rosie walked behind me into his office and used his phone to call for a sheriff's car. His eyes watched her, then came back onto me. He blew pieces of grass out of his mouth.

'She let you muff her?' he said.

We brought him in through the back door of the sheriff's department, fingerprinted and booked him, let him make a phone call to an attorney in Lafayette, then took him down to our interrogation room. Personnel from all over the building were finding ways to get a look at Murphy Doucet.

'You people get back to work,' the sheriff said in the hallway. 'This man is in for assaulting an officer. That's all he's charged with. Have y'all got that?'

'There's three news guys outside your office, sheriff,' a deputy said.

'I'd like to know who called them down here, please,' he said.

'Search me,' the deputy said.

'Will you people get out of here?' he said again to the crowd in the hall. Then he pushed his fingers though his hair and turned to me and Rosie. 'I've got to talk to these reporters before they break a Jack the Ripper story on us. Get what you can from this guy and I'll be right back. Who's his lawyer?'

'Jeb Bonin,' I said.

'We'll still have Doucet till his arraignment in the morning. When are y'all going to search his place?'

'This afternoon,' Rosie said. 'We already sent a deputy over there to sit on it for us.'

'Was the blue Merc out at Spanish Lake?' the sheriff said.

'No, he drives a pickup to work. The Merc must be at his house,' I said.

'All right, get on it. Do it by the numbers, too. We don't want to blow this one.'

The sheriff walked back toward his office. Rosie touched me lightly on the arm.

'Dave, talk with me a second before we go inside,' she said.

'What is it?'

She didn't reply. She went inside our office and waited for me.

'That utility knife you took out of his drawer,' she said. 'He was completely surprised when you found it. That presents a troubling thought for me.'

'It's his knife, Rosie. There's no question about it.'

'Why was he so confident up until that moment?'

'Maybe he just forgot he'd left it there.'

'You got into that security building during the night, removed the knife, then replaced it this morning, didn't you?'

'Time's always on the perp's side, Rosie. While we wait on warrants, they deep-six the evidence.'

'I don't like what I'm hearing you say, Dave.'

'This is our guy. You want him to walk? Because without that knife, he's sure going to do it.'

'I see it differently. You break the rules, you arm the other side.'

'Wait till you meet his lawyer. He's the best in southwest Louisiana. He also peddles his ass to the Teamsters, the mob, and incinerator outfits that burn PCBs. Before he's finished, he'll turn Doucet into a victim and have the jury slobbering on their sleeves.'

Her eyes went back and forth thoughtfully, as though she were asking herself questions and answering them. Then she raised her chin.

'Don't ever do anything like this again, Dave. Not while we're partners,' she said, and walked past me and into the interrogation room, where Murphy Doucet sat in a straight-backed chair at a small table, surrounded by white walls, wreathed in cigarette smoke, scratching at whiskers that grew along the edges of the white chicken's foot embossed on his throat.

I stepped inside the room behind Rosie and closed the door.

'Where's my lawyer at?' he asked.

I took the cigarette from his fingers and mashed it out on the floor.

'You want to make a statement about Cherry LeBlanc?' I said.

'Yeah. I've given it some thought. I remember busting a whore by that name three years ago. So now y'all can tell my why I'd wait three years to kill somebody who'd been in my custody.'

'We think you're a pimp for Julie Balboni, Mr Doucet,' Rosie said. 'We also think you're supplying girls for his pornography operation.'

His eyes went up and down her body.

'Affirmative action?' he said.

'There's something else you don't know about, Murph,' I said. 'We're checking all the unsolved murders of females in areas around highways during the time you were working for the state police. I have a feeling those old logs are going to put you in the vicinity of some bodies you never thought would be connected to you.'

'I don't believe this,' he said.

'I think we've got you dead-bang,' I said.

'You've got a planted knife. This girl here knows it, too. Look at her face.'

'We've not only got the weapon and the photo of you with the victim, we know how it happened and why.'

'What?'

'Cherry LeBlanc told Julie he was a tub of guts and walked out on him. But people don't just walk out on Julie. So he got on the phone and called you up from the motel, didn't he, Murph? You remember that conversation? Would you like me to quote it to you?'

His eyebrows contracted, then his hand went into his pocket for a cigarette.

'No. You can't smoke in here,' I said.

'I got to use the can.'

'It's unavailable now,' I said.

'*She's* here for another reason. It ain't because of a dead hooker,' he said.

'We're all here because of you, Murph. You're going down hard, partner. We haven't even started to talk about Kelly Drummond yet.'

He bit a piece of skin off the ball of his thumb.

'What's the bounce on the pimp beef?' he said.

'You think you're going to cop to a procuring charge when you're looking at the chair? What world are you living in?' I said.

'Ask her. She's here to make a case on Balboni, not a security guard, so clean the shit out of your mouth. What kind of bounce am I looking at?'

'Mr Doucet, you're looking at several thousand volts of electricity cooking your insides. Does that clarify your situation for you?' Rosie said.

He looked into her face.

'Go tell your boss I can put that guinea away for twenty-seven years,' he said. 'Then come back and tell me y'all aren't interested in a deal.'

The sheriff opened the door.

'His lawyer's here,' he said.

'We're going to your house now, Murph,' I said. 'Is there anything else you want to tell us before we leave?'

235

The attorney stepped inside the room. He wore his hair shaved to the scalp, and his tie and shirt collar rode up high on his short neck so that he reminded you of a light-brown hard-boiled egg stuffed inside a business suit.

'Don't say anything more to these people, Mr Doucet,' he said.

I leaned on the table and stared into Murphy Doucet's face. I stared at his white eyebrows, the jittering of his eyeballs, the myriad lines in his skin, the slit of a mouth, the white scar on his throat that could have been layered there with a putty knife.

'What? What the fuck you staring at?' he said.

'Do you remember me?' I said.

'Yeah. Of course. When you were a cop in New Orleans.'

'Look at me. Think hard.'

His eyes flicked away from my face, fastened on his attorney.

'I don't know what he's talking about,' he said.

'Do you have a point, detective?' the attorney said.

'Your hired oil can doesn't have anything to do with this, Murph,' I said. 'It's between me and you now. It's 1957, right after Hurricane Audrey hit. You could smell dead animals all over the marsh. You remember? Y'all made DeWitt Prejean run with a chain locked around his chest, then you blew his leg out from under him. Remember the kid who saw it from across the bay? Look at my face.'

He bit down on his lip, then fitted his chin on top of his knuckles and stared disjointedly at the wall.

'The old jailer gave you guys away when he told me that DeWitt Prejean used to drive a soda-pop truck. Prejean worked for Twinky Lemoyne and had an affair with his wife, didn't he? It seems like there's always one guy still hanging around who remembers more than he should,' I said. 'You still think you're in a seller's market, Murph? How long do you think it's going to be before a guy like Twinky cracks and decides to wash his sins in public?'

'Don't say anything, Mr Doucet,' the attorney said.

'He doesn't have to, Mr Bonin,' I said. 'This guy has been killing people for thirty-five years. If I were you, I'd have some serious reservations about an ongoing relationship with your client. Come on, Rosie.'

The wind swirled dust and grit between the cars in the parking lot, and I could smell rain in the south.

'That was Academy Award stuff, Dave,' Rosie said as we got in my truck.

'It doesn't hurt to make the batter flinch once in a while.'

'You did more than that. You should have seen the lawyer's face when you started talking about the lynching.'

'He's not the kind who's in it for the long haul.'

As I started the truck a gust of wind sent a garbage can clattering down the sidewalk and blew through the oak grove aross the street. A solitary shaft of sunlight broke from the clouds and fell through the canopy, and in a cascade of gold leaves I thought I saw a line of horsemen among the tree trunks, their bodies as gray as stone, their shoulders and their horses' rumps draped with flowing tunics. I pinched the sweat out of my eyes against the bridge of my nose and looked again. The grove was empty except for a black man who was putting strips of tape across the windows of his barbecue stand.

'Dave?' Rosie said.

'Yes?'

'Are you all right?'

'I just got a piece of dirt in my eye.'

When we pulled out on the street I looked into the rearview mirror and saw the detailed image of a lone horseman deep in the trees, a plum-colored plume in his hat, a carbine propped on his thigh. He pushed up the brim of his hat with his gun barrel and I saw that his face was pale and siphoned of all energy and the black sling that held his left arm was sodden with blood.

'*What has opened your wounds, general?*'

'What'd you say?' Rosie asked.

'Nothing. I didn't say anything.'

'You're worried about what Doucet said, aren't you?'

'I'm not following you.'

'You think the Bureau might cut a deal with him.'

'It crossed my mind.'

'This guy's going down, Dave. I promise you.'

'I've made a career of discovering that my priorities aren't the same as those of the people I work for, Rosie. Sometimes the worst ones walk and cops help them do it.'

She looked out the side window, and now it was she whose face seemed lost in an abiding memory or dark concern that perhaps she could never adequately share with anyone.

Murphy Doucet lived in a small freshly-painted white house with a gallery and a raked, tree-shaded lawn across from the golf course on the north side of Lafayette. A bored Iberia Parish deputy and a Lafayette city cop sat on the steps waiting for us, flipping a pocket knife into the lawn. The blue Mercury was parked in the driveway under a chinaberry tree. I unlocked it from the key ring we had taken from Doucet when he was booked; then we pulled out the floor mats, laid them carefully on the grass, searched under the seats, and cleaned out the glove box. None of it was of of any apparent value. We picked up the floor mats by the corners, replaced them on the rugs, and unlocked the trunk.

Rosie stepped back from the odor and coughed into her hand.

'Oh, Dave, it's—' she began.

'Feces,' I said.

The trunk was bare except for a spare tire, a jack, and a small cardboard carton in one corner. The dark-blue rug looked clean, vacuumed or brushed, but twelve inches back from the latch was a dried, tea-colored stain with tiny particles of paper towel embedded in the stiffened fabric.

I took out the cardboard carton, opened the top, and removed a portable spotlight with an extension cord that could be plugged into a cigarette lighter.

'This is what he wrapped the red cellophane around when he picked up the girl hitchhiking down in Vermilion Parish,' I said.

'Dave, look at this.'

She pointed toward the side wall of the trunk. There were a half-dozen black curlicues scotched against the pale blue paint. She felt one of them with two fingers, then rubbed her thumb against the ends of the fingers.

'I think they're rubber heel marks,' she said. 'What kind of shoes was Cherry LeBlanc wearing?'

'Flats with leather soles. And the dead girl in Vermilion didn't have on anything.'

'All right, let's get it towed in and start on the house. We really need—'

'What?'

'Whatever he got careless about and left lying around.'

'Did you call the Bureau yet?'

'No. Why?'

'I was just wondering.'

'What are you trying to say, Dave?'

'If you want a handprint set in blood to make our case, I don't think it's going to happen. Not unless there's some residue on that utility knife we can use for a DNA match. The photograph is a bluff, at least as far as indicting Doucet is concerned. Like you said earlier, everything else we've got so far isn't real strong.'

'So?'

'I think you already know what your boss is going to tell you.'

'Maybe I don't care what he says.'

'I don't want you impairing your career with Fart, Barf, and Itch because you think you have to be hard-nosed on my account, Rosie. Let's be clear on that.'

238

'Cover your own butt and don't worry about mine,' she said, took the key ring out of my hand, and walked ahead of me up the front steps of the house and unlocked the door.

The interior was as neat and squared away as a military barracks. The wood floors were waxed, the stuffed chairs decorated with doilies, the window plants trimmed and watered, the kitchen sink and drainboards immaculate, the pots and pans hung on hooks, the wastebaskets fitted with clean plastic liners, his model planes dusted and suspended on wires from the bedroom ceiling, his bedspread tucked and stretched so tightly that you could bounce a quarter off it.

None of the pictures on the walls dealt with human subjects, except one color photograph of himself sitting on the steps of a cabin with a dead eight-point deer at his feet. Doucet was smiling; a bolt-action rifle with iron sights and a sling lay across his lap.

We searched the house for an hour, searched the garage, then came back and tossed the house again. The Iberia Parish deputy walked through the front door with an ice-cream cone in his hand. He was a dark-haired, narrow-shouldered, wide-hipped man who had spent most of his five years with the department as a crosswalk guard at elementary schools or escorting misdeameanor prisoners to morning arraignment. He stopped eating and wiped the cream out of his mustache with the back of his wrist before he spoke.

'Jesus Christ, Dave, y'all tore the place apart,' he said.

'You want to stay behind and clean it up?' I said.

'Y'all the ones done it, not me.'

'That's right, so you don't have to worry about it,' I said.

'Boy, somebody didn't get enough sleep last night,' he said. When I didn't answer he walked into the center of the room. 'What y'all found in that trunk?'

When I still didn't answer, he peered over my shoulder.

'Oh man, that's a bunch of little girl's underwear, aint it?' he said.

'Yes, it is,' I said.

The deputy cleared his throat.

'That fella been doin' that kind of stuff, too, Dave?'

'It looks like it.'

'Oh, man,' he said. Then his face changed. 'Maybe somebody ought to show him what happens when you crawl over one of them high barbed wire fences.'

'I didn't hear you say that, deputy,' Rosie said.

'It don't matter to me,' he said. 'A fella like that, they's people 'round here get their hands on him, you ain't gonna have to be worryin' about evidence, no. Ax Dave.'

In the trunk we had found eleven small pairs of girls' underwear, children's socks, polka-dot leotards, training bras, a single black patent-leather shoe with a broken strap, a coloring book, a lock of red hair taped to an index card, torn matinee tickets to a local theater, a half-dozen old photographs of Murphy Doucet in the uniform of a Jefferson Parish deputy sheriff, all showing him with children at picnics under moss-hung trees, at a Little League ball game, at a swimming pool filled with children leaping into the air for the camera. All of the clothing was laundered and folded and arranged in a neat pink and blue and white layer across the bottom of the trunk.

After a moment, Rosie said, 'It's his shrine.'

'To *what*?' I said.

'Innocence. He's a psychopath, a rapist, a serial killer, a sadist, maybe a necrophiliac, but he's also a pedophile. Like most pedophiles, he seeks innocence by being among children or molesting them.'

Then she rose from her chair, went into the bathroom, and I heard the water running, heard her spit, heard the water splashing.

'Could you wait outside a minute, Expidee?' I said to the deputy.

'Yeah, sure,' he said.

'We'll be along in a minute. Thanks for your help today.'

'That fella gonna make bail, Dave?'

'Probably.'

'That ain't right,' he said, then he said it again as he went out the door, 'Ain't right.'

The bathroom door was ajar when I tapped on it. Her back was to me, her arms propped stiffly on the basin, the tap still running. She kept trying to clear her throat, as though a fine fish bone were caught in it.

I opened the door, took a clean towel out of a cabinet, and started to blot her face with it. She held her hand up almost as though I were about to strike her.

'Don't touch me with that,' she said.

I set the towel on the tub, tore the top Kleenex from a box, dropped it in the waste can, then pulled out several more, balled them up, and touched at her face with them. She pushed down my wrist.

'I'm sorry. I lost it,' she said.

'Don't worry about it.'

'Those children, that smell in the trunk of the car.'

She made her eyes as wide as possible to hold back the tears, but it didn't work. They welled up in her brown eyes, then rolled in rivulets down her cheeks.

'It's okay, Rosie,' I said, and slipped my arms around her. Her head was buried under my chin. I could feel the length of her body against mine, her back rising and falling under my palms. I could smell the strawberry shampoo in her hair, a heated fragrance like soap in her skin.

The window was open, and the wind blew the curtain into the room. Across the street on a putting green, a red flag snapped straight out on a pole that vibrated stiffly in the cup. In the first drops of rain, which slanted almost parallel to the ground, I saw a figure standing by a stagnant reed-choked pond, a roiling myrtle bush at his back. He held himself erect in the wind with his single crutch, his beard flying about his face, his mouth an **O**, his words lost in distant thunder. The stump of his amputated right leg was wrapped with fresh white bandages that had already turned scarlet with new bleeding.

'*What are you trying to warn me of, general? Why has so much pain come back to you, sir?*'

I felt Rosie twist her face against my chest, then step away from me and walk quickly out the door, picking up her handbag from a chair in one smooth motion so I could not see her face. The screen door slammed behind her.

I put everything from Doucet's trunk into evidence bags, locked the house, and got into the pickup just as a storm of hailstones burst from the sky, clattered on the cab, and bounced in tiny white geysers on the slopes of the golf course as far as the eye could see.

That night the weatherman on the ten o'clock news said that the hurricane was moving again in a northwesterly direction and would probably make landfall sometime late tomorrow around Atchafalaya Bay, just to the east of us. Every offshore drilling rig in the Gulf had shut down, and the low-lying coastal areas from Grand Isle to Sabine Pass were being evacuated.

At eleven the sheriff called.

'Somebody just torched Mikey Goldman's trailers out at Spanish Lake. A gallon milk bottle of gasoline through the window with a truck flare right on top of it,' he said. 'You want to go out there and have a look?'

'Not really. Who's that yelling in the background?'

'Guess. I can't convince him he's lucky he wasn't in the trailer.'

'Let me guess again. He wants Julie Balboni in custody.'

'You must be psychic,' the sheriff said. He paused. 'I've got some bad news. The lab report came in late this evening. That utility knife's clean.'

'Are they sure?'

'They're on the same side as we are, Dave.'

'We can use testimony from the pathologist about the nature of the wounds. We can get an exhumation order if we have to.'

'You're tired. I shouldn't have called tonight.'

'Doucet's a monster, sheriff.'

'Let's talk about it in the morning.'

A sheet of gray rain was moving across my neighbor's sugarcane field toward the house and lightning was popping in the woods behind it.

'Are you there?' he said through the static.

'We've got to pull this guy's plug in a major way.'

'We'll talk with the prosecutor in the morning. Now go to bed, Dave.'

After I replaced the receiver in the cradle I sat for a long time in the chair and stared out the open back door at the rain falling on the duck pond and cattails at the foot of my property. The sky seemed filled with electric lights, the wind resonant with the voices of children.

19

The rain was deafening on the gallery in the morning. When I opened the front door, islands of pecan leaves floated in muddy pools in the yard, and a fine, sweet-smelling, cool mist blew inside the room. I could barely make out the marsh beyond the curtain of rain dancing in a wet yellow light on the bayou's surface. I put on my raincoat and hat and ran splashing through the puddles for the bait shop. Batist and I stacked all the tables, chairs, and umbrellas on the dock in the lee of the building, roped them down, hauled our boats out of the water, and bolted the shutters on the windows. Then we drank a cup of coffee and ate a fried pie together at the counter inside while the wind tried to peel the tin roof off the joists.

In town, Bayou Teche had risen high up on the pilings of the drawbridges and overflowed its banks into the rows of camellia bushes in the city park, and passing cars sent curling brown waves of water and street debris sliding across curbs and lawns all the way to the front steps of the houses along East Main. The air smelled of fish and dead vegetation from storm drains and was almost cold in the lungs, and in front of the courthouse the rain spun in vortexes that whipped at the neck and eyes and seemed to soak your clothes no matter how tightly your raincoat was buttoned. Murphy Doucet arrived at the courthouse in a jail van on a wrist chain with seven other inmates, bare-headed, a cigarette in the center of his mouth, his eyes squinted against the rain, his gray hair pasted down on his head, his voice loud with complaint about the manacle that cut into his wrist.

A black man was locked to the next manacle on the chain. He was epileptic and retarded and was in court every three or four weeks for public drunkenness or disturbing the peace. Inside the foyer, when the bailiff was about to walk the men on the chain to the front of the court room, the black man froze and jerked at the manacle, made a gurgling sound with his mouth while spittle drooled over his bottom lip.

'What the hell's wrong with you?' the bailiff said.

'Want to be on the end of the chain. Want to set on the end of the row,' the black man said.

'He's saying he ain't used to being in the front of the bus,' Doucet said.

'This man been bothering you, Ciro?' the bailiff said.

'No, suh. I just want to set on the end this time. Ain't no white peoples bothered me. I been treated just fine.'

'Hurry up and get this bullshit over with,' Doucet said, wiping his eyes on his sleeve.

'We aim to please. We certainly do,' the bailiff said, unlocked the black man, walked him to the end of the chain, and snapped the last manacle on his wrist.

A young photographer from the *Daily Iberian* raised his camera and began focusing through his lens at Doucet.

'You like your camera, son? . . . I thought so. Then you just keep it poked somewhere else,' Doucet said.

It took fifteen minutes. The prosecutor, a high-strung rail of a man, used every argument possible in asking for high bail on Doucet. Over the constant interruptions and objections of Doucet's lawyer, he called him a pedophile, a psychopath, a menace to the community, and a ghoul.

The judge had silver hair and a profile like a Roman soldier. During World War II he had received the Congressional Medal of Honor and at one time had been a Democratic candidate for governor. He listened patiently with one hand on top of another, his eyes oblique, his head tilted at an angle like a priest feigning attentiveness to an obsessed penitent's ramblings.

Finally the prosecutor pointed at Doucet, his finger trembling, and said, 'Your honor, you turn this man loose, he kills somebody else, goddamn it, the blood's going to be on our hands.'

'Would counsel approach the bench, please? You, too, Detective Robicheaux,' the judge said. Then he said, 'Can you gentlemen tell me what the hell is going on here?'

'It's an on-going investigation, your honor. We need more time,' I said.

'That's not my point,' the judge said.

'I object to the treatment of my client, your honor. He's been bullied, degraded in public, slandered by these two men here. He's been—' Doucet's lawyer said.

'I've heard enough from you today, sir. You be quiet a minute,' the judge said. 'Is the prosecutor's office in the process of filing new charges against the defendant?'

'Your honor, we think this man may have been committing rape and homicide for over three decades. Maybe he killed a policeman in Lafayette. We don't even know where to begin,' the prosecutor said.

'Your sincerity is obvious, sir. So is your lack of personal control,' the judge said. 'And neither is solving our problem here. We have to deal with the charge at hand, and you and Detective Robicheaux both know it. Excuse my impatience, but I don't want y'all dragging "what should be" in here rather than "what is." Now all of you step back.'

Then he said, 'Bail is set at ten thousand dollars. Next case,' and brought his gavel down.

A few minutes later I stood on the portico of the courthouse and watched Murphy Doucet and his lawyer walk past me, without interrupting their conversation or registering my presence with more than a glance, get into the lawyer's new Chrysler, and drive away in the rain.

I went home for lunch but couldn't finish my plate. The back door was opened to the small screened-in porch, and the lawn, the mimosa tree, and the willows along the coulee were dark green in the relentless downpour, the air heavy and cold-smelling and swirling with mist.

Alafair was looking at me from across the table, a lump of unchewed sandwich in her jaw. Bootsie had just trimmed her bangs, and she wore a yellow T-shirt with a huge red and green Tabasco bottle on the front. Bootsie reached over and removed my fingers from my temple.

'You've done everything you could do,' she said. 'Let other people worry about it for a while.'

'He's going to walk. With some time we can round up a few of his girls from the Airline Highway and get him on a procuring beef, along with the resisting arrest and assault charge. But he'll trade it all off for testimony against Julie Balboni. I bet the wheels are already turning.'

'Then that's their decision and their grief to live with, Dave,' Bootsie said.

'I don't read it that way.'

'What's wrong?' Alafair said.

'Nothing, little guy,' I said.

'Is the hurricane going to hit here?' she said.

'It might. But we don't worry about that kind of stuff. Didn't you know coonasses are part duck?'

'My teacher said "coonass" isn't a good word.'

'Sometimes people are ashamed of what they are, Alf,' I said.

'Give it a break, Dave,' Bootsie said.

The front door opened suddenly and a gust of cool air swelled through the house. Elrod came through the hallway folding an umbrella and wiping the water off his face with his hand.

'Wow!' he said. 'I thought I saw Noah's ark out there on the bayou. It could be significant.'

'Ark? What's an ark?' Alafair said.

'El, there's a plate for you in the icebox,' Bootsie said.

'Thanks,' he said, and opened the icebox door, his face fixed with a smile, his eyes studiously carefree.

'What's an ark?' Alafair said.

'It's part of a story in the Bible, Alf,' I said, and watched Elrod as he sat down with a plate of tuna-fish sandwiches and potato salad in his hand. 'What's happening out at the lake, El?'

'Everything's shut down till this storm blows over,' he said. He bit into his sandwich and didn't look up from his plate.

'That'd make sense, wouldn't it?' I said.

He raised his eyes.

'I think it's going to stay shut down,' he said. 'There's only a couple of scenes left to shoot. I think Mikey wants to do them back in California.'

'I see.'

Now it was Alafair who was watching Elrod's face. His eyes focused on his sandwich.

'You leaving, Elrod?' she asked.

'In a couple of days maybe,' he answered. 'But I'm sure I'll be back this way. I'd really like to have y'all come visit, too.'

She continued to stare at him, her face round and empty.

'You could bring Tripod,' he said. 'I've got a four-acre place up Topanga Canyon. It's right up from the ocean.'

'You said you were going to be here all summer,' she said.

'I guess it just hasn't worked out that way. I wish it had,' he said. Then he looked at me. 'Dave, maybe I'm saying the wrong thing here, but y'all come out to LA, I'll get Alafair cast in five minutes. That's a fact.'

'We'll talk it over,' Bootsie said, and smiled across the table at him.

'I could be in the movies where you live?' Alafair said.

'You bet,' Elrod said, then saw the expression on my face. 'I mean, if that's what you and your family wanted.'

'Dave?' She looked up at me.

'Let's see what happens,' I said, and brushed at her bangs with my fingers. Elrod was about to say something else, but I interrupted him. 'Where's Balboni?'

'He doesn't seem to get the message. He keeps hanging around his trailer with his greaseballs. I think he'll still be sitting there when the set's torn down,' Elrod said.

'His trailer might get blown in the lake,' I said.

'I think he has more than one reason for being out there,' Elrod said.

I waited for him to finish, but he didn't. A few minutes later we went out on the gallery. The cypress planks of the steps and floor were dark with rain that had blown back under the eaves. Across the bayou the marsh looked smudged and indistinct in the gray air. Down at the dock Batist was deliberately sinking his pirogue in the shallows so it wouldn't be whipped into a piling by the wind.

'What were you trying to tell me about Balboni?' I said.

'He picks up young girls in town and tells them he's going to put them in a movie. I've heard he's had two or three in there in the last couple of days.'

'That sounds like Julie.'

'How's that?'

'When we were kids he never knew who he was unless he was taking his equipment out of his pants.'

He stared at the rain.

'Maybe there's something I ought to tell you, Dave, not that maybe you don't already know it,' he said. 'When people like us, I'm talking about actors and such, come into a community, everybody gets excited and thinks somehow we're going to change their lives. I'm talking about romantic expectations, glamorous relationships with celebrities, that kind of stuff. Then one day we're gone and they're left with some problems they didn't have before. What I'm saying is they become shamed when they realize how little they always thought of themselves. It's like turning on the lights inside the theater when the matinee is over.'

'Our problems are our own, El. Don't give yourself too much credit.'

'You cut me loose on a DWI and got me sober, Dave. Or at least I got a good running start at it. What'd you get for it? A mess of trouble you didn't deserve.'

'Extend a hand to somebody else. That way you pass on the favor,' I said.

I put my hand on the back of his neck. I could feel the stiff taper of his hair under my palm.

'I think about Kelly most when it rains. It's like she was just washed away, like everything that was her was dissolved right into the earth, like she wasn't ever here,' he said. 'How can a person be a part of your life twenty-four hours a day and then just be gone? I can't get used to it.'

'Maybe people live on inside of us, El, and then one day we get to see them again.'

He leaned one hand against a wood post and stared at the rain. His face was wet with mist.

'It's coming to an end,' he said. 'Everything we've been doing, all the things that have happened, it's fixing to end,' he said.

'You're not communicating too well, partner.'

'I saw them back yonder in that sugarcane field last night. But this time it was different. They were furling their colors and loading their wagons. They're leaving us.'

Why now? I heard my voice say inside myself.

He dropped his arm from the post and looked at me. In the shadows his brown skin was shiny with water.

'Something bad's fixing to happen, Dave,' he said. 'I can feel it like a hand squeezing my heart.'

He tapped the flat of his fist against the wood post as though he were trying to reassure himself of its physical presence.

Late that afternoon the sheriff called me on my extension.

'Dave, could you come down to my office and help me with something?' he said.

When I walked through his door he was leaned back in his swivel chair, watching the treetops flattening the wind outside the window, pushing against his protruding stomach with stiffened fingers as though he were discovering his weight problem for the first time.

'Oh, there you are,' he said.

'What's up ?'

'Sit down.'

'Do we have a problem?'

He brushed at his round, cleft chin with the backs of his fingers.

'I want to get your reaction to what some people might call a developing situation,' he said.

'Developing situation?'

'I went two years to USL, Dave. I'm not the most articulate person in the world. I just try to deal with realities as they are.'

'I get the feeling we're about to sell the ranch.'

'It's not a perfect world.'

'Where's the heat coming from?' I said.

'There're a lot of people who want Balboni out of town.'

'Which people?'

'Business people.'

'They used to get along with him just fine.'

'People loved Mussolini until it came time to hang him upside down in a filling station.'

'Come on, cut to it, sheriff. Who are the other players?'

'The feds. They want Balboni bad. Doucet's lawyer says his client can put Julie so far down under the penal system they'll have to dig him up to bury him.'

'What's Doucet get?'

'He cops to resisting arrest and procuring, one year max on an honor farm. Then maybe the federal witness protection program, psychological counseling, ongoing supervision, all that jazz.'

'Tell them to go fuck themselves.'

'Why is it I thought you might say that?'

'Call the press in. Tell them what kind of bullshit's going on here. Give them the morgue photos of Cherry LeBlanc.'

'Be serious. They're not going to run pictures like that. Look, we can't indict with what we have. This way we get the guy into custody and permanent supervision.'

'He's going to kill again. It's a matter of time.'

'So what do you suggest?'

'Don't give an inch. Make them sweat ball bearings.'

'With what? I'm surprised his lawyer even wants to accept the procuring charge.'

'They think I've got a photo of Doucet with Balboni and Cherry LeBlanc in Biloxi.'

'*Think?*'

'Doucet's face is out of focus. The man in the picture looks like bread dough.'

'Great.'

'I still say we should exhume the body and match the utility knife to the slash wounds.'

'All an expert witness can do is testify that the wounds are consistent with those that might have been made with a utility knife. At least that's what the prosecutor's office says. Doucet will walk and so will Balboni. I say we take the bird in hand.'

'It's a mistake.'

'You don't have to answer to people, Dave. I do. They want Julie out of this parish and they don't care how we do it.'

'Maybe you should give some thought about having to answer to the family of Doucet's next victim, sheriff.'

He picked up a chain of paper clips and trailed them around his blotter.

'I don't guess there's much point in continuing this conversation, is there?' he said.

'I'm right about this guy. Don't let him fly.'

'Wake up, Dave. He flew this morning.' He dropped the paper clips into a clean ashtray and walked past me with his coffee cup. 'You'd better take off a little early this afternoon. This hurricane looks to be a real frog stringer.'

It hit late that evening, pushing waves ahead of it that curled over houseboats and stilt cabins at West Cote Blanche Bay and flattened them like a huge fist. In the south the sky was the color of burnt pewter, then rain-streaked, flumed with thunderheads. You could see tornadoes dropping like suspended snakes from the clouds, filling with water and splintered trees from the marshes, and suddenly breaking apart like whips snapping themselves into nothingness.

I heard canvas popping loose on the dock, billowing against the ropes Batist and I had tried to secure it with, then bursting free and flapping end over end among the cattails. The windows swam with water, lightning exploded out of the gray-green haze of swamp, and in the distance, in the roar of wind and thunder that seemed to clamp down on us like an enormous black glass bell, I thought I could hear the terrified moaning of my neighbor's cattle as they fought to find cover in a woods where mature trees were whipped out of the soft ground like seedlings.

By midnight the power was gone, the water off, and half the top of an oak tree had crashed on the roof and slid down the side of the house, covering the windows with tangles of branches and leaves.

I heard Alafair cry out in her sleep. I lit a candle, placed it in a saucer on top of her bookcase which was filling with her collection of Curious George and Baby Squanto Indian books, and got in bed beside her. She wore her Houston Astros baseball cap and had pulled the sheet up to her chin. Her brown eyes moved back and forth as though she were searching out the sounds of the storm that seeped through the heavy cypress planks in the roof. The candlelight flickered on all the memorabilia she had brought back from our vacations or that we had saved as private signposts of the transitions she had made since I had pulled her from the submerged upside-down wreck of a plane off Southwest Pass: conch shells and dried starfish from Key West, her red tennis shoes embossed with the words *Left* and *Right* on the toes, a Donald Duck cap with a quacking bill from Disneyworld, her yellow T-shirt printed with a smiling purple whale on the front and the words *Baby Orca* that she had fitted over the torso of a huge stuffed frog.

'Dave, the field behind the house is full of lightning,' she said. 'I can hear animals in the thunder.'

'It's Mr Broussard's cattle. They'll be all right, though. They'll bunch up in the coulee.'

'Are you scared?'

'Not really. But it's all right to be scared a little bit if you want to.'

'If you're scared, you can't be standup.'

'Sure you can. Standup people don't mind admitting they're scared sometimes.'

Then I saw something move under the sheet by her feet.

'Alf?'

'What?' Her eyes flicked about the ceiling as though she were watching a bird fly from wall to wall.

I worked the sheet away from the foot of the bed until I was staring at Tripod's silver-tipped rump and black-ringed tail.

'I wonder how this fellow got in your bed, little guy,' I said.

'He probably got out of his cage on the back porch.'

'Yeah, that's probably it. He's pretty good at opening latched doors, isn't he?'

'I don't think he should go back out there, do you, Dave? He gets scared in the thunder.'

'We'll give him a dispensation tonight.'

'A dis— What?'

'Never mind. Let's go to sleep, little guy.'

'Goodnight, big guy. Goodnight, Tripod. Goodnight, Frogger. Goodnight, Baby Squanto. Goodnight, Curious George. Goodnight, Baby Orca. Goodnight, sea shells. Goodnight—'

'Cork it, Alf, and go to sleep.'

'All right. Goodnight, big guy.'

'Goodnight, little guy.'

In my sleep I heard the storm pass overhead like freight trains grinding down a grade, then suddenly we were in the storm's eye, the air as still as if it had been trapped inside a jar; leaves drifted to the ground from the trees, and I could hear the cries of seabirds wheeling overhead.

The bedroom windows shine with an amber light that might have been aged inside oak. I slip on my khakis and loafers and walk out into the cool air that smells of salt and wet woods, and I see the general's troops forming into long columns that wind their way into other columns that seem to stretch over an infinitely receding landscape of hardwood forests fired with red leaves, peach orchards, tobacco acreage, rivers covered with steam, purple mountain ridges and valleys filled with dust from ambulance and ammunition wagons and wheeled artillery pieces, a cornfield churned into stubble by horses' hooves and men's boots, a meandering limestone wall and a sunken road where wild hogs graze on the bodies of the dead.

The general sits on a cypress stump by my coulee, surrounded by enlisted men and his aides. A blackened coffeepot boils amidst a heap of burning sticks by his foot. The officers as well as enlisted men are eating honeycombs peeled from inside a dead oak tree. The general's tunic is buttoned over his bad arm. A civilian in checkered trousers, high-top shoes, braces, and a straw hat is setting up a big box camera on a tripod in front of the group.

The general tips his hat up on his forehead and waves me toward him.

'A pip of a storm, wasn't it?' he says.

'Why are you leaving?'

'Oh, we're not gone just yet. Say, I want to have your photograph taken with us. That gentleman you see yonder is the correspondent for the Savannah Republican. He writes an outstanding story, certainly as good as this Melville fellow, if you ask me.'

'I don't understand what's happening. Why did your wounds open, what were you trying to warn me of?'

'It's my foolishness, son. Like you, I grieve over what I can't change. Was it Bacon that talked about keeping each cut green?'

'Change what?'

'Our fate. Yours, mine. Care for your own. Don't try to emulate me. Look at what I invested my life in. Oh, we were always honorable – Robert Lee, Jackson, Albert Sidney Johnston, A. P. Hill – but we served venal men and a vile enterprise. How many lives would have been spared had we not lent ourselves to the defense of a repellent cause like slavery?'

'People don't get to choose their time in history, general.'

'Well said. You're absolutely right.' He swings the flat of his right hand and hits me hard on the arm, then rises on his crutch and straightens his tunic. 'Now, gentlemen, if y'all will take the honeycombs out of your faces, let's be about this photographing business. I'm amazed at what the sciences are producing these days.'

We stand in a group of eight. The enlisted men have Texas accents, powder-blackened teeth, and beards that grow like snakes on their faces. I can smell horse sweat and wood smoke on their clothes. Just as the photographer removes his straw hat and ducks his head under a black cloth at the back of the camera, I look down the long serpentine corridor of amber light again and see thousands of troops advancing on distant fields, their blue and red and white flags bent into the fusillade, their artillery crews laboring furiously at the mouths of smoking cannon, and I know the place names without their ever being spoken – Culp's Hill, Corinth, the Devil's Den, Kennesaw Mountain, the Bloody Lane – and a collective sound that's like no other in the world rises in the wind and blows across the drenched land.

The photographer finishes and stoops under his camera box and lifts the tripod up on his shoulder. The general looks into the freshening breeze, his eyes avoiding me.

'You won't tell me what's at hand, sir?' I say.

'What does it matter as long as you stay true to your principles?'

'Even the saints might take issue with that statement, general.'

'I'll see you directly, lieutenant. Be of good heart.'

'Don't let them get behind you,' I say.

'Ah, the admonition of a veteran.' Then his aides help him onto his horse and he waves his hat forward and says, 'Hideeho, lads,' but there is no joy in his voice.

The general and his mounted escort move down the incline toward my neighbor's field, the tails of their horses switching, the light arcing over them as bright and heated and refractive as a glass of whiskey held up to the sun.

When I woke in the morning the rain was falling evenly on the trees in the yard and a group of mallards were swimming in the pond at the foot of my property. The young sugarcane in my neighbor's field was pounded flat into the washed-out rows as though it had been trampled by livestock. Above the treeline in the north I saw a small tornado drop like a spring from the sky, fill with mud and water from a field, then burst apart as though it had never been there.

I worked until almost eight o'clock that evening. Power was still off in parts of the parish; traffic signals were down; a rural liquor store had been burglarized during the night; two convenience stores had been held up; a drunk set fire to his own truck in the middle of a street; a parolee two days out of Angola beat his wife almost to death; and a child drowned in a storm drain.

Rosie had spent the day with her supervisor in New Orleans and had come back angry and despondent. I didn't even bother to ask her why. She had the paperwork on our case spread all over her desk, as though somehow rereading it and rearranging it from folder to folder would produce a different result, namely, that we could weld the cell door shut on Murphy Doucet and not have to admit that we were powerless over the bureaucratic needs of others.

Just as I closed the drawers in my desk and was about to leave, the phone rang.

'Dave, I think I screwed up. I think you'd better come home,' Elrod said.

'What's wrong?'

'Bootsie went to town and asked me to watch Alafair. Then Alafair said she was going down to the bait shop to get us some fried pies.'

'Get it out, Elrod. What is it?' I saw Rosie looking at me, her face motionless.

'I forgot Batist had already closed up. I should have gone with her.'

I tried to hold back the anger that was rising in my throat.

'Listen, Elrod—'

'I went down there and she was gone. The door's wide open and the key's still in the lock—'

'How long's it been?'

'A half hour.'

'*A half hour?*'

'You don't understand. I checked down at Poteet's first. Then I saw Tripod running loose on his chain in the road.'

'What was she wearing?'

'A yellow raincoat and a baseball cap.'

'Where's Bootsie?'

'Still in town.'

'All right, stay by the phone and I'll be there in a few minutes.'

'Dave, I'm sorry, I don't know what to say, I—'

'It's not your fault.' I replaced the phone receiver in the cradle, my ears whirring with a sound like wind inside a sea shell, the skin of my face as tight as a pumpkin's.

20

Before Rosie and I left the office I told the dispatcher to put out an all-car alert on Alafair and to contact the state police.

All the way to the house I tried to convince myself that there was an explanation for her disappearance other than the one that I couldn't bear to hold in the center of my mind for more than a few seconds. Maybe Tripod had simply gotten away from her while she was in the bait shop and she was still looking for him, I thought. Or maybe she had walked down to the general store at the four-corners, had forgotten to lock the door, and Tripod had broken loose from the clothesline on his own.

But Alafair never forgot to lock up the bait shop and she wouldn't leave Tripod clipped to the clothesline in the rain.

Moments after I walked into the bait shop, all the images and fears that I had pushed to the edges of my consciousness suddenly became real and inescapable, in the same way that you wake from a nightmare into daylight and with a sinking of the heart realize that the nightmare is part of your waking day and has not been manufatured by your sleep. Behind the counter I saw her Astros baseball cap, where it had been flattened into the duckboards by someone's muddy shoe or boot. Elrod and Rosie watched me silently while I picked it up and placed it on top of the counter. I felt as though I were deep under water, past the point of depth tolerance, and something had popped like a stick and pulled loose in my head. Through the screen I saw Bootsie's car turn into the drive and park by the house.

'I should have figured him for it,' I said.

'Doucet?' Rosie said.

'He was a cop. He's afraid to do time.'

'We're not certain it's Doucet, Dave,' she said.

'He knows what happens to cops inside mainline jails. Particularly to a guy they make as a short-eyes. I'm going up to talk to Bootsie. Don't answer the phone, okay?'

Rosie's teeth made white marks on her bottom lip.

'Dave, I want to bring in the Bureau as soon as we have evidence that it's a kidnapping,' she said.

'So far nothing official we do to this guy works. It's time both of us hear that, Rosie,' I said, and went out the screen door and started up the dock.

I hadn't gone ten yards when I heard the telephone ring behind me. I ran back through the rain and jerked the receiver out of the cradle.

'You sound out of breath,' the voice said.

Don't blow this one.

'Turn her loose, Doucet. You don't want to do this,' I said. I looked into Rosie's face and pointed toward the house.

'I'll make it simple for both of us. You take the utility knife and the photo out of the evidence locker. You put them in a Ziploc bag. At eight o'clock tomorrow morning you leave the bag in the trash can on the corner of Royal and St Ann in New Orleans. I don't guess you ought to plan on getting a lot of sleep tonight.'

Rosie had eased the screen door shut behind her and was walking fast up the incline toward the house in the fading light.

'The photo's a bluff. It's out of focus,' I said. 'You can't be identified in it.'

'Then you won't mind parting with it.'

'You can walk, Doucet. We can't make the case on you.'

'You lying sonofabitch. You tore up my house. Your tow truck scratched up my car. You won't rest till you fuck me up in every way you can.'

'You're doing this because your *property* was damaged?'

'I'll tell you what else I'm going to do if you decide to get clever on me. No, that's not right. It won't be me, because I never hurt a child in my life. You got that?'

He stopped speaking and waited for me. then he said it again: 'You got that, Dave?'

'Yes,' I said.

'But there's a guy who used to work in Balboni's movies, a guy who spent eleven years in Parchman for killing a little nigger girl. You want to know how it went down?'

Then he told me. I stared out the screen door at my neighbor's dark green lawn, at his enormous roses that had burst in the rain and were now scattered in the grass like pink tear drops. A dog began barking, and then I heard it cry out sharply as though it had been whipped across the ribs with a chain.

'Doucet—' I broke in. My voice was wet, as though my vocal cords were covered with membrane.

'You don't like my description? You think I'm just trying to scare you? Get a hold of one of his snuff films. You'll agree he's an artist.'

'Listen to me carefully. If you hurt my daughter, I'll get to you one way or another, in or out of jail, in the witness protection program, it won't matter, I'll take you down in pieces, Doucet.'

'You've said only one thing right today. I'm ging to walk, and you're going to help me, unless you've let that affirmative-action bitch fuck most of your brains out. By the way, forget the trace. I'm at a phone booth and you've got shit on your nose.'

The line went dead.

I was trembling as I walked up the slope to the house. Rosie opened the screen door and came out on the gallery with Bootsie behind her. The skin of Bootsie's face was drawn back against the bone, her throat ruddy with color as though she had a windburn.

'He hung up too soon. We couldn't get it,' Rosie said.

'Dave, my God. What—' Bootsie said. Her pulse was jumping in her neck.

'Let's go inside,' I said, and put my arm around her shoulder. 'Rosie, I'll be out in just a minute.'

'No, talk to me right here,' Bootsie said.

'Murphy Doucet has her. He wants the evidence that he thinks can put him in jail.'

'What for?' she said. 'You told me yesterday that he'll probably get out of it.'

'He doesn't know that. He's not going to believe anybody who tells him that, either.'

'Where is she?'

'I don't know, Boots. But we're going to get her back. If the sheriff calls, don't tell him anything. At least not right now.'

I felt Rosie's eyes on the side of my face.

'What are you doing, Dave?' Bootsie said.

'I'll call you in a little while,' I said. 'Stay with Elrod, okay?'

'What if that man calls back?'

'He won't. He'll figure the line's open.'

Before she could speak again, I went inside and opened the closet door in the bedroom. From under some folded blankets on the top shelf I took out a box of twelve-gauge shells and the Remington pump shotgun whose barrel I had sawed off in front of the pump handle and whose sportsman's plug I had removed years ago. I shook the shells, a mixture of deer slugs and double-ought buckshot, out on the bed and pressed them one by one into the magazine until I felt the spring come snug against the fifth shell. I dropped the rest of the shells into my raincoat pockets.

'Call the FBI, Dave,' Bootsie said behind me.

'No,' I said.

'Then I'll do it.'

'Boots, if they screw it up, he'll kill her. We'll never even find the body.'

Her face was white. I set the shotgun down and pulled her against me. She felt small, her back rounded, inside my arms.

'We've got a few hours,' I said. 'If we can't get her back in that time, I'm going to do what he wants and hope that he turns her loose. I'll bring the sheriff and the FBI in on it, too.'

She stepped back from me and looked up into my face.

'Hope that he—' she said.

'Doucet's never left witnesses.'

She wanted to come with us, but I left her on the gallery with Elrod, staring after us with her hands clenching and unclenching at her sides.

It was almost dark when we turned off the old two-lane highway onto the dirt road that led to Spanish Lake. The rain was falling in the trees and out on the lake and I could see the lights burning in one trailer under the hanging moss by the water's edge. All the way out to the lake Rosie had barely spoken, her small hands folded on top of her purse, the shadows washing across her face like rivulets of rain.

'I have to be honest with you, Dave. I don't know how far I can go along with this,' she said.

'Call in your people now and I'll stonewall them.'

'Do you think that little of us?'

'Not you I don't. But the people you work for are pencil pushers. They'll cover their butts, they'll do it by the numbers, and I'll end up losing Alafair.'

'What are you going to do if you catch Doucet?'

'That's up to him.'

'Is that straight, Dave?'

I didn't answer.

'I saw you put something in your raincoat pocket when you were coming out of the bedroom,' she said. 'I got the impression you were concealing it from Bootsie. Maybe it was just my imagination.'

'Maybe you're thinking too much about the wrong things, Rosie.'

'I want your word this isn't a vigilante mission.'

'You're worried about *procedure* . . . In dealing with a man like this? What's the matter with you?'

'Maybe you're forgetting who your real friends are, Dave.'

I stopped the truck at the security building, rolled down my window, and held up my badge for the man inside, who was leaned back in his chair in front of a portable television set. He put on his hat, came outside, and dropped the chain for me. I could hear the sounds of a war movie through the open door.

'I'll just leave it down for you,' he said.

'Thanks. Is that Julie Balboni's trailer with the lights on?' I said.

'Yeah, that's it.'

'Who's with him?'

The security guard's eyes went past me to Rosie.

'His reg'lar people, I guess,' he said. 'I don't pay it much mind.'

'Who else?'

'He brings out guests from town.' His eyes looked directly into mine.

I rolled up the window, thumped across the chain, and drove into the oak grove by the lake. Twenty yards from Balboni's lighted trailer was the collapsed and blackened shell of a second trailer, its empty windows blowing with rain, its buckled floor leaking cinders into pools of water, the tree limbs above it scrolled with scorched leaves. To one side of Balboni's trailer a Volkswgen and the purple Cadillac with the tinted black windows were parked between two trees. I saw someone light a cigarette inside the Cadillac.

I stepped out of the truck with the shotgun hanging from my right arm and tapped with one knuckle on the driver's window. He rolled the glass down, and I saw the long pink scar inside his right forearm, the boxed hairline on the back of his neck, the black welt like an angry insect on his bottom lip where I had broken off his tooth in the restaurant on East Main. The man in the passenger's seat had the flattened eyebrows and gray scar tissue around his eyes of a prizefighter; he bent his neck down so he could look upward at my face and see who I was.

'What d'you want?' the driver said.

'Both of you guys are fired. Now get out of here and don't come back.'

'Listen to this guy. You think this is Dodge City?' the driver said.

'Didn't you learn anything the first time around?' I said.

'Yeah, that you're a prick who blindsided me, that I can sue your ass, that Julie's got lawyers who can—'

I lifted the shotgun above the window ledge and screwed the barrel into his cheek.

'Do yourself a favor and visit your family in New Orleans,' I said.

His knuckles whitened on the steering wheel as he tried to turn his head away from the pressure of the shotgun barrel. I pressed it harder into the hollow of his cheek.

'Fuck it, do what the man says. I told you the job was turning to shit when Julie run off Cholo,' the other man said. 'Hey, you hear me, man,

259

back off. We're neutral about any personal beefs you got, you understand what I'm saying? You ought to do something about that hard-on you got, knock it down with a hammer or something, show a little fucking control.'

I stepped back and pulled the shotgun free of the window. The driver stared at my hand wrapped in the trigger guard.

'You crazy sonofabitch, you had the safety off,' he said.

'Happy motoring,' I said.

I waited until the taillights of the Cadillac had disappeared through the trees, then I walked up onto the trailer's steps, turned the door knob, and flung the door back into the wall.

A girl not over nineteen, dressed only in panties and a pink bra, was wiggling into a pair of jeans by the side of two bunk beds that had been pushed together in the middle of the floor. Her long hair was unevenly peroxided and looked like twisted strands of honey on her freckled shoulders; for some reason the crooked lipstick on her mouth made me think of a small red butterfly. Julie Balboni stood at an aluminum sink, wearing only a black silk jockstrap, his salt-and-pepper curls in his eyes, his body covered with fine black hair, a square bottle of Scotch poised above a glass filled with cracked ice. His eyes dropped to the shotgun that hung from my right hand.

'You finally losing your mind, Dave?' he said.

I picked up the girl's blouse from the bed and handed it to her.

'Are you from New Iberia?' I asked.

'Yes, sir,' she said, her eyes fastened on mine as she pushed her feet into a pair of pumps.

'Stay away from this man,' I said. 'Women who hang around him end up dead.'

Her frightened face looked at Julie, then back at me.

Rosie put her hands on the girl's shoulders and turned her toward the door.

'You can go now,' she said. 'Listen to what Detective Robicheaux tells you. This man won't put you in the movies, not unless you want to work in pornographic films. Are you okay?'

'Yes, ma'm.'

'Here's your purse. Don't worry about what's happening here. It doesn't have anything to do with you. Just stay away from this man. He's in a lot of trouble,' Rosie said.

The girl looked again at Julie, then went quickly out the door and into the dark. Julie was putting on his trousers now, with his back to us. The walls were covered with felt paintings of red-mouthed tigers and boa constrictors wrapped around the bodies of struggling unicorns. By the door was the canvas bag filled with baseballs, gloves, and metal bats.

Julie's skin looked brown and rubbed with oil in the glow from a bedside lava lamp.

'It looks like you did a real number on Mikey Goldman's trailer,' I said.

He zipped his fly. 'Like most of the time, you're wrong,' he said. 'I don't go around setting fires on my own movie set. That's Cholo Manelli's work.'

'Why does he want to hurt Mikey Goldman?'

'He don't. He thought it was my trailer. He's got his nose bent out of joint about some imaginary wrong I done to him. The first thing Cholo does in the morning is stick his head up his hole. You guys ought to hang out together.'

'Why do you think I'm here, Julie?'

'How the fuck should I know? Nothing you do makes sense to me anymore, Dave. You want to toss the place, see if that little chippy left a couple of 'ludes in the sheets?'

'You think this is some chickenshit roust, Julie?'

He combed his curls back over his head with his fingers. His navel looked like a black ball of hair above his trousers.

'You take yourself too serious,' he said.

'Murphy Doucet has my daughter.' I watched his face. He put his thumbnail into a molar and picked out a piece of food with it. 'Did you hear what I said?'

He poured three fingers of scotch into his glass, then dropped a lemon rind into the ice, his face composed, his eyes glancing out the window at a distant flicker of lightning.

'Too bad,' he said.

'Too bad, huh?'

'Yeah. I don't like to hear stuff like that. It upsets me.'

'Upsets you, does it?'

'Yeah. That's why I don't watch that show *Unsolved Mysteries*. It upsets me. Hey, maybe you can get her face on one of those milk cartons.'

As he drank from his highball, I could see the slight tug at the corner of his mouth, the smile in his eyes. He picked up his flowered shirt from the back of a chair and began putting it on in front of a bathroom door mirror as though we were not there.

I handed Rosie the shotgun, put my hands on my hips, and studied the tips of my shoes. Then I slipped an aluminum bat out of the canvas bag, choked up on the taped handle, and ripped it down across his neck and shoulders. His forehead bounced off the mirror, pocking and spiderwebbing the glass like it had been struck with a ball bearing. He turned back toward me, his eyes and mouth wide with disbelief, and I hit him again, hard, this time across the middle of the face. He crashed headlong into the toilet tank, his nose roaring blood, one side of his mouth drooping as though all the muscle endings in it had been severed.

I leaned over and cuffed both of his wrists around the bottom of the stool. His eyes were receded and out of focus, close-set like a pig's. The water in the bowl under his chin was filling with drops of dark color like pieces of disintegrating scarlet cotton.

I nudged his arm with the bat. His eyes clicked up into my face.

'Where is she, Julie?' I said.

'I cut Doucet loose. I don't have nothing to do with what he does. You get off my fucking case or I'm gonna square this, Dave. It don't matter if you're a cop or not, I'll put out an open contract, I'll cowboy your whole fucking family. I'll—'

I turned around and took the shotgun out of Rosie's hands. I could see words forming in her face, but I didn't wait for her to speak. I bent down on the edge of Julie's vision.

'Your window of opportunity is shutting down, Feet.'

He blew air out of his nose and tried to wipe his face on his shoulder.

'I'm telling you the truth. I don't know nothing about what that guy does,' he said. 'He's a geek . . . I don't hire geeks, I run them off . . . I got enough grief without crazy people working for me.'

'You're lying again, Julie,' I said, stepped back, leveled the shotgun barrel above his head, and fired at an angle into the toilet tank. The double-ought buckshot blew water and splintered ceramic all over the wall. I pumped the spent casing out on the floor. Julie jerked the handcuffs against the base of the stool, like an animal trying to twist itself out of a metal trap.

I touched the warm tip of the barrel against his eyebrow.

'Last chance, Feet.'

His eyes closed; he broke wind uncontrollably in his pants; water and small chips of ceramic dripped out of his hair.

'He's got a camp south of Bayou Vista,' he said. 'It's almost to Atchafalaya Bay. The deed ain't in his name, nobody knows about it, it's like where he does all his weird stuff. It's right where the dirt road ends at the salt marsh. I seen it once when we were out on my boat.'

'Is my daughter there?' I said quietly.

'I just told you, it's where he goes to be weird. You figure it out.'

'We'll be back later, Feet. You can make a lot of noise, if you like, but your gumbals are gone and the security guard is watching war movies. If I get my daughter back, I'll have somebody from the department come out and pick you up. You can file charges against me then or do whatever you want. If you've lied to me, that's another matter.'

Then I saw a secret concern working in his eyes, a worry, a fear that had nothing to do with me or the pain and humiliation that I had inflicted upon him. It was the fear that you inevitably see in the eyes of men like Julie and his kind when they realize that through an ironic accident they are now dealing with forces that are as cruel and unchecked by morality as the energies they'd awakened with every morning of their lives.

'Cholo—' he said.

'What about him?' I said.

'He's out there somewhere.'

'I doubt it.'

'You don't know him. He carries a barber's razor. He's got fixations. He don't forget things. He tied parts of a guy all over a ceiling fan once.'

His chest moved up and down with his breathing against the rim of the toilet bowl. His brow was kneaded with lines, his nose a wet red smear against his face, his eyes twitching with a phlegmy light.

I shut off the valve that was spewing water upward into the shattered tank, then found a quilt and a pile of towels in a linen closet and placed the towels under Julie's forearms and the quilt between his knees and the bottom of the stool.

'That's about all I can do for you, Feet. Maybe it's the bottom of the ninth for both of us,' I said.

The front wheels of the truck shimmied on the cement as I wound up the transmission on Highway 90 southeast of town. It had stopped raining, the oaks and palm trees by the road's edge were coated with mist, and the moon was rising in the east like a pale white and mottled-blue wafer trailing streamers of cloud torn loose from the Gulf's horizon.

'I think I'm beyond all my parameters now, Dave,' Rosie said.

'What would you do differently? I'd like for you to tell me that, Rosie.'

'I believe we should have Balboni picked up – suspicion for involvement in a kidnapping.'

'And my daughter would be dead as soon as Doucet heard about it. Don't tell me that's not true, either.'

'I'm not sure you're in control any more, Dave. That remark about the bottom of the ninth—'

'What about it?'

'You're thinking about killing Doucet, aren't you?'

'I can put you down at the four-corners up there. Is that what you want?'

'Do you think you're the only person who cares about your daughter?

Do you think I want to do anything that would put her in worse jeopardy than she's already in?'

'The army taught me what a free-fire zone is, Rosie. It's a place where the winners make up the rules after the battle's over. Anyone who believes otherwise has never been there.'

'You're wrong about all this, Dave. What we don't do is let the other side make us be like them.'

Ahead I could see the lighted, tree-shadowed white stucco walls of a twenty-four-hour filling station that had been there since the 1930s. I eased my foot off the gas pedal and looked across the seat at Rosie.

'Go on,' she said. 'I won't say anything else.'

We drove through Jeanerette and Franklin into the bottom of the Atchafalaya Basin, where Louisiana's wetlands bled into the Gulf of Mexico, not far from where this story actually began with a racial lynching in the year 1957. Rosie had fallen asleep against the door. At Bayou Vista I found the dirt road that led south to the sawgrass and Atchafalaya Bay. The fields looked like lakes of pewter under the moon, the sugarcane pressed flat like straw into the water. Wood farmhouses and barns were cracked sideways on their foundations, as though a gigantic thumb had squeezed down on their roofs, and along one stretch of road the telephone poles had been snapped off even with the ground for a half mile and flung like sticks into distant trees.

Then the road entered a corridor of oaks, and through the trunks I saw four white horses galloping in circles in a mist-streaked pasture, spooking against the barbed-wire fences, mud flying from their hooves, their nostrils dilated, their eyes bright with fear against a backdrop of dry lightning, their muscles rippling under their skin like silvery water sliding over stone. Then I was sure I saw a figure by the side of the road, the palmetto shadows waving behind him, his steel-gray tunic buttoned at his throat, a floppy campaign hat pulled over his eyes.

I hit my bright lights, and for just a moment I saw his elongated milk-white face as though a flashbulb had exploded in front of it. *'What are you doing here?'* I said.

'Don't use those whom you love to justify a dishonorable cause.'

'That's rhetoric.'

'You gave the same counsel to the Sykes boy.'

'It was you who told me to do it under a black flag. Remember? We blow up their shit big time, general.'

'Then you will do it on your own, suh, and without me.'

The truck's front springs bounced in a chuckhole and splashed a sheet of dirty water across the window; then I was beyond the pasture and the horses that wheeled and raced in the moonlight, traveling deep into the tip of the wetlands, with flooded woods on each side of me, blue herons lifting on extended wings out of the canals, the moist air whipped with the smell of salt and natural gas from the oil platforms out in the swamp.

The road bent out of the trees, and I saw the long expanses of sawgrass and mudflats that spread out into the bay, and the network of channels that had been cut by the oil companies and that were slowly poisoning the marshes with salt water. Rosie was awake now, rubbing her eyes with one knuckle, her face still with fatigue.

'I'm sorry. I didn't mean to fall asleep,' she said.

'It's been a long day.'

'Where's the camp?'

'There's some shacks down by the flats, but they look deserted.'

I pulled the truck to the side of the road and cut the lights. The tide was out, and the bay looked flat and gray and seabirds were pecking shellfish out of the wet sand in the moonlight. Then a wind gusted out of the south and bent a stand of willow trees that stood on a small knoll between the marsh and the bay.

'Dave, there's a light back in those trees,' Rosie said.

Then I saw it, too, at the end of a two-lane sandy track that wound through the willows and over the knoll.

'All right, let's do it,' I said, and pushed down on the door handle.

'Dave, before we go in there, I want you to hear something. If we find the wrong thing, if Alafair's not all right, it's not because of anything you did. It's important for you to accept that now. If I had been in your place, I'd have done everything the same way you have.'

I squeezed her hand.

'A cop couldn't have a better partner than Rosie Gomez,' I said.

We got out of the truck and left the doors open to avoid making any unecessary sound, and walked up the sandy track toward the trees. I could hear gulls cawing and wheeling overhead and the solitary scream of a nutria deep in the marsh. Humps of garbage stood by the sides of the track, and then I realized that it was medical waste – bandages, hypodermic vials, congealed bags of gelatin, sheets that were stiff with dried fluids.

We moved away from the side of the road and into the trees. I walked with the shotgun at port arms, the .45 heavy in the right-hand pocket of my raincoat. Rosie had her chrome-plated .357 magnum gripped with both hands at an upward angle, just to the right of her cheek. Then the wind bent the trees again and blew a shower of wet leaves into a clearing, where we could see a tin-roofed cabin with a small gallery littered with cane poles, crab traps, and hand-throw fishnets, and a Coleman lantern hissing whitely on a wood table in the front room. In the back were an outhouse and a pirogue set up on sawhorses, and behind the outhouse was Murphy Doucet's blue Mercury.

A shadow moved across the window, then a man with his back to us sat down at the table with a coffee pot and a thick white mug in his hands. Even through the rusted screen I could see his stiff, gray military haircut and the deeply tanned skin of his neck whose tone and texture reminded me of a cured tobacco leaf.

We should have been home free. But then I saw the moonlight glint on the wire that was stretched across the two-lane track, three inches above the sand. I propped the shotgun against a tree, knelt down in the wet leaves, and ran my fingers along the wire until I touched two empty Spam cans that were tied with string to the wire, then two more, then two more after that. Through the underbrush, against the glow of moonlight in the clearing, I could make out a whole network of nylon fishing line strung between tree trunks, branches, roots, and underbrush, and festooned with tin cans, pie plates, and even a cow bell.

I was sweating heavily inside my raincoat now. I wiped the salt out of my eyes with my hand.

One lung-bursting rush across the clearing, I thought. *Clear the gallery in one step, bust the door out of the jamb, then park a big one in his brisket and it's over.*

But I knew better. I would sound like a traveling junkyard before I ever made the gallery, and if Alafair was still alive, in all probability he would be holding a pistol at her head.

'We have to wait until it's light or until he comes out,' I whispered to Rosie.

We knelt down in the trees, in the damp air, in the layered mat of black and yellow willow leaves, in the mosquitoes that rose in clouds from around our knees and perched on our faces and the backs of our hands and necks. I saw him get up once, walk to a shelf, then return to the table and read a magazine while he ate soda crackers out of a box. My thighs burned and a band of pain that I couldn't relieve began to spread slowly across my back. Rosie sat with her rump resting on her heels, wiping the mosquitoes off her forearms, her pink skirt hiked up on her thighs, her .357 propped in the fork of a tree. Her neck was shiny with sweat.

Then at shortly after four I could hear mullet jumping in the water, a 'gator flop his tail back in the marsh, a solitary mockingbird singing on the far side of the clearing. The air changed; a cool breeze lifted off the bay and blew the smell of fish and grass shrimp across the flats. Then a pale glow, like cobalt, like the watery green cast of summer light right before a rain, spread under the rim of banked clouds on the eastern horizon, and in minutes I could see the black shapes of jetties extending far out into the bay, small waves white-capping with the incoming tide, the rigging of a distant shrimp boat dropping below a swell.

Then Murphy Doucet wrote the rest of the script for us. He turned down the Coleman lantern, stretched his back, picked up something from the table, went out the front door, and walked behind our line of vision on the far side of the cabin toward the outhouse.

We moved out of the trees into the clearing, stepping over and under the network of can-rigged fishline, then divided in two directions at the corner of the gallery. I could smell a fecund salty odor like dead rats and stagnant water from under the cabin.

The rear windows were boarded with slats from packing boxes and I couldn't see inside or hear any movement. At the back of the cabin I paused, held the shotgun flat against my chest, and looked around the corner. Murphy Doucet was almost to the door of the outhouse, a pair of untied hunting boots flopping on his feet, a silvery object glinting in his right hand. Beyond the outhouse, by the marsh's edge, a bluetick dog was tied to a post surrounded by a ring of feces.

I stepped out from the lee of the cabin, threw the stock of the shotgun to my shoulder, sighted between Doucet's neck and shoulder blades, and felt the words already rising in my throat, like bubbles out of a boiling pot, *Surprise time, motherfucker! Throw it away! Do it now!* when he heard Rosie trip across a fishline that was tied to a cow bell on the gallery.

He looked once over his shoulder in her direction, then leaped behind the outhouse and ran toward the marsh on a long green strip of dry ground covered with buttercups. But five yards before he would have splashed into the willows and dead cypress and perhaps out of our field of fire, his untied boots sank into a pile of rotting medical waste that was matted with the scales of morning-glory vines. A wooden crutch that looked hand-hewn, with a single shaft that fitted into the armrest, sprang from under his boot and hung between his legs like a stick in bicycle spokes.

He turned around helplessly toward Rosie, falling backward off balance now, his blue eyes jittering frantically, his right arm extended toward her, as though it were not too late for her to recognize that his hand held a can of dog food rather than a weapon, just as she let off the first round of her .357 and caught him right in the sternum.

But it didn't stop there. She continued to fire with both hands gripped on the pistol, each soft-nosed slug knocking him backward with the force of a jackhammer, his shirt exploding with scarlet flowers on his bony chest, until the last round in the cylinder hit him in the rib cage and virtually eviscerated him on the water's edge. Then he simply sat down on top of his crumpled legs as though all the bones in his body had been surgically removed.

When she lowered the weapon toward the ground, her cheeks looked like they contained tiny red coals, and her eyes were frozen wide, as though she were staring into a howling storm, one that was filled with invisible forces and grinding winds only she could hear.

But I didn't have time to worry about the line that Rosie had crossed and the grief and knowledge that dark moment would bring with it.

Behind me I heard wood slats breaking loose from the back of the cabin, then I saw metal chair legs crash through the window, and Alafair climbing over the windowsill, her rump hanging in midair, her pink tennis shoes swinging above the damp earth.

I ran to her, grabbed her around the waist, and held her tightly against me. She buried her head under my chin and clamped her legs on my side like a frog, and I could feel the hard resilience of her muscles, the heat in her hands, the spastic breathing in her throat as though she had just burst from deep water into warm currents of salt air and a sunlit day loud with the sound of seabirds.

'Did he hurt you, Squanto?' I said, my heart dropping with my own question.

'I told him he'd better not. I told him what you'd do. I told him you'd rip his nuts out. I told him—'

'Where'd you get this language, Alf?'

A shudder went through her body, as though she had just removed her hand from a hot object, then her eyes squeezed shut and she began to cry.

'It's all right, Baby Squanto. We're going back home now,' I said.

I carried her on my hip back toward the truck, her arms around my neck, her face wet against my shirt.

I heard Rosie walking in the leaves behind me. She dumped the spent brass from the cylinder of her .357 into her palm, looked at them woodenly, then threw them tinkling into the trees.

'Get out of it, Rosie. That guy dealt the play a long time ago.'

'I couldn't stop. Why didn't I stop shooting? It was over and I kept shooting.'

'Because your mind shuts down in moments like that.'

'No, he paid for something that happened to me a long time ago, didn't he?'

'Let the Freudians play with that stuff. They seldom spend time on the firing line. It'll pass. Believe me, it always does.'

'Not hitting a man four times after he was going down. A man armed with a can of dog food.'

I looked at the spreading glow out on the bay and the gulls streaking over the tide's edge.

'He had a piece on him, Rosie. You just don't remember it right now,' I said, and handed Alafair to her.

I went back into the trees, found my raincoat, and carried it over my arm to the place where Murphy Doucet sat slumped among the buttercups, his torn side draining into the water. I took Lou Girard's .32 revolver from my raincoat pocket, wiped the worn bluing and the taped wooden grips on my handkerchief, fitted it into Doucet's hand, and closed his stiffened fingers around the trigger guard.

On his forearm was a set of teethmarks that looked like they had been put there by a child.

Next time out don't mess with Alafair Robicheaux or the Confederate army, Murph, I thought.

Then I picked up the crutch that had caught between his legs. The wood was old, weathered gray, the shaft shaved and beveled by a knife, the armrest tied with strips of rotted flannel.

The sun broke through the clouds overhead, and under the marsh's green canopy I could see hammered gold leaf hanging in the columns of spinning light, and gray shapes like those of long-dead sentinels, and like a man who has finally learned not to think reasonably in an unreasonable world, I offered the crutch at the air, at the shapes in the trees and at the sound of creatures moving through the water, saying *'Don't you want to take this with you, sir?'*

But if he answered, I did not hear it.

Epilogue

I'd like to tell you that the department and the local prosecutor's office finally made their case against Julie Balboni, that we cleaned our own house and sent him up the road to Angola in waist and leg chains for a twenty- or thirty-year jolt. But that's not what happened. How could it? In many ways Julie was us, just as his father had been when he provided the town its gambling machines and its rows of cribs on Railroad and Hopkins avenues. After Julie had left town on his own to become a major figure in the New Orleans mob, we had welcomed him back, winking our eyes at his presence and pretending he was not what or who he was.

I believe Julie and his father possessed a knowledge about us that we did not possess about ourselves. They knew we were for sale.

Julie finally went down, but in a way that no one expected – in a beef with the IRS. No, that's not quite right, either. That ubiquitous federal agency, the bane of the mob, was only a minor footnote in Julie's denouement. The seed of Julie's undoing was Julie. And I guess Julie in his grandiosity would not have had it any other way.

He should have done easy time, a three-year waltz on a federal honor farm in Florida, with no fences or gunbulls, with two-man rooms rather than cells, tennis courts, and weekend furloughs. But while in federal custody in New Orleans he spit in a bailiff's face, tore the lavatory out of his cell wall, and told an informant planted in his cell that he was putting a hit out on Cholo Manelli, who he believed had turned over his books to the IRS (which I heard later was true).

So they shipped Baby Feet up to a maximum-security unit at Fort Leavenworth, Kansas, a place that in the wintertime makes you believe that the earth has been poisoned with Agent Orange and the subzero winds blow from four directions simultaneously.

Most people are not aware of who comprises the population of a maximum-security lockup. They are usually not men like Baby Feet, who was intelligent and fairly sane for a sociopath. Instead, they are usually psychotic meltdowns, although they are not classified as such, otherwise they would be sent to mental institutions from which they would probably be released in a relatively short time. Perhaps they have the intelligence levels of battery-charged cabbages, housed in six-and-one-half-foot bodies that glow with rut. Often they're momma's boys who wear horn-rimmed glasses and comb their hair out on their frail shoulders like girls, murder whole families, and can never offer more in the way of explanation than a bemused and youthful smile.

But none was a match for Julie. He was a made guy, connected both on the inside and outside, a blockhouse behemoth whose whirling feet could make men bleed from every orifice in their bodies. He took over the dope trade, broke heads and groins in the shower, paid to have a rival shanked in the yard and a snitch drowned in a toilet bowl.

He also became a celebrity wolf among the punk population. They ironed his clothes, shampooed his hair, manicured his nails, and asked him in advance what kind of wigs and women's underthings they should wear when they came to his bunk. He encouraged jealousies among them and watched as an amused spectator while they schemed and fought among themselves for his affections and the reefer, pills, and prune-o he could provide to his favorites.

Perhaps he even found the adoration and submission that had always eluded him from the time he used to visit Mabel White's mulatto brothel in Crowley until he had Cherry LeBlanc murdered.

At least the psychologist at Fort Leavenworth who told me this story thought so. He said Julie actually seemed happy his first and final spring on the yard, hitting flyballs to his boys in the outfield, ripping the bat from deep in the box with the power and grace of a DiMaggio, the fine black hair on his shoulders glazed with sweat, his black silk shorts hanging on his hips with the confident male abandon of both a successful athlete and lover, snapping his wrists as he connected with the ball, lifting it higher into the blue sky than anyone at Leavenworth had ever done before, while all around him other cons touched themselves and nodded with approval.

Maybe he was still thinking about these things on the Sunday evening he came in from the diamond, showered, and went to the empty cell of his current lover to take a nap under a small rubber-bladed fan with the sheet over his head. Maybe in his dreams he was once again a movie producer on the edge of immense success, a small-town boy whose story would be recreated by biographers and become the stuff of legends in Hollywood, a beneficient but feared mogul in sunglasses and a two-thousand-dollar white tropical suit who strolled with elegance and grace through the bougainvillea and palm trees and the clink of champagne glasses at Beverly Hills lawn parties.

Or maybe, for just a moment, when a pain sharper than any he had ever thought possible entered his consciousness like a red shard of glass, he saw the face of his father contorted like a fist as the father held him at gunpoint and whipped the nozzle end of a garden hose across Julie's shivering back.

The Molotov cocktail thrown by a competitor for Julie's affections burst on the stone wall above the bunk where Julie was sleeping and covered his entire body with burning paraffin and gasoline. He erupted from the bunk, flailing at the air, the sheet dissolving in black holes against his skin. He ran blindly through the open cell door, wiping at his eyes and mouth, his disintegrating shape an enormous cone of flame now, and with one long bellowing cry he sprang over the rail of the tier and plunged like a meteor three stories to the cement floor below.

What happened to Twinky Hebert Lemoyne?

Nothing. Not externally. He's still out there, a member of a generation whose metamorphosis never quite takes place.

Sometimes I see his picture on the business page of the Lafayette newspaper. You can count on him to be at fund-raiser kick-off breakfasts for whatever charity is in fashion with the business community. In all probability he's even sincere. Once or twice I've run into him at a crab boil or fish fry in New Iberia. He doesn't do well, however, in a personal encounter with the past. His manners are of course gentlemanly, his pink skin and egg-shaped head and crinkling seersucker suit images that you associate with a thoughtful and genteel southern barrister but in the steady and trained avoidance that his eyes perform when you look into his face, you see another man, one whose sense of self-worth was so base that he would participate in a lynching because he had been made a cuckold by one of his own black employees.

No, that's not quite fair to him.

Perhaps, just like Julie Balboni, Twinky Hebert is us. He loathed his past so much that he could never acknowledge it, never expiate his sin, and never forgive himself, either. So, like Proteus rising from the sea and forever reshaping his form, Twinky Hebert Lemoyne made a contract of deceit with himself and consequently doomed himself to relive his past every day of his life.

At the crab boil in the park on Bayou Teche he inadvertently sat down at a wood table under the pavilion not three feet away from me, Bootsie, and Alafair. He had just started to crack the claws on a crab when he realized who sat across from him.

'What are *you* doing here?' he asked, his mouth hanging open.

'I live in New Iberia. I was invited to attend.'

'Are you trying to harass me?'

'I closed the file on the summer of 1957, Mr Lemoyne. Why don't you?'

There was a painful light, like a burning match, deep in his eyes. He tried to break open a crab claw with a pair of nutcrackers, then his hand slipped and sprayed juice on his shirt front.

'Tell a minister about it, tell a cop, get on a plane and tell somebody you never saw before,' I said. 'Just get rid of it once and for all and lose the Rotary Club doodah.'

But he was already walking rapidly toward the men's room, scrubbing at his palms with a paper towel, his change rattling in his pants' pockets, twisting his neck from side to side as though his tie and stiff collar were a rope against his skin.

We took our vacation that year in California and stayed with Elrod in his ranch home built on stilts high up on a cliff in Topanga Canyon, overlooking the Pacific Coast Highway and the ocean that was covered each morning with a thick bluish-white mist, inside which you could hear the waves crashing like avalanches into the beach.

For two weeks Alafair acted in a picture out at Tri-Star with Mikey Goldman and Elrod, and in the evenings we ate cherrystone clams at Gladstone's on the beach and took rides in Mikey Goldman's pontoon plane out to Catalina Island. As the late sun descended into the ocean, it seemed to trail ragged strips of black cloud with it, like a burning red planet settling into the Pacific's water green rim. When the entire coastline was awash in a pink light you could see almost every geological and floral characteristic of the American continent tumbling from the purple crests of the Santa Monica Mountains into the curling line of foam that slid up onto the beaches: dry hills of chaparral, mesquite and scrub oak, clumps of eucalyptus and bottlebrush trees, torrey and ponderosa pine growing between blue-tiled stucco houses, coral walls overgrown with bougainvillea, terraced hillside gardens filled with oleander, yucca plants, and trellises dripping with passion vine, and orange groves whose irrigation ditches looked like quicksilver in the sun's afterglow.

Then millions of lights came on in the canyons, along the freeways, and through the vast sweep of the Los Angeles basin, and it was almost as if you were looking down upon the end point of the American dream, a geographical poem into which all our highways eventually led, a city of illusion founded by conquistadors and missionaries and consigned to the care of angels, where far below the spinning propellers of our seaplane black kids along palm-tree-lined streets in Watts hunted each other with automatic weapons.

I thought in the morning mists that rolled up the canyon I might

273

once again see the noble and chivalric John Bell Hood. Just a glimpse, perhaps, a doff of his hat, the kindness of his smile, the beleaguered affection that always seemed to linger in his face. Then as the days passed and I began to let go of all the violent events of that summer, I had to accept the fact that the general, as Bootsie had said, was indeed only a hopeful figment of my fantasies, a metaphorical and mythic figure probably created as much by the pen of Thomas Mallory or Walter Scott as the LSD someone had put in my drink out at Spanish Lake.

Then two nights before we returned home, Alafair was sitting on the coral wall that rimmed Elrod's terrace, flipping the pages in one of the library books Bootsie had checked out on the War Between the States.

'What you doing in here, Dave?' she said.

'In what? What are you talking about, little guy?'

She continued to stare down at a page opened in her lap.

'You're in the picture. With that old man Poteet and I saw in the corn patch. The one with BO,' she said, and turned the book around so I could look at it.

In the photograph, posed in the stiff attitudes of nineteenth-century photography, were the general and seven of his aides and enlisted men.

'Standing in the back. The one without a gun. That's you, Dave,' she said. Then she stared up at me with a confused question mark in the middle of her face. 'Ain't it?'

'Don't say "ain't," little guy.'

'What are you doing in the picture?'

'That's not me, Alf. Those are Texas soldiers who fought alongside John Bell Hood. I bet they were a pretty good bunch,' I said, and rubbed the top of her head.

'How do you know they're from Texas? It doesn't say that here.'

'It's just a guess.'

She looked at the photograph again and back at me, and her face became more confused.

'Let's get Elrod and Bootsie and go down to the beach for some ice cream,' I said.

I slipped the book from her hand and closed it, picked her up on my hip, and walked through the canopy of purple trumpet vine toward the patio behind the house, where Bootsie and Elrod were clearing off the dishes from supper. Down the canyon, smoke from meat fires drifted through the cedar and mesquite trees, and if I squinted my eyes in the sun's setting, I could almost pretend that Spanish soldiers in silver chest armor and bladed helmets or a long-dead race of hunters were encamped on those hillsides. Or maybe even old compatriots in butternut brown wending their way in and out of history – gallant,

Arthurian, their canister-ripped colors unfurled in the roiling smoke, the fatal light in their faces a reminder that the contest is never quite over, the field never quite ours.

CADILLAC JUKEBOX

For Russ and Jayne Piazza

1

Aaron Crown should not have come back into our lives. After all, he had never really been one of us, anyway, had he? His family, shiftless timber people, had come from north Louisiana, and when they arrived in Iberia Parish, they brought their ways with them, occasionally stealing livestock along river bottoms, poaching deer, perhaps, some said, practicing incest.

I first saw Aaron Crown thirty-five years ago when, for a brief time, he tried to sell strawberries and rattlesnake watermelons out on the highway, out of the same truck he hauled cow manure in.

He seemed to walk sideways, like a crab, and wore bib overalls even in summertime and paid a dollar to have his head lathered and shaved in the barber shop every Saturday morning. His thick, hair-covered body gave off an odor like sour milk, and the barber would open the front and back doors and turn on the fans when Aaron was in the chair.

If there was a violent portent in his behavior, no one ever saw it. The Negroes who worked for him looked upon him indifferently, as a white man who was neither good nor bad, whose moods and elliptical peckerwood speech and peculiar green eyes were governed by thoughts and explanations known only to himself. To entertain the Negroes who hung around the shoeshine stand in front of the old Frederick Hotel on Saturday mornings, he'd scratch matches alight on his clenched teeth, let a pool of paraffin burn to a waxy scorch in the center of his palm, flip a knife into the toe of his work boot.

But no one who looked into Aaron Crown's eyes ever quite forgot them. They flared with a wary light for no reason, looked back at you with a reptilian, lidless hunger that made you feel a sense of sexual ill ease, regardless of your gender.

Some said he'd once been a member of the Ku Klux Klan, expelled from it for fighting inside a Baptist church, swinging a wood bench into the faces of his adversaries.

But that was the stuff of poor-white piney woods folklore, as remote from our French-Catholic community as tales of lynchings and church bombings in Mississippi.

How could we know that underneath a live oak tree hung with moss and spiderwebs of blue moonlight, Aaron Crown would sight down the barrel of a sporterized Mauser rifle, his body splayed out comfortably like an infantry marksman's, the leather sling wrapped tightly around his left forearm, his loins tingling against the earth, and drill a solitary round through a plate glass window into the head of the most famous NAACP leader in Louisiana?

It took twenty-eight years to nail him, to assemble a jury that belonged sufficiently to a younger generation that had no need to defend men like Aaron Crown.

Everyone had always been sure of his guilt. He had never denied it, had he? Besides, he had never been one of us.

It was early fall, an election year, and each morning after the sun rose out of the swamp and burned the fog away from the flooded cypress trees across the bayou from my bait shop and boat-rental business, the sky would harden to such a deep, heart-drenching blue that you felt you could reach up and fill your hand with it like bolls of stained cotton. The air was dry and cool, too, and the dust along the dirt road by the bayou seemed to rise into gold columns of smoke and light through the canopy of oaks overhead. So when I glanced up from sanding the planks on my dock on a Saturday morning and saw Buford LaRose and his wife, Karyn, jogging through the long tunnel of trees toward me, they seemed like part of a photograph in a health magazine, part of an idealized moment caught by a creative photographer in a depiction of what is called the New South, rather than an oddity far removed from the refurbished plantation home in which they lived twenty-five miles away.

I convinced myself they had not come to see me, that forcing them to stop their run out of reasons of politeness would be ungenerous on my part, and I set down my sanding machine and walked toward the bait shop.

'Hello!' I heard Buford call.

Your past comes back in different ways. In this case, it was in the form of Karyn La Rose, her platinum hair sweat-soaked and piled on her head, her running shorts and purple-and-gold Mike the Tiger T-shirt glued to her body like wet Kleenex.

'How y'all doin'?' I replied, my smile as stiff as ceramic.

'Aaron Crown called you yet?' Buford asked, resting one hand on the dock railing, pulling one ankle up toward his muscular thigh with the other.

'How'd you know?' I said.

'He's looking for soft-hearted guys to listen to his story.' Buford grinned, then winked with all the confidence of the eighty-yard passing quarterback he'd been at LSU twenty years earlier. He was still lean-stomached and narrow-waisted, his chest flat like a prizefighter's, his smooth, wide shoulders olive with tan, his curly brown hair bleached on the tips by the sun. He pulled his other ankle up behind him, squinting at me through the sweat in his eyebrows.

'Aaron's decided he's an innocent man,' he said. 'He's got a movie company listening to him. Starting to see the big picture?'

'He gets a dumb cop to plead his cause?' I said.

'I said "soft-hearted," ' he said, his face beaming now.

'Why don't you come see us more often, Dave?' Karyn asked.

'That sounds good,' I said, nodding, my eyes wandering out over the water.

She raised her chin, wiped the sweat off the back of her neck, looked at the sun with her eyelids closed and pursed her lips and breathed through them as though the air were cold. Then she opened her eyes again and smiled good-naturedly, leaning with both arms on the rail and stretching her legs one at a time.

'Y'all want to come in for something to drink?' I asked.

'Don't let this guy jerk you around, Dave,' Buford said.

'Why should I?'

'Why should he call you in the first place?'

'Who told you this?' I asked.

'His lawyer.'

'Sound like shaky legal ethics to me,' I said.

'Give me a break, Dave,' he replied. 'If Aaron Crown ever gets out of Angola, the first person he's going to kill is his lawyer. That's after he shoots the judge. How do we know all this? Aaron called up the judge, collect, mind you, and told him so.'

They said good-bye and resumed their jog, running side by side past the sprinklers spinning among the tree trunks in my front yard. I watched them grow smaller in the distance, all the while feeling that somehow something inappropriate, if not unseemly, had just occurred.

I got in my pickup truck and caught up with them a quarter mile down the road. They never broke stride.

'This bothers me, Buford,' I said out the window. 'You wrote a book about Aaron Crown. It might make you our next governor. Now you want to control access to the guy?'

'Bothers you, huh?' he said, his air-cushioned running shoes thudding rhythmically in the dirt.

'It's not an unreasonable attitude,' I said.

Karyn leaned her face past him and grinned at me. Her mouth was bright red, her brown eyes happy and charged with energy from her run.

'You'll be bothered a lot worse if you help these right-wing cretins take over Louisiana in November. See you around, buddy,' he said, then gave me the thumbs-up sign just before he and his wife poured it on and cut across a shady grove of pecan trees.

She called me that evening, not at the house but at the bait shop. Through the screen I could see the lighted gallery and windows in my house, across the dirt road, up the slope through the darkening trees.

'Are you upset with Buford?' she said.

'No.'

'He just doesn't want to see you used, that's all.'

'I appreciate his concern.'

'Should I have not been there?'

'I'm happy y'all came by.'

'Neither of us was married at the time, Dave. Why does seeing me make you uncomfortable?'

'This isn't turning into a good conversation,' I said.

'I'm not big on guilt. It's too bad you are,' she replied, and quietly hung up.

The price of a velvet black sky bursting with stars and too much champagne, a grassy levee blown with buttercups and a warm breeze off the water, I thought. Celibacy was not an easy virtue to take into the nocturnal hours.

But guilt over an impulsive erotic moment wasn't the problem. Karyn LaRose was a woman you kept out of your thoughts if you were a married man.

Aaron Crown was dressed in wash-faded denims that were too tight for him when he was escorted in leg and waist chains from the lockdown unit into the interview room.

He had to take mincing steps, and because both wrists were cuffed to the chain just below his rib cage he had the bent appearance of an apelike creature trussed with baling wire.

'I don't want to talk to Aaron like this. How about it, Cap?' I said to the gunbull, who had been shepherding Angola convicts under a double-barrel twelve gauge for fifty-five years.

The gunbull's eyes were narrow and valuative, like a man constantly measuring the potential of his adversaries, the corners webbed with wrinkles, his skin wizened and dark as a mulatto's, as if it had been smoked in a fire. He removed his briar pipe from his belt, stuck it in his

282

mouth, clicking it dryly against his molars. He never spoke while he unlocked the net of chains from Aaron Crown's body and let them collapse around his ankles like a useless garment. Instead, he simply pointed one rigid callus-sheathed index finger into Aaron's face, then unlocked the side door to a razor-wire enclosed dirt yard with a solitary weeping willow that had gone yellow with the season.

I sat on a weight lifter's bench while Aaron Crown squatted on his haunches against the fence and rolled a cigarette out of a small leather pouch that contained pipe tobacco. His fingernails were the thickness and mottled color of tortoiseshell. Gray hair grew out of his ears and nose; his shoulders and upper chest were braided with knots of veins and muscles. When he popped a lucifer match on his thumbnail and cupped it in the wind, he inhaled the sulfur and glue and smoke all in one breath.

'I ain't did it,' he said.

'You pleaded nolo contendere, partner.'

'The shithog got appointed my case done that. He said it was worked out.' He drew in on his hand-rolled cigarette, tapped the ashes off into the wind.

When I didn't reply, he said, 'They give me forty years. I was sixty-eight yestiday.'

'You should have pleaded out with the feds. You'd have gotten an easier bounce under a civil rights conviction,' I said.

'You go federal, you got to cell with colored men.' His eyes lifted into mine. 'They'll cut a man in his sleep. I seen it happen.'

In the distance I could see the levee along the Mississippi River and trees that were puffing with wind against a vermilion sky.

'Why you'd choose me to call?' I asked.

'You was the one gone after my little girl when she got lost in Henderson Swamp.'

'I see . . . I don't know what I can do, Aaron. That was your rifle they found at the murder scene, wasn't it? It had only one set of prints on it, too – yours.'

'It was stole, and it didn't have no *set* of prints on it. There was one thumbprint on the stock. Why would a white man kill a nigger in the middle of the night and leave his own gun for other people to find? Why would he wipe off the trigger and not the stock?'

'You thought you'd never be convicted in the state of Louisiana.'

He sucked on a tooth, ground out the ash of his cigarette on the tip of his work boot, field-stripped the paper and let it all blow away in the wind.

'I ain't did it,' he said.

'I can't help you.'

He raised himself to his feet, his knees popping, and walked toward the lockdown unit, the silver hair on his arms glowing like a monkey's against the sunset.

2

The flooded cypress and willow trees were gray-green smudges in the early morning mist at Henderson Swamp. My adopted daughter, Alafair, sat on the bow of the outboard as I swung it between two floating islands of hyacinths and gave it the gas into the bay. The air was moist and cool and smelled of schooled-up *sac-a-lait*, or crappie, and gas flares burning in the dampness. When Alafair turned her face into the wind, her long Indian-black hair whipped behind her in a rope. She was fourteen now, but looked older, and oftentimes grown men turned and stared at her when she walked by, before their own self-consciousness corrected them.

We traversed a long, flat bay filled with stumps and abandoned oil platforms, then Alafair pointed at a row of wood pilings that glistened blackly in the mist. I cut the engine and let the boat float forward on its wake while Alafair slipped the anchor, a one-foot chunk of railroad track, over the gunwale until it bit into the silt and the bow swung around against the rope. The water in the minnow bucket was cold and dancing with shiners when I dipped my hand in to bait our lines.

'Can you smell the *sac-a-lait*? There must be thousands in here,' she said.

'You bet.'

'This is the best place in the whole bay, isn't it?'

'I don't know of a better one,' I said, and handed her a sandwich after she had cast her bobber among the pilings.

It had been almost nine years since I had pulled her from the submerged and flooded wreckage of a plane that had been carrying Salvadoran war refugees. Sometimes in my sleep I would relive that moment when I found her struggling for breath inside the inverted cabin, her face turned upward like a guppy's into the wobbling and diminishing bubble of air above her head, her legs scissoring frantically above her mother's drowned form.

But time has its way with all of us, and today I didn't brood upon water as the conduit into the world of the dead. The spirits of villagers, their mouths wide with the concussion of airbursts, no longer whispered to me from under the brown currents of the Mekong, either, nor did the specter of my murdered wife Annie, who used to call me up long-distance from her home under the sea and speak to me through the rain.

Now water was simply a wide, alluvial flood plain in the Atchafalaya Basin of south Louisiana that smelled of humus and wood smoke, where mallards rose in squadrons above the willows and trailed in long black lines across a sun that was as yellow as egg yolk.

'You really went to see that man Aaron Crown at Angola, Dave?' Alafair asked.

'Sure did.'

'My teacher said he's a racist. He assassinated a black man in Baton Rouge.'

'Aaron Crown's an ignorant and physically ugly man. He's the kind of person people like to hate. I'm not sure he's a killer, though, Alf.'

'Why not?'

'I wish I knew.'

Which was not only an inadequate but a disturbing answer.

Why? Because Aaron Crown didn't fit the profile. If he was a racist, he didn't burn with it, as most of them did. He wasn't political, either, at least not to my knowledge. So what was the motivation, I asked myself. In homicide cases, it's almost always money, sex, or power. Which applied in the case of Aaron Crown?

'Whatcha thinking about, Dave?' Alafair asked.

'When I was a young cop in New Orleans, I was home on vacation and Aaron Crown came to the house and said his daughter was lost out here in a boat. Nobody would go after her because she was fourteen and had a reputation for running off and smoking dope and doing other kinds of things, you with me?'

She looked at her bobber floating between the pilings.

'So I found her. She wasn't lost, though. She was in a houseboat, right across the bay there, with a couple of men. I never told Aaron what she had been doing. But I think he knew.'

'You believe he's innocent?'

'Probably not. It's just one of those strange deals, Alf. The guy loved his daughter, which means he has emotions and affections like the rest of us. That's something we don't like to think about when we assign a person the role of assassin and community geek.'

She thought the word *geek* was funny and snorted through her nose.

It started to sprinkle, and we hung raincoats over our heads like cloistered monks and pulled *sac-a-lait* out of the pilings until midmorning, then layered them with crushed ice in the cooler and headed for home just as a squall churned out of the south like smoke twisting inside a bottle.

We gutted and half-mooned the fish at the gills and scaled them with spoons under the canvas tarp on the dock. Batist, the black man who worked for me, came out of the bait shop with an unlit cigar stuck in his jaw. He let the screen slam behind him. He was bald and wore bell-bottomed blue jeans and a white T-shirt that looked like rotted cheesecloth on his barrel chest.

'There's a guard from the prison farm inside,' he said.

'What's he want?' I said.

'I ain't axed. Whatever it is, it don't have nothing to do with spending money. Dave, we got to have these kind in our shop?'

Oh boy, I thought.

I went inside and saw the old-time gunbull from the lockdown unit I had visited at Angola just yesterday. He was seated at a back table by the lunch meat cooler, his back stiff, his profile carved out of teak. He wore a fresh khaki shirt and trousers, a hand-tooled belt, a white straw hat slanted over his forehead. His walking cane, whose point was sheathed in a six-inch steel tube, the kind road gang hacks used to carry, was hooked by the handle over the back of his chair. He had purchased a fifty-cent can of soda to drink with the brown paper bag of ginger snaps he had brought with him.

'How's it goin', Cap?' I said.

'Need your opinion on something,' he replied. His accent was north Louisiana hill country, the vowels phlegmy and round and deep in the throat, like speech lifted out of the nineteenth century.

His hands, which were dotted with liver spots, shook slightly with palsy. His career reached back into an era when Angola convicts were beaten with the black Betty, stretched out on anthills, locked down in sweatboxes on Camp A, sometimes even murdered by guards on a whim and buried in the Mississippi levee. In the years I had known him I had never seen him smile or heard him mention any form of personal life outside the penitentiary.

'Some movie people is offered me five thousand dollars for a interview about Crown. What do you reckon I ought to do?' he said.

'Take it. What's the harm?'

He bit the edge off a ginger snap.

'I got the feeling they want me to say he don't belong up there on the farm, that maybe the wrong man's in prison.'

'I see.'

'Something's wrong, ain't it?'

'Sir?'

'White man kills a black man down South, them Hollywood people don't come looking to get the white man off.'

'I don't have an answer for you, Cap. Just tell them what you think and forget it.' I looked at the electric clock on the wall above the counter.

'What I think is the sonofabitch's about half-human.' My eyes met his. 'He's got a stink on him don't wash off. If he ain't killed the NAACP nigger, he done it to somebody else.'

He chewed a ginger snap dryly in his jaw, then swallowed it with a small sip of soda, the leathery skin of his face cobwebbed with lines in the gloom.

Word travels fast among the denizens of the nether regions.

On Tuesday morning Helen Soileau came into my office at the Iberia Parish Sheriff's Department and said we had to pick up and hold a New Orleans hoodlum named Mingo Bloomberg, who was wanted as a material witness in the killing of a police officer in the French Quarter.

'You know him?' she asked. She wore a starched white shirt and blue slacks and her badge on her gunbelt. She was a blonde, muscular woman whose posture and bold stare always seemed to anticipate, even relish, challenge or insult.

'He's a button man for the Giacano family,' I said.

'We don't have that.'

'Bad communications with NOPD, then. Mingo's specialty is disappearing his victims. He's big on fish chum.'

'That's terrific. Expidee Chatlin is baby-sitting him for us.'

We checked out a cruiser and drove into the south part of the parish on back roads that were lined with sugarcane wagons on their way to the mill. Then we followed a levee through a partially cleared field to a tin-roofed fish camp set back in a grove of persimmon and pecan trees. A cruiser was parked in front of the screened-in gallery, the front doors opened, the radio turned off.

Expidee Chatlin had spent most of his law-enforcement career as a crossing guard or escorting drunks from the jail to guilty-court. He had narrow shoulders and wide hips, a tube of fat around his waist, and a thin mustache that looked like grease pencil. He and another uniformed deputy were eating sandwiches with Mingo Bloomberg at a plank table on the gallery.

'What do you think you're doing, Expidee?' Helen asked.

'Waiting on y'all. What's it look like?' he replied.

'How's it hanging, Robicheaux?' Mingo Bloomberg said.

'No haps, Mingo.'

He emptied his beer can and put an unlit cigarette in his mouth. He was a handsome man and wore beltless gray slacks and loafers and a long-sleeve shirt printed with flowers. His hair was copper-colored and combed straight back on his scalp, his eyes ice blue, as invasive as a dirty finger when they locked on yours.

He opened his lighter and began to flick the flint dryly, as though we were not there.

'Get out of that chair and lean against the wall,' Helen said.

He lowered the lighter, his mouth screwed into a smile around his cigarette. She pulled the cigarette out of his mouth, threw it over her shoulder, and aimed her nine millimeter into the middle of his face.

'Say something wise, you fuck. Go ahead. I want you to,' she said.

I pulled him to his feet, pushed him against the wall, and kicked his ankles apart. When I shook him down I tapped a hard, square object in his left pocket. I removed a .25 caliber automatic, dropped the magazine, pulled the slide back on the empty chamber, then tossed the pistol into Expidee's lap.

'Nobody told me. I thought the guy was suppose to be a witness or something,' he said.

Helen cuffed Mingo's wrists behind him and shoved him toward the screen door.

'Hey, Robicheaux, you and the lady take your grits off the stove,' he said.

'It's up to you, Mingo,' I said.

We were out front now, under a gray sky, in the wind, in leaves that toppled out of the trees on the edge of the clearing. Mingo rolled his eyes. 'Up to me? You ought to put a cash register on top of y'all's cruiser,' he said.

'You want to explain that?' I said.

He looked at Helen, then back at me.

'Give us a minute,' I said to her.

I walked him to the far side of our cruiser, opened the back door and sat him down behind the wire-mesh screen. I leaned one arm on the roof and looked down into his face. An oiled, coppery strand of hair fell down across his eyes.

'You did the right thing with this guy Crown. You do the right thing, you get taken care of. Something wrong with that?' he said.

'Yeah. I'm not getting taken care of.'

'Then that's your fucking problem.'

'When you get back to the Big Sleazy, stay there, Mingo,' I said, and closed the car door.

'I got a permit for the piece you took off me. I want it back,' he said through the open window.

I waited for Helen to get behind the wheel, drumming my fingers on the cruiser's roof, trying to conceal the disjointed expression in my face.

If you seriously commit yourself to alcohol, I mean full-bore, the way you take up a new religion, and join that great host of revelers who sing and lock arms as they bid farewell to all innocence in their lives, you quickly learn the rules of behavior in this exclusive fellowship whose dues are the most expensive in the world. You drink down. That means you cannot drink in well-lighted places with ordinary people because the psychological insanity in your face makes you a pariah among them. So you find other drunks whose condition is as bad as your own, or preferably even worse.

But time passes and you run out of geography and people who are in some cosmetic way less than yourself and bars where the only admission fee is the price of a 6 A.M. short-dog.

That's when you come to places like Sabelle Crown's at the Underpass in Lafayette.

The Underpass area had once been home to a dingy brick hotel and row of low-rent bars run by a notorious family of Syrian criminals. Now the old bars and brick hotel had been bulldozed into rubble, and all that remained of the city's last skidrow refuge was Sabelle's, a dark, two-story clapboard building that loomed above the Underpass like a solitary tooth.

It had no mirrors, and the only light inside came from the jukebox and the beer signs over the bar. It was a place where the paper Christmas decorations stayed up year-round and you never had to see your reflection or make an unfavorable comparison between yourself and others. Not unless you counted Sabelle, who had been a twenty-dollar whore in New Orleans before she disappeared up north for several years. She was middle-aged now, with flecks of gray in her auburn hair, but she looked good in her blue jeans and V-necked beige sweater, and her face retained a kind of hard beauty that gave fantasies to men who drank late and still believed the darkness of a bar could resurrect opportunities from their youth.

She opened a bottle of 7-Up and set it in front of me with a glass of ice.

'You doin' all right, Streak?' she said.

'Not bad. How about you, Sabelle?'

'I hope you're not here for anything stronger than 7-Up.'

I smiled and didn't reply. The surface of the bar stuck to my wrists. 'Why would a New Orleans gumball named Mingo Bloomberg have an interest in your father?' I said.

'You got me.'

'I went over everything I could find on Aaron's case this afternoon. I think he could have beat it if he'd had a good lawyer,' I said.

She studied my face curiously. The beer sign on the wall made tiny red lights, like sparks, in her hair.

'The big problem was Aaron told some other people he did it,' I said.

She put out her cigarette in the ashtray, then set a shot glass and a bottle of cream sherry by my elbow and walked down the duckboards and around the end of the bar and sat down next to me, her legs hooked in the stool's rungs.

'You still married?' she said.

'Sure.'

She didn't finish her thought. She poured sherry into her shot glass and drank it. 'Daddy went to the third grade. He hauled manure for a living. Rich people on East Main made him go around to their back doors.'

I continued to look into her face.

'Look, when this black civil rights guy got killed with Daddy's rifle, he started making up stories. People talked about him. He got to be a big man for a while,' she said.

'He lied about a murder?'

'How'd you like to be known as white trash in a town like New Iberia?'

'Big trade-off,' I said.

'What isn't?'

She gestured to the bartender, pointed to a shoebox under the cash register. He handed it to her and walked away. She lifted off the top.

'You were in the army. See what you recognize in there. I don't know one medal from another,' she said.

It was heavy and filled with watches, rings, pocket-knives, and military decorations. Some of the latter were Purple Hearts; at least two were Silver Stars. It also contained a .32 revolver with electrician's tape wrapped on the grips.

'If the medal's got a felt-lined box, I give a three-drink credit,' she said.

'Thanks for your time,' I said.

'You want to find out about my father, talk to Buford LaRose. His book sent Daddy to prison.'

'I might do that.'

'When you see Buford, tell him—' But she shook her head and didn't finish. She pursed her lips slightly and kissed the air.

I went home for lunch the next day, and as I came around the curve on the bayou I saw Karyn LaRose's blue Mazda convertible back out of my drive and come toward me on the dirt road. She stopped abreast of me and removed her sunglasses. Her teeth were white when she smiled, her tanned skin and platinum hair dappled with sunlight that fell through the oak trees.

'What's up, Karyn?'

'I thought this would be a grand time to have y'all out.'

'I beg your pardon?'

'Oh, stop all this silliness, Dave.'

'Listen, Karyn—'

'See you, kiddo,' she said, shifted into first, and disappeared in my rearview mirror, her hair whipping in the wind.

I pulled into our dirt drive and parked by the side of the house, which had been built out of notched and pegged cypress during the Depression by my father, a huge, grinning, hard-drinking Cajun who was killed on the salt in an oil well blowout. Over the years the tin roof on the gallery had turned purple with rust and the wood planks in the walls had darkened and hardened with rain and dust storms and smoke from stubble fires. My wife, Bootsie, and I had hung baskets of impatiens from the gallery, put flower boxes in the windows, and planted the beds with roses, hibiscus, and hydrangeas, but in the almost year-round shade of the live oaks and pecan trees, the house had a dark quality that seemed straight out of the year 1930, as though my father still held claim to it.

Bootsie had fixed ham and onion sandwiches and iced tea and potato salad for lunch and we set the kitchen table together and sat down to eat. I kept waiting for her to mention Karyn's visit. But she didn't.

'I saw Karyn LaRose out on the road,' I said.

'Oh, yes, I forgot. Tomorrow evening, she wants us to come to a dinner and lawn party.'

'What did you tell her?'

'I didn't think we had anything planned. But I said I'd ask you.' She had stopped eating. I felt her eyes on my face. 'You don't want to go?'

'Not really.'

'Do you have a reason? Or do we just tell people to drop dead arbitrarily?'

'Buford's too slick for me.'

'He's a therapist and a university professor. Maybe the state will finally have a governor with more than two brain cells.'

'Fine, let's go. It's not a problem,' I said.

'Dave . . .'

'I'm looking forward to it.'

Finally her exasperation gave way to a smile, then to a laugh.

'You're too much, Streak,' she said.

I wiped at my mouth with my napkin, then walked around behind her chair, put my arms on her shoulders, and kissed her hair. It was the color of dark honey and she brushed it in thick swirls on her head, and it always smelled like strawberry shampoo. I kissed her along the cheek and touched her breasts.

'You doin' anything?' I said.

'You have to go back to work.'

'The perps will understand.'

She reached behind the chair and fitted her hand around the back of my thigh.

The curtains in the bedroom, which were white and gauzy and printed with tiny flowers, puffed and twisted in the wind that blew through the trees in the yard. When Bootsie undressed, her body seemed sculpted, glowing with light against the window. She had the most beautiful complexion of any woman I ever knew; when she made love it flushed with heat, as though she had a fever, and took on the hue of a new rose petal. I kissed her breasts and took her nipples in my mouth and traced my fingers down the flatness of her stomach, then I felt her reach down and take me in her palm.

When I entered her she hooked her legs in mine and laced the fingers of one hand in my hair and placed the other hard in the small of my back. I could feel her breath against the side of my face, the perspiration on her stomach and inside her thighs, then her tongue on my neck, the wetness of her mouth near my ear. I wanted to hold it, to give more satisfaction than I received, but that terrible moment of male pleasure and solitary indulgence had its way.

'Boots—' I said hoarsely.

'It's all right, Dave. Go ahead,' she whispered.

She ran both palms down my lower back and pushed me deeper inside, then something broke like a dam and melted in my loins and I closed my eyes and saw a sailfish rise from a cresting wave, its mouth torn with a hook, its skin blue and hard, its gills strung with pink foam. Then it disappeared into the wave again, and the groundswells were suddenly flat and empty, dented with rain, sliding across the fire coral down below.

It should have been a perfect afternoon. But on my way out Bootsie asked, almost as an afterthought, 'Was there any other reason you didn't want to go to the LaRoses'?'

'No, of course not.'

I tried to avert my eyes, but it was too late. I saw the recognition in her face, like a sharp and unexpected slap.

'It was a long time ago, Boots. Before we were married.'

She nodded, her thoughts concealed. Then she said, her voice flat, 'We're all modern people these days. Like you say, Streak, no problem.'

She walked down to the pond at the back of our property by herself, with a bag of bread crusts, to feed the ducks.

3

At sunrise the next day, while I was helping Batist open up the bait shop before I went to work, the old-time gunbull called me long-distance from Angola.

'You remember I told you about them movie people come see me? There's one ain't gonna be around no more,' he said.

'What happened, Cap?'

'My nephew's a uniform at NOPD in the First District. They thought it was just a white man interested in the wrong piece of jelly roll. That's till they found the camera,' he said.

After I hung up the phone I filled minnow buckets for two fishermen, put a rental outboard in the water, and pulled the tarp on guy wires over the spool tables on the dock in case it rained. Batist was sprinkling hickory chips on the coals in the barbecue pit, which we had fashioned from a split oil drum to cook chickens and links of sausage for our midday customers.

'That was that old man from up at the prison farm?' he asked.

'I'm afraid so.'

'I ain't going to say it but once, no. It don't matter what that kind of man bring into your life, it ain't no good.'

'I'm a police officer, podna. I can't always be selective about the people I talk to.'

He cut his head and walked away.

I left a message for the nephew at NOPD and drove to the office just as it started to mist. He returned my call two hours later, then turned over the telephone to a Homicide detective. This is how I've reconstructed the story that was told to me.

Vice had identified the hooker as Brandy Grissum, a black twenty-five-year-old heroin addict who had done a one-bit in the St John the Baptist jail for sale and possession.

She worked with three or four pimps and Murphy artists out of the

Quarter. The pimps were there for the long-term regular trade. The Murphy artists took down the tourists, particularly those who were drunk, married, respectable, in town on conventions, scared of cops and their employers.

It was an easy scam. Brandy would walk into a bar, well dressed, perhaps wearing a suit, sit at the end of the counter, or by herself in a booth, glance once into the john's face, her eyes shy, her hands folded demurely in front of her, then wait quietly while her partner cut the deal.

This is the shuck: 'My lady over there ain't a reg'lar, know what I'm sayin'? Kind of like a schoolgirl just out on the town.' Here he smiles. 'She need somebody take her 'round the world, know what I'm sayin'? I need sixty dollars to cover the room, we'll all walk down to it, I ain't goin' nowhere on you. Then you want to give her a present or something, that's between y'all.'

The difference in this scenario this time was the john had his own room as well as agenda.

His name was Dwayne Parsons, an Academy Award nominee and two-time Emmy winner for his documentary scripts. But Dwayne Parsons had another creative passion, too, one that was unknown to the hooker and the Murphy artist and a second black man who was about to appear soon – a video camera set up on a tripod in his closet, the lens pointed through a crack in the door at the waterbed in his leased efficiency apartment a block off Bourbon.

Parsons and the woman were undressed, on top of black satin sheets, when the hard, insistent knock came at the door. The man's head jerked up from the pillow, his face at first startled, then simply disconcerted and annoyed.

'They'll go away,' he said.

He tried to hold her arms, hold her in place on top of him, but she slid her body off his.

'It's my boyfriend. He don't let me alone. He's gonna break down the do',' she said. She began to gather her clothes in front of her breasts and stomach.

'Hey, I look like a total schmuck to you?' Parsons said. 'Don't open that door . . . Did you hear me . . . Listen, you fucking nigger, you're not hustling me.'

She slid back the deadbolt on the door, and suddenly the back and conked and side-shaved head of a gargantuan black man were in the lens. Whoever he was, he was not the man Brandy Grissom had expected. She swallowed as though she had a razor blade in her throat.

But Dwayne Parsons was still not with the script.

'You want to rob me, motherfucker, just take the money off the dresser. You get the gun at the Screen Actors Guild?' he said.

The black man with the gun did not speak. But the terror in the woman's face left no doubt about the decision she saw taking place in his.

'I ain't seen you befo', bitch. You trying to work independent?' he said.

'No . . . I mean yes, I don't know nobody here. I ain't from New Orleans.' She pressed her clothes against her breasts and genitalia. Her mouth was trembling.

One block away, a brass street band was playing on Bourbon. The man thought some more, then jerked the barrel of his automatic toward the door. She slipped her skirt and blouse on, wadded up her under-garments and shoes and purse and almost flew out the door.

Dwayne Parson's face had drained. He started to get up from the bed.

'No, no, my man,' the black man said, approaching him, blocking off the camera's view of Parson's face. 'Hey, it comes to everybody. You got it on with the sister. It could be worse. I said don't move, man. It's all gonna come out the same way. They ain't no need for suffering.'

He picked up a pillow, pressed it down in front of him, his upper arm swelling to the diameter and hardness of a fireplug while Dwayne Parson's body flopped like a fish's. The man with the gun stepped back quickly and fired two shots into the pillow – *pop, pop* – and then went past the camera's lens, one grizzled Cro-Magnon jaw and gold tooth flashing by like a shark's profile in a zoo tank.

In the distance the street band thundered out 'Fire House Blues.' Dwayne Parson's body, the head still covered by the pillow, looked like a broken white worm in the middle of the sheet.

The LaRose plantation was far out in the parish, almost to St Martinville. The main house had been built in 1857 and was the dusty color of oyster shells, its wide, columned front porch scrolled by live oak trees that grew to the third floor. A row of shacks in back that had once been slaves quarters was now stacked with baled hay, and the old brick smithy had been converted into a riding stable, the arched windows sealed by the original iron shutters, which leaked orange rust as though from a wound.

Bootsie and I drove past the LaRose company store, with its oxidized, cracked front windows and tin-roofed gallery, where barrels of pecans sat by the double screen doors through which thousands of indebted tenants had passed until the civil rights era of the 1960s brought an end to five-dollar-a-day farm labor; then we turned into a white-fenced driveway that led to the rear of the home and the lawn party that was already in progress against a backdrop of live oaks and Spanish moss and an autumnal rose-stippled sky that seemed to reassure us all that the Indian summer of our lives would never end.

While the buffet was being laid out on a row of picnic tables, Buford organized a touch football game and prevailed even upon the most reluctant guests to put down their drinks and join one team or another. Some were from the university in Lafayette but most were people well known in the deceptively lighthearted and carnival-like atmosphere of Louisiana politics. Unlike their counterparts from the piney woods parishes to the north, they were bright, educated, openly hedonistic, always convivial, more concerned about violations of protocol than ideology.

They were fun to be with; they were giddy with alcohol and the exertion of the game, their laughter tinkling through the trees each time the ball was snapped and there was a thumping of feet across the sod and a loud pat of hands on the rump.

Then a white-jacketed black man dinged a metal triangle and everyone filed happily back toward the serving tables.

'Run out, Dave! Let me throw you a serious one!' Buford hollered, the football poised in his palm. He wore tennis shoes, pleated white slacks, the arms of his plum-colored sweater tied around his neck.

'That's enough for me,' I said.

'Don't give me that "old man" act,' he said and cocked his arm to fire a bullet, then smiled and lofted an easy, arching pass that dropped into my hands as though he had plopped it into a basket.

He caught up to me and put his hand on my shoulder.

'Wow, you feel like a bag of rocks. How much iron do you pump?' he said.

'Just enough to keep from falling apart.'

He slipped the football out of my hands, flipped it toward the stable. He watched it bounce and roll away in the dusk, as though he were looking at an unformed thought in the center of his mind.

'Dave, I think we're going to win next month,' he said.

'That's good.'

'You think you could live in Baton Rouge?'

'I've never thought about it.'

Someone turned on the Japanese lanterns in the trees. The air smelled of pecan husks and smoke from a barbecue pit dug in the earth. Buford paused.

'How'd you like to be head of the state police?' he asked.

'I was never much of an administrator, Buford.'

'I had a feeling you'd say something like that.'

'Oh?'

'Dave, why do you think we've always had the worst state government

298

in the union? It's because good people don't want to serve in it. Is the irony lost on you?'

'I appreciate the offer.'

'You want to think it over?'

'Sure, why not?'

'That's the way,' he said, and then was gone among his other guests, his handsome face glowing with the perfection of the evening and the portent it seemed to represent.

Karyn walked among the tree trunks toward me, a paper plate filled with roast duck and venison and dirty rice in one hand, a Corona bottle and cone-shaped glass with a lime slice inserted on the rim gripped awkwardly in the other. My eyes searched the crowd for Bootsie.

'I took the liberty,' Karyn said, and set the plate and glass and beer bottle down on a table for me.

'Thank you. Where'd Boots go?'

'I think she's in the house.'

She sat backward on the plank bench, her legs crossed. She had tied her hair up with a red bandanna and had tucked her embroidered denim shirt tightly into her blue jeans. Her face was warm, still flushed from the touch football game. I moved the Corona bottle and glass toward her.

'You don't drink at all anymore?' she said.

'Nope.'

'You want a Coke?'

'I'm fine, Karyn.'

'Did Buford talk to you about the state police job?'

'He sure did.'

'Gee, Dave, you're a regular blabbermouth, aren't you?'

I took a bite of the dressing, then rolled a strip of duck meat inside a piece of French bread and ate it.

Her eyes dilated. 'Did he offend you?' she said.

'Here's the lay of the land, Karyn. A hit man for the New Orleans mob, a genuine sociopath by the name of Mingo Bloomberg, told me I did the right thing by not getting involved with Aaron Crown. He said I'd get taken care of. Now I'm offered a job.'

'I don't believe you.'

'Believe what?'

'*You.* Your fucking presumption and self-righteousness.'

'What I told you is what happened. You can make of it what you want.'

She walked away through the shadows, across the leaves and molded pecan husks to where her husband was talking to a group of people. I saw them move off together, her hands gesturing while she spoke, then his face turned toward me.

A moment later he was standing next to me, his wrists hanging loosely at his sides.

'I'm at a loss, Dave. I have a hard time believing what you told Karyn,' he said.

I lay my fork in my plate, wadded up my paper napkin and dropped it on the table.

'Maybe I'd better go,' I said.

'You've seriously upset her. I don't think it's enough just to say you'll go.'

'Then I apologize.'

'I know about your and Karyn's history. Is that the cause of our problem here? Because I don't bear a resentment about it.'

I could feel a heat source inside me, like someone cracking open the door on a woodstove.

'Listen, partner, a guy like Mingo Bloomberg isn't an abstraction. Neither is a documentary screenwriter who just got whacked in the Quarter,' I said.

His expression was bemused, almost doleful, as though he were looking down at an impaired person.

'Good night to you, Dave. I believe you mean no harm,' he said, and walked back among his guests.

I stared at the red sun above the sugarcane fields, my face burning with embarrassment.

4

It was raining hard and the traffic was heavy in New Orleans when I parked off St Charles and ran for the colonnade in front of the Pearl. The window was steamed from the warmth inside, but I could see Clete Purcel at the counter, a basket of breadsticks and a whiskey glass and a schooner of beer in front of him, reading the front page of the *Times-Picayune.*

'Hey, big mon,' he said, folding his paper, grinning broadly when I came through the door. His face was round and Irish, scarred across the nose and through one eyebrow. His seersucker suit and blue porkpie hat looked absurd on his massive body. Under his coat I could see his nylon shoulder holster and blue-black .38 revolver. 'Mitch, give Dave a dozen,' he said to the waiter behind the counter, then turned back to me. 'Hang on a second.' He knocked back the whiskey glass and chased it with beer, blew out his breath, and widened his eyes. He took off his hat and mopped his forehead on his coat sleeve.

'You must have had a rocky morning,' I said.

'I helped repossess a car because the guy didn't pay the vig on his bond. His wife went nuts, said he wouldn't be able to get to work, his kids were crying in the front yard. It really gives you a sense of purpose. Tonight I got to pick up a skip in the Iberville Project. I've got another one hiding out in the Desire. You want to hear some more?'

The waiter set a round, metal tray of raw oysters in front of me. The shells were cold and slick with ice. I squeezed a lemon on each oyster and dotted it with Tabasco. Outside, the green-painted iron streetcar clanged on its tracks around the corner of Canal and headed up the avenue toward Lee Circle.

'Anyway, run all this Mingo Bloomberg stuff by me again,' Clete said.

I told him the story from the beginning. At least most of it.

'What stake would Bloomberg have in a guy like Aaron Crown?' I said.

He scratched his cheek with four fingers. 'I don't get it, either.

301

Mingo's a made guy. He's been mobbed-up since he went in the reformatory. The greaseballs don't have an interest in peckerwoods, and they think the blacks are cannibals. I don't know, Streak.'

'What's your take on the murdered scriptwriter?'

'Maybe wrong place, wrong time.'

'Why'd the shooter let the girl slide?' I said.

'Maybe he didn't want to snuff a sister.'

'Come on, Clete.'

'He knew she couldn't turn tricks in the Quarter without permission of the Giacano family. Which means she's producing a weekly minimum for guys you don't mess with.'

'Which means the guy's a pro,' I said.

He raised his eyebrows and lit a cigarette. 'That might be, noble mon, but it all sounds like a pile of shit you don't need,' he said. When I didn't answer, he said, 'So why are you putting your hand in it?'

'I don't like being the subject of Mingo Bloomberg's conversation.'

His green eyes wandered over my face.

'Buford LaRose made you mad by offering you a job?' he asked.

'I didn't say that.'

'I get the feeling there's something you're not telling me. What was that about his wife?' His eyes continued to search my face, a grin tugging at the corner of his mouth.

'Will you stop that?'

'I'm getting strange signals here, big mon. Are we talking about memories of past boom-boom?'

I put an oyster in my mouth and tried to keep my face empty. But it was no use. Even his worst detractors admitted that Clete Purcel was one of the best investigative cops NOPD ever had, until his career went sour with pills and booze and he had to flee to Central America on a homicide warrant.

'So now she's trying to work your crank?' he said.

'Do you have to put it that way? . . . Yeah, okay, maybe she is.'

'What for? . . . Did you know your hair's sweating?'

'It's the Tabasco. Clete, would you ease up, please?'

'Look, Dave, this is the basic lesson here – don't get mixed up with rich people. One way or another, they'll hurt you. The same goes for this civil rights stuff. It's a dead issue, leave it alone.'

'Do you want to go out and talk to Jimmy Ray Dixon or not?' I said.

'You've never met him?'

'No.'

'Jimmy Ray is a special kind of guy. You meet him once and you never quite forget the experience.'

I waited for him to finish but he didn't.

'What do I know?' he said, flipped his breadstick into the straw basket, and began putting on his raincoat. 'There's nothing wrong with the guy a tube of roach paste couldn't cure.'

We drove through the Garden District, past Tulane and Loyola universities and Audubon Park and rows of columned antebellum homes whose yards were filled with trees and flowers. The mist swirled out of the canopy of oak limbs above St Charles, and the neon tubing scrolled on corner restaurants and the empty outdoor cafes looked like colored smoke in the rain.

'Was he in Vietnam?' I asked.

'Yeah. So were you and I. You ever see his sheet?' Clete said.

I shook my head.

'He was a pimp in Chicago. He went down for assault and battery and carrying a concealed weapon. He even brags on it. Now you hear him talking on the radio about how he got reborn. The guy's a shithead, Dave.'

Jimmy Ray Dixon owned a shopping center, named for his assassinated brother, out by Chalmette. He also owned apartment buildings, a nightclub in the Quarter, and a five-bedroom suburban home. But he did business in a small unpainted 1890s cottage hung with flower baskets in the Carrollton district, down by the Mississippi levee, at the end of St Charles where the streetcar turned around. It was a neighborhood of palm trees and green neutral grounds, small restaurants, university students, art galleries and bookstores. It was a part of New Orleans unmarked by spray cans and broken glass in the gutters. In five minutes you had the sense Jimmy Ray had chosen the role of the thumb in your eye.

'You're here to ask me about the cracker that killed my brother? You're kidding, right?'

He chewed and snapped his gum. He wore a long-sleeve blue-striped shirt, which hid the apparatus that attached the metal hook to the stump of his left wrist. His teeth were gold-filled, his head mahogany-colored, round and light-reflective as a waxed bowling ball. He never invited us to sit down, and seemed to make a point of swiveling his chair around to talk to his employees, all of whom were black, in the middle of a question.

'Some people think he might be an innocent man,' I said.

'You one of them?' He grinned.

'Your humor's lost on me, sir.'

'It took almost thirty years to put him in Angola. He should have got the needle. Now the white folks is worried about injustice.'

'A kid in my platoon waited two days at a stream crossing to take out

303

a VC who killed his friend. He used a blooker to do it. Splattered him all over the trees,' I said.

'Something I ain't picking up on?'

'You have to dedicate yourself to hating somebody before you can lay in wait for him. I just never made Aaron Crown for that kind of guy,' I said.

'Let me tell you what I think of Vietnam and memory lane, Jack. I got this' – he tapped his hook on his desk blotter – 'clearing toe-poppers from a rice paddy six klicks out of Pinkville. You want to tell war stories, the DAV's downtown. You want to spring that cracker, that's your bidness. Just don't come around here to do it. You with me on this?'

Clete looked at me, then lit a cigarette.

'Hey, don't smoke in here, man,' Jimmy Ray said.

'*Adios,*' Clete said to me and went out the door and closed it behind him.

'Have any of these documentary movie people been to see you?' I asked.

'Yeah, I told them the right man's in jail. I told them that was his rifle lying out under the tree. I told them Crown was in the KKK. They turned the camera off while I was still talking.' He glanced at the dial on his watch, which was turned around on the bottom of his wrist. 'I don't mean you no rudeness, but I got a bidness to run.'

'Thanks for your help.'

'I ain't give you no help. Hey, man, me and my brother Ely wasn't nothing alike. He believed in y'all. Thought a great day was coming. You know what make us all equal?' He pulled his wallet out of his back pocket, splayed it open with his thumb, and picked a fifty-dollar bill out of it with his metal hook. 'Right here, man,' he said, wagging the bill on the desk blotter.

Late the next day, after we ate supper, I helped Bootsie wash and put away the dishes. The sun had burned into a red ember inside a bank of maroon-colored clouds above the treeline that bordered my neighbor's cane field, and through the screen I could smell rain and ozone in the south. Alafair called from the bait shop, where she was helping Batist close up.

'Dave, there's a man in a boat who keeps coming back by the dock,' she said.

'What's he doing?'

'It's like he's trying to see through the windows.'

'Is Batist there?'

'Yes.'

'Put him on, would you?'

When Batist came on the line, I said, 'Who's the man in the boat?'

'A guy puts earrings.'

As was Batist's way, he translated French literally into English, in this case using the word *put* for *wear*.

'Is he bothering y'all?' I said.

'He ain't gonna bother *me*. I'm fixing to lock up.'

'What's the problem, then?'

'They ain't one, long as he's gone when I go out the do'.'

'I'll be down.'

The air was heavy and wet-smelling and crisscrossed with birds when I walked down the slope toward the dock, the sky over the swamp the color of scorched tin. Batist and Alafair had collapsed the Cinzano umbrellas set in the center of the spool tables and turned on the string of overhead lights. The surface of the bayou was ruffling in the wind, and against the cypress and willows on the far side I could see a man sitting in an outboard, dressed in a dark-blue shirt and a white straw hat.

I walked to the end of the dock and leaned against the railing.

'Can I help you with something?' I asked.

He didn't reply. His face was shadowed, but I could see the glint of his gold earrings in the light from the dock. I went inside the bait shop.

'Turn on the flood lamps, Alf,' I said.

When she hit the toggle switch, the light bloomed across the water with the brilliance of a pistol flare. That's when I saw his eyes.

'Go on up to the house, Alafair,' I said.

'You know him?' she said.

'No, but we're going to send him on his way just the same. Now, do what I ask you, okay?'

'I don't see why I—'

'Come on, Alf.'

She lifted her face, her best pout in place, and went out the screen door and let it slam behind her.

Batist was heating a pot of coffee on the small butane stove behind the counter. He bent down and looked out the window at the bayou again, a cigar in the centre of his mouth.

'What you want to do with that fella, Dave?' he said.

'See who he is.'

I went outside again and propped my hands on the dock railing. The flood lamps mounted on the roof of the bait shop burned away the shadows from around the man in the boat. His hair was long, like a nineteenth-century Indian's, his cheeks unshaved, the skin dark and grained as though it had been rubbed with black pepper. His arms were wrapped with scarlet tattoos, but like none I had ever seen before.

Unlike jailhouse art, the ink ran in strings down the arms, webbed in bright fantails, as though all of his veins had been superimposed on the skin's surface.

But it was the eyes that caught and impaled you. They were hunter's eyes, chemical green, rimmed with a quivering energy, as though he heard the sounds of hidden adversaries in the wind.

'What's your business here, podna?' I asked.

He seemed to think on it. One hand opened and closed on an oar.

'I ain't eat today,' he said. The accent was vaguely Spanish, the tone flat, disconnected from the primitive set of the jaw.

Batist joined me at the rail with a cup of coffee in his hand.

'Come inside,' I said.

Batist's eyes fixed on mine.

The man didn't start his engine. Instead, he used one oar to row across the bayou to the concrete ramp. He stepped into the water, ankle-deep, lifted the bow with one hand and pulled the boat up until it was snug on the ramp. Then he reached behind him and lifted out a stiff bedroll that was tied tightly with leather thongs.

His work boots were loud on the dock as he walked toward us, his Levi's high on his hips, notched under his rib cage with a wide leather belt and brass buckle.

'You oughtn't to ax him in, Dave. This is our place,' Batist said.

'It's all right.'

'No, it surely ain't.'

The man let his eyes slide over our faces as he entered the bait shop. I followed him inside and for the first time smelled his odor, like charcoal and kerosene, unwashed hair, mud gone sour with stagnant water. He waited expectantly at the counter, his bedroll tucked under his arm. His back was as straight as a sword.

I fixed him two chili dogs on a paper plate and set them in front of him with a glass of water. He sat on the stool and ate with a spoon, gripping the handle with his fist, mopping the beans and sauce and ground meat with a slice of bread. Batist came inside and began loading the beer cooler behind the counter.

'Where you from?' I said.

'El Paso.'

'Where'd you get the boat?'

He thought about it. 'I found it two weeks back. It was sunk. I cleaned it up pretty good.' He stopped eating and watched me.

'It's a nice boat,' I said.

His face twitched and his eyes were empty again, the jawbones chewing.

'You got a rest room?' he asked.

306

'It's in the back, behind those empty pop cases.'

'How much your razor blades?' he said to Batist.

'This ain't no drug sto'. What you after, man?' Batist said.

The man wiped his mouth with the flats of his fingers. The lines around his eyes were stretched flat.

Batist leaned on his arms, his biceps flexing like rolls of metal washers.

'Don't be giving me no truck,' he said.

I eased along the counter until the man's eyes left Batist and fixed on me.

'I'm a police officer. Do you need directions to get somewhere?' I said.

'I got a camp out there. That's where I come from. I can find it even in the dark,' he said.

With one hand he clenched his bedroll, which seemed to have tent sticks inside it, and walked past the lunch meat coolers to the small rest room in back.

'Dave, let me ax you somet'ing. You got to bring a 'gator in your hog lot to learn 'gators eat pigs?' Batist said.

Ten minutes passed. I could hear the man splashing water behind the rest room door. Batist had gone back out on the dock and was chaining up the rental boats for the night. I walked past the cooler and tapped with one knuckle on the bolted door.

'We're closing up, podna. You have to come out,' I said.

He jerked open the door, his face streaming water. His dark-blue shirt was unbuttoned, and on his chest I could see the same scarlet network of lines that was tattooed on his arms. The pupils in his eyes looked broken, like India ink dropped on green silk.

'I'd appreciate your cleaning up the water and paper towels you've left on the floor. Then I'd like to have a talk with you,' I said.

He didn't answer. I turned and walked back up front.

I went behind the counter and started to stock the candy shelves for tomorrow, then I stopped and called the dispatcher at the department.

'I think I've got a meltdown in the shop. He might have a stolen boat, too,' I said.

'The governor in town?'

'Lose the routine, Wally.'

'You hurt my feelings . . . You want a cruiser, Dave?'

I didn't have the chance to answer. The man in the white straw hat came from behind me, his hand inserted in the end of his bedroll. I looked at his face and dropped the phone and fell clattering against the shelves and butane stove as he flung the bedroll and the sheath loose from the machete and ripped it through the air, an inch from my chest.

The honed blade sliced through the telephone cord and sunk into the counter's hardwood edge. He leaned over and swung again, the blade whanging off the shelves, dissecting cartons of worms and dirt, exploding a jar of pickled sausage.

Batist's coffee pot was scorched black and boiling on the butane fire. The handle felt like a heated wire across my bare palm. I threw the coffee, the top, and the grinds in the man's face, saw the shock in his eyes, his mouth drop open, the pain rise out of his throat like a broken bubble.

Then I grabbed the tattooed wrist that held the machete and pressed the bottom of the pot down on his forearm.

He flung the machete from his hand as though the injury had come from it rather than the coffee pot. I thought I was home free. I wasn't.

He hit me harder than I'd ever been struck by a fist in my life, the kind of blow that fills your nose with needles, drives the eye deep into the socket.

I got to my feet and tried to follow him out on the dock. One side of my face was already numb and throbbing, as though someone had held dry ice against it. The man in the white straw hat had leaped off the dock onto the concrete ramp and mounted the bow of his boat with one knee and was pushing it out into the current, his body haloed with humidity and electric light.

Batist came out of the tin shed in the willows where we stored our outboard motors, looked up at me, then at the fleeing man.

'Batist, no!' I said.

Batist and I both stood motionless while the man jerked the engine into a roar with one flick of the forearm, then furrowed a long yellow trough around the bend into the darkness.

I used the phone at the house to call the department again, then walked back down to the dock. The moon was veiled over the swamp; lightning forked out of a black sky in the south.

'How come you ain't want me to stop him, Dave?' Batist said.

'He's deranged. I think it's PCP,' I said. But he didn't understand. 'It's called angel dust. People get high on it and bust up brick walls with their bare hands.'

'He knowed who you was, Dave. He didn't have no interest in coming in till he seen you . . . this started wit' that old man from the penitentiary.'

'What are you talking about?'

'That guard, the one you call Cap'n, the one probably been killing niggers up at that prison farm for fifty years. I tole you not to have his kind in our shop. You let his grief get on your front porch, it don't stop there, no. It's gonna come in your house. But you don't never listen.'

He pulled his folded cap out of his back pocket, popped it open, and fitted it on his head. He walked down the dock to his truck without saying goodnight. The tin roof on the bait shop creaked and pinged against the joists in the wind gusting out of the south.

5

Monday morning the sky was blue, the breeze warm off the Gulf when I drove to the University of Southwestern Louisiana campus in Lafayette to talk with Buford LaRose. Classes had just let out for the noon hour, and the pale green quadrangle and colonnaded brick walkways were filled with students on their way to lunch. But Buford LaRose was not in his office in the English department, nor in the glassed-in campus restaurant that was built above a cypress lake behind old Burke Hall.

I called his office at the Oil Center, where he kept a part-time therapy practice, and was told by the receptionist I could find him at Red Lerille's Health and Racquet Club off Johnson Street.

'Are you sure? We were supposed to go to lunch,' I said.

'Dr LaRose always goes to the gym on Mondays,' she answered.

Red's was a city-block-long complex of heated swimming pools, racquet ball and clay tennis courts, boxing and basketball gyms, indoor and outdoor running tracks, and cavernous air-conditioned rooms filled with hundreds of dumbbells and weight benches and exercise machines.

I looked for Buford a half hour before I glanced through the narrow glass window in the door of the men's steam room and saw him reading a soggy newspaper, naked, on the yellow tile stoop.

I borrowed a lock from the pro shop, undressed, and walked into the steam room and sat beside him.

His face jerked when he looked up from his paper. Then he smiled, almost fondly.

'You have a funny way of keeping appointments,' I said.

'You didn't get my message?'

'No.'

'I waited for you. I didn't think you were coming,' he said.

'That's peculiar. I was on time.'

'Not by my watch,' he said, and smiled again.

'I wanted to tell you again I was sorry for my remarks at your party.'

'You went to a lot of trouble to do something that's unnecessary.'

The thermostat kicked on and filled the air with fresh clouds of steam. I could feel the heat in the tiles climb through my thighs and back. I wiped the sweat out of my eyes with my hand.

'Your jaw's bruised,' he said.

'We had a visitor at the bait shop this weekend. NOPD thinks he's a Mexican carnival worker who got loose from a detox center.'

He nodded, gazed with interest at the tile wall in front of us, pushed down on the stoop with the heels of his hands and worked the muscles in his back, his brown, hard body leaking sweat at every pore. I watched the side of his face, the handsome profile, the intelligent eyes that seemed never to cloud with passion.

'You have PhD degrees in both English and psychology, Buford?' I said.

'I received double credits in some areas, so it's not such a big deal.'

'It's impressive.'

'Why are you here, Dave?'

'I have a feeling I may have stuck my arm in the garbage grinder. You know how it is, you stick one finger in, then you're up to your elbow in the pipe.'

'We're back to our same subject, I see,' he said.

Other men walked back and forth in the steam, swinging their arms, breathing deeply.

'How do you know Aaron Crown's daughter?' I asked.

'Who says I do?'

'She does.'

'She grew up in New Iberia. If she says she knows me, fine . . . Dave, you have no idea what you're tampering with, how you may be used to undo everything you believe in.'

'Why don't you explain it to me?'

'This is hardly the place, sir.'

We showered, then went into an enclosed, empty area off to one side of the main locker room to dress. He dried himself with a towel, put on a pair of black nylon bikini underwear and flipflops, and began combing his hair in the mirror. The muscles in his back and sides looked like tea-colored water rippling over stone.

'I've got some serious trouble, Dave. These New York film people want to make a case for Aaron Crown's innocence. They can blow my candidacy right into the toilet,' he said.

'You think they have a vested interest?'

'Yeah, making money . . . Wake up, buddy. The whole goddamn country is bashing liberals. These guys ride the tide. A white man unjustly convicted of killing a black civil rights leader? A story like that is made in heaven.'

I put on my shirt and tucked it in my slacks, then sat on the bench and slipped on my loafers.

'Nothing to say?' Buford asked.

'Your explanations are too simple. The name Mingo Bloomberg keeps surfacing in the middle of my mind.'

'This New Orleans mobster?'

'That's the one.'

'I've got a fund-raiser in Shreveport at six. Come on the plane with me,' he said.

'What for?'

'Take leave from your department. Work for me.'

'Not interested.'

'Dave, I'm running for governor while I teach school. I have no machine and little money. The other side does. Now these sonsofbitches from New York come down here and try to cripple the one chance we've had for decent government in decades. What in God's name is wrong with you, man?'

Maybe Buford was right, I thought as I drove down the old highway through Broussard into New Iberia. I sometimes saw design where there was none, and I had maintained a long and profound distrust of all forms of authority, even the one I served, and the LaRose family had been vested with wealth and power since antebellum days.

But maybe it was also time to have another talk with Mingo Bloomberg, provided I could find him.

As irony would have it, I found a message from Mingo's lawyer in my mailbox when I got back to the department. Mingo would not be hard to find, after all. He was in New Orleans' City Prison and wanted to see me.

Late Tuesday morning I was at the barred entrance to a long corridor of individual cells where snitches and the violent and the incorrigible were kept in twenty-three-hour lockdown. The turnkey opened Mingo's cell, cuffed him to a waist chain, and led him down the corridor to me. While a second turnkey worked the levers to slide back the door on the lockdown area, I could see handheld mirrors extended from bars all the way down the series of cells, each reflecting a set of disembodied eyes.

Both turnkeys escorted us into a bare-walled interview room that contained a scarred wood table and three folding chairs. They were powerful, heavyset men with the top-heavy torsos of weight lifters.

'Thanks,' I said.

But they remained where they were.

'I want to be alone with him. I'd appreciate your unhooking him, too,' I said.

The turnkeys looked at each other. Then the older one used his key on each of the cuffs and said, 'Suit yourself. Bang on the door when you're finished. We won't be far.'

After they went out, I could still see them through the elongated, reinforced viewing glass in the door.

'It looks like they're coming down pretty hard on you, Mingo. I thought you'd be sprung by now,' I said.

'They say I'm a flight risk.'

He was clean-shaved, his jailhouse denims pressed neatly, his copper hair combed back on his scalp like a 1930s leading man's. But his eyes looked wired, and a dry, unwashed odor like sweat baked on the skin by a radiator rose from his body.

'I don't get it. Your people don't protect cop killers,' I said.

He propped one elbow on the table and bit his thumbnail.

'It's the other way around. At least that's what the prosecutor's office thinks. That's what those clowns you used to work with at First District think,' he said.

'You've lost me.'

'You remember the narc who got capped in the Quarter last year? I was in the cage at First District when the cops brought in the boon who did it. Somebody, and I said *somebody*, stomped the living shit out of him. They cracked his skull open on a cement floor and crushed his, what do you call it, his thorax. At least that's what people say. I don't know, because I didn't see it. But the dead boon's family is making a big stink and suing the city of New Orleans for fifty million dollars. Some cops might end up at Angola, too. You ever see a cop do time? Think about the possibilities for his food before he puts a fork in it.'

I kept my eyes flat, waited a moment, removed my sunglasses from their case and clicked them in my palm.

'What are you trying to trade?' I asked.

'I want out of here.'

'I don't have that kind of juice.'

'I want out of lockdown.'

'Main pop may not be a good place for you, Mingo.'

'You live on Mars? I'm safe in main pop. I got problems when I'm in lockdown and cops with blood on their shoes think I'm gonna rat 'em out.'

'You're a material witness. There's no way you're going into the main population, Mingo.'

The skin along his hairline was shiny with perspiration. He screwed a cigarette into his mouth but didn't light it. His blue eyes were filled with light when they stared into mine.

'You worked with those guys. You get a word to them, I didn't see anything happen to the boon. I'll go down on a perjury beef if I have to,' he said.

I let my eyes wander over his face. There were tiny black specks in the blueness of his eyes, like pieces of dead flies, like microscopic traces of events that never quite rinse out of the soul. 'How many people have you pushed the button on?' I asked.

'What? Why you ask a question like that?'

'No reason, really.'

He tried to reconcentrate his thoughts. 'A Mexican guy was at your place, right? A guy with fried mush. It wasn't an accident he was there.'

'Go on.'

'He was muleing tar for the projects. They call him Arana, that means "Spider" in Spanish. He's from a village in Mexico that's got a church with a famous statue in it. I know that because he was always talking about it.'

'That sure narrows it down. Who sent him to my bait shop?'

'What do I get?'

'We can talk about federal custody.'

'That's worse. People start thinking Witness Protection Program.'

'That's all I've got.'

He tore a match from a book and struck it, held the flame to his cigarette, never blinking in the smoke and heat that rose into his handsome face.

'There's stuff going on that's new, that's a big move for certain people. You stumbled into it with that peckerwood, the one who killed Jimmy Ray Dixon's brother.'

'What stuff?'

He tipped his ashes in a small tin tray, his gaze focused on nothing. His cheeks were pooled with color, the fingers of his right hand laced with smoke from the cigarette.

'I don't think you've got a lot to trade, Mingo. Otherwise, you would have already done it.'

'I laid it out for you. You don't want to pick up on it . . .' He worked the burning end of the cigarette loose in the ashtray and placed the unsmoked stub in the package. 'You asked me a personal question a minute ago. Just for fun, it don't mean anything, understand, I'll give you a number. Eleven. None of them ever saw it coming. The guy with the fried head at your place probably wasn't a serious effort.

'I say "probably." I'm half-Jewish, half-Irish, I don't eat in Italian restaurants. I'm outside the window looking in a lot of the time. Hey, you're a bright guy, I know you can connect on this.'

'Enjoy it, Mingo,' I said, and hit on the door with the flat of my fist for the turnkey to open up.

Later that same day, just before I was to sign out of the office, the phone on my desk rang.

It was like hearing the voice of a person who you knew would not go away, who would always be hovering around you like a bad memory, waiting to pull you back into the past.

'How's life, Karyn?' I said.

'Buford will be in Baton Rouge till late tonight. You and I need to talk some things out.'

'I don't think so.'

'You want me to come to your office? Or out to your house? I will, if that's what it takes.'

I left the office and drove south of New Iberia toward my home. I tried to concentrate on the traffic, the red sky in the wet, the egrets perched on the backs of cattle in the fields, the cane wagons being towed to the sugar mill. I wasn't going to give power to Karyn LaRose, I told myself. I owed her nothing. I was sure of that.

I was still trying to convince myself of my freedom from the past when I made an illegal U-turn in the middle of the road and drove to the LaRose plantation.

She wore a yellow sundress, with her platinum hair braided up on her head, a Victorian sapphire brooch on a gold chain around her neck.

'Why'd you park in back?' she said when she opened the door.

'I didn't give it much thought,' I said.

'I bet.'

'Let's hear what you have to say, Karyn. I need to get home.'

She smiled with her eyes, turned and walked away without speaking. When I didn't immediately follow, she paused and looked back at me expectantly. I followed her through the kitchen, a den filled with books and glass gun cases and soft leather chairs, down a darkened cypress-floored hallway hung with oil paintings of Buford's ancestors, into a sitting room whose windows and French doors reached to the ceiling.

She pulled the velvet curtains on the front windows.

'It's a little dark, isn't it?' I said. I stood by the mantel, next to a bright window that gave onto a cleared cane field and a stricken oak tree that stood against the sky like a clutch of broken fingers.

'There's a horrid glare off the road this time of day,' she said. She put

315

ice and soda in two glasses at a small bar inset in one wall and uncorked a bottle of Scotch with a thick, red wax seal embossed on it.

'I don't care for anything, thanks,' I said.

'There's no whiskey in yours.'

'I said I don't want anything.'

The phone rang in another room.

'Goddamn it,' she said, set down her glass, and went into a bedroom.

I looked at my watch. I had already been there ten minutes and had accomplished nothing. On the mantel piece was a photograph of a U.S. Army Air Corps aviator who was sitting inside the splintered Plexiglas nose of a Flying Fortress. The photo must have been taken at high altitude, because the fur collar on his jacket was frozen with his sweat, like a huge glass necklace. His face was exhausted, and except for the area around his eyes where his goggles had been, his skin was black with the smoke of *ack-ack* bursts.

I could hear Karyn's voice rising in the next room: 'I won't sit still for this again. You rent a car if you have to . . . I'm not listening to that same lie . . . You're not going to ruin this, Buford . . . You listen . . . No . . . No . . . No, you listen . . . '

Then she pushed the door shut.

When she came out of the room her eyes were electric with anger, the tops of her breasts rising against her sundress. She went to the bar and drank off her Scotch and soda and poured another one. I looked away from her face.

'Admiring the photo of Buford's father?' she said. 'He was one of the bombardiers who incinerated Dresden. You see the dead oak tree out by the field? Some of Buford's other family members, gentlemen in the Knights of the White Camellia, hanged a Negro and a white carpet-bagger there in 1867. If you live with Buford, you get to hear about this sort of thing every day of your life.'

She drank three fingers of Scotch on ice, her throat swallowing methodically, her mouth wet and cold-looking on the edge of the glass.

'I'd better get going, Karyn. I shouldn't have bothered you,' I said.

'Don't be disingenuous. I brought you here, Dave. Sometimes I wonder how I ever got mixed up with you.'

'You're not mixed up with me.'

'Your memory is selective.'

'I'm sorry it happened, Karyn. I've tried to indicate that to you. It's you and your husband who keep trying to resurrect the past or bring me into your lives.'

'You say "it." What do you mean by "it"?'

'That night by the bayou. I'm sorry. I don't know what else to say.'

'You don't remember coming to my house two weeks later?'

'No.'

'Dave?' Her eyes clouded, then looked into mine, as though she were searching for a lie. 'You have no memory of that afternoon, or the next?'

I felt myself swallow. 'No, I don't. I don't think I saw you again for a year,' I said.

She shook her head, sat in a deep leather chair that looked out onto the dead tree.

'That's hard to believe. I never blamed you for the worry and anxiety and pain I had to go through later, because I didn't make you take precautions. But when you tell me—'

Unconsciously I touched my brow.

'I had blackouts back then, Karyn. I lost whole days. If you say something happened, then—'

'Blackouts?'

'I'd get loaded at night on Beam and try to sober up in the morning with vodka.'

'How lovely. What if I told you I had an abortion?'

The skin of my face flexed against the bone. I could feel a weakness, a sinking in my chest, as though weevil worms were feeding at my heart.

'I didn't. I was just late. But no thanks to you, you bastard . . . Don't just look at me,' she said.

'I'm going now.'

'Oh no, you're not.' She rose from the chair and stood in front of me. 'My husband has some peculiar flaws, but he's still the best chance this state has and I'm not letting you destroy it.'

'Somebody tried to open me up with a machete. I think it had to do with Aaron Crown. I think I don't want to ever see you again, Karyn.'

'Is that right?' she said. The tops of her breasts were swollen and hard, veined with blue lines. I could smell whiskey on her breath, perfume from behind her ears, the heat she seemed to excrete from her sun-browned skin. She struck me full across the face with the flat of her hand.

I touched my cheek, felt a smear of blood where her fingernail had torn the skin.

'I apologize again for having come to your home,' I said.

I walked stiffly through the house, through the kitchen to the backyard and my parked pickup truck. When I turned the ignition, I looked through the windshield and saw her watching me through the back screen, biting the corner of her lip as though her next option was just now presenting itself.

6

It rained all that night. At false dawn a white ground fog rolled out of the swamp, and the cypress trees on the far bank of the bayou looked as black and hard as carved stone. Deep inside the fog you could hear bass flopping back in the bays. When the sun broke above the horizon, like a red diamond splintering apart between the tree trunks, Batist and I were still bailing out the rental boats with coffee cans. Then we heard a car on the road, and when we looked up we saw a purple Lincoln Continental, with Sabelle Crown in the passenger's seat, stop and back up by our concrete boat ramp.

It wasn't hard to figure out which American industry the driver served. He seemed to consciously dress and look the part – elk hide halftop boots, pleated khakis, a baggy cotton shirt that was probably tailored on Rodeo Drive, tinted rimless glasses, his brown hair tied in a ponytail.

As he walked down the ramp toward me, the wind-burned face, the cleft chin, the Roman profile, became more familiar, like images rising from the pages of *People* or *Newsweek* magazine or any number of television programs that featured film celebrities.

His forearms and wrists were thick and corded with veins, the handshake disarmingly gentle.

'My name's Lonnie Felton, Mr Robicheaux,' he said.

'You're a movie director.'

'That's right.'

'How you do, sir?'

'I wonder if we could go inside and talk a few minutes.'

'I'm afraid I have another job to go to when I finish this one.'

Sabelle stood by the fender of the Lincoln, brushing her hair, putting on makeup from her purse.

'Some people are giving Aaron Crown a rough time up at the pen,' he said.

'It's a bad place. It was designed as one.'

'You know what the BGLA is?'

'The Black Guerrilla Liberation Army?'

'Crown's an innocent man. I think Ely Dixon was assassinated by a couple of Mississippi Klansmen. Maybe one of them was a Mississippi highway patrolman.'

'You ought to tell this to the FBI.'

'I got *this* from the FBI. I have testimony from two ex-field-agents.'

'It seems the big word in this kind of instance is always "ex," Mr Felton', I said.

He coughed out a laugh. 'You're a hard-nose sonofabitch, aren't you?' he said.

I stood erect in the boat where I'd been bailing, poured the water out of the can into the bayou, idly flicked the last drops onto the boat's bow.

'I don't particularly care what you think of me, sir, but I'd appreciate your not using profanity around my home,' I said.

He looked off into the distance, suppressing a smile, watching a blue heron lift from an inlet and disappear into the fog.

'We had a writer murdered in the Quarter,' he said. 'The guy was a little weird, but he didn't deserve to get killed. That's not an unreasonable position for me to take, is it?'

'I'll be at the sheriff's department by eight. If you want to give us some information, you're welcome to come in.'

'Sabelle told me you were an intelligent man. Who do you think broke the big stories of our time? My Lai, Watergate, CIA dope smuggling. Reagan's gun deals in Nicaragua? It was always the media, not the government, not the cops. Why not lose the "plain folks" attitude?'

I stepped out of the boat into the shallows and felt the coldness through my rubber boots. I set the bailing can down on the ramp, wrapped the bow chain in my palm and snugged the boat's keel against the waving moss at the base of the concrete pad, and cleared an obstruction from my throat.

He slipped his glasses off his face, dropped them loosely in the pocket of his baggy shirt, smiling all the while. 'Thanks for coming by,' I said.

I walked up the ramp, then climbed the set of side stairs onto the dock. I saw him walk toward his car and shake his head at Sabelle.

A moment later she came quickly down the dock toward me. She wore old jeans, a flannel shirt, pink tennis shoes, and walked splay-footed like a teenage girl.

'I look like hell. He came by my place at five this morning,' she said.

'You look good, Sabelle. You always do,' I said.

'They've moved Daddy into a cellhouse full of blacks.'

'That doesn't sound right. He can request isolation.'

'He'll die before he'll let anybody think he's scared. In the meantime they steal his cigarettes, spit in his food, throw pig shit in his hair, and nobody does anything about it.' Her eyes began to film.

'I'll call this gunbull I know.'

'They're going to kill him, Dave. I know it. It's a matter of time.'

Out on the road, Lonnie Felton waited behind the steering wheel of his Lincoln.

'Don't let this guy Felton use you,' I said.

'*Use* me? Who else cares about us?' Even with makeup, her face looked stark, as shiny as ceramic, in the lacy veil of sunlight through the cypress trees. She turned and walked back up the dock, her pink underwear winking through a small thread-worn hole in the rump of her jeans.

The sheriff was turned sideways in his swivel chair, his bifocals mounted on his nose, twisting strips of pink and white crepe paper into the shape of camellias. On his windowsill was a row of potted plants, which he watered daily from a hand-painted teakettle. He looked like an aging greengrocer more than a law officer, and in fact had run a dry cleaning business before his election to office, but he had been humble enough to listen to advice, and over the years we had all come to respect his judgment and integrity.

Only one door in his life had remained closed to us, his time with the First Marine Division at the Chosin Reservoir during the Korean War, until last year, when he suffered a heart attack and told me from a bed in Iberia General, his breath as stale as withered flowers, of bugles echoing off frozen hills and wounds that looked like roses frozen in snow.

I sat down across from him. His desk blotter was covered with crepe paper camellias.

'I volunteered to help decorate the stage for my granddaughter's school play. You any good at this?' he said.

'No, not really. A movie director, a fellow named Lonnie Felton, was out at my place with Sabelle Crown this morning. They say some blacks are trying to re-create the Garden of Gethsemane for Aaron Crown. I called Angola, but I didn't get any help.'

'Don't look for any. We made him the stink on shit.'

'I beg your pardon?'

'A lot of us, not everybody, but a lot of us, treated people of color pretty badly. Aaron represents everything that's vile in the white race. So he's doing our time.'

'You think these movie guys are right, he's innocent?'

'I didn't say that. Look, human beings do bad things sometimes, particularly in groups. Then we start to forget about it. But there's always one guy hanging around to remind us of what we did or what we used to be. That's Aaron. He's the toilet that won't flush . . . Did I say something funny?'

'No, sir.'

'Good, because what I've got on my mind isn't funny. Karyn LaRose and her attorney were in here earlier this morning.' He set his elbows on his desk blotter, flipped an unfinished paper flower to the side. 'Guess what she had to tell me about your visit last night at her house?'

'I won't even try to.'

'They're not calling it rape, if that makes you feel any better.' He opened his desk drawer and read silently from a clipboard. 'The words are "lascivious intention," "attempted sexual battery," and "indecent liberties." What do you have to say?' His gaze moved away from my face, then came back and stayed there.

'Nothing. It's a lie.'

'I wish the court would just accept my word on the perps. I wish I didn't have to offer any evidence. Boy, that'd be great.'

I told him what had happened, felt the heat climbing into my voice, wiped the film of perspiration off my palms onto my slacks.

His eyes lingered on the scratch Karyn had put on my cheek.

'I think it's a lie, too,' he said. He dropped the clipboard inside the drawer and closed it. 'But I have to conduct an internal investigation just the same.'

'I go on the desk?'

'No. I'm not going to have my department manipulated for someone's political interests, and that's what this is about. You're getting too close to something in this Aaron Crown business. But you stay away from her.'

I still had my morning mail in my hand. On the top was a pink memo slip with a message from Bootsie, asking me to meet her for lunch.

'How public is this going to get?' I asked.

'My feeling is she doesn't intend it to be public. Aside from the fact I know you, that was the main reason I didn't believe her. Her whole account is calculated to be vague. Her charges don't require her to offer physical evidence – vaginal smears, pubic hair, that kind of stuff. This is meant as a warning from the LaRose family. If I have to, I'll carry this back to them on a dung fork, podna.'

He folded his hands on the desk, his face suffused with the ruddy glow of his hypertension.

Way to go, skipper, I thought.

Most people in prison deserve to be there. Old-time recidivists who are down on a bad beef will usually admit they're guilty of other crimes, perhaps much worse ones than the crimes they're down for.

There're exceptions, but not many. So their burden is of their own creation. But it is never an easy one, no matter how modern the facility or how vituperative the rhetoric about country club jails.

You're a nineteen-year-old fish, uneducated, frightened, with an IQ of around 100. At the reception center you rebuff a trusty wolf who works in records and wants to introduce you to jailhouse romance, so the trusty makes sure you go up the road with a bad jacket (the word is out, you snitched off a solid con and caused him to lose his good-time).

You just hit main pop and you're already jammed up, worried about the shank in the chow line, the Molotov cocktail shattered inside your cell, the whispered threat in the soybean field about the experience awaiting you in the shower that night.

So you make a conscious choice to survive and find a benefactor, 'an old man,' and become a full-time punk, one step above the yard bitches. You mule blues, prune-o, and Afghan skunk for the big stripes; inside a metal toolshed that aches with heat, you participate in the savaging of another fish, who for just a moment reminds you of someone you used to know.

Then a day comes when you think you can get free. You're mainline now, two years down with a jacket full of goodtime. You hear morning birdsong that you didn't notice before; you allow your mind to linger on the outside, the face of a girl in a small town, a job in a piney woods timber mill that smells of rosin and hot oil on a ripsaw, an ordinary day not governed by fear.

That's when you tell your benefactor thanks for all his help. He'll understand. Your next time up before the board, you've got a real chance of entering the world again. Why blow it now?

That night you walk into the shower by yourself. A man who had never even glanced at you before, a big stripe, hare-lipped, flat-nosed, his naked torso rife with a raw smell like a freshly uprooted cypress, clenches your skull in his fingers, draws you into his breath, squeezes until the cracking sound stops and you hear the words that he utters with a lover's trembling fondness an inch from your mouth: *I'm gonna take your eyes out with a spoon.*

It was late afternoon when the gunbull drove me in his pickup down to the Mississippi levee, where Aaron Crown, his face as heated as a baked apple under a snap-brim cap, was harrowing an open field, the tractor's engine running full bore, grinding the sun-hardened rows into loam, twisting the tractor's wheel back through the haze of cinnamon-colored dust, reslicing the already churned soil as though his work were an excuse to avenge himself and his kind upon the earth.

At the edge of the field, by a grove of willows, four black inmates, stripped to the waist, were heaping dead tree branches on a fire.

'Y'all ought to have Aaron in isolation, Cap,' I said.

He cut the ignition and spit tobacco juice out the window.

'When he asks,' he replied.

'He won't.'

'Then that's his goddamn ass.'

The captain walked partway out in the field on his cane and raised the hook and held it motionless in the air. Aaron squinted out of the dust and heat and exhaust fumes, then eased the throttle back without killing the engine, as though he could not will himself to separate entirely from the mechanical power that had throbbed between his thighs all day.

Aaron walked toward us, wiping his face with a dirty handkerchief, past the group of blacks burning field trash. Their eyes never saw him; their closed circle of conversation never missed a beat.

He stood by the truck, his body framed by the sun that hung in a liquid yellow orb over the Mississippi levee.

'Yes, sir?' he said to the captain.

'Water it and piss it, Aaron,' the captain said. He limped on his cane to the shade of a gum tree and lit his pipe, turned his face into the breeze off the river.

'I understand you've having some trouble,' I said.

'You ain't heered me say it.'

He walked back to the watercooler belted with bungee cord to the wall of the pickup bed. He filled a paper cup from the cooler and drank it, his gaze fixed on the field, the dust devils swirling in the wind.

'Is it the BGLA?' I asked.

'I don't keep up with colored men's organizations.'

'I don't know if you're innocent or guilty, Aaron. But up there at Point Lookout, the prison cemetery is full of men who had your kind of attitude.'

'That levee yonder's got dead men in it, too. It's the way it is.' He wadded up the paper cup by his side, kneaded it in his hand, a piece of cartilage working against his jawbone.

'I'm going to talk to a civil rights lawyer I know in Baton Rouge. He's a black man, though. Is that going to be a problem?'

'I don't give a shit what he is. I done tole you, I got no complaint, long as I ain't got to cell with one of them.'

'They'll eat you alive, partner.'

He stepped toward me, his wrists seeming to strain against invisible wires at his sides.

'A man's got his own rules. I ain't ask for nothing except out . . . Goddamn it, you tell my daughter she ain't to worry,' he said, his eyes rimming with water. The top of his denim shirt was splayed tightly against his chest. He breathed through his mouth, his fists gathered into impotent rocks, his face dilated with the words his throat couldn't form.

I got back home at dark, then I had to go out again, this time with Helen Soileau to a clapboard nightclub on a back road to investigate a missing person's report.

'Sorry to drag you out, Dave, but the grandmother has been yelling at me over the phone all day,' Helen said. 'I made a couple of calls, and it looks like she's telling the truth. The girl's not the kind to take off and not tell anybody.'

A black waitress had left the club with a white man the night before; she never returned home, nor did she report to work the next day. The grandmother worked as a cook in the club's kitchen and lived in a small frame house a hundred yards down the road. She was a plump, gray-haired woman with a strange skin disease that had eaten white and pink discolorations in her hands, and she was virtually hysterical with anger and grief.

'We'll find her. I promise you,' Helen said as we stood in the woman's dirt yard, looking up at her on her tiny, lighted gallery.

'Then why ain't you looking right now? How come it takes all day to get y'all out here?' she said.

'Tell me what the man looked like one more time,' I said.

'Got a brand-new Lincoln car. Got a pink face shaped like an egg. Got hair that ain't blond or red, somewhere in between, and he comb it straight back.'

'Why did she go off with him?' I asked.

''Cause she's seventeen years old and don't listen. 'Cause she got this on her hands, just like me, and reg'lar mens don't pay her no mind. That answer your question?'

Helen drove us back down the dirt road through the fields to the state highway. The night was humid, layered with smoke from stubble fires, and the stars looked blurred with mist in the sky. We passed the LaRose company store, then the plantation itself. All three floors of the house were lighted, the columned porch decorated with pumpkins and scarecrows fashioned from cane stalks and straw hats. In a back pasture, behind a railed fence, horses were running in the moonlight, as though spooked by an impending storm or the rattle of dry poppy husks in the wind.

'What's on your mind?' Helen asked.

'The description of the white man sounds like Mingo Bloomberg.'

'I thought he was in City Prison in New Orleans.'

'He is. Or at least he was.'

'What would he be doing back around here?'

'Who knows why these guys do anything, Helen? I'll get on it in the morning.'

I looked back over my shoulder at the LaRose house, the glitter of a chandelier through velvet curtains, a flood-lighted gazebo hooded with Confederate jasmine and orange trumpet vine.

'Forget those people. They wouldn't spit on either one of us unless we had something they wanted. Hey, you listening to me, Streak?' Helen said, and hit me hard on the arm with the back of her hand.

I got up early the next morning, left a message on Clete Purcel's answering machine, then drove back to the grandmother's house by the nightclub. The girl, whose name was Barbara Lavey, had still not returned home. I sat in my truck by the front of the grandmother's house and looked at the notes in my notebook. For some reason I drew a circle around the girl's name. I had a feeling I would see it on a case file for a long time.

The grandmother had gone back inside and I had forgotten her. Suddenly she was at the passenger door window. Her glasses fell down on her nose when she leaned inside.

'I'm sorry I was unpolite yestiday. I know you working on it. Here's somet'ing for you and the lady,' she said. She placed a brown paper bag swollen with pecans in my hand.

The sun was still low in the eastern sky when I approached the LaRose plantation. I saw Buford, naked to the waist, in a railed lot by the barn, with a half dozen dark-skinned men who were dressed in straw hats coned on the brims and neckerchiefs and cowboy boots and jeans molded to their buttocks and thighs.

I knew I should keep going, not put my hand again into whatever it was that drove Karyn and Buford's ambitions, not fuel their anger, not give them a handle on an Internal Affairs investigation, but I was never good at taking my own counsel and I could feel the lie she had told turning in my chest like a worm.

I turned into the drive, passed a row of blue-green poplars on the side of the house, and parked by the back lot. A balmy wind, smelling of rain, was blowing hard across the cane acreage, and a dozen roan horses with brands burned deep into the hair were running in the lot, turning against one another, rattling against the railed fence, their manes twisted with fire in the red sunrise.

When I stepped out of the truck, Buford was smiling at me. His skin-tight white polo pants were flecked with mud and tucked inside his polished riding boots. His eyes looked serene, his face pleasant and cool with the freshness of the morning.

I almost extended my hand.

He looked at the sunrise over my shoulder.

' "Red sky at dawn, sailor be forewarned," ' he said. But he was smiling when he said it.

'I shouldn't be here, but I needed to tell you to your face the charges your wife made are fabricated. That's as kind as I can say it.'

'Oh, that stuff. She's dropping it, Dave. Let's put that behind us.'

'Excuse me?'

'It's over. Come take a look at my horses.'

I looked at him incredulously.

'She slandered someone's name,' I said.

He blew out his breath. 'You and my wife were intimate. She probably still bears you a degree of resentment. The god Eros was never a rational influence, Dave. At the same time she doesn't want to see my campaign compromised because you've developed this crazy notion about Aaron Crown being railroaded. So she let both her imagination and her impetuosity cause her to do something foolish. We're sorry for whatever harm we've done you.'

I cupped my hand on a fence rail, felt the hardness of the wood in my palm, tried to see my thoughts in my head before I spoke.

'I get the notion I'm in a therapy session,' I said.

'If you were, you'd get a bill.'

The back door of the house opened, and a slender, white-haired man with a pixie face, one wrinkled with the parchment lines of a chronic cigarette smoker, stepped out into the wind and waved at Buford. He wore a navy blue sports jacket with brass buttons and a champagne-colored silk scarf. I knew the face but I couldn't remember from where.

'I'll be just a minute, Clay,' Buford called. Then to me, 'Would you like to join us for breakfast?'

'No, thanks.'

'How about a handshake, then?'

Two of the wranglers were yelling at each other in Spanish as the horses swirled around them in the lot. One had worked a hackamore over a mare's head and the other was trying to fling a blanket and saddle on her back.

'No? Stay and watch me get my butt thrown, then,' Buford said.

'You were born for it.'

'I beg your pardon?'

'The political life. You've got ice water in your veins,' I said.

'You see that dead oak yonder? Two men were lynched there by my

326

ancestors. When I went after Aaron Crown, I hoped maybe I could atone a little for what happened under that tree.'

'It makes a great story.'

'You're a classic passive-aggressive, Dave, no offense meant. You feign the role of liberal and humanist, but Bubba and Joe Bob own your heart.'

'So long, Buford,' I said, and walked back to my truck. The wind splayed and flattened the poplar trees against Buford's house. When I looked back over my shoulder, he was mounted on the mare's back, one hand twisted in the mane, the hackamore sawed back in the other, his olive-tan torso anointed with the sun's cool light, sculpted with the promise of perfection that only Greek gods know.

Later, Clete Purcel returned my call and told me Mingo Bloomberg had been sprung from City Prison three days ago by attorneys who worked for Jerry Joe Plumb, also known as Short Boy Jerry, Jerry Ace, and Jerry the Glide.

But even as I held the receiver in my hand, I couldn't concentrate on Clete's words about Mingo's relationship to a peculiar player in the New Orleans underworld. The dispatcher had just walked through my open door and handed me a memo slip with the simple message written on it: *Call the Cap up at the zoo re: Crown. He says urgent.*

It took twenty minutes to get him on the phone.

'You was right. I should have listened to you. A bunch of the black boys caught him in the tool shack this morning,' the captain said.

He'd had to walk from the field and he breathed hard into the telephone.

'Is he dead?' I asked.

'You got it turned around. He killed two of them sonsofbitches with his bare hands and liked to got a third with a cane knife. That old man's a real shitstorm, ain't he?'

327

7

Bootsie, Alafair and I were eating supper in the kitchen that evening when the phone rang on the counter. Bootsie got up to answer it. Outside, the clouds in the west were purple and strung with curtains of rain.

Then I heard her say, 'Before I give the phone to Dave, could you put Karyn on? I left her a couple of messages, but she probably didn't have time to call . . . I see . . . When will she be back? . . . Could you ask her to call me, Buford? I've really wanted to talk with her . . . Oh, you know, those things she said about Dave to the sheriff . . . Hang on now, here's Dave.'

She handed me the phone.

'Buford?' I said.

'Yes.' His voice sounded as though someone had just wrapped a strand of piano wire around his throat.

'You all right?' I said.

'Yes, I'm fine, thanks . . . You heard about Crown?' he said.

'A guard at the prison told me.'

'Does this give you some idea of his potential?'

'I hear they were cruising for it.'

'He broke one guy's neck. He drowned the other one in a barrel of tractor oil,' he said.

'I couldn't place your friend this morning. He's Clay Mason, isn't he? What are you doing with him, partner?'

'None of your business.'

'That guy was the P. T. Barnum of the acid culture.'

'As usual, your conclusions are as wrong as your information.'

He hung up the phone. I sat back down at the table.

'You really called Karyn LaRose?' I asked.

'Why? Do you object?' she said.

'No.'

She put a piece of chicken in her mouth and looked at me while she chewed. My stare broke.

'I wish I hadn't gone out to see her, Boots.'

'He's mixed up with that guru from the sixties?' she said.

'Who knows? The real problem is one nobody cares about.'

She waited.

'Aaron Crown had no motivation to kill Ely Dixon. I'm more and more convinced the wrong man's in prison,' I said.

'He was in the Klan, Dave.'

'They kicked him out. He busted up a couple of them with a wood bench inside a Baptist church.'

But why, I thought.

It was a question that only a few people in the Louisiana of the 1990s could answer.

His name was Billy Odom and he ran a junkyard on the stretch of state highway west of Lafayette. Surrounded by a floodplain of emerald green rice fields, the junkyard seemed an almost deliberate eyesore that Billy had lovingly constructed over the decades from rusted and crushed car bodies, mountains of bald tires, and outbuildings festooned with silver hubcaps.

Like Aaron Crown, he was a north Louisiana transplant, surrounded by papists, blacks who could speak French, and a historical momentum that he had not been able to shape or influence or dent in any fashion. His face was as round as a moonpie under his cork sun helmet, split with an incongruous smile that allowed him to hide his thoughts while he probed for the secret meaning that lay in the speech of others. A Confederate flag, almost black with dirt, was nailed among the yellowed calendars on the wall of the shed where he kept his office. He kept licking his lips, leaning forward in his chair, his eyes squinting as though he were staring through smoke.

'A fight in a church? I don't call it to mind,' he said.

'You and Aaron were in the same klavern, weren't you?'

His eyes shifted off my face, studied the motes of dust spinning in a shaft of sunlight. He cocked his head philosophically but said nothing.

'Why'd y'all run him off?' I asked.

''Cause the man don't have the sense God give an earthworm.'

'Come on, Billy.'

'He used to make whiskey and put fertilizer in the mash. That's where I think he got that stink at. His old woman left him for a one-legged blind man.'

'You want to help him, Billy, or see him hung out to dry at Angola?'

His hands draped over his thighs. He studied the backs of them.

'It was 'cause of the girl. His daughter, what's her name, Sabelle, the one runs the bar down at the Underpass.'

'I don't follow you.'

'The meeting was at a church house. She wasn't but a girl then, waiting outside in the pickup truck. Two men was looking out the window at her. They didn't know Crown was sitting right behind them.

'One goes, "I hear that's prime."

'The other goes, "It ain't bad. But you best carry a ball of string to find your way back out."

'That's when Crown put the wood to them. Then he tore into them with his boots. It taken four of us to hold him down.'

'You kicked him out of the Klan for defending his daughter?' I said.

Billy Odom pried a pale splinter out of his grease-darkened desk and scratched lines in his skin with it.

'When they're young and cain't keep their panties on, the old man's in it somewhere,' he said.

'*What?*'

'Everybody had suspicioned it. Then a woman from the welfare caught him at it and told the whole goddamn town. That's how come Crown moved down here.'

'Aaron and his daughter?' I said.

The man who had seen the accident did not report it for almost three days, not until his wife was overcome with guilt herself and went to a priest and then with her husband to the St Martin Parish sheriff's office.

Helen Soileau and I stood on the levee by a canal that rimmed Henderson Swamp and watched a diver in a wetsuit pull the steel hook and cable off the back of a wrecker, wade out into the water by a row of bridge pilings, sinking deeper into a balloon of silt, then disappear beneath the surface. The sky was blue overhead, the moss on the dead cypress lifting in the breeze, the sun dancing on the sandbars and the deep green of the willow islands. When a uniformed sheriff's deputy kicked the winch into gear and the cable clanged tight on the car's frame, a gray cloud of mud churned to the surface like a fat man's fist.

Helen walked up on the wood bridge that spanned the canal, rubbed her shoes on one unrailed edge, and walked back down on the levee again. The front tires of the submerged car, which lay upside down, broke through a tangle of dead hyacinths.

The man who had seen the accident sat on the levee with his wife at his side. He wore a greasy cap, with the bill pulled low over his eyes.

'Go through it again,' I said.

He had to crane his head upward, into the sunlight, when he spoke.

'It was dark. I was walking back to the camp from that landing yonder. There wasn't no moon. I didn't see everything real good,' he replied. His wife looked at the steel cable straining against the automobile's weight, her face vaguely ashamed, the muscles collapsed.

'Yes, you did,' I said.

'He fishtailed off the levee when he hit the bridge, and the car went in. The headlights was on, way down at the bottom of the canal.'

'Then what happened?' I said.

He flexed his lips back on his teeth, as though he were dealing with a profound idea.

'The man floated up in the headlights. Then he come up the levee, right up to the hard road where I was at. He was all wet and walking fast.' He turned his face out of the sunlight again, retreated back into the shade of his cap.

I tapped the edge of my shoe against his buttock.

'You didn't report an accident. If we find anything in that car we shouldn't, you'd better be in our good graces. You with me on this?' I said.

His wife, who wore a print-cotton dress that bagged on her wide shoulders, whispered close to his face while her hand tried to find his.

'He tole me to forget what I seen,' the man said. 'He put his mout' right up against mine when he said it. He grabbed me. In a private place, real hard.' The flush on the back of his neck spread into his hairline.

'What did he look like?' Helen said.

'He was a white man, that's all I know. He'd been drinking whiskey. I could smell it on his mout'. I ain't see him good 'cause the moon was down.'

'You see that power pole there? There's a light on it. It comes on every night,' I said.

The diver walked out of the shallows next to the overturned Lincoln as the winch slid it up on the mud bank. All the windows were closed, and the interior was filled from the roof to the floor with brown water. Then, through the passenger's side, we saw a brief pink-white flash against the glass, like a molting fish brushing against the side of a dirty aquarium.

The diver tried to open the door, but it was wedged into the mud. He got a two-handed ball peen hammer, with a head the size of a brick, and smashed in the passenger window.

The water burst through the folded glass, peppering the levee with crawfish, leeches, a nest of ribbon-thin cottonmouths that danced in the grass as though their backs were broken. But those were not the images that defined the moment.

A woman's hand, then arm, extended itself in the rushing stream, as though the person belted to the seat inside were pointing casually to an object in the grass. The fingers were ringed with costume jewelry, the nails painted with purple polish, the skin eaten by a disease that had robbed the tissue of color.

I squatted down next to the man who had seen the accident and extended my business card on two fingers.

'He didn't try to pull her out. He didn't call for help. He let her drown, alone in the darkness. Don't let him get away with this, podna,' I said.

Clete called the bait shop Saturday morning, just as I was laying out a tray of chickens and links on the pit for our midday fishermen.

'You got a boat for rent?' he asked.

'Sure.'

'Can you rent the guy with me some gear?'

'I have a rod he can borrow.'

'It's a fine day for it, all right.'

'Where are you?'

'Right up the road at the little grocery store. The guy's sitting out in my car. But he doesn't like to go where he's not invited, know what I'm saying, Dave? You want Mingo? Anytime I got to run down a skip, all I got to do is talk to the guy in my car. In this case, he feels a personal responsibility. Plus, y'all go back, right?'

'Clete, you didn't bring Jerry Joe Plumb here?' I said.

He was notorious by the time he was expelled from high school in his senior year – a kid who'd grin just before he hit you, a bouree player who won high stakes from grown men at the saloon downtown, the best dancer in three parishes, the hustler who cast aluminium replicas of brass knuckles in the metal shop foundry and sold them for one dollar apiece with the ragged edges unbuffed so they could stencil daisy chains of red flowers on an adversary's face.

But all that happened after Jerry Joe's mother died in his sophomore year. My memory was of a different boy, from a different, earlier time.

In elementary school we heard his father had been killed at Wake Island, but no one was really sure. Jerry Joe was one of those boys who came to town and left, entered and withdrew from school as his mother found work wherever she could. They used to live in a shack on the edge of a brickyard in Lafayette, then for several years in a trailer behind a welding shop south of New Iberia. On Sundays and the first Fridays of the month we would see him and his mother walking long distances to church, in both freezing weather and on one-hundred-degree afternoons. She was a pale woman, with a pinched and fearful light in her face, and she made him walk on the inside, as though the passing traffic were about to bolt across the curb and kill them both.

For a time his mother and mine worked together in a laundry, and Jerry Joe would come home from school with me and play until my mother and his came down the dirt road in my father's lopsided pick-up. We owned a hand-crank phonograph, and Jerry Joe would root in a dusty pile of 78s and pull out the old scratched recordings of the Hackberry Ramblers and Iry LeJeune and listen to them over and over again, dancing with himself, smiling elfishly, his shoulders and arms cocked like a miniature prizefighter's.

One day after New Year's my father came back unexpectedly from offshore, where he worked as a derrick man, up on the monkey board, high above the drilling platform and the long roll of the Gulf. He'd been fired after arguing with the driller, and as he always did when he lost his job, he'd spent his drag-up check on presents for us and whiskey at Provost's Bar, as though new opportunity and prosperity were just around the corner.

But Jerry Joe had never seen my father before and wasn't ready for him. My father stood silhouetted in the doorway, huge, grinning, irreverent, a man who fought in bars for fun, the black hair on his chest bursting out of the two flannel shirts he wore.

'You dance pretty good. But you too skinny you. We gone have to fatten you up. Y'all come see what I brung,' he said.

At the kitchen table, he began unloading a canvas drawstring bag that was filled with smoked ducks, pickled okra and green tomatoes, a fruit cake, strawberry preserves, a jar of cracklings, and bottle after long-necked bottle of Jax beer.

'Your mama work at that laundry, too? . . . Then that's why you ain't eating right. You tell your mama like I tell his, the man own that place so tight he squeak when he walk,' my father said. 'Don't be looking at me like that, Davie. That man don't hire white people lessen he can treat them just like he do his colored.'

Jerry Joe went back in the living room and sat in a stuffed chair by himself for a long time. The pecan trees by the house clattered with ice in the failing light. Then he came back in the kitchen and told us he was sick. My father put a jar of preserves and two smoked ducks in a paper bag for him and stuck it under his arm and we drove him home in the dark.

That night I couldn't find the hand crank to the phonograph, but I thought Jerry Joe had simply misplaced it. The next day I had an early lesson about the nature of buried anger and hurt pride in a child who had no one in whom he could confide. When the school bus stopped on the rock road where Jerry Joe lived, I saw a torn paper bag by the ditch, the dog-chewed remains of the smoked ducks, the strawberry preserves congealed on the edges of the shattered Mason jar.

He never asked to come to our house again, and whenever I saw him he always conveyed the feeling I had stolen something valuable from him rather than he from us.

Clete parked his dinged, chartreuse Cadillac convertible by the boat ramp and walked down the dock with Jerry Joe toward the bait shop. Jerry Joe was ebullient, enthused by the morning and the personal control he brought to it. His taut body looked made of whipcord, his hair thick and blond and wavy, combed in faint ducktails in back. He wore oxblood tasseled loafers, beige slacks, a loose-fitting navy blue sports shirt with silver thread in it. I said he walked down the dock. That's not true. Jerry Joe rolled, a Panama hat spinning on his finger, his thighs flexing against his slacks, change and keys ringing in his pockets, the muscles in his shoulders as pronounced as oiled rope.

'*Comment la vie*, Dave? You still sell those ham-and-egg sandwiches?' he said, and went through the screen door without waiting for an answer.

'Why'd you do this, Clete?' I said.

'They're worst guys in the life,' he replied.

'Which ones?'

Jerry Joe bought a can of beer and a paper plate of sliced white boudin at the counter and sat at a table in back.

'You're sure full of sunshine, Dave,' he said.

'I'm off the clock. If this is about Mingo, you should take it to the office,' I said.

He studied me. At the corner of his right eye was a coiled white scar. He speared a piece of boudin with a toothpick and put it in his mouth.

'I'm bad for business here, I'm some kind of offensive presence?' he asked.

'We're way down different roads, Jerry Joe.'

'Pull my jacket. Five busts, two convictions, both for operating illegal gambling equipment. This in a state that allows cock fighting . . . You got a jukebox here?'

'No.'

'I heard about the drowned black girl. Mingo's dirty on this?'

'That's the name on the warrant.'

'He says his car got boosted.'

'We've got two witnesses who can put him together with the car and the girl.'

'They gotta stand up, though. Right?' he asked.

'Nobody had better give them reason not to.'

He pushed his plate away with the heel of his hand, leaned forward on his elbows, rolling the toothpick across his teeth. Under the bronze hair of his right forearm was a tattoo of a red parachute and the words *101st Airborne.*

'I hire guys like Mingo to avoid trouble, not to have it. But to give up one of my own people, even though maybe he's a piece of shit, I got to have . . . what's the term for it . . . compelling reasons, yeah, that's it,' he said.

'How does aiding and abetting sound, or conspiracy after the fact?'

He scratched his face and glanced around the bait shop. His eyes crinkled at the corners. 'You like my tattoo? Same outfit as Jimi Hendrix,' he said.

I pushed a napkin and a pencil stub toward him. 'Write down an address, Jerry Joe. NOPD will pick him up. You won't be connected with it.'

'Why don't you get a jukebox? I'll have one of my vendors come by and put one in. You don't need no red quarters. You keep a hundred percent,' he said. 'Hey, Dave, it's all gonna work out. It's a new day. I guarantee it. Don't get tied up with this Aaron Crown stuff.'

'What?'

But he drank his beer, winked at me as he fitted on his Panama hat, then walked out to the Cadillac to wait for Clete.

8

Monday morning, when I went into work, I walked past Karyn LaRose's blue Mazda convertible in the parking lot. She sat behind the wheel, in dark glasses with a white scarf tied around her hair. When I glanced in her direction, she picked up a magazine from the seat and began reading it, a pout on her mouth.

'There's a guy talks like a college professor waiting to see you, Dave,' Wally, the dispatcher, said. His great weight caused a perpetual flush in his neck and cheeks, as though he had just labored up a flight of stairs, and whenever he laughed, usually at his own jokes, his breath wheezed deep in his chest.

I looked through the doorway of the waiting room, then pointed my finger at the back of a white-haired man.

'That gentleman there?' I asked Wally.

'Let's see, we got two winos out there, a bondsman, a woman says UFOs is sending electrical signals through her hair curlers, the black guy cleans the johns, and the professor. Let me know which one you t'ink, Dave.' His face beamed at his own humor.

Clay Mason, wearing a brown narrow-cut western coat with gold and green brocade on it, a snap-button turquoise shirt, striped vaquero pants, and yellow cowboy boots on his tiny feet, sat in a folding chair with a high-domed pearl Stetson on his crossed knee.

I was prepared to dislike him, to dismiss him as the Pied Piper of hallucinogens, an irresponsible anachronism who refused to die with the 1960s. But I was to learn that psychedelic harlequins don't survive by just being psychedelic harlequins.

'Could I help you, sir?' I asked.

'Yes, thank you. I just need a few minutes,' he said, turning to look up at me, his thought processes broken. He started to rise, then faltered. I placed my hand under his elbow and was struck by his fragility, the lightness of his bones.

A moment later I closed my office door behind us. His hair was as fine as white cornsilk, his lined mouth and purple lips like those of an old woman. When he sat down in front of my desk his attention seemed to become preoccupied with two black trusties mowing the lawn.

'Yes, sir?' I said.

'I've interposed myself in your situation. I hope you won't take offense,' he said.

'Are we talking about the LaRoses?' I tried to smile when I said it.

'She's contrite about her behavior, even though I think she needs her rear end paddled. In lieu of that, however, I'm passing on an apology for her.' The accent was soft, deep in the throat, west Texas perhaps. Then I remembered the biographical sketches, the pioneer family background, the inherited oil fortune, the academic scandals that he carried with him like tattered black flags.

'Karyn lied, Dr Mason. With forethought and malicious intent. You don't get absolution by sending a surrogate to confession.'

'That's damn well put. Will you walk with me into the parking lot?'

'No.'

'Your feelings are your feelings, sir. I wouldn't intrude upon them.' His gaze went out the window. He flipped the back of his hand at the air. 'It never really changes, does it?'

'Sir?'

'The black men in prison clothes. Still working off their indenture to the white race.'

'One of those guys molested his niece. The other one cut his wife's face with a string knife.'

'Then they're a rough pair and probably got what's coming to them,' he said, and rose from his chair by holding on to the edge of my desk.

I walked him to the back door of the building. When I opened the door the air was cool, and dust and paper were blowing in the parking lot. Karyn looked at us through the windshield of her car, her features muted inside her scarf and dark glasses. Clay Mason waved his Stetson at the clouds, the leaves spinning in the wind.

'Listen to it rumble, by God. It's a magic land. There's a thunder of calvary in every electric storm,' he said.

I asked a deputy to walk Clay Mason the rest of the way.

'Don't be too hard on the LaRoses,' Mason said as the deputy took his arm. 'They put me in mind of Eurydice and Orpheus trying to flee the kingdom of the dead. Believe me, son, they could use a little compassion.'

Keep your eye on this one, I thought.

Karyn leaned forward and started her car engine, wetting her mouth as she might a ripe cherry.

*

337

Helen Soileau walked into my office that afternoon, anger in her eyes.

'Pick up on my extension,' she said.

'What's going on?'

'Mingo Bloomberg. Wally put him through to me by mistake.'

I punched the lighted button and placed the receiver to my ear. 'Where are you, Mingo?' I said.

'You got Short Boy Jerry to jam me up,' he said.

'Wrong.'

'Don't tell me that. The bondsman pulled my bail. I got that material witness beef in my face again.' A streetcar clanged in the background, vibrated and squealed on the tracks.'

'What do you want?' I said.

'Something to come in.'

'Sorry.'

'I don't like being made everybody's fuck.'

'You let that girl drown. You're calling the wrong people for sympathy.'

'She wanted some ribs. I went inside this colored joint in St Martinville. I come back out and the car's gone.'

I could hear him breathing in the silence.

'I delivered money to Buford LaRose's house,' he said.

'How much?'

'How do I know? It was locked in a satchel. It was heavy, like it was full of phone books.'

'If that's all you're offering, you're up Shit's Creek.'

'The guy gonna be governor is taking juice from Jerry Ace, that don't make your berries tingle?'

'We don't monitor campaign contributions, Mingo. Call us when you're serious. Right now I'm busy,' I said. I eased the receiver down in the cradle and looked at Helen, who was sitting with one haunch on the corner of my desk.

'You going to leave him out there?' she said.

'It's us or City Prison in New Orleans. I think he'll turn himself in to us, then try to get to our witnesses.'

'I hope so. Yes, indeedy.'

'What'd he say to you?'

'Oh, he and I will have a talk about it sometime.' She opened a book that was on my desk. 'Why you reading Greek mythology?'

'That fellow Clay Mason compared the LaRoses to Orpheus and Eurydice . . . They're characters out of Greek legend,' I said. She flipped through several pages in the book, then looked at me again. 'Orpheus went down into the Underworld to free his dead wife. But he couldn't pull it off. Hades got both of them.'

'Interesting stuff,' she said. She popped the book closed, stood up, and tucked her short-sleeve white shirt into her gunbelt with her thumbs. 'Bloomberg goes down for manslaughter, Dave, leaving the scene of a fatal accident, abduction, anything we can hang on him. No deals, no slack. He gets max time on this one.'

'Why would it be otherwise?'

She leaned on the desk and stared directly into my face. Her upper arms were round and hard against the cuffs of her sleeves.

'Because you've got a board up your ass about Karyn LaRose,' she said.

That night, in my dreams, Victor Charles crawled his way once again through a moonlit rice field, his black pajamas glued to his body, his triangular face as bony and hard as a serpent's. But even though he himself was covered with mud and human feces from the water, the lenses on the scope of his French rifle were capped and dry, the bolt action and breech oiled and wiped clean, the muzzle of the barrel wrapped with a condom taken off a dead GI. He was a very old soldier who had fought the Japanese, the British, German-speaking French Legionnaires, and now a new and improbable breed of neo-colonials, blue-collar kids drafted out of slums and rural shitholes that Victor Charles would not be able to identify with his conception of America.

He knew how to turn into a stick when flares popped over his head, snip through wire hung with tin cans that rang like cowbells, position himself deep in foliage to hide the muzzle flash, count the voices inside the stacked sandbags, wait for either the black or white face that flared wetly in a cigarette lighter's flame.

With luck he would always get at least two, perhaps three, before he withdrew backward into the brush, back along the same watery route that had brought him into our midst, like the serpent constricting its body back into its hole while its enemies thundered past it.

That's the way it went down, too. Victor Charles punched our ticket and disappeared across the rice field, which was now sliced by tracers and geysered by grenades. But in the morning we found his scoped, bolt-action rifle, with leather sling and cloth bandoliers, propped in the wire like a monument to his own denouement.

Even in my sleep I knew the dream was not about Vietnam.

The next day I called Angola and talked to an assistant warden. Aaron Crown was in an isolation unit, under twenty-three-hour lockdown. He had just been arraigned on two counts of murder.

'You're talking about first-degree murder? The man was attacked,' I said.

'Stuffing somebody upside down in a barrel full of oil and clamping down the top isn't exactly the system's idea of self-defense,' he replied.

I called Buford LaRose's campaign office in New Iberia and was told he was giving a speech to a convention of land developers in Baton Rouge at noon.

I took the four-lane into Lafayette, then caught I-10 across the Atchafalaya swamp. The cypress and willows were thick and pale green on each side of the elevated highway, the bays wrinkled with wind in the sunlight. Then the highway crossed through meadowland and woods full of palmettos, and up ahead I saw the Mississippi bridge and the outline of the capitol building and the adjacent hotel where Buford was speaking.

He knew his audience. He was genteel and erudite, but he was clearly one of them, respectful of the meretricious enterprises they served and the illusions that brought them together. They shook his hand after his speech and touched him warmly on the shoulders, as if they drew power from his legendary football career, the radiant health and good looks that seemed to define his future.

At the head table, behind a crystal bowl filled with floating camellias, I saw Karyn LaRose watching me.

The dining room was almost empty when Buford chose to recognize me.

'Am I under arrest?'

'Just one question: Why did Crown leave his rifle behind?'

'A half dozen reasons.'

'I've been through your book with a garden rake. You never deal with it.'

'Try he panicked and ran.'

'It was the middle of the night. No one else was around.'

'People tend to do irrational things when they're killing other people.'

The waiters were clearing the tables and the last emissary from the world of Walmart had said his farewell and gone out the door.

'Take a ride up to Angola with me and confront Crown,' I said.

He surprised me. I saw him actually think about it. Then the moment went out of his eyes. Karyn got up from her chair and came around the table. She wore a pink suit with a corsage pinned above the breast.

'Crown might get a death sentence for killing those two inmates,' I said, looking back at Buford.

'Anything's possible,' he replied.

'That's it? A guy you helped put in prison, maybe unjustly, ends up injected, that's just the breaks?'

'Maybe he's a violent, hateful man who's getting just what he deserves.'

I started to walk away. Then I turned.

'I'm going to scramble your eggs,' I said.

I was so angry I walked the wrong way in the corridor and went outside into the wrong parking lot. When I realized my mistake I went back through the corridor toward the lobby. I passed the dining room, then a short hallway that led back to a service elevator. Buford was leaning against the wall by the elevator door, his face ashen, his wife supporting him by one arm.

'What happened?' I said.

The elevator door opened.

'Help me get him up to our room,' Karyn said.

'I think he needs an ambulance.'

'No! We have our own physician here. Dave, help me, *please*. I can't hold him up.'

I took his other arm and we entered the elevator. Buford propped the heel of his hand against the support rail on the back wall, pulled his collar loose with his fingers, and took a deep breath.

'I did a five-minute mile this morning. How about that?' he said, a smile breaking on his mouth.

'You better ease up, partner,' I said.

'I just need to lie down. One hour's sleep and I'm fine.'

I looked at Karyn's face. It was composed now, the agenda, whatever it was, temporarily back in place.

We walked Buford down to a suite on the top floor and put him in bed and closed the door behind us.

'He's talking to a state police convention tonight,' Karyn said, as though offering an explanation for the last few minutes. Through the full-glass windows in the living room you could see the capitol building, the parks and boulevards and trees in the center of the city, the wide sweep of the Mississippi River, the wetlands to the west, all the lovely urban and rural ambiance that came with political power in Louisiana.

'Is Buford on uppers?' I asked.

'No. It's . . . He has a prescription. He gets overwrought sometimes.'

'You'd better get him some help, Karyn.'

I walked through the foyer to the door.

'You're going?' she said.

She stood inches from me, her face turned up into mine. The exertion of getting Buford into the room had caused her to perspire, and her platinum hair and tanned skin took on a dull sheen in the overhead light. I could smell her perfume in the enclosure, the heat from her body. She leaned her forehead into my chest and placed her hands lightly on my arms.

'Dave, it wasn't just the alcohol, was it? You liked me, didn't you?'

She tapped my hips with her small fists, twisted her forehead back and forth on my chest as though an unspoken conclusion about her life was trying to break from her throat.

I put one hand on her arm, then felt behind me for the elongated door handle. It was locked in place, rigid across the sweating cup of my palm.

9

A day later Clete Purcel's chartreuse Cadillac convertible, the top down, pulled up in front of the sheriff's department with Mingo Bloomberg in the passenger's seat. Clete and Mingo came up the walk, through the waiting room, and into my office. Mingo stood in front of my desk in white slacks and a lemon yellow shirt with French cuffs. He rotated his neck, as though his collar were too tight, then put a breath mint in his mouth.

'My lawyer's getting me early arraignment and recognizance. I'm here as a friend of the court, so you got questions, let's do it now, okay?' he said. He snapped the mint in his molars.

'Mingo, I don't think that's the way to start out the day here,' Clete said.

'What's going on, Clete?' I said.

Clete stepped out into the hall and waited for me. I closed the door behind me.

'Short Boy Jerry gave me two hundred bucks to deliver the freight. Don't let Mingo take you over the hurdles. Jerry Joe and NOPD both got their foot on his chain,' he said.

I opened the door and went back in.

'How you feel, Mingo?' I said.

'My car was boosted. I didn't drown a black girl. So I feel okay.'

'You a stand-up guy?' I said.

'What's that mean?'

'Jerry Ace is giving us an anchovy so we don't come back for the main meal. You comfortable with that, Mingo? You like being an hors d'oeuvre?' I said.

'What I don't like is being in New Orleans with a target painted on my back. I'm talking about the cops in the First District who maybe stomped a guy's hair all over the cement . . . I got to use the john. Purcel wouldn't stop the car.'

He looked out the glass partition, then saw the face looking back at him.

'Hey, keep her away from me,' he said.

'You don't like Detective Soileau?' I said.

'She's a muff-diver. I told her over the phone, she ought to get herself a rubber schlong so she can whip it around and spray trees or whatever she wants till she gets it out of her system.'

Helen was coming through the door now. I put my hand on her shoulder and walked her back into the corridor.

'Jerry Joe Plumb made him surrender,' I said.

'Why?' she said, her eyes still fastened on Mingo.

'He's tied up somehow with Buford LaRose and doesn't want us in his face. Mingo says he's getting out on his own recognizance. I think he's going to head for our witnesses.'

'Like hell he is. Has he been Mirandized?'

'Not yet.'

She opened the door so abruptly the glass rattled in the frame.

A half hour later she called me from the jail.

'Guess what? Shithead attacked me. I'll have the paperwork ready for the court in the morning,' she said.

'Where is he?'

'Iberia General. He fell down a stairs. He also needed twelve stitches where I hit him with a baton. Forget recognizance, baby cakes. He's going to be with us awhile.'

'Helen?'

'The paperwork is going to look fine. I went to Catholic school. I have beautiful penmanship.'

Clete and I ate lunch at an outdoor barbecue stand run by a black man in a grove of oak trees. The plank table felt cool in the shade, and you could smell the wet odor of green cordwood stacked under a tarp next to the stand.

'Because I was up early anyway, I happened to turn on the TV and catch "Breakfast Edition," you know, the local morning show in New Orleans,' he said. His eyes stayed on my face. 'What the hell you doing, Streak?'

'Aaron Crown bothers me.'

'You went on television, Dave, with this Hollywood character, what's-his-name, Felton, whatever.'

'I was taped here while he interviewed me on the phone, then it was spliced into the show.'

'Forget the technical tour. Why don't you resign your job while you're at it? What's your boss have to say?'

'I don't think he's heard about it yet.'

'You don't take police business to civilians, big mon. To begin with, they don't care about it. They'll leave you hanging in the breeze, then your own people rat-fuck you as a snitch.'

'Maybe that's the way it's supposed to shake out,' I said.

He drank from a bottle of Dixie beer, one eye squinting over the bottle at me. 'Something else is involved here, mon,' he said.

'Don't make it a big deal, Clete.'

'It's the broad, isn't it?' he said.

'No.'

'You got into the horizontal bop once with her and you're worried you're going to do it again. So you got rid of temptation with a baseball bat. In the meantime maybe you just splashed your career into the bowl . . . Wait a minute, you didn't pork her again, did you?'

'No . . . Will you stop talking like that?'

'Dave, rich guys don't marry mud women from New Guinea. She's one hot-ass piece of work. We all got human weaknesses, noble mon. All I got to do is see her on TV and my Johnson starts barking.'

'You were a fugitive on a homicide warrant,' I said. 'The victim was a psychopath, and his death was a mistake, but the point is you killed him. What if you hadn't beat it? What if you were put away for life unjustly?'

He wiped a smear of barbecue sauce off his palm with a napkin, looked out at the sunlight on the street.

'This guy Crown must mean a lot to you . . . I think I'm going to Red's in Lafayette, take a steam, start the day over again,' he said.

An hour later the sheriff buzzed my extension and asked me to walk down to his office. By now I was sure he had heard about my appearance on 'Morning Edition,' and all the way down the corridor I tried to construct a defense for conduct that, in police work, was traditionally considered indefensible. When I opened the door he was staring at a sheet of lined notebook paper in his hand, rubbing his temple with one finger. His venetian blinds were closed, and his windowsill was green with plants.

'Why is everything around here hard? Why can't we just take care of the problems in Iberia Parish? Can you explain that to me?' he said.

'If you're talking about my being on "Morning Edition," I stand behind what I said, Sheriff. Aaron Crown didn't have motivation. I think Buford LaRose is building a political career on another man's broken back.'

'You were on "Morning Edition"?'

The room was silent. He opened the blinds, and an eye-watering light fell through the window.

'Maybe I should explain,' I said.

'I'd appreciate that.'

When I finished he picked up the sheet of notebook paper and looked at it again.

'I wish you hadn't done that,' he said.

'I'm sorry you feel that way.'

'You don't understand. I wanted to believe the Mexican with the machete was simply a deranged man, not an assassin. I wanted to believe he had no connection with the Crown business.'

'I'm not with you.'

'I don't want to see you at risk, for God's sake. We got two calls from Mexico this morning, one from a priest in some shithole down in the interior, the other from a Mexican drug agent who says he's worked with the DEA in El Paso . . . The guy with the spiderweb tattoos, the lunatic, some *rurales* popped holes all over him. He's dying and he says you will too . . . He says "for the *bugarron*". What's a *bugarron*?'

'I don't know.'

'There's a storm down there. I got cut off before I could make sense out of this drug agent . . . Get a flight this afternoon. Take Helen with you. Americans with no backup tend to have problems down there.'

'We have money for this?'

'Bring me a sombrero.'

10

We flew into El Paso late that night. By dawn of the next day we were on a shuttle flight to a windswept dusty airport set among brown hills five hundred miles into Mexico. The Mexican drug agent who met us wore boots and jeans, a badge on his belt and a pistol and a sports coat over a wash-faded blue golf shirt. His name was Heriberto, and he was unshaved and had been up all night.

'The guy try to kill you, huh?' he said, as he unlocked the doors to the Cherokee in the parking lot.

'That's right,' I said.

'I wouldn't want a guy like that after me. *Es indio*, man, know what I mean? Guy like that will cook your heart over a fire,' he said. He looked at Helen. '*Gringita*, you want to use the rest room? Where we going, there ain't any bushes along the road.'

He looked indolently at the flat stare in her face.

'What did you call her?' I asked.

'Maybe you all didn't get no sleep last night,' he said. 'You can sleep while I drive. I never had a accident on this road. Last night, with no moon, I come down with one headlight.'

The sun rose in an orange haze above hills that looked made of slag, with cactus and burnt mesquite and chaparral on the sides. The dirt road twisted through a series of arroyos where the sandstone walls were scorched by grass fires, then we forded a river that splayed like coffee-stained milk over a broken wood dam and overflowed the banks into willows and rain trees and a roofless mud brick train station by tracks that seemed to disappear into a hillside.

'You were looking at where those tracks go?' Heriberto said. 'The mine company had a tunnel there. The train's still inside.'

'Inside?' I said.

'Pancho Villa blew the mountain down on the tunnel. When a train full of Huerta's jackals was coming through. They're still in there, man. They ain't coming out.'

I took my notebook out of my shirt pocket and opened it.

'What's *bugarron* mean?' I asked.

Helen had fallen asleep in back, her head on her chest.

'It's like *maricon*, except the *bugarron* considers himself the guy.'

'You're talking about homosexuals? I don't get it.'

'He's *adicto*, man. Guy's got meth and lab shit in his head. Those double-ought buckshots in him don't help his thinking too good, either.'

'What lab shit?'

He concentrated on the road, ignoring my question, and swerved around an emaciated dog.

'Why'd you bring us down here?' I said, trying to keep the frustration out of my voice.

'The priest is my wife's cousin. He says you're in danger. Except what he knows he knows from the confession. That means he can't tell it himself. You want to go back to the airport, man, tell me now.'

The sun rose higher in an empty cobalt sky. We crossed a flat plain with sloughs and reeds by the roadside and stone mountains razored against the horizon and Indian families who seemed to have walked enormous distances from no visible site in order to beg by the road. Then the road began to climb and the air grew cooler. We passed an abandoned ironworks dotted with broken windows, and went through villages where the streets were no more than crushed rock and the doors to all the houses were painted either green or blue. The mountains above the villages were gray and bare and the wind swept down the sheer sides and blew dust out of the streets.

'It's all Indians here. They think you paint the door a certain color, evil spirits can't walk inside,' Heriberto said.

Helen was awake now and looking out the window.

'This is what hell must look like,' she said.

'I grew up here. I tell you something, we don't got guys like Arana here. He's from Jalisco. I tell you something else, they don't even got guys like Arana *there*. Guys like him got to go to the United States to get like that, you understand what I'm saying?'

'No,' she answered, looking at the back of his neck.

'My English ain't too good. It's a big problem I got,' he said.

We pulled into a village that was wedged like a toothache in a steep-sided, narrow canyon strewn with the tailings from a deserted open-pit mine on the mountain above. Some of the houses had no outbuildings, only a piece of concrete sewer pipe inserted vertically into the dirt yard for a community toilet. Next to the cantina was the police station, a squat, white-washed building with green shutters that were latched shut on the windows. A jeep carrying three *rurales* and a civilian with a bloody ear and hair like a lion's mane came up the road in a flume of dust from the direction of the mine and parked in front. The three *rurales* wore dirty brown uniforms and caps with lacquered brims and World War I thumb-buster U.S. Army .45 revolvers. The civilian's clothes were in rags and his hands were roped behind him. The *rurales* took him inside the building and closed the door.

'Are these the guys who popped Arana?' I asked.

'Yeah, man, but you don't want to be asking them no questions about it, know what I'm saying?' Heriberto said.

'No, I don't.'

He scratched his nose, then told me a story.

The village had been visited by a carnival that featured a pedal-operated Ferris wheel, a donkey with a fifth leg that grew like a soft carrot out of its side, a concessionaire who sold hand-corked bottles of mescal that swam with thread worms, and Arana, the Spider, a magical man who swallowed flame and blew it like a red handkerchief into the air, whose scarlet, webbed tattoos, Indian-length hair, blackened mouth, and chemical green eyes could charm mountain women from their marital beds. His sexual energies were legendary.

'Arana was in the sack with the wrong man's wife?' I said.

'They gonna tell you that. You go away with that, take that story back home, everything's gonna be fine. You don't, you keep asking questions, maybe we got a problem. You see that guy they just took in? You don't want to go in there today.'

'What'd he do?' Helen asked.

'Two children went in those empty buildings up at the mines and didn't come back. See, where all those pieces of tin are flapping in the wind. He lives in there by himself, he don't ever take a bath, comes down at night and steals food from people.'

'Why'd they shoot Arana?' I said.

'Look, man, how I'm gonna tell you? This ain't no *marijuanista* we're talking about. This guy takes high-powered stuff into the States sometimes. These local guys know that. It's called *la mordita*, you got to pay the bite, man, or maybe you have a shitload of trouble. Like the guy behind those green shutters now. He don't want to see nobody light a cigar.'

The infirmary had been built by an American mining company in the oblong shape of a barracks on a bench above the main street of the village. The lumber had warped the nails out of the joists, and the windows were covered with ragged plastic sheets that popped in the wind. In back, a gasoline-powered generator throbbed next to a water well that had been dug in the middle of a chicken yard.

Inside, the beds were in rows, squared away, either a slop jar or spittoon under each one, the steel gray blankets taut with a military tuck. The woodstove was unlighted, the open door congealed with dead ash. The bare walls and floors seemed enameled with cold.

But the man named Arana needed no heat source other than his own.

He lay on top of the sheet, naked except for a towel across his loins, the scarlet tattoos on his skin emblazoned with sweat. His chest was peppered with wounds that had been dressed with squares of gauze and tape and a yellow salve that smelled like an engine lubricant. But that was not where the offensive odor came from. His right thigh was twice the size it should have been, the shiny reddish black color of an eggplant.

The priest who had called the sheriff brought us chairs to sit by the bed. He was a thin, pale man, dressed in a windbreaker, flannel shirt, khaki pants and work boots that were too big for his ankles, his black hair probably scissor-cropped at home. He put his hand on my arm and turned me aside before I sat down. His breath was like a feather that had been dipped in brandy.

'Arana has absolution but no rest. He believes he served evil people who are going to hurt you,' he said. 'But I'm not sure of anything he says now.'

'What's he told you?'

'Many things. Few of them good.'

'Father, I'm not asking you to violate the seal of the confessional.'

'He's made himself insane with injections. He talks of his fears for young people. It's very confusing.'

I waited. There was a pained glimmer in the priest's eyes. 'Sir?' I said.

'The man some think killed children up at the mines is his relative,' the priest said. 'Or maybe he was talking about what he calls the bugarron. I don't know.'

Helen and I sat down next to the bed. Helen took a tape recorder out of her purse and clicked it on. The man who was named Arana let his eyes wander onto my face.

'You know me, partner?' I said.

He tilted his chin so he could see me better, breathed hard through his nostrils. Then he spoke in a language I didn't recognize.

'It's an Indian dialect,' the priest said. 'No one speaks it here, except his relative, the crazy one who lives inside the mines.'

'Who sent you to New Iberia, Arana?' I said.

But my best attempts at reaching inside his delirium seemed to be of no avail. I tried for a half hour, then felt my own attention start to wander. The priest left and came back. Helen yawned and straightened her back. 'Sorry,' she said. She took one cartridge out of the recorder and put in another.

Then, as though Arana had seen me for the first time, his hand cupped around my wrist and squeezed it like a vise.

'The *bugarron* ride a saddle with flowers cut in it. I seen him at the ranch. You messing everything up for them. They gonna kill you, man,' he said.

'Who's this guy?'

'He ain't got no name. He got a red horse and a silver saddle. He like Indian boys.'

Inadvertently, his hand drew mine against his gangrenous thigh. I saw the pain jump in his face, then anger replace the recognition that had been in his eyes.

'What's this man look like?' I said.

But I had become someone else now, perhaps an old enemy who had come aborning with the carrion birds.

Helen and I walked outside with the priest. The sunlight was cold inside the canyon. Heriberto waited for us in the Cherokee.

'I have no authority here, Father. But I'm worried about the fate of the man from the mines, the one inside the police station,' I said.

'Why?'

'Heriberto says the *rurales* are serious men.'

'Heriberto is corrupt. He takes money from drug smugglers. The *rurales* are Indians. It's against their way to deliberately injure an insane person.'

'I see. Thank you for your goodwill, Father.'

That night Helen and I boarded a four-engine plane for the connection flight back to El Paso. She looked out the window as we taxied onto the runway. Heriberto was standing by a hangar, one hand lifted in farewell.

'How do you read all that?' she said, nodding toward the glass.

'What?'

'Everything that happened today.'

'It's an outdoor mental asylum,' I said.

Later, she fell asleep with her head on my shoulder. I watched the clouds blowing through the propellers, then the sky was clear again and far below I saw the lights of a city spread through a long valley and the Rio Grande River glowing under the moon.

11

Monday morning Karyn LaRose walked through the department's waiting room and paused in front of the dispatcher's office. She didn't need to speak. Wally took one look at her and, without thinking, rose to his feet (and later could not explain to himself or anyone else why he did).

'Yes, ma'am?' he said.

She wore a snug, tailored white suit, white hose, and a wide-brim straw hat with a yellow band.

'Can Dave see me?' she asked.

'Sure, Ms LaRose. You bet. I'll call him and tell him you're on your way.'

He leaned out his door and watched her all the way down the hall.

When I opened the door for her I could feel a flush of color, like windburn, in my throat. Two deputies passing in the hall glanced at us, then one said something to the other and looked back over his shoulder again.

'You look flustered,' she said.

'How you doin', Karyn?' I said.

She sat down in front of my desk. Her hat and face were slatted with sunlight.

'Clay said I have to do this. I mean apologize . . . here . . . in your office. To the sheriff, too. Otherwise, he says I'll have no serenity,' she said. She smiled. Her platinum hair was tucked inside her hat. She looked absolutely beautiful.

'Why are you hanging around with Clay Mason?' I said.

'He was a guest of the university. He's a brilliant man. He's a very good poet, too.'

'I heard he blew his wife's head off at a party in Mexico.'

'It was an accident,' she said.

I let my eyes drop to my watch.

'I'm sorry that I wronged you, Dave. I don't know what else to say.'

She took a breath. 'Why do you have to treat me with fear and guilt? Is it because of the moment there in the hotel room? Did you think I wanted to seduce you with my husband sleeping a few feet away, for God's sakes?'

'There's only one issue here, Karyn. Buford's not the man people think he is. He's taking money from Jerry Joe Plumb. The guy who delivered it to y'all's house was Mingo Bloomberg.'

'Who?'

'He kills people. Right now he's in custody for leaving a black girl to drown in a submerged automobile in Henderson Swamp.'

'I never heard of him. I doubt if Buford has, either.'

'Jerry Joe's mobbed-up. Why do mobbed-up guys want your husband in Baton Rouge?'

'I can't understand you. What are you trying to do to us? Buford's opponents are the same people who supported David Duke.'

'So what? Y'all have made a scapegoat out of Aaron Crown.'

'Dave, you've let yourself become the advocate of a misanthropic degenerate who molested his daughter and murdered the bravest civil rights leader in Louisiana.'

'How do you know he molested Sabelle?'

'I'm sorry, I'm not going to discuss a man like that.'

I looked out the window, fiddled with a paper clip on my blotter.

'You're committed to lost and hopeless causes,' she said. 'I don't think it's because you're an idealist, either. It's pride. You get to be the iconoclast among the Philistines.'

'I used to buy into psychobabble myself, Karyn. It's a lot of fun.'

'I guess there's not much point in any of this, is there?' she said. Her skirt was tight against her body when she gathered up her purse and rose from her chair. 'I wish it had been different, Dave. I wish the grog hadn't gotten you. I wish I'd been able to help. I can't say for sure I loved you, but I loved being with you. Be good to yourself, kiddo.'

With that, she went out the door. I could hear my ears ring in the silence.

Just before lunch the sheriff came into my office.

'This morning I've had a call from the mayor's office, one from the chamber of commerce, and one from the New Iberia Historical Preservation Society,' he said. 'Did you know Jerry Joe Plumb just bought an acre lot right down from the Shadows?'

'No.'

'He also bought a bunch of rural property south of the city limits. How well do you get along with him?'

'All right.'

'Find out what he's up to. I don't want any more phone calls.'

'Where is he?'

'Watching a bulldozer level the house that's on the lot by the Shadows.'

I drove down East Main under the arched live oaks that spanned the street, toward the Shadows, a red brick and white-columned antebellum home built in 1831 on Bayou Teche. The acre Jerry Joe had purchased was located between two Victorian homes and went all the way back to the bayou and was shaded by oaks that were over one hundred years old. I drove through the piked gate and parked next to a salvage truck and an earth grader, where a group of workmen were eating lunch. Down by the bayou was a huge pile of splintered cypress boards, twisted pipe, crushed plaster powdering in the wind, and a flattened gazebo with the passion vine still clinging to the lattice work.

'Y'all couldn't move it instead?' I said.

'The termites was too heavy to get on the truck. That's a pure fact,' a man in a yellow hard hat with a jaw full of bread and Vienna sausage said. He and his friends laughed.

'Where's Jerry Joe? I'll tell him how effective you are at doing PR with the sheriff's department.'

It was a short drive to Mulate's in Breaux Bridge. As soon as I stepped through the door I heard Clifton Chenier's 'Hey Tite Fille' on the jukebox and saw Jerry Joe out on the polished wood floor, dancing with a waitress. His elbows were tucked close to his ribs, his fingers pointed at angles like a 1940s jitterbugger, his oxblood loafers glinting. His whole body seemed animated with rhythm. His shoulders titled and vibrated; he jiggled and bopped and created an incredible sense of energy and movement without ever stepping out of a twelve-inch radius, and all the while his face beamed at the waitress with genuine pleasure and affection.

I ordered a 7-Up at the bar and waited for him to sit down. When he finished dancing he squeezed the waitress's hand, walked past me, his eyes fixed on the black bar man, and said, 'Bring my friend the same order I got.'

'Don't do that, Jerry Joe,' I said to his back.

He pulled out a chair at a table covered with a red-and-white checkered cloth. 'You got it whether you want it or not . . . Catfish filet with étoufée on the top. This is food you expect only in the after-life,' he said. He twisted another chair out. 'What's the haps?'

'Some people want to know why you just bulldozed down a house that George Washington Cable once lived in.'

'Who?'

'A famous writer.'

354

'Because it had an asbestos roof, because the floors were like walking on wet cardboard, because there were vampire bats in the drainpipes.'

'Why not work with people, Jerry Joe, explain that to them, instead of giving them heart failure?'

'Because the problem is not what I'm tearing down, it's what they think I'm going to build. Like maybe a pink elephant in the middle of the historical district.' He put a stuffed mushroom in his mouth. '*What?* Oh, I get it. They got reason to have those kind of concerns?'

'I didn't say that.'

'What are we talking about, then? I got it. It's not the house, it's me.'

'No one can accuse you of being a Rotarian.'

'I told you, my sheet's an embarrassment. I'm on a level with unlicensed church bingo.'

'You and some others guys hit a fur truck. You also stuffed a building contractor into a cement mixer.'

'He was taking scabs through our picket. Besides, I pulled him back out.'

'Why are you buying property south of town?'

He patted his palm on top of his forearm, glanced toward the sound of someone dropping coins inside the jukebox. 'Maybe I want out. Maybe I'm tired of New Orleans, being in the life, all that jazz. So maybe I got a chance and I'm taking it.'

'I'm not with you.'

'Buford LaRose is good for business . . . turn on your brain for a minute, Dave . . . What if these peckerwoods get in Baton Rouge? New Orleans will be a worst toilet than it already is.'

'A Mexican guy tried to take me out. Your man Mingo says it was a hit. Why do mobbed-up people in New Orleans care about a cop in Iberia Parish?'

Jerry Joe scratched the red tattoo of a parachute on his forearm.

'Number one, Mingo's not my man. Number two, times are changing, Dave. Dope's gonna be out one day. The smart money is looking for a new home . . . Listen, to that . . . "La Jolie Blon" . . . Boy, I love that song. My mom taught me to dance to it.'

'Where'd the hit come from?'

'I don't know. That's the honest-to-God truth. Just leave this civil rights garbage alone and watch yourself with Karyn LaRose.'

'How did you—'

'You want to ask me where she's got a certain birthmark?' He pressed his hands flat on the tablecloth and looked at them. 'Try a little humility, Dave. I hate to tell you this, but some broads ain't any different from men. They like to screw down and marry up. She ever talk about marriage to you?'

He raised his eyes and started to grin. Then his face became embarrassed and he grimaced and looked around the room. The coiled white scar at the corner of his eye was bunched in a knot.

'You want a breadstick?' he asked.

Our jailer, Kelso Andrepont, was a three-hundred-pound bisexual black man who pushed his way through life with the calm, inert certitude of a glacier sliding downhill. The furrows in his neck gave off an oily shine and were dotted with moles that looked like raisins pasted on his skin, and his glasses magnified his eyes into luminous orbs the size of oysters.

He stared up at me from his cluttered desk.

'So why are we holding the guy here if he's got a negligent homicide beef in St Martin Parish?'

'We're treating the case as an abduction. The abduction happened inside Iberia Parish,' I said. 'We're working with St Martin on the other charge.'

'Yeah, shit rolls downhill, too. And I'm always downhill from you, Robicheaux.'

'I'm sorry to hear you take that attitude.'

'This guy was born for Camp J. He don't belong here. I got enough racial problems as it is.'

'How about starting over, Kelso?'

'He complains he's being discriminated against, get this, because he's Jewish and we're making him eat pork. So he throws his tray in a trusty's face. Then he says he wants isolation because maybe there's a black guy coming in here to whack him out.

'I go, "What black guy?"

'He goes, "How the fuck should I know? Maybe the guy I just threw the food at."

'I go, "Your brain's been doing too many push-ups, Bloomberg. You ought to give it a rest."

'He goes, "I come in here on my own and a dyke blindsides me with a baton and charges me with assault. No wonder you got a jail ninety percent cannibal. No one else would live in a shithole like this."'

'You've got him in isolation now?' I asked.

'A guy who uses words like *cannibal* to a black man? No, I got him out there in the yard, teaching aerobics to the brothers. This job would drive me to suicide if it wasn't for guys like you, Robicheaux.'

Five minutes later I checked my weapon with a guard who sat inside a steel-mesh cage, and a second guard unlocked a cell at the end of a sunlit corridor that rang with all the sounds of a jailhouse – clanging doors and mop buckets, a dozen radios tuned to a half dozen stations, shouted voices echoing along the ceilings. Mingo Bloomberg sat in his boxer undershorts on a bunk that was suspended from the wall with chains. His body was pink, hairless, without either fat or definition, as though it had been synthetically manufactured. The stitches above his ear looked like a fine strand of black barbed wire embedded in his scalp.

'Kelso says you're being a pain in the ass,' I said.

He let a towel dangle between his legs and bounced it idly on top of his bare toes.

'Did your lawyer tell you our witnesses are going to stand up?' I said.

I expected anger, another run at manipulation. Instead, he was morose, his attention fixed on the sounds out in the corridor, as though they held meaning that he had never quite understood before.

'Did you hear me?' I said.

'I talked to my cousin last night. The wrong people think you got dials on me. There's a black guy, out of Miami, a freelance 'cause Miami's an open city. He's supposed to look like a six-and-a-half-foot stack of apeshit. The word is, maybe he's the guy did this screenwriter in the Quarter. My cousin says the Miami guy's got the whack and is gonna piece it off to some boons inside the jail.'

'You're the hit?'

He stared at the floor, put his little finger in his ear as though there were water in it.

'I never broke no rules. It feels funny,' he said.

'Who's setting it up, Mingo?'

'How many guys could I put inside? You figure it out.'

'You ever hear of a *bugarron*?' I asked.

'No . . . Don't ask me about crazy stuff I don't know anything about. I'm not up for it.' His shoulders were rounded, his chest caved-in. 'You've read a lot, haven't you, I mean books in college, stuff like that?'

'Some.'

'I read something once, in the public library, up on St Charles. It said . . . in your life you end up back where you started, maybe way back when you were little. The difference is you understand it the second time around. But it don't do you no good.'

'Yes?'

'That never made sense to me before.'

That night a guard escorted Mingo Bloomberg down to the shower in his flipflops and skivvies. The guard ate a sandwich and read a magazine on a wood bench outside the shower wall. The steam billowed out on the concrete, then the sound of the water became steady and uninterrupted on the shower floor. The guard put down his magazine and peered around the opening in the wall. He looked at Mingo's face and the rivulets of water running down it, dropped the sandwich, and ran back down the corridor to get the count man from the cage.

12

It was sunrise when I turned into Buford LaRose's house the next morning. I saw him at the back of his property, inside a widely spaced stand of pine trees, a gray English riding cap on his head, walking with a hackamore in his hand toward a dozen horses that were bolting and turning in the trees. The temperature had dropped during the night, and their backs steamed like smoke in the early light. I drove my truck along the edge of a cleared cane field and climbed through the railed fence and walked across the pine needles into the shade that smelled of churned sod and fresh horse droppings.

I didn't wait for him to greet me. I took a photograph from my shirt pocket and showed it to him.

'You recognize this man?' I asked.

'No. Who is he, a convict?'

'Mingo Bloomberg. He told me he delivered money to your house for Jerry Joe Plumb.'

'Sorry. I don't know him.'

I took a second photograph from my pocket, a Polaroid, and held it out in my palm.

'That was taken last night,' I said. 'We had him in lockup for his own protection. But he hanged himself with a towel in the shower.'

'You really know how to get a jump start on the day, Dave. Look, Jerry Joe's connected to a number of labor unions. If I refuse his contribution, maybe I lose several thousand union votes in Jefferson and Orleans parishes.'

'It sure sounds innocent enough.'

'I'm sorry it doesn't fit into your moral perspective . . . Don't go yet. I want to show you something.'

He walked deeper into the trees. Even though there had been frost on the cane stubble that morning, he wore only a T-shirt with his khakis and half-topped boots and riding cap. His triceps looked thick and hard and were ridged with flaking skin from his early fall redfishing trips out on West Cote Blanche Bay. He turned and waited for me.

'Come on, Dave. You made a point of bringing your photographic horror show to my house. You can give me five more minutes of your time,' he said.

The land sloped down through persimmon trees and palmettos and a dry coulee bed that was choked with leaves. I could hear the horses nickering behind us, their hooves thudding on the sod. Ahead, I could see the sunlight on the bayou and the silhouette of a black marble crypt surrounded by headstones and a carpet of mushrooms and a broken iron fence. The headstones were green with moss, the chiseled French inscriptions worn into faint tracings.

Buford pushed open the iron gate and waited for me to step inside.

'My great-grandparents are in that crypt,' he said. He rubbed his hand along the smooth stone, let it stop at a circular pinkish white inlay that was cracked across the center. 'Can you recognize the flower? My great-grandfather and both his brothers rode with the Knights of the White Camellia.'

'Your wife told me.'

'They weren't ashamed of it. They were fine men, even though some of the things they did were wrong.'

'What's the point?'

'I believe it's never too late to atone. I believe we can correct the past, make it right in some way.'

'You're going to do this for the Knights of the White Camellia?'

'I'm doing it for my family. Is there something wrong with that?' he said. He continued to look at my face. The water was low and slow moving in the bayou and wood ducks were swimming along the edge of the dead hyacinths. 'Dave?'

'I'd better be going,' I said.

He touched the front of my windbreaker with his fingers. But I said nothing.

'I was speaking to you about a subject that's very personal with me. You presume a great deal,' he said. I looked away from the bead of light in his eyes. 'Are you hard of hearing?' He touched my chest again, this time harder.

'Don't do that,' I said.

'Then answer me.'

'I don't think they were fine men.'

'Sir?'

'Shakespeare says it in *King Lear*. The Prince of Darkness is a gentleman. They terrorized and murdered people of color. Cut the bullshit, Buford.'

I walked out the gate and back through the trees. I heard his feet in the leaves behind me. He grabbed my arm and spun me around.

'That's the last time you'll turn your back on me, sir,' he said.

'Go to hell.'

His hands closed and opened at his sides, as though they were kneading invisible rubber balls. His forearms looked swollen, webbed with veins.

'You fucked my wife and dumped her. You accuse me of persecuting an innocent man. You insult my family. I don't know why I ever let a piece of shit like you on my property. But it won't happen again. I guarantee you that, Dave.'

He was breathing hard. A thought, like a dark bird with a hooked beak, had come into his eyes, stayed a moment, then left. He slipped his hands stiffly into his back pockets.

The skin of my face felt tight, suddenly cold in the wind off the bayou. I could feel a dryness, a constriction in my throat, like a stick turned sideways. I tried to swallow, to reach for an adequate response. The leaves and desiccated twigs under my feet crunched like tiny pieces of glass.

'You catch me off the clock and repeat what you just said . . . ' I began.

'You're a violent, predictable man, the perfect advocate for Aaron Crown,' he said, and walked through the pines toward the house. He flung the hackamore into a tree trunk.

That night I lay in the dark and looked at the ceiling, then sat on the side of the bed, my thoughts like spiders crawling out of a paper bag I didn't know how to get rid of. A thick, low fog covered the swamp, and under the moon the dead cypress protruded like rotted pilings out of a white ocean.

'What is it?' Bootsie said.

'Buford LaRose.'

'This morning?'

'I want to tear him up. I don't think I've ever felt like that toward anyone.'

'You've got to let it go, Dave.'

I rubbed my palms on my knees and let out my breath.

'Why does he bother you so much?' she asked.

'Because you never let another man talk to you like that.'

'People have said worst to you.' She lay her hand on my arm. 'Put the covers over you. It's cold.'

'I'm going to fix something to eat.'

'Is it because of his background?'

'I don't know.'

She was quiet for a long time.

'Say it, Boots.'

'Or is it Karyn?' she asked.

I went into the kitchen by myself, poured a glass of milk, and stared out the window at my neighbor's pasture, where one of his mares was running full-out along the fence line, her breath blowing, her muscles working rhythmically, as though she were building a secret pleasure inside herself that was about to climax and burst.

The next morning I parked my truck on Decatur Street, on the edge of the French Quarter, and walked through Jackson Square, past St Louis Cathedral, and on up St Ann to the tan stucco building with the arched entrance and brick courtyard where Clete Purcel kept his office. It had rained before dawn, and the air was cool and bright, and bougainvillea hung through the grillwork on the balcony upstairs. I looked through his window and saw him reading from a manila folder on top of his desk, his shirt stretched tight across his back, his glasses as small as bifocals on his big face.

I opened the door and stuck my head inside.

'You still mad?' I said.

'Hey, what's goin' on, big mon?'

'I'll buy you a beignet,' I said.

He thought about it, made a rolling, popping motion with his fingers and hands, then followed me outside.

'Just don't talk to me about Aaron Crown and Buford LaRose,' he said.

'I won't.'

'What are you doing in New Orleans?'

'I need to check out Jimmy Ray Dixon again. His office says he's at his pool hall out by the Desire.'

He tilted his porkpie hat on his head, squinted at the sun above the rooftops.

'Did you ever spit on baseballs when you pitched American Legion?' he said.

We had beignets and coffee with hot milk at an outdoor table in the Cafe du Monde. Across the street, sidewalk artists were painting on easels by the iron fence that bordered the park, and you could hear boat horns out on the river, just the other side of the levee. I told him about Mingo Bloomberg's death.

'It doesn't surprise me. I think it's what they all look for,' he said.

'What?'

'The Big Exit. If they can't get somebody to do it for them, they do it

362

themselves. Most of them would have been better off if their mothers had thrown them away and raised the afterbirth.'

'You want to take a ride?'

'That neighborhood's a free-fire zone, Streak. Let Jimmy Ray slide. He's a walking ad for enlistment in the Klan.'

'See you later, then.'

'Oh, your ass,' he said, and caught up with me on the sidewalk, pulling on his sports coat, a powdered beignet in his mouth.

The pool room was six blocks from the Desire welfare project. The windows were barred, the walls built of cinder blocks and scrolled with spray-painted graffiti. I parked by the curb and stepped up on the sidewalk, unconsciously looked up and down the street.

'We're way up the Mekong, Dave. Hang your buzzer out,' Clete said.

I took out my badge holder and hooked it through the front of my belt, listened to somebody shatter a tight rack and slam the cue stick down on the table's edge, then walked through the entrance into the darkness inside.

The low ceiling seemed to crush down on the pool shooters like a fist. The bar and the pool tables ran the length of the building, a tin-hooded lamp creating a pyramid of smoky light over each felt rectangle. No one looked directly at us; instead, our presence was noted almost by osmosis, the way schooled fish register and adjust to the proximity of a predator, except for one man, who came out of the rest room raking at his hair with a steel comb, glanced toward the front, then slammed out of a firedoor.

Jimmy Ray Dixon was at a card table in back, by himself, a ledger book, calculator, a filter-tipped cigar inside an ashtray, and a stack of receipts in front of him. He wore a blue suit and starched pink shirt with a high collar, a brown knit tie and gold tie pin with a red stone in it.

'I seen you on TV, still frontin' points for the man killed my brother,' he said, without looking up from his work. He picked up a receipt with his steel hook and set it down again.

'I need your help,' I said. I waited but he went on with his work. 'Sir?' I said.

'What?'

'Can we sit down?'

'Do what you want, man.'

Clete went to the bar and got a shot and a beer, then twisted a chair around and sat down next to me.

'Somebody put a hit on Mingo Bloomberg,' I said.

'I heard he hung himself from a water pipe in y'all's jail,' Jimmy Ray said.

'Word gets around fast.'

'A dude like that catch the bus, people have parades.'

'He told me a black guy out of Miami had a contract on him. He said a guy who looks like a six-and-a-half-foot stack of apeshit.'

Clete scraped a handful of peanuts from a bowl on the next table, his eyes drifting down the bar.

'Maybe you ought to give some thought to where you're at,' Jimmy Ray said.

'You heard about a mechanic out of Miami?' I said.

'I tell you how I read this sit'ation. You put a snitch jacket on a guy and jammed him up so he didn't have no place to run. So maybe somebody's conscience bothering him, know what I mean?' he said.

'I think the same hitter popped Lonnie Felton's scriptwriter.'

'Could be. But ain't my bidness.'

'What is your business?'

'Look, man, this is what it is. A smart man got his finger in lots of pies. Don't mean none of them bad. 'Cause this guy's a brother, you ax me if I know him. I don't like to give you a short answer, but you got a problem with the way you think. It ain't much different than that cracker up at Angola.'

Clete leaned forward in his chair, cracked the shell off a peanut, and threw the peanut in his mouth.

'You still pimp, Jimmy Ray?' he asked, his eyes looking at nothing.

'You starting to burn your ticket, Chuck.'

'I count eight bail skips in here. I count three who aren't paying the vig to the Shylock who lent them the bail. The guy who went out the door with his hair on fire snuffed one of Dock Green's hookers in Algiers,' Clete said.

'You want to use the phone, it's a quarter,' Jimmy Ray said.

'No black hitter works the town without permission. Why let him get the rhythm while you got the blues?' Clete said.

'All my blues is on the jukebox, provided to me by Mr Jerry Joe Plumb, boy you grew up with,' Jimmy Ray said to me.

'Crown has to stay down for Buford LaRose to go to Baton Rouge. Tell me you're not part of this, Jimmy Ray,' I said.

He looked up at the clock over the bar. 'The school kids gonna be out on the street. Y'all got anything in your car you want to keep? . . . Excuse me, I got to see how much collards I can buy tonight.'

He began tapping figures off a receipt onto his calculator.

That evening, under a gray sky, Alafair and I raked out the shed and railed horse lot where she kept her Appaloosa. Then we piled the straw and dried-out green manure in a wheelbarrow and buried it in the compost pile by our vegetable garden. The air was cool, flecked with rain, and smelled like gas and chrysanthemums.

'Who's that man down on the dock, Dave?' Alafair said.

He was squatted down on his haunches, with his back to us. He wore a fedora, dark-brown slacks, and a scuffed leather jacket. He was carving a stalk of sugarcane, notching thick plugs out of the stalk between his thumb and the knife blade, feeding them off the blade into his mouth.

'He was in the shop this afternoon. He has a red parachute tattooed on his arm,' she said.

I propped my foot on the shovel's blade and rested my arm across the end of the shaft. 'Jerry Joe Plumb,' I said.

'Is he a bad man?'

'I was never sure, Alf. Tell Bootsie I'll be along in a minute.'

I walked down to the end of the dock and leaned my palms on the rail. Jerry Joe continued to look out at the brown current from under the brim of his fedora. He folded his pocketknife against the heel of his hand. The blade was the dull color of an old nickel.

'You figure I owe you?'

'What for?'

'I took something out of your house a long time ago.'

'I don't remember it.'

'Yeah, you do. I resented you for it.'

'What's up, partner?'

The scar at the corner of his eye looked like bunched white string.

'My mom used to clean house for Buford LaRose's parents . . . The old man could be a rotten bastard, but he gave me a job rough-necking in West Texas when I was just seventeen and later on got me into the airborne. It was the way the old man treated Buford that always bothered me, maybe because I was part responsible for it. You think they won't take you off at the neck because they're rich? It's not enough they win; somebody's got to lose. What I'm saying is, everybody's shit flushes. You're no exception, Dave.'

'You're not making any sense.'

'They'll grind you up.'

What follows is my best reconstruction of Jerry Joe's words.

13

By San Antone I'd run out of bus and food money as well as confidence in dealing with the Texas highway patrol, who believed patching tar on a country road was a cure for almost anything. So I walked five miles of railroad track before I heard a doubleheader coming up the line and took off running along the gravel next to a string of empty flat wheelers, that's boxcars with no springs, my duffle bag banging me in the back, the cars wobbling across the switches and a passenger train on the next track coming up fast, but I worked the door loose, running full-out, flung my duffle on the floor, and crawled up inside the warm smell of grain sacks and straw blowing in the wind and the whistle screaming down the line.

It was near dawn when I woke up, and I knew we were on a trestle because all you could hear was the wheels pinching and squealing on the rails and there wasn't any echo off the ground or the hillsides. The air was cold and smelled like mesquite and blackjack and sage when it's wet, like no one had ever been there before, no gas-driven machines, no drovers fording the river down below, not even Indians in the gorges that snaked down to the bottoms like broken fingers and were cluttered with yellow rocks as big as cars.

There were sand flats in the middle of the river, with pools of water in them that were as red as blood, and dead deer that turkey buzzards had eaten from the topside down so that the skeletons stuck out of the hides and the buzzards used the ribs for a perch. Then we were on a long plateau, inside an electric storm, and I begin to see cattle pens and loading chutes and busted windmills that were wrapped with tumble-weed, adobe houses with collapsed walls way off in the lightning, a single-track dirt road and wood bridge and a state sign that marked the Pecos, where the bottom was nothing but baked clay that would crack and spiderweb under your boots.

The old man, Jude LaRose, told me the name of the town but not how to get to it. That was his way. He drew lines in the dirt, and if you fit between them, he might be generous to you. Otherwise, you didn't exist. The problem was you never knew where the lines were.

I hadn't realized I'd climbed aboard a hotshot, a straight-through that doesn't stop till it reaches its destination. I dropped off on an upgrade, just before another trestle, hit running, and slid all the way down a hill into a wet sand flat flanged with willows that had once been a riverbed and was pocked with horses hooves and deer tracks that were full of rainwater. I walked all day in the rain, crossed fences with warning signs on them in Spanish and English, saw wild horses flowing like shadows down the face of a ridge, worked my way barefoot across a green river with a soap-rock bottom and came out on a dirt road just as a flatbed truck boomed down with drill pipe and loaded with Mexicans sleeping under a tarp ground through a flooded dip in the road and stopped so the man leaning against the top of the cab with an M-1 carbine could say, 'Where you think you goin', man?'

I guess I looked like a drowned cat. I hadn't eaten in two days, and my boots were laced around my neck and the knees were tore out of my britches. He had on a blue raincoat and a straw hat, with water sluicing off the brim, and his beard was silky and black and pointed like a Chinaman's.

'Jude LaRose's place. It's somewhere around here, ain't it?' I said.

'You on it now, man.'

'Where's he live at?'

'Why you want to know that?'

'I'm a friend of his. He told me to come out.'

He leaned down to the window of the cab and said to the Mexicans inside, '*Dice que es amigo del Señor LaRose.*' They laughed. The ones in back had the tarp pushed up over their heads so they could see me, and two of them were eating refried beans and tortillas they had folded into big squares between their fingers. But they were a different sort, not the kind to laugh at other people.

'You know where his house is at?' I said.

He'd already lost interest. He hit on the roof with his fist, and they drove off in the rain, with the drill pipe flopping off the back of the bed and the Mexicans in back looking out at me from under the tarp.

I found Jude LaRose's town that evening. It was nothing more than a dirt crossroads set in a cup of hills that had gone purple and red in the sunset. It had a shutdown auction barn and slaughterhouse, a dried-out hog feeder lot next to a railroad bed with no track and a wood water tank that had rotted down on itself, and a shingle-front two-storey saloon and cafe, where a little black girl was laying out steaks on a mesquite fire in back. The sidewalk was almost higher than the pickups and horses in front of it, iron-stained with the rusted cusps of tethering

367

rings and pooled with the blood of a cougar someone had shot that day and had hung with wire around the neck from the stanchion of an electric Carta Blanca sign that was the same blue as the glow above the hills.

The inside of the saloon had a stamped tin ceiling, card and domino tables in back, a long bar with old-time towel rings and a wall mirror and brass rail and spittoons, and antlers nailed all over the support posts. A dozen cowboys and oil field roughnecks were playing five-card stud and sipping shots with Pearl and Grand Prize on the side.

The menu was on a chalkboard over the bar. The bartender wore a red chin beard, and his eyes were hollowed deep in his face and his arms were as thick as hams. A fat black woman set a platter of barbecue sandwiches in the service window and rang a bell. The bread was gold and brown with butter and grill marks and soft in the center from the barbecue sauce that had soaked through. The bartender put four bottles of Pearl on the tray and carried it to the card table.

'How much is just the lima bean soup without the sandwich?' I asked. I had to keep my hands flat on the bar when I said it, too, because there was a wood bowl full of crackers and pickles right at the end of my fingers.

'Twenty cents,' he said.

'How much for just a cup?'

'Where you from, boy?'

'Louisiana.'

'Go around back and I'll tell the nigger to fix you something.'

'I ain't ask for a handout.'

He pulled up his apron, took a lighter out of his blue jeans, and lit a cigarette. He smoked it and spit a piece of tobacco off the tip of his tongue. He picked up the bowl of crackers and pickles and set it on the counter behind him with the bottles of whiskey and rum and tequila.

'You cain't hang around here,' he said.

It had started to rain again, and I could see the water dripping off the Carta Blanca sign on the face of the dead cougar. Its eyes were seamed shut, like it had gone to sleep. A man opened the front door and the rain blew across the floor.

'How far is it to the LaRose house?' I said.

'What you want out there?'

'Mr LaRose told me to come out.'

The cigarette smoke trailed out of the side of his mouth. A shadow had come into his face, like a man who's caught between fear and suspicion and anger at himself and an even greater fear you'll see all these things going on inside him.

He walked down the duckboards and used the phone on the counter.

When he put the receiver back down his eyes wouldn't stay fixed on mine.

'Mr LaRose says for you to order up. He'll be along when it quits raining,' he said. He set the bowl of pickles and crackers back in front of me, then pried off the top of a Barge's root beer on a wall opener and set it next to the bowl.

'How about a steak and eggs and those stewed tomatoes?' I said.

'Anything else?'

'How about some fried potatoes?'

'What else?'

'How come a Mexican would carry a M-1 carbine on a pipe truck?' I asked.

He leaned on the bar. I could smell soap and sweat in his clothes. 'Where you seen it?' he asked.

'Coming north of the river.'

'You ever heard of no God or law west of the Pecos?'

'No.'

'It means you see wets, you forget it.'

'I don't understand.'

'It's a subject you'd best carry on the end of a shit fork,' he said.

An hour later the sky was empty and dry and pale behind the hills and you could see the sage for miles when Jude LaRose pulled up next to the sidewalk in a wood-paneled Ford station wagon, leaned over and popped open the passenger door and looked at me from under the brim of his Stetson with those blue eyes you didn't ever forget. He was a handsome man in every respect – tall, with a flat stomach, his gray hair cropped GI, his skin sun-browned the shade of a cured tobacco leaf – but I never saw beautiful eyes like that on a man before or since. They were the dark blue you see in patches of water down in the Keys, when the day's hot and bright before a storm and a cloud of perfect blue darkness floats across the reef, and you almost think you can dip your hand into the color and rub it on your skin, like you would ink, but for some reason, down below that perfect piece of color, down in those coral canyons, you know a school of hammer-heads are shredding the bonito into pink thread.

I sat down next to him, with my duffle between my legs, and closed the door. The seats were made from rolled yellow leather, and the light from the mahogany dashboard shone on the leather and reflected up in Jude's face.

'They want you?' he asked.

'Sir?'

'You know what I mean.'

'There're ain't any warrant.'

'What was it?'

'A man whipped me with his belt behind Provost's saloon. Another man held me while he done it.'

'What else?'

'I caught him later that night. When he was by himself. It worked out different this time.'

He unsnapped the button on his shirt pocket and took a Camel out and fitted it in his mouth without ever letting go of my eyes.

'You're not lying about the warrant, are you?' he said.

'I wouldn't lie about something like that.'

'What would you lie about?'

'Sir?'

When we drove away I saw the little black girl who had been laying steaks on the mesquite fire run out from the side of the building and wave at the station wagon.

That night I slept on a bare mattress on the floor of a stucco cottage full of garden tools behind the main house. I dreamed I was on a flat-wheeler freight, high up on a trestle above a canyon, and the trestle's supports were folding under the train's weight and the wheels were squealing on the rail as they gushed sparks and fought to gain traction.

The main house was three-storey purple brick, with white balconies and widow's walks and poplar trees planted as windbreaks around the yard. There was a bunkhouse with a tar paper roof for the fieldhands, rows of feeder lots and corrugated water tanks and windmills for the livestock, a red barn full of baled hay you could stuff a blimp in, a green pasture with hot fences for Jude's thoroughbreds, a scrap yard that was a museum of steam tractors and Model T flatbed trucks, a hundred irrigated acres set aside for vegetables and melons and cantaloupes, and through a long, sloping valley that fanned into a bluff above the river, deer and Spanish bulls mixed in together, belly-deep in grass.

Every fence had a posted sign on it, and for those who couldn't read, animals and stray wetbacks, Jude's foreman had nailed dead crows or gutted and salted coyotes to the cedar posts.

The lights in the main house went on at 4 A.M. when Mrs LaRose, a black-haired German lady with red cheeks and big arms Jude had brought back from the war, read her Book of Mormon at the kitchen table, then walked down to the open-air shed by the bunkhouse and fired the wood cook stove.

By 7 A.M. my first day I was wearing bradded work gloves and a hard hat and steel-toe boots and wrestling the drill bit on the floor of an oil rig right above the Rio Grande, the drill motor roaring, tongs clanging, the chain whipping on the pipe, and drilling mud and salt water flooding out of the hole like we'd punched into an underground lake.

After a week Jude walked down to my cottage and stood in the doorway with Buford, who was just seven years old then and the miniature of his daddy in short pants.

'You got any questions about how things run?' he said.

'No, sir.'

He nodded. 'You sure about that?'

'I'm getting along real fine. I like it here.'

'That's good.' He turned and looked off at the sun on the hills. His eyes were close-set, almost violet, like they were painted with eye shadow. 'Sometimes the Mexican boys talk. They forget what it was like down in the bean field in Chihuahua.'

'I don't pay it no mind.'

'Pay what no mind?'

'They talk in Spanish. So I don't waste my time listening.'

'I see.' He cupped his hand on Buford's head. 'I want you to take him to work in the tomato field tomorrow.'

'I'm supposed to be on the rig.'

'I want Buford to start learning work habits. Come up to the house and get him at six.'

'Yes, sir, if that's what you want.'

'My foreman said you asked about the wages the Mexican boys were making.'

'I guess I don't recall it,' I said.

He studied the side of my face, all the time his fingers rubbing a little circle in Buford's hair.

'Next time you bring your questions to me,' he said.

I looked at the floor and tried not to let him see the swallow in my throat.

You didn't have to roughneck long in Jude's oil patch to find out what was going on. You could hear the trucks at night, grinding across the riverbed. Jude's foreman had moved all the cattle to the upper pasture and dropped the fences along the riverbank so the trucks could cross when the moon was down and catch the dirt road that wound into the ranch next door, where another oil man, a bigger one than Jude, was running the same kind of economics.

A white man got two dollars an hour on the floor of a rig and two twenty-seven up on the monkey board. Wetbacks would do it for four bits and their beans. They'd drill into pay sands with no blowout preventers on the wellhead; work on doodlebug crews in an electric storm, out on a bald prairie, with dynamite and primers and nitro caps in the truck, all those boys strung out along a three-hundred-foot steel tape, handling steel chaining pins and a range pole that might as well have been a lightning rod. I had a suspicion it made for a religious moment.

I saw boys on the rig pinch their fingers off with pipe chains, get their forearms snapped like sticks by the tongs, and find out they weren't taking anything back to Mexico for it but a handshake.

The ranch next door was even worse. I heard a perforating gun blew up and killed a wet on the rig floor. A deputy sheriff helped bury him in a mesquite grove, and an hour later the floor was hosed down and pipe was singing down the hole.

That's not all of it, either. Jude and some of his friends had a special crew of higher-paid wets and white boys who'd been in Huntsville and on the pea farm at Sugarland that were slant drilling, which is when you drill at an angle into somebody else's pool or maybe a company storage sand and you pay off whoever is supposed to be watching the pressure gauges. They'd siphon it out like soda through a straw, cap the well, call it a duster, and be down in Saucillo, drinking Dos X's and mescal before the Texaco Company knew they'd been robbed blind.

I had no complaint, though. Jude paid me a white person's wage, whether I was clanging pipe or watching over Buford in the field. He was a cute little guy in his short pants and cowboy hat. We'd hitch a mule to the tomato sled, set four baskets on it, and pick down one row and up the other, and I'd always let him drive the mule and see how far he could fling the tomatoes that had gotten soft.

The second month I was there, Buford and me started pulling melons at the back end of the field, where a black family lived in a shack by a grove of dried-up mesquite trees. Jude rode his horse out in the field and stretched in the saddle and leaned his arms on the pommel and pushed his hat up on his brow with his thumb. Buford was slapping the reins on the mule's butt and gee-hawing him in a circle at the end of the row.

'How's he doing?' Jude said.

'He's a worker,' I said.

'That's good.' He looked over at the black family's shack. A little girl was playing with a doll on the gallery. 'Y'all been working straight through?'

'Yes, sir, haven't missed a beat,' I said.

'I don't want him playing with anybody back here.'

I tried to keep my focus on Buford and the sled at the end of the row, let the words pass, like it wasn't really important I hear them.

'You understand what I'm saying?' Jude said.

'Yes, sir. You're pretty clear.'

'You bothered by what I'm telling you?'

'That's the little girl who works with her mom at the cafe, ain't it?'

'Don't look at something else when you talk to me, Jerry Joe.'

I raised my eyes up to his. He looked cut out of black cloth against the sun. My eyes burned in the heat and dust.

'It's time the boy learns the difference, that's all,' he said.

'I'm not here to argue, Mr Jude.'

'You may intend to be polite, Jerry Joe. But don't ever address a white man as a person of color would.'

Jude knew how to take your skin off with an emery wheel.

I liked Mrs LaRose. She cooked big breakfasts of eggs and smokehouse ham and refried beans and grits for all the hands and was always baking pies for the evening meal. But she seemed to have a blind spot when it came to Jude. Maybe it was because he was a war hero and her father died in one of Hitler's ovens and Jude brought her here from a displaced persons camp in Cyprus. What I mean is, he wasn't above a Saturday night trip down into Mexico with his foreman, a man who'd been accused of stealing thoroughbred semen from a ranch he worked over in Presidio. One Sunday morning, when the foreman was still drunk from the night before and we were driving out to the rig, he said, 'Y'all sure must grow 'em randy where you're from.'

'Beg your pardon?' I said.

'Bringing back a German heifer ain't kept Jude from milking a couple at a time through the fence.'

Later, he caught me alone in the pipe yard. He was quiet a long time, cleaning his nails with a penknife, still breathing a fog of tequila and nicotine. Then he told me I'd better get a whole lot of gone between me and the ranch if I ever repeated what he'd said.

Don't misunderstand, I looked up to Jude in lots of ways. He told me how scared he'd been when they flew into German *ack-ack*. He said it was like a big box of torn black cotton, and there was no way to fly over or around or under it. They'd just have to sit there with their sweat freezing in their hair while the plane shook and bounced like it was breaking up on a rock road. Right after Dresden a piece of shrapnel the size and shape of a twisted teaspoon sliced through his flight jacket and rib cage so he could actually put his hand inside and touch the bones.

I blame myself for what happened next.

Buford and me were hoeing weeds in the string beans at the end of the field, when this old Mexican hooked one wheel of the pump truck off the edge of the irrigation ditch and dropped the whole thing down on the axle. I left Buford alone and got the jack and some boards out of the cab, and the old man and me snugged them under the frame and started jacking the wheel up till we could rock it forward and get all four wheels on dirt again. Then I looked through the square of light under the truck and saw Buford across the field, playing under a shade tree with the little black girl just as Jude came down the road in his station wagon.

I felt foolish, maybe cowardly, too, for a reason I couldn't explain, lying on my belly, half under the truck, while Jude got out of his station wagon and walked toward his son with a look that made Buford's face go white.

He pulled Buford by his hand up on the black family's gallery, went right through their door with no more thought than he would in kicking open a gate on a hog lot, and a minute later came back outside with one of the little girl's dresses wadded up in his hand.

First, he whipped Buford's bare legs with a switch, then pulled the dress down over his head and made him stand on a grapefruit crate out in the middle of the field, with all the Mexicans bent down in the rows, pretending they didn't see it.

I knew I was next.

He drove out to where the pump truck, was still hanging on the jack, and stared out the car window at me like I was some dumb animal he knew would never measure up.

'You didn't mind your priorities. What you see yonder is the cost of it,' he said.

'Then you should have took it out on me.'

'Don't be a hypocrite on top of it. If you had any guts, you'd have spoken up before I whipped him.'

I could feel my eyes watering, the words quivering in my mouth. 'I think you're a sonofabitch, Jude.'

'He's a LaRose. That's something you won't ever understand, Jerry Joe. You come from white trash, so it's not your fault. But you've got a chance to change your life here. Don't waste it.'

He dropped the transmission in first gear, his face as empty of feeling as a skillet, and left me standing in the weeds, the dust from his tires pluming in a big cinnamon cloud behind his car.

I'd like to tell you I drug up that night, but I didn't. Jude's words burned in my cheeks just like a slap, like only he knew, of all the people in the world, who I really was.

It's funny how you can become the reflection you see in the eyes of a man you admire and hate at the same time. The family went back to Louisiana in the fall, and I stayed on and slant drilled, brought wets across the river, killed wild horses for a dog food company, and fell in love every Saturday night down in Chihuahua. Those boys from

Huntsville pen and the pea farm at Sugarland didn't have anything on me.

When he died of lung cancer ten years later, I thought I'd go to the funeral and finally make my peace with him. I made it as far as the door, where two guys told me Mr LaRose had left instructions the service was to be attended only by family members.

Ole Jude really knew how to do it.

14

It was dark now and rain was falling on the bayou and the tin roof of the bait shop. Jerry Joe drank out of a thick white coffee cup across the table from me. A bare electric light bulb hung over our heads, and his face was shadowed by his fedora.

'What's the point?' I said.

'You're a parish cop in a small town, Dave. When's the last time you turned the key on a rich guy?'

'A DWI about twenty years ago.'

'So am I getting through here?'

'It doesn't change anything.'

'I saw Buford pitch in a college game once. A kid slung the bat at him on a scratch single. The kid's next time up, Buford hit him in the back with a forkball. He acted sorry as hell about it while the kid was writhing around in the dirt, but after the game I heard him tell his catcher, "Looks like we made a Christian today." '

'Buford's not my idea of a dangerous man.'

'It's a way of mind. They don't do things to people, they let them happen. Their hands always stay clean.'

'If you're letting the LaRoses use you, that's your problem, Jerry Joe.'

'Damn, you make me mad,' he said. He clicked his spoon on the handle of his cup and looked out at the rain falling through the glare of the flood lamps. His leather jacket was creased and pale with wear, and I wondered how many years ago he had bought it to emulate the man who had helped incinerate the Florence of northern Europe.

'Take care of what you got, Dave. Maybe deep-six the job, I'll get you on the union. It's easy. You get a pocketful of ballpoint pens and a clipboard and you can play it till you drop,' he said.

'You want to come up and eat with us?'

'That sounds nice . . . ' His face looked melancholy under his fedora. 'Another time, though. I've got a gal waiting for me over in Lafayette. I was never good at staying married, know what I mean? . . .

Dave, the black hooker who saw the screenwriter popped, you still want to find her, she works for Dock Green . . . Hey, tomorrow I'm sending you a jukebox. It's loaded, podna – Lloyd Price, Jimmy Clanton, Warren Storm, Dale and Grace Broussard, Iry LeJeune . . . Don't argue.'

And he went out the screen door into the rain. The string of electric bulbs overhead made a pool of yellow light around his double shadow, like that of a man divided against himself at the bottom of a well.

Dock Green was an agitated, driven, occasionally vicious, ex-heavy-equipment operator, who claimed to have been kidnapped from a construction site near Hue by the Viet Cong and buried alive on the banks of the Perfume River. His face was hard-edged, as though it had been layered from putty that had dried unevenly. It twitched constantly, and his eyes had the lidless intensity of a bird's focusing frenetically upon you, or the person behind you, or the inanimate object next to you, all with the same degree of wariness.

He owned a construction company, a restaurant, and half of a floating casino, but Dock's early money had come from prostitution. Whether out of an avaricious fear that his legitimate businesses would dry up, or the satisfaction he took in controlling the lives of others, he had never let go of the girls and pimps who worked the New Orleans convention trade and kicked back 40 percent to him.

He had married into the Giacano family but soon became an embarrassment to them. Without warning, in a restaurant or in an elevator, Dock's voice would bind in his throat, then squeeze into a higher register, like a man on the edge of an uncontrollable rage. During these moments, his words would be both incoherent and obscene, hurled in the faces of anyone who tried to console or comfort him.

He had a camp and acreage off of old Highway 190 between Opelousas and Baton Rouge, right by the levee and the wooded mudflats that fronted the Atchafalaya River. His metallic gray frame house, with tin roof and screened gallery, was surrounded by palm and banana trees, and palmettos grew in the yard and out in his pasture, where his horses had snubbed the winter grass down to the dirt. Clete and I drove down the service road in Clete's convertible and stopped at the cattleguard. The gate was chain-locked to the post.

A man in khakis and a long-sleeve white shirt with roses printed on it was flinging corn cobs out of a bucket into a chicken yard. He stopped and stared at us. Clete blew the horn.

'What are you doing?' I said.

'He's crazy. Give him something to work with.'

'How about waiting here, Clete?'

'The guy's got syphilis of the brain. I wouldn't go in his house unless I put Kleenex boxes over my shoes first.'

'It's Tourette's syndrome.'

'Sure, that's why half of his broads are registered at the VD clinic.'

I climbed through the barbed wire fence next to the cattleguard. Dock Green was motionless, the bale of the bucket hooked across his palm as if it had been hung from stone. His thin brown hair was cut short and was wet and freshly combed. I saw the recognition come into his eyes, a tic jump in his face.

But the problem in dealing with Dock Green was not his tormented and neurotic personality. It was his intuitive and uncannily accurate sense about other people's underlying motivations, perhaps even their thoughts.

'Who told you I was here?' he said.

'You've got a lot of respect around here, Dock. The St Landry sheriff's office likes to know when you're in town.'

'Who's in the shit machine?'

'Clete Purcel.'

He put down the bucket, cupped one hand to his mouth, the other to his genitalia, and shouted, 'Hey, Purcel, I got your corndog hanging!'

'Dock, I'm looking for a black hooker by the name of Brandy Grissum.'

'An addict, the one saw the screenwriter get capped?'

'That's right.'

'I don't know anything about her. Why's he parked out there?'

'You just said—'

'NOPD already talked to me. That's how I know.' The skin under his eye puckered, like paint wrinkling in a bucket. 'Short Boy Jerry put you here?'

'Why would he do that?' I smiled and tried to keep my eyes flat.

'Y'all went to school together. Now he's moving back to New Iberia. Now you're standing on my property. It don't take a big brain to figure it out.'

'Give me the girl, Dock. I'll owe you one.'

'You looking for a black whore or a black hit man, you should be talking to Jimmy Ray Dixon.'

'I'm firing in the well, huh?' I said. The wind puffed the willow trees that grew on the far side of the levee. 'You've got a nice place here.'

'Don't give me that laid-back act, Robicheaux. I'll tell you what this is about. Short Boy Jerry thought he could throw up some pickets on my jobs and run me under. It didn't work. So now he's using you to put some boards in my head. I think he dimed me with NOPD, too.'

378

'You're pretty fast, Dock.'

His eyes focused on the front gate.

'I can't believe it. Purcel's taking a leak in my cattleguard. I got neighbors here,' Dock said.

'You and the Giacanos aren't backing Buford LaRose, are you?' I asked.

For the first time he smiled, thin-lipped, his eyes slitted inside the hard cast of his face.

'I never bet on anything human,' he said. 'Come inside. I got to get a Pepto or something. Purcel's making me sick.'

The pine walls of his front room were hung with the stuffed heads of antelope and deer. A marlin was mounted above the fireplace, its lacquered skin synthetic-looking and filmed with dust. On a long bookshelf was a line of jars filled with the pickled, yellowed bodies of rattlesnakes and cottonmouth moccasins, a hairless possum, box turtles, baby alligators, a nutria with its paddlelike feet webbed against the glass.

Dock went into the kitchen and came back with a beer in his hand. He offered me nothing. Behind him I saw his wife, one of the Giacano women, staring at me, hollow-eyed, her raven hair pulled back in a knot, her skin as white as bread flour.

'Purcel gets under my skin,' Dock said.

'Why?'

'Same reason you do.'

'Excuse me?'

'You make a guy for crazy, you think you can drop some coins in his slot, turn him into a monkey on a wire. The truth is, I've been down in a place where your eye sockets and your ears and your mouth are stuffed with mud, where there ain't any sound except the voices of dead people inside your head . . . You learn secrets down there you don't ever forget.'

'I was over there, too, Dock. You don't have a franchise on the experience.'

'Not like I was. Not even in your nightmares.' He drank from his beer can, wiped his mouth on the inside of his wrist. His eyes seemed to lose interest in me, then his face flexed with an idle thought, as though a troublesome moth had swum into his vision.

'Why don't you leave me alone and go after that Klansman before he gets the boons stoked up again. At least if he ain't drowned. We got enough race trouble in New Orleans as it is,' he said.

'Who are you talking about?'

He looked at me for a long moment, his face a bemused psycho-drama, like a metamorphic jigsaw puzzle forming and reforming itself.

'That guy Crown, the one you were defending on TV, he jumped into the Mississippi this morning,' he said. 'Your shit machine don't have a radio?'

He drank from his beer can and looked at me blankly over the top of it.

15

It was raining and dark the next morning when Clete let me off in front
of the Iberia Parish Sheriff's Department, then made an illegal U-turn
into the barbecue stand across the street. Lightning had hit the
department's building earlier, knocking out all the electricity except
the emergency lights. When I went into the sheriff's office, he was
standing at his window, in the gloom, with a cup of coffee in his hand,
looking across the street.

'Why's Purcel in town?' he asked.

'A couple of days' fishing.'

'So he drives you to work?'

'My truck's in the shop.'

'He's a rogue cop, Dave.'

'Too harsh, skipper.'

'He has a way of writing his name with a baseball bat. That's not
going to happen here, my friend.'

'You made your point, sir,' I said.

'Good.'

Then he told me about yesterday's events at Angola and later at a
sweet potato farm north of Morganza.

Aaron Crown had vomited in his cell, gone into spasms on the floor,
like an epileptic during a seizure or a man trying to pass gallstones. He
was put in handcuffs and leg chains and placed in the front seat of a van,
rather than in the back, a plastic sick bag in his lap, and sent on his way
to the infirmary, with a young white guard driving.

The guard paid little attention, perhaps even averted his eyes, when
Aaron doubled over with another coughing spasm, never seeing the
bobby pin that Aaron had hidden in his mouth and that he used to pick
one manacle loose from his left wrist, never even thinking of Aaron as an
escape risk within the rural immensity of the farm, nor as an inmate
whose hostility and violence would ever become directed at a white man.

Not until they rounded a curve by the river and Aaron's left arm wrapped around the guard's neck and Aaron's right fist, the loose handcuff whipping from the wrist, smashed into the guard's face and splintered his jawbone.

Then he was hobbling through gum trees and a soybean field, over the levee, down into the willows along the mudflat, where he waded out through the backwater and the reeds and cattails and plunged into the current, his ankles raw and bleeding and still chained together.

By all odds he should have drowned, but later a group of West Feliciana sheriff's deputies with dogs would find a beached tangle of uprooted trees downstream, with a piece of denim speared on a root, and conclude that Aaron had not only grabbed onto the floating island of river trash but had wedged himself inside its branches like a muskrat and ridden the heart of the river seven miles without being seen before the half-submerged trees bumped gently onto a sandspit on the far side and let Aaron disembark into the free people's world as though he had been delivered by a specially chartered ferry.

Then he was back into the piney woods, hard-shell fundamentalist country in which he had been raised, that he took for granted would never change, where a white man's guarantees were understood, so much so that when he entered the barn of a black farmer that night and began clattering through the row of picks and mattocks and scythes and axes and malls hung on the wall to find a tool sharp and heavy enough to cut the chain on his ankles, he never expected to be challenged, much less threatened at gunpoint.

The black man was old, barefoot, shirtless, wearing only the overalls he had pulled on when he had heard Aaron break into his barn.

'What you doin', old man?' he said, and leveled the dogleg twenty gauge at Aaron's chest.

'It's fixing to storm. I come out of it.' Aaron held his right wrist, with the manacle dangling from it, behind his back.

The lightning outside shook like candle flame through the cracks in the wall.

'You got a chain on your feet,' the black man said.

'Cut it for me.'

'Where you got out of?'

'They had me for something I ain't did. Cut the chain. I'll come back and give you some money.'

'You the one they looking for, the one that killed that NAACP man, ain't you?'

'It's a goddamn lie they ruint my life over.'

'Now, I ain't wanting to harm you . . . You stand back, I said you—'

Aaron tore the shotgun from the black man's hand and clutched his throat and squeezed until the black man's knees collapsed, then he wrapped him to a post with baling wire, tore the inside of his house apart, and looted his kitchen.

Five minutes later Aaron Crown disappeared into the howling storm in the black man's pickup truck, the shotgun and a cigar box filled with pennies and a bag of groceries on the seat beside him.

'Where you think he's headed?' I said.

'He got rid of the pickup in Baton Rouge late last night. A block away a Honda was stolen out of a filling station. Guess what? Crown's lawyer, the one who pled him guilty, has decided to go to Europe for a few weeks.'

'How about the judge who sent him up?'

'The state police are guarding his house.' He watched my face. 'What's on your mind?'

'If I were Aaron Crown, my anger would be directed at somebody closer to home.'

'I guess you picked my brain, Dave.'

'I don't like the drift here, Sheriff.'

'The next governor is not going to get murdered in our jurisdiction.'

'Not me. No, sir.'

'If you don't want to be around the LaRoses personally, that's your choice. But you're going to have to coordinate the surveillance on their house . . . Look, the election's Tuesday. Then the sonofabitch will probably be governor. That's the way we've always gotten rid of people we don't like – we elect them to public office. Go with the flow.'

'Wrong man.'

'Karyn LaRose doesn't think so. She called last night and asked for you specifically . . . Could you be a little more detailed on y'all's history?'

'It all seems kind of distant, for some reason.'

'I see . . . ' He sucked a tooth. 'Okay, one other thing . . . Lafayette PD called a little earlier. Somebody broke into a pawnshop about five this morning. He took only one item – a scoped .303 Enfield rifle with a sling. You ever hear of a perp breaking into a pawnshop and stealing only one item? . . . I saw British snipers use those in Korea. They could bust a silhouette on a ridge from five hundred yards . . . Don't treat this as a nuisance assignment, Dave.'

Lonnie Felton's purple Lincoln Continental was parked under a dripping oak in my drive when Clete dropped me off from work that evening. I ran through the rain puddles in the yard, onto the gallery, and smelled the cigarette smoke drifting through the screen.

He sat on the divan, tipping his ashes in a glass candy dish. Even relaxed, his body had the muscular definition of a gymnast, and with his cleft chin and Roman profile and brown ponytail that was shot with gray, he could have been either a first-rate charismatic confidence man, second-story man, or the celebrity that he actually was.

'How do you do, sir?' I said.

'I feel old enough without the "sir,"' he said. His teeth were capped and white, and, like most entertainment people I had met, he didn't allow his eyes to blink, so that they gave no indication of either a hidden insecurity or the presence or absence of an agenda.

'I'm trying to get Mr Felton to stay for dinner,' Bootsie said.

I took off my raincoat and hat and put them on the rack in the hall. 'Sure, why don't you do that?' I said.

'Thanks, another night. I'll be around town a week or so.'

'Oh?'

'I want to use Aaron Crown's old place, you know, that Montgomery Ward brick shack on the coulee, and juxtapose it with the LaRose plantation.'

'It seems like you'd have done that early on,' I said, and sat down on the stuffed chair at the end of the coffee table.

His eyes looked amused. The *Daily Iberian* was folded across the middle on top of the table. I flipped it open so he could see the front page. A three-column headline read: 'LOCAL MAN ESCAPES ANGOLA.'

'The end of your documentary might get written in New Iberia,' I said.

'How's that?'

'You tell me,' I said.

'I have a hard time following your logic. You think the presence of a news camera caused Jack Ruby to kill Lee Harvey Oswald?'

Bootsie got up quietly and went into the kitchen and began fixing coffee on a tray. His eyes stayed on her as she left the room, dropping for a split second to her hips.

'What do you want from me, sir?' I asked.

'You're an interesting man. You had the courage to speak out on Crown's behalf. I'd like for you to narrate two or three closing scenes. I'd like to be with you during the surveillance of LaRose's house.'

'I think you want gunfire on tape, sir.'

He put on his glasses and craned his head around so he could see the wall area next to the window behind him.

'Is that where the bullet holes were?' he asked.

'*What?*'

'I did some deep background on you. This is where your wife killed another woman, isn't it? You didn't have media all over you after she splattered somebody's brains on your wallpaper?'

384

'My wife saved my life. And you get out of our house, Mr Felton.'

Bootsie stood framed in the kitchen doorway, frozen, the tray motionless between her hands.

Felton put out his cigarette in the candy dish and got to his feet slowly, unruffled, indifferent.

'If I were you, I'd spike Buford LaRose's cannon while I had the chance. I think he's a believer in payback,' he said. He turned toward Bootsie. 'I'm sorry for any inconvenience, Ms Robicheaux.'

'If my husband told you to get out, he meant it, bubba,' she said.

A year ago I had stripped the paper from the wall next to the window, put liquid wood filler in the two bullet holes there, then sanded them over and repapered the cypress planks. But sometimes in an idle moment, when my gaze lingered too long on the wall, I remembered the afternoon that an assassin had pointed a .22 caliber Ruger at the side of my face, when I knew that for me all clocks everywhere were about to stop and I could do nothing about it but cross my arms over my eyes, and Bootsie, who had never harmed anyone in her life, had stepped out into the kitchen hallway and fired twice with a nine-millimeter Beretta.

Lonnie Felton backed his Lincoln into the road, then drove toward the drawbridge through the mist puffing out of the tree tunks along the bayou's edge.

'There goes your Hollywood career, Streak,' Bootsie said.

'Somehow I don't feel the less for it.'

'You think Aaron Crown is back?'

'It's too bad if he is. Say, you really shook up Felton's cookie bag.'

'You like that hard gal stuff, huh? Too bad for whom?'

'I think Buford's hooked up with some New Orleans wiseguys. Maybe Aaron won't make the jail . . . Come on, forget this stuff. Let's take the boat down the bayou this evening.'

'In the rain?'

'Why not?'

'What's bothering you, Dave?'

'I have to baby-sit Buford. His plane comes back in from Monroe at ten.'

'I see.'

'It'll be over Tuesday.'

'No it won't,' she said.

'Don't be that way,' I said, and put my hands on her shoulders.

'Which way is that?' Then her eyes grew bright and she said it again,' Which way is that, Dave?'

Later that night Helen Soileau and I met Buford's private plane at the

Lafayette airport and followed him back to the LaRose plantation in a cruiser. Then we parked by his drive in the dark and waited for the midnight watch to come on. The grounds around the house, the slave quarters now filled with baled hay, the brick, iron-shuttered riding stable, were iridescent in the humidity and glare of the security flood lamps that burned as brightly as phosphorous flares. One by one the lights went off inside the house.

'Can you tell me why an assignment like this makes me feel like a peon with a badge?' Helen said.

'Search me,' I said.

'If you were Crown and you wanted to take him out, where would you be?'

'Inside that treeline, with the sun rising behind me in the morning.'

'You want to check it out?'

'It's not morning.'

'Casual attitude.'

'Maybe Buford should have the opportunity to face his sins.'

'I'll forget you said that.'

The next morning, Saturday, just before sunrise, I dressed in the cold, with Bootsie still asleep, and drove back to the LaRose plantation and walked the treeline from the road back to the bayou. In truth, I expected to find nothing. Aaron had no military background, was impetuous, did not follow patterns, and drew on a hill country frame of reference that was as rational as a man stringing a crowning forest fire around his log house.

However, I had forgotten that Aaron was a lifetime hunter, not for sport or even for personal dominion over the land but as one who viewed armadillos and deer, possums and ducks, squirrels and robins, even gar that could be shot from a boat, as food for his table, adversaries that he slew in order to live, none any better or worse or more desirable than another, and he went about it as thoroughly and dispassionately as he would butcher chickens and hogs on a block.

On second consideration, I thought the best trained military sniper could probably take a lesson from Aaron Crown.

One hundred yards from Buford's backyard, with a clear view of the converted carriage house, the driveway, the parked automobiles, I saw the broken gray leaves, the knee and boot marks in the soft ground behind a persimmon tree, an empty Vienna sausage can, crumbs from saltine crackers, the detritus of field-stripped hand-rolled cigarettes.

Then I thought I heard feet running, a shadow flowing between trees, dipping down into a dry coulee bed, racing past the black marble crypt in the center of the LaRose cemetery. But in the muted pink softness of the morning, in the rain that continued to tumble like crystal needles out of the sunlight, I looked again and saw only red horses turning among the tree trunks, divots of impacted layered leaves exploding from their hooves, their backs aura-ed with vapor from their bodies.

I took a Ziploc bag from my coat pocket and began picking up the torn cigarette papers and the Vienna sausage can with the tip of a ballpoint pen just as Buford came out his back door, dressed in jeans, cowboy boots, charcoal suede jacket, and gray Stetson hat, his face raised toward the dawn and the special portent that it seemed to contain.

I wondered if he had ever envisioned his face locked down inside a telescopic sight, just before a toppling .303 round was about to scissor a keyhole through the middle of it.

Maybe he had. Or maybe my fantasy indicated a level of abiding resentment that I did not want to recognize.

That afternoon Clete parked his Cadillac by the boat ramp and walked down the dock and into the bait shop, where I was stacking the chairs and mopping the floor. He poured a cup of coffee for himself at the counter and drank it.

'You looked like you got rained on today,' I said.

'I did.'

'You catch anything?'

'Nope. The water's getting too cool. I found Brandy Grissum, though.'

I fitted a chair upside down on a table and put down my mop.

'My main meal ticket is still running down bail skips for Nig Rosewater and Wee Willie Bimstine,' he said. 'So I checked in with Nig this afternoon to see if he had anything for me, and out of nowhere he tells me a black broad named Brandy Grissum skipped on a prostitution charge and left Nig and Willie holding the bond. But because most of the lowlifes consider Nig a fairly decent guy for a bondsman, Brandy calls him up from a halfway house in Morgan City and says she's scared shitless to come back to New Orleans, and can Nig square her beef with the court and renew her bond.

'Can you imagine the faith these people put in a bondsman? I used to miss my shield. Now I think I'll get me one of those little cinder block offices with a neon sign down by the City Prison.'

'She's in a halfway house?' I said.

'Not for long. She's about to get kicked out. Y'all got a snitch fund?'

'We're lucky to pay the light bill.'

'I wouldn't put that on the top of the discussion.'

*

387

The two-storey halfway house was painted canary yellow and decorated with flower boxes on a shell road that paralleled a canal lined with banana trees and wild elephant ears. The leaves of the elephant ears were withered and streaked white from the water splashed out of potholes by passing automobiles. A rotted-out shrimp boat was half submerged on the far side of the canal, and gars were feeding on something dead that streamed off one of the scuppers. The gallery of the halfway house was cluttered with green plants and straight-back wood chairs, on which both black and white people sat, most of them in mismatched clothes, and smoked cigarettes and looked at nothing or at their shoes or watched the passing of an automobile, until it finally turned onto the highway that led back into Morgan City, which seemed painted with an electric glow against the evening sky.

Brandy Grissum sat with us at a picnic table strewn with children's toys under a Chinaberry tree. She wore lip gloss and rouge high on her cheekbones and a hair net with sequins in it, and jeans and purple cloth slippers and a long-sleeve denim shirt with lace sewn on the cuffs. The whites of her eyes were threaded with blood vessels.

'You can get me some money?' she said.

'Depends on what you've got, Brandy,' I said.

'They gonna put me out tomorrow. I ain't got nowhere to go. He know where my family's at.'

'The shooter?' I said.

'He found me twice. He took me out in the woods . . . he made me do things in the back of his car.' Her eyes flicked away from my face.

'Who's the guy, Brandy?' Clete said.

'He call himself Mookie. He says he's from Miami. But he talks French and he know all about fishing in the bayous up I-10.'

'Mookie what?' I said.

'I don't want to even be knowing his first name. I just want to get my li'l boy from my mother's house and go somewheres else.'

'Why are they putting you out?'

She kneaded the top of her forearm and looked out at the shell road in the twilight.

'They said my urine was dirty when I come back to the house the other day. I say you can look at my arm, I ain't got no new tracks. The proctor, she says I'm skin popping in my thighs, the other women halfways seen it in the shower. I ain't skin popped, though, that's the troot, and I ain't smoked no rock in thirty-seven days.'

'How'd you UA dirty, then?' Clete said.

She picked at her earlobe and raised her eyebrows. 'Don't ax me,' she said.

'Why'd Mookie kill your john?' I asked.

'He said he was doing it to hep out some friends. He said the guy didn't have no bidness messing around with black women, anyway.'

'You work for Dock Green, Brandy?' I asked.

'I got a street manager.'

'You got a Murphy artist,' Clete said.

Her jawbone flexed along one cheek.

'Why'd Mookie let you slide?' I asked.

'He said he liked me. He said I could have China white, all the rock, all the tar I want, all I gotta do is ax. He was smoking rock in his car. He got a look in his face that makes me real scared. Suh, I gotta get out of Lou'sana or he's gonna find me again.'

'You've got to give me more information, Brandy,' I said.

'You the po-liceman from New Iberia?'

'That's right.'

'He know all about you. He know about this one wit' you, too.'

Clete had started to light a cigarette. He took it out of his mouth and looked at her.

'He was saying, now this is what he say, this ain't my words, "If the fat one come around again where he ain't suppose to be, I got permission to burn his kite."'

'When was this?' I said.

'A week ago. Maybe two weeks ago. I don't remember.'

'Is there a way I can get a message to this guy?' Clete asked.

'I don't know no more. I ain't axed for none of this. Y'all gonna give me train fare for me and my li'l boy?'

I pulled an envelope from my back pocket and handed it to her.

'This ain't but two hundred dollars,' she said.

'My piggy bank's tapped out,' I said.

'That means it's out of the man's pocket,' Clete said.

'It don't seem very much for what I tole y'all.'

'I think I'll take a walk, throw some rocks at the garfish. Blow the horn when you're ready to boogie. Don't you love being around the life?' Clete said.

The night before the election I lay in the dark and tried to think my way through the case. Why had the gargantuan black man with the conked hair hung around New Orleans after the hit on the screenwriter? Unless it was to take out Mingo Bloomberg? Or even Clete?

But why expect reasonable behavior of a sociopath?

The bigger question was who did he work for? Brandy Grissum had said the black man had made a threat on Clete one or two weeks ago, which was before we visited Dock Green. But Dock had probably already heard we'd been bumping the furniture around, so the time frame was irrelevant.

Also, I was assuming that Brandy Grissum was not lying. The truth is, most people who talk with cops – perps, lowlifes of any stripe, traffic violators, crime victims, witnesses to crime, relatives of crime victims, or irritable cranks who despise their neighbors' dogs – feel at some point they have to lie, either to protect themselves, somebody else, or to ensure that someone is punished. The fact that they treat you as a credulous moron seems to elude them.

I was still convinced the center of the case lay on the LaRose plantation. The three avenues into it led through Jimmy Ray Dixon, Dock Green, and Jerry Joe Plumb. The motivation that characterized all the players was greed.

It wasn't a new scenario.

But the presence of power and celebrity gave it a glittering mask. The LaRoses were what other people wanted to be, and their sins seemed hardly worthy of recognition.

Except to one man, whose ankles were marbled with bruises from leg chains and whose thoughts flared without respite like dry boards being fed into a furnace.

16

Buford won.

The northern portion of the state was split by a third-party racist candidate, while the southern parishes voted as a bloc for one of their own, a Catholic bon vivant football hero who was descended from Confederate cavalry officers but whose two PhDs and identification with the New South would never allow his constituency to be embarrassed.

The celebration that night in Baton Rouge received the kind of network coverage that one associates with Mardi Gras.

Wednesday night the celebration moved to the LaRose plantation in New Iberia. The moist air smelled of flowers and meat fires, and as if the season had wanted to cooperate with Buford's political ascendancy, a full yellow moon had risen above the bayou and the cleared fields and the thoroughbreds in the pasture, all that seemed to define the LaRose family's historical continuity. First a Dixieland, then a zydeco band played on top of a flatbed truck in the backyard. Hundreds of guests ate okra and sausage gumbo and barbecued chicken wings off of paper plates and lined up at the crystal bowls filled with whiskey-sour punches. They behaved with the cheerful abandon of people who knew their time had come; the crushed flowerbeds, the paper cups strewn on the grass, the red-faced momentary coarseness, were just part of the tribute they paid to their own validation.

Helen Soileau and I walked the treeline along the back fields, talked to two state policemen who carried cut-down pump shotguns, shined our flashlights in storage sheds and the barn and the stables, and then walked back down the drive toward our cruiser in front. It was going to be a long night.

Clay Mason was smoking a cheroot cigar between two parked automobiles, one booted foot propped on a bumper, looking wistfully at the cleared fields and the yellow moon that had filled the branches of a moss-hung oak.

'Ah, Mr Robicheaux, how are you?' he asked.

'Are you visiting, sir?' I said.

'Just long enough to extend congratulations. By God, what an event! I'm surprised Buford's father didn't get up out of the grave for it.'

'I hear he was quite a guy.'

'If that's how you spell "sonofabitch," he was.'

'How'd you know his father?'

'They owned the ranch next to my family's, out west of the Pecos.'

'I see.'

'My father used to say it takes sonsofbitches to build great countries. What do you think about a statement like that?' He puffed on his cigar.

'I wouldn't know.' I saw Helen get in the cruiser and close the door in the dark.

'Son, there's nothing more odious than an intelligent man pretending to be obtuse.'

'I'd better say good night, Dr Mason.'

'Stop acting like a nincompoop. Let's go over here and get a drink.'

'No, thanks.'

He seemed to study the silhouette of the oak branches against the moon.

'I understand y'all matched the fingerprints of that Klansman, Crown, is that his name, to some tin cans or cigarette papers you found in the woods,' he said.

'That's right.'

He flipped his cigar sparking into a rosebed. 'You catch that racist bastard, Mr Robicheaux.'

'I don't think Aaron Crown's a racist.'

He placed his hand, which had the contours of a claw, on my arm. An incisor tooth glinted in his mouth when he grinned.

'A Ku Klux Klansman? Don't deceive yourself. A man like that will rip your throat out and eat it like a pomegranate,' he said.

The breeze blew his fine, white cornsilk hair against his scalp.

Fifteen minutes later I had to use the rest room.

'Go inside,' Helen said.

'I'd like to avoid it.'

'You want to take the cruiser down the road?'

'Bad form.'

'I guess you get to go inside,' she said.

I walked through the crowds of revelers in the yard, past the zydeco musicians on the flatbed truck, who were belting out 'La Valse Negress' with accordion and fiddle and electric guitars, and with one man raking thimbles up and down a replicated aluminum washboard that was molded like soft body armor to his chest. The inside of the house was filled with people, too, and I had to go up the winding stairs to the second floor to find an empty bathroom.

Or one that was almost empty.

The door was ajar. I saw a bare male thigh, the trousers dropped below the knee, a gold watch on a hairy wrist. Decency should have caused me to step back and wait by the top of the stairs. But I had seen something else too – the glassy cylindrical shape between two fingers, the thumb resting on the plunger, the bright squirt of fluid at the tip of the needle.

I pushed open the door the rest of the way.

When Buford connected with the vein, his eyes closed and opened and then glazed over, his lips parted indolently and a muted sound rose from his throat, as though he were sliding onto the edge of orgasm.

Then he heard me.

'Oh . . . Dave,' he said. He put the needle on the edge of the lavatory and swallowed dryly, his eyes flattening, the pupils constricting with the hit.

'Bad shit, Buford,' I said.

He buttoned his trousers and tried to fix his belt.

'Goat glands and vitamins. Not what you think, Dave,' he said.

'So that's why you shoot it up in your thighs?'

'John Kennedy did it.' He smiled wanly. 'Are you going to cuff the governor-elect in his home?'

'It wouldn't stick. Why not talk to somebody you trust about this, before you flame out?'

'It might make an interesting fire.'

'I never met a hype who was any different from a drunk. I'm talking about myself, Buford. We're all smart-asses.'

'You missed your historical period. You should have sat at the elbow of St Augustine. You were born for the confessional. Come on, a new day is at hand, sir, if you would just lend me yours for a moment.'

I helped him sit down on top of the toilet seat lid, then I watched, almost as a voyeur would, as the color came back in his face, his breathing seemed to regulate itself, his shoulders straightened, his eyes lifted merrily into mine.

'We glide on gilded wings above the abyss,' he said. 'The revellers wait—'

I shattered his syringe in the toilet bowl.

'Mark one off to bad manners,' I said.

Early the next morning the sheriff called me into his office.

'Lafayette PD wants us to help with security at the Hotel Acadiana on Pinhook Road,' he said.

'Buford again?'

'The guy's turned the governor's office into a rolling party. We're probably going to be stuck with it a little while.'

'I want off it, skipper.'

'I want my old hairline back.'

'He's a hype.'

'You're telling me we just elected a junkie?'

I told him what had happened the night before. He blew out his breath.

'You're sure he's not diabetic or something like that?' he asked.

'I think it's speed.'

'You didn't want to take him down?'

'Busting a guy in his bathroom with no warrant?'

He rubbed his temple.

'I hate to say this, but I'm still glad he won rather than one of those other shitheads,' he said. He waited. 'No comment?'

'He's bad news. We'll pay for it down the line.'

'God, you're a source of comfort,' he said.

I picked up my morning mail and went into my office just as my phone rang. Dock Green must have hit the floor running.

'You tell that Irish prick he wants to get in my face, I'll meet him in the street, in an alley, out on a sandbar in the middle of the Atchafalaya. Somebody should have busted his spokes a long time ago,' he said.

'Which Irish prick?' I said.

'Duh,' he answered. 'He caused a big scene at my casino. Customers were going out the doors like it was a fire drill. He threw a pool ball into a guy's head at my restaurant'.

'Tell him yourself.'

'I would. Except I can't find him. He's too busy wiping his shit all over the city.'

'Clete's a one-on-one-type guy, Dock.'

'Yeah? Well, I'm a civilized human being. Jimmy Ray Dixon ain't. Your friend's been down in Cannibal Town, saying they give up this black ape been making threats against him or he's going to staple somebody's dork to the furniture. I hope they cook him in a pot.'

'The shooter we want is a guy named Mookie. He's telling people he has permission to take Purcel out. Who'd give him that kind of permission, Dock?'

'Try to fit this into your head, Robicheaux—'

Then I heard a woman's voice and hands scraping on the receiver, as though someone were pulling it from Dock's grasp.

'Mr Robicheaux?'

'Yes.'

'This is Persephone Green. I met you years ago when my name was Giacano.'

'Yes, I remember,' I said, although I didn't.

'Are you sure? Because you were drunk at the time.'

I cleared my throat.

'My husband is trying to say, we don't have anything to do with problems in New Orleans' black community,' she said. 'You leave us alone. You tell your friend the same thing.'

'Your husband's a pimp.'

'And you're an idiot, far out of his depth,' she said, and hung up the phone.

Either the feminists had reached into the mob or the New Orleans spaghetti heads had spawned a new generation.

I used my overtime to take the afternoon off and went to Red Lerille's Health and Racquet Club in Lafayette. I did four sets of curls and military and bench presses with free weights, then went into the main workout room, which had a glass wall that gave onto a shady driveway and the adjacent tennis courts and was lined with long rows of exercise machines. Because it was still early in the day, there were few people on the machines. A half dozen off-duty steroid-pumped Lafayette cops were gathered around a pull-down bar, seemingly talking among themselves.

But their eyes kept drifting to the end of the room, where Karyn LaRose lay on a bench at an inverted angle, her calves and ankles hooked inside two cylindrical vinyl cushions while she raised herself toward her knees, her fingers laced behind her head, her brown thighs shiny with sweat, her breasts as swollen as grapefruit against her Harley motorcycle T-shirt.

I sat down on a Nautlius leg-lift machine, set the pin at 140, and raised the bar with the tops of my feet until my ankles were straight out from my knees and I could feel a burn grow in my thighs.

I felt her on the corner of my vision. She flipped her sweat towel against my leg like a wet kiss.

'Our bodyguard isn't speaking these days?' she said.

'Hello, Karyn.'

She wiped her neck and the back of her hair. Her black shorts were damp and molded to her body.

'You still mad?' she said.

'I never worry about yesterday's box score.'

Her mouth fell open.

'Sorry, bad metaphor,' I said.

'If you aren't a handful.'

'How about requesting me off y'all's security?' I asked.

'You're stuck, baby love.'

'Why?'

'Because you're a cutey, that's why.' She propped her forearm on top of the machine. She let her thigh touch mine.

'Sounds like control to me,' I said.

'That's what it's all about, sweetie.' She bumped me again.

'Stop playing games with people, Karyn. Aaron Crown's out there. He doesn't care about clever rhetoric.'

'Then go find him.'

'I think he'll find us. It won't be a good moment, either.'

She looked down the aisle through the machines. The off-duty Lafayette cops had turned their attention to a dead-lift bar stacked with one-hundred-pound plates. Karyn sucked on her index finger, her eyes fastened on mine, then touched it to my lips.

Later, I drove to Sabelle Crown's bar down by the Lafayette Underpass. Even though the day was bright, the bar's interior was as dark as the inside of a glove. Sabelle was in a back storage shed, her body crisscrossed with the sunlight that fell through the board walls, watching two black men load vinyl bags bursting with beer cans onto a salvage truck.

'I wondered when you'd be around,' she said.

'Oh?'

'He wouldn't come here. I don't know where he is, either.'

'I don't believe you.'

'Suit yourself . . . ' She turned to the black men. 'Okay, you guys got it all? Next week I want you back here on time. No more "My gran'mama been sick, Miz Sabelle" stuff. There're creatures with no eyes living under the garbage I got back here.'

She watched the truck, its slatted sides held in place with baling wire, lumber down the alley. 'God, what a life,' she said. She sat down on a folding chair next to the brick wall and took a sandwich out of a paper bag. A crazy network of wood stairs and rusted fire escapes zigzagged to the upper stories of the building. She pushed another chair toward me with her foot. 'Sit down, Dave, you're making me nervous.'

I looked at a smear of something sticky on the seat and remained standing.

'There's only one person in the world he cares about. Don't tell me he hasn't tried to contact you,' I said.

'You want a baloney sandwich?'

'We can still turn it around. But not if he hurts Buford.'

'Buford was born with a mammy's pink finger up his butt. Let him get out of his own problems for a change.'

'How about your father?'

'Nobody will ever change Daddy's mind about anything.'

Her expression was turned inward, heated with an unrelieved anger.

'What did Buford do to you?' I asked.

'Who said he did? I love the business I run, fighting with colored can recyclers, mopping out the john after winos use it. Tell Buford to drop by. I'll buy him a short-dog.'

'He said he didn't know you.'

Her eyes climbed into my face. 'He did? Wipe off the chair and sit down. I'll tell you a story about our new governor.'

She started to rewrap her sandwich, then she simply threw it in an oil barrel filled with smoldering boards.

That evening it was warm enough to eat supper in the backyard.

'You have to work in Lafayette tonight?' Bootsie said.

'Worse. Buford has a breakfast there in the morning. I'll probably have to stay over.'

'They're really making their point, aren't they?'

'You'd better believe it.'

'You mind if I come over?'

'I think it's a swell idea.'

'Oh, I forgot. Somebody left a letter in the mailbox with no stamp on it.'

'Who put it in there?'

'Batist said he saw a black man on a bicycle stop out on the road . . . It's on the dining-room table.'

I went inside and came back out again. My name and address were printed in pencil, in broken letters, on the envelope. Bootsie watched my face while I read the note inside.

'It's from *him*, isn't it?'

I lay the sheet of Big Chief notebook paper on the picnic table so she could read it.

I killed the two blak boys in the tool bin cause they wuldnt let me be. But I still aint to blame for the first one. Tell that bucket of shit done me all this grief he aint going make Baton Rouge. You was good to me. So don't be standing betwix me and a man that is about to burn in hell wich is where he shud have been sent a long time ago.

Yours truly,
Aaron Jefferson Crown

'He uses a funny phrase. He's says he "ain't to blame" rather than "innocent," ' I said.

'He probably can't spell the word.'

'No, I remember, he always said "I ain't did it." '

'Forget the linguistics, Dave. Pay attention to the last sentence. I'm not going to let you take one for Buford LaRose.'

'It's not going to happen.'

'You've got that right. I'm going to have a talk with our friend Karyn.'

'Don't complicate it, Boots.'

'She's a big girl. She can handle it.'

'When the sheriff wants me off, he'll pull me off.'

'Nice Freudian choice, Streak. Because that's what she's doing – fucking this whole family.'

I still had a half hour before I had to drive to the Hotel Acadiana on the Vermilion River, where Buford and Karyn were being hosted by a builders' association. I sat at the picnic table and took apart my 1911 model U.S. Army .45 automatic that I had bought for twenty-five dollars in Saigon's Bring Cash Alley. It felt cool and heavy in my hand, and my fingers left delicate prints in the thin film of oil on the blueing. I ran the bore brush through the barrel, wiped the breech and the outside of the slide free of the burnt powder left from my last visit to the practice range, slid each hollow-point round out of the magazine, oiled the spring, then replaced them one at a time until the eighth round snugged tight under my thumb.

But guns and the sublimated fantasies that went along with cleaning them were facile alternatives for thinking through complexities. The main problem with this case lay in the fact that many of the players were not professional criminals.

Sabelle's story was not an unusual one. In small southern towns, since antebellum times, the haves and the have-nots may have either despised or feared one another in daylight, but at night both sexual need and the imperious urge had a way of dissolving the social differences that were so easily defined in the morning hours.

I say it wasn't an exceptional story. But that doesn't mean it is any less an indicator of the people we were. I just didn't know if it had a bearing on the case.

He had never really noticed her at New Iberia High. She had been one grade behind him, one of those girls who wore a homemade tattoo on her hand and clothes from the dry goods section of the five-and-dime and trailed rumors behind her that were too outrageous to be believed. She was arrested for shoplifting, then she left school in the eleventh grade and became a waitress in the drive-in and bowling alley at the end of East Main. The summer of his graduation he had gone to the drive-in for beers in his metallic green Ford convertible with three other ballplayers after an American Legion game. He was unshowered, his face flushed with victory and the pink magic of the evening, his uniform grass stained, his spikes clicking on the gravel when he walked to the service window and saw her wiping the moisture off a long-necked Jax with her cupped hand.

She leaned over the beer box and smiled and looked into his eyes and at the grin at the corner of his mouth and knew that he would be back later.

He drove his friends home and bathed and changed clothes and sat at one of the plank tables under the live oaks and drank beer and listened to the music that was piped from the jukebox into loudspeakers nailed in the tree limbs, until she finally walked out in the humid glare of the electric lights at midnight and got into his car and reached over and blew his horn to say good night to the other waitresses who stood giggling behind the drive-in's glass window. He took no notice of her presumption and seemingly proprietary display; he even grinned good-naturedly. No one else was in the lot except an elderly Negro picking up trash and stuffing it in a gunny sack.

They did it the first time on a back road by Lake Martin, in the way that she expected him to, on the backseat, the door open, his pants and belt around his ankles, his body trembling and awkward with his passion, his jaws already going slack and his voice a weak and hoarse whisper before he had fully penetrated her.

Three nights later he went by her home, the Montgomery Ward brick house on the coulee, and convinced her to call in sick at work. This time they drove down the Teche toward Jeanerette and did it in the caretaker's cottage of a plantation built on the bayou by West Indian slaves in 1790, which Buford's father had bought not because of its iron-scrolled verandas or oak-canopied circular drive or wisteria-entwined gazebos or the minié balls drilled in its window frames by Yankee soldiers but simply as a transitory real estate investment for which he wrote a check.

As the summer passed, Buford and Sabelle's late-night routine became almost like that of an ordinary young couple who went steady or who were engaged or whose passion was so obviously pure in its heat and intensity that the discrepancy in their family backgrounds seemed irrelevant.

In her mind the summer had become a song that would have no end. She looked at calendar dates only as they indicated the span of her periods. The inept boy who had trembled on top of her that first night by Lake Martin, and who had sat ashamed in the dark later, his pants still unbuttoned over his undershorts while she held his hand and assured him that it had been a fine moment for her, had gradually transformed into a confident lover, realizing with the exhalation of her breath, the touch of her hands in certain places, the motion of her hips, what gave her the most pleasure, until finally he knew all the right things to do, without being told, and could make her come before he did and then a second time with him.

His triangular back was corded with muscle, his buttocks small and hard under her palms, his mouth always gentle on her body. From the bed in the caretaker's cottage she could look down the corridor of oaks that gave onto the Teche, the limbs and moss and leaves swelling in the wind, and through the dark trunks she could see the moon catch on the water like a spray of silver coins, and it made her think of a picture she had once seen in a children's book of biblical stories.

The picture was titled the *Gates of Eden*. As a child she had thought of it as a place of exodus and exclusion. Now, as she held Buford between her legs and pressed him deeper inside, she knew those gates were opening for her.

But in August he began to make excuses. He had to begin early training for the football season, to be asleep early, to go to Baton Rouge for his physical, to meet with coaches from Tulane and Ole Miss and the University of Texas who were still trying to lure him away from LSU.

On the last Saturday of the month, a day that he had told her he would be in New Orleans, she saw his convertible parked outside Slick's Club in St Martinville, with three girls in it, sitting up on the sides, drinking vodka collins that a Negro waiter brought them from inside.

She was in her father's car. One headlight was broken and the passenger window was taped over with cardboard and the body leaked rust at every seam. She drove around the block twice, her hands sweating on the wheel, her heart beating, then she pulled up at an angle to the convertible and got out, her words like broken Popsicle sticks in her throat.

'What?' one of the girls said.

'Where is Buford? You're with Buford, aren't you? This is his car,' Sabelle said. But her voice was weak, apart from her, outside of her skin, somehow shameful.

The girls looked at one another.

'Buford the Beautiful?' one of them said. The three of them started to laugh, then looked back at her and fluttered their eyes and blew their cigarette smoke at upward angles into the warm air.

Then a huge, redheaded crewcut boy, his hair stiff as metal with butch wax, with whiskey-flushed cheeks, in a gold and purple LSU T-shirt, erupted out the door of the club with someone behind him.

The crewcut boy, who had been an All-State center at New Iberia High, took one look at Sabelle and turned, his grin as wide and obscene as a jack-o'-lantern's, and held up his palms to the person behind him, saying, 'Whoa, buddy! Not the time to go outside. Not unless you want the family jewels on her car aerial.'

She saw Buford's face in the neon light, then it was gone.

She couldn't remember driving home that night. She lay in the dark in her bedroom and listened to the frogs in the woods, to her father getting up to urinate, to her neighbor, a trash hauler, crushing tin cans in the bed of his truck. She watched an evangelist preacher on the black-and-white television set in her tiny living room, then a movie about nuclear war. The movie made use of U.S. Army footage that showed the effects of radiation burns on living animals that had been left in pens five hundred yards from an atomic explosion.

As she listened to the bleating of the animals, she wanted everyone in the movie to die. No, that wasn't it. She believed for the first time she understood something about men that she had never understood before, and she wanted to see a brilliant white light ripple across the sky outside her window, burn it away like black cellophane, yes, a perfect white flame that could superheat the air, eat the water out of the bayou, and instantly wither a corridor of oaks that in the moonlight had become biblical gates in a children's book.

But her anger and the relief it gave her melted away to fatigue, and when the dawn finally came it was gray and wet and the rain ran down inside the walls of the house, and when she heard the trash hauler's wife yelling at her children next door, then striking one of them with a belt, viciously, the voice rising with each blow, Sabelle knew that her future was as linear and as well defined as the nailheads protruding from the buckled linoleum at her feet.

I hadn't watched the time. I went to get in my truck and head for Lafayette, but Bootsie's Toyota was parked behind me. I heard her open Alafair's bedroom window behind me.

'Take my car,' she said. 'I can use the truck.'

'See you in Lafayette,' I said.

'What's your room number?'

'I don't know. Ask at the desk.'

I backed out into the dirt road and looked once again at my truck parked in the opening of the old barn that we used as a garage. I almost went back and got it, but it had been running fine since I had gotten it out of the shop.

And I was running late.

What a bitter line to remember.

17

Years ago Pinhook Road in Lafayette had been a tree-lined two-lane road that led out of town over the Vermilion River into miles of sugarcane acreage. Just before the steel drawbridge that spanned the river was an antebellum home with arbors of pecan trees in the yard. The river was yellow and high in the spring, and the banks were green and heavily wooded. Feral hogs foraged among the trees. The only businesses along the river were a drive-in restaurant called the Skunk, where college and high school kids hung out, and the American Legion Club on the far side of the bridge, where you could eat blue-point crabs and drink pitcher beer on a screened porch that hung on stilts above the water.

But progress and the developers had their way. The oaks were sawed down, the root systems ground into pulp by road graders, the banks of the river covered with cement for parking lots. Overlooking all this new urban environment was the Hotel Acadiana, where builders and developers and union officials from all over the state had come to pay a three-hundred-dollar-a-plate homage to their new governor.

'Do you hear little piggy feet running toward the trough?' Helen Soileau said. We were standing like posts by one side of the banquet-room entrance. A jazz combo was playing inside. Helen kept stoking her own mood.

'What a bunch . . . Did you see Karyn in the bar? I think she's half in the bag,' she said.

'I don't think she's entirely comfortable with her new constituency.'

'Not in the daylight, anyway . . . Check out who just came in the door.'

Persephone Green wore a black see-through evening dress and a sapphire and diamond necklace around her throat. Her shoulders were as white and smooth as moonstone.

'How do you know Dock Green's wife?' I said.

'I was in uniform with NOPD when she shot a prowler at her home in the Garden District. She shot him five times.'

Persephone Green paused by the banquet room door, her black sequined bag dangling from her wrist by a spidery cord.

'You get around,' she said to me. Her hair was pulled straight back and threaded with a string of tiny diamonds.

'Looking after the common good, that sort of thing,' I said.

'We'll all sleep more secure, I'm sure.' Her gaze roved indolently over Helen's face. 'You have a reason for staring at me, madam?'

'No, ma'am.'

'I know you?'

'I was the first officer at the scene when you popped that black guy by your swimming pool. I pulled his head out of the water,' Helen said.

'Oh yes, how could I forget? You're the charm school graduate who made some accusations.'

'Not really. I probably have poor night vision. I was the only one who saw a powder burn by the guy's eyebrow,' Helen said.

'That's right, you made quite a little squeaking noise, didn't you?'

'The scene investigator probably had better eyesight. He's the one took early retirement the same year and bought a liquor store out in Metairie,' Helen said.

'My, what a clever sack of potatoes.'

Persephone Green walked on inside the banquet room. The back of her evening dress was an open V that extended to the lower tip of her vertebrae.

'I'm going up on the roof,' Helen said.

'Don't let her bother you.'

'Tomorrow I'm off this shit. The old man doesn't like it, he can have my shield.'

I watched her walk through the crowd toward the service elevator, her back flexed, her arms pumped, her expression one that dissipated smiles and caused people to glance away from her face.

I walked through the meeting rooms and the restaurant and bar area. Karyn LaRose was dancing by the bandstand with Jerry Joe Plumb. Her evening dress looked like frozen pink champagne poured on her body. She pulled away from him and came up to me, her face flushed and hot, her breath heavy with the smell of cherries and bourbon.

'Dance with me,' she said.

'Can't do it on the job.'

'Yes you will.' She slipped her hand into mine and held it tightly between us. She tilted her chin up; a private thought, like a self-indulgent memory, seemed to light her eyes.

'It looks like you're enjoying yourself,' I said.

'I know of only one moment that feels as good as winning,' she said. She smiled at the corners of her mouth.

'Better have some coffee, Karyn.'

'You're a pill. But you're going to end up in Baton Rouge just the same honey bunny.'

'*Adios*,' I said, and pulled loose from her and went out the side door and into the parking lot.

It was warm and muggy outside, and the moon was yellow and veiled inside a rain ring. There were Lafayette city cops in the parking lot and state police with rifles on the roof. I walked all the way around the hotel and talked with a state policeman and a black security guard at the back door, then checked the opposite side of a hedge that bordered the parking lot, and, finally, for want of anything else to do, walked down toward the river.

Where would Aaron Crown be, I asked myself.

Not in a town or city, I thought. Even before he had been a hunted man, Aaron was one of those who sought out woods and bogs not only as a refuge of shadow and invisibility but as a place where no concrete slab would separate the whirrings in his chest from the power that he instinctively knew lay inside rotted logs and layers of moldy leaves and caves that were as dark as a womb.

Maybe in the Atchafalaya Basin, I thought, holed up in a shack on stilts, smearing his skin with mud to protect it from mosquitoes, eating nutria or coon or gar or whatever bird he could knock from a tree with a club, his ankles lesioned with sores from the leg chains he had run in.

If he tried to get Buford tonight, in all probability it would have to be from a distance, I thought. He could come down the Vermilion, hide his boat under a dock, perhaps circle the hotel, and hunch down in the shrubbery behind the parking lot. With luck Buford would appear under a canvas walkway, or between parked automobiles, and Aaron would wind the leather sling as tightly as a tourniquet around his left forearm, sight the scope's crosshairs on the man who had not only sent him to prison but had used and discarded his daughter as a white overseer would a field woman, then grind his back teeth with an almost sexual pleasure while he squeezed off the round and watched the world try to deal with Aaron Crown's handiwork.

But he had to get inside the perimeter to do it.

I used the pay phone in a restaurant on the riverbank to call Bootsie. While I listened to my own voice on the answering machine, I gazed out the window at the parking lot and the four-lane flow of headlights on Pinhook. A catering truck turned into the hotel, a rug cleaning van driven by a woman, a white stretch limo filled with revelers, a half dozen taxi cabs.

I hung up the phone and went back outside. It was almost 9 P.M. Where was Bootsie?

I went back inside the hotel and rode the service elevator up to the roof. The wind was warm and smelled of rain, and there were yellow slicks of moonlight, like patches of oil paint, floating on the river's surface.

Down below, at the service entrance, the caterers were carrying in stainless steel containers of food, and a blonde woman in a baggy gray dress was pulling a hamper loaded with rug cleaning equipment from her van. A drunk man in a hat and a raincoat wandered through the parked cars, then decided to work his way into the hedge at the back of the lot, simultaneously unzipping his fly. The state policeman at the service door walked out into the lot and paused under a light, his hands on his hips, then stepped close in to the hedge, raised on his toes, and tried to see the man in the raincoat. The state policeman disappeared into the shadows.

'What is it?' Helen said.

'A state trooper went after a drunk in the hedge. I don't see either one of them now . . . Get on the portable, will you?'

'What y'all got down there?' she said into her radio.

'Ain't got nothing,' the voice of a black man said.

'Who is this?'

'The security guard.'

'Put an officer on.'

'They ain't one.'

'What's going on with the guy in the hedge?'

'What guy?'

'The drunk the state trooper went after. Look, find an officer and give him the radio.'

'I done tried to tell you, they ain't nothing going on. Except somebody down here don't have no bidness working in a hotel.'

'What are you talking about?' Helen said.

'Somebody down here got BO could make your nose fall off, that's what I'm talking about. That clear enough?' There was a pause. The security guard was still transmitting but he was speaking to someone else now: 'I told you, you got to have some ID . . . You ain't suppose to be inside here . . . Hey, don't you be coming at me like that . . .'

The portable radio struck the floor.

Helen and I ran for the service elevator.

By the time we got down to the first floor a Lafayette city cop and a state policeman were running down the hallway ahead of us toward the service entrance. Through the glass I could see the catering truck and the rug cleaning van in the parking lot.

'There ain't anybody here,' the city cop said, looking at the empty hallway, then outside. He wore sideburns and his hat was too large for his head. He sniffed the air and made a face. 'Man, what's that smell? It's like somebody rubbed shit on the walls.'

The hallway made a left angle toward the kitchen. Halfway down it were two ventilated wood doors that were closed on a loud humming sound inside. A clothes hamper loaded with squeegee mops and a rug-cleaning machine and bottles of chemicals rested at an angle against the wall. I opened one of the doors and saw, next to the boilers, a thin black man, with a mustache, in the uniform of a security guard, sitting against a pile of crumpled cardboard cartons, his knees drawn up before him, his hands gripping his loins, his face dilated with shock.

'What happened to you, partner?' I said.

'The woman done it,' he answered.

'The woman?'

'I mean, she was dressed like a woman. She come at me. I ain't wanted to do it, but I hit her with my baton. It didn't even slow her up. That's when she grabbed me. Down here. She twisted real hard. She kept saying, "Tell me where LaRose at or I tear it out." ' He swallowed and widened his eyes.

'We'll get the paramedics. You're going to be all right,' I said. I heard Helen go back out the door.

'I ain't never had nothing like this happen,' he said. His face flinched when he tried to change the position of his legs. 'It was when I seen her socks. That's what started it, see. I wouldn't have paid her no mind.'

'Her socks?' I said.

'The catering guys went in the kitchen with all the food. I thought it was one of them stinking up the place. Then I looked at the woman's feet 'cause she was tracking the rug. She had on brogans and socks with blood on them. I axed her to show me some ID. She say it's in the van, then y'all called me on the radio.'

'Where'd this person go?' I said.

'I don't know. Back outside, maybe. She was kicking around in these cartons, looking for something. I think she dropped it when I hit her. It was metal-looking. Maybe a knife.'

Helen came back through the door.

'Check this. It was out in the lot,' she said, and held up a fright wig by one ropy blond strand.

'You did fine,' I said to the security guard. 'Maybe you saved the governor's life tonight.'

'Yeah? I done that?'

'You bet,' I said. Then I saw a piece of black electrician's tape and a glint of metal under a flattened carton. I knelt on one knee and lifted up

406

the carton and inserted my ballpoint pen through the trigger guard of a revolver whose broken wood grips were taped to the steel frame.

'It looks like a thirty-two,' Helen said.

'It sure does.'

'What, that means something?' she asked.

'I've seen it before. In a shoebox full of military decorations at Sabelle Crown's bar,' I said.

An hour later, a half mile away, somebody reported a grate pried off a storm drain. A Lafayette city cop used his flashlight and crawled down through a huge slime-encrusted pipe that led under the streets to a bluff above the Vermilion River. The bottom of the pipe was trenched with the heavy imprints of a man's brogans or work boots. The prints angled off the end of the pipe through the brush and meandered along the mudbank, below the bluff and an apartment building where people watched the late news behind their sliding glass doors, oblivious to the passage of a man who could have stepped out of a cave at the dawn of time.

Aaron found a powerboat locked with a chain to a dock, tore the chain and the steel bolt out of the post, then discovered a hundred yards downstream he had no gas. He climbed up the bank with a can, flung the dress in the brush, and followed a coulee to a lighted boulevard, climbed through a corrugated pipe, and walked into a filling station, wearing only his trousers and brogans, his hairy, mud-streaked torso glowing with an odor that made the attendant blanch.

Aaron opened his calloused palm on a bone-handle pocketknife.

'How much you give me for this?' he asked.

'I don't need one,' the attendant replied, and tried to smile. He was young, his black hair combed straight back; he wore a tie that attached to the collar of his white shirt with a cardboard hook.

'I'll take six dollars for it. You can sell it for ten.'

'No, sir, I really don't need no knife.'

'I just want five dollars gas and a bag of them pork rinds. That's an honest deal.'

The attendant's eyes searched the empty pavilion outside. The rain was slanting across the fluorescent lights above the gas pumps.

'You're trying to make me steal from the man I work for,' he said.

'I ain't got a shirt on my back. I ain't got food to eat. I come in out of the rain and ask for hep and you call me a thief. I won't take that shit.'

'I'll call my boss and ax him. Maybe you can talk to him.'

The attendant lifted the telephone receiver off the hook under the counter. But Aaron's huge hand closed on his and squeezed, then squeezed harder, splaying the fingers, mashing the knuckles like bits of bone against the plastic, his eyes bulging with energy and power an inch from the attendant's face, his grip compressing the attendant's hand into a ball of pain until a cry broke from the attendant's throat and his free hand flipped at the power switch to an unleaded pump.

Aaron left the pocketknife on top of the counter.

'My name's Aaron Crown. I killed two niggers in Angola kept messing with me. You tell anybody I robbed you, I'll be back,' he said.

But the party at the Acadiana never slowed down. The very fact that Aaron had failed so miserably in attempting to penetrate the govenor-elect's security, like an insect trying to fight its way out of a glass bell, was almost a metaphorical confirmation that a new era had begun, one in which a charismatic southern leader and his beautiful wife danced like college sweethearts to a Dixieland band and shared their own aura with such a generosity of spirit that even the most hard-bitten self-made contractor felt humbled and ennobled to be in their presence.

But I was worn out when I got back from the search for Aaron Crown and didn't care anymore about the fortunes of the LaRose family and just wanted to go to sleep. There was a message from Bootsie at the desk when I picked up my room key: *The truck broke down by Spanish Lake and I had to wait for the wrecker. I'm borrowing my sister's car but will be there quite late.*

I left a note for Bootsie with the room number on it and started toward the elevator.

'Mr Robicheaux, you have another message,' the clerk said.

I took the piece of paper from his hand and read it.

Streak, I got the gen on our man Mookie. We're talking about your mainline subhuman here. I'll fill you in later. Let's ROA at the bar. Dangle easy, big mon – Clete.

'I'm a little confused. This is my friend's handwriting. He's here at the hotel?' I said.

The clerk took the slip of paper out of my hand and looked at it.

'Oh yes, he's here. He is certainly here, sir.'

'Excuse me?'

'I think there was a problem about his invitation. He didn't seem to have it with him. Someone tried to put his hand on your friend's arm and walk him to the door.'

'That must have made an interesting show.'

'Oh it was, sir. Definitely.' The clerk was laughing to himself now.

I went into the bar and restaurant, looked on the dance floor and in the banquet and meeting rooms. Normally tracking Clete Purcel's progress through a given area was like following the path of a wrecking ball, but I saw no sign of him and I rode the elevator up to the top floor, where I had been given a room at the end of the hall from Buford and Karyn's, unlocked the door, undressed, and lay down on the bed in the dark.

It was storming outside now, and through the wide glass window I could see the flow of traffic across the bridge and the rain falling out of the electric light into the water. At one time this area had been called Vermilionville, and in 1863 Louisiana's boys in butternut had retreated up the Teche, exhausted, malnourished, their uniforms in rags, often barefoot, and had fought General Banks' federal troops, right here, on the banks of the river, to keep open the flow of supplies from Texas to the rest of the Confederacy.

As I fell onto the edges of sleep I saw sugarcane fields and houses burning and skies that were plum-colored with smoke and heard the popping of small-arms fire and the clatter of muskets and bayonets as a column of infantry ran down the dirt road toward an irrigation ditch, and I had no doubt which direction my sleep was about to take.

This time the sniper was not Victor Charles.

I was trapped in the middle of the dirt road, my feet unable to run. I saw a musket extend itself from a clump of violent green brush, saw the stiffness of its barrel rear in the sunlight, and in my mind, as though I had formed a contract between the condemned and the executioner, the sniper and I became one, joined irrevocably together as co-participants in my death, and just before the .58 caliber round exploded from the barrel I could feel him squeeze the musket in his hands, as though it was really I who cupped its wet hardness in my palms.

In my sleep I heard the door to the hotel room open, then close, heard someone set down a key on the nightstand and close the curtains, felt a woman's weight on the side of the bed and then her hand on my hip, and I knew Bootsie had arrived at the hotel safely.

I lay on my back, with the pillow across my face, and heard her undressing in the dark. She lay beside me, touched my stomach, then moved across my loins, her thighs spread, and put my sex between her legs. Then she leaned close to me, pushed the pillow from my face, and kissed my cheek and put her tongue inside my mouth and placed my sex inside her.

Her tongue tasted like candy, like cherries that had been soaked in bourbon. She raised herself on her arms, the tops of her swollen breasts half-mooned with tan.

I stared upward into the face of Karyn LaRose, who smiled lazily and said, 'Tell me you don't like it, Dave. Tell me. See if you can tell me that . . . Tell me . . . tell me . . . tell me . . . '

18

I found Clete Purcel at the bar. He was drinking a shot of tequila, with a Corona and a saucer of salted limes on the side, his porkpie hat cocked over one eye. The band was putting away its instruments and the bar was almost empty.

'Where you been, noble mon? You look a couple of quarts down,' he said.

'A long day.' I sat next to him and rubbed my face. My skin felt cold, dead to the touch.

'I thought I saw Boots go out the lobby.'

'You did.'

'What's going on?'

'Don't worry about it. What'd you find out about this guy Mookie?'

His eyes seemed to go inside mine, then he tipped back the shot and drank from the bottle of Corona.

'The black broad, Brandy Grissum, came into Nig's office hysterical today. Dig this, she used the two yards you gave her to score a shitload of rock and get wiped out. So while she was on the nod at her mother's house in St John the Baptist, our man Mookie tools on up for some more R&R. Guess what? Mookie decided he wasn't interested in a stoned-out twenty-buck street whore. So he sodomized her little sister.'

He put a Lucky Strike in his mouth and fiddled with his Zippo, as though he were trying to remove an image from his mind, then dropped the Zippo on the bar without lighting the cigarette.

'His last name is Zerrang,' he said. 'He used to be a leg breaker for a couple of shylocks on the Mississippi coast, then he made the big score as a hit man for the greaseballs in Miami. He must be pretty slick, though. I had a friend at NOPD punch on the computer. He's never been down.'

'Who's he working for now?'

'Brandy doesn't know. This time I think she's telling the truth . . . You don't look good, Streak. What's troubling you, mon?'

I told him. We were the only people at the bar now. Clete listened, his face empty of expression. He rubbed his thumb against his cheekbone, and I could see white lines inside the crow's feet at the corner of his eye.

He made a coughing sound in his throat.

'That's quite a story,' he said.

I picked up one of the salted limes from his saucer, then set it down again.

'Bootsie walked in on it?' he asked.

'When Karyn was dressing.'

'How did the LaRose broad get in?'

'She got a pass key from the maid.'

'Dave, you were throwing her out. Bootsie doesn't know that?'

'I didn't have a chance to tell her. I'll call her when she's back home.'

'Man.' He breathed through his nose, his lips crimped together. 'You told Karyn LaRose to peddle her bread somewhere else, though?'

'Something like that.' A scrolled green and red Dixie beer sign was lit over the row of whiskey bottles behind the bar. I felt tired all over and my palms were stiff and dry when I closed and opened them.

'You didn't do anything wrong. You just got to make Boots see that. Right? This isn't a big deal,' he said. He watched me rub the salt in the saucer with the tip of my finger. 'Let's find a late-night joint and get a steak.'

'I'm going to take a shower and go to bed,' I said.

'I'm going up with you.'

'The hell you are.'

'I *know* you, Streak. You're going to get inside your own head and build a case against yourself. The slop chute is closing. For you it's closed permanently. You got that, big mon?'

'There's no problem here, Clete.'

'Yeah, I bet. That broad couldn't buy you, so she decided to fuck your head.' He stood up from the barstool, then grimaced slightly. 'I feel like an upended bottle. Come on, let's get out of here. Remind me in the future to drink in low-class dumps that aren't full of the right people.'

'You're the best, Cletus.'

He put his arm on my shoulder, and we walked together toward the elevator like two impaired Siamese twins trying to get in sync with each other.

The next morning I was part of the caravan that escorted Karyn and Buford back to their home on the Teche. It was balmy and gray after the rain, and you could smell the wet earth in the fields and hear the clanging of the sugarcane refinery down the bayou. It was a fine, late-fall

411

morning, disjointed from the events of last night, as though I had experienced them only in a drunken dream.

From my car I watched Karyn and her husband enter their front door, their faces opaque, perhaps still numb from the alcohol of the night before, or perhaps masking the secrets they waited to share or the buried anger they would vent on each other once inside.

Bootsie was in the backyard, at the redwood picnic table, with a cup of coffee and a cigarette when I parked in the drive. She wore sandals and a terrycloth red shirt and a pair of khakis high on her hips.

'Hi,' I said.

Her legs were crossed, and she tipped her ashes in an inverted preserve jar cap and looked at the ducks skittering across our pond.

'You don't smoke,' I said.

'I'm starting.'

I sat down across from her. Her eyes moved up to meet mine.

'I told you the truth last night,' I said.

'For some reason that doesn't make it any easier.'

'Why?'

'How'd she come to have this obsession with you? What's your end of it?'

'I didn't want to go out to their house when we were first invited there. I tried to avoid her.'

'Who are you putting on?'

I felt my throat close. My eyes burned, as though I were looking into a watery glare.

She threw her cigarette in a flowerbed full of dead leaves by the back wall of the house. Her cheeks were hot and streaked with color. Before I went into the house, I removed the burning cigarette from the leaves and mashed it out in the jar cap in front of her, my gesture as foolish as my words were self-serving.

The wall phone was ringing in the kitchen. I picked it up, my eyes fixed on Bootsie's back through the window. Her hair was thick and woven with gold in the gray light.

'Aaron Crown dumped the boat down by Maurice,' the sheriff said.

'Did anybody see him?'

'No, just the boat.'

'He'll be back.'

'You say that almost with admiration.'

'Like an old gunbull said, Aaron's a traveling shit storm.'

'Anyway, you got your wish. You're off it.'

When I didn't reply, he said, 'You're not going to ask me why?'

'Go ahead, Sheriff.'

412

'Buford called and said you're resentful about the assignment. He said you don't need to come around his house again.'

'He did, did he?'

'That's not all. He said you made a pass at his wife last night.'

'He's a liar.'

'I believe you. But why did he decide to make up a story about you now?'

'Ask him.'

'I will . . . Dave, you still there?'

'I'll talk to you later, Sheriff. I have to go somewhere.'

'I always knew this job would bring me humility . . . Say, you're not going out to get in Buford LaRose's face, are you?'

I drove Bootsie's Toyota to the mechanic's garage, exchanged it for my truck, and asked the mechanic to drive the Toyota back to my house, then I headed out to the LaRose plantation.

But I was not the only person who had a grievance with Buford that day. Jerry Joe Plumb's blue Buick was pulled at an angle to the old LaRose company store, and Jerry Joe stood on the gallery between the two wooden pecan barrels that framed the double front doors, his hands on his hips, speaking heatedly into Buford's face.

I crunched across the shell parking lot and cut my engine. They both looked at me, then stepped inside the double doors with the oxidized and cracked windows and continued their argument, Jerry Joe jabbing his finger in the air, his cheeks pooling with color.

But I could still hear part of it.

'You're shorting me. Your old man wouldn't do this, Buford.'

'You'll get your due.'

'Three of the jobs you promised me are already let to Dock Green.'

'I gave you my word. You stop trying to cadge favors because you knew my family.'

'Persephone let you put your head up her dress?'

Jerry Joe's back was to me. His shoulders looked stiff, rectangular, his triceps swollen with tubes of muscle, like a prizefighter's while he waits for the referee to finish giving instructions before the bell.

But Buford turned away from the insult and lit a cigar, cupping and puffing it in the gloom as though Jerry Joe was not there.

Jerry Joe's leather-soled oxblood loafers were loud on the gallery when he came out the double doors.

'What's the haps, Jerry?' I said.

He balanced on his soles, his face still glowing.

'He asks me the haps? Here's a lesson. You take up with piranha fish, don't expect them to go on a diet.'

413

'Buford stiffed you?'

'That guy don't have the lead in his Eversharp to stiff anybody. Hey, keep your hammer in your pants or get you a full-body condom,' he said, and got into his Buick and started the engine.

I got out of my truck and put my hand on his door window. He rolled it down with the electric motor.

'Spell it out,' I said.

'You're in the way. She knows how to combine business and pleasure. Don't pretend you're a dumb shit.' He pushed the window button again and scorched two lines in the shell parking lot out to the state highway.

I picked a handful of pecans out of one of the barrels by the door and went inside the store.

'You again. Like bubble gum under the shoe,' Buford said.

The store was dark, the cypress floor worn as smooth as wood inside a feed bin, the half-filled shelves filmed with cobwebs. I put a half dollar for the pecans next to the brass cash register on the counter and cracked two of them together in my palm.

'Why are you telling lies about me to the sheriff?' I said.

'You propositioned Karyn at the Acadiana. What do you expect?'

'Who told you this?'

'Karyn, of course.'

'Bad source. Your wife's a pathological liar.'

'Your job's finished here. Go back to doing whatever you do, Dave. Just stay off my property.'

'Wrong. As long as Aaron Crown is running loose, I'll come here anytime I want, Buford.'

He combed his thick, curly hair back with his fingernails, a dark knowledge forming in his face.

'You want to bring me down, don't you?' he said.

'You're a fraud.'

'What did I ever do to you? Can you answer that simple question for me?'

'You and your wife use each other to injure other people . . . You know what a *bugarron* is?'

The skin trembled along the lower rim of his right eye.

'Are you calling me a—' he began.

'You serve a perversity of some kind. I just don't know what it is.'

'The next time you come here, I'll break your jaw. That's a promise.'

He turned and walked down the length of the counter, past the display shelves that were covered with dust, and out the back screen door into the light. The screen slammed behind him like the crack of a rifle.

*

414

I took the rest of the day off and raked piles of wet leaves and pecan husks out of the lawn. The wind was still warm out of the south and the tops of the trees in the swamp were a soft green against the sky, and the only sound louder than my own thoughts was Tripod, Alafair's three-legged coon, running up and down on his chain in the side yard. I burned the leaves in the coulee, then I showered, took a nap, and didn't wake until after sunset. While I was dressing, the phone rang in the kitchen. Bootsie answered it and walked to the bedroom door.

'It's Batist,' she said.

'What's he want?'

'He didn't say.' She went into the living rom, then out on the gallery and sat on the swing.

'That movie fella get a hold of you?' Batist asked.

'No. What's up?'

'He was down here wit' a truck and some people wit' cameras. I tole him he ought to talk to you about what he was doing. I seen him talking on one of them cordless phones. He ain't called you?'

'This man's not a friend, Batist. Is he there now?'

'No. He ain't the reason I called you. It's that big black man. He ain't up to no good.'

'Which black man?'

'The biggest one I ever seen around here.'

'I'll be down in a minute.'

I went out on the gallery. Bootsie still sat in the swing, pushing it back and forth with one foot.

'I need to go down to the dock for a few minutes,' I said.

'Right.'

'Boots, you've got to cut me some slack.'

'You don't see it.'

'What?'

'You hate the LaRoses and what they stand for. That's the power they have over you.'

'I'm a police officer. They're corrupt.'

'You say they are. Nobody else does.' She went inside. The swing twisted emptily on its chains under the bug light.

I walked down the slope through the trees to the dock. The string of lights was turned on over the dock, and you could see bream night-feeding off the insects that fell into the water. Batist was cleaning out the coffee urn inside the bait shop.

'Tell me about the black guy,' I said.

Batist looked up from his work and studied my face. His head was tilted, one eyebrow arched.

'What you mad about?' he asked.

'Nothing.'

'I can see that, all right . . . That movie fella rented a boat and took pictures up and down the bayou. That's when I first seen this black man up the road in a pickup truck, watching the bayou out the window. Later he come on in and axed if a movie's getting made here.

'I say that's what it looks like. He axed me if it's a movie about this white man broke out of Angola, the one killed that black civil rights man in Baton Rouge a long time ago. When I tole him I don't know, he said he's got a story he can give this movie fella, if he gets any money for it, he's gonna give me some, but he's got to find out where the movie man's staying at first.

'I said, "What you want here?"

'He had on this straw hat, with a colored band around it. He took it off and the side of his head was shaved down to the scalp. He goes, "I'm so strong I got muscles in my shit, old man. I'd watch what I say." All the time smiling with gold all over his teet'.

'I go, "I'm fixing to clean up. You want to buy somet'ing?"

'Dave, this man's arms was big as my thigh. His shoulders touched both sides of that do' when he come in. He goes, "You sure that movie fella ain't tole you where he stay at?"

'I go, "It ain't my bidness. Ain't nobody else's here, either."

'He kept looking at me, grinning, messing with the salt shaker on top of the counter, like he was fixing to do somet'ing.

'So I said, "Nigger, don't prove your mama raised a fool."

'He laughed and picked up a ham sandwich and crumpled up a five-dollar bill and t'rew it on the counter and walked out. Just like that. Man didn't no more care if I insulted him than a mosquito was flying round his head.'

'Call me if you see him again. Don't mess with him.'

'Who he is, Dave?'

'He sounds like a guy named Mookie Zerrang. He's a killer, Batist.'

He started to wipe down the counter, then flipped his rag into the bucket.

'They ain't nothing for it, is they?' he said.

'Beg your pardon?'

'They out there, they in here. Don't nobody listen to me,' he said, and waved his arm toward the screened windows, the floodlighted bayou, the black wall of shadows on the far bank. 'It ain't never gonna be like it use to. What for we brought all this here, Dave?'

He turned his back to me and began dropping the board shutters on the windows and latching them from the inside.

19

Early Saturday morning I made coffee and fixed a bowl of Grape-Nuts and blueberries in the bait shop and ate breakfast by myself at the counter and watched the sun rise over the swamp. It had rained, then cleared during the night, and the bayou was yellow with mud and the dock slick with rainwater. A week ago Jerry Joe's vending machine company had delivered a working replica of a 1950s Wurlitzer jukebox while I wasn't in the shop; it sat squat and heavy in the corner, its plastic casing marbled with orange and red and purple light, the rows of 45 rpm records arrayed in a shiny black semi-circle inside the viewing glass. I had resolved to have Jerry Joe's people remove it.

I still hadn't made the phone call.

I punched Jimmy Clanton's 'Just a Dream,' Harry Choates's 1946 recording of 'La Julie Blon,' Nathan Abshire's 'Pine Grove Blues.'

Their voices and music were out of another era, one that we thought would never end. But it did, incrementally, in ways that seemed inconsequential at the time, like the unexpected arrival at the front gate of a sun-browned oil lease man in khaki work clothes who seemed little different from the rest of us.

I unplugged the jukebox from the wall. The plastic went dead and crackled like burning cellophane in the silence of the room.

Then I drove to the University of Southwestern Louisiana library in Lafayette.

Buford's bibliography was impressive. He had published historical essays on the Knights of the White Camellia and the White League and the violent insurrection they had led against the federal occupation of the War Between the States. The articles were written in the neutral and abstruse language of academic journals, but his sentiments were not well disguised: the night riders who had lynched and burned had their roles forced upon them.

His other articles were in psychological and medical journals. They seemed to be diverse, with no common thread, dealing with various kinds of phobias and depression as well as hate groups that could not tolerate a pluralistic society.

But in the last five years he seemed to have changed his professional focus and begun writing about the science of psychopharmacology and its use in the cure of alcoholics.

I returned the magazines and journals to the reference desk and was about to leave. But it wasn't quite yet noon, and telling myself I had nothing else to do, I asked the librarian for the student yearbooks from the early 1970s, the approximate span when Karyn LaRose attended USL.

She hadn't been born into Buford's LaRose's world. Her father had been a hard-working and likable man who supplied gumballs and novelties, such as plastic monster teeth and vampire fingernails, for dimestore vending machines. The family lived in a small frame house on the old St Martinville road, and the paintless and desiccated garage that fronted the property was rimmed along the base with a rainbow of color from the gumballs that had rotted inside and leaked through the floor. If you asked Karyn what her father did for a living, she always replied that he was in the retail supply business.

Most of us who attended USL came from blue-collar, French-speaking families or could not afford to attend LSU or Tulane. Most of us commuted from outlying parishes, and as a result the campus was empty and quiet and devoid of most social life on the weekends.

But not for Karyn. She made the best of her situation, and her name and photograph appeared again and again in the yearbooks that covered her four years at USL. She made the women's tennis team and belonged to a sorority and the honor society; she was a maid of honor to the homecoming queen one year, and homecoming queen the next. In her photographs her face looked modest and radiant, like that of a person who saw only goodness and promise in the world.

I was almost ready to close the last yearbook and return the stack to the reference desk when I looked again at a group photograph taken in front of Karyn's sorority house, then scanned the names in the cutline.

The coed on the end of the row, standing next to Karyn, was Persephone Giacano. Both of them were smiling, their shoulders and the backs of their wrists touching.

I began to look for Persephone's name in other yearbooks. I didn't find it. It was as though she had appeared for one group photograph in front of the sorority house, then disappeared from campus life.

The administration building was still open. I used the librarian's phone and called the registrar's office.

'We have a Privacy Act, you know?' the woman who answered said.

'I just want to know which years she was here,' I said.

'You're a police officer?'

'That's correct.'

I heard her tapping on some computer keys.

'Nineteen seventy-two to nineteen seventy-three,' she said.

'She dropped out or she transferred to another school?' I asked.

She was quiet a moment. Then she said, 'If I were you, I'd look through some of the campus newspapers for that period. Who knows what you might find?'

It took a while. The story was brief, no more than four column inches with a thin caption on page three of a late spring 1973 issue of the *Vermilion*, written in the laconic style of an administrative press handout that does not want to dwell overly long on a university scandal.

A half dozen students had been expelled for stealing tests from the science building. The article stated the tests had been taken from a file cabinet, but the theft had been discovered before the examinations had been given, and the professors whose exams would have been compromised had all been notified.

At the very bottom of the article was the line, *A seventh USL student, Persephone Giacano, voluntarily withdrew from the university before charges were filed against her.*

I called the registrar's office again, and the same woman answered.

'Can I look at an old transcript?' I asked. 'You send those out upon request, anyway, don't you?'

'Why don't you come over here and introduce yourself? You sound like such an interesting person,' she answered.

I walked across the lawn and through the brick archways to the registrar's office and stood at the counter until an elderly, robin-breasted lady with blue hair waited on me. I opened my badge.

'My, you're exactly what you say you are,' she said.

'Does everyone get this treatment?'

'We save it for just a special few.'

I wrote Karyn's maiden name on a scratch pad and slid it across the counter to the woman. She looked at it a long time. The front office area was empty.

'It's important in ways that are probably better left unsaid,' I said.

'Why don't you walk back here?' she answered.

I stood behind her chair while she tapped on the computer's keyboard. Then I saw Karyn's transcript pop up on the blue screen. 'She was here four years and graduated in 1974. See,' the woman said, and slowly rolled Karyn's academic credits down the screen, shifting in her chair so I could have a clear view.

Karyn had been a liberal arts major and had made almost straight *As* in the humanities. But when an accounting class, or a zoology or algebra class rolled across the screen, the grades dropped to Cs, or Ws for 'Withdrew.'

'Could you drop it back to the spring of 1973?' I asked.

The woman in the chair hesitated, then tapped the 'page up' button. She waited only a few seconds before shutting down the screen. But it was long enough.

Karyn had made As in biology and chemistry the same semester that Persephone Giacano had been forced to leave the university.

Karyn was nobody's fall partner.

I parked my truck in the alley behind Sabelle Crown's bar and entered it through the back door. The only light came from the neon beer signs on the wall and the television set that was tuned to the LSU-Georgia Tech game. The air was thick with a smell like unwashed hair and old shoes and sweat and synthetic wine.

Sabelle was mopping out her tiny office in back.

'I need Lonnie Felton's address,' I said.

She stuck her mop in the pail and took a business card out of her desk drawer.

'He rented a condo over the river. Good life, huh?' she said. She resumed her work, her back to me, the exposed muscles in her waist rolling with each motion of her arms.

'Aaron was here, wasn't he?' I said.

'What makes you think that?' she answered, her voice flat.

'He was carrying the thirty-two I saw in that shoebox full of medals you keep behind the bar.'

She stopped mopping and straightened up. Her head was tilted to one side.

'You didn't know that?' I said.

She went out to the bar and returned with the shoebox, slipped the rubber band off the top, and poured the collection of rings and watches and pocketknives and military decorations onto the desk.

Her gaze was turned inward, as though she were reviewing a filmstrip. I could hear her breathing through her nose in the silence. Her fingernails were curled into the heels of her hands.

'I guess I majored in being anybody's fuck,' she said.

'You don't have to be.'

She took a roll of breath mints out of her blue jeans and put one in her mouth with her thumb. 'Lonnie was here. In the middle of the night,' she said. 'He interviewed Daddy right out there at the bar. I went out to get food. When I came back, only Lonnie was here.'

'Felton knew your father had the gun?'

'You tell me,' she said. The skin of her face was shiny and tight against the bone, her eyes swimming with an old knowledge about the nature of susceptibility and betrayal.

I found Lonnie Felton by the swimming pool, in the courtyard of the white brick condominium he had rented above the Vermilion River. The surface of the water was glazed with a slick of suntan lotion and the sunlight that filtered through the moss in the trees overhead. Lonnie Felton lay on a bright yellow double-size plastic lounge chair, with a redheaded girl of eighteen or nineteen beside him. They both wore dark glasses and wet swimsuits, and their bodies looked hard and brown and prickled with cold. Lonnie Felton took a sip from a collins glass and smiled at me, his eyes hidden behind his glasses, his lips spreading back from his teeth. His girlfriend snuggled closer to his side, her knees and elbows drawn up tightly against him.

'You know what aiding and abetting is?' I asked.

'You bet.'

'I can hang it on you.'

He smiled again. His lips were flat and thin against his teeth, his sex sculpted against his swimsuit. 'The Napoleonic Code supersedes the First Amendment?' he said.

'I think Mookie Zerrang was at my bait shop yesterday. He wanted to know where you lived.'

'Who?'

'The black guy who murdered your scriptwriter.'

'Oh yea. Well, keep me informed, will you?'

'It's cold, Lonnie. I want to go inside,' the girl next to him said. She teased the elastic band on his trunks with the tips of her fingers.

'I've got to admire your Kool-Aid. I'd be worried if a guy like that was looking for me,' I said.

'Let me lay it out for you. Dwayne Parsons, that's the great writer we're talking about here, was an over-the-hill degenerate who factored himself into the deal because he filmed some friends doing some nasty things between the sheets. What I'm saying here is, he had a sick karma and it caught up with him. Look, if this black guy comes here to do me, you know what I'm going to tell him? "Thanks for not coming sooner. Thanks for letting me have the life I've lived." I don't argue with my fate, Jack. It's that simple.'

'I have a feeling he won't be listening.'

A cascade of tiny yellow and scarlet leaves tumbled out of the trees into the swimming pool. The redheaded girl rubbed her face against Lonnie Felton's chest and lay her forearm across his loins.

'You don't like us very much, do you?' he said.

'Us?'

'What you probably call movie people.'

'Have a good day, Mr Felton. Don't let them get behind you.'

'What?'

'Go to more movies. Watch a rerun of *Platoon* sometime.'

I drove along the river and caught the four-lane into Broussard, then took the old highway toward Cade and Spanish Lake into New Iberia. The highway was littered with crushed stalks of sugarcane that had fallen off the wagons on their way to the mill, and dust devils spun out of the bare and harrowed fields and in the distance I could see egrets rise like a scattering of white rose petals above a windbreak of poplar trees.

I had lied to Lonnie Felton. It was doubtful that I could make an aiding and abetting charge against him stick. But that might turn out to be the best luck he could have ever had, I thought.

I turned on the radio and listened to the LSU-Georgia Tech game the rest of the way home.

Bootsie was washing dishes when I walked into the kitchen. She wore a pair of straw sandals and white slacks and a purple shirt with green and red flowers printed on it. The tips of her hair were gold in the light through the screen.

'What's going on, boss man?' she said, without turning around.

I put my hand on her back.

'There's an all-you-can-eat crawfish buffet in Lafayette for six-ninety-five,' I said.

'I already started something.'

'I used all the wrong words the last couple of days,' I said.

She rinsed a plate and set it in the rack. She gazed at a solitary mockingbird that stood on the redwood table.

'There're some things a woman has a hard time accepting. It doesn't matter what caused them to happen,' she said.

She picked up another plate and rinsed it. I felt her weight lean forward, away from the touch of my hand.

'You want to go to afternoon Mass?' I said.

'I don't think I have time to change,' she answered.

That night I took Alafair and a friend of hers to a movie in New Iberia and for ice cream afterward. Later, I found things to do in the bait shop, even though the fishing season was almost over and few customers would be there in the morning. Through the black silhouette of trees up the slope, I could see the lighted gallery of our house, the darkened living room, Bootsie's shadow moving on the drawn shades in our bedroom.

I called my AA sponsor, an ex-roughneck and barroom owner named Tee Neg, who'd had seven years sobriety when he walked into a bait and liquor store owned by a black man and had asked for a bucketful of shiners, then on an impulse, with no forethought other than his ongoing resentment over the fingers he'd pinched off on a drill pipe, had changed his order to a quart of whiskey and stayed drunk for the next five years. His next AA meeting was at Angola Prison.

I told him about what had happened between me and Bootsie. I knew what was coming.

'You took a drink over it?' he said.

'No.'

'Hey, you ever get drunk while you was asleep?'

'No.'

'Then go to bed. I'll talk to you in the morning, you.' He hung up.

After all the lights in the house went out, I walked up the slope and went inside and lay down on the living room couch in the dark.

Wally, the dispatcher, called at one in the morning.

'The St Martin Parish sheriff's office is interviewing some hysterical kids at Henderson Swamp. I can't make sense out of it. You want to go up there?' he said.

'Not really.'

'It sounds like Aaron Crown. That's where you think he's hid out at, right?'

'What sounds like Aaron Crown?'

'The one tore up these two people. They say the walls of the houseboat is painted with blood. The guy held the girl while he done the man, then he done it to the girl.'

'You're not making sense, Wally.'

'That's what I said. The deputy called it in didn't make no sense. So how about hauling your ass up there?'

20

Sometimes the least reliable source in reconstructing a violent crime is the eyewitness to it. The blood veins dilate in the brain, the emotions short-circuit, memory shuts down and dulls the images that wish to disfigure the face of the human family.

Seven emergency vehicles were parked along the Henderson levee when I got there. The moon was up and the water and the moss in the cypress were stained the color of pewter. A wood gangplank led from the levee through a stand of flooded willows to a large, motorized houseboat whose decks burned with the floodlights from a sheriff's boat moored next to it.

The witnesses were an elderly man and his partially blind wife, who had been spending the weekend on their own houseboat, and a group of stoned high-school kids who stunk of reefer and keg beer and were trembling at the prospect of what they had stepped into.

Earlier, they had all seen the victims having drinks at a restaurant farther up the levee. Everyone agreed they were a handsome couple, tourists perhaps, pleasant and certainly polite, although the woman seemed a little young for the man; but he was charming, just the same, athletic-looking, friendly toward the kids, a decent sort, obviously in control of things (one of the stoned-out high school students said he 'was kind of like a modern business-type guy, like you see on TV'); the man had wanted to rent fishing gear and hire a guide to take him out in the morning.

The intruder came just before midnight, in a flat-bottomed aluminum outboard, the throttle turned low, the engine muttering softly along the main channel that rimmed the swamp, past the islands of dead hyacinths and the gray cypress that rose wedge-shaped out of the water at the entrance to the bays.

But he knew his destination. In midchannel he angled his outboard toward the houseboat rented by the couple, then cut the gas and let his boat glide on its own wake through a screen of hanging willows and bump softly against the rubber tires that hung from the houseboat's gunnels.

The people inside were still up, eating a late supper on a small table in the galley, a bottle of white wine and a fondue pan set between them. They either didn't hear the intruder, or never had time to react, before he pulled himself by one hand over the rail, lighting on the balls of his feet, his body alive with a sinewy grace that belied his dimensions.

Then he tore the locked hatch out of the jamb with such violence that one hinge came with it.

At first the kids, who were gathered around the tailgate of a pick-up truck on the levee, thought the intruder was a black man, then they realized when he burst into the lighted cabin that he wore dark gloves and a knitted ski mask.

But they had no doubt about what took place next.

When the man they had seen in the restaurant tried to rise from his chair in the galley, the intruder swung a wide-bladed fold-out game dressing knife into the side of his throat and raked it at a downward angle into his rib cage, then struck him about the neck and head again and again, gathering the young woman into one arm, never missing a stroke, whipping the wounded man down lower and lower from the chair to the floor, flinging ropes of blood across the windows.

He paused, as though he was aware he had an audience, stared out of the holes in his mask toward the levee, then opened his mouth, which rang with gold, licked the neck of the screaming young woman he held pinioned against his body with one muscle-swollen arm, and drew the knife across her throat.

I stood just inside the torn hatch with a St Martin Parish homicide detective and the medical examiner. The two bodies lay curled on the floor, their foreheads almost touching.

'You ever see a blood loss like that?' the plainclothes said. He was dressed in a brown suit and a fedora, with a plain blue necktie, and he had clipped the tie inside his shirt. He bit into a candy bar. 'I got a sugar deficiency,' he said.

Two paramedics began lifting the dead man into a body bag. His ponytail had been splayed by someone's shoe and was stuck to the linoleum.

'You okay, Dave?' the plainclothes said.

'Sure.'

'The perp cleaned out their ID.'

'His name was Lonnie Felton. I don't know who the girl was. He was a film director.'

'You know him?'

I nodded and looked at the stare in Felton's eyes.

'I make Aaron Crown for this,' the plainclothes said. 'What do you think? How many we got around here could do something like this? . . . You listening, Dave?'

'What?' I said. The paramedic worked the zipper on the vinyl bag over Felton's face. 'Oh, sorry . . . ' I said to the plainclothes. 'The kids were right the first time. It's a black guy. Mookie Zerrang's his name. It's funny what you said, that's all.'

'Come again?'

'About listening. I told Felton the guy who'd do him wouldn't be a good listener. It seemed like a clever thing to say at the time.'

The plainclothes looked at me strangely, a smear of chocolate on his mouth.

21

After I was discharged from the army, a friend from my outfit and I drove across the country for a fishing vacation in Montana. On July 4 we stopped at a small town in western Kansas that Norman Rockwell could have painted. The streets were brick, lined with Chinese elm trees, and the limestone courthouse on the square rose out of the hardware and feed and farm equipment stores like a medieval castle against a hard blue porcelain sky. Next to our motel was a stucco 3.2 beer tavern that looked like a wedding cake, shaded by an enormous willow that crowned over the eaves. At the end of the street you could see an ocean of green wheat that rippled in the wind as far as the eye could see. The rain that fell that afternoon on the hot sidewalks was the sweetest smell I ever experienced.

What's the point?

For years I thought of this place as an island untouched by the war in Indochina and disconnected from the cities burning at home. When I was a patrolman in uniform in the New Orleans welfare projects, I used to remember the hot, clean airy smell of the rain falling on those sidewalks in 1965.

Then an ex-Kansas cop we picked up drunk on an interstate fugitive warrant told me the town that existed in my fond recollection was the site of Truman Capote's novel *In Cold Blood*, the story of two pathological killers who murdered a whole family for thirty-nine dollars and a radio.

You learn soon or you learn late: There are no islands.

It was Monday morning and no one was in custody for the double homicide in St Martin Parish.

'I'm afraid they're not buying your theory about a black hit man,' the sheriff said.

'Why not?'

'There's no evidence the man was black.'

'He had a mouthful of gold teeth, just like the guy who did the scriptwriter.'

'So what? Maybe Aaron Crown has gold fillings, too.'

'I doubt if Aaron ever bought a toothbrush, much less saw a dentist.'

'You believe somebody was trying to stop Felton from exposing our governor-elect as a moral troglodyte. Maybe you're right. But for a lot of people it's a big reach.'

'Crown didn't do this, Sheriff.'

'Look, the St Martin ME says both victims had been smoking heroin before they got it. Felton's condo had a half kee of China white in it. St Martin thinks maybe the killings are drug related. Robbery's a possible motive, too.'

'Robbery?'

'The killer took the girl's purse and Felton's wallet. Felton was flashing a lot of money around earlier in the evening . . . ' He stopped and returned my stare. 'I haven't convinced you?'

'Where are you trying to go with this, skipper?'

'Nowhere. I don't have to. It's out of our jurisdiction. End of discussion, Dave.'

I opened the morning mail in my office, escorted a deranged woman from the men's room, picked up a parole violator in the state betting parlor out by the highway, helped recover a stolen farm tractor, spent my lunch hour and two additional hours waiting to testify at the courthouse, only to learn the defendant had been granted a continuance, and got back to the office with a headache and the feeling I had devoted most of the day to snipping hangnails in a season of plague.

The state police now had primary responsibility for protecting Buford, and Aaron Crown and my problems with the LaRose family were becoming less and less a subject of interest to anybody else.

But one person, besides Clete, had tried to help me, I thought.

The tattooed carnival worker named Arana.

I inserted the cassette Helen and I had made of his deathbed statement in a tape player and listened to it again in its entirety. But only one brief part of it pointed a finger: 'The *bugarron* ride a saddle with flowers cut in it. I seen him at the ranch. You messing everything up for them. They gonna kill you, man . . . '

'Who's this guy?' my voice asked.

And the man called Arana responded, 'He ain't got no name. He got a red horse and a silver saddle. He like Indian boys.'

I clicked off the tape player and lay the cassette on my desk blotter and looked at it. Puzzle through that, I thought.

Then, just as chance and accident are wont to have their way, I glanced out the window and saw a man blowing his horn at other drivers, forcing his way across two lanes to park in an area designated for the handicapped. His face was as stiff as plaster when he walked across the grass to the front entrance, oblivious to the sprinkler that cut a dark swath across his slacks.

A moment later Wally called me on my extension.

'Dave, we got a real zomboid out here in the waiting room says he wants to see you,' he said.

'Yeah, I know. Send him back.'

'Who is he?'

'Dock Green.'

'That pimp from New Orleans suppose to got clap of the brain?'

'The one and only.'

'Dave, we don't got enough local sick ones? You got to import these guys in here?'

Dock Green wore a beige turtleneck polo shirt tucked tightly into his belt so that the movements of his neck and head seemed even more stark and elliptical, like moving images in a filmstrip that's been abbreviated. He sat down in front of my desk without being asked, his eyes focusing past me out the window, then back on my face again. The skin between his lip and the corner of his nose twitched.

'I got to use your phone,' he said, and picked up the receiver and started punching numbers.

'That's a private . . . Don't worry about it, go ahead,' I said.

'I'll pick you up at six sharp . . . No, out front, Persephone . . . ' he said into the receiver. 'No, I ain't wanted there, I don't like it there, I ain't coming in there . . . Good-bye.'

He hung up and blew his breath up into his face. 'I got a charge to file,' he said.

'What might that be, Dock?'

'I can see you're on top of things. There's another side to Jerry the Glide.'

'Yeah?'

'He went out to my construction site with some of his asswipes and busted up my foreman. He held him down on the ground by his ears and spit in his face.'

'Spit in his face?'

'There's an echo in here?'

I wrote a note on my scratch pad, reminding myself to pick up a half gallon of milk on the way home.

'We'll get right on this, Dock.'

'That's it?'

'Yep.'

'You didn't ask me where.'

'Why don't you let me have that?'

He gave me directions. I fingered the tape cassette containing the deathbed statement of the Mexican carnival worker.

'Let's take a ride and see what Jerry Joe has to say for himself,' I said.

'Right now?'

'You bet.'

The concentration in his eyes made me think of sweat bees pressed against glass.

We drove in a cruiser through the corridor of live oaks on East Main to the site on Bayou Teche where Jerry Joe was building his new home. The equipment was shut down, the construction crew gone.

'I guess we struck out,' I said, and turned across the drawbridge and headed out of town toward the LaRose plantation.

'This ain't the way.'

'It's a nice day for a drive.'

I saw the recognition come together in Dock's face.

'You're trying to piss on my shoes. You know my wife's out at Karyn LaRose's,' he said.

'I've got to check something out, Dock. It doesn't have anything to do with you.'

'Fuck that and fuck you. I don't like them people. I ain't going on their property.'

I pulled off on the shoulder of the road by the LaRose's drive. Dust was billowing out of the fields in back, and the house looked pillared and white and massive against the gray sky.

'Why not?' I asked.

'I got to do business with hypocrites, it don't mean we got to use the same toilet. Hey, you don't think they got shit stripes in their under-wear? They got dead people in the ground here.'

'You're talking about the cemetery in back?'

'I ain't got to see a headstone to smell a grave. There's one by that tree over there. There's another one down by the water. A kid's in it.'

'You know about a murder?'

But he didn't get to answer. A shudder went through him and he sank back into the seat and began to speak unintelligibly, his lips wrinkling back on his teeth as though all of his motors were misfiring, obscenity and spittle rolling off his tongue.

I put the transmission in gear and turned into the drive.

'You going to make it, Dock?' I said.

His breath was as dense as sewer gas. He pressed his palm wetly against his mouth.

'Hang loose, babe,' I said, and walked through the drive and the porte

430

cochere into the backyard, where a state trooper in sunglasses was eating a bowl of ice cream in a canvas lawn chair.

I opened my badge.

'I'd like to check the stables,' I said.

'What for?'

I averted my gaze, stuck my badge holder in my back pocket.

'It's just a funny feeling I have about Crown,' I answered.

'Help yourself.'

I climbed through the rails of the horse lot and entered the open end of the old brick smithy that had been converted into a stable. The iron shutters on the arched windows were closed, and motes of dust floated in the pale bands of light as thickly as lint in a textile mill. The air was warm and sour-sweet with the smells of leather, blankets stiff with horse sweat, chickens that wandered in from outside, the dampness under the plank floors, fresh hay scattered in the stalls, a wheelbarrow stacked with manure, a barrel of dried molasses-and-grain balls.

I went inside the tack room at the far end of the building. Buford's saddles were hung on collapsible two-by-fours that extended outward on screwhooks from the wall. The English saddles were plain, utilitarian, the leather unmarked by the maker's knife. But on the western saddles, with pommels as wide as bulls' snouts, the cantles and flaps and skirts were carved with roses and birds and snakes, and in the back of each cantle was a mother-of-pearl inlay of an opened camellia.

But the man named Arana had said the *bugarron* rode a silver saddle, and there was none here.

'What you looking for in the tack room, Detective Robicheaux?' the trooper said behind me. He leaned against the doorjamb, his arms folded, his expression masked behind his shades. He wore a campaign hat tilted over his eyes, like a DI's, with the leather strap on the back of his head.

'You never can tell what you might trip across.'

'Somehow that don't ring right.'

'I know you?'

'You do now. Ms LaRose says she'd prefer you wasn't on her place.'

'She'll prefer it less if Aaron's her next visitor . . . Have a nice day.'

I walked down the wood floor between the stalls toward the opened end of the building.

'Don't be back in the stable without a warrant, sir,' the trooper said behind me.

I climbed through the rails in the horse lot and walked under the trees in the backyard toward the porte cochere. Karyn LaRose came out the side screen door, a drink in her hand, with Persephone Green behind her. Karyn turned around and lifted her fingers in the air.

431

'Let me talk to Dave a minute, Seph,' she said.

There was a pinched, black light in Persephone Green's face as she glared at me. But she did as she was asked and closed the door and disappeared behind the glass.

'I'm going to drain the blood out of your veins for what you did to me,' Karyn said.

'What I did to you?'

'In front of your wife, in the hotel. You rotten motherfucker.'

'Your problem is with yourself, Karyn. You just don't know it.'

'Save the cheap psychology for your AA meetings. Your life's going to be miserable. I promise.'

'Dock Green says there're dead people under the tree in your side yard.'

'That's marvelous detective work. They were lynched and buried there over a century ago.'

'How about a kid in the unmarked grave by the water?'

Her skin under her makeup turned as pale and dry as paper.

22

The next morning I walked up to Jerry Joe Plumb on his plot of tree-dotted land in the middle of the historical district on East Main. He was watching two cement mixers pour the foundation for his home on a felled tree. He wore khakis and his leather flyer's jacket, and the sunlight through the oaks looked like yellow blades of grass on his face.

'Dock Green says you knocked around his construction foreman,' I said.

'It got a little out of hand.'

'You held him down and spit in his face?'

'I apologized.'

'I bet he appreciated that.'

'I went on a tab for three hundred large to back Buford's campaign. You know what the vig is on three hundred large? Now Dock's wheeling and dealing with Buford while I got building suppliers looking at me with knives and forks.'

'Then quit protecting Buford.'

'You got it wrong . . . But . . . Never mind, come in my trailer and I'll show you something.'

Inside, he spread a roll of architect's plans across a drafting table and weighted down the ends, then combed his hair while he looked admiringly at the sketch of the finished house. 'See, it's turn-of-the-century. It'll fit right in. The brick's purple and comes out of a hundred-year-old house I found over in Mississippi,' he said.

The building was three storeys high, a medieval fortress rather than a house, with balconies and widow's walks and windbreaks that were redundant inside a city, and I thought of Jerry Joe's description of the LaRose home out west of the Pecos, where he had fled at age seventeen.

'You're going to let Buford burn you because of the old man, what was his name, Jude?' I said.

'If it wasn't for Jude, I'd a been majoring in cotton picking on a prison farm.'

'I took Dock out to the LaRose plantation yesterday. He says there's a kid's grave down by the water.'

'Better listen to him, then.'

'Oh?'

'The guy hears voices. It's like he knows stuff people aren't supposed to know. He puts dead things in jars. Maybe he's a ghoul.'

I started to leave. 'Stay away from his construction site, okay?' I said.

'I'm not the problem, Dave. Neither is Dock. You got a disease in this town. The whole state does, and it's right up the bayou.'

'Then stop letting Buford use you for his regular punch,' I said.

Jerry Joe clipped his comb inside his shirt pocket and stepped close to my face, his open hands curved simianlike by his sides, the white scar at the corner of his eye bunching into a knot.

'We're friends, but don't you ever in your life say anything like that to me again,' he said.

After I got back to the department, the sheriff buzzed my extension and asked me to come into his office. He sat humped behind his desk, scraping the bowl of his pipe with a penknife.

'Our health carrier called this morning. They've developed a problem with your coverage,' he said.

'What problem?'

'Your drinking history.'

'Why call about it now?'

'That's the question. You were in therapy a few years back?'

'That's right.'

'After your wife was killed?'

I nodded, my eyes shifting off his.

'The psychologist's file on you went through their fax this morning,' he said. 'It came through ours, too. It also went to the *Daily Iberian*.' Before I could speak, he said, 'I tore it up. But the guy from Blue Cross was a little strung out.'

'Too bad.'

'Dave, you're sober now, but you had two slips before you made it. I guess there was a lot of Vietnam stuff in that file, too. Civilians don't handle that stuff well.' He set the pipe down and looked at the tops of his hands. 'Who sent the fax?'

'The therapist died two years ago.'

'So?'

'I'm not omniscient.'

'We both know what I'm talking about.'

'He had an office in the Oil Center. In the same suite as Buford LaRose's.'

'It wasn't Buford, though, was it?'

'I don't know if Buford's potential has ever been plumbed.'

'Dave, tell me you haven't been out to see Karyn.'

'Yesterday . . . I took Dock Green out there.'

His swivel chair creaked when he leaned back in it. His teeth made a clicking sound in the stem of his dead pipe.

At dawn the next morning I cut the gas on my outboard engine north of the LaRose plantation and let the aluminum boat float sideways in the current past the barbed wire fenceline that extended into the water and marked the edge of Buford's property. The sun was an orange smudge through the hardwood trees, and I could hear horses nickering beyond the mist that rose out of the coulee. I used a paddle to bring the boat out of the current and into the backwater, the cattails sliding off the bow and the sides, then I felt the metal bottom bite into silt.

I could see the black marble crypt and the piked iron fence that surrounded it at the top of the slope, the silhouette of a state trooper who was looking in the opposite direction, a roan gelding tossing its head and backing out of spiderwebs that were spread between two persimmon trunks.

Part of the coulee had caved in, and the runoff had washed over the side and eroded a clutch of wide rivulets in the shape of a splayed hand, down the embankment to the bayou's edge. I pushed the paddle hard into the silt and watched the trees, the palmettos, a dock and boat-house, and the pine-needle-covered, hoof-scarred floor of the woods drift past me.

Then I saw it, in the same way your eye recognizes mortality in a rain forest when birds lift suddenly off the canopy or the wind shifts and you smell an odor that has always lived like a dark thought on the edge of your consciousness.

But in truth it wasn't much – a series of dimples on the slope, grass that was greener than it should have been, a spray of mushrooms with poisonous skirts. Maybe my contention with the LaRoses had broached the confines of obsession. I slipped one of the oar locks, tied a handkerchief through it, and tossed it up on the bank.

Then I drifted sideways with the current into the silence of the next bend, yanked the starter rope, and felt the engine's roar reverberate through my palm like a earache.

At sunset I put on my gym shorts and running shoes and did a mile and a half to the drawbridge, waved at the bridge tender, and turned back toward home, the air like a cool flame on my skin. Ahead of me I saw a Buick pull to the side of the road and park, the front window roll down, then the door open halfway. Jerry Joe remained seated, his arms propped in the window as though he were leaning on a bar, a can of Budweiser in one hand, a pint of whiskey in the other. He looked showered and fresh, and he wore a white suit with an open-collar lavender shirt. A flat cardboard box lay on the leather seat next to him.

'You gonna bust me for an open container?' he said.

'It's a possibility.'

'I'm sorry about getting in your face yesterday.'

'Forget it.'

'You remember my mother?'

'Sure.'

'She used to make me go to confession all the time. I hated it. She was a real coonass, you know, and she'd say, "You feel guilty about you done something to somebody, Jerry Joe, you gonna try to pretend you don't know that person no more 'cause he gonna make you remember who you are and the bad thing you done, or maybe you're gonna try to hurt him, you. So that's why you gotta go to confess, you."'

He tilted the bottle and threaded a thin stream of bourbon into the opening of his beer can. Then he drank from the can, the color in his eyes deepening.

'Yes?' I said.

'People like Karyn and Buford reinvent themselves. It's like my mother said. They don't want mirrors around to remind them of what they used to be.'

'What can I do for you, partner?'

'I ain't lily white. I've been mixed up with the LaRose family a long time. But the deal going down now . . . I don't know . . . It ain't just the money . . . It bothers me.'

'Tell somebody about it, Jerry Joe. Like your mom said.' I tried to smile.

He reached around behind him and picked up the cardboard box from the seat. 'I brought you something belongs to you. It was still buried behind the old house.'

I rested the box on the window and lifted the top. The hand crank to our old phonograph lay in the middle of a crinkled sheet of white wrapping paper. The metal was deformed and bulbous with rust, and the wood handle had been eaten by groundwater.

'So I returned your property and I got no reason to be mad at you,' he said. He was smiling now. He closed his car door and started his engine.

'Stay on that old-time R&B,' I said.

'I never been off it.'

436

I walked the rest of the way home. The sun was gone now and the air was damp and cold, and the last fireflies of the season traced their smoky red patterns in the shadows.

23

When your stitches are popping loose and your elevator has already plummeted past any reasonable bottom and the best your day offers is seeds and stems at sunrise to flatten the kinks or a street dealer's speedball that can turn your heart into a firecracker, you might end up in a piece of geography as follows:

A few blocks off Canal, the building was once a bordello that housed both mulatto and white women; then in a more moral era, when the downtown brothels were closed by the authorities and the girls started working out of taxicabs instead, the building was partitioned into apartments and studios for artists, and finally it became simply a 'hotel,' with no name other than that, the neon letters emblazoned vertically on a tin sign above a picture glass window that looked in upon a row of attached theater seats. Old people seemingly numbed by the calamity that had placed them in these surroundings stared vacantly through the glass at the sidewalk.

The Mexican man had climbed the fire escape onto the peaked roof, then had glided out among the stars. He hit the courtyard with such an impact that he split a flagstone like it was slate.

The corridor was dark and smelled of the stained paper bags filled with garbage that stood by each door like sentinels. Clete opened the dead man's room with a passkey.

'A Vietnamese boat lady owns the place. She found the guy's pay stub and thought I could get his back rent from the state,' he said.

Most of the plaster was gone from the walls. A mattress was rolled on an iron bed frame, and a pile of trash paper, green wine bottles, and frozen TV dinner containers was swept neatly into one corner. A flattened, plastic wallet and a cardboard suitcase and a guitar with twelve tuning pegs and no strings lay on top of a plank table. The sound hole on the guitar was inlaid with green and pink mollusk shell, and the wood below the hole had been cut with scratches that looked like cat's whiskers.

'What was he on?' I said.

'A couple of the wetbrains say he was cooking brown skag with ups. The speed is supposed to give it legs. The mamasan found the wallet under the bed.'

It contained no money, only a detached stub from a pay voucher for ninety-six dollars, with Buford LaRose's name and New Iberia address printed in the upper left-hand corner, and a Catholic holy card depicting a small statue of Christ's mother, with rays of gold and blue light emanating from it. Underneath the statue was the caption *La Virgin de Zapopan.*

I unsnapped the suitcase. His shirts and trousers and underwear were all rolled into tight balls. A pair of boots were folded at the tops in one corner. The toes were pointed and threadbare around the welt, the heels almost flat, the leather worn as smooth and soft as felt in a slipper. Under the boots, wrapped in a towel, was a solitary roweled spur, the cusp scrolled with winged serpents.

'It looks like the guy had another kind of life at one time,' Clete said.

'Does NOPD know he worked for Buford LaRose?'

'The mamasan called them and got the big yawn. They've got New Orleans cops pulling armed robberies. Who's got time for a roof flyer down here in Shitsville?'

'Dock Green says a kid's buried on the LaRose property.'

'You try for a warrant?'

'The judge said insufficient grounds. He seemed to think I had personal motivations as well.'

'You're going about it the wrong way, Streak. Squeeze somebody close to LaRose.'

'Who?'

'That old guy, the poet, the fuckhead left over from the sixties, he was working his scam out at Tulane last night. He's doing a repeat performance up on St Charles this afternoon.'

He drummed the square tips of his fingers on the face of the guitar.

'No grand displays, Clete,' I said.

'Me?'

Clay Mason's poetry reading was in a reception hall above a restaurant in the Garden District. From the second-story French doors you could look down upon a sidewalk cafe, the oaks along the avenue, the iron streetcars out on the neutral ground, a K&B drugstore on the corner whose green and purple neon hung like colored smoke in the rain.

Clete and I sat on folding chairs in the back of the hall. We were lucky to get seats at all. College kids dressed in Seattle grunge lined the walls.

'Can you believe anybody going for this guy's shuck today?' Clete said.

'It's in.'

'Why?'

'They missed all the fun.'

In reality, I probably knew a better answer. But it sounded like a weary one, even to myself, and I left it unsaid. Presidents who had never heard a shot fired in anger vicariously revised the inadequacy of their own lives by precipitating suffering in the lives of others, and they were lauded for it. Clay Mason well understood the nature of public memory and had simply waited for his time and a new generation of intellectual cannon fodder to come round again.

His pretentiousness, his feigned old man's humility and irreverence toward the totems, were almost embarrassing. He had been an academic for years, but he denigrated universities and academics. He spoke of his own career in self-effacing terms but gave the impression he had known the most famous writers of his time. In his eccentric western clothes, a Stetson hat cocked on his white head, a burning cigarette cupped in his small hand, he became the egalitarian spokesman for the Wobblies, the railroad hobos of Woody Guthrie and Hart Crane, the miners killed at Ludlow, Colorado, the girls whose bodies were incinerated like bolts of cloth in the Triangle Shirtwaist Factory fire.

His poems were full of southwestern mesas and peyote cactus, ponies that drank out of blood-red rivers, fields blown with bluebonnets and poppies, hot winds that smelled of burning hemp.

His words seemed to challenge all convention and caution, even his own death, which one poem described in terms of a chemical rainbow rising from the ashes of his soul.

The audience loved it.

Clete craned forward in his seat.

'Check it out by the door, big mon,' he said.

Karyn LaRose was dressed in a pale blue suit and white hose, with a white scarf about her neck, her legs crossed, listening attentively to Clay Mason. The horn-rimmed glasses she wore only added to her look of composure and feminine confidence. Two state troopers stood within five feet of her, their hands folded behind them, as though they were at parade rest.

'Why do I feel like a starving man looking at a plate of baked Alaska?' Clete said. 'You think I could interest her in some private security?'

A middle-aged woman in front of us turned and said, 'Would you kindly be quiet?'

'Sorry,' Clete said, his face suddenly blank.

After Clay Mason finished reading his last poem, the audience rose to its feet and applauded and then applauded some more. Clete and I worked our way to the front of the hall, where a cash drink bar was open and a buffet was being set up.

'Watch out for the Smokies. It looks like they're working on their new chevrons,' Clete said.

Clay Mason stood with a group by Karyn's chair, his weight resting on his cane. When he saw me, the parchment lines in his pixie face seem to deepen, then he smiled quickly and extended his hand out of the crowd. It felt like a twig in mine.

'I'm flattered by your presence, sir,' he said.

'It's more business than pleasure. A Mexican kid who worked for Buford took a dive off a flophouse roof,' I said.

'Yeah, definitely bad shit. They had to put the guy's brains back in his head with a trowel,' Clete said.

I gave Clete a hard stare, but it didn't register.

'I'm sorry to hear about this,' Clay Mason said.

On the edge of my vision I could see Karyn LaRose seated not more than two feet from us.

'What's happening, Karyn?' I said, without looking at her.

'You gentlemen wouldn't contrive to turn a skunk loose at a church social, would you?' Clay Mason said, a smile wrinkling at the corner of his mouth.

I took the pay stub from my shirt pocket and looked at it. 'The guy's name was Fernando Spinoza. You know him?' I asked.

'No, can't say that I do,' Clay Mason said.

'How about you, Karyn?' I asked.

The redness in her cheeks looked like arrowpoints. But her eyes were clear with purpose and she didn't hesitate in her response.

'This man is a detective with the Iberia Parish Sheriff's Department,' she said to the two troopers. 'He's annoyed me and my husband in every way he can. It's my belief he has no other reason for being here.'

'Is that right, sir?' one of the troopers said, his eyes slightly askance, rising slightly on the balls of his feet, his hands still folded behind him.

'I'm here because of a kid who had to be blotted off a flagstone,' I said.

'You have some kind of jurisdiction in New Orleans? How about y'all get something to eat over at the buffet table?' the trooper said. His face was lumpy, not unpleasant or hostile or dumb, just lumpy and obsequious.

'Here's today's flash, buddy,' Clete said. 'This old guy you're a doorman for, he popped his own wife. Shot an apple off her head at a party with a forty-four Magnum down in Taco Ticoville. Except he was stinking drunk and left her hair all over the wallpaper. Maybe we should be telling that to these dumb kids who listen to his bullshit.'

The conversation around us died as though someone had pulled the plug on a record player. I looked over at Clete and was never prouder of him.

But our moment with Clay Mason wasn't over. Outside, we saw him walk from under the blue canvas awning at the front entrance of the restaurant toward a waiting limo, Karyn LaRose at his side, leaning on his cane, negotiating the peaked sidewalk where the roots of oak trees had wedged up the concrete. A small misshaped black and brown mongrel dog, with raised hair like pig bristles, came out of nowhere and began barking at Mason, its teeth bared and its nails clicking on the pavement, advancing and retreating as fear and hostility moved it. Mason continued toward the limo, his gaze fixed ahead of him. Then, without missing a step, he suddenly raised his cane in the air and whipped it across the dog's back with such force that the animal ran yipping in pain through the traffic as though its spine had been broken.

The next evening, at sunset, I drove my truck up the state road that paralleled Bayou Teche and parked in a grove across the water from Buford's plantation. Through my Japanese field glasses I could see the current flowing under his dock and boathouse, the arched iron shutters on the smithy, the horses in his fields, the poplars that flattened in the wind against the side of his house. Then I moved the field glasses along the bank, where I had thrown the oar lock tied with my handkerchief. The oar lock was gone, and someone had beveled out a plateau on the slope and had poured a concrete pad and begun construction of a gazebo there.

I propped my elbows on the hood of my truck and moved the glasses through the trees, and in the sun's afterglow, which was like firelight on the trunks, I saw first one state trooper, then a second, then a third, all of them with scoped and leather-slung bolt-action rifles. Each trooper sat on a chair in the shadows, much like hunters positioning themselves in a deer stand.

I heard a boot crack a twig behind me.

'Hep you with something?' a trooper asked.

He was big and gray, close to retirement age, his stomach protruding like a sack of gravel over his belt.

I opened my badge holder.

'On the job,' I said.

'Still ain't too good to be here. Know what I mean?' he said.

'I don't.'

'This morning they found work boot prints on the mudbank. Like boots a convict might wear.'

442

'I see.'

'If he comes in, they don't want him spooked out,' the trooper said. We looked at each other in the silence. There was a smile in his eyes.

'It looks like they know their work,' I said.

'Put it like you want. Crown comes here, he's gonna have to kill his next nigger down in hell.'

The backyard was dim with mist when I fixed breakfast in the kitchen the next morning. I heard Bootsie walk into the kitchen behind me. The window over the sink was open halfway and the radio was playing on the windowsill.

'Are you listening to the radio?' she said.

'Yeah, I just clicked it on.'

'Alafair's still asleep.'

'I wasn't thinking. I'll turn it off.'

'No, just turn it down.'

'All right,' I said. I walked to the sink and turned down the volume knob. I looked out the window at the yard until I was sure my face was empty of expression, then I sat down again and we ate in silence.

We were both happy when the phone rang on the wall.

'You have the news on?' the sheriff asked.

'No.'

'I wouldn't call so early but I thought it'd be better if you heard it from me . . . '

'What is it, skipper?'

'Short Boy Jerry. NOPD found his car by the Desire welfare project a half hour ago . . . He was beaten to death . . . '

I felt a tick jump in my throat. I pressed my thumb hard under my ear to clear a fluttering sound, like a wounded butterfly, out of my hearing. I saw Bootsie looking at me, saw her put down her coffee cup gently and her face grow small.

'You there, podna?' the sheriff said.

'Who did it?'

'NOPD thinks a gang of black pukes. I'll tell you up front, Dave, he went out hard.'

'I need the plane,' I said.

24

The sun was pale, almost white, like a sliver of ice hidden behind clouds above Lake Pontchartrain, when Clete Purcel met me at the New Orleans airport and drove us back down I-10 toward the city.

'You really want to go to the meat locker, Streak?' he asked.

'You know another place to start?'

'It was just a question.'

Morgues deny all the colors the mind wishes to associate with death. The surfaces are cool to the touch, made of aluminum and stainless steel, made even more sterile in appearance by the dull reflection of the fluorescent lighting overhead. The trough and the drains where an autopsy was just conducted are spotless; the water that wells across and cleanses the trough's bottom could have issued from a spring.

But somehow, in the mind, you hear sounds behind all those gleaming lockers, like fluids dripping, a tendon constricting, a lip that tightens into a sneer across the teeth.

The assistant wore a full-length white lab coat that looked like a nineteenth-century duster. He paused with his hand on the locker door. He had a cold and kept brushing at his nose with the back of his wrist.

'The guy's hands are bagged. Otherwise, he's like they found him,' he said.

'This place is an igloo in here. Let's see it, all right?' Clete said.

The assistant looked at Clete oddly and then pulled out the drawer. Clete glanced down at Jerry Joe, let out his breath, then lifted his eyes to mine.

'When it's this bad, it usually means a tire iron or maybe a curb button. The uniforms found him on the pavement, so it's hard to tell right now,' the assistant said. 'You knew the guy?'

'Yeah, he knew the guy,' Clete answered.

'I was just wondering what he was doing in that neighborhood at night, that's all,' the assistant said. 'If a white guy's down there at night, it's usually for cooze or rock. We on the same side here?'

Most of Jerry Joe's teeth had been broken off. One of his eyes looked like a tea-stained egg. The other was no longer an eye. I lifted his left hand. It felt like a heavy piece of old fruit inside the plastic bag.

'Both of them are broken. I don't know anything about this guy, but my bet is, he went the whole fifteen before they clicked off his switch,' the attendant said.

'Thank you, sir, for your time,' I said, and turned and walked outside.

I talked with the scene investigator at the District from a filling station pay phone. He had a heavy New Orleans blue-collar accent, which is far closer to the speech of Brooklyn than to the Deep South; he told me he had to go to a meeting and couldn't talk to me right now.

'When can you talk?' I asked.

'When I get out of the meeting.'

'When is that?'

'Leave your number.'

We pulled back into the traffic. Clete's window was down and the wind whipped the hair on his head. He kept looking across the seat at me.

'Streak, you're making me tense,' he said.

'You buy kids did this?' I asked.

'I think that's how it's going to go down.'

'You didn't answer my question.'

He took a swizzle stick off his dashboard and put it in his mouth. A neutral ground with palm trees on it streamed past his window. 'I can't see Jerry Ace getting taken down by pukes. Not like this, anyway. Maybe if he got capped—'

'Why would he be down by the Desire?'

'He dug R&B. He was a paratrooper. He thought he had magic painted on him . . . Dave, don't try to make sense out of it. This city's in flames. You just can't see them.'

Jerry Joe's blue Buick had already been towed to the pound. A uniformed cop opened the iron gate for us and walked with us past a row of impounded cars to the back of the lot. The Buick was parked against a brick wall, its trunk sprung, its dashboard ripped out, the glove box rifled, the leather door panels pried loose, the stereo speakers gouged with screwdrivers out of the headliner. A strip of torn yellow crime scene tape was tangled around one wheel, flapping in the wind.

'Another half hour and they would have had the engine off the mounts,' Clete said.

'How do you read it?' I said.

'A gang of street rats got to it after he was dead.'

'It looks like they had him made for a mule.'

445

'The side panels? Yeah. Which means they didn't know who he was.'

'But they wouldn't have hung around to strip the car if they'd killed him, would they?' I said.

'No, their consciences were clean. You hook them up, that's what they'll tell you. Just a harmless night out, looting a dead man's car. I think I'm going to move to East Los Angeles,' he said.

We went to the District and caught the scene investigator at his desk. He was a blond, tall, blade-faced man named Cramer who wore a sky blue sports coat and white shirt and dark tie with a tiny gold pistol and chain fastened to it. The erectness of his posture in the chair distracted the eye from his paunch and concave chest and the patina of nicotine on his fingers.

'Do we have anybody in custody? No. Do we have any suspects? Yeah. Every gangbanger in that neighborhood,' he said.

'I think it was a hit,' I said.

'You think a hit?' he said.

'Maybe Jerry Joe was going to dime some people, contractors lining up at the trough in Baton Rouge,' I said.

'You used to be at the First District, right?'

'Right.'

'Tell me when I say something that sounds wrong – a white guy down by the Desire at night isn't looking to be shark meat.'

'Come on, Cramer. Kids aren't going to kill a guy and peel the car with the body lying on the street,' I said.

'Maybe they didn't know they'd killed him. You think of that?'

'I think you're shit-canning the investigation,' I said.

'I punched in at four this morning. A black kid took a shot at another kid in the Desire. He missed. He killed a three-month-old baby instead. Short Boy Jerry was a mutt. You asking me I got priorities? Fucking "A" I do.'

His phone rang. He picked it up, then hit the 'hold' button.

'Y'all get a cup of coffee, give me ten minutes,' he said.

Clete and I walked down the street and ate a hot dog at a counter where we had to stand, then went back to the District headquarters. Cramer scratched his forehead and looked at a yellow legal pad on his blotter.

'That was the ME called,' he said. 'Short Boy Jerry had gravel and grains of concrete in his scalp, but it was from a fall, not a blow. There were pieces of leather in the wounds around his eyes, probably from gloves the hitter was wearing or a blackjack. Death was caused by a broken rib getting shoved into the heart.'

He lit a cigarette and put the paper match carefully in the ashtray with two fingers, his eyes veiled.

446

'What's the rest of it?' I asked.

'The M.E. thinks the assailant or assailants propped Short Boy Jerry up to prolong the beating. The bruises on the throat show a single hand held him up straight while he was getting it in the stomach. The brain was already hemorrhaging when the rib went into the heart . . . '

'What's that numeral at the bottom of the page?' I asked.

'The blows in the ribs were from a fist maybe six inches across.'

'You got a sheet on a gangbanger that big?' I said.

'That doesn't mean there's not one.'

'Start looking for a black mechanic named Mookie Zerrang,' I said.

'Who?' he said.

'He looks like a stack of gorilla shit with gold teeth in it. Feel flattered. He gets ten large a whack in Miami. I'm surprised he'd be seen in a neighborhood like this. No kidding, they say the guy's got rigid standards,' Clete said, fixing his eyes earnestly on Cramer's face.

That evening I let Batist go home early and cleaned the bait shop and the tables on the dock by myself. The air was cool, the sky purple and dense with birds, the dying sun as bright as an acetylene flame on the horizon. I could see flights of ducks in V formations come in low over the swamp, then circle away and drop beyond the tips of the cypress into the darkness on the other side.

I plugged in Jerry Joe's jukebox and watched the colored lights drift through the plastic casing like smoke from marker grenades. There were two recordings of 'La Jolie Blon' in the half-moon rack, one by Harry Choates and the other by Iry LeJeune. I had never thought about it before, but both men's lives seemed to be always associated with that haunting, beautiful song, one that was so pure in its sense of loss you didn't have to understand French to comprehend what the singer felt. 'La Jolie Blon' wasn't about a lost love. It was about the end of an era.

Iry LeJeune was killed on the highway, changing a tire, and Harry Choates died in alcoholic madness in the Austin city jail, either after beating his head bloody against the bars or being beaten unmercifully by his jailers.

Maybe their tragic denouements had nothing to do with a song that had the power to break the heart. Maybe such a conclusion was a product of my own alcoholic mentality. But I had to grieve just a moment on their passing, just as I did for Jerry Joe, and maybe for all of us who tried to hold on to a time that was quickly passing away.

Jerry the Glide had believed in Wurlitzer jukeboxes and had secretly worshipped the man who had helped burn Dresden. What a surrogate, I thought, then wondered what mine was.

A car came down the road in the dusk, then slowed, as though the driver might want to stop, perhaps for a beer on the way home. I turned off the outside flood lamps, then the string of lights over the dock, then the lights inside the shop, and the car went past the boat ramp and down the road and around the curve. I leaned with my forearm against the jukebox's casing and started to punch a selection. But you can't recover the past with a recording that's forty years old, nor revise all the moments when you might have made life a little better for the dead.

I could feel the blood beating in my wrists. I jerked the plug from the wall, sliced the cord in half with my pocketknife, and wheeled the jukebox to the back and left it in a square of moonlight, face to the wall.

25

Early Sunday morning I parked my pickup in the alley behind Sabelle Crown's bar in Lafayette. The alley was littered with bottles and beer cans, and a man and woman were arguing on the landing above the back entrance to the bar. The woman wore an embroidered Japanese robe that exposed her thick calves, and her chestnut hair was unbrushed and her face without makeup. The man glanced down at me uncertainly, then turned back to the woman.

'You t'ink you wort' more, go check the mirror, you,' he said. He walked down the wood stairs and on down the alley, stepping over a rain puddle, without looking at me. The woman went back inside.

I climbed the stairs to the third story, where Sabelle lived by herself at the end of a dark hallway that smelled of insecticide and mold.

'It's seven in the morning. You on a drunk or something?' she said when she opened the door. She wore only a T-shirt without a bra and a pair of blue jeans that barely buttoned under her navel.

'You still have working girls here, Sabelle?' I said.

'We're all working girls, honey. Y'all just haven't caught on.' She left the door open for me and walked barefoot across the linoleum and took a coffee pot off her two-burner stove.

'I want you to put me with your father.'

'Like meet with him, you're saying?'

'However you want to do it.'

'So you can have him executed?'

'I believe Buford LaRose is setting him up to be killed.'

She set the coffee pot back on the stove without pouring from it.

'How do you know this?' she said.

'I was out to his place. Those state troopers aren't planning to take prisoners.'

She sucked in her bottom lip.

'What are you offering?' she asked.

'Maybe transfer to a federal facility.'

'Daddy hates the federal government.'

'That's a dumb attitude.'

'Thanks for the remark. I'll think about it.'

'There're only a few people who've stood in Buford's way, Sabelle. The scriptwriter and Lonnie Felton were two of them. Jerry Joe Plumb was another. He was killed yesterday morning. That leaves your dad.'

'Jerry Joe?' she said. Her face was blank, like that of someone who has been caught unawares by a photographer's flash.

'He was methodically beaten to death. My guess is by the same black guy who killed Felton and his girlfriend and the scriptwriter.'

She sat down at her small kitchen table and looked out the window across the rooftops.

'The black guy again?' she said.

'That means something to you?'

'What do I know about black guys? They pick up the trash. They don't drink in my bar.'

'Get a hold of your old man, Sabelle.'

'Say, you're wrong about one thing.'

'Oh?'

'Daddy's not the only guy in Buford's way. Take it from a girl who's been there. When he decides to fuck somebody, he doesn't care if it's male or female. Keep your legs crossed, sweetie.'

I looked at the glint in her eye, and at the anger and injury it represented, and I knew that her friendship with me had always been a presumption and vanity on my part and that in reality Sabelle Crown had long ago consigned me, unfairly or not, to that arm of male violators and users who took and never gave.

Monday an overweight man in a navy blue suit with hair as black as patent leather tapped on my office glass. There was a deep dimple in his chin.

'Can I help you?' I said.

'Yeah, I just kind of walked myself back here. This is a nice building y'all got.' His right hand was folded on a paper bag. I waited. 'Oh, excuse me,' he said. 'I'm Ciro Tauzin, state police, Baton Rouge. You got a minute, suh?'

His thighs splayed on the chair when he sat down. His starched dress shirt was too small for him and the collar button had popped loose under the knot in his necktie.

'You know what I got here?' he asked, putting his hand in the paper bag. 'An oar lock with a handkerchief tied through it. That's a strange thing for somebody to find on their back lawn, ain't it?'

'Depends on who the person is.'

'In this case, it was one of my men found it on Buford LaRose's place. So since an escaped convict is trying to assassinate the governor-elect, we didn't want to take nothing for granted and we took some prints off it and ran them through AFIS, you know, the Automatic Fingerprint Identification System. I tell you, podna, what a surprise when we found out who those prints belonged to. Somebody steal an oar lock off one of your boats, suh?'

'Not to my knowledge.'

'You just out throwing your oar locks on people's lawn?'

'It was just an idle speculation on my part. About a body that might have been buried there.'

'Is that right? I declare. Y'all do some fascinating investigative work in Iberia Parish.'

'You're welcome to join us.'

'Ms LaRose says you got an obsession, that you're carrying out a vendetta of some kind. She thinks maybe you marked the back of the property for Aaron Crown.'

'Karyn has a creative mind.'

'Well, you know how people are, suh. They get inside their heads and think too much. But one of my troopers told me you were knocking around in the stables, where you didn't have no bidness. What you up to, Mr Robicheaux?'

'I think Aaron's a dead man if he gets near your men.'

'Really? Well, suh, I won't bother you any more today. Here's your oar lock back. You're not going to be throwing nothing else up in their yard, are you?'

'I'm not planning on it. Tell me something.'

'Yes, suh?'

'Why would the LaRoses decide to put in a gazebo right where I thought there might be an unmarked burial?'

'You know, I thought about that myself. So I checked with the contractor. Mr LaRose put in the order for that gazebo two months ago.'

He rose and extended his hand.

I didn't take it.

'You're fronting points for a guy who's got no bottom, Mr Tauzin. No offense meant,' I said.

That night I went to bed early, before Bootsie, and was almost asleep when I heard her enter the room and begin undressing. She brushed her teeth and stayed in the bathroom a long time, then clicked off the bathroom light and lay down on her side of the bed with her head turned toward the wall. I placed my palm on her back. Her skin was warm through her nightgown.

She looked up into the darkness.

'You all right?' she said.

'Sure.'

'About Jerry Joe, I mean?'

'I was okay today.'

'Dave?'

'Yes?'

'No . . . I'm sorry. I'm too tired to talk about it tonight.'

'About what?'

She didn't reply at first, then she said, 'That woman . . . I hate her.'

'Come on, Boots. See her for what she is.'

'You're playing her game. It's a rush for both of you. I'm not going to say any more . . .' She sat on the side of the bed and pushed her feet in her slippers. 'I can't take this, Dave,' she said, and picked up her pillow and a blanket and went into the living room.

The moon was down, the sky dark, when I was awakened at five the next morning by a sound out in the swamp, wood knocking against wood, echoing across the water. I sat on the edge of the bed, my head still full of sleep, and heard it again through the half-opened window, an oar striking a log perhaps, the bow sliding off a cypress stump. Then I saw the light in the mist, deep in the flooded trees, like a small halo of white phosphorous burning against the dampness, moving horizontally four feet above the waterline.

I put on my khakis and loafers and flannel shirt, took a flashlight out of the nightstand and my .45 automatic out of the dresser drawer and walked to the end of the dock.

The light out in the trees was gone. The air was gray with mist, the bayou dimpled by the rolling backs of gars.

'Who are you?' I called.

It was quiet, as though the person in the trees was considering my question, then I heard a paddle or an oar dipping into water, raking alongside a wood gunnel.

'Tell me who you are!' I called. I waited. Nothing. My words sounded like those of a fool trapped by his own fears.

I unlocked the bait shop and turned on the flood lamps, then unchained an outboard by the end of the concrete ramp, set one knee on the seat, and shoved out into the bayou. I cranked the engine and went thirty yards downstream and turned into a cut that led back into a dead bay surrounded by cypress and willows. The air was cold and thick with fog, and when I shut off the engine I heard a bass flop its tail in the shallows. Nutrias perched on every exposed surface, their eyes as red as sapphires in the glow of my flashlight.

Then, at the edge of the bay, I saw the path a boat had cut in the layer of algae floating between two stumps. I shined my light deep into the trees and saw a moving shape, the shadow of a hunched man, a flash of dirty gold water flicked backward as a pirogue disappeared beyond a mudbank that was overgrown with palmettos.

'Aaron?' I asked the darkness.

But no one responded.

I tried to remember the images in my mind's eye – the breadth of the shoulders, a hand pulling aside a limb, a neck that seemed to go from the jaws into the collarbones without taper. But the reality was I had seen nothing clearly except a man seated low in a pirogue and –

A glistening, thin object in the stern. It was metal, I thought. A chain perhaps. The barrel of a rifle.

My flannel shirt was sour with sweat. I could hear my heart beating in the silence of the trees.

I came home for lunch that day. Alafair was at school and Bootsie was gone. There was no note on the corkboard where we left messages for one another. I fixed a ham and onion sandwich and a glass of iced tea and heated a bowl of dirty rice and ate at the kitchen table. Batist called from the bait shop.

'Dave, there's a bunch of black mens here drinking beer and using bad language out on the dock,' he said.

'Who are they?' I asked.

'One's got a knife instead of a hook on his hand.'

'A what?'

'Come see, 'cause I'm fixing to run 'em down the road.'

I walked down the slope through the trees. A new Dodge Caravan was parked by the concrete boat ramp, and five black men stood on the end of the dock, their shirtsleeves rolled in the warm air, drinking can beer while Jimmy Ray Dixon gutted a two-foot yellow catfish he had gill-hung from a nail on a light post.

A curved and fine-pointed knife blade, honed to the blue thinness of a barber's razor, was screwed into a metal and leather cup that fitted over the stump of Jimmy Ray's left wrist. He drew the blade's edge around the catfish's gills, then cut a neat line down both sides of the dorsal fin and stripped the skin back with a pair of pliers in his right hand. He sliced the belly from the apex of the V where the gills met to the anus and let the guts fall out of the cavity like a sack of blue and red jelly.

The tops of his canvas shoes were speckled with blood. He was grinning.

'I bought it from a man caught it in a hoop net at Henderson,' he said.

'Y'all want to rent a boat?'

'I hear the fishing here ain't any good.'

'It's not good anywhere now. The water's too cool.'

'I got a problem with a couple of people bothering me. I think you behind it,' he said.

'You want to lose the audience?' I said.

'Y'all give me a minute,' he said to the other men. They were dressed in tropical shirts, old slacks, shoes they didn't care about. But they weren't men who fished. Their hands squeezed their own sex, almost with fondness; their eyes followed a black woman walking on the road; they whispered to one another, even though their conversation was devoid of content.

They started to go inside the shop.

'It's closed,' I said.

'Hey, Jim, we ain't here to steal your watermelons,' Jimmy Ray said.

'I'd appreciate it if you didn't call me a racial name,' I said.

'Y'all open the cooler. I'll be along,' he said to his friends. He watched them drift in a cluster down the dock toward the van.

'Here's what it is,' he said. 'That cracker Cramer, yeah, you got it, white dude from Homicide, smells like deodorant, is down at my pool hall, axing if I know why Jerry the Glide was in the neighbourhood when somebody broke all his sticks.'

Not bad, Cramer, I thought.

'Then your friend, Purcel, hears from this pipehead street chicken Mookie Zerrang's got permission to burn his kite, so he blames me. I ain't got time for this, Jack.'

'Why *was* Jerry Joe in your neighbourhood?'

'It ain't my neighbourhood, I got a bidness there. I don't go in there at night, either.' He brushed the sack of fish guts off the dock with his shoe and watched it float away in the current. 'Why you got to put your hand in this shit, man?'

'You know how it is, a guy's got to do something for kicks.'

'I hear it's 'cause you was fucking some prime cut married to the wrong dude. That's your choice, man, but I don't like you using my brother to do whatever you doing. Give my fish to the old man in there,' he said, and started to walk away.

I walked after him and touched his back with the ball of my finger. I could feel his wingbone through the cloth of his shirt, see the dark grain of his whiskers along the edge of his jaw, smell the faint odor of sweat and talcum in his skin.

'Don't use profanity around my home, please,' I said.

'You worried about language round your home? Man put a bullet in mine and killed my brother. That's the difference between us. Don't let it be lost on you, Chuck.'

454

He got in the front passenger's seat of the van, slid a metal sheath over the knife blade attached to his stump, then unscrewed the blade and drank from a bottle of Carta Blanca, his throat working smoothly until the bottle was empty. The bottle made a dull, tinkling sound when it landed in the weeds by the roadside.

The next day I got the warrant to search the grounds of the LaRose plantation. Helen Soileau parked the cruiser in the driveway, and I got out and knocked on the front door.

Karyn was barefoot and wore only a pair of shorts and a halter, with a thick towel around her neck, when she opened the door. In the soft afternoon light her tan took on the dark tint of burnt honey. The momentary surprise went out of her face, and she leaned an arm against the doorjamb and brushed back her hair with her fingers.

'What are we here for today?' she said.

'Here's the warrant. We'll be looking at some things back on the bayou.'

'How did you—' she began, then stopped.

'All I had to do was tell the judge the state police warned me off y'all's property. He seemed upset about people intruding on his jurisdiction.'

'Then you should scurry on with your little errand, whatever in God's name it is.'

'Does Jerry Joe's death bother you at all?'

Her mouth grew small with anger.

'There're days when I wish I was a man, Dave. I'd honestly love to beat the living shit out of you.' The door clicked shut.

Helen and I walked through the coolness of the porte cochere into the backyard. The camellias were in bloom and the backyard was filled with a smoky gold light. I could see Karyn inside the glassed-in rear corner of the house, touching her toes in a crisscross motion, her thighs spread, the back of her neck slick with a necklace of sweat.

'You ever read anything about the Roman Coliseum? When gladiators fought on lakes of burning oil, that kind of stuff?' Helen said.

'Yeah, I guess.'

'I have a feeling Karyn LaRose was in the audience.'

We walked past the stables and through the hardwoods to the sloping bank of the Teche. A heavyset black state trooper sat in a folding chair, back among the trees, eating cracklings from a jar. His scoped rifle was propped against a pine trunk. He glanced at my badge holder hanging from my coat pocket and nodded.

'Crown hasn't tried to get through your perimeter, huh?' I said, and smiled.

'You ax me, he's been spooked out,' he answered.

'How's that?' I asked.

'Man's smart. See the mosquitoes I been swatting all day?'

'They're bad after a rain,' I said.

'They're bad in these trees anytime. Man don't see nobody out yonder on the bank, he knows what's waiting for him inside the woods. *That*, or somebody done tole him.'

'You take it easy,' I said.

Helen and I walked along the bank toward the spot where I had thrown the oar lock. I could feel her eyes on me, watching.

'You're damn quiet,' she said.

'Sorry, I didn't mean to be.'

'*Dave?*'

'What's up?'

'I'm getting a bad sense here.'

'What's that?' I said, my eyes focused on the gazebo that two carpenters were hammering and sawing on around the bayou's bend.

'What that trooper said. Did you warn Crown?'

'We don't execute people in Iberia Parish. We want the man in custody, not in a box.'

'We didn't have this conversation, Streak.'

The carpenters were on all fours atop the gazebo's round, peaked roof, their nail bags swinging from their stomachs.

'That's quite a foundation. Y'all always pour a concrete pad under a gazebo?' I said.

'High water will rot it out if you don't,' one man answered.

'What did y'all do with the dirt you excavated?'

'Some guy work for Mr LaRose, I guess.'

'Y'all did the excavation?'

'No, sir. Mr LaRose done that hisself. He got his own backhoe.'

'I see. Y'all doin' all right?'

'Yes, sir. Anyt'ing wrong?'

'Not a thing,' I said.

I walked down on the grassy bank, which was crisscrossed with the deep prints of cleated tires and dozer tracks. A fan of mud and torn divots of grass lay humped among the cattails at the bayou's edge. I poked at it with a stick and watched it cloud and drift away in the current.

'You want to bag some of it?' Helen said.

'It's a waste of time. Buford beat us to it.'

'It was a long shot,' Helen said. 'You've got to consider the source, too, Dave. Dock Green's nuts.'

'No, he's not. He's just different.'

'That's a new word for it.'

I didn't say anything. We walked up the slope and through the trees toward the house. The air was filled with gold shafts of light inside the trees, and you could smell the water in the coulee and the fecund odor of wet fern and the exposed root systems that trailed in the current like torn cobweb.

'Can I get out of line a minute?' Helen said.

I looked at her and waited. She kept walking up the incline, her face straight ahead, her shoulders slightly bent, her masculine arms taut-looking with muscle.

'The homicides you're worried about took place out of our jurisdiction. The Indian guy who tried to mess you over with the machete is dead. We don't have a crime connected with the LaRoses to investigate in Iberia Parish, Dave,' she said.

'They're both dirty.'

'So is the planet,' she said.

We took a shorter route back and exited the woods by a cleared field and passed the brick stables and an adjacent railed lot where a solitary bay gelding stood like a piece of stained redwood in a column of dust-laden sunlight. The brand on his flank was shaped in the form of a rose, burned deep into the hair like calcified ringworm.

'They sure leave their mark on everything, don't they?' I said.

'What should they use, spray cans? Give it a break,' Helen said.

'I'll tell them we're leaving now,' I said.

'Don't do it, Dave.'

'I'll see you in the car, Helen.'

She continued on through the field toward the driveway. I walked through the backyard toward the porte cochere, then glanced through a screen of bamboo into the glassed-in rear of the house where Karyn had been doing her aerobic exercises. We stared into each other's face with a look of mutual and surprised intimacy that went beyond the moment, beyond my ability to define or guard against, that went back into a deliberately forgotten image of two people looking nakedly upon each other's faces during intercourse.

I had caught her unawares in front of a small marble-topped bar with a champgne glass and a silver ice bucket containing a green bottle of Cold Duck on it. But Karyn was not one to be undone by an unexpected encounter with an adversary. With her eyes fastened on my face, a pout on her mouth like an adolescent girl, she unhooked her halter and let it drop from her breasts and unbuttoned her shorts and pushed them and her panties down over her thighs and knees and stepped out of them. Then she pulled the pins from her platinum hair and shook it out on her shoulders and put the glass of Cold Duck to her mouth, her eyes fixed on mine, as empty as death.

26

Jimmy Ray Dixon was one of those in-your-face people who insult and demean others with such confidence that you always assume they have nothing to hide themselves.

It's a good ruse. Just like offering a lie when no one has challenged your integrity. For example, lying about how you lost a hand in Vietnam.

After Jimmy Ray and his entourage had left the dock, I'd called a friend at the Veterans Administration in New Orleans.

The following day, when I got back to the department from the LaRose plantation, my friend called and read me everything he had pulled out of the computer on Jimmy Ray Dixon.

He didn't lose a hand clearing toe-poppers from a rice paddy outside Pinkville. A gang of Chinese thieves, his business partners in selling stolen PX liquor on the Saigon black market, cut it off.

A cross-referenced CID report also indicated Jimmy Ray may have been involved in smuggling heroin home in GI coffins.

So he lied about his war record, I thought. But who wouldn't, with a file like that?

That was not what had bothered me.

At the dock Jimmy Ray had said somebody had shot into his home and had killed his brother.

His home.

I went to the public library and the morgue at the *Daily Iberian* and began searching every piece of microfilm I could find on the assassination of Ely Dixon.

Only one story, in *Newsweek* magazine, mentioned the fact that Ely was killed in a two-bedroom house he rented for fifty dollars a month from his brother, Jimmy Ray, to whom the article referred as a disabled Vietnam war veteran.

I drove back to the department and went into the sheriff's office.

'What if the wrong man was killed?' I said.

'I have a feeling my interest is about to wane quickly,' he said.

'It was the sixties. Church bombings in Birmingham and Bogalusa, civil-rights workers lynched in Mississippi. Everybody assumed Ely Dixon was the target.'

'You're trying to figure out the motivation on a homicide that's twenty-eight years old? Who cares? The victim doesn't. He's dead just the same.'

He could barely contain the impatience and annoyance in his voice. He turned his swivel chair sideways so he wouldn't have to look directly at me when he spoke.

'I like you a lot, Dave, but, damn it, you don't listen. Leave the LaRoses alone. Let Aaron Crown fall in his own shit.'

'I told Helen we don't execute people in Iberia Parish.'

'Don't be deluded. That's because the electric chair doesn't travel anymore.'

He began fiddling with a file folder, then he put it in his desk drawer and rose from his chair and looked out the window until he heard me close the door behind me.

Batist went home sick with a cold that evening, and before supper Alafair and I drove down to his house with a pot of soup. His wife had died the previous year, and he lived with his three bird dogs and eight cats on a dirt road in an unpainted wood house with a sagging gallery and a peaked corrugated roof, a truck garden in a side lot and a smoke-house in back. The sparse grass in his yard was raked clean, his compost pile snugged in by chicken wire, his crab traps stacked next to a huge iron pot in the backyard where he cooked cracklings in the fall.

Over the years, in early spring, when he broke the thatched hard-pan on his garden, his single-tree plow had furrowed back bits of square nails, the rusted shell of a wagon spring, .58 caliber minié balls, a corroded tin of percussion caps, a molded boot, a brass buckle embossed with the letters *CSA*, the remains from a Confederate encampment that had probably been overrun by federals in 1863.

I first met Batist when I was a little boy and he was a teenager, a blacksmith's helper in a rambling, red barnlike structure on a green lot out on West Main. Batist worked for a frail, very elderly man named Mr Antoine, one of the last surviving Confederate veterans in the state of Louisiana. Every day Mr Antoine sat in the wide doors of his smithy, to catch the breeze, in red suspenders and straw hat, the skin under his throat distended like an inverted cock's comb.

Anyone who wished could drop by and listen to his stories about what he called 'the War.'

Few did.

But I'll never forget one he told me and Batist.

It was during Jubal Early's last assault on the federals before the surrender at Appomattox. A fourteen-year-old drummer boy from Alabama was the only unwounded survivor of his outfit. Rather than surrender or run, he tied a Confederate battle flag to an empty musket and mounted a horse and charged the union line. He rode two hundred yards through a bullet-cropped cornfield littered with southern dead, his colors raised above his head all the while, he eyes fixed on the stone wall ahead of him where five thousand federals waited and looked at him in disbelief.

Not one of them fired his weapon.

Instead, when the boy's horse labored up the slope and surged through a gap in the wall, three federal soldiers pulled him from the saddle and took his colors and pinioned him to the ground. The boy flailed and kicked until one soldier in blue said, 'Son, you ain't got to study on it no more. You're over on the Lord's side now.'

Mr Antoine slapped his thigh and howled at the implications of his story, whatever they were.

Later, I would read a similar account about Cemetery Ridge. Maybe it was all apocryphal. But if you ever doubted Mr Antoine's authority as a veteran of the Civil War, he would ask you to feel the cyst-encrusted pistol ball that protruded like a sparrow's egg below his right elbow.

The irony was the fact that the man who probably knew more first-hand accounts of Mr Antoine's War, and the man who grew food in the detritus of a Confederate encampment, was a descendant of slaves and did not know how to read and write and consequently was never consulted as a source of information by anyone.

He sat down with the soup at the kitchen table in a pair of slippers and surplus navy dungarees and a denim shirt buttoned at the throat. The sun glimmered off the bayou through the trees behind his house.

'Fat Daddy Babineau brought me some pork chops, but they ain't good for you when you got a stomach upsetness. I didn't want to hurt his feelings, though,' he said.

'You going to be all right by yourself?' I said.

'I'm gonna be fine.' He looked at Alafair, who was examining some minié balls on his kitchen shelf. Then he looked back at me.

'What is it?' I asked.

'Fat Daddy just left. I was fixing to call you.' He kept his eyes on my face.

'Alf, you want to take the truck to the four corners and get a half gallon of milk?' I said.

'Pretty slick way of getting rid of me. But . . . okay,' she said, one palm extended for the keys, the other on her hip.

460

'Fat Daddy seen this man bring his pirogue out of the swamp.' Batist said after Alafair had gone out the door. 'Him and his wife was fishing on the bank, and this big nigger wit' one side of his head shaved paddled out of the trees. It was the same morning you seen that man wit' a light out past our dock, Dave.

'Fat Daddy said this big nigger had gold teet' and arms thick as telephone pole. There was a gun up in the bow, and when Fat Daddy seen it, the nigger give him such a mean look Fat Daddy's wife wanted to get in the car. It's the same man come to our shop, ain't it?'

'It sounds like him.'

'That ain't all of it, no. Fat Daddy and his wife was walking down the levee when they seen the same nigger again, this time busting out the bottom of the pirogue with his foot. He smashed big holes all over it and sunk it right in the canal. Why he want to do somet'ing like that?'

'Who knows? Maybe he didn't want to leave his fingerprints around.'

'That ain't all of it. He seen them watching him and he walked up on the levee and got between Fat Daddy and Fat Daddy's car and says, "Why you following me around?"'

'Fat Daddy says, "We come here to fish, not to mind nobody else's bidness."'

'The nigger says, "You gonna tell somebody you seen a man leave us alone. We ain't give you no truck."'

'The nigger smiles then. He says, "You a nice fat man. You know why I bust up my pirogue? 'Cause it got leaks in it." All the time he was squeezing his hand on his privates, like he got an itch, like he didn't care there was a woman there. Fat Daddy said when you looked into that nigger's face, you didn't have no doubt what was on his mind. He wanted you to say just one t'ing wrong so he could let out all his meanness on you.

'Fat Daddy's wife got in the car, not moving an inch, not hardly breathing she was so scared, praying all the time Fat Daddy would just come on and get them out of there.

'Then the nigger takes Fat Daddy's pole and his bucket out of his hand and puts them in the backseat and opens the front door and helps Fat Daddy get behind the wheel. He says, "I'm gonna show y'all somet'ing I ain't sure I can still do. Y'all watch, now."

'He hooked his hands under the front bumper and started straining, like all the veins in his face was gonna pop out of his skin, grinning with them gold teet', snuff running out of his mout'. Then the car come up in the air, and the back wheels started rolling off the levee, just befo' he let it crash on the ground again.

'He come around to the window, still grinning, like he done some'ing

461

great, and let spit drip out of his mout' on his finger. He took Fat Daddy's sun helmet off his head and put his finger in Fat Daddy's ear and then dropped his hat back on his head again. Didn't say one word. Just rubbed spit in po' Fat Daddy's ear and walked off.

'What kind of man do t'ings like that, Dave? It makes me feel real bad. I wish I'd done somet'ing to stop that man when he come in our shop. Lawd God, I do.'

Batist shook his head, his spoon forgotten by the side of his soup bowl.

A therapist once told me that dreams are not a mystery. They simply represent our hopes and fears, he said. But unfortunately I was never good at distinguishing between the two.

I see an arbor atop the grassy slope of Bayou Teche. The tree trunks look hard and white under the moon, stonelike yet filled with power, as though the coldness in the light has trapped a trembling energy inside the bark. Inside the arbor is a wicker picnic basket filled with grapes and bananas, a corked green bottle of burgundy, a bottle of black label Jack Daniel's wrapped in a soft towel, a bucket of shaved ice with two chrome cups chilling inside it.

I can taste the charcoal and the oak in the whiskey, as weightless as liquid smoke on the back of the tongue. I can feel its heat spread from my stomach into my chest and my loins. But my system is dry, as though my glands have become dust, and the real rush doesn't come until the second hit, a long deep swallow of sugar and shaved ice and mint leaves and bourbon, then it reaches every nerve in my body, just as if someone had struck a sulfurous match across the base of the brain.

But this time the dream is not just about the charcoal-filtered product of Lynchburg, Tennessee. She's on her knees inside the arbor, her bottom resting on her heels, eating a sandwich with both hands, somehow vulnerable and reminiscent of a wartime photo of a frightened and starving child. She smiles when she sees me, as she would greet an old friend, and she gathers her dress in her hands and works it over her head. Her tan body seems glazed with moonglow, her breasts swollen and hard, her face innocent of any agenda except the welcoming press of her thighs around mine. In the dream I know it's wrong, that I've reached a place where I can't turn it around, just like the whiskey that lights old fires and once again claims a landscape inside me I'd long forgotten. Her mouth is on mine, her fingers on my hips, then kneading the small of my back, and I feel something break inside me, like water bursting through the bottom of a paper bag, and when I look into her face, my body trembling with the moment, I see a tangle of platinum

462

hair and eyes like black glass and a self-indulgent lazy smile that ends in a kiss of contempt upon the cheek.

I woke and sat on the side of the bed, my fingers clenched on my knees, my loins aching like those of an adolescent boy trapped inside the unrelieved fantasies of his masturbation.

Outside, I heard Tripod running on his chain and wind coursing through the trees and dead leaves swirling across the yard. When the wind dropped, the night was silent for only a moment, then I heard leaves again, this time breaking under someone's foot.

I looked out the window and saw Tripod sitting on top of his hutch, motionless, his face pointed toward the backyard.

I slipped on a pair of blue jeans and my tennis shoes, took my .45 out of the dresser and the flashlight from the nightstand, and checked the lock on the front door. Bootsie was asleep on the couch, her arm across her eyes, a magazine splayed on the floor by her. I turned on the flood lamp in the mimosa tree and stepped out into the yard.

The wind blew plumes of ash out of my neighbor's field and ruffled the starlight's reflection on the duck pond by my fence line. I searched the side yard, the horse lot and stable, the aluminum tool-shed where we still kept my father's old tractor, then I walked along the edge of the coulee toward the duck pond.

The batteries in my flashlight grew weaker and I turned them off and started back toward the house. I heard the shrill, hysterical-like cry of a nutria out in the swamp.

A man with the sinewy proportions of an atavistic throwback moved out quickly from behind a stand of banana trees and shoved the blunt, round end of a hard object into the centre of my back.

'I could have used a telephone. I come here in trust. Don't mess it up,' he said.

'What do you want, Aaron?'

'Give me your pistol . . . I'll give it back. I promise. I ain't gonna harm nobody, either.'

His hand moved down my arm and slipped the .45 free from my fingers. He smelled like humus and wool clothes full of wood smoke and dried sweat.

'I got you! Sonofabitch if I didn't! Slickered you good!' he said. He squatted and roared at his own humor, slapped his thigh with one hand. 'Didn't have nothing but this old corncob pipe I got out of a garbage can! How you like that!'

'Why don't you act your age?'

'Did y'all use the same kind of smarts against them Viet Cong?' He danced like an ape under the overhang of withered banana leaves.

'You going to give me my piece back?' I said.

'Can't do *that*.' Then his face went as blank and stark as a sheet of tin under the starlight. 'I want you to set up my surrender to Buford LaRose.'

When I didn't reply, he said, 'You deaf? Just set it up. Out in the country somewheres. He'll go for it. It'll make him a big man.'

'I don't know if I trust what you've got in mind, partner.'

'They sent a little pisspot Eye-talian after me. Man I was in jail with and knowed where my camp was at. Some people is cursed by their knowledge.'

'What are you saying?'

His eyes were wide, lidless, burning with certainty about the adversarial nature of the world.

'You might say I talked to his conscience. He said me and you are the shit on somebody's nose and it's suppose to get wiped off before a certain governor gets sworn in. He was at a point in his life he didn't want to keep no secrets.'

'I don't like what you're telling me, Aaron.'

'They treated me worsen they would a nigger rapist. You think I give a fuck about what you don't like? . . . We got a mutual interest here.'

'No, we don't.'

He put the .45 under my jaw. 'Then you walk to the shed.'

'You're starting to seriously piss me off, Aaron.'

He pushed the barrel harder into my throat. 'LaRose used my daughter and throwed her away. Then he sent me to the penitentiary. You side with them, then you're my enemy.'

His face was bloodless, his dilated nostrils radiating gray hair. He wasn't a bizarre old man anymore, or even a pitiful and ignorant victim. For some reason, as I stared into the vacuity of his eyes, I was absoutely convinced he would have found reason to wage war against Buford LaRose's world even if Buford LaRose had never existed.

'I'm not going in that shed, Aaron. It ends here,' I said.

He breathed loudly in the darkness. His tongue looked like a gray biscuit inside his mouth.

'I done cut your phone line already. I'll give you back this later. But don't come after me,' he said.

'You're a foolish man, sir.'

'No, I'm a dead one. That's what they call people in the Death House, the Dead Men. Wait till you feel that big nigger's hand on you. Or one of yourn up at the house. See how goddamn liberal you are then.'

'What did you say?'

But he was gone, running like a crab through the trees, his prison work boots crashing in the leaves.

I sat on the floor by the couch where Bootsie slept. Her eyes opened into mine.

'What is it?' she said.

'Aaron Crown was outside . . .' I placed my hand on her arm before she could get up. 'It's all right. He's gone now. But he cut the phone line.'

'Crown was—'

'I'm giving it up, Boots. Aaron, the LaRose family, whatever they're into, it's somebody else's responsibility now.'

She raised herself on one elbow.

'What happened out there?' she asked.

'Nothing. That's the point. Nothing I do will ever change the forces these people represent.'

Her eyes steadied on mine and seemed to look inside me.

'You want to fix something to eat?' she said.

'That'd be swell. I'll use the phone in the bait shop to call the department.'

When I locked the front door behind me, I could see her in the kitchen, shredding a raw potato on a grater to make hash browns, her robe cinched around her hips, just as though we were waking to an ordinary dawn and the life we'd had before I'd allowed the fortunes of Aaron Crown and the LaRose family to grow like a tentacle into our own.

In the morning Batist found my .45 wrapped in a Kentucky Fried Chicken bag under the doormat on his gallery.

27

'We've got a real prize in the holding cell,' Helen said.

I followed her down the corridor to the lockup area and waited for the deputy to open the cell. The biker inside had a gold beard and head of hair like a lion's mane. His eyes reminded me of Lifesavers, pushed deep into folds of skin that were raw from windburn or alcohol or blood pressure that could probably blow an automobile gasket.

His name was Jody Hatcher. A year and a half ago the court had released him to the Marine Corps, in hopes, perhaps, that the whole Hatcher family would simply disappear from Iberia Parish. His twin sister achieved a brief national notoriety when she was arrested for murdering seven men who picked her up hitchhiking on the Florida Turnpike. The mother, an obese, choleric woman with heavy facial hair, was interviewed by CBS on the porch of the shack where the Hatcher children were raised. I'll never forget her words: 'It ain't my fault. She was born that way. I whipped her every day when she was little. It didn't do no good.'

'They treating you all right, Jody?' I said after the deputy locked me and Helen inside.

'I don't like the echoes, man. I can't tell what's out in the hall and what's inside,' he said, grinning, pointing at his head. He wore skin-tight black jeans and a black leather vest with no shirt. His face seemed filled with a merry, self-ironic glow, like a man who's become an amused spectator at the dissolution of his own life.

Helen and I sat down on the wood bench against the far wall. In the center of the cell was a urine-streaked drain hole.

'They say your saddlebags were full of crystal meth,' I said.

'Yeah, dude I lent my Harley to probably really messed me over. Wow, I hate it when they do that to you.'

I nodded, as though we were all listening to a sad truth.

'I thought you were in Haiti,' I said.

'Got cut loose, man. You saw that on TV about the firefight at the police station? That was my squad. See, this native woman was cheering us up on a balcony and an attaché busted her upside the head with a baton. That's why we was down at the police station. We camied-up and set up a perimeter 'cause we didn't want these guys hurting the people no more. The Corps is peace makers, not peace keepers, a lot of civilians don't understand that. We got the word these guys was gonna light us up, so this one dude comes outside and starts to turn toward us with an Uzi in his hand, and *pow*, man, I see the tracer come out of the lieutenant's gun, and then shit storm is flying through the air and before I knew it I burned a whole magazine on just one guy, like chickens was pecking him to death against the wall. I wasn't up for it, man. That's some real cruel shit to watch.'

He was seated on a wood bench, his wrists crossed on his knees, his fists clenched, his face staring disjointedly into space.

'Tell Detective Robicheaux about the Mexican cowboy,' Helen said.

'We already covered that, ain't we? I don't like remembering stuff like that.' He puckered his mouth like a fish's.

'You got to work with us, Jody, you want some slack on the meth,' Helen said.

'It was right before I went in the Crotch. I met the Mexican guys in a bar in Loreauville. I was doing dust and rainbows and drinking vodka on top of it, and we all ended up out in a woods somewhere. It was a real weirded-out hot night, with fireflies crawling all over the trees and bullfrogs croaking and nutrias screaming out on the water. These guys had some beautiful meth, high-grade clean stuff that don't foul your blood. But this one cowboy tied off and slapped a vein till it was purple as a turnip, then he spikes into it and *whoop*, he doubles over and crumples on the ground, with the rubber tourniquet flopping in his teeth like a snake with its head cut off.

'It's not like skag. You don't drop the guy in cold water or a snowbank. The guy's eyes rolled, all kind of stuff came out of his mouth, his knees started jerking against his chest. What are you gonna do, man? I was wasted. Jesus, it was like watching a guy drown when you can't do nothing about it.'

'Is that all of it, Jody?' I asked.

'Tell him,' Helen said.

'They dug a hole and buried him,' he said.

'Who?' I asked.

'Everybody. I run off in the trees. I couldn't watch it . . . Maybe he wasn't dead . . . That's what keeps going through my head . . . They didn't get a doctor or nothing . . . They should have put a mirror in front of his nose or something . . .'

'Who was there, Jody?' I asked.

'The guy who just got elected governor.'

'You're sure?' I said.

'He was strung out, crying like a little kid. There was some other Americans there had to take care of him.'

'Who?' I asked.

'I don't know, man. I blacked out. I couldn't take it. I can't even tell you where I was at. I woke up behind a colored bar in St Martinville with dogs peeing on me.'

His face was swollen, glazed like the red surfaces on a lollipop, decades older than his years. He wiped his eyes with the heel of his hand.

Back in my office, Helen said, 'What do you think?'

'Take his statement. Put it in the file,' I answered.

'That's it?'

'Somebody snipped Jody's brain stem a long time ago.'

'You don't believe him?'

'Yeah I do. But it won't stand up. Buford LaRose won't go down until he gets caught in bed with a dead underage male prostitute.'

'Too much,' she said, and walked out the door.

Saturday morning Clete Purcel drove in from New Orleans, fished for two hours in a light mist, then gave it up and drank beer in the bait shop while I added up my receipts and tried to figure my quarterly income tax payment. He spoke little, gazing out the window at the rain, as though he was concentrating on a conversation inside his head.

'Say it,' I said.

'After I got to Vietnam, I wished I hadn't joined the Corps,' he said.

'So?'

'You already rolled the dice, big mon. You can't just tell these cocksuckers you don't want to play anymore.'

'Why not?'

'Because I keep seeing Jerry Joe's face in my dreams, that's why . . . That's his jukebox back there?'

'Yeah.'

'What's on it?'

'Forties and fifties stuff. Every one of them is a Cadillac.'

'Give me some quarters.'

'I sliced the cord in half.'

'That's a great way to deal with the problem, Streak.'

A half hour later the phone rang. It was Buford LaRose. I walked with the phone into the back of the shop.

'Meet me at the Patio restaurant in Loreauville,' he said.

468

'No, thanks,' I said.

'Goddamn it, Dave, I want to get this mess behind us.'

'Good. Resign your office.'

'Crown's a killing machine,' he said.

'If he is, you helped make him that way.'

'You don't know, do you?'

'What?'

'About the guy who was just fished out of Henderson Swamp.'

'That's St Martin Parish. It's not my business. Good-bye, Buford.' I hung up the phone.

'That was dickhead?' Clete said.

'Yep.'

'What did he want?'

I told him.

'You're just going to let it slide down the bowl?'

'That about sums it up.'

'Mistake. Stay in their faces, Streak. Don't let them blindside you. I'll back your plan, mon.'

He turned toward me on the counter stool, his scarred face as flat and round as a pie tin, his eyes a deep green under his combed, sandy hair.

'Listen to me for once,' he said. 'That was Mookie Zerrang you saw in the pirogue. You want the button man out of your life, you got to find his juice.'

The bayou seemed to dance with yellow light in the rain. I wiped down the counter, carried out the trash, stocked the cooler in back, then finally quit a foolish dialogue inside myself and dialed Buford's answering service in Lafayette so I wouldn't have to call him at home.

'This is Dave Robicheaux. Tell Mr LaRose I'll be in my office at eight Monday morning.'

He was in at ten, with Ciro Tauzin from the state police at his side. The St Martin Parish sherrif's report on a body recovered from Henderson Swamp lay on my desk.

'You starting to get a better picture of Aaron Crown now?' Buford said.

'Not really,' I said.

'Not really? The victim's stomach was slit open and filled with rocks. What kind of human being would do something like that?' Buford said.

'I have a better question, Buford. What was a New Orleans gumball, a hit man for the Giacano family, doing at Henderson Swamp?' I said.

'He celled with Crown,' Buford said.

'So why would Crown want to kill his cell partner?' I asked.

'Maybe he was gonna turn Aaron in. The guy had some weapons

charges against him. Criminals ain't big on loyalty, no,' Tauzin said, and smiled.

'I think he was there to whack Crown and lost. What's your opinion on that, Mr Tauzin?' I asked.

The coat of his blue suit looked like it was buttoned crookedly on his body. There were flecks of dandruff inside the oil on his black hair. He rubbed the cleft in his chin with his thumb.

'Men like Crown will kill you for the shoes on your feet, the food in your plate. I don't believe they're a hard study, suh,' he said.

'You get in touch with him through his daughter,' Buford said. 'If he'll surrender to me, I'll guarantee his safety and I promise he won't be tried for a capital offense . . .' He paused a moment, then raised his hands off the arms of the chair. 'Maybe down the road, two or three years maximum, he can be released because of his age.'

'Pretty generous,' I said.

Buford and Ciro Tauzin both waited. I picked up a paper clip and dropped it on my blotter.

'Dave?' Buford said.

'He bears you great enmity,' I answered.

'You've talked with him.' He said it as a statement, not as a question. I could almost hear the analytical wheels turning in his head. I saw a thought come together in his eyes. There was no denying Buford's level of intelligence. 'He wants a meet? He's told you he'll try to kill me?'

'Make peace with his daughter. Then he might listen to you.'

Buford's eyes wrinkled at the corners as he tried to peel the meaning out of my words.

'A short high school romance? That's what you're talking about now?' he said.

But before I could speak, Ciro Tauzin said, 'Here's the deal, Mr Robicheaux. You can help us if you want, or you can tell everybody else what their jobs is. But if Aaron Crown don't come in, I'm gonna blow his liver out. Is that clear enough, suh?'

I held his stare.

'Should I pass on your remarks, Mr Tauzin?' I answered.

'I'd appreciate it if you would. It's quite an experience doing bidness with you, suh. Your reputation doesn't do you justice.'

I made curlicues with a ballpoint pen on a yellow legal pad until they had left the room.

Two minutes later, Buford came back alone and opened the door, his seersucker coat over his shoulder, his plaid shirt rolled on his veined forearms. His curly hair hung on his forehead, and his cheeks were as bright as apples.

'You'll never like me, Dave. Maybe I can't blame you. But I give you

470

my solemn word, I'll protect Aaron Crown and I'll do everything I can to see him die a free man,' he said.

For just a moment I saw the handsome, young LSU quarterback of years ago who could be surrounded by tacklers, about to be destroyed, his bones crushed into the turf, his very vulnerability bringing the crowd to its feet, and then rocket an eighty-yard pass over his tacklers' heads and charm it into the fingers of a forgotten receiver racing across the goal line.

Some Saturday-afternoon heroes will never go gently into that good night. At least not this one, I thought.

Probably over 90 percent of criminal investigations are solved by accident or through informants. I didn't have an informant within Buford's circle, but I did have access to a genuine psychotic whose dials never failed to entertain if not to inform.

I called his restaurant in New Orleans and two of his construction offices and through all the innuendo and subterfuge concluded that Dock Green was at his camp on the Atchafalaya River.

The sky was gray and the wide expanse of the river dimpled with rain when I pulled onto the service road and headed toward the cattle guard at the front of his property. I could see Dock, in a straw hat and black slicker, burning what looked like a pile of dead trees by the side of the house. But that was not what caught my eye. Persephone Green had just gotten into her Chrysler and was roaring down the gravel drive toward me, dirt clods splintering like flint from under the tires. I had to pull onto the grass to avoid being hit.

A moment later, when I walked up to the trash fire, I saw the source of Persephone's discontent. Two stoned-out women, oblivious to the weather, floated on air mattresses in a tall, cylindrical plastic pool, fed by a garden hose, in the backyard.

'Unexpected visit from the wife, Dock?' I asked.

'I don't know why she's got her head up her hole. She's filing for divorce, anyway.'

He poked at the fire with a blackened rake. The wind shifted and suddenly the smell hit me. In the center of burning tree limbs and a bed of white ash was the long, charred shape of an alligator.

'It got stuck in my culvert and drowned. A gator don't know how to back up,' he said.

'Why don't you bury it?'

'Animals would dig it up. What d' you want here?'

'You've been out in front of me all the time, Dock. I respect that,' I said.

'What?'

471

'About the body on the LaRose plantation and any number of other things. It's hard to float one by you, partner.'

His face was smeared by charcoal, warm with the heat of the fire. He watched me as he would a historical enemy crossing field and moat into his enclave.

'I spent some time in the courthouse this afternoon. You've got state contracts to build hospitals,' I said.

'So?'

'The contracts are already let. You're going to be a rich man. Eventually Buford's going to take a fall. Why go down with him?'

'Good try, no cigar.'

'Tell me, Dock, you think he'll have Crown popped if I set up Crown's surrender?'

'Who gives a shit?'

'A grand jury.'

He brushed at his nose with one knuckle, huffed air out a nostril, flicked his eyes off my face to the women in the pool, then looked at nothing, all with the same degree of thought or its absence.

'You're dumb,' he said.

'I see.'

'You're worried about a worthless geezer and nigger-trouble that's thirty years old. LaRose'll put a two-by-four up your ass.'

'How?'

'He wants company.'

'Sorry, Dock, I don't follow your drift.'

His thick palm squeezed dryly on the hoe handle.

'Why don't people want to step on graves? Because they care about the stiffs that's down there? If he gets his hand on your ankle, he'll pull you in the box with him,' he said.

My lips, the skin around my mouth, moved wordlessly in the wind.

Bootsie and I did the dishes together after supper. It had stopped raining, and the sky outside was a translucent blue and ribbed with purple and red clouds.

'You're going to set it up?' she asked.

'Yes.'

'Why?'

'I want to cut the umbilical cord.'

'What's the sheriff say?'

' "Do it." '

'What's the problem, then?'

'I don't trust Buford LaRose.'

'Oh, Dave,' she said, her breath exhaling, her eyes closing then opening. She put her hands on my arms and lay her forehead awkwardly on my shoulder, her body not quite touching mine, like someone who fears her embrace will violate propriety.

In the morning I called Sabelle Crown and told her of Buford's offer. Two hours later the phone on my desk rang.

'I can be out in two or three years?' the voice said.

'Aaron?'

'Is that the deal?' he asked.

'I'm not involved. Use an attorney.'

'It's lawyers sold my ass down the river.'

'Don't call here again. Understand? I've got nothing more to do with your life.'

'You goddamn better hope you don't,' he said, and hung up.

The rest of the workweek passed, and I heard nothing more about Aaron Crown. Friday had been a beautiful December day, and the evening was just as fair. The wind was off the Gulf, and you could smell salt and distant rain and night-blooming flowers and ozone in the trees, and you had to remind yourself it was winter and not spring. Bootsie and I decided to go Christmas shopping in Lafayette, and I aked Batist to close the bait shop and stay up at the house with Alafair until we returned.

It wasn't even necessary. She was playing at the neighbor's house next door. When we drove away, Batist was standing in our front yard, his overalls straps notched into his T-shirt, the smooth, saddle-gold texture of his palm raised to say good-bye.

28

The man in the floppy hat and black rubber big-button raincoat came at sunset, from a great distance, where at first he was just a speck on the horizon, walking across my neighbor's burned sugarcane acreage, ash powdering around his boots, the treeline etched with fire behind him. He could have been a fieldhand looking for a calf stuck in the coulee, a tenant farmer shortcutting home from his rental acreage, or perhaps a hobo who had swung down from a SP freight, except for the purpose in his gait, the set of his jaw, the switch in his gloved hand that he whipped against his leg. When clouds covered the sun and lightning struck in the field, the man in the raincoat never broke stride. My neighbor's cow swirled like water out of his path.

Batist had been watching television in the living room. He went back into the kitchen to refill his coffee cup, burned his lips with the first sip, then poured it into the saucer and blew on it while he looked out the kitchen window at the ash lifting in the fields, the rain slanting like glass across the sun's last spark in the west.

The window was open and he heard horses running on the sod and cattle lowing in the coulee, and only when he squinted his eyes did he see the hatted and coated shape of the man who whipped the switch methodically against his leg.

Batist rubbed his eyes, went back into the living room for his glasses, returned to the window and saw a milky cloud of rain and dust rising out of the field and no hatted man in a black coat but a solitary Angus heifer standing in our yard.

Batist stepped out into the yard, into the sulfurous smell blowing out of the fields, then walked to the duck pond and down the fence line until he saw the fence post that had been wedged sideways in the hole and the three strands of barbed wire that had been stomped out of the staples into the ground.

'Somebody out here?' he called.

The wind was like a watery insect in his ears.

He latched the screen door behind him, walked to the front of the house and stepped out on the gallery, looked into the yard and the leaves spinning in vortexes between the tree trunks, the shadows of overhead limbs thrashing on the ground. Down by the bayou, one of our rental boats clanked against its chain, thumping against the pilings on the dock.

He thought about his dogleg twenty gauge down in the bait shop. The bait shop looked small and distant and empty in the rain, and he wished he had turned on the string of electric lights over the dock, then felt foolish and embarrassed at his own thoughts.

He stood in the center of the living room, the wind seeming to breathe through the front and back screens, filling the house with a cool dampness that he couldn't distinguish from the sheen of sweat on his skin.

He pulled aside a curtain and looked across the driveway at the neighbor's house. The gallery was lighted and a green wreath and pinecones wrapped with scarlet ribbon hung on the front door; a Christmas tree, a blue spruce shimmering with tinsel, stood in a window. A sprinkler fanned back and forth in the rain, fountaining off the tree trunks in the yard.

He picked up the phone and started to dial a number, then realized he wasn't even certain about whom he was dialing. He set the receiver back in the cradle, ashamed of the feeling in his chest, the way his hands felt stiff and useless at his sides.

He wiped his face on his sleeve, smelled a sour odor rising from his armpit, then stood hesitantly at the front door again. In his mind's eye he saw himself walking down to the bait shop and returning up the slope with a shotgun like a man who finally concedes that his fears have always been larger than his courage. He unlatched the screen and pushed it open with the flat of his hand and breathed the coolness of the mist blowing under the gallery eaves, then stepped back inside and blew out his breath.

Batist never heard the intruder in the black rubber raincoat, not until he cinched his arm under Batist's throat and squeezed as though he were about to burst a walnut. He wrenched Batist's head back into his own, drawing Batist's body into his loins, a belt buckle that was as hard-edged as a stove grate, impaling him against his chest, his unshaved jaw biting like emery paper into the back of Batist's neck.

The intruder's floppy hat fell to the floor. He seemed to pause and look at it, as he would at a distraction from the linear and familiar course of things and the foregone conclusion that had already been decided for him and his victim.

From the corner of his eye Batist saw a gold-tipped canine tooth that the intruder licked with the bottom of his tongue. Then the arm snapped tight under Batist's chin again, and through the front screen Batist saw the world as a place where trees torn from their roots floated upside down in the rain.

'I'm fixing to pinch off your pipe for good, old man. That mean you don't get no more air. You'll just gurgle on the floor like a dog been run over across the t'roat . . . Where Robicheaux at?' the intruder said.

When Batist woke up, he was on his side, in the middle of the living room floor, his knees drawn up before him. The house was quiet, and he could see rain blowing through the screen, wetting the cypress planks in the floor, and he thought the hatted man in the rubber coat was gone.

Then he felt the intruder's gloved hand close on the bottom of his chin and tilt his face toward him, as though the intruder were arranging the anatomical parts on a store dummy.

'You went to sleep on me, old man. That's 'cause I shut off the big vein that goes up to your brain,' the intruder said. He was squatted on his haunches, sipping from a half-pint bottle of apricot brandy, His eyes were turquoise, the scalp above his ears shaved bare, the color of putty.

'You best get out of here, nigger, while you still can,' Batist said.

The intruder drank from the bottle, let the brandy roll on his tongue, settle in his teeth, as though he were trying to kill an abscess in his gum.

Batist raised himself into a sitting position, waiting for the intruder to react. But he didn't. He sipped again from the brandy, nestled one buttock more comfortably against the heel of his boot. His shirt and the top of his coat were unbuttoned, and a necklace of blue shark's teeth was tattooed across his collarbones and around his upper chest. Cupped in his right hand was a banana knife, hooked at the tip, the edge filed into a long silver thread.

'Fishing any good here?' he asked.

He reached out with one finger and touched Batist on the end of his nose, then tilted the brandy again, his eyes closing with the pleasure the liquor gave him.

Batist drove the bottle into the intruder's mouth with the flat of his hand, shattering the glass against the teeth, bursting the lips into a torn purple flower.

The intruder's face stiffened with shock, glistened with droplets of brandy and saliva and blood. But instead of reeling from the room in pain and rage, he rose to his feet and his right foot exploded against the side of Batist's head. He cleaned bits of glass out of his mouth with his fingers, spitting, as though there were peanut brittle on his tongue, his gashed lip finally reforming into a smile.

He bent over, the hooked point of the banana knife an inch from

Batist's eye. He started to speak, then paused, pressed his mouth against his palm, looked at it, and wiped his hand on his raincoat.

'Now you made me work for free. You ain't got nowhere to go for a while, do you?' he said, and thumbed the buttons loose on his coat.

29

Forty miles away, in the Atchafalaya Basin, the same night the intruder came to my house, Aaron Crown threaded an outboard through a nest of canals until he reached a shallow inlet off the river, where a steel-bottomed oyster boat lay half-sunk in the silt. The decks and hull were the color of a scab, the cabin eaten to the density of aged cork by termites and worms. The entrance to the inlet was narrow, the willows on each side as thick as hedges, the river beyond it running hard and fast and yellow with foam.

He sat on a wood stool inside the cabin, his skin slathered with mud, the stolen Enfield rifle propped between his legs, his eyes fixed on the river, which they would have to cross. The light was perfect. He could see far into the distance, like a creature staring out of a cave, but they in turn could not see him. He had told them no helicopters, not even for the news people. If he heard helicopters, he would be gone deep into the canopy of the swamp before anyone could reach the entrance to the inlet.

The state-police administrator had said it was all a simple matter. Aaron only had to wade into the sunlight, his rifle over his head. No one would harm him. Television cameras would record the moment, and that night millions of people would be forced to acknowledge the struggle of one man against an entire state.

He remembered his original arrest for the murder of the NAACP leader and the national attention it brought him. How many men were allowed to step into history twice?

The state policeman had confirmed the arrangement: two or three years in a federal old folks' facility, no heavy work, no lockdown, good food, a miniature golf course, a television and card room, long-distance access to news reporters whenever he wanted.

But what if it went down wrong tonight? Even that could be an acceptable trade-off. Buford LaRose would be out there somewhere. Aaron squeezed the stock of the Enfield a little tighter in his palms, the dried mud on his palms scraping softly on the wood, his loins stirring at the thought.

He opened a can of potted meat and dipped a saltine cracker into it and chewed the cracker and meat slowly and then drank from a hot can of Coca-Cola. When the potted meat was almost gone, he split a cracker in half and furrowed out the meat from the seams at the bottom of the can, not missing a morsel, and lay the cracker on his tongue and drank the last of his Coca-Cola. He started to roll a cigarette, then saw a curtain of rain moving across the river's surface toward him, and inside the rain he saw three large powerboats with canvas tarps behind the cabins and the faces of uniformed men behind the water-beaded windows.

But where was the boat with the news people on it?

He rose to his feet and let the tobacco roll off his cupped cigarette paper and stick to his pants legs and prison work boots. The wind was blowing harder now, whipping the willow and cypress trees, capping the river's surface. The uniformed men in the boats hadn't seen him yet and had cut back their throttles and were drifting in the chop, the canvas tarps flapping atop the decks.

South of the squall, the sky was filled with purple and yellow clouds, like smoke ballooning out of an industrial fire. He squinted into the rain to see more clearly. What were they doing? The state police adminis-trator, what was his name, Tauzin, should have been out on the deck with a bullhorn, to tell him what to do, to take control, to make sure the news people filmed Aaron wading out of the swamp, his rifle held high above his head, a defiant hill-country man whose surrender had been personally negotiated by the governor of the state.

Something was wrong. One, two, three, then a total of four men had come out the cabin doors onto the decks of their boats, cautious not to expose themselves, the bills of their caps turned backward on their heads.

It couldn't be what he thought. The offer had come through a man he trusted in the Iberia Parish Sheriff's Department. The state policeman had given his word, also. And where was that damn Buford LaRose? Aaron knew Buford would never miss an opportunity like this one, to stand before the cameras, with a wetlands background, his aristocratic face softened by the lights of humanity and conscience.

Then a terrible thought appeared in a bright, clear space in the center of his mind with such vividness that his face burned once again with a memory that was sixty years out of his past, a little boy in rent overalls being shoved into a school yard puddle by a boy whose father owned the cotton gin, the words hurled down at him, *Aaron, you're dumber than a nigger trying to hide in a snowbank.* It was the old recognition that his best efforts always turned out the same: he was the natural-born victim of his betters. In this case the simple fact was that Buford LaRose had already been elected. He didn't have to prove anything to anybody. Aaron Crown was nothing more than a minor nuisance of whom the world had finally tired and was about to dispose of as you would an insect with a Flit can.

Aaron saw this thought as clearly as he saw the face of the man with the inverted cap working his way forward on the lead boat, between the gunnel and cabin. They were like two bookends facing each other now. But Aaron refused to wince or cower, to let them see the fear that made his bowels turn to water. *You'd like to do it, yessiree Bob, blow hair and bone all over the trees, but you're one of them kind won't drop his britches and take a country squat till somebody tells you it's all right.* Aaron's hand crushed the aluminum soda can in his palm, the bottom glinting like a heliograph.

He was wrong.

The muzzle of the M-16 rifle flashed in the rain just as the boat's bow rose in the chop, and the .223 round thropped past Aaron's ear, punching a neat hole in the wall behind him, its trajectory fading deep in the swamp. A second later the other uniformed men cut loose in unison, firing tear gas and M-16's on full automatic and twelve-gauge pump Remingtons loaded with double-ought buckshot.

But Aaron was running now, and not where they thought he would. While gas shells hissed on the deck and buckshot and .223 rounds perforated the oyster boat's cabin, criss-crossing the gloomy interior with tubular rays of light, he slid down the ladder inside the ship's steel hull, his rifle inverted on its sling, then exited the boat through the far side, where the plates had been stripped from a spar by a salvager. As he ran through a chain of sandbars and stagnant pools of water, he could hear the steady dissection of the cabin, glass breaking, bullets whanging off metal surfaces, shattered boards spinning out into the trees like sticks blown from a forest fire.

He glanced once over his shoulder after he kicked over the outboard. *Fire.* He hadn't imagined it. Their magazines had been loaded with tracers, and the oyster boat's cabin was liquid with flames.

Inside the caked patina of mud on Aaron's face, his eyes were as pink as Mercurochrome, filmed with the reflected glow of what he knew now had been the final demonstrable evidence of the lifetime conspiracy directed at him and his family. Somehow that gave him a satisfaction and feeling of confirmation that was like being submerged and bathed in warm water. He bit down on his molars with an almost sexual pleasure but could not tell himself why.

Late that same night, a voice with a peckerwood accent that did not identify itself left a message on my recording machine: 'Buford got to you. I don't know how. But I'd just as lief cut the equipment off two shithogs as one.'

30

The account of Aaron Crown's escape from the state police is my re-creation of the story as it was related to me by a St Martin Parish deputy in the waiting room down the hall from Batist's room at Iberia General. Clete Purcel and I watched the deputy get into the elevator and look back at us blank-faced while the doors closed behind him.

'What are you thinking?' Clete asked.

'It's no accident Mookie Zerrang came to my house the same night Crown was set up for a whack.'

Clete leaned forward in his chair and rubbed one hand on the other, picked at a callus, his green eyes filled with thought. He had driven from New Orleans in two and a half hours, steam rising from the hood of his Cadillac like vapor off dry ice when he pulled under the electric arc lamps in the hospital parking lot.

'Zerrang's got to go off-planet, Streak,' he said.

'He will.'

'It won't happen. Not unless you or I do it. This guy's juice is heavy-voltage, mon.'

I didn't answer.

'You know I'm right. When they deal it down and dirty, we take it back to them under a black flag,' he said.

'Wrong discussion, wrong place.'

'There's a geek in Jefferson Parish. A real sicko. Even the wiseguys cross the street when they see him coming. But he owes five large to Nig. I can square the debt. Mookie Zerrang will be walking on stumps . . . Are you listening?'

I went to the cold drink machine, then put my change back in my pocket and kept on walking to the nurses' station.

'I have to talk to my friend,' I said.

'Sorry, not until the doctor comes back,' the nurse said. She smiled and did not mean to be impolite.

'I apologize, then,' I said, and went past her and into Batist's room.

He was turned on his side, facing the opposite wall, his back layered with bandages. The intruder had used a type of ASP, a steel bludgeon, sold in police supply stores, that telescopes out of a handle. The one used by the intruder was modified with an extension that operated like a spring or whip, with a steel ball the size of a small marble attached to the tip. The paramedics had to cut away Batist's overalls and T-shirt with scissors and peel the cloth off his skin like cobweb.

His head jerked on the pillow when he heard me behind him.

'It's okay, partner,' I said, and walked around the foot of the bed.

His right eye was swollen shut, his nose broken and X-ed with tape.

'I ain't felt a lot of it, Dave. He hit me upside the head first, 'cause I raised up and caught him another one in the mout',' he said.

I sat down on a chair by his bedside.

'I promise we'll get this guy,' I said.

'It ain't your fault, no.'

'I helped set up Aaron Crown, Batist. I didn't know it, but I was giving somebody permission to wipe me off the slate, too.'

'Who been doing all this, Dave? What we done to them?'

'They're right up there on the Teche. Buford and Karyn LaRose.'

His eyes closed and opened as though he were on the edge of sleep or looking at a thought inside his mind.

'It ain't their way,' he said.

'Why?'

'Their kind don't never see bad t'ings, Dave. Any black folk on a plantation tell you that. The white folk up in the big house don't ever want to know what happen out in the field or down in the quarters. They got people to take care of that for them.'

The nurse and the doctor came through the door and looked at us silently.

'You going to be all right for a while?' I said.

'Sure. They been treating me good,' Batist said.

'I'm sorry for this,' I said.

He moved his fingers slightly on the sheet and patted the top of my hand as my father might have done.

Clete followed me home and went to sleep in our guest room. I lay in the dark next to Bootsie, with my arm over my eyes, and heard rainwater ticking out of the trees into the beds of leaves that tapered away from the tree trunks. I tried to organize my thoughts, then gave it up and fell asleep when the stars were still out. I didn't wake until after sunrise. The room, the morning itself, seemed empty and stark, devoid of memory, as it used to be when I'd wake from alcoholic blackouts. Then the events of the previous night came back like a slap.

Batist's first reaction when he had seen me in the hospital had been to prevent me from worrying about his pain. He'd had no thought of himself, no desire for revenge, no sense of recrimination toward me or the circumstances that placed him in the path of a sadist like Mookie Zerrang.

I spent ten months in Vietnam and never saw a deliberate atrocity, at least not one committed by Americans. Maybe that was because most of my tour was over before the war really warmed up. I saw a ville after the local chieftain had called in the 105s on his own people, and I saw some Kit Carsons bind the wrists of captured Viet Cong and wrap towels around their faces and pour water onto the cloth a canteen at a time until they were willing to trade their own families for a teaspoon of air. Someone always had an explanation for these moments, one that allowed you to push the images out of your mind temporarily. It was the unnecessary cruelty, the kind that was not even recognized as such, that hung in the mind like an unhealed lesion.

A mental picture postcard that I could never find a proper postage stamp for: The mamasan is probably over seventy. Her dugs are withered, her skin as shriveled as a dried apple's. She and her grand-daughter clean hooches for a bunch of marines, wash their clothes, burn the shit barrels at the latrine. Two enlisted men fashion a sign from cardboard and hang it around her neck and pose sweaty and barechested with her while a third marine snaps their photo with a Polaroid camera. The sign says MISS NORTH DAKOTA. If the mamasan comprehends the nature of the insult, it does not show in the cracked parchment of her face. The marines are grinning broadly in the photo.

Voltaire wrote about the cruelty he saw in his neighbor who was the torturer at the Bastille. He described the impulse as insatiable, possessing all the characteristics of both lust and addiction to a drug. Had he not been hired by the state, the neighbor would have paid to continue his tasks in those stone rooms beneath the streets of Paris.

Mookie Zerrang was not simply a hit man on somebody's payroll. He was one of those who operated on the edges of the human family, waiting for the halt and the lame or those who had no voice, his eyes smiling with anticipation when he knew his moment was at hand.

I couldn't swallow my food at breakfast. I went into the living room and finished cleaning the spot on the floor where we had found Batist. I stuffed the throw rug he had lain on and the paper towels I had used to scrub the cypress planks into a vinyl garbage bag.

'I'm going down to the bait shop,' I said to Bootsie.

'Close it up for today,' she replied.

'It's Saturday. There might be a few customers by.'

'No, you want to make a private phone call. Do it here. I'll leave,' she said.

'We didn't get much sleep, Boots. It's not a day to hurt each other.'

'Tell it to yourself.'

There was nothing for it. I unlocked the bait shop and dialed Buford LaRose's home number.

'Hello?' Karyn said.

'Where's Buford?'

'In the shower.'

'Put him on the phone.'

'Leave him alone, Dave. Go away from us.'

'Maybe I should catch him another time. Would the inauguration ball be okay?'

'It's by invitation. You won't be attending . . .' She paused, as though she were enjoying a sliver of ice on her tongue. 'By the way, since you're a conservationist, you'll enjoy this. I talked to someone about the swamp area around your bait shop being turned into a wilderness preserve. Of course, that will mean commercial property like yours will be acquired by the state or federal government. Oh, Buford's toweling off now. Have a nice day, Dave.'

She sat the phone down on a table and called out in a lilting voice, 'Guess who?'

I heard Buford scrape the receiver up in his hand.

'Don't tell me,' he said.

'Shut up, Buford—'

'No, this time you shut up, Dave. Aaron Crown didn't do what he was told. He was supposed to throw his rifle in the water. Instead, he flashed a soda can or something in a window and a trooper started shooting. I tried to stop it.'

'You were there?'

'Yes, of course.'

'I think you're lying,' I said. But his explanation was disarming.

'It's what happened. Check it out.'

'The black man who works for me was almost beaten to death last night.'

'I'm sorry. But what does that have to do with me?'

I felt my anger and confidence wane. I rubbed at one eye with the heel of my hand and saw concentric circles of red light receding into my brain. My hands felt cold and thick and I could smell my own odor. I started to speak but the words wouldn't come.

'Dave, are you okay?' he said. His voice was odd, marked with sympathy.

I hung up and sat at the counter and rested my forearms on the counter, my head bent forward, and felt a wave of exhaustion and a sense of personal impotence wash through me like the first stages of amoebic dysentery. Through the window I heard Bootsie's car back into the road, then I saw her and Alafair drive away through the long corridor of oaks toward town. A small metallic mirror hung on a post behind the counter. The miniature face of the man reflected inside it did not look like someone I knew.

31

Clete and I went back to Iberia General to visit Batist, then drove to Red Lerille's Gym in Lafayette. Clete ordered a baked potato smothered with cheese and sour cream and bacon strips and green onions at the cafe outside the weight room and ate it at a table by the glass wall and watched me while I worked out for a half hour on the machines. Then he put on a pair of trunks and swam outside in the heated pool and later met me in the steam room.

'How you feel?' he said.

'All right. It's just a touch of the mosquito.'

A man sitting next to us folded the newspaper he was reading and lay it on the tile stoop and went out. Clete waited until the man closed the door behind him.

'You're beating up on yourself unfairly, big mon,' he said.

'People are dead. No one's in custody. A man like Batist is attacked by a degenerate. Tell me what I've done right.'

'You listen to me,' he said, and raised his finger in my face. The skin of his massive shoulders and chest looked boiled and red in the steam. 'You're a police officer. You can't ignore what you see happening around you. If you fuck up, that's the breaks. In a firefight you stomp ass and take names and let somebody else add up the arithmetic. Get off your own case.'

'One day we're going to get your shield back,' I said.

He cupped his hand around the back of my neck. I could feel the moisture and grease ooze out from under his palm and fingers. 'If I had to play by the rules, I couldn't cover my old podjo's back,' he said.

His smile was as gentle as a girl's.

I dropped him off at a motel by the four-lane in New Iberia and drove home alone. I waved at the deputy parked in a cruiser by the bait shop and turned into our dirt driveway and cut the engine and listened to it cool and tick while I looked at Bootsie's car and the doves that rose out

487

of my neighbor's field against the late sun and then at Bootsie's face in the middle of a windy swirl of curtains at a window in the rear of the house before she turned away as though I were not there.

I started toward the back door, forming words in my mind to address problems I couldn't even define, then stopped, the way you do when thinking doesn't work anymore, and walked down the slope to the bait shop, into the green, gaslike odor of the evening, the pecan husks breaking under my shoes, as though I could walk beyond the box of space and time and loveless tension that my father's handhewn cypress house had become.

The string of electric lights was turned on over the dock and I could hear music through the screens.

'What are you doing, Alf?' I said.

'I got the key to the jukebox out of the cash register. Is that all right?'

'Yeah, that's fine.'

She had wheeled Jerry Joe Plumb's jukebox away from the wall, where I had pushed it front end first, and unlocked the door and stacked the 45 rpm records on top of a soft towel on the counter.

'I'm playing each one of them on my portable and recording them on tape. I've already recorded fifteen of them,' she said. 'You like all these, don't you?'

I nodded, my eyes gazing out the window at the lighted gallery of the house. 'That's great, Alf,' I said.

'Who's the buttwipe who cut the electric cord on the box?'

'Beg your pardon?'

'The buttwipe who sliced off the cord. What kind of person would do that?'

'How about it on the language?'

'Big deal,' she said. She slid a record off her machine and replaced it with another, her face pointed downward so that her hair hid her expression.

'Why are you so angry?' I asked.

'You and Bootsie, Dave. Why don't y'all stop it?'

I sat down on a stool next to her.

'I made some mistakes,' I said.

'Then unmake them. You're my father. You're supposed to fix things. Not break the jukebox 'cause you're mad at it.'

I crimped my lips and tried to find the right words. If there were any, I didn't know them.

'Everything's messed up in our house. I hate it,' she said, her eyes shining, then brimming with tears.

'Let's see what we can do about it, then,' I said, and walked up the slope, through the trees, across the gallery and into the stillness of the house.

Bootsie was at the kitchen table, drinking a cup of coffee. She wore a pair of straw sandals and white slacks and a stonewashed denim shirt. The surfaces of her face looked as cool and shiny as alabaster.

'The job's not worth it anymore. It's time to hang it up,' I said.

'Is that what you want?'

'I can always do some PI stuff with Clete if we get jammed up.'

'No.'

'I thought you'd approve.'

'I had to go to confession this afternoon,' she said.

'What for?'

'I went to see Batist at the hospital. When I left I wanted to kill the man who did that to him. I wanted to see something even worse happen to Karyn and Buford. I told Father Pitre my feelings probably won't go away, either. He said it was all right, it's natural to feel what I do . . . But it's not going to be all right, not until those people are punished. Nobody can be allowed to get away with what they've done.'

Her neck bloomed with color. I stood behind her chair and put my hands on her shoulders and kneaded my thumbs on her spine, then leaned over and pressed my cheek against her hair. I felt her reach up over my head and touch the back of my neck, arching her head against mine, rubbing her hair against my skin. Then she rose from her chair and pressed herself against me, no holding back now, her breasts and flat stomach and thighs tight against me, her mouth like a cold burn on my throat.

Through the screen I could hear Alafair playing 'La Jolie Blon' on her record player.

No Duh Dolowitz was a Jersey transplant and old-time pete man who had been dented too many times in the head with a ball peen hammer, which didn't diminish his talents as a safecracker but for some reason did develop in him a tendency for bizarre humor, finally earning him the nickname among cops of the Mob's Merry Prankster. He backed up a truck to the home of a contractor in the Poconos and filled his wet bar and basement game room to the ceiling with bituminous coal, stole a human head from the Tulane medical school and put it in a government witness's bowling ball bag, and sabotaged the family-day promotion of a floating casino by smuggling a group of black transvestites on board to do the stage show.

Also, in terms of information about the underworld, he was the human equivalent of flypaper.

Sunday morning Clete and I found him in his brother-in-law's saloon and poolroom by the Industrial Canal in New Orleans. He wore a maroon shirt, white suspenders, knife-creased gray slacks, and a biscuit-colored derby hat. His face was tan and lean, his mustache as black as grease. He sat with us at a felt-covered card table, sipping black coffee from a demitasse with a tiny silver spoon in it. The poolroom had a stamped tin ceiling, a railed bar, wood floors, and big glass windows painted with green letters that gave a green cast to the inside of the room. It was still early, and the poolroom was closed.

'Give No Duh a beer and a shot. Put it on my tab,' Clete called to the bartender, then said to Dolowitz, 'You're looking very copacetic, No Duh.'

'Shitcan the beer and the shot,' Dolowitz said. 'Why the squeeze?'

'We're looking for a guy named Mookie Zerrang,' I said.

'A cannibal looks like King Kong?' he said.

'He hurt a friend of mine real bad. I think he killed Short Boy Jerry, too,' I said.

His brown eyes looked without expression at a point on the far wall.

'I hear you're on the outs with the Giacanos,' Clete said.

Dolowitz shook his head nonchalantly, his face composed.'

'You and Stevie Gee got nailed on that pawnshop job. You made bond first and creeped Stevie's house,' Clete said.

'He mentioned he boosted my mother's new car?' Dolowitz said.

'You've got bad markers all over town and you're four weeks back on the vig to Wee Willie Bimstine,' Clete said.

'I'd tell you "No duh," Purcel, but I'm not interested in defending myself or having trouble with either one of yous. You want to play some nine ball? A dollar on the three, the six, and the nine.'

'Dave can get you a few bucks from his department. I can get Wee Willie off your back. How about it?' Clete said.

'Zerrang's freelance,' Dolowitz said. 'Look, check my jacket. I burned a safe or two and did some creative favors for a few people. Zerrang blows heads. He's a sicko, too. He likes being cruel when he don't have to be.'

'Three names I want you to think about, No Duh,' I said. 'Jimmy Ray Dixon, Dock Green, and his wife, Persephone.'

He was motionless in his chair, the names registering in his eyes in ways you couldn't read. Then the skin at the side of his mouth ticked slightly. His eyes hardened and his upper lip filmed with moisture, as though the room had suddenly become close and warm.

'Here's the rest of it,' Clete said. 'You come up with the gen on these guys, I'll make you righteous with Wee Willie. But you shine us off and miss another week on the vig, you better get your skinny ass back up to the Jersey Shore, find a hole, and pull it in after you.'

When we left him, his confidence had drained like water out of a sink and his face was filled with the conflict of a hunted animal.

Clete and I stood on the sidewalk under the dilapidated wood colonnade that shaded the front of the poolroom. It was cool in the shade, and the sunlight looked bright and hard on the neutral ground and the palm trees.

'I can't do this, Clete,' I said.

'Don't screw it up, mon.'

I tapped on the door glass for the bartender to open up.

'Do what you feel comfortable with, No Duh. Nobody's going to twist you,' I said.

'Go play with your worms. Blimpo out there gets off on this. I hope in the next life both yous come back a guy like me, see how you like it,' he replied.

32

As a police officer you accept the fact that, in all probability, you will become the instrument that delivers irreparable harm to a variety of individuals. Granted, they design their own destinies, are intractable in their attitudes, and live with the asp at their breasts; but the fact remains that it is you who will appear at some point in their lives, like the headsman with his broad ax on the medieval scaffold, and serve up a fate to them that has the same degree of mercy as that dealt out by your historical predecessor.

An image or two: A soft-nosed .45 round that skids off a brick wall and topples before it finds its mark; a baton swung too high that crushes the windpipe; or salting the shaft on a killer of children, a guy you could never nail legitimately, a guy who asks to see you on his last night, but instead of finding peace you watch him vomit his food into a stainless steel chemical toilet and weep uncontrollably on the side of his bunk while a warden reads his death warrant and two opaque-faced screws unlock the death cage.

So the job becomes easier if you think of them in either clinical or jailhouse language that effectively separates them from the rest of us: sociopaths, pukes, colostomy bags, lowlifes, miscreants, buckets of shit, street mutts, recidivists, greaseballs, meltdowns, maggots, gorillas in the mist. Any term will do as long as it indicates that the adversary is pathologically different from yourself.

Then your own single-minded view of the human family is disturbed by a chance occurrence that leads you back into the province of the theologian.

Early Monday morning three land surveyors in a state boat set up a transit instrument on a sandpit in the flooded woods across from the bait shop and began turning angles with it, measuring the bayou frontage with a surveyor's chain, and driving flagged laths at odd intervals into the mudbank.

'You mind telling me what y'all are doing?' I said from the end of the dock.

The transit operator, in folded-down hip waders and rain hat, swiped mosquitoes out of his face and replied, 'The state don't have a recent plat.'

'Who cares?'

'You got a problem with it, talk to my boss in Lafayette. You think we're putting a highway through your house?'

I thought about it. 'Yeah, it's a possibility,' I said.

I called his supervisor, a state civil engineer, and got nowhere. Then I called the sheriff's department, told Wally I'd be in late, and drove to Lafayette.

I was on Pinhook Road, down in the old section, which was still tree lined and unmarked by strip malls, when I saw Karyn LaRose three cars ahead of me, driving a waxed yellow Celica convertible. One lane was closed and the traffic was heavy at the red light, but no one honked, no one tried to cut off another driver.

Except Karyn.

She pulled onto the shoulder, drove around a construction barrier, a cloud of dust drifting off her wheels through the windows of the other cars, and then cut back into the line just before the intersection.

She changed the angle of her rearview mirror and looked at her reflection, tilted up her chin, removed something from the corner of her mouth with her fingernail, oblivious to everyone around her. The oak limbs above her flickered with a cool gold-green light. She threw back her hair and put on her sunglasses and tapped her ring impatiently on the steering wheel, as though she were sitting reluctantly on a stage before an audience that had not quite earned her presence.

An elderly black woman, bent in the spine like a knotted turnip, with glasses as thick as quartz, was laboring down a sidestreet with a cane, working her way toward the bus stop, waving a handkerchief frantically at the bus that had just passed, her purse jiggling from her wrist. She wore a print cotton dress and untied, scuffed brown shoes that exposed the pale, calloused smoothness of her lower foot each time she took a step.

Karyn stared at her from behind her sunglasses, then turned out of the traffic and got out of her convertible and listened without speaking while the old woman gestured at the air and vented her frustration with the Lafayette bus system. Then Karyn knelt on one knee and tied the woman's shoes and held her cocked elbow while the old woman got into the passenger seat of the convertible, and a moment later the two of them drove through the caution light and down the boulevard like old friends.

I'm sure she never saw me. Nor was her act of kindness a performance for passers-by, as it was already obvious she didn't care what they thought of her. I only knew it was easier for me to think of

Karyn LaRose in one-dimensional terms, and endowing her with redeeming qualities was a complexity I didn't need.

Twenty minutes later the state engineer told me an environmental assessment was being made of the swamp area around my dock and bait shop.

'What's that mean?' I said.

'Lyndon Johnson didn't like some of his old neighbors and had their property turned into a park . . . That's a joke, Mr Robicheaux . . . Sir, I'd appreciate your not looking at me like that.'

Helen Soileau happened to glance up from the watercooler when I came through the back door of the department from the parking lot. She straightened her back and tucked her shirt into her gunbelt with her thumbs and grinned.

'What's funny?' I said.

'I've got a great story for you about Aaron.'

'He's not my idea of George Burns, Helen. Let me get my mail first.'

I picked up my messages and my mail from my pigeonhole and stopped by the cold drink machine for a Dr Pepper. On the top of the stack was an envelope addressed to me in pencil, postmarked in Lafayette, with no zip code. I had no doubt who had sent it.

I sat down in a chair by the cold drink machine and opened the envelope with one finger, like peeling away a bandage on a wound. The letter was printed on a paper towel.

> *Dear Mr Roboshow,*
>
> *I thought you was honest but you have shit on me just like them others. Thank God I am old and have got to the end of my row and cant be hurt by yall no more. But that dont mean I will abide your pity either, no sir, it dont, I have seen the likes of yall all my life and know how you think so dont try to act like you are better than me. Also tell that prissy pissant Buford LaRose I will settel some old bidness then finish with him too.*
>
> *You have permission to pass this letter on to people in the press.*
> *Sinserely yours,*
> *a loyal democrat who voted for John Kennedy,*
> *Aaron Jefferson Crown*

Helen was waiting for me inside my office.

'Crown went after Jimmy Ray Dixon. Can you believe it?' she said.

I looked again at the letter in my hand. 'What's his beef with Jimmy Ray?'

'If Jimmy Ray knows, he's not saying. He seems to have become an instant law-and-order man, though.'

She repeated the story to me as it had been told to her by NOPD. You didn't have to be imaginative to re-create the scene. The images were like those drawn from a surreal landscape, where a primitive and half-formed creature rose from a prehistoric pool of genetic soup into a world that did not wish to recognize its origins.

Jimmy Ray had been at his fish camp with three of his employees and their women out by Bayou Lafourche. The night was humid, the dirt yard illuminated by an electric mechanic's lamp hung in a dead pecan tree, and Jimmy Ray was on a creeper under his jacked-up truck, working with a wrench on a brake drum, yelling at a second man to get him a beer from inside the shack. When the man didn't do it fast enough, Jimmy Ray went inside to get the beer himself, and another man, bored for something to do, took his place on the creeper.

Aaron Crown had been crouched on a cypress limb by the bayou's edge, listening to the voices inside the lighted center of the yard, unable to see past a shed at who was speaking but undoubtedly sure that it was Jimmy Ray yelling orders at people from under the truck.

He released his grasp on the limb and dropped silently into the yard, dressed in a seersucker suit two sizes too small for him that he had probably taken from a washline or a Salvation Army Dumpster, and brand-new white leather basketball shoes with layers of mud as thick as waffles caked around the soles.

One of Jimmy Ray's employees was smoking a cigarette, staring at the mist rising from the swamp, perhaps yawning, when he smelled an odor from behind him, a smell that was like excrement and sour milk and smoke from a meat fire. He started to turn, then a soiled hand clamped around his mouth, the calluses as hard as dried fish scale against his lips, and he felt himself pulled against the outline of Crown's body, into each curve and contour, moulded against the phallus and thighs and whipcord stomach, suspended helplessly insde the rage and sexual passion of a man he couldn't see, until the blood flow to his brain stopped as if his jugular had been pinched shut with pliers.

The man under the truck saw the mud-encrusted basketball shoes, the shapeless seersucker pants that hung on ankles scarred by leg manacles, and knew his last night on earth had begun even before Aaron began to rock the truck back and forth on the jack.

The man on the creeper almost made it completely into the open when the truck toppled sideways and fell diagonally across his thighs. After the first red-black rush of pain that arched his head back in the dirt, that seemed to seal his mouth and eyes and steal the air from his lungs, he felt himself gradually float upward from darkness to the top of a warm pool, where two powerful hands released themselves from his face and allowed light into his brain and breath into his body. Then he saw Aaron bending over him, his hands propped on his knees, staring at him curiously.

'Damn if I can ever get the right nigger or white man, either one,' Aaron said.

He looked up at a sound from the shack, shadows across a window shade, a car loaded with revelers bounding down a rutted road through the trees toward the clearing. His face was glazed with sweat, glowing in the humidity, his eyes straining into the darkness, caught between an unsatisfied bloodlust that was within his grasp and the knowledge that his inability to think clearly had always been the weapon his enemies had used against him.

Then, as silently as he had come, he slunk away in the shadows, like a thick-bodied crab moving sideways on mechanical extensions.

'How do you figure it?' Helen said.

'It doesn't make sense. What was it he said to the man under the truck?'

She read from her notepad: ' "Damn if I can ever get the right nigger or white man, either one." '

'I think Aaron has an agenda that none of us has even guessed at,' I said.

'Yeah, war with the human race.'

'That's not it,' I answered.

'What is?'

It's the daughter, I thought.

I visited Batist in the hospital that afternoon, then picked up three pounds of frozen peeled crawfish and a carton of potato salad in town, so Bootsie would not have to cook, and drove down the dirt road toward the house. The bayou was half in shadow and the sunlight looked like gold thread in the trees. Dust drifted out on the bayou's surface and coated the wild elephant ears that grew in dark clumps in the shallows. My neighbor was stringing Christmas lights on his gallery while his rotating hose sprinkler clattered a jet of water among the myrtle bushes and tree trunks in his yard. It was the kind of perfect evening that seemed outside of time, so gentle and removed from the present that you would not be surprised if a news carrier on a bike with balloon tires threw a rolled paper onto your lawn with a headline announcing victory over Japan.

But its perfection dissipated as soon as I pulled into the drive and saw a frail priest in a black suit and Roman collar step out of his parked car and glare at me as though I had just risen from the Pit.

'Could I help you, Father?' I said.

496

'I want to know why you've been tormenting Mr Dolowitz,' he said. His face called to mind a knotted, red cauliflower.

I stooped down so I could see the man in the passenger seat. He kept his face straight ahead, his biscuit-colored derby hat like a bowl on his head.

'No Duh?' I said.

'I understand you're a practicing Catholic,' the priest said.

'That's correct.'

'Then why have you forced this man to commit a crime? He's terrified. What the hell's the matter with you?'

'There's a misunderstanding here, Father.'

'Then why don't you clear things up for me, sir?'

I took his hand and shook it, even though he hadn't offered it. It was as light as balsa sticks in my palm and didn't match the choleric heat in his face. His name was Father Timothy Mulcahy, from the Irish Channel in New Orleans, and he was the pastor of a small church off Magazine whose only parishioners were those too poor or elderly to move out of the neighborhood.

'I didn't threaten this man, Father. I told him he could do what was right for himself,' I said. Then I leaned down to the driver's window. 'No Duh, you tell Father Mulcahy the truth or I'm going to mop up the yard with you.'

'Ah, it's clear you're not a violent man,' the priest said.

'No Duh, now is not the time—' I began.

'It was the other guy, that animal Purcel, Father. But Robicheaux was with him,' No Duh said.

The priest cocked one eyebrow, then tilted his head, made a self-deprecating smile.

'Well, I'm sorry for my rashness,' he said. 'Nonetheless, Mr Dolowitz shouldn't have been forced to break into someone's home,' he said.

'Would you give us a few minutes?' I said.

He nodded and started to walk away, then touched my arm and took me partway with him.

'Be easy with him. This man's had a terrible experience,' he said.

I went back to the priest's car and leaned on the window jamb. Dolowitz took off his hat and set it on his knees. His face looked small, waxlike, devoid of identity. He touched nervously at his mustache.

'What happened?' I asked.

'I creeped Dock Green's house. Somebody left the key in the lock. I stuck a piece of newspaper under the door and knocked the key out and caught it on the paper and pulled it under the door. They got me going back out. They didn't know I'd been inside. If they had, I wouldn't be alive,' he said.

'Who got you?'

'Persephone Green and a button guy works for the Giacanos and some other pervert gets off hurting people.' For the first time his eyes lifted into mine. They possessed a detachment that reminded me of that strange, unearthly look we used to call in Vietnam the thousand-yard stare.

'What they'd do to you, partner?'

The fingers of one hand tightened on the soft felt of his hat. 'Buried me alive . . . ,' he said. 'What, you surprised? You think only Dock's got this thing about graves and talking with dead people under the ground? Him and Persephone are two of a kind. She thought it was funny. She laughed while they put a garden hose in my mouth and covered me over with a front-end loader. It was just like being locked in black concrete, with no sound, with just a little string of dirty air going into my throat. They didn't dig me up till this morning. I went to the bathroom inside my clothes.'

'I'm sorry, No Duh. But I didn't tell you to creep Dock's house.'

'My other choice is I miss the vig again with Wee Willie Bimstine and get fed into an airplane propeller? Thanks for your charitable attitudes.'

'I've got a room behind the bait shop. You can stay here till we square you with Wee Willie.'

'You'd do that?'

'Sure.'

'It's full of snakes out there. You want the gen on Dock? Persephone eighty-sixed him after she caught him porking his broads.'

'That's old news, No Duh.'

'I got in his desk. It's full of building plans for hospitals. Treatment places for drunks and addicts. There was canceled checks from Jimmy Ray Dixon. Go figure.'

'Figure what?'

'Dock supplies broads for every gash-hound in the mob. That's the only reason they let a crazy person like him come around. But he don't cut no deal he don't piece off to the spaghetti heads. When'd the mob start working with colored? You think it's a mystery how the city got splashed in the bowl?'

'Who set up Jerry Joe Plumb, No Duh?'

'*He* did.'

'Jerry Joe set himself up?'

'He was always talking about you, how your mothers use to work together, how he use to listen to all your phonograph records over at your house. At the same time he was wheeling and dealing with the Giacanos, washing money for them, pretending he could walk on both sides of the line . . . You don't get it, do you? You know what will get you killed in New Orleans? When they look in your eyes and know you ain't like them, when they know you ain't willing to do things most people won't even think about. That's when they'll cut you from your package to your throat and eat a sandwich while they're doing it.'

I took my grocery sack of frozen crawfish and potato salad out of the truck and glanced at the priest, who stood at the end of my dock, watching a flight of ducks winnow across the tops of the cypress trees. His hair was snow white, his face windburned in the fading light. I wondered if his dreams were troubled by the confessional tales that men like Dolowitz brought from the dark province in which they lived, or if sleep came to him only after he granted himself absolution, too, and rinsed their sins from his memory, undoing the treachery that had made him the repository of their evil.

I walked up the drive, through the deepening shadows, into the back door of my house.

33

At sunrise Clete Purcel and I sat in my truck on the side street next to Persephone and Dock Green's home in the Garden District. The morning was cold, and clouds of mist almost completely blanketed the two-story antebellum house and the white brick wall that surrounded the backyard. Clete ate from a box of jelly-filled doughnuts and drank out of a large Styrofoam cup of coffee.

'I can't believe I got up this early just to pull No Duh's butt out of the fire,' he said. When I didn't reply, he said, 'If you think you're going to jam up Persephone Green, you're wrong. Didi Gee was her old man, and she's twice as smart as he was and just as ruthless.'

'She'll go down just like he did.'

'The Big C killed Didi. We never touched him.'

'It doesn't matter how you get to the boneyard.'

'What, we got an exemption?' he said, then got out of the truck and strolled across the street to the garden wall. The palms that extended above the bricks were dark green inside the mist. I heard a loud splash, then saw Clete lean down and squint through the thick grillwork on the gate. He walked back to the truck, picked up another doughnut and coffee off the floor and sat down in the seat. He shook an image out of his thoughts.

'What is it?' I said.

'It's forty-five degrees and she's swimming in the nude. She's got quite a stroke . . .' He drank out of his coffee cup and looked at the iron gate in the wall. He pursed his mouth, obviously not yet free from an image that hovered behind his eyes. 'Damn, I'm not kidding you, Streak, you ought to see the gagongas on that broad.'

'Look out front,' I said.

A gray stretch limo with a rental U-Haul truck behind it pulled to the curb. Dock Green got out of the back of the limo and strode up the front walk.

'Show time,' Clete said. He removed my Japanese field glasses from the glove box and focused them on the limo's chauffeur, who was wiping the water off the front windows. 'Hey, it's Whitey Zeroski,' Clete said. 'Remember, the wetbrain used to own a little pizza joint in the Channel? He ran for city council and got a megaphone and put VOTE FOR WHITEY signs all over his car and drove into colored town on Saturday night. He couldn't figure out why he got all his windows broken.'

A moment later we heard Dock and Persephone Green's voices on the other side of the garden wall.'

'It don't have to shake out like this,' he said.

'You milked through the fence too many times, hon. I hope they were worth it,' she replied.

'It's over. You got my word . . . Come out of the water and talk. We can go have breakfast somewhere.'

'Bye, Dock.'

'We're a team, Seph. Ain't nothing going to separate us. Believe it when I say it.'

'I hate to tell you this but you're a disappearing memory. I've got to practice my backstroke now . . . Keep your eyes somewhere else, Dock . . . You don't own the geography anymore.'

We heard her body weight push off from the side of the pool and her arms dipping rhythmically into the water.

'Let's 'front both of them,' Clete said, and started to get out of the truck.

'No, that'll just get No Duh into it deeper.'

'Where's your head, Dave? That guy wouldn't piss on you if you were on fire. The object is to flush Mookie Zerrang out in the open and then take him off at the neck.'

'We have to wait, Cletus.'

I saw the frustration and anger in his face. I put my hand on his shoulder. It was as hard as a cured ham. When he didn't speak, I took my hand away.

'I appreciate your coming with me,' I said.

'Oh hell yeah, this is great stuff. You know why I was a New Orleans cop? Because we could break all the rules and get away with it. This town's problems aren't going to end until we run all these fuckers back under the sewer grates where they belong.'

'I think Persephone got to you, partner,' I said.

'You're right. I should have been a criminal. It's a simpler life.'

For a half hour Dock and two workmen carried out his office furniture, his computer, his files, and a huge glass bottle, the kind mounted on water coolers, filled with an amber-tinted liquid and the embalmed body of a bobcat. The bobcat's paws were pressed against the glass, as though it were drowning.

Then the three of them drove away without the limo. Clete and I got out of the truck and walked to the gate. Through the grillwork and the banana fronds I could see steam rising off the turquoise surface of the pool and hear her feet kicking steaily with her long stroke.

'It's Dave Robicheaux. How about opening up, Persephone?' I said.

'Dream on,' she replied from inside the steam.

'You stole a test for Karyn LaRose and got expelled from college. Why let her take you down again?'

'Excuse me?'

'Try this as a fantasy, Seph. You and all your friends are on an airliner with Karyn and Buford LaRose. Karyn and Buford are at the controls. The plane is on fire. There are only two parachutes on board . . . Who's going to end up with the parachutes?'

I could hear her treading water in the stillness, then rising from the pool at the far end.

She appeared at the gate in a white robe and sandals, a towel wrapped around her hair. She unlocked the gate and pulled it back on its hinges, then turned and walked to an iron table without speaking, the long, tapered lines of her body molded against the cloth of her robe.

She combed her hair back with her towel, her face regal at an angle to us, seemingly indifferent to our presence.

'What's on your mind?' she said. Her voice was throaty, her cheeks pale and slightly sunken, her mouth the same shade as the red morning glories that cascaded down the wall behind her.

Clete kept staring at her.

'Has he been fed?' she asked.

'You got to pardon me. I was thinking you look like Cher, the movie actress. You even have a tattoo,' he said.

'My, you have busy eyes,' she said.

'Yeah, I was noticing the hole over there by the compost pile. Is that where y'all buried No Duh Dolowitz?' he said.

'The little man with the grease mustache? That's what this is about?' she asked.

'He shouldn't have come here, Persephone. He thought he was doing something for me. It was a mistake,' I said.

'I see. I'm going to have him hurt?'

'You're a tough lady,' I said.

'I have no interest in your friends, *Dave*. You don't mind if I call you "Dave," do you, since you call me by my first name without asking?'

'Mookie Zerrang is a bad button man, Seph. He doesn't do it for money. That means you've got no dials on him.'

'Did you ever have this kind of conversation with my father, or do you speak down to me just because I'm a woman?'

'In honesty, I guess I did.'

'What Streak means is, he beat the shit out of Didi Gee with a canvas money bag filled with lug nuts. He did this because your old man had his half-brother shot. You might say y'all have a tight family history,' Clete said.

Clete's mouth was hooked downward at the corners, his face heated, the scar tissue through his eyebrow and across his nose flexed tight against the skull. She tried to meet his gaze, then looked away at the tongues of vapor rising from her swimming pool.

'What was that about?' I asked him in the truck.

'I told you, I'm tired of being patient with lowlifes. You know what our finest hour was? The day we popped that drug dealer and his bodyguard in the back of their Caddy. The seats looked like somebody had thrown a cow through a tree shredder. Admit it, it was a grand afternoon.'

'Bad way to think, Cletus.'

'One day you're going to figure out you're no different from me, Dave.'

'Yeah?'

'Then you're going to shoot yourself.'

He tried to hold the seriousness in his face, but I saw his eyes start to smile.

'You'll never change, Streak,' he said, his expression full of play again.

I turned the ignition, then looked through the front window and saw Whitey Zeroski, the limo driver, walking toward us. He wore a gray chauffeur's uniform, with brass buttons and a gray cap that sat low, military style, over his white eyebrows.

'What are you guys doing here?' he said through my window, his eyes focusing on the doughnut Clete was about to put in his mouth.

'You want a doughnut, Whitey?' Clete said.

'I don't mind . . . Thanks, Purcel . . . I'm stuck here . . . Dock says I should hang around in case his wife wants to meet him up at Copeland's for breakfast.'

'Dock better do a reality check,' Clete said.

'That fight, you mean? It goes on all the time. Dock might give up lots of things, but his wife ain't gonna be one of them.'

'Oh yeah?' Clete said.

'Dock's nuts, but he ain't so nuts he forgot his wife's got the brains in the family.'

'It's the stuff of great love affairs,' Clete said.

'Who built the big casino downtown?' Whitey said. 'Mobbed-up guys with real smarts from Chicago and Vegas, right? Where do they build it? Between Louis Armstrong Park and the Iberville welfare project, the two most dangerous areas in downtown New Orleans. If you win at the table, you just walk outside and hand your money over to the muggers. How's that for fucking smarts? You think the lesson is lost on the local schmucks?'

Clete and I looked at each other.

Twenty minutes later we were on I-10, speeding past Lake Pontchartrain. Fog puffed out of the trees on the north shore of the lake, and the rain was falling on the lake's surface inside the fog.

'She's the funnel for the wiseguys and Jimmy Ray Dixon into LaRose's administration, isn't she?' Clete said.

'That's the way I'd read it.'

'I don't think I'm going to survive having a wetbrain like Whitey Zeroski explain that to me,' he said.

Early the next morning I went to Sabelle Crown's bar at the Underpass in Lafayette. The black bartender told me I'd find her at the city golf course on the northside.

'The golf course?' I said.

'That's where she go when she want to be alone,' he said.

He was right. I found her sitting on a bench under a solitary oak tree by the first fairway, a scarf tied around her head, flipping bread crusts from a bag at the pigeons. The sky was gray, and leaves were blowing out of the trees in the distance.

'Your old man tried to drop a car frame on top of Jimmy Ray Dixon,' I said.

'The things you learn,' she said.

'Who got you started in the life, Sabelle?'

'You know, I have a total blackout about all that stuff.'

'You left New Iberia for New Orleans, then disappeared up north.'

'This is kind of a private place for me, Dave. Buford LaRose tried to have Daddy killed out on the Atchafalaya River. Haven't you done enough?'

'Were you in Chicago?' I asked.

She brushed the bread crumbs off her hands and walked to her parked automobile, the back of her scarf lifting in the wind.

After I returned to the office, I got a telephone call from the sheriff.

'I'm in Vermilion Parish. Drop what you're doing and come over for a history lesson,' he said.

'What's up?'

'You said this character Mookie Zerrang was a leg breaker on the Mississippi coast and a button man in Miami?'

'That's the word.'

'Think closer to home.'

I signed out of the office and met the sheriff on a dirt road that fed into a steel-and-wood bridge over the Vermilion River ten miles south of Lafayette. He was leaning against his cruiser, eating from a roll of red boudin wrapped in wax paper. The sky had cleared, and the sunlight on the water looked like hammered gold leaf. The sheriff wiped his mouth with his wrist.

'Man, I love this stuff,' he said. 'My doctor says my arteries probably look like the sewer lines under Paris. I wonder what he means by that.'

'What are we doing here, skipper?' I said.

'That name, "Zerrang", it kept bouncing around in my head. Then I remembered the story of that Negro kid back during World War II. You remember the one? Same name.'

'No.'

'Yeah, you do. He was electrocuted. He was fourteen years old and probably retarded. He was too small for the chair, or the equipment didn't work right, I forget which. But evidently what happened to him was awful.'

His face became solemn. He lay the waxpaper and piece of boudin on the cruiser's hood and slipped his hands in his pockets and gazed at the river.

'I was a witness at only one execution. The guy who got it was depraved and it never bothered me. But whenever I think of that Zerrang kid back in '43, I wonder if the human race should be on the planet . . . Take a walk with me,' he said.

We crossed an irrigation ditch on a board plank and entered a stand of hackberry and persimmon trees on the riverbank. Up ahead, through the foliage, I could see three spacious breezy homes on big green lots. But here, inside the tangle of trees and air vines and blackberry bushes, was Louisiana's more humble past – a cypress shack that was only a pile of boards now, some of them charred, a privy that had collapsed into the hole under it, a brick chimney that had toppled like broken teeth into the weeds.

'This is where the boy's family lived, at least until a bunch of drunks set their shack on fire. The boy had one brother, and the brother had a son named Mookie. What do you think of that?' he said.

'Where'd you get all this, Sheriff?' I asked.

'From my dad, just this morning. He's ninety-two years old now. However, his memory is remarkable. Sometimes it gives him no rest.'

The sheriff turned over a blackened board with the toe of his half-topped boot.

'Did your father grow up around here?'

The sheriff rubbed the calluses of one palm on the backs of his knuckles.

'Sir?' I said.

'He was one of the drunks who burned them out. We can't blame Mookie Zerrang on the greaseballs in Miami. He's of our own making, Dave.'

34

Batist had been released from the hospital that day, and after work I shopped for him at the grocery in town and then drove out to his house.

He was sitting in a soft, stuffed chair on the gallery, wearing a flannel shirt over the bandages that were taped on his shoulders. His daughter, a large, square woman who looked more Indian than black, was in the side yard, hammering the dust out of a quilt with an old tennis racquet.

I told Batist the story about the Zerrang family, the fourteen-year-old boy who was cooked alive in the electric chair, the drunks who burned his home.

Batist's face was impassive while I spoke. His broad hands were motionless on his thighs, the knuckles like carved wood.

'My daddy got killed by lightning working for twenty cents an hour,' he said. 'The white man owned the farm knowed mules draw lightning, but he sat on his gallery while it was storming all over the sky and tole my daddy to keep his plow turned in the field, not to come out till he'd cut the last row. That's what he done to my daddy. But I ain't growed up to hate other people for it, no.'

'You need anything else, partner?'

'That nigger's out yonder in the swamp. Fat Daddy's wife had a dream about him. He was wading through the water, with a big foldout knife in his hand, the kind you dress deer with.'

'Don't believe in that stuff, Batist.'

'Nigger like that come out of hell, Dave. Don't say he cain't go in your dreams.'

I walked back out to my truck, trying not to think about his words, or the fact that Fat Daddy's wife had somehow seen in her dream the type of wide-bladed, foldout game dressing knife that Mookie Zerrang had used to murder Lonnie Felton and his girlfriend at Henderson Swamp.

Early the next morning I called an old friend of mine named Minos Dautrieve at the DEA in New Orleans. Then I called Buford at his house.

'Meet me in City Park,' I said.

'Considering our track record, that seems inappropriate, Dave,' he said.

'Persephone Green is destroying your life. Is that appropriate?'

A half hour later I was sitting at a picnic table when I saw him get out of his car by the old brick fire station in the park and walk through the oak trees toward me. He wore a windbreaker over a LSU T-shirt and white pleated slacks without a belt. His curly hair was damp and freshly combed and he had shaved so closely that his cheeks glowed with color. He sat down at the plank table and folded his hands. I pushed a Styrofoam cup of coffee toward him and opened the top of a take-out container.

'Sausage and eggs from Victor's,' I said.

'No thanks.'

'Suit yourself,' I said, and wrapped a piece of French bread around a sausage paddy and dipped it in my coffee. Then I put it back in my plate without eating it. 'Persephone Green is the bag lady for the Giacano family and Jimmy Ray Dixon and every other New Orleans lowlife who put money into your campaign. The payback is the chain of state hospitals for drunks and addicts,' I said.

'The contracts are all going to legitimate corporations, Dave. I don't know all their stockholders. Why should I?'

'Stockholders? Dock tried to squeeze out Short Boy Jerry. When Jerry Joe wouldn't squeeze, they had him beaten to death. Is that what stockholders do?'

'Is this why you got me out here?'

'No. I couldn't figure why you kept this sixties character, Clay Mason, around. Then I remembered you'd published some papers on psycho-pharmacology, you know, curing drunks with drugs and all that jazz.'

'You belong to AA. You know only one point of view. It's not your fault. But there're other roads to recovery.'

'That's why you're on the spike yourself?'

I saw the hurt in his face, the stricture in his throat.

'I talked to a friend in the DEA this morning,' I said. 'His people think Mason's got money in your hospital chain. They also think he's involved with some crystal meth labs down in Mexico. That's mean shit, Buford. Bikers dig it for gangbangs, stomping people's ass, stuff like that.'

'Do you get a pleasure out of this? Why do you have this obsession with me and my wife? Can't you leave us in peace?'

'Maybe I've been in the same place you are.'

'You're going to save me? . . .' He shook his head, then his eyes grew close together and filmed over. He sat very still for a long time, like a man who imagined himself riding a bicycle along the rim of a precipice. 'It's Karyn they own.'

His face darkened with anger. He stared at the bayou, as though the reflected sunlight he saw there could transport him out of the moment he had just created for himself.

'How?' I asked. 'The cheating back in college? Persephone had been blackmailing her over something that happened twenty years ago?'

'You know how many educational and honor societies she belongs to? She'd be disgraced. The irony is she didn't need to cheat. She was a good student on her own.'

But not number one, I thought.

He studied my eyes and seemed to see the thought buried there.

'If you tell anybody this, I'll sue you for libel. Then I'll personally kick your ass,' he said.

'I'm not your problem.'

His face was puffed, naked, the eyes like brown marbles in a pan of water.

I picked up my coffee and the sausage paddy I'd wrapped in a piece of French bread and walked to my truck. The sunlight looked like yellow smoke through the trees. Buford still sat at the plank table, his forehead on his palm, oblivious to the camellias that were in full bloom along the banks of Bayou Teche.

I didn't tell Buford all the content of my conversation with my friend Minos Dautrieve at the DEA in New Orleans. Minos and his colleagues were about to raid the ranch of Clay Mason seven hundred miles below the Texas border, in the state of Jalisco.

And Helen Soileau and I were invited.

35

We flew into Guadalajara at noon with Minos and two other DEA agents. Minos was a tall, lean, cynical, good-natured man with blond close-cropped hair that was starting to whiten. When he had played forward for LSU years ago, sportswriters had nicknamed him 'Dr Dunkenstein' for the ferocious rim-jarring slam dunks that were his trademark. As we taxied toward the hangar, he pulled back the curtain on the charter plane's window and looked at the hills in the distance, then at a parked van with three wide backseats and, leaning against it, an unshaved man in blue jeans and a maroon football jersey with a holstered pistol and a gold shield clipped onto his belt.

'There's our ride,' he said.

Helen stared out the window.

'I don't believe it. It's that smart-ass, what's-his-name, Heriberto, the one looks like his hair was cut with garden clippers,' she said.

'You know that guy?' Minos asked.

'He's a Mexican drug agent. A priest up in the mountains told us he's dirty,' I said.

'They all are. One of our guys got sold out here and tortured to death,' Minos said. 'This guy's fairly harmless.'

'Great character reference,' Helen said.

We drove out of the city and through the small village of Zapopan. In the center of the village square was a gazebo, surrounded by rain trees, where a band was playing and children were firing out of milk bottles rockets that popped high in the sky. On one side of the square was a grayish pink eighteenth-century cathedral whose stone steps had been worn smooth and cupped down the center by the knees of thousands of penitents who worked themselves painfully up the steps on their birthdays, simultaneously saying a rosary.

'That's a famous church. The statue of the Virgin of Zapopan's in there. There been a lot of miracles here, man,' Heriberto said.

'This is the place,' I said to Helen.

'What place?' she said.

'Mingo Bloomberg told me the guy named Arana was from a village in Jalisco that had a famous religious statue in it,' I said.

Heriberto steered around a parked bus, on top of which sat two soldiers in camouflage fatigues and steel pots. A third soldier was urinating in the street. The street sign on the corner said EMILIANO ZAPATA.

'The guy the *rurales* shot by the mines? Yeah, he should have gone to church a lot more. But was *Indio*, you know. One day they're in church, the next day they're drunk, chasing *puta*, causing a lot of shit with the government. See, man, their real problem is they ain't big on work,' he said.

Helen leaned forward from the seat behind us. 'How about shutting the fuck up?' she said.

'*Gringita*, I ain't got nothing against these people. But in the south they been killing our soldiers. You want to see what happens?' Heriberto said, lifting a shoe box of photographs from under the seat.

The photos were black and white, creased and hand-soiled around the edges, as though they had been passed around for viewing many times. In one photo three dead rebels lay by the side of a road, their bandannas still tied over the lower half of their faces. They had on U.S. Army web gear and bandoliers and looked like they had been killed while running. Several other photos showed another scene from different angles; a half dozen male corpses had been strung up by their feet from an adobe colonnade, their fingers inches above the dirt, their faces featureless with dried blood.

'The old guy we gonna see this afternoon? He encourages these guys, gives them money for guns, gets them killed. The guy comes from your country, *Gringita*,' Heriberto said.

'If I were you, I wouldn't say any more,' I said.

He opened his fingers in the air, as though he were releasing an invisible bird from them, and drove out of the village toward the mountains and a place that could have been sawed out of the revolutionary year of 1910.

We drove on a high switchback rock road through dead trees and a boulder-strewn landscape and rain that covered the windows like running plastic, then crested a ridge that was blackened by a forest fire, dancing with lightning, and dropped down out of the storm into sunlight again and a long cultivated valley with green hills in the distance and a volcano that was beveled across the top as though it had been sheared by tin snips. The road followed a river with wide, red clay alluvial banks that were scissored with the tracks of livestock, then we were inside another village, this one with cobblestone streets, buff-colored colonnades, a stone watering trough in front of the *cervecería*, a tiny open-air market where bees' combs and uncured meat were sold off wood carts that were boxed with screens to keep out the blowflies.

The streets and walkways under the colonnades were filled with soldiers. They were all young and carried World War II M-1 rifles and M-16s. Some of the M-16s had a knob welded onto the bolt, which meant they were early Vietnam-era issue, notorious among grunts for the bolt that often jammed and had to be driven into the chamber with the heel of the hand.

We stood in the street while Minos talked with a collection of Mexican drug agents gathered around the tailgate of an army six-by. The air was shining and cool after the rain, and you could see for miles. Heriberto stared off in the distance at a rambling white ranch house with a blue tile roof on the slope of a hill. His legs were spread slightly, his expression contemplative.

'Big day for the *Tejano*. We gonna fuck him up good, man,' he said.

'That's where he lives? You think maybe he's seen us coming?' I asked.

'We cut his phone. He ain't going nowhere.'

I took Minos aside.

'What are they expecting to find up there, the Russian Army?' I said.

'A lot of these guys speak English, Dave.'

'They've blown the operation.'

'Not in their mind. This is how they say "get out of town" to people they normally can't touch. Mason should be flattered.'

'You don't like him?'

'My sister was a flowerchild back in the sixties. She thought this guy was a great man. She got loaded on hash and acid and floated out on the sunset from a ten-storey window.'

We followed a caravan of six army trucks down a winding dirt road to the walled compound that surrounded Clay Mason's ranch. The walls were topped with broken glass and spirals of razor wire, and the wood gates at the entrance were chain-locked and barred with a cross-beam inside. The lead truck, which was fronted with a plow-shaped dozer blade, gained speed, roaring across the potholes, the soldiers in back rocking back and forth, then crashed through the gates and blew them off their hinges.

The soldiers trashed the house, fanned out into the yards and out-buildings, kicked chickens out of their way like exploding sacks of feathers, and for no apparent reason shot a pig running from a barn and threw it down the well.

'Can you put a stop to this bullshit?' I said to Minos.

'You see that fat slob with the Sam Browne belt on? He's a graduate of the School of the Americas at Fort Benning. He also owns a whorehouse. He knocked the glass eye out of a girl for sassing him. No, thanks.'

While his house was being torn apart, Clay Mason leaned against a cedar post on his front porch and smoked a hand-rolled cigarette, his pixie eyes fixed on me and Minos. His hair extended like white straw under his domed Stetson hat.

'Karyn warned me you're a vindictive man,' he said.

'I'm sorry about your place. It's not my doing,' I said.

'Like hell it isn't.' Then a yellow tooth glinted behind his lip and he added, 'You little pisspot.'

He flipped his cigarette away, walked to the corner of his house on his cane, and urinated in the yard, audibly passing gas with his back turned to us, shaking his penis; a small, hatted, booted man, in a narrow, ratty coat, whose power had touched thousands of young lives.

Helen and I walked behind the ranch house, where the soldiers had forced five field hands to lean spread-eagled against the stone wall of the barn. The field hands were young and frightened and kept turning their heads to see if guns were being pointed at their backs. The soldiers shook them down but kept them leaning on their arms against the wall.

'I don't like being in on this one, Dave,' Helen said.

'Don't watch it. We'll be out of here soon,' I said.

We walked inside the barn. The loft was filled with hay, the horse stalls slatted with light, the dirt floor soft as foam rubber with dried manure. Through the doors at the far end I could see horses belly-deep in grass against a blue mountain.

Hanging from pegs on a wood post, like a set used by only one man, were a pair of leather chaps, a bridle, a yellow rain slicker, a sleeveless knitted riding vest, flared gloves made from deer hide, and two heavy Mexican spurs with rowels as big as half dollars. I rotated one of the rowels with my thumb. The points were sticky, coated with tiny pieces of brown hair.

Behind the post, a silver saddle was splayed atop a sawhorse. I ran my hand across the leather, the cool ridges of metal, the seared brand of a Texas cattle company on one flap. The cantle was incised with roses, and in the back of the cantle was a mother-of-pearl inlay of an opened camellia.

'What is it?' Helen said.

'Remember, the guy named Arana said the *bugarron* rode a silver saddle carved with flowers? I think Clay Mason's our man.'

'What can you do about it?'

'Nothing.'

'That's it?'

'Who knows?' I said.

We walked back into the sun's glare and the freshness of the day and the wind that smelled of water and grass and horses in the fields.

But the young field hands spread-eagled against the stone wall of the barn were not having a good day at all. The shade was cool in the lee of the barn, but they were sweating heavily, their arms trembling with tension and exertion. One boy had a dark inverted V running down his pants legs, and the soldiers were grinning at his shame.

'School of the Americas?' I said to the fat man in the Sam Browne belt. I tried to smile.

He wore tinted prescription glasses and stood taller than I. His eyes looked at me indolently, then moved to Helen, studying her figure.

'What you want?' he said.

'How about cutting these guys some slack? They're not traffickers, they're just *camposinos*, right?' I said.

'We decide what they are. You go on with the woman . . . Is *guapa*, huh? Is maybe lesbian but *puta* is *puta*.' He held out his palms and cupped them, as though he were holding a pair of cantaloupes.

'What'd you say?' Helen asked.

'He didn't say anything,' I said.

'Yeah he did. Say it again, you bucket of bean shit, and see what happens.'

The officer turned away, a wry smile on his mouth, a light in the corner of his eye.

She started to step toward him, but I moved in front of her, my eyes fastened on hers. The anger in her gaze shifted to me, like a person breaking glassware indiscriminately, then I saw it die in her face. I walked with her toward the ranch house, the backs of my fingers touching her hand. She widened the space between us.

'Next time don't interfere,' she said.

'Those kids would have taken our weight.'

'Oh yeah? . . . Well . . . I'm sure you're right . . . You swinging dicks are always right . . . Let's close it down here. I've had my share of the tomato patch for today.'

She walked ahead of me through the open front door of the house into the living room, where Clay Mason sat in a deep deer-hide chair amid a litter of shattered glass, antique firearms stripped from the walls, splayed books, and overturned furniture. On one stucco wall, pinned inside a broken viewing case, was a sun-faded flag of the Texas republic.

Mason's hands were folded on top of his cane, his eyes narrow and liquid with resentment.

'Don't get up . . . I just need to use your john . . . Such a gentleman . . . ,' she said, and continued on into the back of the house, without ever slowing her step.

'Looks like you're going to skate,' I said.

'My family earned every goddamn inch of this place. We'll be here when the rest of you are dust.'

An upper corner of the Texas flag had fallen loose from the blue felt backboard it was pinned to. I reached through the broken glass and smoothed the cloth flat and replaced the pin. Faded strips of butternut cloth, inscribed in almost illegible ink with the names of Civil War battles, were sewn around the flag's borders.

'This flag belonged to the Fourth Texas. Those were John Bell Hood's boys,' I said.

'My great-grandfather carried that flag.'

'It was your family who lived on the ranch next to the LaRoses', west of the Pecos, wasn't it? Jerry Joe Plumb told me how y'all slant drilled and ran wets across the river.'

'Do you read newspapers? There's a revolution being fought here. Everything you're doing helps those men out there kill Mayan Indians.'

'Men like you always have a banner, Dr Mason. The truth is, you live vicariously through the suffering of other people.'

'Get out . . .' He flicked at the air with the backs of his fingers, as though he were dispelling a bad odor.

I tried to think of a rejoinder, but I had none. Clay Mason had spent a lifetime floating above the wreckage he had precipitated, seemingly immune to all the Darwinian and moral laws that affected the rest of us, and my rhetoric sounded foolish compared to the invective he had weathered for decades.

I stepped across the broken glass on the oak floor toward the open doorway. Outside, the soldiers were loading up in the six-bys.

'Hold on, Streak,' Helen said behind me. 'It looks like our friend flushed the candy store down the commode. Except it backed up on him. Guess what got stuck under the rim?'

She dipped the tip of her little finger into a child's balloon and held the white powder up in a column of sunlight, then wiped her finger on a piece of tissue paper.

'It's a little wet. Can you call that fat guy in, see if he wants to do the taste test?' she said.

36

I should have seen it coming but I didn't.

The morning after our return from Guadalajara the sheriff opened the door to my office and leaned inside.

'That was Lafayette PD. You'd better get over there. Sabelle Crown's pinned inside a car on the Southern Pacific tracks.'

'What happened?'

'She was abducted from the city golf course by this guy Zerrang. What was she doing on a golf course?'

'She feeds the pigeons there.'

'Anyway, Zerrang must have taken her somewhere. Evidently it was pretty bad. When he was finished, he left her unconscious in her car on the train tracks. Why's Zerrang after Sabelle Crown?'

'He wants her father,' I said.

'I don't get it.'

'Mookie Zerrang works for Persephone Green and Jimmy Ray Dixon. Jimmy Ray knows sooner or later Aaron's going to kill him.'

'What for?'

'I think it has to do with Sabelle.'

'To tell you the truth, Dave, I really don't give a damn about any of these people's motivations. It's like figuring out why shit stinks. I just wish they'd stay the hell out of our parish. Get over there, will you?'

The sheriff brushed something out of his eye, then he said, 'Except why would this guy torture a woman, then leave her on the train tracks? Why didn't he just kill her and put her out of her misery?'

'Because he hurts a lot more people this way,' I said.

Helen Soileau and I drove in a cruiser on the four-lane to Lafayette. Emergency flares burned inside the fog when we arrived at the railroad crossing where the freight locomotive had struck Sabelle's gas-guzzler broadside and pushed it fifty yards down the rails in a spray of sparks.

We parked on the shoulder of the road and walked through the weeds to the car's wreckage by the side of the tracks. It lay upside down, the engine block driven through the firewall, the roof mashed against the steering column. Lafayette firemen had covered the outside metal, the engine, and gas tank with foam and were trying to wedge open the driver's window with a hydraulic jack.

A paramedic had worked his way on his stomach through the inverted passenger's window, and I could hear him talking inside. A moment later he crawled back out. His shirt and both of his latex gloves were spotted with blood.

He sat in the grass, his hands on his thighs. A fireman put a plug of tobacco in the paramedic's mouth to bite off, then helped him up by one arm.

'How's it look?' I said.

'The car didn't burn. Otherwise, that lady don't have a whole lot of luck,' he replied. He looked into my eyes and saw the unanswered question still there. He shook his head.

I took off my coat, slipped my clip-on holster off my belt, and squeezed through the passenger's window into the car's interior. I could smell gas and the odor of musty cushions and old grease and burnt electrical wires.

Sabelle's head and upper torso were layered with crumpled metal, so that she had virtually no mobility. I couldn't see the lower portion of her body at all. She coughed, and I felt the spray touch my face like a warm mist.

'What'd he do to you, kiddo?' I said.

'Everything.'

'Those guys out there are the best. They'll have you out of here soon.'

'When I close my eyes I can feel the world turning. If I don't open them quickly. I won't get back . . . I betrayed Daddy, Dave.'

'It's not your fault.'

'Mookie Zerrang knows where he is.'

'There's still time to stop it. If you'll trust me.'

Her eyes went out of focus, then settled on mine again. One cheek was marbled with broken veins. The rent metal around her head looked like an aura fashioned out of warped pewter.

She told me where to look.

'Jimmy Ray Dixon was your pimp in New Orleans, wasn't he? Then he took you north, to work for him in Chicago.'

'I made my own choices. I got no kick coming.'

'Your father murdered Ely Dixon, didn't he?'

'Wipe my nose, Streak. My hands are caught inside something.'

I worked my handkerchief from my back pocket and touched at her upper lip with it. She coughed again, long and hard this time, gagging in her throat, and I tried to hold her chin so she wouldn't cut it on a strip of razored metal that was wrapped across her chest. The handkerchief came away with a bright red flower in the middle of it.

'I have to go now,' I said.

'Tell Daddy I'm sorry,' she said.

'You're the best daughter a father could have, Sabelle.'

I thought her eyes wrinkled at the corners. But they didn't. Her eyes were haunted with fear, and my words meant nothing.

I backed out of the passenger window onto the grass. I could smell water in a ditch, the loamy odor of decayed pecan husks in an orchard, taste the fog on my tongue, hear the whirring sound of automobile tires out on the paved road. I walked away just as a team of firemen and uniformed Lafayette cops used the Jaws of Life to wrench open one side of the wrecked car. The sprung metal sounded just like a human scream.

Helen and I drove down I-10 toward the Atchafalaya River. It was misting, and the fields and oak and palm trees along the roadside were gray and wet-looking, and up ahead I could see the orange and blue glow of a filling station inside the fog that rolled off the river.

'What are you worrying about?' Helen said.

I touched the brake on the cruiser.

'I've got to do something.' I said.

'What?'

'Maybe Zerrang didn't head right for the Basin. Maybe there's another way to pull his plug.'

'You don't look too happy about it, whatever it is,' she said.

'How would you like to save Buford LaRose's career for him?' I said.

I called his house from the filling station pay phone. Through the glass I could see the willows on the banks of the Atchafalaya, where we were to meet two powerboats from the St Martin Parish Sheriff's Department.

'Buford?' I said.

'What is it?'

'Sabelle Crown's dead.'

'Oh man, don't tell me that.'

'She was tortured, then left on a train track in her car by Mookie Zerrang.'

I could hear him take the receiver away from his ear, hear it scrape against a hard surface. Then I heard him breathing in the mouthpiece again.

'You were right about Aaron Crown,' I said. 'He killed Ely Dixon. But it was a mistake. He went to the house to kill Jimmy Ray. He didn't know that Jimmy Ray had moved out and rented it to his brother.'

'Why would he want to kill Jimmy Ray Dixon?'

'Jimmy Ray got Sabelle started in the life . . . You're vindicated, Buford. That means you get word to Persephone Green to call Mookie Zerrang off.'

'Are you insane? Do you think I control these people? What in God's name is the matter with you?'

'No, they control you.'

'Listen, I just had that ghoul beating on my front door. I ran him off my property with a pistol.'

'Which ghoul?'

'Who else, Dock Green. His wife dumped him. He accused me and Karyn of being involved in a ménage à trois with her. I guess that's her style.'

'It seems late to be righteous,' I said.

'What's that mean?'

'You treated Sabelle Crown like shit.'

He was silent for what seemed a long time. Then he said, 'Yeah, I didn't do right by her . . . I wish I could change it . . . Good-bye, Dave.'

He quietly hung up the phone.

Helen and I sat in the cabin of the St Martin Parish sheriff's boat. The exhaust pipes idled at the waterline while a uniformed deputy smoked a cigarette in the open hatchway and waited for the boat skipper to return from his truck with a can of gasoline.

I could feel Helen's eyes on my face.

'What is it?' I said.

'I don't like the way you look.'

'It hasn't been a good day.'

'Maybe you shouldn't be in on this one,' she said.

'Is that right?'

'Unless he deals it, Mookie Zerrang comes back alive, Streak.'

'Well, you never know how things are going to work out,' I said.

Her lips were chapped, and she rubbed them with the ball of her finger, her eyes glazed over with hidden thoughts.

We went down the Atchafalaya, with the spray blowing back across the bow, then we entered a side channel and a bay that was surrounded by flooded woods. Under the sealed sky, the water in the bay was an unnatural, luminous yellow, as though it were the only element in its environment that possessed color. Up ahead, in the mist, I could see the shiny silhouette of an abandoned oil platform, then a canal through the woods and inside the tangle of air vines and cypress and willow trees a shack built on wood pilings.

'That's it,' I said to the boat pilot.

He cut back on the throttle, stared through the glass at the woods, then reversed the engine so we didn't drift into the shore.

'You want to go head-on in there?' he asked.

'You know another way to do it?' I said.

'Bring in some SWAT guys on a chopper and blow that shack into toothpicks,' he replied.

A St Martin Parish plainclothes homicide investigator who was on the other boat walked out on the bow and used a bullhorn, addressing the shack as though he did not know who its occupants were.

'We want to talk to y'all that's inside. You need to work your way down that ladder with one hand on your head. There won't nobody get hurt,' he said.

But there was no sound, except the idling boat engines and the rain that had started falling in large drops on the bay's surface. The plainclothes wiped his face with his hand and tried again.

'Aaron, we know you in there. We afraid somebody's come out here to hurt you, podna. Ain't it time to give it up?' he said.

Again, there was silence. The plainclothes' coat was dark with rain and his tie was blown back across his shirt. He looked toward our boat, shrugged his shoulders, and went inside the cabin.

'Let's do it, skipper,' I said to the pilot.

He pushed the throttle forward and took our boat into the canal. The wake from our boat receded back through the trees, gathering with it sticks and dead hyacinths, washing over logs and finally disappearing into the flooded undergrowth. The second boat eased into the shallows behind us until its hull scraped on the silt.

Helen and I dropped off the bow into the water and immediately sank to our thighs, clouds of gray mud ballooning around us. She carried a twelve-gauge Remington shotgun, with the barrel sawed off an inch above the pump. I pulled back the slide on my .45, chambered the top round in the magazine, and set the safety.

A flat-bottom aluminum boat with an outboard engine was tied to a piling under the shack. Helen and I waded through the water, ten yards apart, not speaking, our eyes fixed on the shack's shuttered windows and the ladder that extended upward to an open door with a gunny sack curtain blowing in the door frame.

On my left, the St Martin plainclothes and three uniformed deputies were spread out in a line, breaking their way through a stand of willows.

Helen and I walked under the shack and listened. I cupped my hand on a piling to feel for movement above.

Nothing.

Helen held the twelve-gauge at port arms, her knuckles white on the stock and pump. Her faded blue jeans were drenched up to her rump.

The air was cold and felt like damp flannel against the skin, and I could smell an odor like bleached gars and gas from a sewer main.

Then I felt something tick against my face, like a mild irritant, a wet leaf, a blowfly. Unconsciously, I wiped at it with my hand, then I felt it again, harder this time, against my eyebrow, my forehead, in my hair, directly in my face as I stared upward at the plank floor of the shack.

Helen's mouth was parted wide, her face white.

I wiped my face on my coat sleeve and stared at the long red smear across the cloth.

I felt a revulsion go through my body as though I had been spat upon. I tore off my coat, soaked it in the water at my knees, and wiped my face and hair with it, my hand trembling.

Above me, strings of congealed blood hung from the planks and lifted and fell in the wind.

I moved out from under the shack, slipped the safety off the .45, and began climbing the ladder, which was set at a gradual angle, almost like stairs. Helen moved out into the water, away from the shack, and aimed the twelve gauge at the door above my head, then, just before I went inside, swung the barrel away and followed me.

I reached the top rung and paused, my hand on the doorjamb. The gunny sack curtain billowed back on the nails it hung from, exposing a rusted icebox without power, a table and chair, a solitary wood bunk, a coon hide that someone had been fleshing with a spoon.

I pulled myself up and went inside, tearing away the curtain, kicking back the door against the wall.

Except it did not fly back against the wall.

I felt the wood knock into meat and bone, a massive and dense weight that did not surrender space.

I clenched the .45 in both hands and pointed it at the enormous black shape behind the door, my finger slick with sweat inside the trigger guard.

My eyes wouldn't assimilate the naked man in front of me. Nor the fact that he was upside down. Nor what had been done to him.

The fence wire that had been looped around his ankles and notched into the roof beam was buried so deeply in his ankles that it was nearly invisible.

Helen lumbered into the room, her shotgun pointed in front of her. She lowered it to her side and looked at the hanging man.

'Oh boy,' she said. She propped open the shutter on a window and cleared her throat and spit. She looked back at me, then blew out her breath. Her face was discolored, as though she had been staring into a cold wind. 'I guess he got his,' she said. Then she went to the window again, with the back of her wrist to her mouth. But this time she collected herself, and when she looked at me again her face was composed.

'Come on, we can still nail him,' I said.

The plainclothes homicide investigator and two of the uniformed deputies were waiting for us at the bottom of the ladder.

'What's up there?' the plainclothes said. His eyes tried to peel meaning out of our faces. '*What*, it's some kind of company secret?'

'Go look for yourself. Be careful what you step in,' Helen said.

'Crown killed Mookie Zerrang. He couldn't have gone far,' I said.

'He ain't gone far at all,' the third deputy said, sloshing toward us from the opposite side of the woods. 'Look up yonder through that high spot.'

We all stared through the evenly spaced tree trunks at a dry stretch of compacted silt that humped out of the water like the back of a black whale. It was covered with palmettos and crisscrossed with the webbed tracks of nutria, and in the middle of the palmettos, squatting on his haunches, smoking a hand-rolled cigarette, was Aaron Crown.

We waded toward him, our guns still drawn. If he heard or saw us, or even cared if we were in his proximity, he showed no sign.

His body and clothes were painted with blood from his pate to the mud-encrusted basketball shoes he wore. His eyes, which were finally drained of all the heat and energy that had defined his life, seemed to look out of a scarlet mask. We stood in a circle around him, our weapons pointed at the ground. In the damp air, smoke hung at the corner of his mouth like wisps of cotton.

'You know about Sabelle?' I asked.

'That 'un in yonder couldn't talk about nothing else before he died,' he replied.

'You're an evil man, Aaron Crown,' I said.

'I reckon it otherwise.' He rubbed the cigarette's hot ash between his fingers until it was dead. 'If them TV people is out there, I need to wash up.'

He looked up at our faces, his lidless eyes waiting for an answer.

37

On Christmas morning I sat at the kitchen table and looked at a photograph in the *Daily Iberian* of Buford and Karyn dancing together at the country club. They looked like people who would live forever.

Bootsie paused behind me, her palm resting on my shoulder.

'What are you thinking about?' she asked.

'Jerry Joe Plumb . . . No journalist will ever mention his name in association with theirs, but he paid their dues for them.'

'He paid his own, too, Dave.'

'Maybe.'

The window was open and a balmy wind blew from my neighbor's pasture and swelled the curtains over the sink. I filled a cup with coffee and hot milk and walked outside in the sunshine. Alafair sat at the redwood picnic table, playing with Tripod in her lap and listening to the tape she had made of the records on Jerry Joe's jukebox. She flipped Tripod on his back and bounced him gently up and down by pulling his tail while he pushed at her forearm with his paws.

'Thanks for all the presents. It's a great Christmas,' she said.

'Thanks for everything you gave me, too,' I said.

'Can Tripod have some more eggnog ice cream?'

'Sure.'

'Those creeps are gone, aren't they?'

'Yeah, the worst of the lot are. The rest get it somewhere down the road. We just don't see it.'

I thought perhaps I might have to explain my remark, but I didn't. She had actually lived through more than I had in her young life, and her comprehension of the world was oftentimes far better than mine.

She went inside the house with Tripod under her arm, then came back out on the step.

'I forgot. We ate it all,' she said.

'There's some in the freezer down at the shop. I'll get it,' I said.

I walked down the slope through the leaves drifting out of the oak and pecan branches overhead. I had strung Christmas lights around boughs and holly and red ribbon on the weathered cypress walls, and Alafair had glued a Santa Claus made from satin wrapping paper to the door. The bayou was empty of boats, and the sound of my shoes was so loud on the dock that it echoed off the water and sent a cloud of robins clattering out of the trees.

I had gotten the ice cream from the game freezer and was about to lock up again when I saw Dock Green park a black Lincoln by the boat ramp and walk toward me.

'It's Christmas. We're closed,' I said.

'LaRose has got my wife up at his house,' he said.

'I don't believe that's true. Even if it is, she's a big girl and can make her own choices.'

'I can give you that guy, diced and fried.'

'Not interested.'

'It ain't right.'

He sat down at a spool table and stared out at the bayou. His neck was as stiff as a chunk of sewer pipe. A muscle jumped in his cheek.

'I think you were involved with Jerry Joe's death. I just can't prove it. But I don't have to talk with you, either. So how about getting out of here?' I said.

He rubbed the heel of his hand in one eye.

'I never killed nobody. I need Persephone back. It ain't right he can steal my wife, pull a gun on me, I can't do nothing about it . . . I told Seph this is how it'd be if we messed with people was born with money . . . They take, they don't give,' he said.

Then I realized he was drunk.

'Get a motel room or go back to your camp, Dock. I'll get somebody to drive you,' I said.

He rose to his feet, as though from a trance, and said, more to the wind than to me, 'He controls things above the ground, but he don't hear the voices that's down in the earth . . . They can call me a geek, it don't matter, her and me are forever.'

I went back into the shop and called for a cruiser. When I came outside again, he was gone.

That night Alafair and Bootsie and I went out to eat, then drove down East Main, through the corridor of live oaks, looking at the lights and decorations on the nineteenth-century homes along Bayou Teche. We passed the city hall and library, the flood-lit grotto, which contained a statue of Christ's mother, where the home of George Washington Cable had once stood, the darkened grounds and bamboo border around the

Shadows, and in the center of town the iron-and-wood drawbridge over the Teche.

I drove past the old Southern Pacific station and up the St Martinville road, and, without thinking, like a backward glance at absolved guilt, I let my eyes linger on the abandoned frame house where Karyn LaRose had grown up. The garage that had contained her father's boxes of gumballs and plastic monster teeth and vampire fingernails still stood at the front of the property, the doors padlocked, and I wondered when she drove past it if she ever saw the little girl who used to play there in the yard, her hands sticky with the rainbow seepage from the gum that mildewed and ran through the cracks inside.

'Look, up the road, y'all, it's a fire,' Alafair said.

Beyond the next curve you could see the reddish orange bloom in the sky, the smoke that trailed back across the moon. We pulled to the side of the road for a firetruck to pass.

'Dave, it's Buford and Karyn's house,' Bootsie said.

We came around the curve, and across the cleared acreage the house looked like it was lit from within by molten metal. Only one pump truck had arrived, and the firemen were pulling a hose from the truck toward the front porch.

I stopped on the opposite side of the road and ran toward the truck. I could already feel the heat from the house against my skin.

'Is anybody in there?' I said. The faces of the firemen looked like yellow tallow in the light from the flames.

'Somebody was at the window upstairs but they couldn't make it out,' a lieutenant said. 'You're from the sheriff's department, aren't you?'

'Right.'

'There's a trail of gasoline from the back of the house out to the stables. What the hell kind of security did y'all have out here?'

'Buford worried about Aaron Crown, not Dock Green,' I said.

'Who?' he said.

Another pump truck came up the road, but the heat had punched holes in the roof now, the poplars against the side wall were wrapped with fire, and the glow through the collapsing shingles bloomed in an ever-widening circumference, defining everything in red-black shapes that was Buford's – the brick stables and tack rooms, the fields that had already been harrowed for next year's planting, the company store with the barrels of pecans on each side of the front doors, the stark and leafless tree that his ancestors in the Knights of the White Camellia had used to lynch members of the carpetbag government, the horses with Mexican brands that spooked and thudded through the rolling hard-woods as though they had never been bridled or broken.

Then I saw Buford come through the front door, a water-soaked blanket held in a cone over his head.

He tore the blanket away and flung it aside, as though the blanket itself contained the heat that had scalded his body. He smelled like ashes and charcoal and scorched hair, and smoke rose in dirty strings from his clothes.

'Where is she?' he said, staring wild-eyed at the firemen in his yard.

'Who? Who else is in there?' a fireman said.

'Where is she, Dave?'

'I don't know, Buford,' I replied.

'She was on the stairs, right next to me . . .'

'She didn't make it out, partner,' I said.

I reached out to take his arm in my hand. I felt the smooth hardness of his triceps brush my palm, then he was gone, running toward the rectangle of flame beyond the Greek pillars on the front porch. A fireman in a canvas coat and a big hat tried to tackle him and hit hard and empty-armed against the brick walkway.

Buford went up the steps, his arms in front of his face, wavering for just a moment in the heat that withered his skin and chewed apart the interior of his house, then he crossed his forearms over his eyes and went through the flames and disappeared inside.

I heard a fireman yell, 'Pour it on him, pour it on him, pour it on him, goddamn it!'

The pressurized spray of water caromed off the doorway and dissected the vortex of fire that was dissolving the stairway, filling the chandeliers with music, eating the floor away, blowing windows out into the yard.

Then we saw them, just for a moment, like two featureless black silhouettes caught inside a furnace, joined at the hip, their hands stretched outward, as though they were offering a silent testimony about the meaning of their own lives before they stepped backward into the burning lake that had become their new province.

Epilogue

Spring didn't come for a long time that year. The days were cold well into March, the swamp gray with winterkill. Batist would run his trotlines each morning at sunrise, his pirogue knocking against the swollen base of the cypress trunks. I would watch him from the bait shop window while he retrieved each empty hook and rebaited it and dropped it back in the water, wiping the coldness off his hand on his trousers, the mist rising about his bent shoulders. Then he would come back inside, shivering unduly inside his quilted jacket, and we would drink coffee together and prepare the chickens and sausage links for a few fishermen or tourists who might be in that day.

Persephone and Dock Green were never seen again; some say they fled the country, perhaps to South America. The irony was that even though a filling station attendant in St Martinville identified Dock as the man who had bought gas in a can from him on the night Buford and Karyn died, the gas can found on the LaRose plantation had no fingerprints on it, and without an eyewitness to the arson Dock would have never been convicted.

The greater truth was that Dock Green's strain of madness had always served a function, just as Aaron Crown's had, and the new governor of Louisiana, a practical-minded businessman, was not given to brooding over past events and letting them encumber his vision of the future.

Jimmy Ray Dixon?

He has a late-hour radio talk show in New Orleans now, and with some regularity he tells his listeners that his brother's spirit has finally been laid to rest. Why now? He doesn't answer that question. He's not comfortable with the mention of Mookie Zerrang's name, and when he hears it, his rhetoric becomes more religious and abstruse.

Dock Green's girls still work the same bars and street corners, Jimmy Ray jerks his listeners around and they love him for it, and Aaron Crown sits in a maximum security unit at Angola, denying his guilt to European journalists who have done front-page features on him.

The players don't change, just the audience.

But maybe that's just a police officer's jaded interpretation of things, since few seem interested in the death of Short Boy Jerry, a man who everyone knew operated by choice on the edge of the New Orleans underworld and hence invited his fate.

No draconian sword fell into the life of Clay Mason, either. He was expelled from Mexico and his property seized, but in a short while he was visiting college campuses again, being interviewed on the Internet, selling his shuck on TV. A patron of the arts bought him a home in the hills outside Santa Fe, where his proselytes and fellow revelers from the 1960s gathered and a famous New York photographer caught him out on the terrace, his face as craggy and ageless as the blue ring of mountains behind him, a sweat-banded Stetson crimped on his head, his pixie eyes looking directly into the camera. The cutline under the photo read, 'A Lion in Winter.'

But I think I've learned not to grieve on the world's ways, at least not when spring is at hand.

It rained hard the third week in March, then the sky broke clear and one morning the new season was upon us and the swamp was green again, the new leaves on the flooded stands of trees rippling in the breeze off the Gulf, the trunks of the cypress painted with lichen.

Alafair and I rode her Appaloosa bareback down the road, like two wooden clothespins mounted on its spine, and put up a kite in the wind. The kite was a big one, the paper emblazoned with an American flag, and it rose quickly into the sky, higher and higher, until it was only a distant speck above the sugarcane fields to the north.

In my mind's eye I saw the LaRose plantation from the height of Alafair's kite, the rolling hardwoods and the squared fields where Confederate and federal calvary had charged and killed one another and left their horses screaming and disemboweled among the cane stubble, and I wondered what Darwinian moment had to effect itself before we devolved from children flying paper flags in the sky to half-formed creatures thundering in a wail of horns down the road to Roncevaux.

That night we ate crawfish at Possum's in St Martinville and went by the old church in the center of town and walked under the Evangeline Oaks next to the Teche where I first kissed Bootsie in the summer of 1957 and actually felt the tree limbs spin over my head. Alafair was out on the dock behind the church, dropping pieces of bread in a column of electric light onto the water's surface. Bootsie slipped her arm around my waist and bumped me with her hip.

'What are you thinking about, slick?' she said.

'You can't ever tell,' I said.

That night she and I ate a piece of pecan pie on the picnic table in the backyard, then, like reaching your hand into the past, like giving yourself over to the world of play and nonreason that takes you outside of time, I punched on Alafair's stereo player that contained the taped recording of all the records on Jerry Joe's jukebox.

We danced to 'Jolie Blon' and 'Tes Yeux Bleu,' then kicked it up into overdrive with 'Bony Maronie,' 'Long Tall Sally,' and 'Short Fat Fanny.' Out in the darkness, beyond the glow of the flood lamp in the mimosa tree, my neighbor's cattle were bunching in the coulee as an electric storm veined the sky with lightning in the south. The air was suddenly cool and thick with the sulfurous smell of ozone, the wind blowing dust out of the new cane, the wisteria on our garage flattening against the board walls while shadows and protean shapes formed and reformed themselves, like Greek players on an outdoor stage beckoning to us, luring us from pastoral chores into an amphitheater by the sea, where we would witness once again the unfinished story of ourselves.

SUNSET LIMITED

For Bill and Susan Nelson

I would like to thank the following attorneys for all the legal information they have provided me in the writing of my books over the years: my son James L. Burke, Jr., and my daughter Alafair Burke and my cousins Dracos Burke and Porteus Burke.

I would also like once again to thank my wife Pearl, my editor Patricia Mulcahy, and my agent Philip Spitzer for the many years they have been on board.

I'd also like to thank my daughters Pamela McDavid and Andree Walsh, from whom I ask advice on virtually everything.

1

I had seen a dawn like this one only twice in my life: once in Vietnam, after a Bouncing Betty had risen from the earth on a night trail and twisted its tentacles of light around my thighs, and years earlier outside of Franklin, Louisiana, when my father and I discovered the body of a labor organizer who had been crucified with sixteen-penny nails, ankle and wrist, against a barn wall.

Just before the sun broke above the Gulf's rim, the wind, which had blown the waves with ropes of foam all night, suddenly died and the sky became as white and brightly grained as polished bone, as though all color had been bled out of the air, and the gulls that had swooped and glided over my wake lifted into the haze and the swells flattened into an undulating sheet of liquid tin dimpled by the leathery backs of stingrays.

The eastern horizon was strung with rain clouds and the sun should have risen out of the water like a mist-shrouded egg yolk, but it didn't. Its red light mushroomed along the horizon, then rose into the sky in a cross, burning in the center, as though fire were trying to take the shape of a man, and the water turned the heavy dark color of blood.

Maybe the strange light at dawn was only coincidence and had nothing to do with the return to New Iberia of Megan Flynn, who, like a sin we had concealed in the confessional, vexed our conscience, or worse, rekindled our envy.

But I knew in my heart it was not coincidence, no more so than the fact that the man crucified against the barn wall was Megan's father and that Megan herself was waiting for me at my dock and bait shop, fifteen miles south of New Iberia, when Clete Purcel, my old Homicide partner from the First District in New Orleans, and I cut the engines on my cabin cruiser and floated through the hyacinths on our wake, the mud billowing in clouds that were as bright as yellow paint under the stern.

It was sprinkling now, and she wore an orange silk shirt and khaki slacks and sandals, her funny straw hat spotted with rain, her hair dark

533

red against the gloom of the day, her face glowing with a smile that was like a thorn in the heart.

Clete stood by the gunnel and looked at her and puckered his mouth. 'Wow,' he said under his breath.

She was one of those rare women gifted with eyes that could linger briefly on yours and make you feel, rightly or wrongly, you were genuinely invited into the mystery of her life.

'I've seen her somewhere,' Clete said as he prepared to climb out on the bow.

'Last week's *Newsweek* magazine,' I said.

'That's it. She won a Pulitzer Prize or something. There was a picture of her hanging out of a slick,' he said. His gum snapped in his jaw.

She had been on the cover, wearing camouflage pants and a T-shirt, with dog tags round her neck, the downdraft of the British helicopter whipping her hair and flattening her clothes against her body, the strap of her camera laced around one wrist, while, below, Serbian armor burned in columns of red and black smoke.

But I remembered another Megan, too: the in-your-face orphan of years ago, who, with her brother, would run away from foster homes in Louisiana and Colorado, until they were old enough to finally disappear into that wandering army of fruit pickers and wheat harvesters whom their father, an unrepentant IWW radical, had spent a lifetime trying to organize.

I stepped off the bow onto the dock and walked toward my truck to back the trailer down the ramp. I didn't mean to be impolite. I admired the Flynns, but you paid a price for their friendship and proximity to the vessel of social anger their lives had become.

'Not glad to see me, Streak?' she said.

'Always glad. How you doin', Megan?'

She looked over my shoulder at Clete Purcel, who had pulled the port side of the boat flush into the rubber tires on my dock and was unloading the cooler and rods out of the stern. Clete's thick arms and fire-hydrant neck were peeling and red with fresh sunburn. When he stooped over with the cooler, his tropical shirt split across his back. He grinned at us and shrugged his shoulders.

'That one had to come out of the Irish Channel,' she said.

'You're not a fisher, Meg. You out here on business?'

'You know who Cool Breeze Broussard is?' she asked.

'A house creep and general thief.'

'He says your parish lockup is a toilet. He says your jailer is a sadist.'

'We lost the old jailer. I've been on leave. I don't know much about the new guy.'

534

'Cool Breeze says inmates are gagged and handcuffed to a detention chair. They have to sit in their own excrement. The U.S. Department of Justice believes him.'

'Jails are bad places. Talk to the sheriff, Megan. I'm off the clock.'

'Typical New Iberia. Bullshit over humanity.'

'See you around,' I said, and walked to my truck. Rain was pinging in large, cold drops on the tin roof of the bait shop.

'Cool Breeze said you were stand-up. He's in lockdown now because he dimed the jailer. I'll tell him you were off the clock,' she said.

'This town didn't kill your father.'

'No, they just put me and my brother in an orphanage where we polished floors with our knees. Tell your Irish friend he's beautiful. Come out to the house and visit us, Streak,' she said, and walked across the dirt road to where she had parked her car under the trees in my drive.

Up on the dock, Clete poured the crushed ice and canned drinks and speckled trout out of the cooler. The trout looked stiff and cold on the board planks.

'You ever hear anything about prisoners being gagged and cuffed to chairs in the Iberia Parish Prison?' I asked.

'That's what that was about? Maybe she ought to check out what those guys did to get in there.'

'She said you were beautiful.'

'She did?' He looked down the road where her car was disappearing under the canopy of oaks that grew along the bayou. Then he cracked a Budweiser and flipped me a can of diet Dr. Pepper. The scar over his left eyebrow flattened against his skull when he grinned.

The turnkey had been a brig chaser in the Marine Corps and still wore his hair buzzed into the scalp and shaved in a razor-neat line on the back of his neck. His body was lean and braided with muscle, his walk as measured and erect as if he were on a parade ground. He unlocked the cell at the far end of the corridor, hooked up Willie Cool Breeze Broussard in waist and leg manacles, and escorted him with one hand to the door of the interview room, where I waited.

'Think he's going to run on you, Top?' I said.

'He runs at the mouth, that's what he does.'

The turnkey closed the door behind us. Cool Breeze looked like two hundred pounds of soft black chocolate poured inside jailhouse denims. His head was bald, lacquered with wax, shiny as horn, his eyes drooping at the corners like a prizefighter's. It was hard to believe he was a second-story man and four-time loser.

'If they're jamming you up, Cool Breeze, it's not on your sheet,' I said.

'What you call Isolation?'

'The screw says you asked for lockdown.'

His wrists were immobilized by the cuffs attached to the chain around his waist. He shifted in his chair and looked sideways at the door.

'I was on Camp J up at Angola. It's worse in here. A hack made a kid blow him at gunpoint,' he said.

'I don't want to offend you, Breeze, but this isn't your style.'

'What ain't?'

'You're not one to rat out anybody, not even a bad screw.'

His eyes shifted back and forth inside his face. He rubbed his nose on his shoulder.

'I'm down on this VCR beef. A truckload of them. What makes it double bad is I boosted the load from a Giacano warehouse in Lake Charles. I need to get some distance between me and my problems, maybe like in the islands, know what I saying?'

'Sounds reasonable.'

'No, you don't get it. The Giacanos are tied into some guys in New York City making dubs of movies, maybe a hundred t'ousand of them a week. So they buy lots of VCRs, cut-rate prices, Cool Breeze Midnight Supply Service, you wit' me?'

'You've been selling the Giacanos their own equipment? You're establishing new standards, Breeze.'

He smiled slightly, but the peculiar downward slope of his eyes gave his expression a melancholy cast, like a bloodhound's. He shook his head.

'You still don't see it, Robicheaux. None of these guys are that smart. They started making dubs of them kung fu movies from Hong Kong. The money behind them kung fus comes from some very bad guys. You heard of the Triads?'

'We're talking about China White?'

'That's how it gets washed, my man.'

I took out my business card and wrote my home number and the number of the bait shop on the back. I leaned across the table and slipped it in his shirt pocket.

'Watch your butt in here, Breeze, particularly that ex-jarhead.'

'Meet the jailer. It's easy to catch him after five. He like to work late, when they ain't no visitors around.'

Megan's brother Cisco owned a home up Bayou Teche, just south of Loreauville. It was built in the style of the West Indies, one story and rambling, shaded by oaks, with a wide, elevated gallery, green, ventilated window shutters, and fern baskets hanging from the eaves. Cisco and his friends, movie people like himself, came and went with the seasons, shooting ducks in the wetlands, fishing for tarpon and speckled trout in the Gulf. Their attitudes were those of people who used geographical areas and social cultures as playgrounds and nothing more. Their glittering lawn parties, which we saw only from the road through the myrtle bushes and azalea and banana trees that fringed his property, were the stuff of legend in our small sugarcane town along the Teche.

I had never understood Cisco. He was tough, like his sister, and he had the same good looks they had both inherited from their father, but when his reddish-brown eyes settled on yours, he seemed to search inside your skin for something he wanted, perhaps coveted, yet couldn't define. Then the moment would pass and his attention would wander away like a balloon on the breeze.

He had dug irrigation ditches and worked the fruit orchards in the San Joaquin and had ended up in Hollywood as a road-wise, city-library-educated street kid who was dumbfounded when he discovered his handsome face and seminal prowess could earn him access to a movie lot, first as an extra, then as a stuntman.

It wasn't long before he realized he was not only braver than the actors whose deeds he performed but that he was more intelligent than most of them as well. He co-wrote scripts for five years, formed an independent production group with two Vietnam combat veterans, and put together a low-budget film on the lives of migrant farmworkers that won prizes in France and Italy.

His next film opened in theaters all over the United States.

Now Cisco had an office on Sunset Boulevard, a home in Pacific Palisades, and membership in that magic world where bougainvillea and ocean sun were just the token symbols of the health and riches that southern California could bestow on its own.

It was late Sunday evening when I turned off the state road and drove up the gravel lane toward his veranda. His lawn was blue-green with St. Augustine grass and smelled of chemical fertilizer and the water sprinklers twirling between the oak and pine trees. I could see him working out on a pair of parallel bars in the side yard, his bare arms and shoulders cording with muscle and vein, his skin painted with the sun's late red light through the cypresses on the bayou.

As always, Cisco was courteous and hospitable, but in a way that made you feel his behavior was learned rather than natural, a barrier rather than an invitation.

'Megan? No, she had to fly to New Orleans. Can I help you with something?' he said. Before I could answer, he said, 'Come on inside. I need something cold. How do you guys live here in the summer?'

All the furniture in the living room was white, the floor covered with straw mats, blond, wood-bladed ceiling fans turning overhead. He stood shirtless and barefooted at a wet bar and filled a tall glass with crushed ice and collins mix and cherries. The hair on his stomach looked like flattened strands of red wire above the beltline of his yellow slacks.

'It was about an inmate in the parish prison, a guy named Cool Breeze Broussard,' I said.

He drank from his glass, his eyes empty. 'You want me to tell her something?' he asked.

'Maybe this guy was mistreated at the jail, but I think his real problem is with some mobbed-up dudes in New Orleans. Anyway, she can give me a call.'

'Cool Breeze Broussard. That's quite a name.'

'It might end up in one of your movies, huh?'

'You can't ever tell,' he replied, and smiled.

On one wall were framed still shots from Cisco's films, and on a side wall photographs that were all milestones in Megan's career: a ragged ditch strewn with the bodies of civilians in Guatemala, African children whose emaciated faces were crawling with blowflies, French Legionnaires pinned down behind sandbags while mortar rounds geysered dirt above their heads.

But, oddly, the color photograph that had launched her career and had made *Life* magazine was located at the bottom corner of the collection. It had been shot in the opening of a storm drain that bled into the Mississippi just as an enormous black man, in New Orleans City Prison denims strung with sewage, had burst out of the darkness into the fresh air, his hands raised toward the sun, as though he were trying to pay tribute to its energy and power. But a round from a sharpshooter's rifle had torn through his throat, exiting in a bloody mist, twisting his mouth open like that of a man experiencing orgasm.

A second framed photograph showed five uniformed cops looking down at the body, which seemed shrunken and without personality in death. A smiling crew-cropped man in civilian clothes was staring directly at the camera in the foreground, a red apple with a white hunk bitten out of it cupped in his palm.

'What are you thinking about?' Cisco asked.

'Seems like an inconspicuous place to put these,' I said.

'The guy paid some hard dues. For Megan and me, both,' he said.

'Both?'

'I was her assistant on that shot, inside the pipe when those cops decided he'd make good dog food. Look, you think Hollywood's the only meat market out there? The cops got citations. The black guy got to rape a sixteen-year-old white girl before he went out. I get to hang his picture on the wall of a seven-hundred-thousand-dollar house. The only person who didn't get a trade-off was the high school girl.'

'I see. Well, I guess I'd better be going.'

Through the French doors I saw a man of about fifty walk down the veranda in khaki shorts and slippers with his shirt unbuttoned on his concave chest. He sat down in a reclining chair with a magazine and lit a cigar.

'That's Billy Holtzner. You want to meet him?' Cisco said.

'Who?'

'When the Pope visited the studio about seven years ago, Billy asked him if he had a script. Wait here a minute.'

I tried to stop him but it was too late. The rudeness of his having to ask permission for me to be introduced seemed to elude him. I saw him bend down toward the man named Holtzner and speak in a low voice, while Holtzner puffed on his cigar and looked at nothing. Then Cisco raised up and came back inside, turning up his palms awkwardly at his sides, his eyes askance with embarrassment.

'Billy's head is all tied up with a project right now. He's kind of intense when he's in preproduction.' He tried to laugh.

'You're looking solid, Cisco.'

'Orange juice and wheat germ and three-mile runs along the surf. It's the only life.'

'Tell Megan I'm sorry I missed her.'

'I apologize about Billy. He's a good guy. He's just eccentric.'

'You know anything about movie dubs?'

'Yeah, they cost the industry a lot of money. That's got something to do with this guy Broussard?'

'You got me.'

When I walked out the front door the man in the reclining chair had turned off the bug light and was smoking his cigar reflectively, one knee crossed over the other. I could feel his eyes on me, taking my measure. I nodded at him, but he didn't respond. The ash of his cigar glowed like a hot coal in the shadows.

2

The jailer, Alex Guidry, lived outside of town on a ten-acre horse farm devoid of trees or shade. The sun's heat pooled in the tin roofs of his outbuildings, and grit and desiccated manure blew out of his horse lots. His oblong 1960s red-brick house, its central-air-conditioning units roaring outside a back window twenty-four hours a day, looked like a utilitarian fortress constructed for no other purpose than to repel the elements.

His family had worked for a sugar mill down toward New Orleans, and his wife's father used to sell Negro burial insurance, but I knew little else about him. He was one of those aging, well-preserved men with whom you associate a golf photo on the local sports page, membership in a self-congratulatory civic club, a charitable drive that is of no consequence.

Or was there something else, a vague and ugly story years back? I couldn't remember.

Sunday afternoon I parked my pickup truck by his stable and walked past a chain-link dog pen to the riding ring. The dog pen exploded with the barking of two German shepherds who caromed off the fencing, their teeth bared, their paws skittering the feces that lay baked on the hot concrete pad.

Alex Guidry cantered a black gelding in a circle, his booted calves fitted with English spurs. The gelding's neck and sides were iridescent with sweat. Guidry sawed the bit back in the gelding's mouth.

'What is it?' he said.

'I'm Dave Robicheaux. I called earlier.'

He wore tan riding pants and a form-fitting white polo shirt. He dismounted and wiped the sweat off his face with a towel and threw it to a black man who had come out of the stable to take the horse.

'You want to know if this guy Broussard was in the detention chair? The answer is no,' he said.

'He says you've put other inmates in there. For days.'

'Then he's lying.'

'You have a detention chair, though, don't you?'

'For inmates who are out of control, who don't respond to Isolation.'

'You gag them?'

'No.'

I rubbed the back of my neck and looked at the dog pen. The water bowl was turned over and flies boiled in the door of the small doghouse that gave the only relief from the sun.

'You've got a lot of room here. You can't let your dogs run?' I said. I tried to smile.

'Anything else, Mr. Robicheaux?'

'Yeah. Nothing better happen to Cool Breeze while he's in your custody.'

'I'll keep that in mind, sir. Close the gate on your way out, please.'

I got back in my truck and drove down the shell road toward the cattle guard. A half dozen Red Angus grazed in Guidry's pasture, while snowy egrets perched on their backs.

Then I remembered. It was ten or eleven years back, and Alex Guidry had been charged with shooting a neighbor's dog. Guidry had claimed the dog had attacked one of his calves and eaten its entrails, but the neighbor told another story, that Guidry had baited a steel trap for the animal and had killed it out of sheer meanness.

I looked into the rearview mirror and saw him watching me from the end of the shell drive, his legs slightly spread, a leather riding crop hanging from his wrist.

Monday morning I returned to work at the Iberia Parish Sheriff's Department and took my mail out of my pigeonhole and tapped on the sheriff's office.

He tilted back in his swivel chair and smiled when he saw me. His jowls were flecked with tiny blue and red veins that looked like fresh ink on a map when his temper flared. He had shaved too close and there was a piece of bloody tissue paper stuck in the cleft in his chin. Unconsciously he kept stuffing his shirt down over his paunch into his gunbelt.

'You mind if I come back to work a week early?' I asked.

'This have anything to do with Cool Breeze Broussard's complaint to the Justice Department?'

'I went out to Alex Guidry's place yesterday. How'd we end up with a guy like that as our jailer?'

'It's not a job people line up for,' the sheriff said. He scratched his forehead. 'You've got an FBI agent in your office right now, some gal named Adrien Glazier. You know her?'

'Nope. How'd she know I was going to be here?'

'She called your house first. Your wife told her. Anyway, I'm glad you're back. I want this bullshit at the jail cleared up. We just got a very weird case that was thrown in our face from St. Mary Parish.'

He opened a manila folder and put on his glasses and peered down at the fax sheets in his fingers. This is the story he told me.

Three months ago, under a moon haloed with a rain ring and sky filled with dust blowing out of the sugarcane fields, a seventeen-year-old black girl named Sunshine Labiche claimed two white boys forced her car off a dirt road into a ditch. They dragged her from behind the wheel, walked her by each arm into a cane field, then took turns raping and sodomizing her.

The next morning she identified both boys from a book of mug shots. They were brothers, from St. Mary Parish, but four months earlier they had been arrested for a convenience store holdup in New Iberia and had been released for lack of evidence.

This time they should have gone down.

They didn't.

Both had alibis, and the girl admitted she had been smoking rock with her boyfriend before she was raped. She dropped the charges.

Late Saturday afternoon an unmarked car came to the farmhouse of the two brothers over in St. Mary Parish. The father, who was bedridden in the front room, watched the visitors, unbeknown to them, through a crack in the blinds. The driver of the car wore a green uniform, like sheriff's deputies in Iberia Parish, and sunglasses and stayed behind the wheel, while a second man, in civilian clothes and a Panama hat, went to the gallery and explained to the two brothers they only had to clear up a couple of questions in New Iberia, then they would be driven back home.

'It ain't gonna take five minutes. We know you boys didn't have to come all the way over to Iberia Parish just to change your luck,' he said.

The brothers were not cuffed; in fact, they were allowed to take a twelve-pack of beer with them to drink in the back seat.

A half hour later, just at sunset, a student from USL, who was camped out in the Atchafalaya swamp, looked through the flooded willow and gum trees that surrounded his houseboat and saw a car stop on the levee. Two older men and two boys got out. One of the older men wore a uniform. They all held cans of beer in their hands; all of them urinated off the levee into the cattails.

Then the two boys, dressed in jeans and Clorox-stained print shirts with the sleeves cut off at the armpits, realized something was wrong.

542

They turned and stared stupidly at their companions, who had stepped backward up the levee and were now holding pistols in their hands.

The boys tried to argue, holding their palms outward, as though they were pushing back an invisible adversary. Their arms were olive with suntan, scrolled with reformatory tattoos, their hair spiked in points with butch wax. The man in uniform raised his gun and shouted an unintelligible order at them, motioning at the ground. When the boys did not respond, the second armed man, who wore a Panama hat, turned them toward the water with his hand, almost gently, inserted his shoe against the calf of one, then the other, pushing them to their knees, as though he was arranging manikins in a show window. Then he rejoined the man in uniform up the bank. One of the boys kept looking back fearfully over his shoulder. The other was weeping uncontrollably, his chin tilted upward, his arms stiff at his sides, his eyes tightly shut.

The men with guns were silhouetted against a molten red sun that had sunk across the top of the levee. Just as a flock of ducks flapped across the sun, the gunmen clasped their weapons with both hands and started shooting. But because of the fading light, or perhaps the nature of their deed, their aim was bad.

Both victims tried to rise from their knees, their bodies convulsing simultaneously from the impact of the rounds.

The witness said, 'Their guns just kept popping. It looked like somebody was blowing chunks out of a watermelon.'

After it was over, smoke drifted out over the water and the shooter in the Panama hat took close-up flash pictures with a Polaroid camera.

'The witness used a pair of binoculars. He says the guy in the green uniform had our department patch on his sleeve,' the sheriff said.

'White rogue cops avenging the rape of a black girl?'

'Look, get that FBI agent out of here, will you?'

He looked at the question in my face.

'She's got a broom up her ass.' He rubbed his fingers across his mouth. 'Did I say that? I'm going to go back to the laundry business. A bad day used to be washing somebody's golf socks,' he said.

I looked through my office window at the FBI agent named Adrien Glazier. She sat with her legs crossed, her back to me, in a powder-blue suit and white blouse, writing on a legal pad. Her handwriting was filled with severe slants and slashes, with points in the letters that reminded me of incisor teeth.

When I opened the door she looked at me with ice-blue eyes that could have been taken out of a Viking's face.

'I visited William Broussard last night. He seems to think you're going to get him out of the parish prison,' she said.

'Cool Breeze? He knows better than that.'

'Does he?'

I waited. Her hair was ash-blond, wispy and broken on the ends, her face big-boned and adversarial. She was one of those you instinctively know have a carefully nursed reservoir of anger they draw upon as needed, in the same way others make use of daily prayer. My stare broke.

'Sorry. Is that a question?' I said.

'You don't have any business indicating to this man you can make deals for him,' she said.

I sat down behind my desk and glanced out the window, wishing I could escape back into the coolness of the morning, the streets that were sprinkled with rain, the palm fronds lifting and clattering in the wind.

I picked up a stray paper clip and dropped it in my desk drawer and closed the drawer. Her eyes never left my face or relented in their accusation.

'What if the prosecutor's office does cut him loose? What's it to you?' I said.

'You're interfering in a federal investigation. Evidently you have a reputation for it.'

'I think the truth is you want his *cojones* in a vise. You'll arrange some slack for him after he rats out some guys you can't make a case against.'

She uncrossed her legs and leaned forward. She cocked her elbow on my desk and let one finger droop forward at my face.

'Megan Flynn is an opportunistic bitch. What she didn't get on her back, she got through posing as the Joan of Arc of oppressed people. You let her and her brother jerk your pud, then you're dumber than the people in my office say you are,' she said.

'This has to be a put-on.'

She pulled a manila folder out from under her legal pad and dropped it on my desk blotter.

'Those photos are of a guy named Swede Boxleiter. They were taken in the yard at the Colorado state pen in Canon City. What they don't show is the murder he committed in broad daylight with a camera following him around the yard. That's how good he is,' she said.

His head and face were like those of a misshaped Marxist intellectual, the yellow hair close-cropped on the scalp, the forehead and brainpan too large, the cheeks tapering away to a mouth that was so small it looked obscene. He wore granny glasses on a chiseled nose, and a rotted and torn weight lifter's shirt on a torso that rippled with cartilage.

The shots had been taken from an upper story or guard tower with a zoom lens. They showed him moving through the clusters of convicts in the yard, faces turning toward him the way bait fish reflect light when a barracuda swims toward their perimeter. A fat man was leaning against the far wall, one hand squeezed on his scrotum, while he told a story to a half circle of his fellow inmates. His lips were twisted with a word he was forming, purple from a lollypop he had been eating. The man named Swede Boxleiter passed an inmate who held a tape-wrapped ribbon of silver behind his back. After Swede Boxleiter had walked by, the man whose palm seemed to have caught the sun like a heliograph now had his hands stuffed in his pockets.

The second-to-last photo showed a crowd at the wall like early men gathered on the rim of a pit to witness the death throes and communal roasting of an impaled mammoth.

Then the yard was empty, except for the fat man, the gash across his windpipe bubbling with saliva and blood, the tape-wrapped shank discarded in the red soup on his chest.

'Boxleiter is buddies with Cisco Flynn. They were in the same state home in Denver. Maybe you'll get to meet him. He got out three days ago,' she said.

'Ms. Glazier, I'd like to—'

'It's Special Agent Glazier.'

'Right. I'd like to talk with you, but . . . Look, why not let us take care of our own problems?'

'What a laugh.' She stood up and gazed down at me. 'Here it is. Hong Kong is going to become the property of Mainland China soon. There're some people we want to put out of business before we have to deal with Beijing to get at them. Got the big picture?'

'Not really. You know how it is out here in the provinces, swatting mosquitoes, arresting people for stealing hog manure, that sort of thing.'

She laughed to herself and dropped her card on my desk, then walked out of my office and left the door open as though she would not touch anything in our department unless it was absolutely necessary.

At noon I drove down the dirt road by the bayou toward my dock and bait shop. Through the oak trees that lined the shoulder I could see the wide gallery and purple-streaked tin roof of my house up the slope. It had rained again during the morning, and the cypress planks in the walls were stained the color of dark tea, the hanging baskets of impatiens blowing strings of water in the wind. My adopted daughter Alafair, whom I had pulled from a submerged plane wreck out on the salt when she was a little girl, sat in her pirogue on the far side of the bayou, fly-casting a popping bug into the shallows.

I walked down on the dock and leaned against the railing. I could smell the salty odor of humus and schooled-up fish and trapped water out in the swamp. Alafair's skin was bladed with the shadows of a willow tree, her hair tied up on her head with a blue bandanna, her hair so black it seemed to fill with lights when she brushed it. She had been born in a primitive village in El Salvador, her family the target of death squads because they had sold a case of Pepsi-Cola to the rebels. Now she was almost sixteen, her Spanish and early childhood all but forgotten. But sometimes at night she cried out in her sleep and would have to be shaken from dreams filled with the marching boots of soldiers, peasants with their thumbs wired together behind them, the dry ratcheting sound of a bolt being pulled back on an automatic weapon.

'Wrong time of day and too much rain,' I said.

'Oh, yeah?' she said.

She lifted the fly rod into the air, whipping the popping bug over her head, then laying it on the edge of the lily pads. She flicked her wrist so the bug popped audibly in the water, then a goggle-eye perch rose like a green-and-gold bubble out of the silt and broke the surface, its dorsal fin hard and spiked and shiny in the sunlight, the hook and feathered balsa-wood lure protruding from the side of its mouth.

Alafair held the fly rod up as it quivered and arched toward the water, retrieving the line with her left hand, guiding the goggle-eye between the islands of floating hyacinths, until she could lift it wet and flopping into the bottom of the pirogue.

'Not bad,' I said.

'You had another week off. Why'd you go back to work?' she said.

'Long story. See you inside.'

'No, wait,' she said, and set her rod down in the pirogue and paddled across the bayou to the concrete boat ramp. She stepped out into the water with a stringer of catfish and perch wrapped around her wrist, and climbed the wood steps onto the dock. In the last two years all the baby fat had melted off her body, and her face and figure had taken on the appearance of a mature woman's. When she worked with me in the bait shop, most of our male customers made a point of focusing their attention everywhere in the room except on Alafair.

'A lady named Ms. Flynn was here. Bootsie told me what happened to her father. You found him, Dave?' she said.

'My dad and I did.'

'He was crucified?'

'It happened a long time ago, Alf.'

'The people who did it never got caught? That's sickening.'

'Maybe they took their own fall down the road. They all do, one way or another.'

546

'It's not enough.' Her face seemed heated, pinched, as though by an old memory.

'You want some help cleaning those fish?' I asked.

Her eyes looked at me again, then cleared. 'What would you do if I said yeah?' she asked. She swung the stringer so it touched the end of my polished loafer.

'Megan wants me to get her inside the jail to take pictures?' I said to Bootsie in the kitchen.

'She seems to think you're a pretty influential guy,' she replied.

Bootsie was bent over the sink, scrubbing the burnt grease off a stove tray, her strong arms swollen with her work; her polo shirt had pulled up over her jeans, exposing the soft taper of her hips. She had the most beautiful hair I had ever seen in a woman. It was the color of honey, with caramel swirls in it, and its thickness and the way she wore it up on her head seemed to make the skin of her face even more pink and lovely.

'Is there anything else I can arrange? An audience with the Pope?' I said.

She turned from the drainboard and dried her hands on a towel.

'That woman's after something else. I just don't know what it is,' she said.

'The Flynns are complicated people.'

'They have a way of finding war zones to play in. Don't let her take you over the hurdles, Streak.'

I hit her on the rump with the palm of my hand. She wadded up the dish towel and threw it past my head.

We ate lunch on the redwood table under the mimosa tree in the back yard. Beyond the duck pond at the back of our property my neighbor's sugarcane was tall and green and marbled with the shadows of clouds. The bamboo and periwinkles that grew along our coulee rippled in the wind, and I could smell rain and electricity in the south.

'What's in that brown envelope you brought home?' Bootsie asked.

'Pictures of a mainline sociopath in the Colorado pen.'

'Why bring them home?'

'I've seen the guy. I'm sure of it. But I can't remember where.'

'Around here?'

'No. Somewhere else. The top of his head looks like a yellow cake but he has no jaws. An obnoxious FBI agent told me he's pals with Cisco Flynn.'

'A head like a yellow cake? A mainline con? Friends with Cisco Flynn?'

'Yeah.'

'Wonderful.'

That night I dreamed of the man named Swede Boxleiter. He was crouched on his haunches in the darkened exercise yard of a prison, smoking a cigarette, his granny glasses glinting in the humid glow of lights on the guard towers. The predawn hours were cool and filled with the smells of sage, water coursing over boulders in a canyon riverbed, pine needles layered on the forest floor. A wet, red dust hung in the air, and the moon seemed to rise through it, above the mountain's rim, like ivory skeined with dyed thread.

But the man named Swede Boxleiter was not one to concern himself with the details of the alpine environment he found himself in. The measure of his life and himself was the reflection he saw in the eyes of others, the fear that twitched in their faces, the unbearable tension he could create in a cell or at a dining table simply by not speaking.

He didn't need a punk or prune-o or the narcissistic pleasure of clanking iron in the yard or even masturbation for release from the energies that, unsatiated, could cause him to wake in the middle of the night and sit in a square of moonlight as though he were on an airless plateau that echoed with the cries of animals. Sometimes he smiled to himself and fantasized about telling the prison psychologist what he really felt inside, the pleasure that climbed through the tendons in his arm when he clasped a shank that had been ground from a piece of angle iron on an emery wheel in the shop, the intimacy of that last moment when he looked into the eyes of the hit. The dam that seemed to break in his loins was like water splitting the bottom of a paper bag.

But prison shrinks were not people you confided in, at least if you were put together like Swede Boxleiter and ever wanted to make the street again.

In my dream he rose from his crouched position, reached up and touched the moon, as though to despoil it, but instead wiped away the red skein from one corner with his fingertip and exposed a brilliant white cup of light.

I sat up in bed, the window fan spinning its shadows on my skin, and remembered where I had seen him.

Early the next morning I went to the city library on East Main Street and dug out the old *Life* magazine in which Megan's photos of a black rapist's death inside a storm drain had launched her career. Opposite the full-page shot of the black man reaching out futilely for the sunlight was the group photo of five uniformed cops staring down at his body. In the foreground was Swede Boxleiter, holding a Red Delicious apple with a white divot bitten out of it, his smile a thin worm of private pleasure stitched across his face.

*

But I wasn't going to take on the Flynns' problems, I told myself, or worry about a genetic misfit in the Colorado pen.

I was still telling myself that late that night when Mout' Broussard, New Iberia's legendary shoeshine man and Cool Breeze's father, called the bait shop and told me his son had just escaped from the parish prison.

3

Cajuns often have trouble with the *th* sound in English, and as a result they drop the *h* or pronounce the *t* as a *d*. Hence, the town's collectively owned shoeshine man, Mouth Broussard, was always referred to as Mout'. For decades he operated his shoeshine stand under the colonnade in front of the old Frederic Hotel, a wonderful two-story stucco building with Italian marble columns inside, a ballroom, a saloon with a railed mahogany bar, potted palms and slot and racehorse machines in the lobby, and an elevator that looked like a polished brass birdcage.

Mout' was built like a haystack and never worked without a cigar stub in the corner of his mouth. He wore an oversized gray smock, the pockets stuffed with brushes and buffing rags ribbed with black and oxblood stains. The drawers under the two elevated chairs on the stand were loaded with bottles of liquid polish, cans of wax and saddle soap, toothbrushes and steel dental picks he used to clean the welts and stitches around the edges of the shoe. He could pop his buffing rags with a speed and rhythm that never failed to command a silent respect from everyone who watched.

Mout' caught all the traffic walking from the Southern Pacific passenger station to the hotel, shined all the shoes that were set out in the corridors at night, and guaranteed you could see your face in the buffed point of your shoe or boot or your money would be returned. He shined the shoes of the entire cast of the 1929 film production of *Evangeline*; he shined the shoes of Harry James's orchestra and of U.S. Senator Huey Long just before Long was assassinated.

'Where is Cool Breeze now, Mout'?' I said into the phone.

'You t'ink I'm gonna tell you that?'

'Then why'd you call?'

'Cool Breeze say they gonna kill him.'

'Who is?'

'That white man run the jail. He sent a nigger try to joog him in the ear with a wire.'

'I'll be over in the morning.'

'The morning? Why, t'ank you, suh.'

'Breeze went down his own road a long time ago, Mout'.'

He didn't reply. I could feel the late-summer heat and the closeness of the air under the electric light.

'Mout'?' I said.

'You right. But it don't make none of it easier. No suh, it surely don't.'

At sunrise the next morning I drove down East Main, under the canopy of live oaks that spanned the street, past City Hall and the library and the stone grotto and statue of Christ's mother, which had once been the site of George Washington Cable's home, and the sidewalks cracked by tree roots and the blue-green lawns filled with hydrangeas and hibiscus and philodendron and the thick stand of bamboo that framed the yard of the 1831 plantation manor called The Shadows, and finally into the business district. Then I was on the west side of town, on back streets with open ditches, railroad tracks that dissected yards and pavement, and narrow paintless houses, in rows like bad teeth, that had been cribs when nineteenth-century trainmen used to drink bucket beer from the saloon with the prostitutes and leave their red lanterns on the gallery steps when they went inside.

Mout' was behind his house, flinging birdseed at the pigeons that showered down from the telephone wires into his yard. He walked bent sideways at the waist, his eyes blue with cataracts, one cheek marbled pink and white by a strange skin disease that afflicts people of color; but his sloped shoulders were as wide as a bull's and his upper arms like chunks of sewer pipe.

'It was a bad time for Breeze to run, Mout'. The prosecutor's office might have cut him loose,' I said.

He mopped his face with a blue filling-station rag and slid the bag of birdseed off his shoulder and sat down heavily in an old barber's chair with an umbrella mounted on it. He picked up a fruit jar filled with coffee and hot milk from the ground and drank from it. His wide mouth seemed to cup around the bottom of the opening like a catfish's.

'He gone to church wit' me and his mother when he was a li'l boy,' he said. 'He played ball in the park, he carried the newspaper, he set pins in the bowling alley next to white boys and didn't have no trouble. It was New Orleans done it. He lived with his mother in the projects. Decided he wasn't gonna be no shoeshine man, have white folks tipping their cigar ashes down on his head, that's what he tole me.'

Mout' scratched the top of his head and made a sound like air leaving a tire.

'You did the best you could. Maybe it'll turn around for him someday,' I said.

'They gonna shoot him now, ain't they?' he said.

'No. Nobody wants that, Mout'.'

'That jailer, Alex Guidry? He use to come down here when he was in collitch. Black girls was three dollars over on Hopkins. Then he'd come around the shoeshine stand when they was black men around, pick out some fella and keep looking in his face, not letting go, no, peeling the skin right off the bone, till the man dropped his head and kept his eyes on the sidewalk. That's the way it was back then. Now y'all done hired the same fella to run the jail.'

Then he described his son's last day in the parish prison.

The turnkey who had been a brig chaser in the Marine Corps walked down the corridor of the Isolation unit and opened up the cast-iron door to Cool Breeze's cell. He bounced a baton off a leather lanyard that was looped around his wrist.

'Mr. Alex says you going back into Main Pop. That is, if you want,' he said.

'I ain't got no objection.'

'It must be your birthday.'

'How's that?' Cool Breeze said.

'You'll figure it out.'

'I'll figure it out, huh?'

'You wonder why you people are in here? When you think an echo is a sign of smarts?'

The turnkey walked him through a series of barred doors that slid back and forth on hydraulically operated steel arms, ordered him to strip and shower, then handed him an orange jumpsuit and locked him in a holding cell.

'They gonna put Mr. Alex on suspension. But he's doing you right before he goes out. So that's why I say it must be your birthday,' the turnkey said. He bounced the baton on its lanyard and winked. 'When he's gone, I'm gonna be jailer. You might study on the implications.'

At four that afternoon Alex Guidry stopped in front of Cool Breeze's cell. He wore a seersucker suit and red tie and shined black cowboy boots. His Stetson hung from his fingers against his pant leg.

'You want to work scrub-down detail and do sweep-up in the shop?' he asked.

'I can do that.'

'You gonna make trouble?'

'Ain't my style, suh.'

'You can tell any damn lie you want when you get out of here. But if I'm being unfair to you, you tell me to my face right now,' he said.

'People see what they need to.'

Alex Guidry turned his palm up and looked at it and picked at a callus with his thumb. He started to speak, then shook his head in disgust and walked down the corridor, the leather soles of his boots clicking on the floor.

Cool Breeze spent the next day scrubbing stone walls and side-walks with a wire brush and Ajax, and at five o'clock reported to the maintenance shop to begin sweep-up. He used a long broom to push steel filings, sawdust, and wood chips into tidy piles that he shoveled onto a dustpan and dumped into a trash bin. Behind him a mulatto whose golden skin was spotted with freckles the size of dimes was cutting a design out of a piece of plywood on a jigsaw, the teeth ripping a sound out of the wood like an electrified scream.

Cool Breeze paid no attention to him, until he heard the plywood disengage from the saw. He turned his head out of curiosity just as the mulatto balled his fist and tried to jam a piece of coat-hanger wire, sharpened to a point like an ice pick and driven vertically through the wood handle off a lawn-mower starter rope, through the center of Cool Breeze's ear and into his brain.

The wire point laid open Cool Breeze's cheek from the jawbone to the corner of his mouth.

He locked his attacker's forearm in both his hands, spun with him in circles, then walked the two of them toward the saw that hummed with an oily light.

'Don't make me do it, nigger,' he said.

But his attacker would not give up his weapon, and Cool Breeze drove first the coat hanger, then the balled fist and the wood plug gripped inside the palm into the saw blade, so that bone and metal and fingernails and wood splinters all showered into his face at once.

He hid inside the barrel of a cement mixer, where by all odds he should have died. He felt the truck slow at the gate, heard the guards talking outside while they walked the length of the truck with mirrors they held under the frame.

'We got one out on the ground. You ain't got him in your barrel, have you?' a guard said.

'We sure as hell can find out,' the truck driver said.

Gears and cogs clanged into place, then the truck vibrated and shook and giant steel blades began turning inside the barrel's blackness, lifting curtains of wet cement into the air like cake dough.

'Get out of here, will you? For some reason that thing puts me in mind of my wife in the bathroom,' the guard said.

Two hours later, on a parish road project south of town, Cool Breeze climbed from inside the cement mixer and lumbered into a cane field like a man wearing a lead suit, his lacerated cheek bleeding like a flag, the cane leaves edged with the sun's last red light.

'I don't believe it, Mout',' I said.

'Man ain't tried to joog him?'

'That the jailer set it up. He's already going on suspension. He'd be the first person everyone suspected.'

''Cause he done it.'

'Where's Breeze?'

Mout' slipped his sack of birdseed over his shoulder and began flinging handfuls into the air again. The pigeons swirled about his waxed bald head like snowflakes.

My partner was Detective Helen Soileau. She wore slacks and men's shirts to work, seldom smiled or put on makeup, and faced you with one foot cocked at an angle behind the other, in the same way a martial artist strikes a defensive posture. Her face was lumpy, her eyes unrelenting when they fixed on you, and her blond hair seemed molded to her head like a plastic wig. She leaned on my office windowsill with both arms and watched a trusty gardener edging the sidewalk. She wore a nine-millimeter automatic in a hand-tooled black holster and a pair of handcuffs stuck through the back of her gunbelt.

'I met Miss Pisspot of 1962 at the jail this morning,' she said.

'Who?'

'That FBI agent, what's her name, Glazier. She thinks we set up Cool Breeze Broussard to get clipped in our own jail.'

'What's your take on it?'

'The mulatto's a pipehead. He says he thought Breeze was somebody else, a guy who wanted to kill him because he banged the guy's little sister.'

'You buy it?' I asked.

'A guy who wears earrings through his nipples? Yeah, it's possible. Do me a favor, will you?' she said.

'What's up?'

Her eyes tried to look casual. 'Lila Terrebonne is sloshed at the country club. The skipper wants me to drive her back to Jeanerette.'

'No, thanks.'

'I could never relate to Lila. I don't know what it is. Maybe it's because she threw up in my lap once. I'm talking about your AA buddy here.'

'She didn't call me for help, Helen. If she had, it'd be different.'

'If she starts her shit with me, she's going into the drunk tank. I don't care if her grandfather was a U.S. senator or not.'

She went out to the parking lot. I sat behind my desk for a moment, then pinged a paper clip in the wastebasket and flagged down her cruiser before she got to the street.

Lila had a pointed face and milky green eyes and yellow hair that was bleached the color of white gold by the sun. She was light-hearted about her profligate life, undaunted by hangovers or trysts with married men, laughing in a husky voice in nightclubs about the compulsions that every two or three years placed her in a hospital or treatment center. She would dry out and by order of the court attend AA meetings for a few weeks, working a crossword puzzle in the newspaper while others talked of the razor wire wrapped around their souls, or staring out the window with a benign expression that showed no trace of desire, remorse, impatience, or resignation, just temporary abeyance, like a person waiting for the hands on an invisible clock to reach an appointed time.

From her adolescent years to the present, I did not remember a time in her life when she was not the subject of rumor or scandal. She was sent off by her parents to the Sorbonne, where she failed her examinations and returned to attend USL with blue-collar kids who could not even afford to go to LSU in Baton Rouge. The night of her senior prom, members of the football team glued her photograph on the rubber machine in Provost's Bar.

When Helen and I entered the clubhouse she was by herself at a back table, her head wreathed in smoke from her ashtray, her unfilled glass at the ends of her fingertips. The other tables were filled with golfers and bridge players, their eyes careful never to light on Lila and the pitiful attempt at dignity she tried to impose on her situation. The white barman and the young black waiter who circulated among the tables had long since refused to look in her direction or hear her order for another drink. When someone opened the front door, the glare of sunlight struck her face like a slap.

'You want to take a ride, Lila?' I said.

'Oh, Dave, how are you? They didn't call you again, did they?'

'We were in the neighborhood. I'm going to get a membership here one day.'

'The same day you join the Republican Party. You're such a riot. Would you help me up? I think I twisted my ankle,' she said.

She slipped her arm in mine and walked with me through the tables, then stopped at the bar and took two ten-dollar bills from her purse. She put them carefully on the bar top.

'Nate, this is for you and that nice young black man. It's always a pleasure to see you all again,' she said.

'Come back, Miss Lila. Anytime,' the barman said, his eyes shifting off her face.

Outside, she breathed the wind and sunshine as though she had just entered a different biosphere. She blinked and swallowed and made a muted noise like she had a toothache.

'Please drive me out on the highway and drop me wherever people break furniture and throw bottles through glass windows,' she said.

'How about home, instead?' I asked.

'Dave, you are a total drag.'

'Better appreciate who your friends are, ma'am,' Helen said.

'Do I know you?' Lila said.

'Yeah, I had the honor of cleaning up your—'

'Helen, let's get Miss Lila home and head back for the office.'

'Oh, by all means. Yes, indeedy,' Helen said.

We drove south along Bayou Teche toward Jeanerette, where Lila lived in a plantation home whose bricks had been dug from clay pits and baked in a kiln by slaves in the year 1791. During the Depression her grandfather, a U.S. senator, used dollar-a-day labor to move the home brick by brick on flatboats up the bayou from its original site on the Chitimacha Indian Reservation. Today, it was surrounded by a fourteen-acre lawn, live oak and palm trees, a sky-blue swimming pool, tennis courts, gazebos hung with orange passion vine, two stucco guest cottages, a flagstone patio and fountain, and gardens that bloomed with Mexicali roses.

But we were about to witness a bizarre spectacle when we turned onto the property and drove through the tunnel of oaks toward the front portico, the kind of rare event that leaves you sickened and ashamed for your fellow human beings. A movie set consisting of paintless shacks and a general store with a wide gallery set up on cinder blocks, put together from weathered cypress and rusted tin roofs and Jax beer and Hadacol signs to look like the quarters on a 1940s corporation farm, had been constructed on the lawn, a dirt road laid out and sprinkled with hoses in front of the galleries. Perhaps two dozen people milled around on the set, unorganized, mostly at loose ends, their bodies shiny with sweat. Sitting in the shade of a live oak tree by a table stacked with catered food was the director, Billy Holtzner, and next to him, cool and relaxed in yellow slacks and white silk shirt, was his friend and business partner, Cisco Flynn.

'Have you ever seen three monkeys try to fuck a football? I'd like to eighty-six the whole bunch but my father has a yen for a certain item. It tends to come in pink panties,' Lila said from the back seat.

'We'll drop you at the porch, Lila. As far as I'm concerned, your car broke down and we gave you a lift home,' I said.

'Oh, stop it. Both of you get down and have something to eat,' she said. Her face had cleared in the way a storm can blow out of a sky and leave it empty of clouds and full of carrion birds. I saw her tongue touch her bottom lip.

'Do you need assistance getting inside?' Helen said.

'Assistance? That's a lovely word. No, right here will do just fine. My, hasn't this all been pleasant?' Lila said, and got out and sent a black gardener into the house for a shaker of martinis.

Helen started to shift into reverse, then stopped, dumbfounded, at what we realized was taking place under the live oak tree.

Billy Holtzner had summoned all his people around him. He wore khaki shorts with flap pockets and Roman sandals with lavender socks and a crisp print shirt with the sleeves folded in neat cuffs on his flaccid arms. Except for the grizzled line of beard that grew along his jawline and chin, his body seemed to have no hair, as though it had been shaved with a woman's razor. His workmen and actors and grips and writers and camera people and female assistants stood with wide grins on their faces, some hiding their fear, others rising on the balls of their feet to get a better look, while he singled out one individual, then another, saying, 'Have you been a good boy? We've been hearing certain rumors again. Come on now, don't be shy. You know where you have to put it.'

Then a grown man, someone who probably had a wife or girlfriend or children or who had fought in a war or who at one time had believed his life was worthy of respect and love, inserted his nose between Billy Holtzner's index and ring fingers and let him twist it back and forth.

'That wasn't so bad, was it? Oh, oh, I see somebody trying to sneak off there. Oh, *Johnny* . . .' Holtzner said.

'These guys are out of a special basement, aren't they?' Helen said.

Cisco Flynn walked toward the cruiser, his face good-natured, his eyes earnest with explanation.

'Have a good life, Cisco,' I said out the window, then to Helen, 'Hit it.'

'You don't got to tell me, boss man,' she replied, her head looking back over her shoulder as she steered, the dark green shadows of oak leaves cascading over the windshield.

4

That night the moon was yellow above the swamp. I walked down to the dock to help Batist, the black man who worked for me, fold up the Cinzano umbrellas on our spool tables and close up the bait shop. There was a rain ring around the moon, and I pulled back the awning that covered the dock, then went inside just as the phone rang on the counter.

'Mout' called me. His son wants to come in,' the voice said.

'Stay out of police business, Megan.'

'Do I frighten you? Is that the problem here?'

'No, I suspect the problem is use.'

'Try this: He's fifteen miles out in the Atchafalaya Basin and snakebit. That's not metaphor. He stuck his arm in a nest of them. Why don't you deliver a message through Mout' and tell him just to go fuck himself?'

After I hung up I flicked off the outside flood lamps. Under the moon's yellow light the dead trees in the swamp looked like twists of paper and wax that could burst into flame with the touch of a single match.

At dawn the wind was out of the south, moist and warm and checkered with rain, when I headed the cabin cruiser across a long, flat bay bordered on both sides by flooded cypress trees that turned to green lace when the wind bent their branches. Cranes rose out of the trees against a pink sky, and to the south storm clouds were piled over the Gulf and the air smelled like salt water and brass drying in the sun. Megan stood next to the wheel, a thermos cup full of coffee in her hand. Her straw hat, which had a round dome and a purple band on it, was crushed over her eyes. To get my attention, she clasped my wrist with her thumb and forefinger.

'The inlet past that oil platform. There's a rag tied in a bush,' she said.

'I can see it, Megan,' I replied. Out of the corner of my eye I saw her face jerk toward me.

'I shouldn't speak or I shouldn't touch? Which is it?' she said.

I eased back the throttle and let the boat rise on its wake and drift into a cove that was overgrown by a leafy canopy and threaded with air vines and dimpled in the shallows with cypress trees. The bow scraped, then snugged tight on a sandspit.

'In answer to your question, I was out at your brother's movie set yesterday. I've decided to stay away from the world of the Big Score. No offense meant,' I said.

'I've always wondered what bank guards think all day. Just standing there, eight hours, staring at nothing. I think you've pulled it off, you know, gotten inside their heads.'

I picked up the first-aid kit and dropped off the bow and walked through the shallows toward a beached houseboat that had rotted into the soft texture of moldy cardboard.

I heard her splash into the water behind me.

'Gee, I hope I can be a swinging dick in the next life,' she said.

The houseboat floor was tilted on top of the crushed and rusted oil drums on which it had once floated. Cool Breeze sat in the corner, dressed in clothes off a wash line, the wound in his cut face stitched with thread and needle, his left arm swollen like a black balloon full of water.

I heard Megan's camera start clicking behind me.

'Why didn't you call the Feds, Breeze?' I asked.

'That woman FBI agent wants me in front of a grand jury. She say I gonna stay in the system, too, till they done wit' me.'

I looked at the electrical cord he had used for a tourniquet, the proud flesh that had turned the color of fish scale around the fang marks, the drainage that had left viscous green tailings on his shirt. 'I tell you what, I'll dress those wounds, hang your arm in a sling, then we'll get a breath of fresh air,' I said.

'You cut that cord loose, the poison gonna hit my heart.'

'You're working on gangrene now, partner.'

I saw him swallow. The whites of his eyes looked painted with iodine.

'You're jail-wise, Breeze. You knew the Feds would take you over the hurdles. Why'd you want to stick it to Alex Guidry?'

This is the story he told me while I used a rubber suction cup to draw a mixture of venom and infection from his forearm. As I listened on one knee, kneading the puncture wounds, feeling the pain in his body flicker like a candle flame under his skin, I could only wonder again at the white race's naïveté in always sending forth our worst members as our emissaries.

Twenty years ago, down the Teche, he owned a dirt-road store knocked together from scrap boards, tin stripped off a condemned rice mill, and Montgomery Ward brick that had dried out and crusted and pulled loose from the joists like a scab. He also had a pretty young wife named Ida, who cooked in a cafe and picked tabasco peppers on a corporate farm. After a day in the field her hands swelled as though they had been stung by bumblebees and she had to soak them in milk to relieve the burning in her skin.

On a winter afternoon two white men pulled up on the bib of oyster shell that served as a parking lot in front of the gallery, and the older man, who had jowls like a bulldog's and smoked a cigar in the center of his mouth, asked for a quart of moonshine.

'Don't tell me you ain't got it, boy. I know the man from Miss'sippi sells it to you.'

'I got Jax on ice. I got warm beer, too. I can sell you soda pop. I ain't got no whiskey.'

'That a fact? I'm gonna walk back out the door, then come back in. One of them jars you got in that box behind the motor oil better be on the counter or I'm gonna redecorate your store.'

Cool Breeze shook his head.

'I know who y'all are. I done paid already. Why y'all giving me this truck?' he said.

The younger white man opened the screen door and came inside the store. His name was Alex Guidry, and he wore a corduroy suit and cowboy hat and western boots, with pointed, mirror-bright toes. The older man picked up a paper bag of deep-fried cracklings from the counter. The grease in the cracklings made dark stains in the paper. He threw the bag to the younger man and said to Cool Breeze, 'You on parole for check writing now. That liquor will get you a double nickel. Your woman yonder, what's her name, Ida? She's a cook, ain't she?'

The man with bulldog jowls was named Harpo Delahoussey, and he ran a ramshackle nightclub for redbones (people who are part French, black, and Indian) by a rendering plant on an oxbow off the Atchafalaya River. When the incinerators were fired up at the plant, the smoke from the stacks filled the nearby woods and dirt roads with a stench like hair and chicken entrails burned in a skillet. The clapboard nightclub didn't lock its doors from Friday afternoon until late Sunday night; the parking lot (layered with thousands of flattened beer cans) became a maze of gas-guzzlers and pickup trucks; and the club's windows rattled and shook with the reverberations of rub board and thimbles, accordion, drums, dancing feet, and electric guitars whose feedback screeched like fingernails on slate.

At the back, in a small kitchen, Ida Broussard sliced potatoes for french fries while caldrons of red beans and rice and robin gumbo boiled on the stove, a bandanna knotted across her forehead to keep the sweat out of her eyes.

But Cool Breeze secretly knew, even though he tried to deny it to himself, that Harpo Delahoussey had not blackmailed him simply to acquire a cook, or even to reinforce that old lesson that every coin pressed into your palm for shining shoes, cutting cane, chopping cotton, scouring ovens, dipping out grease traps, scrubbing commodes, cleaning dead rats from under a house, was dispensed by the hand of a white person in the same way that oxygen could be arbitrarily measured out to a dying hospital patient.

One night she wouldn't speak when he picked her up, sitting against the far door of the pickup truck, her shoulders rounded, her face dull with a fatigue that sleep never took away.

'He ain't touched you, huh?' Cool Breeze said.

'Why you care? You brung me to the club, ain't you?'

'He said the rendering plant gonna shut down soon. That mean he won't be needing no more cook. What you gonna do if I'm in Angola?'

'I tole you not to bring that whiskey in the store. Not to listen to that white man from Miss'sippi sold it to you. Tole you, Willie.'

Then she looked out the window so he could not see her face. She wore a rayon blouse that had green and orange lights in it, and her back was shaking under the cloth, and he could hear her breath seizing in her throat, like hiccups she couldn't control.

He tried to get permission from his parole officer to move back to New Orleans.

Permission denied.

He caught Ida inhaling cocaine off a broken mirror behind the house. She drank fortified wine in the morning, out of a green bottle with a screw cap that made her eyes lustrous and frightening. She refused to help out at the store. In bed she was unresponding, dry when he entered her, and finally not available at all. She tied a perforated dime on a string around her ankle, then one around her belly so that it hung just below her navel.

'Gris-gris is old people's superstition,' Cool Breeze said.

'I had a dream. A white snake, thick as your wrist, it bit a hole in a melon and crawled inside and ate all the meat out.'

'We gonna run away.'

'Mr. Harpo gonna be there. Your PO gonna be there. State of Lou'sana gonna be there.'

He put his hand under the dime that rested on her lower stomach and ripped it loose. Her mouth parted soundlessly when the string razored burns along her skin.

The next week he walked in on her when she was naked in front of the mirror. A thin gold chain was fastened around her hips.

'Where you get that?' he asked.

She brushed her hair and didn't answer. Her breasts looked as swollen and full as eggplants.

'You ain't got to cook at the club no more. What they gonna do? Hurt us more than they already have?' he said.

She took a new dress off a hanger and worked it over her head. It was red and sewn with colored glass beads like an Indian woman might wear.

'Where you got money for that?' he asked.

'Mine to know, yours to find out,' she replied. She fastened a hoop earring to her lobe with both hands, smiling at him while she did it.

He began shaking her by the shoulders, her head whipping like a doll's on her neck, her eyelids closed, her lipsticked mouth open in a way that made his phallus thicken in his jeans. He flung her against the bedroom wall, so hard he heard her bones knock into the wood, then ran from the house and down the dirt road, through a tunnel of darkened trees, his brogans exploding through the shell of ice on the chuckholes.

In the morning he tried to make it up to her. He warmed boudin and fixed cush-cush and coffee and hot milk, and set it all out on the table and called her into the kitchen. The dishes she didn't smash on the wall she threw into the back yard.

He drove his pickup truck through the bright coldness of the morning, the dust from his tires drifting out onto the dead hyacinths and the cattails that had been winter-killed in the bayou, and found Harpo Delahoussey at the filling station he owned in town, playing dominoes with three other white men at a table by a gas stove that hissed with blue flame. Delahoussey wore a fedora, and a gold badge on the pocket of his white shirt. None of the men at the table looked up from their game. The stove filled the room with a drowsy, controlled warmth and the smell of shaving cream and aftershave lotion and testosterone.

'My wife ain't gonna be working at the club no more,' Cool Breeze said.

'Okay,' Delahoussey said, his eyes concentrated on the row of dominoes in front of him.

The room seemed to scream with silence.

'Mr. Harpo, maybe you ain't understood me,' Cool Breeze said.

'He heard you, boy. Now go on about your business,' one of the other men said.

A moment later, by the door of his truck, Cool Breeze looked back through the window. Even though he was outside, an oak tree swelling with wind above his head, and the four domino players were in a small room beyond a glass, he felt it was he who was somehow on display, in a cage, naked, small, an object of ridicule and contempt.

Then it hit him: *He's old. An old man like that, one piece of black jelly roll just the same as another. So who give her the dress and wrap the gold chain around her stomach?*

He wiped his forehead on the sleeve of his canvas coat. His ears roared with sound and his heart thundered in his chest.

He woke in the middle of the night and put on an overcoat and sat under a bare lightbulb in the kitchen, poking at the ashes in the wood stove, wadding up paper and feeding sticks into the flame that wouldn't catch, the cold climbing off the linoleum through his socks and into his ankles, his confused thoughts wrapped around his face like a net.

What was it that tormented him? Why was it he couldn't give it words, deal with it in the light of day, push it out in front of him, even kill it if he had to?

His breath fogged the air. Static electricity crackled in the sleeves of his overcoat and leaped off his fingertips when he touched the stove.

He wanted to blame Harpo Delahoussey. He remembered the story his daddy, Mout', had told him of the black man from Abbeville who broke off a butcher knife in the chest of a white overseer he caught doing it with his wife against a tree, then had spit in the face of his executioner before he was gagged and hooded with a black cloth and electrocuted.

He wondered if he could ever possess the courage of a man like that.

But he knew Delahoussey was not the true source of the anger and discontent that made his face break a sweat and his palms ring as though they had been beaten with boards.

He had accepted his role as cuckold, had even transported his wife to the site of her violation by a white man (and later, from Ida's mother, he would discover the exact nature of what Harpo Delahoussey did to her), because his victimization had justified a lifetime of resentment toward those who had forced his father to live gratefully on tips while their cigar ashes spilled down on his shoulders.

Except his wife had now become a willing participant. Last night she had ironed her jeans and shirt and laid them out on the bed, put perfume in her bathwater, washed and dried her hair and rouged her cheekbones to accentuate the angular beauty of her face. Her skin had seemed to glow when she dried herself in front of the mirror, a tune humming in her throat. He tried to confront her, force the issue, but her eyes were veiled with secret expectations and private meaning that made him ball his hands into fists. When he refused to drive her to the nightclub, she called a cab.

The fire wouldn't catch. An acrid smoke, as yellow as rope, laced with a stench of rags or chemically treated wood, billowed into his face. He opened all the windows, and frost speckled on the wallpaper and kitchen table. In the morning, the house smelled like a smoldering garbage dump.

She dressed in a robe, closed the windows, opened the air lock in the stove by holding a burning newspaper inside the draft, then began preparing breakfast for herself at the drainboard. He sat at the table and stared at her back stupidly, hoping she would reach into the cabinet, pull down a bowl or cup for him, indicate in some way they were still the people they once were.

'He tole me, you shake me again, you going away, Willie,' she said.

'Who say that?'

She walked out of the room and didn't answer.

'Who?' he called after her.

It was the letter that did it.

Or the letter that he didn't read in its entirety, at least not until later.

He had driven the truck back from the store, turned into his yard, and seen her behind the house, pulling her undergarments, jeans, work shirts, socks, and dresses, her whole wardrobe, off the wash line.

A letter written with a pencil stub on a sheet of lined paper, torn from a notebook, lay on the coffee table in the living room.

He could hear his breath rising and falling in his mouth when he picked it up, his huge hand squeezing involuntarily on the bottom of the childlike scrawl.

> *Dear Willie,*
>
> *You wanted to know who the man was I been sleeping with. I am telling you his name not out of meaness but because you will find out anyway and I dont want you to go back to prison. Alex Guidry was good to me when you were willing to turn me over to Mr. Harpo because of some moonshine whisky. You cant know what it is like to have that old man put his hand on you and tell you to come into the shed with him and make you do the things I had to do. Alex wouldnt let Mr. Harpo bother me any more and I slept with him because I wanted to and—*

He crumpled up the paper in his palm and flung it into the corner. In his mind's eye he saw Alex Guidry's fish camp, Guidry's corduroy suit and western hat hung on deer antlers, and Guidry himself mounted between Ida's legs, his muscled buttocks thrusting his phallus into her, her fingers and ankles biting for purchase into his white skin.

Cool Breeze hurled the back screen open and attacked her in the yard. He slapped her face and knocked her into the dust, then picked her up and shook her and shoved her backward onto the wood steps. When she tried to straighten her body with the heels of her hands, pushing herself away from him simultaneously, he saw the smear of blood on her mouth and the terror in her eyes, and realized, for the first time in his life, the murderous potential and level of self-hatred that had always dwelled inside him.

He tore down the wash line and kicked over the basket that was draped with her clothes. The leafless branches of the pecan tree overhead exploded with the cawing of crows. He didn't hear the truck engine start in the front and did not realize she was gone, that he was alone in the yard with his rage, until he saw the truck speeding into the distance, the detritus of the sugarcane harvest spinning in its vacuum.

Two duck hunters found her body at dawn, in a bay off the Atchafalaya River. Her fingers were coated with ice and extended just above the water's surface, the current silvering across the tips. A ship's anchor chain, one with links as big as bricks, was coiled around her torso like a fat serpent. The hunters tied a Budweiser carton to her wrist to mark the spot for the sheriff's department.

A week later Cool Breeze found the crumpled paper he had flung in the corner. He spread it flat on the table and began reading where he had left off before he had burst into the back yard and struck her across the face.

> I slept with him because I wanted to and because I was so mad at you and hurt over what you did to the wife that has always loved you.
> But Alex Guidry dont want a blak girl in his life, at least not on the street in the day lite. I know that now and I dont care and I tole him that. I will leave if you want me to and not blame you for it. I just want to say I am sorry for treating you so bad but it was like you had thrown me away forever.
> Your wife,
> Ida Broussard

Cool Breeze lay on a row of air cushions inside the cabin cruiser, his arm in a sling, his face sweating. When he had finished speaking, Megan looked at me sadly, her eyes prescient with the knowledge that a man's best explanation for his life can be one that will never satisfy him or anybody else.

'Y'all ain't gonna say nothing?' he asked.

'Let go of it, partner,' I said.

'The Man always got the answer,' he replied.

'Your daddy is an honest and decent person. If you're still ashamed of him because he shined shoes, yeah, I think that's a problem, Breeze,' I said.

'*Dave* . . .' Megan said.

'Give it a break, Megan,' I said.

'No . . . Behind us. The G sent us an escort,' she said.

I turned and looked back through the hatch at our wake. Coming hard right up the trough was a large powerboat, its enamel-white bow painted with the blue-and-red insignia of the United States Coast Guard. A helicopter dipped out of the sky behind the Coast Guard boat, yawing, its downdraft hammering the water.

I entered a channel that led to the boat ramp where my truck and boat trailer were parked. The helicopter swept past us and landed in the shell parking area below the levee. The right-hand door opened and the FBI agent named Adrien Glazier stepped out and walked toward us while the helicopter's blades were still spinning.

I waded through the shallows onto the concrete ramp.

'You're out of your jurisdiction, so I'm going to save you a lot of paperwork,' she said.

'Oh?'

'We're taking Mr. William Broussard into our custody. Interstate transportation of stolen property. You want to argue about it, we can talk about interference with a federal law officer in the performance of her duty.'

Then I saw her eyes focus over my shoulder on Megan, who stood on the bow of my boat, her hair blowing under her straw hat.

'You take one picture out here and I'll have you in handcuffs,' Adrien Glazier said.

'Broussard's been snakebit. He needs to be in a hospital,' I said.

But she wasn't listening. She and Megan stared at each other with the bright and intimate recognition of old adversaries who might have come aborning from another time.

5

The next day at lunchtime Clete Purcel picked me up at the office in the chartreuse Cadillac convertible that he had bought from a member of the Giacano crime family in New Orleans, a third-generation miscreant by the name of Stevie Gee who decided to spot-weld a leak in the gas tank but got drunk first and forgot to fill the tank with water before he fired up the welding machine. The scorch marks had faded now and looked like smoky gray tentacles on the back fenders.

The back seat was loaded with fishing rods, a tackle box that was three feet long, an ice chest, air cushions, crushed beer cans, life preservers, crab traps, a hoop net that had been ground up in a boat propeller, and a tangled trot line whose hooks were ringed with dried smelt.

Clete wore baggy white pants without a shirt and a powder-blue porkpie hat, and his skin looked bronzed and oily in the sun. He had been the best cop I ever knew until his career went south, literally, all the way to Central America, because of marriage trouble, pills, booze, hookers, indebtedness to shylocks, and finally a murder warrant that his fellow officers barely missed serving on him at the New Orleans airport.

I went inside Victor's on Main Street for a take-out order, then we crossed the drawbridge over Bayou Teche and drove past the live oaks on the lawn of the gray and boarded-up buildings that used to be Mount Carmel Academy, then through the residential section into City Park. We sat at a picnic table under a tree, not far from the swimming pool, where children were cannonballing off the diving board. The sun had gone behind the clouds and rain rings appeared soundlessly on the bayou's surface, like bream rising to feed.

'That execution in St. Mary Parish . . . the two brothers who got clipped after they raped the black girl? How bad you want the perps?' he said.

'What do you think?'

'I see it as another parish's grief. As a couple of guys who got what they had coming.'

567

'The shooters had one of our uniforms.'

He set down the pork-chop sandwich he was eating and scratched the scar that ran through his left eyebrow.

'I'm still running down skips for Nig Rosewater and Wee Willie Birnstine. Nig went bail for a couple of chippies who work a regular Murphy game in the Quarter. They're both junkies, runny noses, scabs on their thighs, mainlining six and seven balloons a day, sound familiar, scared shitless of detoxing in City Prison, except they're even more scared of their pimp, who's the guy they have to give up if they're going to beat the Murphy beef.

'So they ask Nig if they should go to the prosecutor's office with this story they got off a couple of johns who acted like over-the-hill cops. These guys were talking to each other about capping some brothers out in the Basin. One of the chippies asks if they're talking about black guys. One duffer laughs and says, "No, just some boys who should have kept practicing on colored girls and left white bread alone."'

'Where are these guys out of?'

'They said San Antone. But johns usually lie.'

'What else do the girls know?'

'They're airheads, Dave. The intellectual one reads the shopping guide on the toilet. Besides, they're not interested in dealing anymore. Their pimp decided to plea out, so they're off the hook.'

'Write down their names, will you?'

He took a piece of folded paper from his pants pocket, with the names of the two women and their addresses already written on it, and set it on the plank table. He started eating again, his green eyes smiling at nothing.

'Old lesson from the First District, big mon. When somebody wastes a couple of shit bags . . .' He realized I wasn't listening, that my gaze was focused over his shoulder on the swimming pool. He turned and stared through the tree trunks, his gaze roving across the swimmers in the pool, the parents who were walking their children by the hand to an instruction class a female lifeguard was putting together in the shallow end. Then his eyes focused on a man who stood between the wire enclosure and the bathhouse.

The man had a peroxided flattop, a large cranium, like a person with water on the brain, cheekbones that tapered in an inverted triangle to his chin, a small mouth full of teeth. He wore white shoes and pale orange slacks and a beige shirt with the short sleeves rolled in neat cuffs and the collar turned up on the neck. He pumped a blue rubber ball in his right palm.

'You know that dude?' Clete said.

'His name's Swede Boxleiter.'

'A graduate?'

'Canon City, Colorado. The FBI showed me some photos of a yard job he did on a guy.'

'What's he doing around here?'

Boxleiter wore shades instead of the granny glasses I had seen in the photos. But there was no doubt about the object of his attention. The children taking swim lessons were lined up along the edge of the pool, their swimsuits clinging wetly to their bodies. Boxleiter snapped the rubber ball off the pavement, ricocheting it against the bathhouse wall, retrieving it back into his palm as though it were attached to a magic string.

'Excuse me a minute,' I said to Clete.

I walked through the oaks to the pool. The air smelled of leaves and chlorine and the rain that was sprinkling on the heated cement. I stood two feet behind Boxleiter, who hung on to the wire mesh of the fence with one hand while the other kneaded the rubber ball. The green veins in his forearm were pumped with blood. He chewed gum, and a lump of cartilage expanded and contracted against the bright slickness of his jaw.

He felt my eyes on the back of his neck.

'You want something?' he asked.

'We thought we'd welcome you to town. Have you drop by the department. Maybe meet the sheriff.'

He grinned at the corner of his mouth.

'You think you seen me somewhere?'

I continued to stare into his face, not speaking. He removed his shades, his eyes askance.

'Soooo, what kind of gig are we trying to build here?' he asked.

'I don't like the way you look at children.'

'I'm looking at a swimming pool. But I'll move.'

'We nail you on a short-eyes here, we'll flag your jacket and put you in lockdown with some interesting company. This is Louisiana, Swede.'

He rolled the rubber ball down the back of his forearm, off his elbow, and caught it in his palm, all in one motion. Then he rolled it back and forth across the top of his fingers, the gum snapping in his jaw all the while.

'I went out max time. You got no handle. I got a job, too. In the movies. I'm not shitting you on that,' he said.

'Watch your language, please.'

'My language? Wow, I love this town already.' Then his face tilted, disconcerted, his breath drawing through his nose like an animal catching a scent. 'Why's Blimpo staring at me like that?'

I turned and saw Clete Purcel standing behind me. He grinned and took out his comb and ran it through his sandy hair with both hands. The skin under his arms was pink with sunburn.

'You think I got a weight problem?' he asked.

'No. 'Cause I don't know you. I don't know what kind of problem you got.'

'Then why'd you call me Blimpo?'

'So maybe I didn't mean anything by it.'

'I think you did.'

But Boxleiter turned his back on us, his attention fixed on the deep end of the pool, his right hand opening and closing on the blue rubber ball. The wind blew lines in his peroxided hair, and his scalp had the dead gray color of putty. His lips moved silently.

'What'd you say?' Clete asked. When Boxleiter didn't reply, Clete fitted his hand under Boxleiter's arm and turned him away from the fence. 'You said, "Blow me, Fatso"?'

Boxleiter slipped the ball in his pocket and looked out into the trees, his hands on his hips.

'It's a nice day. I'm gonna buy me a sno'ball. I love the spearmint sno'balls they sell in this park. You guys want one?' he said.

We watched him walk away through the trees, the leaves crunching under his feet like pecan shells, toward a cold drink stand and ice machine a black man had set up under a candy-striped umbrella.

'Like the boy says, he doesn't come with handles,' Clete said.

That afternoon the sheriff called me into his office. He was watering his window plants with a hand-painted teakettle, smoking his pipe at the same time. His body was slatted with light through the blinds, and beyond the blinds I could see the whitewashed crypts in the old Catholic cemetery.

'I got a call from Alex Guidry. You reported him to the Humane Society?' he said.

'He keeps his dogs penned on a filthy concrete slab without shade.'

'He claims you're harassing him.'

'What did the Humane Society say?'

'They gave him a warning and told him they'd be back. Watch your back with this character, Dave.'

'That's it?'

'No. The other problem is your calls to the FBI in New Orleans. They're off our backs for a while. Why stir them up?'

'Cool Breeze should be in our custody. We're letting the Feds twist him to avoid a civil suit over the abuse of prisoners in our jail.'

'He's a four-time loser, Dave. He's not a victim. He fed a guy into an electric saw.'

'I don't think it's right.'

'Tell that to people when we have to pass a parish sales tax to pay off a class action suit, particularly one that will make a bunch of convicts rich. I take that back. Tell it to that female FBI agent. She was here while you were out to lunch. I really enjoyed the half hour I spent listening to her.'

'Adrien Glazier was here?'

It was Friday, and when I drove home that evening I should have been beginning a fine weekend. Instead, she was waiting for me on the dock, a cardboard satchel balanced on the railing under her hand. I parked the car in the drive and walked down to meet her. She looked hot in her pink suit, her ice-blue eyes filmed from the heat or the dust on the road.

'You've got Breeze in lockdown and everybody around here scared. What else do you want, Ms. Glazier?'

'It's Special Agent Gla—'

'Yeah, I know.'

'You and Megan Flynn are taking this to the media, aren't you?'

'No. At least I'm not.'

'Then why do both of you keep calling the Bureau?'

'Because I'm being denied access to a prisoner who escaped from our jail, that's why.'

She stared hard into my face, as though searching for the right dials, her back teeth grinding softly, then said, 'I want you to look at a few more photos.'

'No.'

'What's the matter, you don't want to see the wreckage your gal leaves in her wake?'

She pulled the elastic cord loose from the cardboard satchel and spilled half the contents on a spool table. She lifted up a glossy eight-by-ten black-and-white photo of Megan addressing a crowd of Latin peasants from the bed of a produce truck. Megan was leaning forward, her small hands balled into fists, her mouth wide with her oration.

'Here's another picture taken a few days later. If you look closely, you'll recognize some of the dead people in the ditch. They were in the crowd that listened to Megan Flynn. Where was she when this happened? At the Hilton in Mexico City.'

'You really hate her, don't you?'

I heard her take a breath, like a person who has stepped into fouled air.

'No, I don't hate her, sir. I hate what she does. Other people die so she can feel good about herself,' she said.

I sifted through the photos and news clippings with my fingers. I picked up one that had been taken from the *Denver Post* and glued on a piece of cardboard backing. Adrien Glazier was two inches away from my skin. I could smell perspiration and body powder in her clothes. The news article was about thirteen-year-old Megan Flynn winning first prize in the *Post*'s essay contest. The photo showed her sitting in a chair, her hands folded demurely in her lap, her essay medal worn proudly on her chest.

'Not bad for a kid in a state orphanage. I guess that's the Megan I always remember. Maybe that's why I still think of her as one of the most admirable people I've ever known. Thanks for coming by,' I said, and walked up the slope through the oak and pecan trees on my lawn, and on into my lighted house, where my daughter and wife waited supper for me.

Monday morning Helen Soileau came into my office and sat on the corner of my desk.

'I was wrong about two things,' she said.

'Oh?'

'The mulatto who tried to do Cool Breeze, the guy with the earring through his nipple? I said maybe I bought his story, he thought Breeze was somebody else? I checked the visitors' sheet. A lawyer for the Giacano family visited him the day before.'

'You're sure?'

'Whiplash Wineburger. You ever meet him?'

'Whiplash represents other clients, too.'

'Pro bono for a mulatto who works in a rice mill?'

'Why would the Giacanos want to do an inside hit on a guy like Cool Breeze Broussard?'

She raised her eyebrows and shrugged.

'Maybe the Feds are squeezing Breeze to bring pressure on the Giacanos,' I said, in answer to my own question.

'To make them cooperate in an investigation of the Triads?'

'Why not?'

'The other thing I was going to tell you? Last night Lila Terrebonne went into that new zydeco dump on the parish line. She got into it with the bartender, then pulled a .25 automatic on the bouncer. A couple of uniforms were the first guys to respond. They got her purse from her with the gun in it without any problem. Then one of them brushed against her and she went ape shit.

'Dave, I put my arm around her and walked her out the back door, into the parking lot, with nobody else around, and she cried like a kid in my arms . . . You following me?'

'Yeah, I think so,' I said.

'I don't know who did it, but I know what's been done to her,' she said. She stood up, flexed her back, and inverted the flats of her hands inside the back of her gunbelt. The skin was tight around her mouth, her eyes charged with light. My gaze shifted off her face.

'When I was a young woman and finally told people what my father did to me, nobody believed it,' she said. ' "Your dad was a great guy," they said. "Your dad was a wonderful parent." '

'Where is she now?'

'Iberia General. Nobody's pressing charges. I think her old man already greased the owner of the bar.'

'You're a good cop, Helen.'

'Better get her some help. The guy who'll pay the bill won't be the one who did it to her. Too bad it works out that way, huh?'

'What do I know?' I said.

Her eyes held on mine. She had killed two perps in the line of duty. I think she took no joy in that fact. But neither did she regret what she had done nor did she grieve over the repressed anger that had rescinded any equivocation she might have had before she shot them. She winked at me and went back to her office.

6

With regularity politicians talk about what they call the war against drugs. I have the sense few of them know anything about it. But the person who suffers the attrition for the drug trade is real, with the same soft marmalade-like system of lungs and heart and viscera inherited from a fish as the rest of us.

In this case her name was Ruby Gravano and she lived in a low-rent hotel on St. Charles Avenue in New Orleans, between Lee Circle and Canal, not far from the French Quarter. The narrow front entrance was framed by bare lightbulbs, like the entrance to a 1920s movie theater. But quaint similarities ended there. The interior was superheated and breathless, unlighted except for the glare from the airshaft at the end of the hallways. For some reason the walls had been painted firehouse red with black trim, and now, in the semidarkness, they had the dirty glow of a dying furnace.

Ruby Gravano sat in a stuffed chair surrounded by the litter of her life: Splayed tabloid magazines, pizza cartons, used Kleenex, a coffee cup with a dead roach inside, a half-constructed model of a spaceship that had been stuck back in the box and stepped on.

Ruby Gravano's hair was long and black and made her thin face and body look fuller than they were. She wore shorts that were too big for her and exposed her underwear, and foundation on her thighs and forearms, and false fingernails and false eyelashes and a bruise like a fresh tattoo on her left cheek.

'Dave won't jam you up on this, Ruby. We just want a string that'll lead back to these two guys. They're bad dudes, not the kind you want in your life, not the kind you want other girls to get mixed up with. You can help a lot of people here,' Clete said.

'We did them in a motel on Airline Highway. They had a pickup truck with a shell on it. Full of guns and camping gear and shit. They smelled like mosquito repellent. They always wore their hats. I've seen hogs eat with better table manners. They're johns. What else you want to know?' she said.

'Why'd you think they might be cops?' I asked.

'Who else carries mug shots around?'

'Beg your pardon?' I said.

'The guy I did, he was undressing and he finds these two mug shots in his shirt pocket. So he burns them in an ashtray and that's when his friend says something about capping two brothers.'

'Wait a minute. You were all in the same room?' Clete said.

'They didn't want to pay for two rooms. Besides, they wanted to trade off. Connie does splits, but I wouldn't go along. One of those creeps is sickening enough. Why don't you bug Connie about this stuff?'

'Because she blew town,' Clete said.

She sniffed and wiped her nose with her wrist. 'Look, I'm not feeling too good. Y'all got what you need?' she said.

'Did they use a credit card to pay for the room?' I asked.

'It's a trick pad. My manager pays the owner. Look, believe it or not, I got another life besides this shit. How about it?'

She tried to look boldly into my face, but her eyes broke and she picked up the crushed model of a spaceship from its box on the floor and held it in her lap and studied it resentfully.

'Who hit you, Ruby?' I asked.

'A guy.'

'You have a kid?'

'A little boy. He's nine. I bought him this, but it got rough in here last night.'

'These cops, duffers, whatever they were, they had to have names,' I said.

'Not real ones.'

'What do you mean?'

'The one who burned the pictures, the other guy called him Harpo. I go, "Like that guy in old TV movies who's a dummy and is always honking a horn?" The guy called Harpo goes, "That's right, darlin', and right now I'm gonna honk *your* horn." '

She tried to fit the plastic parts of the model back together. Her right cheek was pinched while she tried to focus, and the bruise on it knotted together like a cluster of blue grapes. 'I can't fix this. I should have put it up in the closet. He's coming over with my aunt,' she said. She pushed hard on a plastic part and it slid sharply across the back of her hand.

'How old a man was Harpo?' I asked.

'Like sixty, when they start acting like they're your father and Robert Redford at the same time. He has hair all over his back . . . I got to go to the bathroom. I'm gonna be in there a while. Look, you want to stay, maybe you can fix this. It's been a deeply fucked-up day.'

'Where'd you buy it?' I asked.

'K&B's. Or maybe at the Jackson Brewery, you know, that mall that used to be the Jax brewery . . . No, I'm pretty sure it wasn't the Brewery.' She bit a hangnail.

Clete and I drove to a K&B drugstore up St. Charles. It was raining, and the wind blew the mist out of the trees that arched over the streetcar tracks. The green-and-purple neon on the drugstore looked like scrolled candy in the rain.

'Harpo was the name of the cop who took Cool Breeze Broussard's wife away from him,' I said.

'That was twenty years ago. It can't be the same guy, can it?'

'No, it's unlikely.'

'I think all these people deserve each other, Streak.'

'So why are we buying a toy for Ruby Gravano's son?'

'I seldom take my own advice. Sound like anybody else you know, big mon?'

On Wednesday I drove a cruiser down the old bayou road toward Jeanerette and Lila Terrebonne's home. As I neared the enormous lawn and the oak-lined driveway, I saw the production crew at work on the set that had been constructed to look like the quarters on a corporation farm, and I kept driving south, toward Franklin and the place where my father and I had discovered a crucifixion.

Why?

Maybe because the past is never really dead, at least not as long as you deny its existence. Maybe because I knew that somehow the death of Cisco and Megan Flynn's father was about to come back into our lives.

The barn was still there, two hundred yards from the Teche, hemmed in by banana trees and blackberry bushes. The roof was cratered with a huge hole, the walls leaning in on themselves, the red paint nothing more than thin strips that hadn't yet been weathered away by wind and sun.

I walked through the blackberry bushes to the north side of the barn. The nail holes were sealed over with dust from the cane fields and water expansion in the wood, but I could still feel their edges with the tips of my fingers and, in my mind's eye, see the outline of the man whose tormented face and broken body and blood-creased brow greeted my father and me on that fiery dawn in 1956.

No grass grew around the area where Jack Flynn died. (But there was no sunlight there, I told myself, only green flies buzzing in the shade, and the earth was hardpan and probably poisoned by herbicides that had been spilled on the ground.) Wild rain trees, bursting with bloodred flowers, stood in the field, and the blackberries on the bushes were fat and moist with their own juices when I touched them. I wondered at the degree of innocence that allowed us to think of Golgotha as an incident trapped inside history. I wiped the sweat off my face with a handkerchief and unbuttoned my shirt and stepped out of the shade into the wind, but it brought no relief from the heat.

I drove back up the bayou to the Terrebonne home and turned into the brick drive and parked by the carriage house. Lila was ebullient, her milky green eyes free of any remorse or memory of pulling a gun in a bar and being handcuffed to a bed in Iberia General Hospital. But like all people who are driven by a self-centered fear, she talked constantly, controlling the environment around her with words, filling in any silent space that might allow someone to ask the wrong question.

Her father, Archer Terrebonne, was another matter. He had the same eyes as his daughter, and the same white-gold hair, but there was no lack of confidence in either his laconic speech or the way he folded his arms across his narrow chest while he held a glass of shaved ice and bourbon and sliced oranges. In fact, his money gave him the kind of confidence that overrode any unpleasant reflection he might see in a mirror or the eyes of others. When you dealt with Archer Terrebonne, you simply accepted the fact that his gaze was too direct and personal, his skin too pale for the season, his mouth too red, his presence too close, as though there were a chemical defect in his physiology that he wore as an ornament and imposed upon others.

We stood under an awning on the back terrace. The sunlight was blinding on the surface of the swimming pool. In the distance a black groundskeeper was using an air blower to scud leaves off the tennis courts.

'You won't come inside?' Archer said. He glanced at his watch, then looked at a bird in a tree. The ring finger of his left hand was missing, sawed off neatly at the palm, so that the empty space looked like a missing key on a piano.

'Thanks, anyway. I just wanted to see that Lila was all right.'

'Really? Well, that was good of you.'

I noticed his use of the past tense, as though my visit had already ended.

'There's no charges, but messing with guns in barrooms usually has another conclusion,' I said.

'We've already covered this territory with other people, sir,' he said.

'I don't think quite enough,' I said.

'Is that right?' he replied.

Our eyes locked on each other's.

'Dave's just being an old friend, Daddy,' Lila said.

'I'm sure he is. Let me walk you to your cruiser, Mr. Robicheaux.'

'*Daddy*, I mean it, Dave's always worrying about his AA friends,' she said.

'You're not in that organization. So he doesn't need to worry, does he?'

I felt his hand cup me lightly on the arm. But I said goodbye to Lila and didn't resist. I walked with him around the shady side of the house, past a garden planted with mint and heart-shaped caladiums.

'Is there something you want to tell me, sir?' he asked. He took a swallow from his bourbon glass and I could feel the coldness of the ice on his breath.

'A female detective saved your daughter from a resisting arrest charge,' I said.

'Yes?'

'She thinks Lila has been sexually molested or violated in some way.'

His right eye twitched at the corner, as though an insect had momentarily flown into his vision.

'I'm sure y'all have many theories about human behavior that most of us wouldn't understand. We appreciate your good intentions. However, I see no need for you to come back,' he said.

'Don't count on it, sir.'

He wagged his finger back and forth, then walked casually toward the rear of the house, sipping his drink as though I had never been there.

The sun was white in the sky and the brick drive was dappled with light as bright as gold foil. Through the cruiser's front window I saw Cisco Flynn walk toward me from a trailer, his palms raised for me to stop.

He leaned down on the window.

'Take a walk with me. I got to keep my eye on this next scene,' he said.

'Got to go, Cisco.'

'It's about Swede Boxleiter.'

I turned off the ignition and walked with him to a canvas awning that was suspended over a worktable and a half dozen chairs. Next to the awning was a trailer whose air-conditioning unit dripped with moisture like a block of ice.

'Swede's trying to straighten out. I think he's going to make it this time. But if he's ever a problem, give me a call,' Cisco said.

'He's a mainline recidivist, Cisco. Why are you hooked up with him?'

'When we were in the state home? I would have been anybody's chops if it hadn't been for Swede.'

'The Feds say he kills people.'

'The Feds say my sister is a Communist.'

The door to the trailer opened and a woman stepped out on the small porch. But before she could close the door behind her, a voice shouted out, 'Goddamnit, I didn't say you could leave. Now, you listen, hon. I don't know if the problem is because your brains are between your legs or because you think you've got a cute twat, but the next time I tell that pissant to rewrite a scene, you'd better not open your mouth. Now you get the fuck back to work and don't you ever contradict me in front of other people again.'

Even in the sunlight her face looked refrigerated, bloodless, the lines twisted out of shape with the humiliation that Billy Holtzner bathed her with. He shot an ugly look at Cisco and me, then slammed the door.

I turned to go.

'There's a lot of stress on a set, Dave. We're three million over budget already. That's other people's money we're talking about. They get mad about it,' Cisco said.

'I remember that first film you made. The one about the migrant farmworkers. It was sure a fine movie.'

'Yeah, a lot of college professors and 1960s leftovers dug it in a big way.'

'The guy in that trailer is a shithead.'

'Aren't we all?'

'Your old man wasn't.'

I got into the cruiser and drove through the corridor of trees to the bayou road. In the rearview mirror Cisco Flynn looked like a miniature man trapped inside an elongated box.

That night, as Bootsie and I prepared to go to bed, dry lightning flickered behind the clouds and the pecan tree outside the window was stiffening in the wind.

'Why do you think Jack Flynn was killed?' Bootsie asked.

'Working people around here made thirty-five cents an hour back then. He didn't have a hard time finding an audience.'

'Who do you think did it?'

'Everyone said it came from the outside. Just like during the Civil Rights era. We always blamed our problems on the outside.'

She turned out the light and we lay down on top of the sheets. Her skin felt cool and warm at the same time, the way sunlight does in the fall.

'The Flynns are trouble, Dave.'

'Maybe.'

'No, no maybe about it. Jack Flynn might have been a good man. But I always heard he didn't become a radical until his family got wiped out in the Depression.'

'He fought in the Lincoln Brigade. He was at the battle of Madrid.'

'Good night,' she said.

She turned toward the far wall. When I spread my hand on her back I could feel her breath rise and fall in her lungs. She looked at me over her shoulder, then rolled over and fit herself inside my arms.

'Dave?' she said.

'Yes?'

'Trust me on this. Megan needs you for some reason she's not telling you about. If she can't get to you directly, she'll go through Clete.'

'That's hard to believe.'

'He called tonight and asked if I knew where she was. She'd left a message on his answering machine.'

'Megan Flynn and Clete Purcel?'

I woke at sunrise the next morning and drove through the leafy shadows on East Main and then five miles up the old highway to Spanish Lake. I was troubled not only by Bootsie's words but also by my own misgivings about the Flynns. Why was Megan so interested in the plight of Cool Breeze Broussard? There was enough injustice in the world without coming back to New Iberia to find it. And why would her brother Cisco front points for an obvious psychopath like Swede Boxleiter?

I parked my truck on a side road and poured a cup of coffee from my thermos. Through the pines I could see the sun glimmering on the water and the tips of the flooded grass waving in the shallows. The area around the lake had been the site of a failed Spanish colony in the 1790s. In 1836 two Irish immigrants who had survived the Goliad Massacre during the Texas Revolution, Devon Flynn and William Burke, cleared and drained the acreage along the lake and built farmhouses out of cypress trees that were rooted in the water like boulders. Later the train stop there became known as Burke's Station.

Megan and Cisco's ancestor had been one of those Texas soldiers who had surrendered to the Mexican army with the expectation of boarding a prison ship bound for New Orleans, and instead had been marched down a road on Palm Sunday and told by their Mexican captors to kneel in front of the firing squads that were forming into position from two directions. Over 350 men and boys were shot, bayoneted, and clubbed to death. Many of the survivors owed their lives to a prostitute who ran from one Mexican officer to the next, begging for the lives of the Texans. Her name and fate were lost to history, but those who escaped into the woods that day called her the Angel of Goliad.

I wondered if Cisco ever thought about his ancestor's story as material for a film.

The old Flynn house still stood by the lake, but it was covered by a white-brick veneer now and the old gallery had been replaced by a circular stone porch with white pillars. But probably most important to Megan and Cisco was the simple fact that it and its terraced gardens and gnarled live oaks and lakeside gazebo and boathouse all belonged to someone else.

Their father was bombed by the Luftwaffe and shot at by the Japanese on Guadalcanal and murdered in Louisiana. Were they bitter, did they bear us a level of resentment we could only guess at? Did they bring their success back here like a beast on a chain? I didn't want to answer my own question.

The wind ruffled the lake and the longleaf pine boughs above my truck. I glanced in the rearview mirror and saw the sheriff's cruiser pull in behind me. He opened my passenger door and got inside.

'How'd you know I was out here?' I asked.

'A state trooper saw you and wondered what you were doing.'

'I got up a little early today.'

'That's the old Flynn place, isn't it?'

'We used to dig for Confederate artifacts here. Camp Pratt was right back in those trees.'

'The Flynns bother me, too, Dave. I don't like Cisco bringing this Boxleiter character into our midst. Why don't both of them stay in Colorado?'

'That's what we did to Megan and Cisco the first time. Let a friend of their dad dump them in Colorado.'

'You'd better define your feelings about that pair. I got Boxleiter's sheet. What kind of person would bring a man like that into his community?'

'We did some serious damage to those kids, Sheriff.'

'*We*? You know what your problem is, Dave? You're just like Jack Flynn.'

'Excuse me?'

'You don't like rich people. You think we're in a class war. Not everybody with money is a sonofabitch.'

He blew out his breath, then the heat went out of his face. He took his pipe from his shirt pocket and clicked it on the window jamb.

'Helen said you think Boxleiter might be a pedophile,' he said.

'Yeah, if I had to bet, I'd say he's a real candidate.'

'Pick him up.'

'What for?'

'Think of something. Take Helen with you. She can be very creative.'

Idle words that I would try to erase from my memory later.

7

I drove back toward the office. As I approached the old Catholic cemetery, I saw a black man with sloping shoulders cross the street in front of me and walk toward Main. I stared at him, dumbfounded. One cheek was bandaged, and his right arm was stiff at his side, as though it pained him.

I pulled abreast of him and said, 'I can't believe it.'

'Believe what?' Cool Breeze said. He walked bent forward, like he was just about to arrive somewhere. The whitewashed crypts behind him were beaded with moisture the size of quarters.

'You're supposed to be in federal custody.'

'They cut me loose.'

'Cut you loose? Just like that?'

'I'm going up to Victor's to eat breakfast.'

'Get in.'

'I don't mean you no disrespect, but I ain't gonna have no more to do with po-licemens for a while.'

'You staying with Mout'?'

But he crossed the street and didn't answer.

At the office I called Adrien Glazier in New Orleans.

'What's your game with Cool Breeze Broussard?' I asked.

'Game?'

'He's back in New Iberia. I just saw him.'

'We took his deposition. We don't see any point in keeping him in custody,' she replied.

I could feel my words binding in my throat.

'What's in y'all's minds? You've burned this guy.'

'Burned him?'

'You made him rat out the Giacanos. Do you know what they do to people who snitch them off?'

'Then why don't you put him in custody yourself, Mr. Robicheaux?'

'Because the prosecutor's office dropped charges against him.'

'Really? So the same people who complain when we investigate their jail want us to clean up a local mess for them?'

'Don't do this.'

'Should we tell Mr. Broussard his friend Mr. Robicheaux would like to see him locked up again? Or will you do that for us?' she said, and hung up.

Helen opened my door and came inside. She studied my face curiously.

'You ready to boogie?' she asked.

Swede Boxleiter had told me he had a job in the movies, and that's where we started. Over in St. Mary Parish, on the front lawn of Lila Terrebonne.

But we didn't get far. After we had parked the cruiser, we were stopped halfway to the set by a couple of off-duty St. Mary Parish sheriff's deputies with American flags sewn to their sleeves.

'Y'all putting us in an embarrassing situation,' the older man said.

'You see that dude there, the one with the tool belt on? His name's Boxleiter. He just finished a five bit in Colorado,' I said.

'You got a warrant?'

'Nope.'

'Mr. Holtzner don't want nobody on the set ain't got bidness here. That's the way it is.'

'Oh yeah? Try this. Either you take the marshmallows out of your mouth or I'll go down to your boss's office and have your ass stuffed in a tree shredder,' Helen said.

'Say what you want. You ain't getting on this set,' he said.

Just then, Cisco Flynn opened the door of a trailer and stepped out on the short wood porch.

'What's the problem, Dave?' he asked.

'Boxleiter.'

'Come in,' he said, making cupping motions with his upturned hands, as though he were directing an aircraft on a landing strip.

Helen and I walked toward the open door. Behind him I could see Billy Holtzner combing his hair. His eyes were pale and watery, his lips thick, his face hard-planed like gray rubber molded against bone.

'Dave, we want a good relationship with everybody in the area. If Swede's done something wrong, I want to know about it. Come inside, meet Billy. Let's talk a minute,' Cisco said.

But Billy Holtzner's attention had shifted to a woman who was brushing her teeth in a lavatory with the door open.

'Margot, you look just like you do when I come in your mouth,' he said.

'Adios,' I said, walking away from the trailer with Helen.

Cisco caught up with us and waved away the two security guards.

'What'd Swede do?' he asked.

'Better question: What's he got on you?' I said.

'What have I done that you insult me like this?'

'Mr. Flynn, Boxleiter was hanging around small children at the city pool. Save the bullshit for your local groupies,' Helen said.

'All right, I'll talk to him. Let's don't have a scene,' Cisco said.

'Just stay out of the way,' she said.

Boxleiter was on one knee, stripped to the waist, tightening a socket wrench on a power terminal. His Levi's were powdered with dust, and black power lines spidered out from him in all directions. His torso glistened whitely with sweat, his skin rippling with sinew each time he pumped the wrench. He used his hand to mop the sweat out of one shaved armpit, then wiped his hand on his jeans.

'I want you to put your shirt on and take a ride with us,' I said.

He looked up at us, smiling, squinting into the sun. 'You don't have a warrant. If you did, you'd have already told me,' he said.

'It's a social invitation. One you really don't want to turn down,' Helen said.

He studied her, amused. Dust swirled out of the dirt street that had been spread on the set. The sky was cloudless, the air moist and as tangible as flame against the skin. Boxleiter rose to his feet. People on the set had stopped work and were watching now.

'I got a union book. I'm like anybody else here. I don't have to go anywhere,' he said.

'Suit yourself. We'll catch you later,' I said.

'I get it. You'll roust me when I get home tonight. It don't bother me. Long as it's legal,' he said.

Helen's cheeks were flushed, the back of her neck damp in the heat. I touched her wrist and nodded toward the cruiser. Just as she turned to go with me, I saw Boxleiter draw one stiff finger up his rib cage, collecting a thick dollop of sweat. He flicked it at her back.

Her hand went to her cheek, her face darkening with surprise and insult, like a person in a crowd who cannot believe the nature of an injury she has just received.

'You're under arrest for assaulting a police officer. Put your hands behind you,' she said.

He grinned and scratched at an insect bite high up on his shoulder.

'Is there something wrong with the words I use? Turn around,' she said.

He shook his head sadly. 'I got witnesses. I ain't done anything.'

'You want to add "resisting" to it?' she said.

'Whoa, mama. Take your hands off me . . . Hey, enough's enough . . . Buddy, yeah, you, guy with the mustache, you get this dyke off me.'

She grabbed him by the shoulders and put her shoe behind his knee. Then he brought his elbow into her breast, hard, raking it across her as he turned.

She slipped a blackjack from her pants pocket and raised it over her shoulder and swung it down on his collarbone. It was weighted with lead, elongated like a darning sock, the spring handle wrapped with leather. The blow made his shoulder drop as though the tendons had been severed at the neck.

But he flailed at her just the same, trying to grab her around the waist. She whipped the blackjack across his head, again and again, splitting his scalp, wetting the leather cover on the blackjack each time she swung.

I tried to push him to the ground, out of harm's way, but another problem was in the making. The two off-duty sheriff's deputies were pulling their weapons.

I tore my .45 from my belt holster and aimed into their faces.

'Freeze! It's over! . . . Take your hand off that piece! Do it! Do it! Do it!'

I saw the confusion and the alarm fix in their eyes, their bodies stiffening. Then the moment died in their faces. 'That's it . . . Now, move the crowd back. That's all you've got to do . . . That's right,' I said, my words like wet glass in my throat.

Swede Boxleiter moaned and rolled in the dirt among the power cables, his fingers laced in his hair. Both my hands were still squeezed tight on the .45's grips, my forearms shining with sweat.

The faces of the onlookers were stunned, stupefied. Billy Holtzner pushed his way through the crowd, turned in a circle, his eyebrows climbing on his forehead, and said, 'I got to tell you to get back to work?' Then he walked back toward his trailer, blowing his nose on a Kleenex, flicking his eyes sideways briefly as though looking at a minor irritant.

I was left staring into the self-amused gaze of Archer Terrebonne. Lila stood behind him, her mouth open, her face as white as cake flour. The backs of my legs were still trembling.

'Do y'all specialize in being public fools, Mr. Robicheaux?' he asked. He touched at the corner of his mouth, his three-fingered hand like that of an impaired amphibian.

The sheriff paced in his office. He pulled up the blinds, then lowered them again. He kept clearing his throat, as though there were an infection in it.

'This isn't a sheriff's department. I'm the supervisor of a mental institution,' he said.

He took the top off his teakettle, looked inside it, and set the top down again.

'You know how many faxes I've gotten already on this? The St. Mary sheriff told me not to put my foot in his parish again. That sonofabitch actually threatened me,' he said.

'Maybe we should have played it differently, but Boxleiter didn't give us a lot of selection,' I said.

'Outside our jurisdiction.'

'We told him he wasn't under arrest. There was no misunderstanding about that,' I said.

'I should have used their people to take him down,' Helen said.

'Ah, a breakthrough in thought. But I'm suspending you just the same, at least until I get an IA finding,' the sheriff said.

'He threw sweat on her. He hit her in the chest with his elbow. He got off light,' I said.

'A guy with twenty-eight stitches in his head?'

'You told us to pick him up, skipper. That guy would be a loaded gun anyplace we tried to take him down. You know it, too,' I said.

He crimped his lips together and breathed through his nose.

'I'm madder than hell about this,' he said.

The room was silent, the air-conditioning almost frigid. The sunlight through the slatted blinds was eye-watering.

'All right, forget the suspension and IA stuff. See me before you go into St. Mary Parish again. In the meantime, you find out why Cisco Flynn thinks he can bring his pet sewer rats into Iberia Parish . . . Helen, you depersonalize your attitude toward the perps, if that's possible.'

'The sewer rats?' I said.

He filled his pipe bowl from a leather pouch and didn't bother to look up until we were out of the room.

That evening Clete Purcel parked his Cadillac convertible under the shade trees in front of my house and walked down to the bait shop. He wore a summer suit and a lavender shirt with a white tie. He went to the cooler and opened a bottle of strawberry soda.

'What, I look funny or something?' he said.

'You look sharp.'

He drank out of the pop bottle and watched a boat out on the bayou.

'I'll treat y'all to dinner at the Patio in Loreauville,' he said.

'I'd better work.'

He nodded, then looked at the newscast on the television set that sat above the counter.

'Thought I'd ask,' he said.

'Who you going to dinner with?'

'Megan Flynn.'

'Another time.'

He sat down at the counter and drank from his soda. He drew a finger through a wet ring on the wood.

'I'm only supposed to go out with strippers and junkies?' he said.

'Did I say anything?'

'You hide your feelings like a cat in a spin dryer.'

'So she's stand-up. But why's she back in New Iberia? We're Paris on the Teche?'

'She was born here. Her brother has a house here.'

'Yeah, he's carrying weight for a psychopath, too. Why you think that is, Clete? Because Cisco likes to rehabilitate shank artists?'

'I hear Helen beat the shit out of Boxleiter with a slapjack. Maybe he's got the message and he'll get out of town.'

I mopped down the counter and tossed the rag on top of a case of empty beer bottles.

'You won't change your mind?' he said.

'Come back tomorrow. We'll entertain the bass.'

He made a clicking sound with his mouth and walked out the door and into the twilight.

After supper I drove over to Mout' Broussard's house on the west side of town. Cool Breeze came out on the gallery and sat down on the swing. He had removed the bandage from his cheek, and the wound he had gotten at the jail looked like a long piece of pink string inset in his skin.

'Doctor said I ain't gonna have no scar.'

'You going to hang around town?' I asked.

'Ain't got no pressing bidness nowheres else.'

'They used you, Breeze.'

'I got Alex Guidry fired, ain't I?'

'Does it make you feel better?'

He looked at his hands. They were wide, big-boned, lustrous with callus.

'What you want here?' he asked.

'The old man who made your wife cook for him, Harpo Delahoussey? Did he have a son?'

'What people done tole you over in St. Mary Parish?'

'They say he didn't.'

He shook his head noncommittally.

'You don't remember?' I said.

.'t my bidness.'

harpo may have executed a couple of kids out in the

s in New Orleans? You know what they do to a black man
off? I'm suppose to worry about some guy blowing away
white trash raped a black girl?'

n those men took away your wife twenty years ago, you couldn't
do anything about it. Same kind of guys are still out there, Breeze. They
function only because we allow them to.'

'I promised Mout' to go crabbing with him in the morning. I best be
getting my sleep,' he said.

But when I got into my truck and looked back at him, he was still in
the swing, staring at his hands, his massive shoulders slumped like a bag
of crushed rock.

It was hot and dry Friday night, with a threat of rain that never came.
Out over the Gulf, the clouds would vein and pulse with lightning, then
the thunder would ripple across the wetlands with a sound like damp
cardboard tearing. In the middle of the night I put my hands inside
Bootsie's nightgown and felt her body's heat against my palms, like the
warmth in a lampshade. Her eyes opened and looked into mine, then
she touched my hardness with her fingertips, her hand gradually
rounding itself, her mouth on my cheek, then on my lips. She rolled
on her back, her hand never leaving me, and waited for me to enter her.

She came before I did, both of her hands pushing hard into the small
of my back, her knees gathered around my thighs, then she came a
second time, with me, her stomach rolling under me, her voice muted
and moist in my ear.

She went into the bathroom and I heard the water running. She
walked toward me out of the light, touching her face with a towel, then
lay on top of the sheet and put her head on my chest. The ends of her
hair were wet and the spinning blades of the window fan made shadows
on her skin.

'What's worrying you?' she asked.

'Nothing.'

She kicked me in the calf.

'Clete Purcel. I think he's going to be hurt,' I said.

'Advice about love and money. Give it to anyone except friends.'

'You're right. You were about Megan, too. I'd thought better of her.'

She ran her fingernails through my hair and rested one ankle across
mine.

Sunday morning I woke at dawn and went down to the bait shop to help

Batist open up. I was never sure of his age, but he had been a teenager during World War II when he had worked for Mr. Antoine, one of Louisiana's last surviving Confederate veterans, at Mr. Antoine's blacksmith shop in a big red barn out on West Main. Mr. Antoine had willed Batist a plot of land and a small cypress home on the bayou, and over the years Batist had truck farmed there, augmented his income by trapping and fishing with my father, buried two wives, and raised five children, all of whom graduated from high school. He was illiterate and sometimes contentious, and had never traveled farther from home than New Orleans in one direction and Lake Charles in the other, but I never knew a more loyal or decent person.

We started the fire in the barbecue pit, which was fashioned from a split oil drum with handles and hinges welded on it, laid out our chickens and sausage links on the grill for our midday customers, and closed down the lid to let the meat smoke for at least three hours.

Batist wore a pair of bell-bottomed dungarees and a white T-shirt with the sleeves razored off. His upper arms bunched like cantaloupes when he moved a spool table to hose down the dock under it.

'I forgot to tell you. That fella Cool Breeze was by here last night,' he said.

'What did he want?'

'I ain't ax him.'

I expected him to say more but he didn't. He didn't like people of color who had jail records, primarily because he believed they were used by whites as an excuse to treat all black people unfairly.

'Does he want me to call him?' I asked.

'I know that story about his wife, Dave. Maybe it wasn't all his fault, but he sat by while them white men ruined that po' girl. I feel sorry for him, me, but when a man got a grief like that against hisself, there ain't nothing you can do for him.'

I looked up Mout's name in the telephone book and dialed the number. While the phone rang Batist lit a cigar and opened the screen on the window and flicked the match into the water.

'No one home,' I said after I hung up.

'I ain't gonna say no more.'

He drew in on his cigar, his face turned into the breeze that blew through the screen.

Bootsie and Alafair and I went to Mass, then I dropped them off at home and drove to Cisco Flynn's house on the Loreauville road. He answered the door in a terry-cloth bathrobe that he wore over a pair of scarlet gym shorts.

'Too early?' I said.

'No, I was about to do a workout. Come in,' he said, opening the door wide. 'Look, if you're here to apologize about that stuff on the set—'

'I'm not.'

'Oh.'

'The sheriff wants to know why the city of New Iberia is hosting a mainline con like your friend Boxleiter.'

We were in the living room now, by the collection of photographs that had made Megan famous.

'You were never in a state home, Dave. How would you like to be seven years old and forced to get up out of bed in the middle of the night and suck somebody's cock? Think you could handle that?'

'I think your friend is a depraved and violent man.'

'*He's* violent? Y'all put him in the hospital over a drop of sweat.'

Through the French doors I could see two dark-skinned people sitting at a glass table under a tree in the back yard. The man was big, slightly overweight, with a space between his front teeth and a ponytail that hung between his shoulder blades. The woman wore shorts and a tank top and had brownish-red hair that reminded me of tumbleweed. They were pouring orange juice into glasses from a clear pitcher. A yellow candle stub was melted to the table.

'Something bothered me the last time I was here. These photos that were in *Life* magazine? Y'all caught the kill from inside the drainpipe, just as the bullet hit the black guy in the neck?'

'That's right.'

'What were you doing in the pipe? How'd you know the guy was coming out at that particular place?'

'We made an arrangement to meet him, that's all.'

'How'd the cops know he was going to be there?'

'I told you. He raped a high school girl. They had an all-points out on him.'

'Somehow that doesn't hang together for me,' I said.

'You think we set it up? We were *inside* the pipe. Bullets were ricocheting and sparking all around us. What's the use? I've got some guests. Is there anything else?'

'Guests?'

'Billy Holtzner's daughter and her boyfriend.'

I looked out the French doors again. I saw a glassy reflection between the fingers of the man's right hand.

'Introduce me.'

'It's Sunday. They're just getting up.'

'Yeah, I can see.'

'Hey, wait a minute.'

But I opened the French doors and stepped outside. The man with the ponytail, who looked Malaysian or Indonesian, cupped the candle stub melted to the table, popping the waxy base loose, and held it behind his thigh. Holtzner's daughter had eyes that didn't fit her fried hair. They were a soapy blue, mindless, as devoid of reason as a drowsy cat's when small creatures run across its vision.

A flat, partially zippered leather case rested on a metal chair between her and her boyfriend.

'How y'all doing?' I asked.

Their smiles were self-indulgent rather than warm, their faces suffused by a chemical pleasure that was working in their skin like flame inside tallow. The woman lowered her wrist into her lap and the sunlight fell like a spray of yellow coins on the small red swelling inside her forearm.

'The officer from the set,' the man said.

'It is,' the woman said, leaning sideways in her chair to see behind me. 'Is that blond lady here? The one with the blackjack. I mean that guy's head. Yuck.'

'We're not in trouble, are we?' the man said. He smiled. The gap in his front teeth was large enough to insert a kitchen match in.

'You from the U.K.?' I said.

'Just the accent. I travel on a French passport,' he said, smiling. He removed a pair of dark glasses from his shirt pocket and put them on.

'Y'all need any medical attention here?'

'No, not today, I don't think,' the man said.

'Sure? Because I can run y'all down to Iberia General. It's no trouble.'

'That's very kind of you, but we'll pass,' the man said.

'What's he talking about?' the woman said.

'Being helpful, that sort of thing, welcoming us to the neighborhood,' the man said.

'Hospital?' She scratched her back by rubbing it against her chair. 'Did anybody ever tell you you look like Johnny Wadd?'

'Not really.'

'He died of AIDS. He was very underrated as an artist. Because he did porno, if that's what you want to call it.' Then her face went out of focus, as though her own words had presented a question inside herself.

'Dave, can I see you?' Cisco said softly behind me.

I left Billy Holtzner's daughter and the man with the ponytail without saying goodbye. But they never noticed, their heads bent toward each other as they laughed over a private joke.

Cisco walked with me through the shade trees to my truck. He had slipped on a golf shirt with his gym shorts, and he kept pulling the cloth away from the dampness of his skin.

'I don't have choices about what people around me do sometimes,' he said.

'Choose not to have them here, Cisco.'

'I work in a bowl of piranhas. You think Billy Holtzner is off the wall? He twists noses. I can introduce you to people who blow heads.'

'I didn't have probable cause on your friends. But they shouldn't take too much for granted.'

'How many cops on a pad have you covered for? How many times have you seen a guy popped and a throw-down put on his body?'

'See you, Cisco.'

'What am I supposed to feel, Dave? Like I just got visited by St. Francis of Assisi? In your ear.'

I walked to my truck and didn't look back at him. I heard the woman braying loudly in the back yard.

When I went down to the bait shop to open up Monday morning, Cool Breeze Broussard was waiting for me at a spool table, the Cinzano umbrella ruffling over his head. The early sun was dark red through the trunks of the cypresses.

'It gonna be another hot one,' he said.

'What's the haps, Breeze?'

'I got to talk . . . No, out here. I like to talk in open space . . . How much of what I tell you other people got to learn about?'

'That depends.'

He made a pained face and looked at the redness of the sun through the trees.

'I went to New Orleans Saturday. A guy up Magazine, Jimmy Fig, Tommy Figorelli's brother, the guy the Giacanos sawed up and hung in pieces from a ceiling fan? I figured Jimmy didn't have no love for the Giacanos 'cause of his brother, and, besides, me and Jimmy was in the Block together at Angola, see. So I t'ought he was the right man to sell me a cold piece,' Cool Breeze said.

'You're buying unregistered guns?' I said.

'You want to hear me or not? . . . So he go, "Willie in your line of work, you don't need no cold piece."

'I go, "This ain't for work. I got in bad wit' some local guys, maybe you heard. But I ain't got no money right now, so I need you to front me the piece."

'He say, "You feeling some heat from somewhere, Breeze?" And he say it wit' this smart-ass grin on his face.

'I say, "Yeah, wit' the same dudes who freeze-wrapped your brother's parts in his own butcher shop. I hear they drank eggnog while he was spinning round over their heads."

'He say, "Well, my brother had some sexual problems that got him into trouble. But it ain't Italians you got to worry about. The word is some peckerwoods got a contract to do a black blabbermouth in New Iberia. I just didn't know who it was."

'I say, "Blabbermouth, huh?"

'He go, "You was ripping off the Giacanos and selling their own VCRs back to them? Then you snitch them off and come to New Orleans figuring somebody's gonna front you a piece? Breeze, nothing racial meant, but you people ought to stick to pimping and dealing rock." '

'Who are these peckerwoods?' I asked.

'When I tole you the story about me and Ida, about how she wrapped that chain round her t'roat and drowned herself, I left somet'ing out.'

'Oh?'

'A year after Ida died, I was working at the Terrebonne cannery, putting up sweet potatoes. Harpo Delahoussey run the security there for Mr. Terrebonne. We come to the end of the season and the cannery shut down, just like it do every winter, and everybody got laid off. So we went on down to the unemployment office and filed for unemployment insurance. Shouldn't have been no problem.

'Except three weeks go by and the state sends us a notice we ain't qualified for no checks 'cause we cannery workers, and 'cause the cannery ain't open, we ain't available to work.

'I went on down to see Mr. Terrebonne, but I never got past Harpo Delahoussey. He's sitting there at a big desk wit' his foot in the wastebasket, sticking a po'boy sandwich in his mout'. He go, "It's been explained to you, Willie. Now, you don't want wait round here till next season, you go on down to New Orleans, get you a job, try to stay out of trouble for a while. But don't you come round here bothering Mr. Terrebonne. He been good to y'all."

''Bout a week later they was a big fire at the cannery. You could smell sweet potatoes burning all the way down to Morgan City. Harpo Delahoussey jumped out a second-story window wit' his clothes on fire. He'da died if he hadn't landed in a mud puddle.'

'You set it?'

'Harpo Delahoussey had a nephew wit' his name. He use to be a city po-liceman in Franklin. Everybody called him Li'l Harpo.'

'You think this is one of the peckerwoods?'

'Why else I'm telling you all this? Look, I ain't running no more.'

'I think you're living inside your head too much, Breeze. The Giacanos use mechanics out of Miami or Houston.'

'Jimmy Fig tole me I was a dumb nigger ought to be pimping and selling crack. What you saying ain't no different. I feel bad I come here.'

He got up and walked down the dock toward his truck. He passed two white fishermen who were just arriving, their rods and tackle boxes gripped solidly in their hands. They walked around him, then glanced over their shoulders at his back.

'That boy looks like his old lady just cut him off,' one of them said to me, grinning.

'We're not open yet,' I said, and went inside the bait shop and latched the screen behind me.

8

You read the jacket on a man like Swede Boxleiter and dismiss him as one of those genetically defective creatures for whom psychologists don't have explanations and let it go at that.

Then he does or says something that doesn't fit the pattern, and you go home from work with boards in your head.

Early Monday morning I called Cisco Flynn's home number and got his answering service. An hour later he returned my call.

'Why do you want Swede's address? Leave him alone,' he said.

'He's blackmailing you, isn't he?'

'I remember now. You fought Golden Gloves. Too many shots to the head, Dave.'

'Maybe Helen Soileau and I should drop by the set again and talk to him there.'

Boxleiter lived in a triplex built of green cinder blocks outside St. Martinville. When I turned into his drive he was throwing a golfball against the cement steps on the side of the building, ricocheting it off two surfaces before he retrieved it out of the air again, his hand as fast as a snake's head, *click-click, click-click, click-click*. He wore blue Everlast boxing trunks and a gauzy see-through black shirt and white high-top gym shoes and leather gloves without fingers and a white bill cap that covered his shaved and stitched head like an inverted cook pan. He glanced at me over his shoulder, then began throwing the ball again.

'The Man,' he said. The back yard had no grass and lay in deep shade, and beyond the tree trunks the bayou shimmered in the sunlight.

'I thought we'd hear from you,' I said.

'How's that?'

'Civil suit, brutality charges, that kind of stuff.'

'Can't ever tell.'

'Give the golf game a break a minute, will you?'

His eyes smiled at nothing, then he flipped the ball out into the yard

595

and waited, his sunken cheeks and small mouth like those of a curious fish.

'I couldn't figure the hold you had on Cisco,' I said. 'But it's that photo that began Megan's career, the one of the black man getting nailed in the storm drain, isn't it? You told the cops where he was coming out. Her big break was based on a fraud that cost a guy his life.'

He cleaned an ear with his little finger, his eyes as empty of thought as glass.

'Cisco is my friend. I wouldn't hurt him for any reason in the world. Somebody try to hurt him, I'll cut them into steaks.'

'Is that right?'

'You want to play some handball?'

'Handball?'

'Yeah, against the garage.'

'No, I—'

'Tell the dyke I got no beef. I just didn't like the roust in front of all them people.'

'Tell the dyke? You're an unusual man, Swede.'

'I heard about you. You were in Vietnam. Anything on my sheet you probably did in spades.'

Then, as though I were no longer there, he did a handstand in the yard and walked on stiffened arms through the shade, the bottoms of his gym shoes extended out like the shoulders of a man with no head.

Clete Purcel sat in the bow of the outboard and drained the foam out of a long-necked bottle of beer. He cast his Rapala between two willow trees and retrieved it back toward him, the sides of the lure flashing just below the surface. The sun was low on the western horizon and the canopy overhead was lit with fire, the water motionless, the mosquitoes starting to form in clouds over the islands of algae that extended out from the flooded cypress trunks.

A bass rose from the silt, thick-backed, the black-green dorsal fin glistening when it broke the water, and knocked the Rapala into the air without taking the treble hook. Clete set his rod on the bow and slapped the back of his neck and looked at the bloody smear on his palm.

'So this guy Cool Breeze is telling you a couple of crackers got the whack on him? One of them is maybe the guy who did these two brothers out in the Atchafalaya Basin?' he said.

'Yeah, that's about it.'

'But you don't buy it?'

'When did the Giacanos start using over-the-hill peckerwoods for button men?'

'I wouldn't mark it off, mon. This greaseball in Igor's was complaining to me about how the Giacano family is falling apart, how they've lost their self-respect and they're running low-rent action like porno joints and dope in the projects. I say, "Yeah, it's a shame. The world's really going to hell," and he says, "You telling me, Purcel? It's so bad we got a serious problem with somebody, we got to outsource."

'I say, "Outsource?"

'He goes, "Yeah, niggers from the Desire, Vietnamese lice-heads, crackers who spit Red Man in Styrofoam cups at the dinner table."

'It's the Dixie Mafia, Dave. There's a nest of them over on the Mississippi coast.'

I drew the paddle through the water and let the boat glide into a cove that was freckled with sunlight. I cast a popping bug with yellow feathers and red eyes on the edge of the hyacinths. A solitary blue heron lifted on extended wings out of the grass and flew through an opening in the trees, dimpling the water with its feet.

'But you didn't bring me out here to talk about wiseguy bullshit, did you?' Clete said.

I watched a cottonmouth extend its body out of the water, curling around a low branch on a flooded willow, then pull itself completely into the leaves.

'I don't know how to say it,' I said.

'I'll clear it up for both of us. I like her. Maybe we got something going. That rubs you the wrong way?'

'A guy gets involved, he doesn't see things straight sometimes,' I said.

'"Involved," like in the sack? You're asking me if I'm in the sack with Megan?'

'You're my friend. You carried me down a fire escape when that kid opened up on us with a .22. Something stinks about the Flynn family.'

Clete's face was turned into the shadows. The back of his neck was the color of Mercurochrome.

'On my best day I kick in some poor bastard's door for Nig Rosewater. Last week a greaseball tried to hire me to collect the vig for a couple of his shylocks. Megan's talking about getting me on as head of security with a movie company. You think that's bad?'

I looked at the water and the trapped air bubbles that chained to the surface out of the silt. I heard Clete's weight turn on the vinyl cushion under him.

'Say it, Dave. Any broad outside of a T&A joint must have an angle if she'd get involved with your podjo. I'm not sensitive. But lay off Megan.'

I disconnected the sections of my fly rod and set them in the bottom of the boat. When I lifted the outboard and yanked the starter rope, the dry propeller whined like a chain saw through the darkening swamp. I didn't speak again until we were at the dock. The air was hot, as though it had been baked on a sheet of tin, the current yellow and dead in the bayou, the lavender sky thick with birds.

Up on the dock, Clete peeled off his shirt and stuck his head under a water faucet. The skin across his shoulders was dry and scaling.

'Come on up for dinner,' I said.

'I think I'm going back to New Orleans tonight.' He took his billfold out of his back pocket and removed a five-dollar bill and pushed it into a crack in the railing. 'I owe for the beer and gas,' he said, and walked with his spinning rod and big tackle box to his car, his love handles aching with fresh sunburn.

The next night, under a full moon, two men wearing hats drove a pickup truck down a levee in Vermilion Parish. On either side of them marshlands and saw grass seemed to flow like a wide green river into the Gulf. The two men stopped their truck on the levee and crossed a plank walkway that oozed sand and water under their combined weight. They passed a pirogue that was tied to the walkway, then stepped on ground that was like sponge under their western boots. Ahead, inside the fish camp, someone walked across the glare of a Coleman lantern and made a shadow on the window. Mout' Broussard's dog raised its head under the shack, then padded out into the open air on its leash, its nose lifted into the wind.

9

Mout' stood in the doorway of the shack and looked at the two white men. Both were tall and wore hats that shadowed their faces. The dog, a yellow-and-black mongrel with scars on its ears, growled and showed its teeth.

'Shut up, Rafe!' Mout' said.

'Where's Willie Broussard at?' one of the men said. The flesh in his throat was distended and rose-colored, and gray whiskers grew on his chin.

'He gone up the levee to the sto'. Coming right back. Wit' some friends to play bouree. What you gentlemens want?' Mout' said.

'Your truck's right yonder. What'd he drive in?' the second man said. He wore a clear plastic raincoat and his right arm held something behind his thigh.

'A friend carried him up there.'

'We stopped there for a soda. It was locked up. Where's your outboard, old man?' the man with whiskers said.

'Ain't got no outboa'd.'

'There's the gas can yonder. There's the cut in the cattails where it was tied. Your boy running a trot line?'

'What y'all want to bother him for? He ain't done you nothing.'

'You don't mind if we come inside, do you?' the man in the raincoat said. When he stepped forward, the dog lunged at his ankle. He kicked his boot sideways and caught the dog in the mouth, then pulled the screen and latch out of the doorjamb.

'You stand over in the corner and stay out of the way,' the man with whiskers said.

The man in the raincoat lifted the Coleman lantern by the bail and walked into the back yard with it. He came back in and shook his head.

The man with whiskers bit off a corner on a tobacco plug and worked it into his jaw. He picked up an empty coffee can out of a trash sack and spit in it.

'I told you we should have come in the A.M. You wake them up and do business,' the man in the raincoat said.

'Turn off the lantern and move the truck.'

'I say mark it off. I don't like guessing who's coming through a door.'

The man with whiskers looked at him meaningfully.

'It's your rodeo,' the man in the raincoat said, and went back out the front door.

The wind blew through the screens into the room. Outside, the moonlight glittered like silver on the water in the saw grass.

'Lie down on the floor where I can watch you. Here, take this pillow,' the man with whiskers said.

'Don't hurt my boy, suh.'

'Don't talk no more. Don't look at my face either.'

'What's I gonna do? You here to kill my boy.'

'You don't know that. Maybe we just want to talk to him . . . Don't look at my face.'

'I ain't lying on no flo'. I ain't gonna sit by while y'all kill my boy. What y'all t'ink I am?'

'An old man, just like I'm getting to be. You can have something to eat or put your head down on the table and take a nap. But don't mix in it. You understand that? You mix in it, we gonna forget you're an old nigra don't nobody pay any mind to.'

The man in the raincoat came back through the door, a sawed-off over-and-under shotgun in his right hand.

'I'm burning up. The wind feels like it come off a desert,' he said, and took off his coat and wiped his face with a handkerchief. 'What was the old man talking about?'

'He thinks the stock market might take a slide.'

'Ask him if there's any stray pussy in the neighborhood.'

The man with whiskers on his chin leaned over and spit tobacco juice into the coffee can. He wiped his lips with his thumb.

'Bring his dog in here,' he said.

'What for?'

'Because a dog skulking and whimpering around the door might indicate somebody kicked it.'

'I hadn't thought about that. They always say you're a thinking man, Harpo.'

The man with the whiskers spit in the can again and looked hard at him.

The man who had worn the raincoat dragged the dog skittering through the door on its leash, then tried to haul it into the air. But the dog's back feet found purchase on the floor and its teeth tore into the man's hand.

600

'Oh, shit!' he yelled out, and pushed both his hands between his thighs.

'Get that damn dog under control, old man, or I'm gonna shoot both of you,' the man with whiskers said.

'Yes, suh. He ain't gonna be no trouble. I promise,' Mout' said.

'You all right?' the man with whiskers asked his friend.

His friend didn't answer. He opened an ice chest and found a bottle of wine and poured it on the wound. His hand was strung with blood, his fingers shaking as though numb with cold. He tied his handkerchief around the wound, pulling it tight with his teeth, and sat down in a wood chair facing the door, the shotgun across his knees.

'This better come out right,' he said.

Mout' sat in the corner, on the floor, his dog between his thighs. He could hear mullet splash out in the saw grass, the drone of a distant boat engine, dry thunder booming over the Gulf. He wanted it to rain, but he didn't know why. Maybe if it rained, no, stormed, with lightning all over the sky, Cool Breeze would take shelter and not try to come back that night. Or if it was thundering real bad, the two white men wouldn't hear Cool Breeze's outboard, hear him lifting the crab traps out of the aluminum bottom, hefting up the bucket loaded with catfish he'd unhooked from the trot line.

'I got to go to the bat'room,' he said.

But neither of the white men acknowledged him.

'I got to make water,' he said.

The man with whiskers stood up from his chair and straightened his back.

'Come on, old man,' he said, and let Mout' walk ahead of him out the back door.

'Maybe you a good man, suh. Maybe you just ain't giving yourself credit for being a good man,' Mout' said.

'Go ahead and piss.'

'I ain't never give no trouble to white people. Anybody round New Iberia tell you that. Same wit' my boy. He worked hard at the bowling alley. He had him a li'l sto'. He tried to stay out of trouble but wouldn't nobody let him.'

Then Mout' felt his caution, his lifetime of deference and obsequiousness and pretense slipping away from him. 'He had him a wife, her name was Ida, the sweetest black girl in Franklin, but a white man said she was gonna cook for him, just like that, or her husband was gonna go to the penitentiary. Then he took her out in the shed and made her get down on her knees and do what he want. She t'rowed up and begged him not to make her do it again, and every t'ree or fo' nights he walked

601

her out in the shed and she tole herself it's gonna be over soon, he gonna get tired of me and then me and Cool Breeze gonna be left alone, and when he got finished wit' her and made her hate herself and hate my boy, too, another white man come along and give her presents and took her to his bed and tole her t'ings to tell Cool Breeze so he'd know he wasn't nothing but a nigger and a nigger's wife is a white man's jelly roll whenever he want it.'

'Shake it off and zip up your pants,' the man with whiskers said.

'You cain't get my boy fair. He'll cut yo' ass.'

'You better shut up, old man.'

'White trash wit' a gun and a big truck. Seen y'all all my life. Got to shove niggers round or you don't know who you are.'

The man with whiskers pushed Mout' toward the shack, surprised at the power and breadth of muscle in Mout's back.

'I might have underestimated you. Don't take that as good news,' he said.

Mout' woke just before first light. The dog lay in his lap, its coat stiff with mud. The two white men sat in chairs facing the front door, their shoulders slightly rounded, their chins dropping to their chests. The man with the shotgun opened his eyes suddenly, as though waking from a dream.

'Wake up,' he said.

'What is it?'

'Nothing. That's the point. I don't want to drive out of here in sunlight.'

The man with whiskers rubbed the sleep out of his face.

'Bring the truck up,' he said.

The man with the shotgun looked in Mout's direction, as if asking a question.

'I'll think about it,' the man with whiskers said.

'It's mighty loose, Harpo.'

'Every time I say something, you got a remark to make.'

The man with the shotgun rewrapped the bloody handkerchief on his hand. He rose from the chair and threw the shotgun to his friend. 'You can use my raincoat if you decide to do business,' he said, and went out into the dawn.

Mout' waited in the silence.

'What do you think we ought to do about you?' the man with whiskers asked.

'Don't matter what happen here. One day the devil gonna come for y'all, take you where you belong.'

'You got diarrhea of the mouth.'

602

'My boy better than both y'all. He outsmarted you. He know y'all here. He out there now. Cool Breeze gonna come after you, Mr. White Trash.'

'Stand up, you old fart.'

Mout' pushed himself to his feet, his back against the plank wall. He could feel his thighs quivering, his bladder betraying him. Outside, the sun had risen into a line of storm clouds that looked like the brow of an angry man.

The man with whiskers held the shotgun against his hip and fired one barrel into Mout's dog, blowing it like a bag of broken sticks and torn skin into the corner.

'Get a cat. They're a lot smarter animals,' he said, and went out the door and crossed the board walkway to the levee where his friend sat on the fender of their pickup truck, smoking a cigarette.

10

'Cool Breeze run out of gas. That's why he didn't come back to the camp,' Mout' said.

It was Wednesday afternoon, and Helen and I sat with Mout' in his small living room, listening to his story.

'What'd the Vermilion Parish deputies say?' Helen asked.

'Man wrote on his clipboa'd. Said it was too bad about my dog. Said I could get another one at the shelter. I ax him, "What about them two men?" He said it didn't make no sense they come into my camp to kill a dog. I said, "Yeah, it don't make no sense 'cause you wasn't listening to the rest of it."'

'Where's Cool Breeze, Mout'?'

'Gone.'

'Where?'

'To borrow money.'

'Come on, Mout',' I said.

'To buy a gun. Cool Breeze full of hate, Mr. Dave. Cool Breeze don't show it, but he don't forgive. What bother me is the one he don't forgive most is himself.'

Back at my office, I called Special Agent Adrien Glazier at the FBI office in New Orleans.

'Two white men, one with the first name of Harpo, tried to clip Willie Broussard at a fish camp in Vermilion Parish,' I said.

'When was this?'

'Last night.'

'Is there a federal crime involved here?'

'Not that I know of. Maybe crossing a state line to commit a felony.'

'You have evidence of that?'

'No.'

'Then why are you calling, Mr. Robicheaux?'

'His life's in jeopardy.'

'We're not unaware of the risk he's incurred as a federal witness. But I'm busy right now. I'll have to call you back,' she said.

'You're busy?'

The line went dead.

A uniformed deputy picked up Cool Breeze in front of a pawnshop on the south side of New Iberia and brought him into my office.

'Why the cuffs?' I said.

'Ask him what he called me when I told him to get in the cruiser,' the deputy replied.

'Take them off, please.'

'By all means. Glad to be of service. You want anything else?' the deputy said, and turned a tiny key in the lock on the cuffs.

'Thanks for bringing him in.'

'Oh, yeah, anytime. I always had aspirations to be a bus driver,' he said, and went out the door, his eyes flat.

'Who you think is on your side, Breeze?' I said.

'Me.'

'I see. Your daddy says you're going to get even. How you going to do that? You know who these guys are, where they live?'

He was sitting in the chair in front of my desk now, looking out the window, his eyes downturned at the corners.

'Did you hear me?' I said.

'You know how come one of them had a raincoat on?' he said.

'He didn't want the splatter on his clothes.'

'You know why they left my daddy alive?'

I didn't reply. His gaze was still focused out the window. His hands looked like black starfish on his thighs.

'Long as Mout's alive, I'll probably be staying at his house,' he said. 'Mout' don't mean no more to them than a piece of nutria meat tied in a crab trap.'

'You didn't answer my question.'

'Them two men who killed the white boys out in the Basin? They ain't did that in St. Mary Parish without permission. Not to no white boys, they didn't. And it sure didn't have nothing to do with any black girl they raped in New Iberia.'

'What are you saying?'

'Them boys was killed 'cause of something they done right there in St. Mary.'

'So you think the same guys are trying to do you, and you're going to find them by causing some trouble over in St. Mary Parish? Sounds like a bad plan, Breeze.'

His eyes fastened on mine for the first time, his anger unmasked. 'I

605

ain't said that. I was telling you how it work round here. Blind hog can find an ear of corn if you t'row it on the ground. But you tell white folks grief comes down from the man wit' the money, they ain't gonna hear that. You done wit' me now, suh?'

Late that same afternoon, an elderly priest named Father James Mulcahy called me from St. Peter's Church in town. He used to have a parish made up of poor and black people in the Irish Channel, and had even known Clete Purcel when Clete was a boy, but he had been transferred by the Orleans diocese to New Iberia, where he did little more than say Mass and occasionally hear confessions.

'There's a lady here. I thought she came for reconciliation. But I'm not even sure she's Catholic,' he said.

'I don't understand, Father.'

'She seems confused, I think in need of counseling. I've done all I can for her.'

'You want me to talk to her?'

'I suspect so. She won't leave.'

'Who is she?'

'Her name is Lila Terrebonne. She says she lives in Jeanerette.'

Helen Soileau got in a cruiser with me and we drove to St. Peter's. The late sun shone through the stained glass and suffused the interior of the church with a peculiar gold-and-blue light. Lila Terrebonne sat in a pew by the confessional boxes, immobile, her hands in her lap, her eyes as unseeing as a blind person's. An enormous replication of Christ on the cross hung on the adjacent wall.

At the vestibule door Father Mulcahy placed his hand on my arm. He was a frail man, his bones as weightless as a bird's inside his skin.

'This lady carries a deep injury. The nature of her problem is complex, but be assured it's of the kind that destroys people,' he said.

'She's an alcoholic, Father. Is that what we're talking about here?' Helen said.

'What she told me wasn't in a sacramental situation, but I shouldn't say any more,' he replied.

I walked up the aisle and sat in the pew behind Lila.

'You ever have a guy try to pick you up in church before?' I asked.

She turned and stared at me, her face cut by a column of sunshine. The powder and down on her cheeks glowed as though illuminated by klieg lights. Her milky green eyes were wide with expectation that seemed to have no source.

'I was just thinking about you,' she said.

'I bet.'

'We're all going to die, Dave.'

'You're right. But probably not today. Let's take a ride.'

'It's strange I'd end up sitting here under the Crucifixion. Do you know the Hanged Man in the Tarot?'

'Sure,' I said.

'That's the death card.'

'No, it's St. Sebastian, a Roman soldier who was martyred for his faith. It represents self-sacrifice,' I said.

'The priest wouldn't give me absolution. I'm sure I was baptized Catholic before I was baptized Protestant. My mother was a Catholic,' she said.

Helen stood at the end of Lila's pew, chewing gum, her thumbs hooked in her gunbelt. She rested three fingers on Lila's shoulders.

'How about taking us to dinner?' she said.

An hour later we crossed the parish line into St. Mary. The air was mauve-colored, the bayou dimpled with the feeding of bream, the wind hot and smelling of tar from the highway. We drove up the brick-paved drive of the Terebonne home. Lila's father stood on the portico, a cigar in his hand, his shoulder propped against a brick pillar.

I pulled the cruiser to a stop and started to get out.

'Stay here, Dave. I'm going to take Lila to the door,' Helen said.

'That isn't necessary. I'm feeling much better now. I shouldn't have had a drink with that medication. It always makes me a bit otherworldly,' Lila said.

'Your father doesn't like us, Lila. If he wants to say something, he should have the chance,' Helen said.

But evidently Archer Terrebonne was not up to confronting Helen Soileau that evening. He took a puff from his cigar, then walked inside and closed the heavy door audibly behind him.

The portico and brick parking area were deep in shadow now, the gold and scarlet four-o'clock flowers in full bloom. Helen walked toward the portico with her arm around Lila's shoulders, then watched her go in the house and close the door. Helen continued to look at the door, working the gum in her jaw, the flat of one hand pushed down in the back of her gunbelt.

She opened the passenger door and got in.

'I'd say leapers and vodka,' I said.

'No odor, fried terminals. Yeah, that sounds right. Great combo for a coronary,' she replied.

I turned around in front of the house and drove toward the service road and the bridge over the bayou. Helen kept looking over the seat through the rear window.

'I wanted to kick her old man's ass. With a baton, broken teeth and bones, a real job,' she said. 'Not good, huh, bwana?'

'He's one of those guys who inspire thoughts like that. I wouldn't worry about it.'

'I had him made for a child molester. I was wrong. That woman's been raped, Dave.'

11

The next morning I called Clete Purcel in New Orleans, signed out of the office for the day, and drove across the elevated highway that spanned the chain of bays in the Atchafalaya Basin, across the Mississippi bridge at Baton Rouge, then down through pasture country and the long green corridor through impassable woods that tapered into palmettos and flooded cypress on the north side of Lake Pontchartrain. Then I was at the French Quarter exit, with the sudden and real urban concern of having to park anywhere near the Iberville Welfare Project.

I left my truck off Decatur, two blocks from the Cafe du Monde, and crossed Jackson Square into the shade of Pirates Alley between the lichen-stained garden of the Cathedral and the tiny bookstore that had once been the home of William Faulkner. Then I walked on down St. Ann, in sunlight again, to a tan stucco building with an arched entrance and a courtyard and a grilled balcony upstairs that dripped bougainvillea, where Clete Purcel kept his private investigation agency and sometimes lived.

'You want to take down Jimmy Fig? How hard?' he said.

'We don't have to bounce him off the furniture, if that's what you mean.'

Clete wore a pressed seersucker suit with a tie, and his hair had just been barbered and parted on the side and combed straight down on his head so that it looked like a little boy's.

'Jimmy Figorelli is a low-rent sleaze. Why waste time on a shit bag?' he said.

'It's been a slow week.'

He looked at me with the flat, clear-eyed pause that always indicated his unbelief in what I was saying. Through the heavy bubbled yellow glass in his doors, I saw Megan Flynn walk down the stairs in blue jeans and a T-shirt and carry a box through the breezeway to a U-Haul trailer on the street.

'She's helping me move,' Clete said.

'Move where?'

'A little cottage between New Iberia and Jeanerette. I'm going to head security at that movie set.'

'Are you crazy? That director or producer or whatever he is, Billy Holtzner, is the residue you pour out of spittoons.'

'I ran security for Sally Dio at Lake Tahoe. I think I can handle it.'

'Wait till you meet Holtzner's daughter and boyfriend. They're hypes, or at least she is. Come on, Clete. You were the best cop I ever knew.'

Clete turned his ring on his finger. It was made of gold and silver and embossed with the globe and anchor of the U.S. Marine Corps.

'Yeah, "was" the best cop. I got to change and help Megan. Then we'll check out Jimmy Fig. I think we're firing in the well, though,' he said.

After he had gone upstairs I looked out the back window at the courtyard, the dry wishing well that was cracked and never retained water, the clusters of untrimmed banana trees, Clete's rust-powdered barbells that he religiously pumped and curled, usually half full of booze, every afternoon. I didn't hear Megan open the door to the breezeway behind me.

'What'd you say to get him upset?' she asked. She was perspiring from her work and her T-shirt was damp and shaped against her breasts. She stood in front of the air-conditioning unit and lifted the hair off the back of her neck.

'I think you're sticking tacks in his head,' I said.

'Where the hell you get off talking to me like that?'

'Your brother's friends are scum.'

'Two-thirds of the world is. Grow up.'

'Boxleiter and I had a talk. The death photo of the black guy in the drainpipe was a setup.'

'You're full of shit, Dave.'

We stared at each other in the refrigerated coolness of the room, almost slit-eyed with antagonism. Her eyes had a reddish-brown cast in them like fire inside amber glass.

'I think I'll wait outside,' I said.

'You know what homoeroticism is? Guys who aren't quite gay but who've got a yen they never deal with?' she said.

'You'd better not hurt him.'

'Oh, yeah?' she said, and stepped toward me, her hands shoved in her back pockets like a baseball manager getting in an umpire's face. Her neck was sweaty and ringed with dirt and her upper lip was beaded with moisture. 'I'm not going to take your bullshit, Dave. You go fuck yourself.' Then her face, which was heart-shaped and tender to look at and burning with anger at the same time, seemed to go out of focus. '*Hurt* him? My father was nailed alive to a board wall. You lecture me on hurting people? Don't you feel just a little bit embarrassed, you self-righteous sonofabitch?'

I walked outside into the sunshine. Sweat was running out of my hair; the backdraft of a passing sanitation truck enveloped me with dust and the smell of decaying food. I wiped my forehead on my sleeve and was repelled by my own odor.

Clete and I drove out of the Quarter, crossed Canal, and headed up Magazine in his convertible. He had left the top down while the car had been parked on the street and the seats and metal surfaces were like the touch of a clothes iron. He drove with his left hand, his right clenched around a can of beer wrapped in a paper sack.

'You want to forget it?' I asked.

'No, you want to see the guy, we see the guy.'

'I heard Jimmy Fig wasn't a bad kid before he was at Khe Sanh.'

'Yeah, I heard that story. He got wounded and hooked on morphine. Makes great street talk. I'll tell you another story. He was the wheelman on a jewelry store job in Memphis. It should have been an easy in-and-out, smash-and-grab deal, except the guys with him decided they didn't want witnesses, so they executed an eighty-year-old Jew who had survived Bergen-Belsen.'

'I apologize to you and Megan for what I said back there.'

'I've got hypertension, chronic obesity, and my own rap sheet at NOPD. What do guys like us care about stuff like that?'

He pressed his aviator glasses against his nose, hiding his eyes. Sweat leaked out of his porkpie hat and glistened on his flexed jaw.

Jimmy Figorelli ran a sandwich shop and cab stand on Magazine just below Audubon Park. He was a tall, kinetic, wired man, with luminous black eyes and black hair that grew in layers on his body.

He was chopping green onions in an apron and never missed a beat when we entered the front door and stood under the bladed ceiling fan that turned overhead.

'You want to know who put a hit on Cool Breeze Broussard? You come to my place of business and ask me a question like that, like you need the weather report or something?' He laughed to himself and raked the chopped onions off the chopping board onto a sheet of wax paper and started slicing a boned roast into strips.

'The guy doesn't deserve what's coming down on him, Jimmy. Maybe you can help set it right,' I said.

'The guys you're interested in don't fax me their day-to-day operations,' he replied.

Clete kept lifting his shirt up from his shoulders with his fingers.

'I got a terrible sunburn, Jimmy. I want to be back in the air-conditioning with a vodka and tonic, not listening to a shuck that might cause a less patient person to come around behind that counter,' Clete said.

Jimmy Figorelli scratched an eyebrow, took off his apron and picked up a broom and began sweeping up green sawdust from around an ancient Coca-Cola cooler that sweated with coldness.

'What I heard is the clip went to some guys already got it in for Broussard. It's nigger trouble, Purcel. What else can I tell you? *Semper fi*,' he said.

'I heard you were in the First Cav at Khe Sanh,' I said.

'Yeah, I was on a Jolly Green that took a RPG through the door. You know what I think all that's worth?'

'You paid dues lowlifes don't. Why not act like it?' I said.

'I got a Purple Heart with a *V* for valor. If I ever find it while I'm cleaning out my garage, I'll send it to you,' he said.

I could hear Clete breathing beside me, almost feel the oily heat his skin gave off.

'You know what they say about the First Cav patch, Jimmy. "The horse they couldn't ride, the line they couldn't cross, the color that speaks for itself,"' Clete said.

'Yeah, well, kiss my ass, you Irish prick, and get out of my store.'

'Let's go,' I said to Clete.

He stared at me, his face flushed, the skin drawn back against the eye sockets. Then he followed me outside, where we stood under an oak and watched one of Jimmy Fig's cabs pick up a young black woman who carried a red lacquered purse and wore a tank top and a miniskirt and white fishnet stockings.

'You didn't like what I said?' Clete asked.

'Why get on the guy's outfit? It's not your way.'

'You got a point. Let me correct that.'

He walked back inside, his hands at his sides, balled into fists as big as hams.

'Hey, Jimmy, I didn't mean anything about the First Cav. I just can't take the way you chop onions. It irritates the hell out of me,' he said.

Then he drove his right fist, lifting his shoulder and all his weight into the blow, right into Jimmy Figorelli's face.

Jimmy held on to the side of the Coca-Cola box, his hand trembling uncontrollably on his mouth, his eyes dilated with shock, his fingers shining with blood and bits of teeth.

Three days later it began to rain, and it rained through the Labor Day weekend and into the following week. The bayou by the dock rose above the cattails and into the canebrake, my rental boats filled with water, and moccasins crawled into our yard. On Saturday night, during a downpour, Father James Mulcahy knocked on our front door.

He carried an umbrella and wore a Roman collar and a rain-flecked gray suit and a gray fedora. When he stepped inside he tried not to breathe into my face.

'I'm sorry for coming out without calling first,' he said.

'We're glad you dropped by. Can I offer you something?' I said.

He touched at his mouth and sat down in a stuffed chair. The rain was blowing against the gallery, and the tin roof of the bait shop quivered with light whenever thunder was about to roll across the swamp.

'Would you like a drink, sir?' I asked.

'No, no, that wouldn't be good. Coffee's fine. I have to tell you about something, Mr. Robicheaux. It bothers me deeply,' he said.

His hands were liver-spotted, ridged with blue veins, the skin as thin as parchment on the bones. Bootsie brought coffee and sugar and hot milk on a tray from the kitchen. When the priest lifted the cup to his mouth his eyes seemed to look through the steam at nothing, then he said, 'Do you believe in evil, Mr. Robicheaux? I don't mean the wicked deeds we sometimes do in a weak moment. I mean evil in the darkest theological sense.'

'I'm not sure, Father. I've seen enough of it in people not to look for a source outside of ourselves.'

'I was a chaplain in Thailand during the Vietnam War. I knew a young soldier who participated in a massacre. You might have seen the pictures. The most unforgettable was of a little boy holding his grandmother's skirts in terror while she begged for their lives. I spent many hours with that young soldier, but I could never remove the evil that lived in his dreams.'

'I don't understand how—' I began.

He raised his hand. 'Listen to me,' he said. 'There was another man, a civilian profiteer who lived on the air base. His corporation made incendiary bombs. I told him the story of the young soldier who had machine-gunned whole families in a ditch. The profiteer's rejoinder was to tell me about a strafing gun his company had patented. In thirty seconds it could tear the sod out of an entire football field. In that moment I think that man's eyes were the conduit into the abyss.'

Bootsie's face wore no expression, but I saw her look at me, then back at the priest.

'Please have dinner with us,' she said.

'Oh, I've intruded enough. I really haven't made my point either. Last night in the middle of the storm a truck stopped outside the rectory. I thought it was a parishioner. When I opened the door a man in a slouch hat and raincoat was standing there. I've never felt the presence of evil so strongly in my life. I was convinced he was there to kill me. I think he would have done it if the housekeeper and Father Lemoyne hadn't walked up behind me.

'He pointed his arm at me and said, "Don't you break the seal." Then he got back in his truck and drove away with the lights off.'

'You mean divulge the content of a confession?' I asked.

'He was talking about the Terrebonne woman. I'm sure of it. But what she told me wasn't under the seal,' he replied.

'You want to tell me about Lila, Father?' I said.

'No, it wouldn't be proper. A confidence is a confidence. Also, she wasn't entirely coherent and I might do her a great disservice,' he said. But his face clouded, and it was obvious his own words did little to reassure him.

'This man in the truck, Father? If his name is Harpo, we want to be very careful of him,' I said.

'His eyes,' the priest said.

'Sir?'

'They were like the profiteer's. Without moral light. A man like that speaking of the confessional seal. It offends something in me in a way I can't describe.'

'Have dinner with us,' I said.

'Yes, that's very kind of you. Your home seems to have a great warmth to it. From outside it truly looked like a haven in the storm. Could I have that drink after all?'

He sat at the table with a glass of cream sherry, his eyes abstract, feigning attention, like those of people who realize that momentary refuge and the sharing of fear with others will not relieve them of the fact that death may indeed have taken up residence inside them.

Monday morning I drove down Bayou Teche through Jeanerette into the little town of Franklin and talked to the chief of police. He was a very light mulatto in his early forties who wore sideburns and a gold ring in his ear and a lacquered-brim cap on the back of his head.

'A man name of Harpo? There used to be a Harpo Delahoussey. He was a sheriff's deputy, did security at the Terrebonne cannery,' the police chief said.

'That's not the one. This guy was maybe his nephew. He was a Franklin police officer. People called him Little Harpo,' I said.

He fiddled with a pencil and gazed out the window. It was still raining, and a black man rode a bicycle down the sidewalk, his body framed against the smoky neon of a bar across the street.

'When I was a kid there was a cop round here name of H. Q. Scruggs.' He wet his lips. 'When he come into the quarters we knew to call him Mr. H.Q. Not Officer. That wasn't enough for this gentleman. But I remember white folks calling him Harpo sometimes. As I recall, he'd been a guard up at Angola, too. If you want to talk about him, I'll give you the name and address of a man might help you.'

'You don't care to talk about him?'

He laid the pencil flat on his desk blotter. 'I don't like to even remember him. Fortunately today I don't have to,' he said.

Clem Maddux sat on his gallery, smoking a cigarette, in a sway-back deer-hide chair lined with a quilt for extra padding. One of his legs was amputated at the torso, the other above the knee. His girth was huge, his stomach pressing in staggered layers against the oversized ink-dark blue jeans he wore. His skin was as pink and unblemished as a baby's, but around his neck goiters hung from his flesh like a necklace of duck's eggs.

'You staring at me, Mr. Robicheaux?' he asked.

'No, sir.'

'It's Buerger's Disease. Smoking worsens it. But I got diabetes and cancer of the prostate, too. I got diseases that'll outlive the one that kills me,' he said, then laughed and wiped spittle off his lips with his wrist.

'You were a gun bull at Angola with Harpo Scruggs?'

'No, I was head of farm machinery. I didn't carry a weapon. Harpo was a tower guard, then a shotgun guard on horseback. That must have been forty years ago.'

'What kind of hack was he?'

'Piss-poor in my opinion. How far back you go?'

'You talking about the Red Hat gang and the men buried under the levee?'

'There was this old fart used to come off a corn-whiskey drunk meaner than a razor in your shoe. He'd single out a boy from his gang and tell him to start running. Harpo asked to get in on it.'

'Asked to kill someone?'

'It was a colored boy from Laurel Hill. He'd sassed the field boss at morning count. When the food truck come out to the levee at noon, Harpo pulled the colored boy out of the line and told him he wasn't eating no lunch till he finished sawing a stump out of the river bottom. Harpo walked him off into some gum trees by the water, then I seen the boy starting off on his own, looking back uncertain-like while Harpo was telling him something. Then I heard it, *pow, pow,* both barrels. Double-ought bucks, from not more than eight or ten feet.'

Maddux tossed his cigarette over the railing into the flower bed.

'What happened to Scruggs?' I asked.

'He done a little of this, a little of that, I guess.'

'That's a little vague, Cap.'

'He road-ganged in Texas a while, then bought into a couple of whorehouses. What do you care anyway? The sonofabitch is probably squatting on the coals.'

'He's squatting—'

'He got burned up with a Mexican chippy in Juárez fifteen years ago. Wasn't nothing left of him except a bag of ash and some teeth. Damn, son, y'all ought to update and get you some computers.'

12

Two days later I sat at my desk, sifting through the Gypsy fortune-telling deck called the Tarot. I had bought the deck at a store in Lafayette, but the instruction book that accompanied it dealt more with the meaning of the cards than with the origins of their iconography. Regardless, it would be impossible for anyone educated in a traditional Catholic school not to recognize the historical associations of the imagery in the Hanged Man.

The phone on my desk buzzed.

'Clete Purcel and Megan Flynn just pulled up,' the sheriff said.

'Yeah?'

'Get him out of here.'

'Skipper . . .'

He hung up.

A moment later Clete tapped on my glass and opened the door, then paused and looked back down the hall, his face perplexed.

'What happened, the john overflow in the waiting room again?' he said.

'Why's that?'

'A pall is hanging over the place every time I walk in. What do those guys do for kicks, watch snuff films? In fact, I asked the dispatcher that. Definitely no sense of humor.'

He sat down and looked around my office, grinned at me for no reason, straightened his back, flexed his arms, bounced his palms up and down on the chair.

'Megan's with you?' I said.

'How'd you know that?'

'Uh, I think the sheriff saw y'all from his window.'

'The sheriff? I get it. He told you to roll out the welcome wagon.' His eyes roved merrily over my face. 'How about we treat you to lunch at Lagniappe Too?'

'I'm buried.'

'Megan gave you her drill-instructor impersonation the other day?'
'It's very convincing.'
He beat out a staccato with his hands on the chair arms.
'Will you stop that and tell me what's on your mind?' I said.
'This cat Billy Holtzner. I've seen him somewhere. Like from Vietnam.'
'Holtzner?'
'So we had nasty little marshmallows over there, too. Anyway, I go, "Were you in the Crotch?" He says, "The Crotch?" I say, "Yeah, the Marine Corps. Were you around Da Nang?" What kind of answer do I get? He sucks his teeth and goes back to his clipboard like I'm not there.'
He waited for me to speak. When I didn't he said, '*What?*'
'I hate to see you mixed up with them.'
'See you later, Streak.'
'I'm coming with you,' I said, and stuck the Hanged Man in my shirt pocket.

We ate lunch at Lagniappe Too, just down from The Shadows. Megan sat by the window with her hat on. Her hair was curved on her cheeks, and her mouth looked small and red when she took a piece of food off her fork. The light through the window seemed to frame her silhouette against the green wall of bamboo that grew in front of The Shadows. She saw me staring at her.
'Is something troubling you, Dave?' she asked.
'You know Lila Terrebonne?'
'The senator's granddaughter?'
'She comes to our attention on occasion. The other day we had to pick her up at the church, sitting by herself under a crucifix. Out of nowhere she asked me about the Hanged Man in the Tarot.'
I slipped the card out of my shirt pocket and placed it on the tablecloth by Megan's plate.
'Why tell me?' she said.
'Does it mean something to you?'
I saw Clete lower his fork into his plate, felt his eyes fix on the side of my face.
'A man hanging upside down from a tree. The tree forms a cross,' Megan said.
'The figure becomes Peter the Apostle, as well as Christ and St. Sebastian. Sebastian was tied to a tree and shot with darts by his fellow Roman soldiers. Peter asked to be executed upside down. You notice, the figure makes a cross with his legs in the act of dying?' I said.
Megan had stopped eating. Her cheeks were freckled with discoloration, as though an invisible pool of frigid air had burned her face.
'What is this, Dave?' Clete said.

618

'Maybe nothing,' I said.

'Just lunch conversation?' he said.

'The Terrebonnes have had their thumbs in lots of pies,' I said.

'Will you excuse me, please?' Megan said.

She walked between the tables to the rest room, her purse under her arm, her funny straw hat crimped across the back of her red hair.

'What the hell's the matter with you?' Clete said.

That evening I drove to Red Lerille's Health & Racquet Club in Lafayette and worked out with free weights and on the Hammer-Strength machines, then ran two miles on the second-story track that overlooked the basketball courts.

I hung my towel around my neck and did leg stretches on the handrail. Down below, some men were playing a pickup basketball game, thudding into one another clumsily, slapping one another's shoulders when they made a shot. But an Indonesian or Malaysian man at the end of the court, where the speed and heavy bags were hung, was involved in a much more intense and solitary activity. He wore sweats and tight red leather gloves, the kind with a metal dowel across the palm, and he ripped his fists into the heavy bag and sent it spinning on the chain, then speared it with his feet, hard enough to almost knock down a kid who was walking by.

He grinned at the boy by way of apology, then moved over to the speed bag and began whacking it against the rebound board, without rhythm or timing, slashing it for the effect alone.

'You were at Cisco's house. You're Mr. Robicheaux,' a woman's voice said behind me.

It was Billy Holtzner's daughter. But her soapy blue eyes were focused now, actually pleasant, like a person who has stepped out of one identity into another.

'You remember me?' she asked.

'Sure.'

'We didn't introduce ourselves the other day. I'm Geraldine Holtzner. The boxer down there is Anthony. He's an accountant for the studio. I'm sorry for our rudeness.'

'You weren't rude.'

'I know you don't like my father. Not many people do. We're not problem visitors here. If you have one, it's Cisco Flynn,' she said.

'Cisco?'

'He owes my father a lot of money. Cisco thinks he can avoid his responsibilities by bringing a person like Swede Boxleiter around.'

She gripped the handrail and extended one leg at a time behind her. Her wild, brownish-red hair shimmered with perspiration.

'You let that guy down there shoot you up?' I asked.

'I'm all right today. Sometimes I just have a bad day. You're a funny guy for a cop. You ever have a screen test?'

'Why not get rid of the problem altogether?'

But she wasn't listening now. 'This area is full of violent people. It's the South. It lives in the woodwork down here. This black man who's coming after the Terrebonnes, why don't you do something about him?' she said.

'Which black man? Are you talking about Cool Breeze Broussard?'

'Which? Yeah, that's a good question. You know the story about the murdered slave woman, the children who were poisoned? If I had stuff like that in my family, I'd jump off a cliff. No wonder Lila Terrebonne's a drunk.'

'It was nice seeing you,' I said.

'Gee, why don't you just say fuck you and turn your back on people?'

Her skin was the color of milk that has browned in a pan, her blue eyes dancing in her face. She wiped her hair and throat with a towel and threw it at me.

'That kick-boxing stuff Anthony's doing? He learned it from me,' she said.

Then she raised her face up into mine, her lips slightly parted, speckled with saliva, her eyes filled with anticipation and need.

On the way back home I stopped in the New Iberia city library and looked up a late-nineteenth-century reminiscence written about our area by a New England lady named Abigail Dowling, a nurse who came here during a yellow fever epidemic and was radicalized not by slavery itself and the misery it visited upon the black race but by what she called its dehumanizing effects on the white.

One of the families about which she wrote in detail was the Terrebonnes of St. Mary Parish.

Before the Civil War, Elijah Terrebonne had been a business partner in the slave trade with Nathan Bedford Forrest and later had ridden at Forrest's side during the battle of Brice's Crossing, where a Minié shattered his arm and took him out of the war. But Elijah had also been below the bluffs at Fort Pillow when black troops who begged on their knees were executed at point-blank range in retaliation for a sixty-mile scorched-earth sweep by Federal troops into northern Mississippi.

'He was of diminutive stature, with a hard, compact body. He sat his horse with the rigidity of a clothes pin,' Abigail Dowling wrote in her journal. 'His countenance was handsome, certainly, of a rosy hue, and it exuded a martial light when he talked of the War. In consideration of his physical stature I tried to overlook his imperious manner. In spite of his propensity for miscegenation, he loved his wife and their twin girls and was unduly possessive about them, perhaps in part because of his own romantic misdeeds.

'Unfortunately for the poor black souls on his plantation, the lamps of charity and pity did not burn brightly in his heart. I have been told General Forrest tried to stop the slaughter of negro soldiers below the bluffs. I believe Elijah Terrebonne had no such redemptive memory for himself. I believe the fits of anger that made him draw human blood with a horse whip had their origins in the faces of dead black men who journeyed nightly to Elijah's bedside, vainly begging mercy from one who had murdered his soul.'

The miscegenation mentioned by Abigail Dowling involved a buxom slave woman named Lavonia, whose husband, Big Walter, had been killed by a falling tree. Periodically Elijah Terrebonne rode to the edge of the fields and called her away from her work, in view of the other slaves and the white overseer, and walked her ahead of his horse into the woods, where he copulated with her in an unused sweet potato cellar. Later, he heard that the overseer had been talking freely in the saloon, joking with a drink in his hand at the fireplace, stoking the buried resentment and latent contempt of other landless whites about the lust of his employer. Elijah laid open his face with a quirt and adjusted his situation by moving Lavonia up to the main house as a cook and a wet nurse for his children.

But when he returned from Brice's Crossing, with pieces of bone still working their way out of the surgeon's incision in his arm, the Teche country was occupied, his house and barns looted, the orchards and fields reduced to soot blowing in the wind. The only meat on the plantation consisted of seven smoked hams Lavonia had buried in the woods before the Federal flotilla had come up the Teche.

The Terrebonnes made coffee out of acorns and ate the same meager rations as the blacks. Some of the freed males on the plantation went to work on shares; others followed the Yankee soldiers marching north into the Red River campaign. When the food ran out, Lavonia was among a group of women and elderly folk who were assembled in front of their cabins by Elijah Terrebonne and then told they would have to leave.

She went to Elijah's wife.

Abigail Dowling wrote in the journal, 'It was a wretched sight, this stout field woman without a husband, with no concept of historical events or geography, about to be cast out in a ruined land filled with night riders and drunken soldiers. Her simple entreaty could not have described her plight more adequately: "I'se got fo' children, Missy. What's we gonna go? What's I gonna feed them with?"'

Mrs. Terrebonne granted her a one-month reprieve, either to find a husband or to receive help from the Freedmen's Bureau.

The journal continued: 'But Lavonia was a sad and ignorant creature who thought guile could overcome the hardness of heart in her former masters. She put cyanide in the family's food, believing they would become ill and dependent upon her for their daily care.

'Both of the Terrebonne girls died. Elijah would have never known the cause of their deaths, except for the careless words of Lavonia's youngest child, who came to him, the worst choice among men, to seek solace. The child blurted out, "My mama been crying, Mas'er. She got poison in a bottle under her bed. She say the devil give it to her and made her hurt somebody with it. I think she gonna take it herself."

'By firelight Elijah dug up the coffins of his children from the wet clay and unwound the wrappings from their bodies. Their skin was covered with pustules the color and shape of pearls. He pressed his hand on their chests and breathed the air trapped in their lungs and swore it smelled of almonds.

'His rage and madness could be heard all the way across the fields to the quarters. Lavonia tried to hide with her children in the swamp, but to no avail. Her own people found her, and in fear of Elijah's wrath, they hanged her with a man's belt from a persimmon tree.'

What did it all mean? Why did Geraldine Holtzner allude to the story at Red's Gym in Lafayette? I didn't know. But in the morning Megan Flynn telephoned me at the dock. Clete Purcel had been booked on a DWI and a black man had started a fire on the movie set in the Terrebonnes' front yard.

She wanted to talk.

'Talk? Clete's in the bag and you want to talk?' I said.

'I've done something terribly wrong. I'm just down the road. Will it bother you if I come by?'

'Yes, it will.'

'Dave?'

'What?'

Then her voice broke.

13

Megan sat at a back table in the bait shop with a cup of coffee and waited for me while I rang up the bill on two fishermen who had just finished eating at the counter. Her hat rested by her elbow and her hair blew in the wind from the fan, but there was a twisted light in her eyes, as though she could not concentrate on anything outside her skin.

I sat down across from her.

'Y'all had a fight?' I asked.

'It was over the black man who started the fire,' she said.

'That doesn't make any sense,' I said.

'It's Cool Breeze Broussard. It has to be. He was going to set fire to the main house but something scared him off. So he poured gasoline under a trailer on the set.'

'Why should you and Clete fight over that?'

'I helped get Cool Breeze out of jail. I knew about all his trouble in St. Mary Parish and his wife's suicide and his problems with the Terrebonne family. I wanted the story. I pushed everything else out of my mind . . . Maybe I planted some ideas in him about revenge.'

'You still haven't told me why y'all fought.'

'Clete said people who set fires deserve to be human candles themselves. He started talking about some marines he saw trapped inside a burning tank.'

'Breeze has always had his own mind about things. He's not easily influenced, Megan.'

'Swede will kill him. He'll kill anybody he thinks is trying to hurt Cisco.'

'That's it, huh? You think you're responsible for getting a black man into it with a psychopath?'

'Yes. And he's not a psychopath. You've got this guy all wrong.'

'How about getting Clete into the middle of it? You think that might be a problem, too?'

'I feel very attached—'

'Cut it out, Megan.'

'I have a deep—'

'He was available and you made him your point man. Except he doesn't have any idea of what's going on.'

Her eyes drifted onto mine, then they began to film. I heard Batist come inside the shop, then go back out.

'Why'd you want to put him on that movie set?' I said.

'My brother. He's mixed up with bad people in the Orient. I think the Terrebonnes are in it, too.'

'What do you know about the Terrebonnes?'

'My father hated them.'

A customer came in and picked a package of Red Man off the wire rack and left the money on the register. Megan straightened her back and touched at one eye with her finger.

'I called the St. Mary Sheriff's Department. Clete will be arraigned at ten,' I said.

'You don't hold me in very high regard, do you?'

'You just made a mistake. Now you've owned up to it. I think you're a good person, Meg.'

'What do I do about Clete?'

'My father used to say never treat a brave man as less.'

'I wish Cisco and I had never come back here.'

But you always do, I thought. *Because of a body arched into wood planks, its blood pooling in the dust, its crusted wounds picked by chickens.*

'What did you say?' she asked.

'Nothing. I didn't say anything.'

'I'm going. I'll be at Cisco's house for a spell.'

She put a half dollar on the counter for the coffee and walked out the screen door. Then, just before she reached her automobile, she turned and looked back at me. She held her straw hat in her fingers, by her thigh, and with her other hand she brushed her hair back on her head, her face lifted into the sunlight.

Batist flung a bucket full of water across one of the spool tables.

'When they make cow eyes at you, it ain't 'cause they want to go to church, no,' he said.

'What?'

'Her daddy got killed when she was li'l. She always coming round to talk to a man older than herself. Like they ain't no other man in New Iberia. You got to go to collitch to figure it out?' he said.

Two hours later Helen and I drove over to Mout' Broussard's house on the west side of town. A black four-door sedan with tinted windows and a phone antenna was parked in the dirt driveway, the back door open.

Inside, we could see a man in a dark suit, wearing aviator glasses, unlocking the handcuffs on Cool Breeze Broussard.

Helen and I walked toward the car as Adrien Glazier and two male FBI agents got out with Cool Breeze.

'What's happenin', Breeze?' I said.

'They give me a ride to my daddy's,' he replied.

'Your business here needs to wait, Mr. Robicheaux,' Adrien Glazier said.

Out of the corner of my eye I saw one of the male agents touch Cool Breeze on the arm with one finger and point for him to wait on the gallery.

'What are you going to do with him?' I asked Adrien Glazier.

'Nothing.'

'Breeze is operating out of his depth. You know that. Why are you leaving the guy out there?' I said.

'Has he complained to you? Who appointed you his special oversight person?' she replied.

'You ever hear of a guy named Harpo Scruggs?' I asked.

'No.'

'I think he's got the contract on Breeze. Except he's supposed to be dead.'

'Then you've got something to work on. In the meantime, we'll handle things here. Thanks for dropping by,' the man who had uncuffed Cool Breeze said. He was olive-skinned, his dark blond hair cut short, his opaque demeanor one that allowed him to be arrogant without ever being accountable.

Helen stepped toward him, her feet slightly spread.

'Reality check, you pompous fuck, this is our jurisdiction. We go where we want. You try to run us off an investigation, you're going to be picking up the soap in our jail tonight,' she said.

'She's the one busted up Boxleiter,' the other male agent said, his elbow hooked over the top of the driver's door, a smile at the edge of his mouth.

'Yes?' she said.

'Impressive . . . Mean shit,' he said.

'We're gone,' Adrien Glazier said.

'Run this guy Scruggs. He was a gun bull at Angola. Maybe he's hooked up with the Dixie Mafia,' I said.

'A dead man? *Right*,' she said, then got in her car with her two colleagues and drove away.

Helen stared after them, her hands on her hips.

'Broussard's the bait tied down under the tree stand, isn't he?' she said.

'That's the way I'd read it,' I said.

Cool Breeze watched us from the swing on the gallery. His brogans were caked with mud and he spun a cloth cap on the tip of his index finger.

I sat down on the wood steps and looked out at the street.

'Where's Mout'?' I asked.

'Staying at his sister's.'

'You're playing other people's game,' I said.

'They gonna know when I'm in town.'

'Bad way to think, podna.'

I heard the swing creak behind me, then his brogans scuffing the boards under him as the swing moved back and forth. A young woman carrying a bag of groceries walked past the house and the sound of the swing stopped.

'My dead wife Ida, I hear her in my sleep sometimes. Talking to me from under the water, wit' that icy chain wrapped round her. I want to lift her up, out of the silt, pick the ice out of her mout' and eyes. But the chain just too heavy. I pull and pull and my arms is like lead, and all the time they ain't no air getting down to her. You ever have a dream like that?' he said.

I turned and looked at him, my ears ringing, my face suddenly cold.

'I t'ought so. You blame me for what I do?' he said.

That afternoon I made telephone calls to Juárez, Mexico, and to the sheriff's departments in three counties along the Tex-Mex border. No one had any information about Harpo Scruggs or his death. Then an FBI agent in El Paso referred me to a retired Texas Ranger by the name of Lester Cobb. His accent was deep down in his breathing passages, like heated air breaking through the top of oatmeal.

'You knew him?' I said into the receiver.

'At a distance. Which was as close as I wanted to get.'

'Why's that?'

'He was a pimp. He run Mexican girls up from Chihuahua.'

'How'd he die?'

'They say he was in a hot pillow joint acrost the river. A girl put one in his ear, then set fire to the place and done herself.'

'They say?'

'He was wanted down there. Why would he go back into Juárez to get laid? That story never did quite wash for me.'

'If he's alive, where would I look for him?'

'Cockfights, cathouses, pigeon shoots. He's the meanest bucket of shit with a badge I ever run acrost . . . Mr. Robicheaux?'

626

'Yes, sir?'

'I hope he's dead. He rope-drug a Mexican behind his Jeep, out through the rocks and cactus. You get in a situation with him . . . Oh, hell, I'm too damn old to tell another lawman his business.'

It rained that evening, and from my lighted gallery I watched it fall on the trees and the dock and the tin roof of the bait shop and on the wide, yellow, dimpled surface of the bayou itself.

I could not shake the images of Cool Breeze's recurring dream from my mind. I stepped out into the rain and cut a half-dozen roses from the bushes in the front garden and walked down the slope with them to the end of the dock.

Batist had pulled the tarp out on the guy wires and turned on the string of electric lights. I stood at the railing, watching the current drift southward toward West Cote Blanche Bay and eventually the Gulf, where many years ago my father's drilling rig had punched into an early pay sand, blowing the casing out of the hole. When the gas ignited, a black-red inferno ballooned up through the tower, all the way to the monkey board where my father worked as a derrick man. The heat was so great the steel spars burned and collapsed like matchsticks.

He and my murdered wife Annie and the dead men from my platoon used to speak to me through the rain. I found saloons by the water, always by the water, where I could trap and control light and all meaning inside three inches of Beam, with a Jax on the side, while the rain ran down the windows and rippled the walls with neon shadows that had no color.

Now, Annie and my father and dead soldiers no longer called me up on the phone. But I never underestimated the power of the rain or the potential of the dead, or denied them their presence in the world.

And for that reason I dropped the roses into the water and watched them float toward the south, the green leaves beaded with water as bright as crystal, the petals as darkly red as a woman's mouth turned toward you on the pillow for the final time.

On the way back up to the house I saw Clete Purcel's chartreuse Cadillac come down the dirt road and turn into the drive. The windows were streaked with mud, the convertible top as ragged as a layer of chicken feathers. He rolled down the window and grinned, in the same way that a mask grins.

'Got a minute?' he said.

I opened the passenger door and sat in the cracked leather seat beside him.

'You doing okay, Cletus?' I asked.

'Sure. Thanks for calling the bondsman.' He rubbed his face. 'Megan came by?'

'Yeah. Early this morning.' I kept my eyes focused on the rain blowing out of the trees onto my lighted gallery.

'She told you we were quits?'

'Not exactly.'

'I got no bad feelings about it. That's how it shakes out sometimes.' He widened his eyes. 'I need to take a shower and get some sleep. I'll be okay with some sleep.'

'Come in and eat with us.'

'I'm keeping the security gig at the set. If you see this guy Broussard, tell him not to set any more fires . . . Don't look at me like that, Streak. The trailer he burned had propane tanks on it. What if somebody had been in there?'

'He thinks the Terrebonnes are trying to have him killed.'

'I hope they work it out. In the meantime, tell him to keep his ass off the set.'

'You don't want to eat?'

'No. I'm not feeling too good.' He looked out into the shadows and the water dripping out of the trees. 'I got in over my head. It's my fault. I'm not used to this crap.'

'She's got strong feelings for you, Clete.'

'Yeah, my temp loves her cat. See you tomorrow, Dave.'

I watched him back out into the road, then shift into low, his big head bent forward over the wheel, his expression as meaningless as a jack-o'-lantern's.

After Bootsie and Alafair and I ate dinner, I drove up the Loreauville road to Cisco Flynn's house. When no one answered the bell, I walked the length of the gallery, past the baskets of hanging ferns, and looked through the side yard. In back, inside a screened pavilion, Cisco and Megan were eating steaks at a linen-covered table with Swede Boxleiter. I walked across the grass toward the yellow circle of light made by an outside bug lamp. Their faces were warm, animated with their conversation, their movements automatic when one or the other wanted a dish passed or his silver wine goblet refilled. My loafer cracked a small twig.

'Sorry to interrupt,' I said.

'Is that you, Dave? Join us. We have plenty,' Cisco said.

'I wanted to see Megan a minute. I'll wait out in my truck,' I said.

The three of them were looking out into the darkness, the tossed salad and pink slices of steak on their plates like part of a nineteenth-century French still life. In that instant I knew that whatever differences defined them today, the three of them were held together by a mutual experience that an outsider would never understand. Then Boxleiter broke the moment by picking up a decanter and pouring wine into his goblet, spilling it like drops of blood on the linen.

Ten minutes later Megan found me in the front yard.

'This morning you told me I had Boxleiter all wrong,' I said.

'That's right. He's not what he seems.'

'He's a criminal.'

'To some.'

'I saw pictures of the dude he shanked in the Canon City pen.'

'Probably courtesy of Adrien Glazier. By the way, the guy you think he did? He was in the Mexican Mafia. He had Swede's cell partner drowned in a toilet . . . This is why you came out here?'

'No, I wanted to tell you I'm going to leave y'all alone. Y'all take your own fall, Megan.'

'Who asked you to intercede on our behalf anyway? You're still pissed off about Clete, aren't you?' she said.

I walked across the lawn toward my truck. The wind was loud in the trees and made shadows on the grass. She caught up with me just as I opened the door to the truck.

'The problem is you don't understand your own thinking,' she said. 'You were raised in the church. You see my father's death as St. Sebastian's martyrdom or something. You believe in forgiving people for what's not yours to forgive. I'd like to take their eyes out.'

'*Their* eyes. Who is *their*, Megan?'

'Every hypocrite in this—' She stopped, stepping back as though retreating from her own words.

'Ah, we finally got to it,' I said.

I got in the truck and closed the door. I could hear her heated breathing in the dark, see her chest rise and fall against her shirt. Swede Boxleiter walked out of the side yard into the glow of light from the front gallery, an empty plate in one hand, a meat fork in the other.

14

The tall man who wore yellow-tinted glasses and cowboy boots and a weathered, smoke-colored Stetson made a mistake. While the clerk in a Lafayette pawnshop and gun store bagged up two boxes of .22 magnum shells for him, the man in the Stetson happened to notice a bolt-action military rifle up on the rack.

'That's an Italian 6.5 Carcano, ain't it? Hand it down here and I'll show you something,' he said.

He wrapped the leather sling over his left arm, opened the bolt, and inserted his thumb in the chamber to make sure the gun was not loaded.

'This is the same kind Oswald used. Now, here's the mathematics. The shooter up in that book building had to get off three shots in five and a half seconds. You got a stopwatch?' he said.

'No,' the clerk said.

'Here, look at my wristwatch. Now, I'm gonna dry-fire it three times. Remember, I ain't even aiming and Oswald was up six stories, shooting at a moving target.'

'That's not good for the firing pin,' the clerk said.

'It ain't gonna hurt it. It's a piece of shit anyway, ain't it?'

'I wish you wouldn't do that, sir.'

The man in the Stetson set the rifle back on the glass counter and pinched his thumb and two fingers inside his Red Man pouch and put the tobacco in his jaw. The clerk's eyes broke when he tried to return the man's stare.

'You ought to develop a historical curiosity. Then maybe you wouldn't have to work the rest of your life at some little pissant job,' the man said, and picked up his sack and started for the front door.

The clerk, out of shame and embarrassment, said to the man's back, 'How come you know so much about Dallas?'

'I was there, boy. That's a fact. The puff of smoke on the grassy knoll?' He winked at the clerk and went out.

The clerk stood at the window, his face tingling, feeling belittled, searching in his mind for words he could fling out the door but knowing he would not have the courage to do so. He watched the man in the Stetson drive down the street to an upholstery store in a red pickup truck with Texas plates. The clerk wrote down the tag number and called the sheriff's department.

On Friday morning Father James Mulcahy rose just before dawn, fixed two sandwiches and a thermos of coffee in the rectory kitchen, and drove to Henderson Swamp, outside of the little town of Breaux Bridge, where a parishioner had given him the use of a motorized houseboat.

He drove along the hard-packed dirt track atop the levee, above the long expanse of bays and channels and flooded cypress and willows that comprised the swamp. He parked at the bottom of the levee, walked across a board plank to the houseboat, released the mooring ropes, and floated out from the willows into the current before he started the engine.

The clouds in the eastern sky were pink and gray, and the wind lifted the moss on the dead cypress trunks. Inside the cabin, he steered the houseboat along the main channel, until he saw a cove back in the trees where the bream were popping the surface along the edge of the hyacinths. When he turned into the cove and cut the engine, he heard an outboard coming hard down the main channel, the throttle full out, the noise like a chain saw splitting the serenity of the morning. The driver of the outboard did not slow his boat to prevent his wake from washing into the cove and disturbing the water for another fisherman.

Father Mulcahy sat in a canvas chair on the deck and swung the bobber from his bamboo pole into the hyacinths. Behind him, he heard the outboard turning in a circle, heading toward him again. He propped his pole on the rail, put down the sandwich he had just unwrapped from its wax paper, and walked to the other side of the deck.

The man in the outboard killed his engine and floated in to the cove, the hyacinths clustering against the bow. He wore yellow-tinted glasses, and he reached down in the bottom of his boat and fitted on a smoke-colored Stetson that was sweat-stained across the base of the crown. When he smiled his dentures were stiff in his mouth, the flesh of his throat red like a cock's comb. He must have been sixty-five, but he was tall, his back straight, his eyes keen with purpose.

'I'm fixing to run out of gas. Can you spare me a half gallon?' he said.

'Maybe your high speed has something to do with it,' Father Mulcahy said.

'I'll go along with that.' Then he reached out for an iron cleat on the houseboat as though he had already been given permission to board. Behind the seat was a paper bag stapled across the top and a one gallon tin gas can.

'I know you,' Father Mulcahy said.

'Not from around here you don't. I'm just a visitor, not having no luck with the fish.'

'I've heard your voice.'

The man stood up in his boat and grabbed the handrail and lowered his face so the brim of his hat shielded it from view.

'I have no gas to give you. It's all in the tank,' Father Mulcahy said.

'I got a siphon. Right here in this bag. A can, too.'

The man in the outboard put one cowboy boot on the edge of the deck and stepped over the rail, drawing a long leg behind him. He stood in front of the priest, his head tilted slightly as though he were examining a quarry he had placed under a glass jar.

'Show me where your tank's at. Back around this side?' he said, indicating the lee side of the cabin, away from the view of anyone passing on the channel.

'Yes,' the priest said. 'But there's a lock on it. It's on the ignition key.'

'Let's get it, then, Reverend,' the man said.

'You know I'm a minister?' Father Mulcahy said.

The man did not reply. He had not shaved that morning, and there were gray whiskers among the red-and-blue veins in his cheeks. His smile was twisted, one eye squinted behind the lens of his glasses, as though he were arbitrarily defining the situation in his own mind.

'You came to the rectory . . . In the rain,' the priest said.

'Could be. But I need you to hep me with this chore. That's our number one job here.'

The man draped his arm across the priest's shoulders and walked him inside the cabin. He smelled of deodorant and chewing tobacco, and in spite of his age his arm was thick and meaty, the crook of it like a yoke on the back of the priest's neck.

'Your soul will be forfeit,' the priest said, because he could think of no other words to use.

'Yeah, I heard that one before. Usually when a preacher was trying to get me to write a check. The funny thing is, the preacher never wanted Jesus's name on the check.'

Then the man in the hat pulled apart the staples on the paper bag he had carried on board and took out a velvet curtain rope and a roll of tape and a plastic bag. He began tying a loop in the end of the rope, concentrating on his work as though it were an interesting, minor task in an ordinary day.

The priest turned away from him, toward the window and the sun breaking through the flooded cypresses, his head lowered, his fingers pinched on his eyelids.

The parishioner's sixteen-gauge pump shotgun was propped just to the left of the console. Father Mulcahy picked it up and leveled the barrel at the chest of the man in the Stetson hat and clicked off the safety.

'Get off this boat,' he said.

'You didn't pump a shell into it. There probably ain't nothing in the chamber,' the man said.

'That could be true. Would you like to find out?'

'You're a feisty old rooster, ain't you?'

'You sicken me, sir.'

The man in yellow-tinted glasses reached in his shirt pocket with his thumb and two fingers and filled his jaw with tobacco.

'Piss on you,' he said, and opened the cabin door to go back outside.

'Leave the bag,' the priest said.

15

The priest called the sheriff's office in St. Martin Parish, where his encounter with the man in the Stetson had taken place, then contacted me when he got back to New Iberia. The sheriff and I interviewed him together at the rectory.

'The bag had a velvet cord and a plastic sack and a roll of tape in it?' the sheriff said.

'That's right. I left it all with the sheriff in St. Martinville,' Father Mulcahy said. His eyes were flat, as though discussing his thoughts would only add to the level of degradation he felt.

'You know why he's after you, don't you, Father?' I said.

'Yes, I believe I do.'

'You know what he was going to do, too. It would have probably been written off as a heart attack. There would have been no rope burns, nothing to indicate any force or violence,' I said.

'You don't have to tell me that, sir,' he replied.

'It's time to talk about Lila Terrebonne,' I said.

'It's her prerogative to talk with you as much as she wishes. But not mine,' he said.

'Hubris isn't a virtue, Father,' I said.

His face flared. 'Probably not. But I'll be damned if I'll be altered by a sonofabitch like the man who climbed on my boat.'

'That's one way of looking at it. Here's my card if you want to put a net over this guy,' I said.

When we left, rain that looked like lavender horse tails was falling across the sun. The sheriff drove the cruiser with the window down and ashes blew from his pipe onto his shirt. He slapped at them angrily.

'I want that guy in the hat on a respirator,' he said.

'We don't have a crime on that houseboat, skipper. It's not even in our jurisdiction.'

'The intended victim is. That's enough. He's a vulnerable old man.

Remember when you lived through your first combat and thought you had magic? A dangerous time.'

A half hour later a state trooper pulled over a red pickup truck with a Texas tag on the Iberia-St. Martin Parish line.

The sheriff and I stood outside the holding cell and looked at the man seated on the wood bench against the back wall. His western-cut pants were ironed with sharp creases, the hard points of his oxblood cowboy boots buffed to a smooth glaze like melted plastic. He played with his Stetson on his index finger.

The sheriff held the man's driver's license cupped in his palm. He studied the photograph on it, then the man's face.

'You're Harpo Scruggs?' the sheriff asked.

'I was when I got up this morning.'

'You're from New Mexico?'

'Deming. I got a chili-pepper farm there. The truck's a rental, if that's what's on your mind.'

'You're supposed to be dead,' the sheriff said.

'You talking about that fire down in Juárez? Yeah, I heard about that. But it wasn't me.'

His accent was peckerwood, the Acadian inflections, if they had ever existed, weaned out of it.

'You terrorize elderly clergymen, do you?' I said.

'I asked the man for a can of gas. He pointed a shotgun at me.'

'You mind going into a lineup?' the sheriff asked.

Harpo Scruggs looked at his fingernails.

'Yeah, I do. What's the charge?' he said.

'We'll find one,' the sheriff said.

'I don't think y'all got a popcorn fart in a windstorm,' he said.

He was right. We called Mout' Broussard's home and got no answer. Neither could we find the USL student who had witnessed the execution of the two brothers out in the Atchafalaya Basin. The father of the two brothers was drunk and contradictory about what he had seen and heard when his sons were lured out of the house.

It was 8 P.M. The sheriff sat in his swivel chair and tapped his fingers on his jawbone.

'Call Juárez, Mexico, and see if they've still got a warrant,' he said.

'I already did. It was like having a conversation with impaired people in a bowling alley.'

'Sometimes I hate this job,' he said, and picked up a key ring off his desk blotter.

Ten minutes later the sheriff and I watched Harpo Scruggs walk into the parking lot a free man. He wore a shirt with purple-and-red flowers on it, and it swelled with the breeze and made his frame look even larger than it was. He fitted on his hat and slanted the brim over his eyes, took a small bag of cookies from his pocket and bit into one of them gingerly with his false teeth. He lifted his face into the breeze and looked with expectation at the sunset.

'See if you can get Lila Terrebonne in my office tomorrow morning,' the sheriff said.

Harpo Scruggs's truck drove up the street toward the cemetery. A moment later Helen Soileau's unmarked car pulled into the traffic behind him.

That night Bootsie and I fixed ham and onion sandwiches and dirty rice and iced tea at the drainboard and ate on the breakfast table. Through the hallway I could see the moss in the oak trees glowing against the lights on the dock.

'You look tired,' Bootsie said.

'Not really.'

'Who's this man Scruggs working for?'

'The New Orleans Mob. The Dixie Mafia. Who knows?'

'The Mob letting one of their own kill a priest?'

'You should have been a cop, Boots.'

'There's something you're not saying.'

'I keep feeling all this stuff goes back to Jack Flynn's murder.'

'The Flynns again.' She rose from the table and put her plate in the sink and looked through the window into the darkness at the foot of our property. 'Why always the Flynns?' she said.

I didn't have an adequate answer, not even for myself when I lay next to Bootsie later in the darkness, the window fan drawing the night air across our bed. Jack Flynn had fought at the battle of Madrid and at Alligator Creek on Guadalcanal; he was not one to be easily undone by company goons hired to break a farmworkers' strike. But the killers had kidnapped him out of a hotel room in Morgan City, beaten him with chains, impaled his broken body with nails as a lesson in terror to any poor white or black person who thought he could relieve his plight by joining a union. To this day not one suspect had been in custody, not one participant had spoken carelessly in a bar or brothel.

The Klan always prided itself on its secrecy, the arcane and clandestine nature of its rituals, the loyalty of its members to one another. But someone always came forward, out of either guilt or avarice, and told of the crimes they committed in groups, under cover of darkness, against their unarmed and defenseless victims.

But Jack Flynn's murderers had probably not only been protected,

636

they had been more afraid of the people they served than Louisiana or federal law.

Jack Flynn's death was at the center of our current problems because we had never dealt with our past, I thought. And in not doing so, we had allowed his crucifixion to become a collective act.

I propped myself up on the mattress with one elbow and touched Bootsie's hair. She was sound asleep and did not wake. Her eyelids looked like rose petals in the moon's glow.

Early Saturday morning I turned into the Terrebonne grounds and drove down the oak-lined drive toward the house. The movie set was empty, except for a bored security guard and Swede Boxleiter, who was crouched atop a plank building, firing a nail gun into the tin roof.

I stood under the portico of the main house and rang the chimes. The day had already turned warm, but it was cool in the shade and the air smelled of damp brick and four-o'clock flowers and the mint that grew under the water faucets. Archer Terrebonne answered the door in yellow-and-white tennis clothes, a moist towel draped around his neck.

'Lila's not available right now, Mr. Robicheaux,' he said.

'I'd very much like to talk to her, sir.'

'She's showering. Then we're going to a brunch. Would you like to leave a message?'

'The sheriff would appreciate her coming to his office to talk about her conversation with Father James Mulcahy.'

'Y'all do business in an extraordinary fashion. Her discussions with a minister are the subject of a legal inquiry?'

'This man was almost killed because he's too honorable to divulge something your daughter told him.'

'Good day, Mr. Robicheaux,' Terrebonne said, and closed the door in my face.

I drove back through the corridor of trees, my face tight with anger. I started to turn out onto the service road, then stopped the truck and walked out to the movie set.

'How's it hangin', Swede?' I said.

He fired the nail gun through the tin roof into a joist and pursed his mouth into an inquisitive cone.

'Where's Clete Purcel?' I asked.

'Gone for the day. You look like somebody pissed in your underwear.'

'You know the layout of this property?'

'I run power cables all over it.'

'Where's the family cemetery?'

'Back in those trees.'

He pointed at an oak grove and a group of whitewashed brick crypts with an iron fence around it. The grass within the fence was freshly mowed and clipped at the base of the bricks.

'You know of another burial area?' I asked.

'Way in back, a spot full of briars and palmettos. Holtzner says that's where the slaves were planted. Got to watch out for it so the local blacks don't get their ovaries fired up. What's the gig, man? Let me in on it.'

I walked to the iron fence around the Terrebonne cemetery. The marble tablet that sealed the opening to the patriarch's crypt was cracked across the face from settlement of the bricks into the softness of the soil, but I could still make out the eroded, moss-stained calligraphy scrolled by a stone mason's chisel: *Elijah Boethius Terrebonne, 1831–1878, soldier for Jefferson Davis, loving father and husband, now brother to the Lord.*

Next to Elijah's crypt was a much smaller one in which his twin girls were entombed. A clutch of wildflowers, tied at the stems with a rubber band, was propped against its face. There were no other flowers in the cemetery.

I walked toward the back of the Terrebonne estate, along the edge of a coulee that marked the property line, beyond the movie set and trailers and sky-blue swimming pool and guest cottages and tennis courts to a woods that was deep in shade, layered with leaves, the tree branches wrapped with morning glory vines and cobweb.

The woods sloped toward a stagnant pond. Among the palmettos were faint depressions, leaf-strewn, sometimes dotted with mushrooms. Was the slave woman Lavonia, who had poisoned Elijah's daughters, buried here? Was the pool of black water, dimpled by dragonflies, part of the swamp she had tried to hide in before she was lynched by her own people?

Why did the story of the exploited and murdered slave woman hang in my mind like a dream that hovers on the edge of sleep?

I heard a footstep in the leaves behind me.

'I didn't mean to give you a start,' Lila said.

'Oh, hi, Lila. I bet you put the wildflowers on the graves of the children.'

'How did you know?'

'Did your father tell you why I was here?'

'No . . . He . . . We don't always communicate very well.'

'A guy named Harpo Scruggs tried to kill Father Mulcahy.'

The blood drained out of her face.

'We think it's because of something you told him,' I said.

When she tried to speak, her words were broken, as though she could not form a sentence without using one that had already been spoken by someone else. 'I told the priest? That's what you're saying?'

'He's taking your weight. Scruggs was going to suffocate him with a plastic bag.'

'Oh, Dave—' she said, her eyes watering. Then she ran toward the house, her palms raised in the air like a young girl.

We had just returned from Mass on Sunday morning when the phone rang in the kitchen. It was Clete.

'I'm at a restaurant in Lafayette with Holtzner and his daughter and her boyfriend,' he said.

'What are you doing in Lafayette?'

'Holtzner's living here now. He's on the outs with Cisco. They want to come by,' he said.

'What for?'

'To make some kind of rental offer on your dock.'

'Not interested.'

'Holtzner wants to make his pitch anyway. Dave, the guy's my meal ticket. How about it?'

An hour later Clete rolled up to the dock in his convertible, with Holtzner beside him and the daughter and boyfriend following in a Lincoln. The four of them strolled down the dock and sat at a spool table under a Cinzano umbrella.

'Ask the waiter to bring everybody a cold beer,' Holtzner said.

'We don't have waiters. You need to get it yourself,' I said, standing in the sunlight.

'I got it,' Clete said, and went inside the shop.

'We'll pay you a month's lease but we'll be shooting for only two or three days,' Anthony, the boyfriend, said. He wore black glasses, and when he smiled the gap in his front teeth gave his face the imbecilic look of a Halloween pumpkin.

'Thanks anyway,' I said.

'*Thanks?* That's it?' Holtzner said.

'He thinks we're California nihilists here to do a culture fuck on the Garden of Eden,' Geraldine, the daughter, said to no one.

'You got the perfect place here for this particular scene. Geri's right, you think we're some kind of disease?' Holtzner said.

'You might try up at Henderson Swamp,' I said.

Clete came back out of the bait shop screen carrying a round tray with four sweating long-neck bottles on it. He set them one by one on the spool table, his expression meaningless.

'Talk to him,' Holtzner said to him.

'I don't mess with Streak's head,' Clete said.

'I hear you got Cisco's father on the brain,' Holtzner said to me. 'His father's death doesn't impress me. My grandfather organized the first garment workers' local on the Lower East Side. They stuck his hands in a stamp press. Irish cops broke up his wake with clubs, took the ice off his body and put it in their beer. They pissed in my grandmother's sink.'

'You have to excuse me. I need to get back to work,' I said, and walked toward the bait shop. I could hear the wind ruffling the umbrella in the silence, then Anthony was at my side, grinning, his clothes pungent with a smell like burning sage.

'Don't go off in a snit, nose out of joint, that sort of thing,' he said.

'I think you have a problem,' I said.

'We're talking about chemical dependencies now, are we?'

'No, you're hard of hearing. No offense meant,' I said, and went inside the shop and busied myself in back until all of them were gone except Clete, who remained at the table, sipping from his beer bottle.

'Why's Holtzner want to get close to you?' he asked.

'You got me.'

'I remembered where I'd seen him. He was promoting USO shows in Nam. Except he was also mixed up with some PX guys who were selling stuff on the black market. It was a big scandal. Holtzner was kicked out of Nam. That's like being kicked out of Hell . . . You just going to sit there and not say anything?'

'Yeah, don't get caught driving with beer on your breath.'

Clete pushed his glasses up on his head and drank from his bottle, one eye squinted shut.

That night, in a Lafayette apartment building on a tree-and-fern-covered embankment that overlooked the river, the accountant named Anthony mounted the staircase to the second-story landing and walked through a brick passageway toward his door. The underwater lights were on in the swimming pool, and blue strings of smoke from barbecue grills floated through the palm and banana fronds that shadowed the terrace. Anthony carried a grocery sack filled with items from a delicatessen, probably obscuring his vision, as evidently he never saw the figure that waited for him behind a potted orange tree.

The knife must have struck as fast as a snake's head, in the neck, under the heart, through the breastbone, because the coroner said Anthony was probably dead before the jar of pickled calf brains in his sack shattered on the floor.

16

Helen Soileau and I met Ruby Gravano and her nine-year-old boy at the Amtrak station in Lafayette Monday afternoon. The boy was a strange-looking child, with his mother's narrow face and black hair but with eyes that were set unnaturally far apart, as though they had been pasted on the skin. She held the boy, whose name was Nick, by one hand and her suitcase by the other.

'Is this gonna take long? Because I'm not feeling real good right now,' she said.

'There's a female deputy in that cruiser over there, Ruby. She's going to take Nick for some ice cream, then we'll finish with business and take y'all to a bed-and-breakfast in New Iberia. Tomorrow you'll be back on your way,' I said.

'Did you get the money bumped up? Houston's a lot more expensive than New Orleans. My mother said I can stay a week free, but then I got to pay her rent,' she said.

'Three hundred is all we could do,' I said.

Her forehead wrinkled. Then she said, 'I don't feel too comfortable standing out here. I don't know how I got talked into this.' She looked up and down the platform and fumbled in her bag for a pair of dark glasses.

'You wanted a clean slate in Houston. You were talking about a treatment program. Your idea, not ours, Ruby,' Helen said.

The little boy's head rotated like a gourd on a stem as he watched the disappearing train, the people walking to their cars with their luggage, a track crew repairing a switch.

'He's autistic. This is all new to him. Don't look at him like that. I hate this shit,' Ruby said, and pulled on the boy's hand as though she were about to leave us, then stopped when she realized she had no place to go except our unmarked vehicle, and in reality she didn't even know where that was.

We put Nick in the cruiser with the woman deputy, then drove to

Four Corners and parked across the street from a sprawling red-and-white motel that looked like a refurbished eighteenth-century Spanish fortress.

'How do you know he's in the room?' Ruby said.

'One of our people has been watching him. In five minutes he's going to get a phone call. Somebody's going to tell him smoke is coming out of his truck. All you have to do is look through the binoculars and tell us if that's the john you tricked on Airline Highway,' I said.

'You really got a nice way of saying it,' she replied.

'Ruby, cut the crap. The guy in that room tried to kill a priest Friday morning. What do you think he'll do to you if he remembers he showed you mug shots of two guys he capped out in the Basin?' Helen said.

Ruby lowered her chin and bit her lip. Her long hair made a screen around her narrow face.

'It's not fair,' she said.

'What?' I asked.

'Connie picked those guys up. But she doesn't get stuck with any of it. You got a candy bar or something? I feel sick. They wouldn't turn down the air-conditioning on the train.'

She sniffed deep in her nose, then wiped her nostrils hard with a Kleenex, pushing her face out of shape.

Helen looked through the front window at one of our people in a phone booth on the corner.

'It's going down, Ruby. Pick up the binoculars,' she said.

Ruby held the binoculars to her eyes and stared at the door to the room rented by Harpo Scruggs. Then she shifted them to an adjacent area in the parking lot. Her lips parted slightly on her teeth.

'What's going on?' she said.

'Nothing. What are you talking about?' I said.

'That's not the guy with the mug shots. I don't know that guy's name. We didn't ball him either,' she said.

'Take the oatmeal out of your mouth,' Helen said.

I removed the binoculars from her hands and placed them to my eyes.

'The guy out there in the parking lot. He came to the diner where the guy named Harpo and the other john were eating with us. He talks like a coon-ass. They went outside together, then he drove off,' she said.

'You never told us this,' I said.

'Why should I? You were asking about johns.'

I put the binoculars back to my eyes and watched Alex Guidry, the fired Iberia Parish jailer who had cuckolded Cool Breeze Broussard, knock on empty space just as Harpo Scruggs ripped open the door and charged outside, barefoot and in his undershirt and western-cut trousers, expecting to see a burning truck.

Later the same afternoon, when the sheriff was in my office, two Lafayette homicide detectives walked in and told us they were picking up Cool Breeze Broussard. They were both dressed in sport clothes, their muscles swollen with steroids. One of them, whose name was Daigle, lit a cigarette and kept searching with his eyes for an ashtray to put the burnt match in.

'Y'all want to go out to his house with us?' he asked, and dropped the match in the wastebasket.

'I don't,' I said.

He studied me. 'You got some kind of objection, something not getting said here?' he asked.

'I don't see how you make Broussard for this guy's, what's his name, Anthony Pollock's murder,' I replied.

'He's got a hard-on for the Terrebonne family. There's a good possibility he started the fire on their movie set. He's a four-time loser. He shanked a guy on Camp J. He mangled a guy on an electric saw in your own jail. You want me to go on?' Daigle said.

'You've got the wrong guy,' I said.

'Well, fuck me,' he said.

'Don't use that language in here, sir,' the sheriff said.

'What?' Daigle said.

'The victim was an addict. He had overseas involvements. He didn't have any connection with Cool Breeze. I think you guys have found an easy dartboard,' I said.

'We made up all that stuff on Broussard's sheet?' the other detective said.

'The victim was stabbed in the throat, heart, and kidney and was dead before he hit the floor. It sounds like a professional yard job,' I said.

'A yard job?' Daigle said.

'Talk to a guy by the name of Swede Boxleiter. He's on lend-lease from Canon City,' I said.

'Swede who?' Daigle said, taking a puff off his cigarette with three fingers crimped on the paper.

The sheriff scratched his eyebrow.

'Get out of here,' he said to the detectives.

A few minutes later the sheriff and I watched through the window as they got into their car.

'At least Pollock had the decency to get himself killed in Lafayette Parish,' the sheriff said. 'What's the status on Harpo Scruggs?'

'Helen said a chippy came to his room in a taxi. She's still in there.'

'What's Alex Guidry's tie-in to this guy?'

'It has something to do with the Terrebonnes. Everything in St. Mary Parish does. That's where they're both from.'

'Bring him in.'

'What for?'

'Tell him he's cruel to animals. Tell him his golf game stinks. Tell him I'm just in a real pissed-off mood.'

Tuesday morning Helen and I drove down Main, then crossed the iron drawbridge close by the New Iberia Country Club.

'You don't think this will tip our surveillance on Harpo Scruggs?' she said.

'Not if we do it right.'

'When those two brothers were executed out in the Basin? One of the shooters had on a department uniform. It could have come from Guidry.'

'Maybe Guidry was in it,' I said.

'Nope, he stays behind the lines. He makes the system work for him.'

'You know him outside the job?' I asked.

'He arrested my maid out on a highway at night when he was a deputy in St. Mary Parish. She's never told anyone what he did to her.'

Helen and I parked the cruiser in front of the country club and walked past the swimming pool, then under a spreading oak to a practice green where Alex Guidry was putting with a woman and another man. He wore light brown slacks and two-tone golf shoes and a maroon polo shirt; his mahogany tan and thick salt-and-pepper hair gave him the look of a man in the prime of his life. He registered our presence in the corner of his eye but never lost his concentration. He bent his knees slightly and tapped the ball with a plop into the cup.

'The sheriff has invited you to come down to the department,' I said.

'No, thank you,' he said.

'We need your help with a friend of yours. It won't take long,' Helen said.

The red flag on the golf pin popped in the wind. Leaves drifted out of the pecan trees and live oaks along the fairway and scudded across the freshly mowed grass.

'I'll give it some thought and ring y'all later on it,' he said, and started to reach down to retrieve his ball from the cup.

Helen put her hand on his shoulder.

'Not a time to be a wise-ass, sir,' she said.

Guidry's golf companions looked away into the distance, their eyes fixed on the dazzling blue stretch of sky above the tree line.

Fifteen minutes later we sat down in a windowless interview room. In the back seat of the cruiser he had been silent, morose, his face dark with anger when he looked at us. I saw the sheriff at the end of the hall just before I closed the door to the room.

'Y'all got some damn nerve,' Guidry said.

'Someone told us you're buds with an ex-Angola gun bull by the name of Harpo Scruggs,' I said.

'I know him. So what?' he replied.

'You see him recently?' Helen asked. She wore slacks and sat with one haunch on the corner of the desk.

'No.'

'Sure?' I said.

'He's the nephew of a lawman I worked with twenty years ago. We grew up in the same town.'

'You didn't answer me,' I said.

'I don't have to.'

'The lawman you worked with was Harpo Delahoussey. Y'all put the squeeze on Cool Breeze Broussard over some moonshine whiskey. That's not all you did either,' I said.

His eyes looked steadily into mine, heated, searching for the implied meaning in my words.

'Harpo Scruggs tried to kill a priest Friday morning,' Helen said.

'Arrest him, then.'

'How do you know we haven't?' I asked.

'I don't. It's none of my business. I was fired from my job, thanks to your friend Willie Broussard,' he said.

'Everyone else told us Scruggs was dead. But you know he's alive. Why's that?' Helen said.

He leaned back in the chair and rubbed his mouth, saying something in disgust against his hand at the same time.

'Say that again,' Helen said.

'I said you damn queer, you leave me alone,' he replied.

I placed my hand on top of Helen's before she could rise from the table. 'You were in the sack with Cool Breeze's wife. I think you contributed to her suicide and helped ruin her husband's life. Does it give you any sense of shame at all, sir?' I said.

'It's called changing your luck. You're notorious for it, so lose the attitude, fucko,' Helen said.

'I tell you what, when you're dead from AIDS or some other disease you people pass around, I'm going to dig up your grave and piss in your mouth,' he said to her.

Helen stood up and massaged the back of her neck. 'Dave, would you leave me and Mr. Guidry alone a minute?' she said.

*

But whatever she did or said after I left the room, it didn't work.

Guidry walked past the dispatcher, used the phone to call a friend for a ride, and calmly sipped from a can of Coca-Cola until a yellow Cadillac with tinted windows pulled to the curb in front.

Helen and I watched him get in on the passenger side, roll down the window, and toss the empty can on our lawn.

'What bwana say now?' Helen said.

'Time to use local resources.'

That evening Clete picked me up in his convertible in front of the house and we headed up the road toward St. Martinville.

'You call Swede Boxleiter a "local resource"?' he said.

'Why not?'

'That's like calling shit a bathroom ornament.'

'You want to go or not?'

'The guy's got electrodes in his temples. Even Holtzner walks around him. Are you listening?'

'You think he did the number on this accountant, Anthony Pollock?'

He thought about it. The wind blew a crooked part in his sandy hair.

'*Could* he do it? In a blink. Did he have motive? You got me, 'cause I don't know what these dudes are up to,' he said. 'Megan told me something about Cisco having a fine career ahead of him, then taking money from some guys in the Orient.'

'Have you seen her?'

He turned his face toward me. It was flat and red in the sun's last light, his green eyes as bold as a slap. He looked at the road again.

'We're friends. I mean, she's got her own life. We're different kinds of people, you know. I'm cool about it.' He inserted a Lucky Strike in his mouth.

'Clete, I'm—'

He pulled the cigarette off his lip without lighting it and threw it into the wind.

'What'd the Dodgers do last night?' he said.

We pulled into the driveway of the cinder-block triplex where Swede Boxleiter lived and found him in back, stripped to the waist, shooting marbles with a slingshot at the squirrels in a pecan tree.

He pointed his finger at me.

'I got a bone to pick with you,' he said.

'Oh?'

'Two Lafayette homicide roaches just left here. They said you told them to question me.'

'Really?' I said.

'They threw me up against the car in front of my landlord. One guy kicked me in both ankles. He put his hand in my crotch with little kids watching.'

'Dave was trying to clear you as a suspect. These guys probably got the wrong signal, Swede,' Clete said.

He pulled back the leather pouch on the slingshot, nests of veins popping in his neck, and fired a scarlet marble into the pecan limbs.

'I want to run a historical situation by you. Then you tell me what's wrong with the story,' I said.

'What's the game?' he asked.

'No game. You're con-wise. You see stuff other people don't. This is just for fun, okay?'

He held the handle of the slingshot and whipped the leather pouch and lengths of rubber tubing in a circle, watching them gain speed.

'A plantation owner is in the sack with one of his slave women. He goes off to the Civil War, comes back home, finds his place trashed by the Yankees, and all his slaves set free. There's not enough food for everybody, so he tells the slave woman she has to leave. You with me?'

'Makes sense, yeah,' Swede said.

'The slave woman puts poison in the food of the plantation owner's children, thinking they'll only get sick and she'll be asked to care for them. Except they die. The other black people on the plantation are terrified. So they hang the slave woman before they're all punished,' I said.

Swede stopped twirling the slingshot. 'It's bullshit,' he said.

'Why?' I asked.

'You said the blacks were already freed. Why are they gonna commit a murder for the white dude and end up hung by Yankees themselves? The white guy, the one getting his stick dipped, he did her.'

'You're a beaut, Swede,' I said.

'This is some kind of grift, right?'

'Here's what it is,' Clete said. 'Dave thinks you're getting set up. You know how it works sometimes. The locals can't clear a case and they look around for a guy with a heavy sheet.'

'We've got a shooter or two on the loose, Swede,' I said. 'Some guys smoked two white boys out in the Basin, then tried to clip a black guy by the name of Willie Broussard. I hate to see you go down for it.'

'I can see you'd be broke up,' he said.

'Ever hear of a dude named Harpo Scruggs?' I asked.

'No.'

'Too bad. You might have to take his weight. See you around. Thanks for the help with that historical story,' I said.

Clete and I walked back to the convertible. The air felt warm and moist, and the sky was purple above the sugarcane across the road. Out of the corner of my eye I saw Swede watching us from the middle of the drive, stretching the rubber tubes on his slingshot, his face jigsawed with thought.

We stopped at a filling station for gas down the road. The owner had turned on the outside lights and the oak tree that grew next to the building was filled with black-green shadows against the sky. Clete walked across the street and bought a sno'ball from a small wooden stand and ate it while I put in the gas.

'What was the plantation story about?' he asked.

'I had the same problem with it as Boxleiter. Except it's been bothering me because it reminded me of the story Cool Breeze told me about his wife's suicide.'

'You lost me, big mon,' Clete said.

'She was found in freezing water with an anchor chain wrapped around her. When they want to leave a lot of guilt behind, they use shotguns or go off rooftops.'

'I'd leave it alone, Dave.'

'Breeze has lived for twenty years with her death on his conscience.'

'There's another script, too. Maybe he did her,' Clete said. He bit into his sno'ball and held his eyes on mine.

Early the next morning Batist telephoned the house from the dock.

'There's a man down here want to see you, Dave,' he said.

'What's he look like?'

'Like somebody stuck his jaws in a vise and busted all the bones. That ain't the half of it. While I'm mopping off the tables, he walks round on his hands.'

I finished my coffee and walked down the slope through the trees. The air was cool and gray with the mist off the water, and molded pecan husks broke under my shoes.

'What's up, Swede?' I said.

He sat at a spool table, eating a chili dog with a fork from a paper plate.

'You asked about this guy Harpo Scruggs. He's an old fart, works out of New Mexico and Trinidad, Colorado. He freelances, but if he's doing a job around here, the juice is coming out of New Orleans.'

'Yeah?'

'Something else. If Scruggs tried to clip a guy and blew it but he's still hanging around, it means he's working for Ricky the Mouse.'

'Ricky Scarlotti?'

'There's two things you don't do with Ricky. You don't blow hits and

648

you don't ever call him the Mouse. You know the story about the horn player?'

'Yes.'

'That's his style.'

'Would he have a priest killed?'

'That don't sound right.'

'You ever have your IQ tested, Swede?'

'No, people who bone you five days a week don't give IQ tests.'

'You're quite a guy anyway. You shank Anthony Pollock?'

'I was playing chess with Cisco. Check it out, my man. And don't send any more cops to my place. Believe it or not, I don't like some polyester geek getting his hand on my crank.'

He rolled up his dirty paper plate and napkin, dropped them in a trash barrel, and walked down the dock to his car, snapping his fingers as though he were listening to a private radio broadcast.

Ricky Scarlotti wasn't hard to find. I went to the office, called NOPD, then the flower shop he owned at Carrollton and St. Charles.

'You want to chat up Ricky the Mouse with me?' I asked Helen.

'I don't think I'd go near that guy without a full-body condom on,' she replied.

'Suit yourself. I'll be back this afternoon.'

'Hang on. Let me get my purse.'

We signed out an unmarked car and drove across the Atchafalaya Basin and crossed the Mississippi at Baton Rouge and turned south for New Orleans.

'So you're just gonna drop this Harpo Scruggs stuff in his lap?' Helen said.

'You bet. If Ricky thinks someone snitched him off, we'll know about it in a hurry.'

'That story about the jazz musician true?' she said.

'I think it is. He just didn't get tagged with it.'

The name of the musician is forgotten now, except among those in the 1950s who had believed his talent was the greatest since Bix Beiderbecke's. The melancholy sound of his horn hypnotized audiences at open-air concerts on West Venice beach. His dark hair and eyes and pale skin, the fatal beauty that lived in his face, that was like a white rose opening to black light, made women turn and stare at him on the street. His rendition of 'My Funny Valentine' took you into a consideration about mutability and death that left you numb.

But he was a junky and jammed up with LAPD, and when he gave up the names of his suppliers, he had no idea that he was about to deal with Ricky Scarlotti.

Ricky had run a casino in Las Vegas, then a race track in Tijuana, before the Chicago Commission moved him to Los Angeles. Ricky didn't believe in simply killing people. He created living object lessons. He sent two black men to the musician's apartment in Malibu, where they pulled his teeth with pliers and mutilated his mouth. Later, the musician became a pharmaceutical derelict, went to prison in Germany, and died a suicide.

Helen and I drove through the Garden District, past the columned nineteenth-century homes shadowed by oaks whose root systems humped under sidewalks and cracked them upward like baked clay, past the iron green-painted streetcars with red-bordered windows clanging on the neutral ground, past Loyola University and Audubon Park, then to the levee where St. Charles ended and Ricky kept the restaurant, bookstore, and flower shop that supposedly brought him his income.

His second-story office was carpeted with a snow-white rug and filled with glass artworks and polished steel-and-glass furniture. A huge picture window gave onto the river and an enormous palm tree that brushed with the wind against the side of the building.

Ricky's beige pinstripe suit coat hung on the back of his chair. He wore a soft white shirt with a plum-colored tie and suspenders, and even though he was nearing sixty, his large frame still had the powerful muscle structure of a much younger man.

But it was the shape of his head and the appearance of his face that drew your attention. His ears were too large, cupped outward, the face unnaturally rotund, the eyes pouched with permanent dark bags, the eyebrows half-mooned, the black hair like a carefully scissored pelt glued to the skull.

'It's been a long time, Robicheaux. You still off the bottle?' he said.

'We're hearing some stuff that's probably all gas, Ricky. You know a mechanic, a freelancer, by the name of Harpo Scruggs?' I said.

'A guy fixes cars?' he said, and grinned.

'He's supposed to be a serious button man out of New Mexico,' I said.

'Who's she? I've seen you around New Orleans someplace, right?' He was looking at Helen now.

'I was a patrolwoman here years ago. I still go to the Jazz and Heritage Festival in the spring. You like jazz?' Helen said.

'No.'

'You ought to check it out. Wynton Marsalis is there. Great horn man. You don't like cornet?' she said.

'What is this, Robicheaux?'

'I told you, Ricky. Harpo Scruggs. He tried to kill Willie Broussard, then a priest. My boss is seriously pissed off.'

'Tell him that makes two of us, 'cause I don't like out-of-town cops 'fronting me in my own office. I particularly don't like no bride of Frankenstein making an implication about a rumor that was put to rest a long time ago.'

'Nobody has shown you any personal disrespect here, Ricky. You need to show the same courtesy to others,' I said.

'That's all right. I'll wait outside,' Helen said, then paused by the door. She let her eyes drift onto Ricky Scarlotti's face. 'Say, come on over to New Iberia sometime. I've got a calico cat that just won't believe you.'

She winked, then closed the door behind her.

'I don't provoke no more, Robicheaux. Look, I know about you and Purcel visiting Jimmy Figorelli. What kind of behavior is that? Purcel smashes the guy in the mouth for no reason. Now you're laying off some hillbilly *cafone* on me.'

'I didn't say he was a hillbilly.'

'I've heard of him. But I don't put out contracts on priests. What d'you think I am?'

'A vicious, sadistic piece of shit, Ricky.'

He opened his desk drawer and removed a stick of gum and peeled it and placed it in his mouth. Then he brushed at the tip of one nostril with his knuckle, huffing air out of his breathing passage. He pushed a button on his desk and turned his back on me and stared out the picture window at the river until I had left the room.

That evening I drove to the city library on East Main. The spreading oaks on the lawn were filled with birds and I could hear the clumps of bamboo rattling in the wind, and fireflies were lighting in the dusk out on the bayou. I went inside the library and found the hardback collection of Megan's photography that had been published three years ago by a New York publishing house.

What could I learn from it? Maybe nothing. Maybe I only wanted to put off seeing her that evening, which I knew I had to do, even though I knew I was breaking an AA tenet by injecting myself into other people's relationships. But you don't let a friend like Clete Purcel swing in the gibbet.

The photographs in her collection were stunning. Her great talent was her ability to isolate the humanity and suffering of individuals who lived in our midst but who nevertheless remained invisible to most passersby. Native Americans on reservations, migrant farm-workers, mentally impaired people who sought heat from steam grates, they looked at the camera with the hollow eyes of Holocaust victims and made the viewer wonder what country or era the photograph had been taken in, because surely it could not have been our own.

Then I turned a page and looked at a black-and-white photo taken on a reservation in South Dakota. It showed four FBI agents in windbreakers taking two Indian men into custody. The Indians were on their knees, their fingers laced behind their heads. An AR-15 rifle lay in the dust by an automobile whose windows and doors were perforated with bullet holes.

The cutline said the men were members of the American Indian Movement. No explanation was given for their arrest. One of the agents was a woman whose face was turned angrily toward the camera. The face was that of the New Orleans agent Adrien Glazier.

I drove out to Cisco's place on the Loreauville road and parked by the gallery. No one answered the bell, and I walked down by the bayou and saw her writing a letter under the light in the gazebo, the late sun burning like a flare beyond the willow trees across the water. She didn't see or hear me, and in her solitude she seemed to possess all the self-contained and tranquil beauty of a woman who had never let the authority of another define her.

Her horn-rimmed glasses gave her a studious look that her careless and eccentric dress belied. I felt guilty watching her without her knowledge, but in that moment I also realized what it was that attracted men to her.

She was one of those women we instinctively know are braver and more resilient than we are, more long-suffering and more willing to be broken for the sake of principle. You wanted to feel tender toward Megan, but you knew your feelings were vain and presumptuous. She had a lion's heart and did not need a protector.

'Oh, Dave. I didn't hear you come up on me,' she said, removing her glasses.

'I was down at the library looking at your work. Who were those Indians Adrien Glazier was taking down?'

'One of them supposedly murdered two FBI agents. Amnesty International thinks he's innocent.'

'There were some other photos in there you took of Mexican children in a ruined church around Trinidad, Colorado.'

'Those were migrant kids whose folks had run off. The church was built by John D. Rockefeller after his goons murdered the families of striking miners up the road at Ludlow.'

'I mention it because Swede Boxleiter told me a hit man named Harpo Scruggs had a ranch around there.'

'He should know. He and Cisco were placed in a foster home in Trinidad. The husband was a pederast. He raped Swede until he bled inside. Swede took it so the guy wouldn't start on Cisco next.'

I sat down on the top step of the gazebo and tossed a pebble into the bayou.

'Clete's my longtime friend, Megan. He says he needs this security job with Cisco's company. I don't think that's why he's staying here,' I said.

She started to speak but gave it up.

'Even though he says otherwise, I don't think he understands the nature of y'all's relationship,' I said.

'Is he drinking?'

'Not now, but he will.'

She rested her cheek on her hand and gazed at the bayou.

'What I did was rotten,' she said. 'I wake up every morning and feel like a bloody sod. I just wish I could undo it.'

'Talk to him again.'

'You want Cisco and me out of his life. That's the real agenda, isn't it?'

'The best cop New Orleans ever had has become a grunt for Billy Holtzner.'

'He can walk out of that situation anytime he wants. How about my brother? Anthony Pollock worked for some nasty people in Hong Kong. Who do you think they're going to blame for his death?'

'To tell you the truth, it's a long way from Bayou Teche. I don't really care.'

She folded her letter and put away her pen and walked up the green bank toward the house, her silhouette surrounded by the tracings of fireflies.

Cisco filmed late that night and did not return home until after 2 A.M. The intruders came sometime between midnight and then. They were big, heavy men, booted, sure of themselves and unrelenting in their purpose. They churned and destroyed the flower beds, where they disabled the alarm system, and slipped a looped wire through a window jamb and released the catch from inside. Each went through the opening with one muscular thrust, because hardly any dirt was scuffed into the bricks below the jamb.

They knew where she slept, and unlike the men who admired Megan for her strength, these men despised her for it. Their hands fell upon her in her sleep, wrenched her from the bed, bound her eyes, hurled her through the door and out onto the patio and down the slope to the bayou. When she pulled at the tape on her eyes, they slapped her to her knees.

But while they forced her face into the water, none of them saw the small memo recorder attached to a key ring she held clenched in her palm. Even while her mouth and nostrils filled with mud and her lungs burned for air as though acid had been poured in them, she tried to keep her finger pressed on the 'record' button.

Then she felt the bayou grow as warm as blood around her neck just as a veined, yellow bubble burst in the center of her mind, and she knew she was safe from the hands and fists and booted feet of the men who had always lived on the edge of her camera's lens.

17

The tape on the small recorder had only a twenty-second capacity. Most of the voices were muffled and inaudible, but there were words, whole sentences, sawed out of the darkness that portrayed Megan's tormenters better than any photograph could:

'Hold her, damnit! This is one bitch been asking for it a long time. You cain't get her head down, get out of the way.'

'She's bucking. When they buck, they're fixing to go under. Better pull her up unless we're going all the way.'

'Let her get a breath, then give it to her again. Ain't nothing like the power of memory to make a good woman, son.'

It was 2:30 A.M. now and the ambulance had already left with Megan for Iberia General. The light from the flashers on our parked cruisers was like a blue, white, and red net on the trees and the bayou's surface and the back of the house. Cisco paced back and forth on the lawn, his eyes large, his face dilated in the glare. Behind him I could see the sheriff squatted under the open window with a flashlight, peeling back the ruined flowers with one hand.

'You know who did it, don't you?' I said to Cisco.

'If I did, I'd have a gun down somebody's mouth,' he replied.

'Give the swinging dick act a break, Cisco.'

'I can't tell you who, I can only tell you why. It's payback for Anthony.'

'Walk down to the water with me,' I said, and cupped one hand on his elbow.

We went down the slope to the bayou, where the mudbank had been imprinted at the water's edge by Megan's bare knees and sliced by heavy boots that had fought for purchase while she struggled with at least three men. An oak tree sheltered us from the view of the sheriff and the uniformed deputies in the yard.

'Don't you lie to me. With these guys payback means dead. They want something. What is it?' I said.

'Billy Holtzner embezzled three-quarters of a million out of the budget by working a scam on our insurance coverage. But he put it on me. Anthony worked for the money people in Hong Kong. He believed what Billy told him. He started twisting my dials and ended up with big leaks in his arteries.'

'Swede?'

'We were playing chess for a lot of the evening. I don't know if he did it or not. Swede's protective. Anthony was a prick.'

'Protective? The victim was a prick? Great attitude.'

'It's complicated. There's a lot of big finance involved. You're not going to understand it.' He saw the look on my face. 'I'm in wrong with some bad guys. The studio's going to file bankruptcy. They want to gut my picture and inflate its value on paper to liquidate their debts.'

The current in the bayou was dead, hazed over with insects, and there was no air under the trees. He wiped his face with his hand.

'I'm telling the truth, Dave. I didn't think they'd go after Megan. Maybe there's something else involved. About my father, maybe. I don't understand it all either . . . Where you going?' he said.

'To find Clete Purcel.'

'What for?'

'To talk to him before he hears about this from someone else.'

'You coming to the hospital?' he asked, his fingers opened in front of him as though the words of another could be caught and held as physical guarantees.

It was still dark when I parked my truck by the stucco cottage Clete had rented outside Jeanerette. I pushed back the seat and slept through a rain shower and did not wake until dawn. When I woke, the rain had stopped and the air was heavy with mist, and I saw Clete at his mailbox in a robe, the *Morning Advocate* under his arm, staring curiously at my truck. I got out and walked toward him.

'What's wrong?' he said, lines breaking across his brow.

I told him of everything that happened at Cisco's house and of Megan's status at Iberia General. He listened and didn't speak. His face had the contained, heated intensity of a stainless-steel pan that had been left on a burner.

Then he said, 'She's going to make it?'

'You bet.'

'Come inside. I already have coffee on the stove.' He turned away from me and pushed at his nose with his thumb.

'What are you going to do, Clete?'

'Go up to the hospital. What do you think?'

'You know what I mean.'

'I'll fix eggs and sausage for both of us. You look like you got up out of a coffin.'

Inside his kitchen I said, 'Are you going to answer me?'

'I already heard about you and Helen visiting Ricky Scar. He's behind this shit, isn't he?'

'Where'd you hear about Scarlotti?'

'Nig Rosewater. He said Ricky went berserk after you left his office. What'd y'all do to jack him up like that?'

'Don't worry about it. You stay out of New Orleans.'

He poured coffee in two cups and put a cinnamon roll in his mouth and looked out the window at the sun in the pine trees.

'Did you hear me?' I said.

'I got enough to do right here. I caught Swede Boxleiter in the Terrebonne cemetery last night. I think he was prizing bricks out of a crypt.'

'What for?'

'Maybe he's a ghoul. You know what for. You planted all that Civil War stuff in his head. I'd love to tell Archer Terrebonne an ex-con meltdown is digging up his ancestors' bones.'

But there was no humor in his face, only a tic at the corner of one eye. He went into the other room and called Iberia General, then came back in the kitchen, his eyes filled with private thoughts, and began beating eggs in a big pink bowl.

'Clete?'

'The Big Sleazy's not your turf anymore, Streak. Why don't you worry about how this guy Scruggs got off his leash? I thought y'all had him under surveillance.'

'He lost the stakeout at the motel.'

'You know the best way to deal with that dude? A big fat one between the eyes and a throw-down on the corpse.'

'You might have your butt in our jail, if that's what it takes,' I said.

He poured hot milk into my coffee cup. 'Not even the perps believe that stuff anymore. You want to go to the hospital with me?' he said.

'You got it.'

'The nurse said she asked for me. How about that? How about that Megan Flynn?'

I looked at the back of his thick neck and huge shoulders as he made breakfast and thought of warning NOPD before he arrived in New Orleans. But I knew that would only give his old enemies in the New Orleans Police Department a basis to do him even greater harm than Ricky Scarlotti might.

We drove back up the tree-lined highway to New Iberia in a corridor of rain.

At Iberia General I sat in the waiting room while Clete went in to see Megan first. Five minutes after we arrived I saw Lila Terrebonne walk down the hall with a spray of carnations wrapped in green tissue paper. She didn't see me. She paused at the open door to Megan's room, her eyelids blinking, her back stiff with apprehension. Then she turned and started hurriedly toward the elevator.

I caught her before she got on.

'You're not going to say hello?' I asked.

I could smell the bourbon on her breath, the cigarette smoke in her hair and clothes.

'Give these to Megan for me. I'll come back another time,' she said.

'How'd you know she was here?'

'It was on the radio . . . Dave, get on the elevator with me.' When the elevator door closed, she said, 'I've got to get some help. I've had it.'

'Help with what?'

'Booze, craziness . . . Something that happened to me, something I've never told anybody about except my father and the priest at St. Peter's.'

'Why don't we sit in my pickup?' I said.

What follows is my reconstruction of the story she told me while the rain slid down the truck's windows and a willow tree by the bayou blew in the wind like a woman's hair.

She met the two brothers in a bar outside Morgan City. They were shooting pool, stretching across the table to make difficult shots, their sleeveless arms wrapped with green-and-red tattoos. They wore earrings and beards that were trimmed in neat lines along the jawbone, jeans that were so tight their genitalia were cupped to the smooth shape of a woman's palm. They sent a drink to her table, and one to an old man at the bar, and one to an oil-field roughneck who had used up his tab. But they made no overture toward her.

She watched them across the top of her gin ricky, the tawdry grace of their movements around the pool table, the lack of attention they showed anything except the skill of their game, the shots they speared into leather side pockets like junior high school kids.

Then one of them noticed her watching. He proffered the cue stick to her, smiling. She rose from her chair, her skin warm with gin, and wrapped her fingers around the cue's thickness, smiling back into the young man's face, seeing him glance away shyly, his cheeks color around the edges of his beard.

They played nine ball. Her father had taught her how to play billiards when she was a young girl. She could walk a cue ball down the rail, put reverse English on it and not leave an opponent an open shot, make a soft bank shot and drop the money balls – the one and the six and the nine – into the pocket with a tap that was no more than a whisper.

The two brothers shook their heads in dismay. She bought them each a bottle of beer and a gin ricky for herself. She played another game and beat them again. She noticed they didn't use profanity in her presence, that they stopped speaking in mid-sentence if she wished to interrupt, that they grinned boyishly and looked away if she let her eyes linger more than a few seconds on theirs.

They told her they built board roads for an oil company, they had been in the reformatory after their mother had deserted the family, they had been in the Gulf War, in a tank, one that'd had its treads blown off by an Iraqi artillery shell. She knew they were lying, but she didn't care. She felt a sense of sexual power and control that made her nipples hard, her eyes warm with toleration and acceptance.

When she walked to the ladies' room, the backs of her thighs taut with her high heels, she could see her reflection in the bar mirror and she knew that every man in the room was looking at the movement of her hips, the upward angle of her chin, the grace in her carriage that their own women would never possess.

The brothers did not try to pick her up. In fact, when the bar started to close, their conversation turned to the transmission on their truck, a stuck gear they couldn't free, their worry they could not make it the two miles to their father's fish camp. Rain streamed down the neon-lighted window in front.

She offered to follow them home. When they accepted, she experienced a strange taste in her throat, like copper pennies, like the wearing off of alcohol and the beginnings of a different kind of chemical reality. She looked at the faces of the brothers, the grins that looked incised in clay, and started to reconsider.

Then the bartender beckoned to her.

'Lady, taxicabs run all night. A phone call's a quarter. If they ain't got it, they can use mine free,' he said.

'There's no problem. But thanks very much just the same. Thank you, truly. You're very nice,' she replied, and hung her purse from her shoulder and let one of the brothers hold a newspaper over her head while they ran for her automobile.

They did it to her in an open-air tractor shed by a green field of sugarcane in the middle of an electric storm. One held her wrists while the other brother climbed between her legs on top of a worktable. After he came his body went limp and his head fell on her breast. His mouth was wet and she could feel it leaving a pattern on her blouse. Then he rose from her and put on his blue jeans and lit a cigarette before clasping her wrists so his brother, who simply unzipped his jeans without taking them off, could mount her.

When she thought it was over, when she believed there was nothing else they could take from her, she sat up on the worktable with her clothes crumpled in her lap. Then she watched one brother shake his head and extend his soiled hand toward her face, covering it like a surgeon's assistant pressing an ether mask on a patient, forcing her back down on the table, then turning her over, his hand shifting to the back of her neck, crushing her mouth into the wood planks.

She saw a bolt of lightning explode in the fork of hardwood tree, saw it split the wood apart and tear the grain right through the heart of the trunk. Deep in her mind she thought she remembered a green felt pool table and a boyish figure shoving a cue like a spear through his bridged fingers.

Lila's face was turned slightly toward the passenger window when she finished her story.

'Your father had them killed?' I said.

'I didn't say that. Not at all.'

'It's what happened, though, isn't it?'

'Maybe I had them killed. It's what they deserved. I'm glad they're dead.'

'I think it's all right to feel that way,' I said.

'What are you going to do with what I've told you?'

'Take you home or to a treatment center in Lafayette.'

'I don't want to go into treatment again. If I can't do it with meetings and working the program, I can't do it at all.'

'Why don't we go to a meeting after work? Then you go every day for ninety days.'

'I feel like everything inside me is coming to an end. I can't describe it.'

'It's called "a world destruction fantasy." It's bad stuff. Your heart races, you can't breathe, you feel like a piano wire is wrapped around your forehead. Psychologists say we remember the birth experience.'

She pressed the heel of her hand to her forehead, then cracked the window as though my words had drawn the oxygen out of the air.

'Lila, I've got to ask you something else. Why were you talking about a Hanged Man?'

'I don't remember that. Not at all. That's in the Tarot, isn't it? I don't know anything about that.'

'I see.'

660

Her skin had gone white under her caked makeup, her eyelashes stiff and black and wide around her milky green eyes.

I walked through the rain into the hospital and rode up in the elevator with Lila's tissue-wrapped spray of carnations in my hand. Helen Soileau was in the waiting room.

'You get anything?' I asked.

'Not much. She says she thinks there were three guys. They sounded like hicks. One guy was running things,' she replied.

'That's got to be Harpo Scruggs.'

'I think we're going about this the wrong way. Cut off the head and the body dies.'

'Where's the head?'

'Beats me,' she said.

'Where's Purcel?'

'He's still in there.'

I walked to the open door, then turned away. Clete was sitting on the side of Megan's bed, leaning down toward her face, his big arms and shoulders forming a tent over her. Her right hand rested on the back of his neck. Her fingers stroked his uncut hair.

The sky cleared that night, and Alafair and Bootsie and I cooked out in the back yard. I had told the sheriff about my conversation with Lila Terrebonne, but his response was predictable. We had established possible motivation for the execution of the two brothers. But that was all we had done. There was no evidence to link Archer Terrebonne, Lila's father, to the homicide. Second, the murders still remained outside our jurisdiction and our only vested interest in solving them was the fact that one of the shooters wore an Iberia Parish deputy sheriff's uniform.

I went with Lila to an AA meeting that night, then returned home.

'Clete called. He's in New Orleans. He said for you not to worry. What'd he mean?' Bootsie said.

661

18

Ricky Scarlotti ate breakfast the next morning with two of his men in his restaurant by St. Charles and Carrollton. It was a fine morning, smelling of the wet sidewalks and the breeze off the river. The fronds of the palm trees on the neutral ground were pale green and lifting in the wind against a ceramic-blue sky; the streetcar was loading with passengers by the levee, the conductor's bell clanging. No one seemed to take notice of a chartreuse Cadillac convertible that turned off St. Charles and parked in front of the flower shop, nor of the man in the powder-blue porkpie hat and seersucker pants and Hawaiian shirt who sat behind the steering wheel with a huge plastic seal-top coffee mug in his hand.

The man in the porkpie hat inserted a dime in the parking meter and looked with interest at the display of flowers an elderly woman was setting out on the sidewalk under a canvas awning. He talked a moment with the woman, then entered the restaurant and stopped by the hot bar and wrapped a cold cloth around the handle of a heavy cast-iron skillet filled with chipped beef. He made his way unobtrusively between the checker-cloth-covered tables toward the rear of the restaurant, where Ricky Scarlotti had just patted his mouth with a napkin and had touched the wrist of one of the men at his side and nodded in the direction of the approaching figure in the porkpie hat.

The man at Ricky Scarlotti's side had platinum hair and a chemical tan. He put down his fork and got to his feet and stood flat-footed like a sentinel in front of Ricky Scarlotti's table. His name was Benny Grogan and he had been a professional wrestler before he had become a male escort for a notorious and rich Garden District homosexual. NOPD believed he had also been the backup shooter on at least two hits for the Calucci brothers.

'I hope you're here for the brunch, Purcel,' he said.

'Not your gig, Benny. Get off the clock,' Clete said.

'Come on, make an appointment. Don't do this. Hey, you deaf?' Then Benny Grogan reached out and hooked his fingers on the back of Clete's shirt collar as Clete brushed past him.

Clete flung the chipped beef into Benny Grogan's face. It was scalding hot and it matted his skin like a papier-mâché mask with slits for the eyes. Benny's mouth was wide with shock and pain and an unintelligible sound that rose out of his chest like fingernails grating on a blackboard. Then Clete whipped the bottom of the skillet with both hands across the side of Benny's head, and backswung it into the face of the man who was trying to rise from his chair on the other side of Ricky Scarlotti, the cast-iron cusp ringing against bone, bursting the nose, knocking him backward on the floor.

Ricky Scarlotti was on his feet now, his mouth twisted, his finger raised at Clete. But he never got the chance to speak.

'I brought you some of your own, Ricky,' Clete said.

He jammed a pair of vise grips into Ricky Scarlotti's scrotum and locked down the handles. Ricky Scarlotti's hands grabbed impotently at Clete's wrists while his head reared toward the ceiling.

Clete began backing toward the front door, pulling Ricky Scarlotti with him.

'Work with me on this. You can do it, Mouse. That a boy. Step lively now. Coming through here, gangway for the Mouse!' Clete said, pushing chairs and tables out of the way with his buttocks.

Out on the street he unhooked Scarlotti from the vise grips and bounced him off the side of a parked car, then slapped his face with his open hand, once, twice, then a third time, so hard the inside of Scarlotti's mouth bled.

'I'm not carrying, Mouse. Free shot,' Clete said, his hands palm up at his sides now.

But Scarlotti was paralyzed, his mouth hanging open, his lips like red Jell-O. Clete grabbed him by his collar and the back of his belt and flung him to the sidewalk, then picked him up, pushed him forward, and flung him down again, over and over, working his way down the sidewalk, clattering garbage cans along the cement. People stared from automobiles, the streetcar, and door fronts but no one intervened. Then, like a man who knows his rage can never be satiated, Clete lost it. He drove Scarlotti's head into a parking meter, smashing it repeatedly against the metal and glass. A woman across the street screamed hysterically and people began blowing car horns. Clete spun Scarlotti around by his bloodied shirtfront and threw him across a laddered display of flowers under the canvas awning.

'Tell these people why this is happening, Ricky. Tell them how you had a guy's teeth torn out, how you had a woman blindfolded and beaten and held underwater,' Clete said, advancing toward him, his shoes crunching through the scattered potting soil.

Scarlotti dragged himself backward, his nose bleeding from both nostrils. But the elderly woman who had set the flowers out on the walk ran from the restaurant door and knelt beside him with her arms stretched across his chest, as though she were preventing him from rising. She screamed in Italian at Clete, her eyes serpentine and liquid.

Benny Grogan, the ex-wrestler, touched Clete on the elbow. Pieces of chipped beef still clung to his platinum hair. He held a ball-peen hammer in his hand, but he tossed it onto a sack of peat moss. For some reason, the elderly woman stopped screaming, as though a curtain had descended on a stage.

'You see a percentage in this, Purcel?' Benny Grogan said.

Clete looked at the elderly woman squatted by her son.

'You should go to church today, burn a candle, Mouse,' he said.

He got in his convertible and drove to the corner, his tailpipe billowing white smoke, and turned down a shady side street toward St. Charles. He took his seal-top coffee mug off the dashboard and drank from it.

19

It was early Saturday morning and Clete was changing a tire in my drive while he talked, spinning a lug wrench on a nut, his love handles wedging over his belt.

'So I took River Road and barrel-assed across the Huey Long and said goodbye to New Orleans for a while,' he said. He squinted up at me and waited. 'What?' he said.

'Scarlotti is a small player in this, Clete,' I said.

'That's why you and Helen were pounding on his cage?' He got to his feet and threw his tools in the trunk. 'I've got to get some new tires. I blew one coming off the bridge. What d' you mean, small player? That pisses me off, Dave.'

'I think he and the Giancano family put the hit on Cool Breeze because he ratted them out to the Feds. But if you wanted to get even for Megan, you probably beat up on the wrong guy.'

'The greaseballs are taking orders, even though they've run the action in New Orleans for a hundred years? Man, I learn something every day. Did you read that article in the *Star* about Hitler hiding out in Israel?'

His face was serious a moment, then he stuck an unlit cigarette in his mouth and the smile came back in his eyes and he twirled his porkpie hat on his finger while he looked at me, then at the sunrise behind the flooded cypresses.

I helped Batist at the bait shop, then drove to Cool Breeze's house on the west side of town and was told by a neighbor he was out at Mout's flower farm.

Mout' and a Hmong family from Laos farmed three acres of zinnias and chrysanthemums in the middle of a sugarcane plantation on the St. Martinville road, and each fall, when football season began, they cut and dug wagonloads of flowers that they sold to florists in Baton Rouge and New Orleans. I drove across a cattle guard and down a white shale road until I saw a row of poplars that was planted as a windbreak and Cool

Breeze hoeing weeds out in the sunlight while his father sat in the shade reading a newspaper by a card table with a pitcher of lemonade on it.

I parked my truck and walked down the rows of chrysanthemums. The wind was blowing and the field rippled with streaks of brown and gold and purple color.

'I never figured you to take up farming, Breeze,' I said.

'I give up on some t'ings. So my father made this li'l job for me, that's all,' he said.

'Beg your pardon?'

'Getting even wit' people, t'ings like that. I ain't giving nobody reason to put me back in jail.'

'You know what an exhumation order is?' I asked.

As with many people of color, he treated questions from white men as traps and didn't indicate an answer one way or another. He stooped over and jerked a weed and its root system out of the soil.

'I want to have a pathologist examine your wife's remains. I don't believe she committed suicide,' I said.

He stopped work and rested his hands on the hoe handle. His hands looked like gnarled rocks around the wood. Then he put one hand inside the top of his shirt and rubbed his skin, his eyes never leaving mine.

'Say again?'

'I checked with the coroner's office in St. Mary Parish. No autopsy was done on Ida's body. It simply went down as a suicide.'

'What you telling me?'

'I don't think she took her life.'

'Didn't nobody have reason to kill her. Unless you saying I . . . Wait a minute, you trying to—'

'You're not a killer, Breeze. You're just a guy who got used by some very bad white people.'

He started working the hoe between the plants again, his breath coming hard in his chest, his brow creased like an old leather glove. The wind was cool blowing across the field, but drops of sweat as big as marbles slid off his neck. He stopped his work again and faced me, his eyes wet.

'What we got to do to get this here order you talking about?' he asked.

When I got home a peculiar event was taking place. Alafair and three of her friends were in the front yard, watching a man with a flattop haircut stand erect on an oak limb, then topple into space, grab a second limb and hang from it by his knees.

I parked my pickup and walked across the yard while Boxleiter's eyes, upside down, followed me. He bent his torso upward, flipped his legs in the air, and did a half-somersault so that he hit the ground on the balls of his feet.

'Alafair, would you guys head on up to the house and tell Bootsie I'll be there in a minute?' I said.

'She's on the gallery. Tell her yourself,' Alafair said.

'*Alf . . .*' I said.

She rolled her eyes as though the moment was more than her patience could endure, then she and her friends walked through the shade toward the house.

'Swede, it's better you bring business to my office,' I said.

'I couldn't sleep last night. I always sleep, I mean dead, like stone. But not last night. There's some heavy shit coming down, man. It's a feeling I get. I'm never wrong.'

'Like what?'

'This ain't no ordinary grift.' He fanned his hand at the air, as though sweeping away cobweb. 'I never had trouble handling the action. You draw lines, you explain the rules, guys don't listen, they keep coming at you, you unzip their package. But that ain't gonna work on this one.' He blotted the perspiration off his face with the back of his forearm.

'Sorry. You're not making much sense, Swede.'

'I don't got illusions about how guys like me end up. But Cisco and Megan ain't like me. I was sleeping in the Dismas House in St. Louis after I finished my first bit. They came and got me. They see somebody jammed up, people getting pushed around, they make those people's problem their problem. They get that from their old man. That's why these local cocksuckers nailed him to a wall.'

'You're going have to watch your language around my home, partner,' I said.

His hand shot out and knotted my shirt in a ball.

'You're like every cop I ever knew. You don't listen. I can't stop what's going on.'

I grabbed his wrist and thrust it away from me. He opened and closed his hands impotently.

'I hate guys like you,' he said.

'Oh?'

'You go to church with your family, but you got no idea what life is like for two-thirds of the human race.'

'I'm going inside now, Swede. Don't come around here anymore.'

'What'd I do, use bad language again?'

'You cut up Anthony Pollock. I can't prove it, and it didn't happen in our jurisdiction, but you're an iceman.'

'If I did it in a uniform, you'd be introducing me at the Kiwanis Club.

I hear you adopted your kid and treated her real good. That's a righteous deed, man. But the rest of your routine is comedy. A guy with your brains ought to be above it.'

He walked down the slope to the dirt road and his parked car. When he was out of the shade he stopped and turned around. His granny glasses were like ground diamonds in the sunlight.

'How many people did it take to crucify Megan and Cisco's old man and cover it up for almost forty years? I'm an iceman? Watch out one of your neighbors don't tack you up with a nail gun,' he yelled up the slope while two fishermen unhitching a boat trailer stared at him open-mouthed.

I raked and burned leaves that afternoon and tried not to think about Swede Boxleiter. But in his impaired way he had put his thumb on a truth about human behavior that eludes people who are considered normal. I remembered a story of years ago about a fourteen-year-old boy from Chicago who was visiting relatives in a small Mississippi town not far from the Pearl River. One afternoon he whistled at a white woman on the street. Nothing was said to him, but that night two Klansmen kidnapped him from the home of his relatives, shot and killed him, and wrapped his body in a net of bricks and wire and sank it in the river.

Everyone in town knew who had done it. Two local lawyers, respectable men not associated with the Klan, volunteered to defend the killers. The jury took twenty minutes to set them free. The foreman said the verdict took that long because the jury had stopped deliberations to send out for soda pop.

It's a story out of another era, one marked by shame and collective fear, but its point is not about racial injustice but instead the fate of those who bear Cain's mark.

A year after the boy's death a reporter from a national magazine visited the town by the Pearl River to learn the fate of the killers. At first they had been avoided, passed by on the street, treated at grocery or hardware counters as though they had no first or last names, then their businesses failed – one owned a filling station, the other a fertilizer yard – and their debts were called. Both men left town, and when asked their whereabouts old neighbors would only shake their heads as though the killers were part of a vague and decaying memory.

The town that had been complicit in the murder ostracized those who had committed it. But no one had been ostracized in St. Mary Parish. Why? What was the difference in the accounts of the black teenager's murder and Jack Flynn's, both of which seemed collective in nature?

Answer: The killers in Mississippi were white trash and economically dispensable.

Sunday afternoon I found Archer Terrebonne on his side patio, disassembling a spinning reel on a glass table top. He wore slippers and white slacks and a purple shirt that was embroidered with his initials on the pocket. Overhead, two palm trees with trunks that were as gray and smooth as elephant hide creaked against a hard-blue sky. Terrebonne glanced up at me, then resumed his concentration, but not in an unpleasant way.

'Sorry to bother you on Sunday, but I suspect you're quite busy during the week,' I said.

'It's no bother. Pull up a chair. I wanted to thank you for the help you gave my daughter.'

You didn't do wide-end runs around Archer Terrebonne.

'It's wonderful to see her fresh and bright in the morning, unharried by all the difficulties she's had, all the nights in hospitals and calls from policemen,' he said.

'I have a problem, Mr. Terrebonne. A man named Harpo Scruggs is running all over our turf and we can't get a net over him.'

'Scruggs? Oh yes, quite a character. I thought he was dead.'

'His uncle was a guy named Harpo Delahoussey. He did security work at y'all's cannery, the one that burned.'

'Yes, I remember.'

'We think Harpo Scruggs tried to kill a black man named Willie Broussard and almost drowned Jack Flynn's daughter.'

He set down the tiny screwdriver and the exposed brass mechanisms of the spinning reel. The tips of his delicate fingers were bright with machine oil. The wind blew his white-gold hair on his forehead.

'But you use the father's name, not the daughter's. What inference should I gather from that, sir? My family has a certain degree of wealth and hence we should feel guilt over Jack Flynn's death?'

'Why do you think he was killed?'

'That's your province, Mr. Robicheaux, not mine. But I don't think Jack Flynn was a proletarian idealist. I think he was a resentful, envious troublemaker who couldn't get over the fact his family lost their money through their own mismanagement. Castle Irish don't do well when their diet is changed to boiled cabbage.'

'He fought Franco's fascists in Spain. That's a peculiar way to show envy.'

'What's your purpose here?'

'Your daughter is haunted by something in the past she can't tell anybody about. It's connected to the Hanged Man in the Tarot. I wonder if it's Jack Flynn's death that bothers her.'

He curled the tips of his fingers against his palm, as though trying to rub the machinist's oil off them, looking at them idly.

'She killed her cousin when she was fifteen. Or at least that's what she's convinced herself,' he said. He saw my expression change, my lips start to form a word. 'We had a cabin in Durango at the foot of a mountain. They found the key to my gun case and started shooting across a snowfield. The avalanche buried her cousin in an arroyo. When they dug her out the next day, her body was frozen upright in the shape of a cross.'

'I didn't know that, sir.'

'You do now. I'm going in to eat directly. Would you care to join us?'

When I walked to my truck I felt like a man who had made an obscene remark in the midst of a polite gathering. I sat behind the steering wheel and stared at the front of the Terrebonne home. It was encased in shadow now, the curtains drawn on all the windows. What historical secrets, what private unhappiness did it hold? I wondered if I would ever know. The late sun hung like a shattered red flame in the pine trees.

20

I remember a Christmas dawn five years after I came home from Vietnam. I greeted it in an all-night bar built of slat wood, the floor raised off the dirt with cinder blocks. I walked down the wood steps into a deserted parking area, my face numb with alcohol, and stood in the silence and looked at a solitary live oak hung with Spanish moss, the cattle acreage that was gray with winter, the hollow dome of sky that possessed no color at all, and suddenly I felt the vastness of the world and all the promise it could hold for those who were still its children and had not severed their ties with the rest of the human family.

Monday morning I visited Megan at her brother's house and saw a look in her eyes that I suspected had been in mine on that Christmas morning years ago.

Had her attackers held her underwater a few seconds more, her body would have conceded what her will would not: Her lungs and mouth and nose would have tried to draw oxygen out of water and her chest and throat would have filled with cement. In that moment she knew the heartbreaking twilight-infused beauty that the earth can offer, that we waste as easily as we tear pages from a calendar, but neither would she ever forget or forgive the fact that her reprieve came from the same hands that did Indian burns on her skin and twisted her face down into the silt.

She was living in the guest cottage at the back of Cisco's house, and the French doors were open and the four-o'clocks planted as borders around the trees were dull red in the shade.

'What's that?' she said.

I lay a paper sack and the hard-edged metal objects inside it on her breakfast table.

'A nine-millimeter Beretta. I've made arrangements for somebody to give you instruction at the firing range,' I said.

She slipped the pistol and the unattached magazine out of the sack and pulled back the slide and looked at the empty chamber. She flipped the butterfly safety back and forth.

'You have peculiar attitudes for a policeman,' she said.

'When they deal the play, you take it to them with fire tongs,' I said.

She put the pistol back in the sack and stepped out on the brick patio and looked at the bayou with her hands in the back pockets of her baggy khaki pants.

'I'll be all right after a while. I've been through worse,' she said.

I stepped outside with her. 'No, you haven't,' I said.

'Excuse me?'

'It only gets so bad. You go to the edge, then you join a special club. A psychologist once told me only about three percent of the human family belongs to it.'

'I think I'll pass on the honor.'

'Why'd you come back?'

'I see my father in my sleep.'

'You want the gun?'

'Yes.'

I nodded and turned to go.

'Wait.' She took her eyeglass case out of her shirt pocket and stepped close to me. There was a dark scrape at the corner of her eye, like dirty rouge rubbed into the grain. 'Just stand there. You don't have to do anything,' she said, and put her arms around me and her head on my chest and pressed her stomach flat against me. She wore doeskin moccasins and I could feel the instep of her foot on my ankle.

The top of her head moved under my chin and against my throat and the wetness of her eyes was like an unpracticed kiss streaked on my skin.

Rodney Loudermilk had lived two weeks on the eighth floor of the old hotel that was not two blocks from the Alamo. The elevator was slow and throbbed in the shaft, the halls smelled bad, the fire escapes leaked rust down the brick sides of the building. But there was a bar and grill downstairs and the view from his window was magnificent. The sky was blue and salmon-colored in the evening, the San Antonio River lighted by sidewalk restaurants and gondolas that passed under the bridges, and he could see the pinkish stone front of the old mission where he often passed himself off as a tour guide and led college girls through the porticoed walkways that were hung with grapevines.

He was blind in one eye from a childhood accident with a BB gun. He wore sideburns and snap-button cowboy shirts with his Montgomery Ward suits. He had been down only once, in Sugarland, on a nickel-and-dime burglary beef that had gone sour because his fall partner, a black man, had dropped a crowbar off the roof through the top of a greenhouse.

But Rodney had learned his lesson: Stay off of roofs and don't try to turn watermelon pickers into successful house creeps.

The three-bit on Sugarland Farm hadn't been a wash either. He had picked up a new gig, one that had some dignity to it, that paid better, that didn't require dealing with fences who took him off at fifteen cents on the dollar. One week off the farm and he did his first hit. It was much easier than he thought. The target was a rancher outside Victoria, a loudmouth fat shit who drove a Cadillac with longhorns for a hood ornament and who kept blubbering, 'I'll give you money, boy. You name the price. Look, my wife's gonna be back from the store. Don't hurt her, okay . . . ' then had started to tremble and messed himself like a child.

'That goes to show you, money don't put no lead in your pencil,' Rodney was fond of telling his friends.

He also said the fat man was so dumb he never guessed his wife had put up the money for the hit. But Rodney let him keep his illusions. Why not? Business was business. You didn't personalize it, even though the guy was a born mark.

Their grief was their own, he said. They owed money, they stole it, they cheated on their wives. People sought justice in different ways. The state did it with a gurney and a needle, behind a viewing glass, while people watched like they were at an X-rated movie. Man, *that* was sick.

Rodney showered in the small tin stall and put on a fresh long-sleeve shirt, one that covered the tattooed chain of blue stars around his left wrist, then looked at his four suits in the closet and chose one that rippled with light like a sheet of buffed tin. He slipped on a new pair of black cowboy boots and fitted a white cowboy hat on his head, pulling the brim at an angle over his blind eye.

All you had to do was stand at the entrance to the Alamo and people came up and asked you questions. Clothes didn't make the person. Clothes *were* the person, he told people. You ever see a gun bull mounted on horseback without a hat and shades? You ever see a construction boss on a job without a clipboard and hard hat and a pocketful of ballpoints? You ever see a hooker that *ain't* made up to look like your own personal pinball machine?

Rodney conducted tours, gave directions around the city, walked tourists to their hotels so they wouldn't be mugged by what he called 'local undesirables we're fixing to get rid of.'

A buddy, a guy he'd celled with at Sugarland, asked him what he got out of it.

'Nothing. That's the point, boy. They got nothing I want.'

Which wasn't true. But how did you explain to a pipehead that walking normals around, making them apprehensive one moment, relieving their fears another, watching them hang on his words about the cremation of the Texan dead on the banks of the river (an account he had memorized from a brochure) gave him a rush like a freight train loaded with Colombian pink roaring through the center of his head?

Or popping a cap on a slobbering fat man who thought he could bribe Rodney Loudermilk.

It was dusk when Rodney came back from showing two elderly nuns where Davy Crockett had been either bayoneted to death or captured against the barracks wall and later tortured. They both had seemed a little pale at the details he used to describe the event. In fact, they had the ingratitude to tell him they didn't need an escort back to their hotel, like he had BO or something. Oh, well. He had more important things on his mind. Like this deal over in Louisiana. He'd told his buddy, the pipehead, he didn't get into a new career so he could go back to strong-arm and B&E bullshit. That whole scene on the bayou had made him depressed in ways he couldn't explain, like somebody had stolen something from him.

She hadn't been afraid. When they're afraid, it proves they got it coming. When they're not afraid, it's like they're spitting in your face. Yeah, that was it. You can't pop them unless they're afraid, or they take part of you with them. Now he was renting space in his head to a hide (that's what he called women) he shouldn't even be thinking about. He had given her power, and he wanted to go back and correct the images that had left him confused and irritable and not the person he was when he gave guided tours in his western clothes.

He looked at the slip of paper he had made a note on when this crazy deal started. It read: *Meet H.S. in New Iberia. Educate a commonist?* A commonist? Republicans live in rich houses, not commonists. Any dumb shit knows that. Why had he gotten into this? He crumpled up the note in his palm and bounced it off the rim of the wastebasket and called the grill for a steak and baked potato, heavy on the cream and melted butter, and a green salad and a bottle of champale.

It was dusk and a purple haze hung on the rooftops when a man stepped out of a hallway window onto a fire escape, then eased one foot out on a ledge and worked his way across the brick side of the building, oblivious to the stares of two winos down in the alley eight floors below. When the ledge ended, he paused for only a moment, then with the agility of a cat, he hopped across empty space onto another ledge and entered another window.

Rodney Loudermilk had just forked a piece of steak into his mouth when the visitor seized him from behind and dragged him out of his chair, locking arms and wrists under Rodney's rib cage, lifting him into the air and simultaneously carrying him to the window, whose curtains swelled with the evening breeze. Rodney probably tried to scream and strike out with the fork that was in his hand, but a piece of meat was lodged like a stone in his throat and the arms of his visitor seemed to be cracking his ribs like sticks.

Then there was a rush of air and noise and he was out above the city, among clouds and rooftops and faces inside windows that blurred past him. He concentrated his vision on the dusky purple stretch of sky that was racing away from him, just like things had always raced away from him. It was funny how one gig led to another, then in seconds the rounded, cast-iron, lug-bolted dome of an ancient fire hydrant rose out of the cement and came at your head faster than a BB traveling toward the eye.

The account of Rodney Loudermilk's death was given us over the phone by a San Antonio homicide investigator named Cecil Hardin, who had found the crumpled piece of notepaper by the wastebasket in Loudermilk's hotel room. He also read us the statements he had taken from the two witnesses in the alley and played a taped recording of an interview with Loudermilk's pipehead friend.

'You got any idea who H.S. is?' Hardin asked.

'We've had trouble around here with an ex-cop by the name of Harpo Scruggs,' I said.

'You think he's connected to Loudermilk's death?' he asked.

'The killer was an aerialist? My vote would go to another local, Swede Boxleiter. He's a suspect in a murder in Lafayette Parish.'

'What are y'all running over there, a school for criminals? Forget I said that. Spell the name, please.' Then he said, 'What's the deal on this guy Boxleiter?'

'He's a psychopath with loyalties,' I said.

'You a comedian, sir?'

I drove up the Loreauville road to Cisco's house. Megan was reading a book in a rocking chair on the gallery.

'Do you know where Swede was on Sunday?' I asked.

'He was here, at least in the morning. Why?'

'Just a little research. Does the name Rodney Loudermilk mean anything to you?'

'No. Who is he?'

'A guy with sideburns, blind in one eye?'

She shook her head.

'Did you tell Swede anything about your attackers, how they looked, what they said?'

675

'Nothing I didn't tell you. I was asleep when they broke in. They wound tape around my eyes.'

I scratched the back of my neck. 'Maybe Swede's not our man.'

'I don't know what you're talking about, Dave.'

'Sunday evening somebody canceled out a contract killer in a San Antonio hotel. He was probably one of the men who broke into your house.'

She closed the book in her lap and looked out into the yard. 'I told Swede about the blue stars on a man's wrist,' she said.

'What?'

'One of them had a string of stars tattooed on his wrist. I told that to one of your deputies. He wrote it down.'

'If he did, the sheriff and I never saw it.'

'What difference does it make?'

'The guy in San Antonio, he was thrown out an eighth-floor window by somebody who knows how to leap across window ledges. He had a chain of blue stars tattooed around his left wrist.'

She tried to hide the knowledge in her eyes. She took her glasses off and put them back on again.

'Swede was here that morning. He ate breakfast with us. I mean, everything about him was normal,' she said, then turned her face toward me.

'Normal? You're talking about Boxleiter? Good try, Meg.'

Helen and I drove to the movie set on the Terrebonne lawn.

'Sunday? I was at Cisco's. Then I was home. Then I went to a movie,' Swede said. He dropped down from the back of a flatbed truck, his tool belt clattering on his hips. His gaze went up and down Helen's body. 'We're not getting into that blackjack routine again, are we?'

'Which movie?' I asked.

'*Sense and Sensibility.* Ask at the theater. The guy'll remember me 'cause he says I plugged up the toilet.'

'Sounds good to me. What about you, Helen?' I said.

'Yeah, I always figured him for a fan of British novels,' she said.

'What am I supposed to have done?'

'Tossed a guy out a window in San Antonio. His head hit a fire hydrant at a hundred twenty miles per. Big mess,' I said.

'Yeah? Who is this fucking guy I supposedly killed?'

'Would you try not to use profanity?' I said.

'Sorry. I forgot, Louisiana is an open-air church. I got a question for you. Why is it guys like me are always getting rousted whenever some barf bag gets marched off with the Hallelujah Chorus? Does Ricky the Mouse do time? Is Harpo Scruggs sitting in your jail? Of course not.

676

You turned him loose. If guys like me weren't around, you'd be out of a job.' He pulled a screwdriver from his belt and began tapping it across his palm, rolling his eyes, chewing gum, rotating his head on his neck. 'Is this over? I got to get to work.'

'We might turn out to be your best friends, Swede,' I said.

'Yeah, shit goes great with frozen yogurt, too,' he said, and walked away from us, his bare triangular back arched forward like that of a man in search of an adversary.

'You going to let him slide like that?' Helen said.

'Sometimes the meltdowns have their point of view.'

'Just coincidence he stops up a toilet in a theater on the day he needs an alibi?'

'Let's go to the airport.'

But if Swede took a plane to San Antonio or rented one, we could find no record of it.

That night the air was thick and close and smelled of chrysanthemums and gas, then the sky filled with lightning and swirls of black rain that turned to hail and clattered and bounced like mothballs on the tin roof of the bait shop.

Two days later I drove to St. Mary Parish with Cool Breeze Broussard to watch the exhumation of his wife's body from a graveyard that was being eaten daily by the Atchafalaya River.

At one time the graveyard had sat on dry ground, fringed by persimmon and gum trees, but almost twenty years ago the Atchafalaya had broken a levee and channeled an oxbow through the woods, flooding the grave sites, then had left behind a swampy knob of sediment strung with river trash. One side of the graveyard dipped toward the river, and each year the water cut more deeply under the bank, so that the top layer hung like the edge of a mushroom over the current.

Most of the framed and spiked name tags that served as markers had been knocked down or stepped on and broken by hunters. The dime-store vases and the jelly glasses used for flower jars lay embedded in sediment. The graduation and wedding and birth pictures wrapped in plastic had been washed off the graves on which they had been originally placed and were now spotted with mud, curled and yellowed by the sun so that the faces on them were not only anonymous but stared incongruously out of situations that seemed to have never existed.

The forensic pathologist and a St. Mary Parish deputy and the two black men hired as diggers and the backhoe operator waited.

'You know which one it is?' I asked Cool Breeze.

'That one yonder, wit' the pipe cross. I welded it myself. The shaft goes down t'ree feet,' he said.

The serrated teeth on the bucket of the backhoe bit into the soft earth and lifted a huge divot of loam and roots and emerald-colored grass from the top of the grave. Cool Breeze's shoulder brushed against mine, and I could feel the rigidity and muted power in his body, like the tremolo that rises from the boiler room of a ship.

'We can wait on the levee until they're finished,' I said.

'I got to look,' he said.

'Beg your pardon?'

'Cain't have nobody saying later that ain't her.'

'Breeze, she's been in the ground a long time.'

'Don't matter. I'll know. What you t'ink I am anyway? Other men can look at my wife, but I'm scared to do it myself?'

'I think you're a brave man,' I said.

He turned his head and looked at the side of my face.

The backhoe was bright yellow against the islands of willow trees between the graveyard and the main portion of the river. The loam in the grave turned to mud as the bucket on the backhoe dipped closer to the coffin. The day was blue-gold and warm and flowers still bloomed on the levee, but the air smelled of humus, of tree roots torn out of wet soil, of leaves that have gone acidic and brown in dead water. At five feet the two black diggers climbed into the hole with spades and began sculpting the coffin's shape, pouring water from a two-gallon can on the edges, wiping the surface and corners slick with rags.

They worked a canvas tarp and wood planks under it, then ran ropes tied to chains under the tarp, and we all lifted. The coffin came free more easily than I had expected, rocking almost weightlessly in the bottom of the canvas loop, a missing panel in one side blossoming with muddy fabric.

'Open it up,' Cool Breeze said.

The pathologist looked at me. He wore red suspenders and a straw hat and had a stomach like a small pillow pushed under his belt. I nodded, and one of the diggers prized the lid loose with a blade screwdriver.

I had seen exhumations before. The view of mortality they present to the living is not easily dismissed. Sometimes the coffin fills with hair, the nails, particularly on the bare feet, grow into claws, the face puckers into a gray apple, the burial clothes contain odors that cause people to retch.

That is not what happened to Ida Broussard.

Her white dress had turned brown, like cheesecloth dipped in tea, but her skin had the smooth texture and color of an eggplant and her hair was shiny and black on her shoulders and there was no distortion in her expression.

Cool Breeze's hand reached out and touched her cheek. Then he walked away from us, without speaking, and stood on the edge of the graveyard and looked out at the river so we could not see his face.

'How do you explain it?' I said to the pathologist.

'An oil company buried some storage tanks around here in the 1930s. Maybe some chemical seepage got in the coffin,' he replied.

He looked back into my eyes. Then he spoke again. 'Sometimes I think they wait to tell us something. There's no need for you to pass on my observation.'

21

Friday evening Bootsie and I dropped Alafair at the show in Lafayette, then ate dinner at a restaurant on the Vermilion River. But as soon as Alafair was not with us, Bootsie became introspective, almost formal when she spoke, her eyes lingering on objects without seeing them.

'What is it?' I said outside the restaurant.

'I'm just tired,' she replied.

'Maybe we should have stayed home.'

'Maybe we should have.'

After Alafair went to bed, we were alone in the kitchen. The moon was up and the trees outside were full of shadows when the wind blew.

'Whatever it is, just say it, Boots.'

'She was at the dock today. She said she couldn't find you at your office. She didn't bother to come up to the house. Of course, she's probably just shy.'

'She?'

'You know who. She finds any excuse she can to come out here. She said she wanted to thank you for the shooting lessons you arranged for her. You didn't want to give them to her yourself?'

'Those guys almost killed her. They might pull it off the next time.'

'Maybe it's her own fault.'

'That's a rough thing to say, Boots.'

'She hides behind adversity and uses it to manipulate other people.'

'I'll ask her not to come here again.'

'Not on my account, please.'

'I give up,' I said, and went out into the yard.

The cane in my neighbor's field was green and dented with channels like rivers when the wind blew, and beyond his tree line I could see lightning fork without sound out of the sky. Through the kitchen window I heard Bootsie clattering dishes into the dishwasher. She slammed the washer door shut, the cups and silverware rattling in the rack. I heard the washer start to hum, then her shadow went past the window and disappeared from view and the overhead light went off and the kitchen and the yard were dark.

We wanted Harpo Scruggs. But we had nothing to charge him with. He knew it, too. He called the dock on Sunday afternoon.

'I want to meet, talk this thing out, bring it to an end,' he said.

'It's not a seller's market, Scruggs.'

'What you got is your dick in your hand. I can clean the barn for you. There's an old nigra runs a barbecue joint next to a motel on State Road 70 north of Morgan City. Nine o'clock,' he said, and hung up.

I went outside the bait shop and hosed down a rental boat a fisherman had just returned, then went back inside without chaining it up and called Helen Soileau at her home.

'You want to do backup on a meet with Harpo Scruggs?' I said.

'Make him come in.'

'We don't have enough to charge him.'

'There's still the college kid, the witness who saw the two brothers executed in the Basin.'

'His family says he's on a walking tour of Tibet.'

'He killed Mout's dog. Vermilion Parish can charge him with endangering.'

'"Mout" says he never got a good look at the guy's face.'

'Dave, we need to work this guy. He doesn't bring the Feds into it, he doesn't plead out. We fit his head in a steel vise.'

'So take a ride with me. I want you to bring a scoped rifle.'

She was silent a moment. Then she said, 'Tell the old man.'

The barbecue place was a rambling, tin-roofed red building, with white trim and screen porches, set back in a grove of pines. Next door was a cinder-block motel that had been painted purple and fringed with Christmas lights that never came down. Through the screen on a side porch I saw Harpo Scruggs standing at the bar, a booted foot on the rail, his tall frame bent forward, his Stetson at an angle on his freshly barbered head. He wore a long-sleeve blue shirt with pink polka dots and an Indian-stitched belt and gray western slacks that flowed like water over the crook in his knee. He tilted back a shot glass of whiskey and sipped from a glass of beer.

I stood by a plank table at the edge of the clearing so he could see me. He put an unlit cigarette in his mouth and opened the screen door and lit the cigarette with a Zippo as he walked toward me.

'You got anybody with you?' he asked.

'You see anyone?'

He sat down at the plank table and smoked his cigarette, his elbows

681

on the wood. The clouds above the pines were black and maroon in the sun's afterglow. He tipped his ashes carefully over the edge of the table so they wouldn't blow back on his shirt.

'I heard about a man got throwed out a window. I think one of two men done it. Swede Boxleiter or that bucket of whale sperm got hisself kicked off the New Orleans police force,' he said.

'Clete Purcel?'

'If that's his name. You can tell them I didn't have nothing to do with hurting that woman.'

'Tell them yourself.'

'All this trouble we been having? It can end in one of two ways. That black boy, Broussard, don't testify against the dagos in New Orleans and some people gets paid back the money they're owed.

'The other way it ends is I get complete immunity as a government witness, all my real estate is sold and the proceeds are put in bearer bonds. Not one dollar of it gets touched by the IRS. Then I retire down in Gautemala. Y'all decide.'

'Who the hell do you think you are?' I said.

A black man brought a bottle of Dixie beer on a metal tray to the table. Scruggs tipped him a quarter and wiped the lip of the bottle with his palm.

'I'm the man got something you want, son. Or you wouldn't be sitting here,' he replied.

'You took money from Ricky Scarlotti, then fucked up everything you touched. Now you've got both the Mob and a crazoid like Boxleiter on your case,' I said.

He drank out of the beer and looked into the pine trees, sucking his false teeth, his expression flat. But I saw the muted change in his eyes, the way heat glows when the wind puffs ash off a coal.

'You ain't so different from me,' he said. 'You want to bring them rich people down. I can smell it in you, boy. A poor man's got hate in his glands. It don't wash out. That's why nigras stink the way they do.'

'You've caused a lot of trouble and pain for people around here. So we've decided in your case it should be a two-way street. I'd hoped you'd provoke a situation here.'

'You got a hideaway on your ankle?'

'My partner has your face in the crosshairs of a scoped .30-06. She'd looked forward to this evening with great anticipation, sir. Enjoy your beer. We'll catch you down the road.'

I walked out to the parking lot and waited for Helen to pull my truck around from the other side of the motel. I didn't look behind me, but I could feel his eyes on my back, watching. When Helen drew to a stop in front of me, the scoped, bolt-action rifle on the gun rack, the dust drifting off the tires, she cocked one finger like a pistol and aimed it out the window at Harpo Scruggs.

Tuesday morning the sheriff called me into his office.

'I just got the surveillance report on Scruggs,' he said. 'He took the Amtrak to Houston, spent the night in a Mexican hot-pillow joint, then flew to Trinidad, Colorado.'

'He'll be back.'

'I think I finally figured out something about wars. A few people start them and the rest of us fight them. I'm talking about all these people who use our area for a bidet. I think this state is becoming a mental asylum, I really do.' Something outside the window caught his attention. 'Ah, my morning wouldn't be complete without it. Cisco Flynn just walked in the front door.'

Five minutes later Cisco sat down in front of my desk.

'You got anything on these guys who attacked Megan?' he asked.

'Yeah. One of them is dead.'

'Did you clear Swede on that deal?'

'You mean did I check out his alibi? He created a memorable moment at the theater. Water flowed out of the men's room into the lobby. At about five in the afternoon.'

'From what I understand, that should put him home free.'

'It might.'

I watched his face. His reddish-brown eyes smiled at nothing.

'Megan felt bad that maybe she made a suspect out of Swede,' he said.

'You can pretend otherwise, but he's a dangerous man, Cisco.'

'How about the cowboy who went out the window? Would you call him a dangerous man?'

I didn't answer. We stared at each other across the desk. Then his eyes broke.

'Good seeing you, Dave. Thanks for giving Megan the gun,' he said.

I watched silently as he opened the office door and went out into the hall.

I propped my forehead on my fingers and stared at the empty green surface of my desk blotter. Why hadn't I seen it? I had even used the term 'aerialist' to the San Antonio homicide investigator.

I went out the side door of the building and caught Cisco at his car. The day was beautiful, and his suntanned face looked gold and handsome in the cool light.

'You called the dead man a cowboy,' I said.

He grinned, bemused. 'What's the big deal?' he said.

'Who said anything about how the guy was dressed?'

'I mean "cowboy" like "hit man." That's what contract killers are called, aren't they?'

'You and Boxleiter worked this scam together, didn't you?'

He laughed and shook his head and got in his car and drove out of the lot, then waved from the window just before he disappeared in the traffic.

The forensic pathologist called me that afternoon.

'I can give it to you over the phone or talk in person. I'd rather do it in person,' he said.

'Why's that?'

'Because autopsies can tell us things about human behavior I don't like to know about,' he replied.

An hour later I walked into his office.

'Let's go outside and sit under the trees. You'll have to excuse my mood. My own work depresses the hell out of me sometimes,' he said.

We sat in metal chairs behind the white-painted brick building that housed his office. The hard-packed earth stayed in shade almost year-round and was green with mold and sloped down to a ragged patch of bamboo on the bayou. Out in the sunlight an empty pirogue that had pulled loose from its mooring turned aimlessly in the current.

'There're abrasions on the back of her head and scrape marks on her shoulder, like trauma from a fall rather than a direct blow,' he said. 'Of course, you're more interested in cause of death.'

'I'm interested in all of it.'

'I mean, the abrasions on her skin could have been unrelated to her death. Didn't you say her husband knocked her around before she fled the home?'

'Yes.'

'I found evidence of water in the lungs. It's a bit complicated, but there's no question about its presence at the time she died.'

'So she was alive when she went into the marsh?'

'Hear me out. The water came out of a tap, not a swamp or marsh or brackish bay, not unless the latter contains the same chemicals you find in a city water supply.'

'A faucet?'

'But that's not what killed her.' He wore an immaculate white shirt, and his red suspenders hung loosely on his concave chest. He snuffed down in his nose and fixed his glasses. 'It was heart failure, maybe brought on by suffocation.'

'I'm not putting it together, Clois.'

'You were in Vietnam. What'd the South Vietnamese do when they got their hands on the Vietcong?'

684

'Water poured on a towel?'

'I think in this case we're talking about a wet towel held down on the face. Maybe she fell, then somebody finished the job. But I'm in a speculative area now.'

The image he had called up out of memory was not one I wanted to think about. I looked at the fractured light on the bayou, a garden blooming with blue-and-pink hydrangeas on the far bank. But he wasn't finished.

'She was pregnant. Maybe two months. Does that mean anything?' he said.

'Yeah, it sure does.'

'You don't look too good.'

'It's a bad story, Doc.'

'They all are.'

22

That evening Clete parked his convertible by the dock and hefted an ice chest up on his shoulder and carried it to a fish-cleaning table by one of the water faucets I had mounted at intervals on a water line that ran the length of the dock's handrail. He poured the ice and at least two dozen sac-a-lait out on the table, put on a pair of cloth gardener's gloves, and started scaling the sac-a-lait with a spoon and splitting open their stomachs and half-mooning the heads at the gills.

'You catch fish somewhere else and clean them at my dock?' I said.

'I hate to tell you this, the fishing's a lot better at Henderson. How about I take y'all to the Patio for dinner tonight?'

'Things aren't real cool at the house right now.'

He kept his eyes flat, his face neutral. He washed the spooned fish scales off the board plank. I told him about the autopsy on Ida Broussard.

When I finished he said. 'You like graveyard stories? How about this? I caught Swede Boxleiter going out of the Terrebonne cemetery last night. He'd used a trowel to take the bricks out of the crypt and pry open the casket. He took the rings from the corpse's fingers, and a pair of riding spurs and a silver picture frame that Archer Terrebonne says held a photo of some little girls a slave poisoned.

'I cuffed Boxleiter to a car bumper and went up to the house and told Terrebonne a ghoul had been in his family crypt. That guy must have Freon in his veins. He didn't say a word. He went down there with a light and lifted the bricks back out and dragged the casket out on the ground and straightened the bones and rags inside and put the stolen stuff back on the corpse, didn't blink an eye. He didn't even look at Boxleiter, like Boxleiter was an insect sitting under a glass jar.'

'What'd you do with Boxleiter?'

'Fired him this morning.'

'*You* fired him?'

'Billy Holtzner tends to delegate authority in some situations. He promised me a two-hundred-buck bonus, then hid in his trailer while I walked Boxleiter off the set. Have you told this Broussard guy his wife was murdered?'

'He's not home.'

'Dave, I'll say it again. Don't let him come around the set to square a beef, okay?'

'He's not a bad guy, Clete.'

'Yeah, they've got a lot of that kind on Camp J.'

Early the next morning I sat with Cool Breeze on the gallery of his father's house and told him, in detail, of the pathologist's findings. He had been pushing the swing at an angle with one foot, then he stopped and scratched his hand and looked out at the street.

'The blow on the back of her head and the marks on her shoulders, could you have done that?' I said.

'I pushed her down on the steps. But her head didn't hit nothing but the screen.'

'Was the baby yours?'

'Two months? No, we wasn't . . . It couldn't be my baby.'

'You know where she went after she left your house, don't you?' I said.

'I do now.'

'You stay away from Alex Guidry. I want your promise on that, Breeze.'

He pulled on his fingers and stared at the street.

'I talked with Harpo Scruggs Sunday night,' I said. 'He's making noise about your testifying against the Giacanos and Ricky Scarlotti.'

'Why ain't you got him in jail?'

'Sooner or later, they all go down.'

'Ex-cop, ex-prison guard, man killed niggers in Angola for fun? They go down when God call 'em. What you done about Ida, it ain't lost on me. T'ank you.'

Then he went back in the house.

I ate lunch at home that day. But Bootsie didn't sit at the kitchen table with me. Behind me, I heard her cleaning the drainboard, putting dishes in the cabinets, straightening canned goods in the cupboard.

'Boots, in all truth, I don't believe Megan Flynn has any romantic interest in an over-the-hill small-town homicide cop,' I said.

'Really?'

'When I was a kid, my father was often drunk or in jail and my mother was having affairs with various men. I was alone a lot of the time, and for some reason I didn't understand I was attracted to people who had something wrong with them. There was a big, fat alcoholic nun

I always liked, and a half-blind ex-convict who swept out Provost's Bar, and a hooker on Railroad Avenue who used to pay me a dollar to bring a bucket of beer to her crib.'

'So?'

'A kid from a screwed-up home sees himself in the faces of excoriated people.'

'You're telling me you're Megan Flynn's pet bête noire?'

'No, I'm just a drunk.'

I heard her moving about in the silence, then she paused behind my chair and let the tips of her fingers rest in my hair.

'Dave, it's all right to call yourself that at meetings. But you're not a drunk to me. And she'd better not ever call you one either.'

I felt her fingers trail off my neck, then she was gone from the room.

Two days later Helen and I took the department boat out on a wide bay off the Atchafalaya River where Cisco Flynn was filming a simulated plane crash. We let the bow of the boat scrape up onto a willow island, then walked out on a platform that the production company had built on pilings over the water. Cisco was talking to three other men, his eyes barely noting our presence.

'No, tell him to do it again,' he said. 'The plane's got to come in lower, right out of the sun, right across those trees. I'll do it with him if necessary. When the plane blows smoke, I want it to bleed into that red sun. Okay, everybody cool?'

It was impressive to watch him. Cisco used authority in a way that made others feel they shared in it. He was one of their own, obviously egalitarian in his attitudes, but he could take others across a line they wouldn't cross by themselves.

He turned to me and Helen.

'Watch the magic of Hollywood at work,' he said. 'This scene is going to take four days and a quarter of a million dollars to shoot. The plane comes in blowing black smoke, then we film a model crashing in a pond. We've got a tail section mounted on a mechanical arm that draws the wreckage underwater like a sinking plane, then we do the rescue dive in the LSU swimming pool. It edits down to two minutes of screen time. What d'you think about that?'

'I ran you through the National Crime Information Center. You and Swede Boxleiter took down a liquor store when you were seventeen,' I said.

'Boy, the miracle of computers,' he said. He glanced out at a boat that was moored in the center of the bay. It was the kind used for swamp tours, wide across the beam, domed with green Plexiglas, its white hull gleaming.

'Where were you Sunday evening, Cisco?' I said.

'Rented a pontoon plane and took a ride out on the Gulf.'

'I have to pass on relevant information about you to a homicide investigator in San Antonio.'

'So why tell me about it?'

'I try to do things in the daylight, at least when it involves people I used to trust.'

'He's saying you're being treated better than you deserve,' Helen said.

'The guy who soared on gilded wings out the hotel window? I think the Jersey Bounce was too easy. You saying I did it? Who cares?' Cisco replied.

'Rough words,' I said.

'Yeah?' He picked up a pair of field glasses from a table and tossed them at me. 'Check out the guys who are on that boat. That's reality out there. I wish it would go away, but I'm stuck with it. So give me a break on the wiseacre remarks.'

I focused the glasses through an open window on a linen-covered table where Billy Holtzner and his daughter and two Asian men were eating.

'The two Chinese are the bean counters. When the arithmetic doesn't come out right, they count the numbers a second time on your fingers. Except your fingers aren't on your hands anymore,' he said.

'I'd get into a new line of work,' I said.

'Dave, I respect you and I don't want you to take this wrong. But don't bother me again without a warrant and in the meantime kiss my royal ass,' Cisco said.

'You only try to get men to kiss your ass?' Helen said.

He walked away from us, both of his hands held in the air, as though surrendering to an irrational world, just as a twin-engine amphibian roared across the swamp at treetop level, a pipe in the stern blowing curds of black smoke across the sun.

That evening I jogged to the drawbridge on the dirt road while heat lightning veined the clouds and fireflies glowed and faded like wet matches above the bayou's surface. Then I did three sets each of push-ups, barbell curls, dead lifts, and military presses in the back yard, showered, and went to bed early.

On the edge of sleep I heard rain in the trees and Bootsie undressing in the bathroom, then I felt her weight next to me on the bed. She turned on her side so that her stomach and breasts were pressed against me, and put one leg across mine and her hand on my chest.

'You're drawn to people who have problems. My problem is I don't like other women making overtures to my husband,' she said.

'I think that's a problem I can live with,' I replied.

She raised her knee and hit me with it. Then her hand touched me and she lifted her nightgown and sat on my thighs and leaned over me and looked into my face.

Outside the window, I could see the hard, thick contours of an oak limb, wrapped with moonlight, glistening with rain.

The next day was Saturday. At false dawn I woke from a dream that lingered behind my eyes like cobweb. The dream was about Megan Flynn, and although I knew it did not signify unfaithfulness, it disturbed me just as badly, like a vapor that congeals around the heart.

In the dream she stood on a stretch of yellow hardpan, a treeless purple mountain at her back. The sky was brass, glowing with heat and dust. She walked toward me in her funny hat, her khaki clothes printed with dust, a tasseled red shawl draped around her shoulders.

But the red around her shoulders was not cloth. The wound in her throat had drained her face of blood, drenching her shirt, tasseling the ends of her fingers.

I went down to the dock and soaked a towel in the melted ice at the bottom of the cooler and held it to my eyes.

It was just a dream, I told myself. But the feeling that went with it, that was like toxin injected into the muscle tissue, wouldn't go away. I had known it in Vietnam when I knew someone's death was at hand, mine or someone for whom I was responsible, and it had taken everything in me to climb aboard a slick that was headed up-country, trying to hide the fear in my eyes, the dryness in my mouth, the rancid odor that rose from my armpits.

But that had been the war. Since then I'd had the dream and the feelings that went with it only once – in my own house, the night my wife Annie was murdered.

Twenty years ago Alex Guidry had owned a steel-gray two-story frame house outside Franklin, with a staircase on the side and a second-floor screened porch where he slept in the hot months. Or at least this is what the current owner, an elderly man named Plo Castile, told me. His skin was amber, wizened, as hairless as a manikin's, and his eyes had the blue rheumy tint of oysters.

'I bought this property fo'teen years ago from Mr. Alex. He give me a good price, 'cause I already owned the house next do',' he said. 'He slept right out yonder on that porch, at least when it wasn't cold, 'cause he rented rooms sometimes to oilfield people.'

The yard was neat, with two palm trees in it, and flowers were planted around the latticework at the base of the main house and in a garden by a paintless barn and around a stucco building with a tin roof elevated above the walls.

'Is that a washhouse?' I said.

'Yes, suh, he had a couple of maids done laundry for them oilfield people. Mr. Alex was a good bidnessman.'

'You remember a black woman named Ida Broussard, Mr. Plo?'

He nodded. 'Her husband was the one been in Angola. He run a li'l sto'.' His eyes looked at a cane field beyond the barbed-wire fence.

'She come around here?'

He took a package of tobacco and cigarette papers out of his shirt pocket. 'Been a long time, suh.'

'You seem like an honest man. I believe Ida Broussard was murdered. Did she come around here?'

He made a sound, as though a slight irritation had flared in his throat.

'Suh, you mean they was a murder here, that's what you saying?' But he already knew the answer, and his eyes looked into space and he forgot what he was doing with the package of tobacco and cigarette papers. He shook his head sadly. 'I wish you ain't come here wit' this. I seen a fight. Yeah, they ain't no denying that. I seen it.'

'A fight?'

'It was dark. I was working in my garage. She drove a truck into the yard and gone up the back stairs. I could tell it was Ida Broussard 'cause Mr. Alex had the floodlight on. But, see, it was cold wet'er then and he wasn't sleeping on the porch, so she started banging on the do' and yelling he better come out.

'I seen only one light go on. All them oilfield renters was gone, they was working seven-and-seven offshore back then. I didn't want to hear no kind of trouble like that. I didn't want my wife to hear it either. So I went in my house and turned on the TV.

'But the fighting stopped, and I seen the inside light go out, then the floodlight, too. I t'ought: Well, he ain't married, white people, colored people, they been doing t'ings together at night they don't do in the day for a long time now, it ain't my bidness. Later on, I seen her truck go down the road.'

'You never told anyone this?'

'No, suh. I didn't have no reason to.'

'After she was found dead in the swamp?'

'He was a policeman. You t'ink them other policemen didn't know he was carrying on wit' a colored woman, they had to wait for me to tell them about it?'

'Can I see the washhouse?'

The inside was cool and dank and smelled of cement and water.

Duckboards covered the floor, and a tin washtub sat under a water spigot that extended from a vertical pipe in one wall. I placed my palm against the roughness of the stucco and wondered if Ida Broussard's cries or strangled breath had been absorbed into the dampness of these same walls.

'I boil crabs out here now and do the washing in my machine,' Mr. Plo said.

'Are those wood stairs out there the same ones that were on the building twenty years ago?' I asked.

'I painted them. But they're the same.'

'I'd like to take some slivers of wood from them, if you don't mind.'

'What for?'

'If you see Alex Guidry, you can tell him I was here. You can also tell him I took evidence from your staircase. Mr. Plo, I appreciate your honesty. I think you're a good man.'

He walked across his yard toward the front door, his face harried with his own thoughts, as wrinkled as a turtle's foot. Then he stopped and turned around.

'Her husband, the one run the li'l sto'? What happened to him?' he asked.

'He went back to prison,' I answered.

Mr. Plo crimped his mouth and opened his screen door and went inside his house.

From his kitchen window Swede Boxleiter could see the bayou through the pecan trees in the yard. It was a perfect evening. A boy was fishing in a green pirogue with a bamboo pole among the lily pads and cattails; the air smelled like rain and flowers; somebody was barbecuing steak on a shady lawn. It was too bad Blimpo nailed him coming out of the graveyard. He liked being with Cisco and Megan again, knocking down good money on a movie set, working out every day, eating seafood and fixing tropical health drinks in the blender. Louisiana had its moments.

Maybe it was time to shake it. His union card was gold in Hollywood. Besides, in California nobody got in your face because you might be a little singed around the edges. Weirded out, your arms stenciled with tracks, a rap sheet you could wallpaper the White House with? That was the bio for guys who wrote six-figure scripts. But he'd let Cisco call the shot. The problem was, the juice was just too big on this one. Taking down punks like Rodney Loudermilk or that accountant Anthony Whatever wasn't going to get anybody out of Shitsville.

He loaded the blender with fresh strawberries, bananas, two raw eggs, a peeled orange, and a can of frozen fruit cocktail, and flicked on the switch. Why was that guy from the power company still messing around outside?

'Hey, you! I told you, disconnect me again, your next job is gonna be on the trash truck!' Swede said.

'That's my day job already,' the utility man replied.

They sure didn't have any shortage of wise-asses around here, Swede thought. How about Blimpo in his porkpie hat hooking him to a car bumper and going up to the Terrebonne house and bringing this guy back down to the crypt, like Swede's the pervert, a dog on a chain, not this fuck Terrebonne crawling around on his hands and knees, smoothing out the bones and rags in the casket, like he's packing up a rat's nest to mail it somewhere.

'What are you doing with my slingshot?' Swede said through the window.

'I stepped on it. I'm sorry,' the utility man said.

'Put it down and get out of here.'

But instead the utility man walked beyond Swede's vision to the door and knocked.

Swede went into the living room, shirtless and barefoot, and ripped open the door.

'It's been a bad week. I don't need no more trouble. I pay my bill through the super, so just pack up your shit and—' he said.

Then they were inside, three of them, and over their shoulders he saw a neighbor painting a steak with sauce on a grill and he wanted to yell out, to send just one indicator of his situation into the waning light, but the door closed quickly behind the men, then the kitchen window, too, and he knew if he could only change two seconds of his life, revise the moment between his conversation with the utility man at the window and the knock on the door, none of this would be happening, that's what two seconds could mean.

One of them turned on the TV, increasing the volume to an almost deafening level, then slightly lowering it. Were the three men smiling now, as though all four of them were involved in a mutually shameful act? He couldn't tell. He stared at the muzzle of the DE25 automatic.

Man, in the bowl, big time, he thought.

But a fellow's got to try.

His shank had a four-inch blade, with a bone-and-brass handle, a brand called Bear Hunter, a real collector's item Cisco had given him. Swede pulled it from his right pocket, ticking the blade's point against the denim fabric, opening the blade automatically as he swung wildly at a man's throat.

It was a clean cut, right across the top of the chest, slinging blood in a diagonal line across the wall. Swede tried to get the second man with the backswing, perhaps even felt the knife arc into sinew and bone, but a sound like a Chinese firecracker popped inside his head, then he was falling into a black well where he should have been able to lie unmolested, looking up at the circle of peering faces far above him only if he wanted.

But they rolled him inside a rug and carried him to a place where he knew he did not want to go. He'd screwed up, no denying it, and they'd unzipped his package. But it should have been over. Why were they doing this? They were lifting him again now, out of a car trunk, over the top of the bumper, carrying him across grass, through a fence gate that creaked on a hinge, unrolling him now in the dirt, under a sky bursting with stars.

One of his eyes didn't work and the other was filmed with blood. But he felt their hands raising him up, molding him to a cruciform design that was foreign to his life, that should not have been his, stretching out his arms against wood. He remembered pictures from a Sunday school teacher's book, a dust-blown hill and a darkening sky and helmeted soldiers whose faces were set with purpose, whose fists clutched spikes and hammers, whose cloaks were the color of their work.

Hadn't a woman been there in the pictures, too, one who pressed a cloth against a condemned man's face? Would she do that for him, too? He wondered these things as he turned his head to the side and heard steel ring on steel and saw his hand convulse as though it belonged to someone else.

23

Helen and I walked through the clumps of banana trees and blackberry bushes to the north side of the barn, where a group of St. Mary Parish plainclothes investigators and uniformed sheriff's deputies and ambulance attendants stood in a shaded area, one that droned with iridescent green flies, looking down at the collapsed and impaled form of Swede Boxleiter. Swede's chest was pitched forward against the nails that held his wrists, his face hidden in shadow, his knees twisted in the dust. Out in the sunlight, the flowers on the rain trees were as bright as arterial blood among the leaves.

'It looks like we got joint jurisdiction on this one,' a plainclothes cop said. His name was Thurston Meaux and he had a blond mustache and wore a tweed sports coat with a starched denim shirt and a striped tie. 'After the photographer gets here, we'll take him down and send y'all everything we have.'

'Was he alive when they nailed him up?' I asked.

'The coroner has to wait on the autopsy. Y'all say he took the head wound in his apartment?' he said.

'That's what it looks like,' I replied.

'You found brass?'

'One casing. A DE25.'

'Why would somebody shoot a guy in Iberia Parish, then nail him to a barn wall in St. Mary?' Meaux said.

'Another guy died here in the same way forty years ago,' I said.

'This is where that happened?'

'I think it's a message to someone,' I said.

'We already ran this guy. He was a thief and a killer, a suspect in two open homicide cases. I don't see big complexities here.'

'If that's the way you're going to play it, you won't get anywhere.'

'Come on, Robicheaux. A guy like that is a walking target for half the earth. Where you going?'

Helen and I walked back to our cruiser and drove through the weeds, away from the barn and between two water oaks whose leaves were starting to fall, then back out on the state road.

'I don't get it. What message?' Helen said, driving with one hand, her badge holder still hanging from her shirt pocket.

'If it was just a payback killing, the shooters would have left his body in the apartment. When we met Harpo Scruggs at the barbecue place? He said something about hating rich people. I think he killed Swede and deliberately tied Swede's murder to Jack Flynn's to get even with somebody.'

She thought about it.

'Scruggs took the Amtrak to Houston, then flew back to Colorado,' she said.

'So he came back. That's the way he operates. He kills people over long distances.'

She looked over at me, her eyes studying my expression.

'But something else is bothering you, isn't it?' she said.

'Whoever killed Swede hung him up on the right side of where Jack Flynn died.'

She shook a half-formed thought out of her face.

'I like working with you, Streak, but I'm not taking any walks inside your head,' she said.

Alex Guidry was furious. He came through the front door of the sheriff's department at eight o'clock Monday morning, not slowing down at the information desk or pausing long enough to knock before entering my office.

'You're getting Ida Broussard's case reopened?' he said.

'You thought there was a statute of limitations on murder?' I replied.

'You took splinters out of my old house and gave them to the St. Mary Parish sheriff's office?' he said incredulously.

'That about sums it up.'

'What's this crap about me suffocating her to death?'

I paper-clipped a sheaf of time sheets together and stuck them in a drawer.

'A witness puts you with Ida Broussard right before her death. A forensic pathologist says she was murdered, that water from a tap was forced down her nose and mouth. If you don't like what you're hearing, Mr. Guidry, I suggest you find a lawyer,' I said.

'What'd I ever do to you?'

'Sullied our reputation in Iberia Parish. You're a bad cop. You bring discredit on everyone who carries a badge.'

'You better get your own lawyer, you sonofabitch. I'm going to twist a two-by-four up your ass,' he said.

I picked up my phone and punched the dispatcher's extension.

'Wally, there's a man in my office who needs an escort to his automobile,' I said.

Guidry pointed one stiffened finger at me, without speaking, then strode angrily down the hallway. A few minutes later Helen came into my office and sat on the edge of my desk.

'I just saw our ex-jailer in the parking lot. Somebody must have spit on his toast this morning. He couldn't get his car door open and he ended up breaking off his key in the lock.'

'Really?' I said.

Her eyes crinkled at the corners.

Four hours later our fingerprint man called. The shell casing found on the carpet of Swede Boxleiter's apartment was clean and the apartment contained no identifiable prints other than the victim's. That same afternoon the sheriff called Helen and me into his office.

'I just got off the phone with the sheriff's department in Trinidad, Colorado. Get this. They don't know anything about Harpo Scruggs, except he owns a ranch outside of town,' he said.

'Is he there now?' Helen said.

'That's what I asked. This liaison character says, "Why you interested in him?" So I say, "Oh, we think he might be torturing and killing people in our area, that sort of thing." ' The sheriff picked up his leather tobacco pouch and flipped it back and forth in his fingers.

'Scruggs is a pro. He does his dirty work a long way from home,' I said.

'Yeah, he also crosses state lines to do it. I'm going to call that FBI woman in New Orleans. In the meantime, I want y'all to go to Trinidad and get anything you can on this guy.'

'Our travel budget is pretty thin, skipper,' I said.

'I already talked to the Parish Council. They feel the same way I do. You keep crows out of a cornfield by tying a few dead ones on your fence wire. That's a metaphor.'

Early the next morning our plane made a wide circle over the Texas panhandle, then we dropped through clouds that were pooled with fire in the sunrise and came in over biscuit-colored hills dotted with juniper and pine and pinyon trees and landed at a small windblown airport outside Raton, New Mexico.

The country to the south was as flat as a skillet, hazed with dust in the early light, the monotony of the landscape broken by an occasional mesa. But immediately north of Raton the land lifted into dry, pinyon-covered, steep-sided hills that rose higher and higher into a mountainous plateau where the old mining town of Trinidad, once home to the Earps and Doc Holliday, had bloomed in the nineteenth century.

We rented a car and drove up Raton Pass through canyons that were still deep in shadow, the sage on the hillsides silvered with dew. On the left, high up on a grade, I saw a roofless church, with a facade like that of a Spanish mission, among the ruins and slag heaps of an abandoned mining community.

'That church was in one of Megan's photographs. She said it was built by John D. Rockefeller as a PR effort after the Ludlow massacre,' I said.

Helen drove with one hand on the steering wheel. She looked over at me with feigned interest in her eyes.

'Yeah?' she said, chewing gum.

I started to say something about the children and women who were suffocated in a cellar under a burning tent when the Colorado militia broke a miners' strike at Ludlow in 1914.

'Go on with your story,' she said.

'Nothing.'

'You know history, Streak. But it's still the good guys against the shit bags. We're the good guys.'

She put her other hand on the wheel and looked at me and grinned, her mouth chewing, her bare upper arms round and tight against the short sleeves of her shirt.

We reached the top of the grade and came out into a wide valley, with big mountains in the west and the old brick and quarried rock buildings of Trinidad off to the right, on streets that climbed into the hills. The town was still partially in shadow, the wooded crests of the hills glowing like splinters of black-green glass against the early sun.

We checked in with the sheriff's department and were assigned an elderly plainclothes detective named John Nash as an escort out to Harpo Scruggs's ranch. He sat in the back seat of our rental car, a short-brim Stetson cocked on the side of his head, a pleasant look on his face as he watched the landscape go by.

'Scruggs never came to y'all's attention, huh?' I said.

'Can't say that he did,' he replied.

'Just an ordinary guy in the community?'

'If he's what you say, I guess we should have taken better note of him.' His face was sun-browned, his eyes as blue as a butane flame, webbed with tiny lines at the corners when he smiled. He looked back out the window.

'This definitely seems like a laid-back place, yessiree,' Helen said, her eyes glancing sideways at me. She turned off the state highway onto a dirt road that wound through an arroyo layered with exposed rock.

'What do you plan to do with this fellow?' John Nash said.

'You had a shooting around here in a while?' Helen said.

John Nash smiled to himself and stared out the window again. Then he said, 'That's it yonder, set back against that hill. It's a real nice spot here. Not a soul around. A Mexican drug smuggler pulled a gun on me down by that creek once. I killed him deader than hell.'

Helen and I both turned around and looked at John Nash as though for the first time.

Harpo Scruggs's ranch was rail-fenced and covered with sage, bordered on the far side by low hills and a creek that was lined with aspens. The house was gingerbread late Victorian, gabled and paintless, surrounded on four sides by a handrailed gallery. We could see a tall figure splitting firewood on a stump by the barn. Our tires thumped across the cattle guard. John Nash leaned forward with his arms on the back of my seat.

'Mr. Robicheaux, you're not hoping for our friend out there to do something rash, are you?' he said.

'You're an interesting man, Mr. Nash,' I said.

'I get told that a lot,' he replied.

We stopped the car on the edge of the dirt yard and got out. The air smelled like wet sage and wood smoke and manure and horses when there's frost on their coats and they steam in the sun. Scruggs paused in his work and stared at us from under the flop brim of an Australian bush hat. Then he stood another chunk of firewood on its edge and split it in half.

We walked toward him through the side yard. Coffee cans planted with violets and pansies were placed at even intervals along the edge of the gallery. For some reason John Nash separated himself from us and stepped up on the gallery and propped his hands on the rail and watched us as though he were a spectator.

'Nice place,' I said to Scruggs.

'Who's that man up on my gallery?' he said.

'My boss man's brought the Feds into it, Scruggs. Crossing state lines. Big mistake,' I said.

'Here's the rest of it. Ricky Scar is seriously pissed because a poor-white-trash peckerwood took his money and then smeared shit all over southwest Louisiana,' Helen said.

'Plus you tied a current homicide to one that was committed forty years ago,' I said.

'The real mystery is why the Mob would hire a used-up old fart who thinks bedding hookers will stop his johnson from dribbling in the toilet bowl three times a night. That Mexican hot-pillow joint you visited in Houston? The girl said she wanted to scrub herself down with peroxide,'

Helen said. When Scruggs stared at her, she nodded affirmatively, her face dramatically sincere.

Scruggs leaned the handle of his ax against the stump and bit a small chew off a plug of tobacco, his shoulders and long back held erect inside his sun-faded shirt. He turned his face away and spit in the dirt, then rubbed his nose with the back of his wrist.

'You born in New Iberia, Robicheaux?' he asked.

'That's right.'

'You think with what I know of past events, bodies buried in the levee at Angola, troublesome people killed in St. Mary Parish, I'm going down in a state court?'

'Times have changed, Scruggs,' I said.

He hefted the ax in one hand and began splitting a chunk of wood into long white strips for kindling, his lips glazed with a brown residue from the tobacco in his jaw. Then he said, 'If y'all going down to Deming to hurt my name there, it won't do you no good. I've lived a good life in the West. It ain't never been dirtied by nigra trouble and rich people that thinks they can make white men into nigras, too.'

'You were one of the men who killed Jack Flynn, weren't you?' I said.

'I'm fixing to butcher a hog, then I got a lady friend coming out to visit. I'd like for y'all to be gone before she gets here. By the way, that man up on the gallery ain't no federal agent.'

'We'll be around, Scruggs. I guarantee it,' I said.

'Yeah, you will. Just like a tumblebug rolling shit balls.'

We started toward the car. Behind me I heard his ax blade splitting a piece of pine with a loud snap, then John Nash called out from the gallery, 'Mr. Scruggs, where's that fellow used to sell you cordwood, do your fence work and such, the one looks like he's got clap on his face?'

'He don't work for me no more,' Scruggs said.

'I bet he don't. Being as he's in a clinic down in Raton with an infected knife wound,' John Nash said.

In the back seat of the car Nash took a notebook from his shirt pocket and folded back several pages.

'His name's Jubal Breedlove. We think he killed a trucker about six years ago over some dope but we couldn't prove it. I put him in jail a couple of times on drunk charges. Otherwise, his sheet's not remarkable,' he said.

'You found this guy on your own?' I said.

'I started calling hospitals when you first contacted us. Wait till you see his face. People tend to remember it.'

'Can you get on the cell phone and make sure Breedlove isn't allowed any phone calls in the next few minutes?' I said.

'I did that early this morning.'

'You're a pretty good cop, Mr. Nash.'

He grinned, then his eyes focused out the window on a snowshoe rabbit that was hopping through grass by an irrigation ditch. 'By the way, I told you only what was on his sheet. About twenty years ago a family camping back in the hills was killed in their tents. The man done it was after the daughter. When I ran Jubal Breedlove in on a drunk charge, I found the girl's high school picture in his billfold.'

Less than an hour later we were at the clinic in Raton. Jubal Breedlove lay in a narrow bed in a semiprivate room that was divided by a collapsible partition. His face was tentacled with a huge purple-and-strawberry birthmark, so that his eyes looked squeezed inside a mask. Helen picked up his chart from the foot of the bed and read it.

'Boxleiter put some boom-boom in your bam-bam, didn't he?' she said.

'What?' he said.

'Swede slung your blood all over the apartment. He might as well have written your name on the wall,' I said.

'Swede who? I was robbed and stabbed behind a bar in Clayton,' he said.

'That's why you waited until the wound was infected before you got treatment,' I said.

'I was drunk for three days. I didn't know what planet I was on,' he replied. His hair was curly, the color of metal shavings. He tried to concentrate his vision on me and Helen, but his eyes kept shifting to John Nash.

'Harpo wouldn't let you get medical help down in Louisiana, would he? You going to take the bounce for a guy like that?' I asked.

'I want a lawyer in here,' he said.

'No, you don't,' Nash said, and fitted his hand on Breedlove's jaws and gingerly moved his head back and forth on the pillow, as though examining the function of Breedlove's neck. 'Remember me?'

'No.'

He moved his hand down on Breedlove's chest, flattening it on the panels of gauze that were taped across Breedlove's knife wound.

'Mr. Nash,' I said.

'Remember the girl in the tent? I sure do.' John Nash felt the dressing on Breedlove's chest with his fingertips, then worked the heel of his hand in a slow circle, his eyes fixed on Breedlove's. Breedlove's mouth opened as though his lower lip had been jerked downward on a wire, and involuntarily his hands grabbed at Nash's wrist.

'Don't be touching me, boy. That'll get you in a lot of trouble,' Nash said.

'Mr. Nash, we need to talk outside a minute,' I said.

'That's not necessary,' he replied, and gathered a handful of Kleenex from a box on the nightstand and wiped his palm with it. 'Because everything is going to be just fine here. Why, look, the man's eyes glisten with repentance already.'

We had one suspect in Trinidad, Colorado, now a second one in New Mexico. I didn't want to think about the amount of paperwork and the bureaucratic legal problems that might lie ahead of us. After we dropped John Nash off at the sheriff's office, we ate lunch in a cafe by the highway. Through the window we could see a storm moving into the mountains and dust lifting out of the trees in a canyon and flattening on the hardpan.

'What are you thinking about?' Helen asked.

'We need to get Breedlove into custody and extradite him back to Louisiana,' I said.

'Fat chance, huh?'

'I can't see it happening right now.'

'Maybe John Nash will have another interview with him.'

'That guy can cost us the case, Helen.'

'He didn't seem worried. I had the feeling Breedlove knows better than to file complaints about local procedure.' When I didn't reply, she said, 'Wyatt Earp and his brothers used to operate around here?'

'After the shoot-out at the O.K. Corral they hunted down some other members of the Clanton gang and blew them into rags. I think this was one of the places on their route.'

'I wonder what kind of salary range they have here,' she said.

I paid the check and got a receipt for our expense account.

'That story Archer Terrebonne told me about Lila and her cousin firing a gun across a snowfield, about starting an avalanche?' I said.

'Yeah, you told me,' Helen said.

'You feel like driving to Durango?'

We headed up through Walsenburg, then drove west into the mountains and a rainstorm that turned to snow when we approached Wolf Creek Pass. The juniper and pinyon trees and cinnamon-colored country of the southern Colorado plateau were behind us now, and on each side of the highway the slopes were thick with spruce and fir and pine that glistened with snow that began melting as soon as it touched the canopy.

At the top of Wolf Creek we pulled into a rest stop and drank coffee from a thermos and looked out on the descending crests of the mountains. The air was cold and gray and smelled like pine needles

702

and wet boulders in a streambed and ice when you chop it out of a wood bucket in the morning.

'Dave, I don't want to be a pill . . .' Helen began.

'About what?'

'It seems like I remember a story years ago about that avalanche, I mean about Lila's cousin being buried in it and suffocating or freezing to death,' she said.

'Go on.'

'I mean, who's to say the girl wasn't frozen in the shape of a cross? That kind of stuff isn't in an old newspaper article. Maybe we're getting inside our heads too much on this one.'

I couldn't argue with her.

When we got to the newspaper office in Durango it wasn't hard to find the story about the avalanche back in 1967. It had been featured on the first page, with interviews of the rescuers and photographs of the slide, the lopsided two-story log house, a barn splintered into kindling, cattle whose horns and hooves and ice-crusted bellies protruded from the snow like disembodied images in a cubist painting. Lila had survived because the slide had pushed her into a creekbed whose overhang formed itself into an ice cave where she huddled for two days until a deputy sheriff poked an iron pike through the top and blinded her with sunlight.

But the cousin died under ten feet of snow. The article made no mention about the condition of the body or its posture in death.

'It was a good try and a great drive over,' Helen said.

'Maybe we can find some of the guys who were on the search and rescue team,' I said.

'Let it go, Dave.'

I let out my breath and rose from the chair I had been sitting in. My eyes burned and my palms still felt numb from involuntarily tightening my hands on the steering wheel during the drive over Wolf Creek Pass. Outside, the sun was shining on the nineteenth-century brick buildings along the street and I could see the thickly timbered, dark green slopes of the mountains rising up sharply in the background.

I started to close the large bound volume of 1967 newspapers in front of me. Then, like the gambler who can't leave the table as long as there is one chip left to play, I glanced again at a color photograph of the rescuers on a back page. The men stood in a row, tools in their hands, wearing heavy mackinaws and canvas overalls and stocking caps and cowboy hats with scarves tied around their ears. The snowfield was sunlit, dazzling, the mountains blue-green against a cloudless sky. The men were unsmiling, their clothes flattened against their bodies in the wind, their faces pinched with cold. I read the cutline below the photograph.

'Where you going?' Helen said.

I went into the editorial room and returned with a magnifying glass.

'Look at the man on the far right,' I said. 'Look at his shoulders, the way he holds himself.'

She took the magnifying glass from my hand and stared through it, moving the depth of focus up and down, then concentrating on the face of a tall man in a wide-brim cowboy hat. Then she read the cutline.

'It says "H. Q. Skaggs." The reporter misspelled it. It's Harpo Scruggs,' she said.

'Archer Terrebonne acted like he knew him only at a distance. I think he called him "quite a character," or something like that.'

'Why would they have him at their cabin in Colorado? The Terrebonnes don't let people like Scruggs use their indoor plumbing,' she said. She stared at me blankly, then said, as though putting her thoughts on index cards, 'He did scut work for them? He's had something on them? Scruggs could be blackmailing Archer Terrebonne?'

'They're joined at the hip.'

'Is there a Xerox machine out there?' she asked.

24

We got back to New Iberia late the next day. I went to the office before going home, but the sheriff had already gone. In my mailbox he had left a note that read: 'Let's talk tomorrow about Scruggs and the Feds.'

That evening Bootsie and Alafair and I went to a restaurant, then I worked late at the dock with Batist. The moon was up and the water in the bayou looked yellow and high, swirling with mud, between the deep shadows of the cypress and willow trees along the banks.

I heard a car coming too fast on the dirt road, then saw Clete Purcel's convertible stop in front of the boat ramp, a plume of dust drifting across the canvas top. But rather than park by the ramp, he cut his lights and backed into my drive, so that the car tag was not visible from the road.

I went back into the bait shop and poured a cup of coffee. He walked down the dock, looking back over his shoulder, his print shirt hanging out of his slacks. He grinned broadly when he came through the door.

'Beautiful night. I thought I might get up early in the morning and do some fishing,' he said.

'The weather's right,' I said.

'How was Colorado?' he asked, then opened the screen door and looked back outside.

I started to pour him a cup of coffee, but he reached in the cooler and twisted the top off a beer and drank it at the end of the counter so he could see the far end of the dock.

'You mind if I sleep here tonight? I don't feel like driving back to Jeanerette,' he said.

'What have you done, Clete?'

He ticked the center of his forehead with one fingernail and looked into space.

'A couple of state troopers almost got me by Spanish Lake. I'm not supposed to be driving except for business purposes,' he said.

'Why would they be after you?'

'This movie gig is creeping me out. I went up to Ralph & Kacoo's in Baton Rouge,' he said. 'All right, here it is. But I didn't start it. I was eating oysters on the half-shell and having a draft at the bar when Benny Grogan comes up to me – you know, Ricky the Mouse's bodyguard, the one with platinum hair, the wrestler and part-time bone smoker.

'He touches me on the arm, then steps away like I'm going to swing on him or something. He says, "We got a problem, Purcel. Ricky's stinking drunk in a back room."

'I say, "No, *we* don't got a problem. You got a problem."

'He goes, "Look, he's got some upscale gash in there he's trying to impress, so everything's gonna be cool. Long as maybe you go somewhere else. I'll pay your tab. Here's a hundred bucks. You're our guest somewhere else tonight."

'I say, "Benny, you want to wear food on your face again, just put your hand on my arm one more time."

'He shrugs his shoulders and walks off and I thought that'd be the end of it. I was going to leave anyway, right after I took a leak. So I'm in the men's room, and they've got this big trough filled with ice in it, and of course people have been pissing in it all night, and I'm unzipping my pants and reading the newspaper that's under a glass up on the wall and I hear the door bang open behind me and some guy walking like the deck is tilting under his feet.

'He goes, "I got something for you, Purcel. They say it hits your guts like an iron hook."

'I'm not kidding you, Dave, I didn't think Ricky Scar could make my heart seize up, but that's what happened when I looked at what was in his hand. You ever see the current thread between the prongs on a stun gun? I go, "Dumb move, Ricky. I was just leaving. I consider our troubles over."

'He goes, "I'm gonna enjoy this."

'Just then this biker pushes open the door and brushes by Ricky like this is your normal, everyday rest-room situation. When Ricky turned his head I nailed him. It was a beaut, Dave, right in the eye. The stun gun went sailing under the stalls and Ricky fell backward in the trough. This plumber's helper was in the corner, one of these big, industrial-strength jobs for blowing out major toilet blockage. I jammed it over Ricky's face and shoved him down in the ice and held him under till I thought he might be more reasonable, but he kept kicking and flailing and frothing at the mouth and I couldn't let go.

'The biker says, "The dude try to cop your stick or something?"

'I go, "Find a guy named Benny Grogan in the back rooms. Tell him Clete needs some help. He'll give you fifty bucks."

'The biker goes, "Benny Grogan gives head, not money. You're on your own, Jack."

'That's when Benny comes through the door and sticks a .38 behind my ear. He says, "Get out of town, Purcel. Next time, your brains are coming out your nose."

'I didn't argue, mon. I almost made the front door when I hear the Mouse come roaring out of the can and charge down the hallway at me, streaming ice and piss and toilet paper that was stuck all over his feet.

'Except a bunch of people in a side dining room fling open this oak door, it must be three inches thick with wrought iron over this thick yellow glass panel in it, and they slam it right into the Mouse's face, you could hear the metal actually ding off his skull.

'So while Ricky's rolling around on the carpet, I eased on outside and decided to cruise very copacetically out of Baton Rouge and leave the greaseballs alone for a while.'

'Why were state troopers after you? Why were you out by Spanish Lake instead of on the four-lane?'

His eyes clicked sideways, as though he were seriously researching the question.

'Ummm, I kept thinking about begging off from the Mouse when he put his stun gun on snap, crackle, and pop. So out there in the parking lot were about eight or nine chopped-down Harleys. They belonged to the same bunch the Gypsy Jokers threatened to kill for wearing their colors. I still had all my repo tools in the trunk, so I found the Mouse's car and slim-jimmed the door and fired it up. Then I propped a board against the gas pedal, pointed it right into the middle of the Harleys, and dropped it into low.

'I cruised around for five minutes, then did a drive-by and watched it all from across the street. The bikers were climbing around on Ricky's car like land crabs, kicking windows out, slashing the seats and tires, tearing the wires out of the engine. It was perfect, Dave. When the cops got there, it was even better. The cops were throwing bikers in a van, Ricky was screaming in the parking lot, his broad trying to calm him down, Ricky swinging her around by her arm like she was a stuffed doll, people coming out every door in the restaurant like the place was on fire. Benny Grogan got sapped across the head with a baton. Anyway, it'll all cool down in a day or so. Say, you got any of those sandwiches left?'

'I just can't believe you,' I said.

'What'd I do? I just wanted to eat some oysters and have a little peace and quiet.'

'Clete, one day you'll create a mess you won't get out of. They're going to kill you.'

'Scarlotti is a punk and a rodent and belongs under a sewer grate. Hey, the Bobbsey Twins from Homicide spit in their mouths and laugh it off, right? Quit worrying. It's only rock 'n' roll.'

His eyes were green and bright above the beer bottle while he drank, his face flushed and dilated with his own heat.

Just after eight the next morning the sheriff came into my office. He stood at the window and propped his hands on the sill. His sleeves were rolled to his elbows, his forearms thick and covered with hair.

'I talked with that FBI woman, Glazier, about Harpo Scruggs. She's a challenge to whatever degree of civility I normally possess,' he said.

'What'd she say?'

'She turned to an ice cube. That's what bothers me. He's supposed to be mixed up with the Dixie Mafia, but there's nothing in the NCIC computer on him. Why this general lack of interest?'

'Up until now his victims have been low profile, people nobody cared about,' I said.

'That woman hates Megan Flynn. Why's it so personal with her?'

We looked at each other. 'Guilt?' I said.

'Over what?'

'Good question.'

I walked down to Helen's office, then we both signed out for New Orleans.

We drove to New Orleans and parked off Carondelet and walked over to the Mobil Building on Poydras Street. When we sat down in her office, she rose from her chair and opened the blinds, as though wishing to create an extra dimension in the room. Then she sat back down in a swivel chair and crossed her legs, her shoulders erect inside her gray suit, her ice-blue eyes fixed on something out in the hallway. But when I turned around, no one was there.

Then I saw it in her face, the dryness at the corner of the mouth, the skin that twitched slightly below the eye, the chin lifted as though to remove a tension in the throat.

'We thought y'all might want to help bring down this guy Scruggs. He's going back and forth across state lines like a ping-pong ball,' I said.

'If you don't have enough grounds for a warrant, why should we?' she said.

'Every cop who worked with him says he was dirty. Maybe he even murdered convicts in Angola. But there's no sheet on him anywhere,' I said.

'You're saying somehow that's our fault?'

708

'No, we're thinking Protected Witness Program or paid federal informant,' Helen said.

'Where do you get your information? You people think—' she began.

'Scruggs is the kind of guy who would flirt around the edges of the Klan. Back in the fifties you had guys like that on the payroll,' I said.

'You're talking about events of four decades ago,' Adrien Glazier said.

'What if he was one of the men who murdered Jack Flynn? What if he committed that murder while he was in the employ of the government?' I said.

'You're not going to interrogate me in my own office, Mr. Robicheaux.'

We stared mutely at each other, her eyes watching the recognition grow in mine.

'That's it, isn't it? You *know* Scruggs killed Megan Flynn's father. You've known it all along. That's why you bear her all this resentment.'

'You'll either leave now or I'll have you removed from the building,' she said.

'Here's a Kleenex. Your eyes look a little wet, ma'am. I can relate to your situation. I used to work for the NOPD and had to lie and cover up for male bozos all the time,' Helen said.

We drove into the Quarter and had beignets and coffee and hot milk at the Cafe du Monde. While Helen bought some pralines for her nephew, I walked across the street into Jackson Square, past the sidewalk artists who had set up their easels along the piked fence that surrounded the park, past the front of St. Louis Cathedral where a string band was playing, and over to a small bookstore on Toulouse.

Everyone in AA knows that his survival as a wet drunk was due partly to the fact that most people fear the insane and leave them alone. But those who are cursed with the gift of Cassandra often have the same fate imposed upon them. Gus Vitelli was a slight, bony Sicilian ex-horse trainer and professional bouree player whose left leg had been withered by polio and who had probably read almost every book in the New Orleans library system. He was obsessed with what he called 'untold history,' and his bookstore was filled with material on conspiracies of every kind.

He told anyone who would listen that the main players in the assassinations of both John Kennedy and Martin Luther King came from the New Orleans area. Some of the names he offered were those of Italian gangsters. But if the Mob was bothered by his accusations, they didn't show it. Gus Vitelli had long ago been dismissed in New Orleans as a crank.

The problem was that Gus was a reasonable and intelligent man. At least in my view.

He was wearing a T-shirt that exclaimed 'I Know Jack Shit,' and wrote prices on used books while I told him the story about the murder of Jack Flynn and the possible involvement of an FBI informant.

'It wouldn't surprise me that it got covered up. Hoover wasn't any friend of pinkos and veterans of the Lincoln Brigade,' he said. He walked to a display table and began arranging a pile of paperback books, his left leg seeming to collapse and then spring tight again with each step. 'I got a CIA manual here that was written to teach the Honduran army how to torture people. Look at the publication date, 1983. You think people are gonna believe that?' He flipped the manual at me.

'Gus, have you heard anything about a hit on a black guy named Willie Broussard?'

'Something involving the Giacanos or Ricky Scarlotti?'

'You got it.'

'Nothing about a hit. But the word is Ricky Scar's sweating ball bearings 'cause he might have to give up some Asian guys. The truth is, I'm not interested. People like Ricky give all Italians a bad name. My great-grandfather sold bananas and pies out of a wagon. He raised thirteen kids like that. He got hung from a streetlamp in 1890 when the police commissioner was killed.'

I thanked him for his time and started to leave.

'The guy who was crucified against the barn wall?' he said. 'The reason people don't buy conspiracy theories is they think "conspiracy" means everybody's on the same program. That's not how it works. Everybody's got a different program. They just all want the same guy dead. Socrates was a gadfly, but I bet he took time out to screw somebody's wife.'

I had worried that Cool Breeze Broussard might go after Alex Guidry. But I had not thought about his father.

Mout' and two of his Hmong business partners bounced their stake truck loaded with cut flowers into the parking lot of the New Iberia Country Club. Mout' climbed down from the cab and asked the golf pro where he could find Alex Guidry. It was windy and bright, and Mout' wore a suit coat and a small rainbow-colored umbrella that clamped on his head like an elevated hat.

He began walking down the fairway, his haystack body bent forward, his brogans rising and falling as though he were stepping over plowed rows in a field, a cigar stub in the side of his mouth, his face expressionless.

He passed a weeping willow that was turning gold with the season, and a sycamore whose leaves looked like flame, then stopped at a polite distance from the green and waited until Alex Guidry and his three friends had putted into the cup.

'Mr. Guidry, suh?' Mout' said.

Guidry glanced at him, then turned his back and studied the next fairway.

'Mr. Guidry, I got to talk wit' you about my boy,' Mout' said.

Guidry pulled his golf cart off the far slope of the green. But his friends had not moved and were looking at his back now.

'Mr. Guidry, I know you got power round here. But my boy ain't coming after you. Suh, please don't walk away,' Mout' said.

'Does somebody have a cell phone?' Guidry asked his friends.

'Alex, we can go over here and have a smoke,' one of them said.

'I didn't join this club to have an old nigger follow me around the golf course,' Guidry replied.

'Suh, my boy blamed himself twenty years for Ida's death. I just want you to talk wit' me for five minutes. I apologize to these gentlemen here,' Mout' said.

Guidry began walking toward the next tee, his golf cart rattling behind him.

For the next hour Mout' followed him, perspiration leaking out of the leather brace that held his umbrella hat in place, the sun lighting the pink-and-white discoloration that afflicted one side of his face.

Finally Guidry sliced a ball into the rough, speared his club angrily into his golf bag, walked to the clubhouse, and went into the bar.

It took Mout' twenty minutes to cover the same amount of ground and he was sweating and breathing heavily when he came inside the bar. He stood in the center of the room, amid the felt-covered card tables and click of poker chips and muted conversation, and removed his umbrella hat and fixed his blue, cataract-frosted eyes on Guidry's face.

Guidry kept signaling the manager with one finger.

'Mr. Robicheaux say you held a wet towel over Ida's nose and mout' and made her heart stop. He gonna prove it, so that mean my boy don't have to do nothing, he ain't no threat to you,' Mout' said.

'Somebody get this guy out of here,' Guidry said.

'I'm going, suh. You can tell these people here anyt'ing you want. But I knowed you when you was buying black girls for t'ree dol'ars over on Hopkins. So you ain't had to go after Ida. You ain't had to take my boy's wife, suh.'

The room was totally quiet. Alex Guidry's face burned like a red lamp. Mout' Broussard walked back outside, his body bent forward at the middle, his expression as blank as the grated door on a woodstove.

25

Late Friday afternoon I received a call from John Nash in Trinidad.

'Our friend Jubal Breedlove checked out of the clinic in Raton and is nowhere to be found,' he said.

'Did he hook up with Scruggs?' I asked.

'It's my feeling he probably did.'

The line was silent.

'Why do you feel that, Mr. Nash?' I asked.

'His car's at his house. His clothes seem undisturbed. He didn't make a withdrawal from his bank account. What does that suggest to you, Mr. Robicheaux?'

'Breedlove's under a pile of rock?'

'Didn't Vikings put a dog at the foot of a dead warrior?' he asked.

'Excuse me?'

'I was thinking about the family he murdered in the campground. The father put up a terrific fight to protect his daughter. I hope Breedlove's under a pile of rock by that campground.'

After work I had to go after a boat a drunk smashed into a stump and left with a wrenched propeller on a sandbar. I tilted the engine's housing into the stern of the boat and was about to slide the hull back into the water when I saw why the drunk had waded through the shallows to dry land and walked back to his car: the aluminum bottom had a gash in it like a twisted smile.

I wedged a float cushion into the leak so I could pull the boat across the bayou into the reeds and return with a boat trailer to pick it up. Behind me I heard an outboard come around the corner and then slow when the man in the stern saw me standing among the flooded willows.

'I hope you don't mind my coming out here. The Afro-American man said it would be all right,' Billy Holtzner said.

'You're talking about Batist?'

'Yes, I think that's his name. He seems like a good fellow.'

He cut his engine and let his boat scrape up on the sandbar. When he walked forward the boat rocked under him and he automatically stooped over to grab the gunnels. He grinned foolishly.

'I'm not very good at boats,' he said.

My experience has been that the physical and emotional transformation that eventually comes aborning in every bully never takes but one form. The catalyst is fear and its effects are like a flame on candle wax. The sneer around the mouth and the contempt and disdain in the eyes melt away and are replaced by a self-effacing smile, a confession of an inconsequential weakness, and a saccharine affectation of goodwill in the voice. The disingenuousness is like oil exuded from the skin; there's an actual stink in the clothes.

'What can I do for you?' I said.

He stood on the sandbar in rolled denim shorts and tennis shoes without socks and a thick white shirt sown with a half dozen pockets. He looked back down the bayou, listening to the drone of an outboard engine, his soft face pink in the sunset.

'Some men might try to hurt my daughter,' he said.

'I think your concern is for yourself, Mr. Holtzner.'

When he swallowed, his mouth made an audible click.

'They've told me I either pay them money I don't have or they'll hurt Geri. These men take off heads. I mean that literally,' he said.

'Come down to my office and make a report.'

'What if they find out?' he asked.

I had turned to chain the damaged hull to the back of my outboard. I straightened up and looked into his face. The air itself seemed fouled by his words, his self-revelation hanging in the dead space between us like a dirty flag. His eyes went away from me.

'You can call me during office hours. Whatever you tell me will be treated confidentially,' I said.

He sat down in his boat and began pushing it awkwardly off the sandbar by shoving a paddle into the mud.

'Did we meet somewhere before?' he asked.

'No. Why?'

'Your hostility. You don't hide it well.'

He tried to crank his engine, then gave it up and drifted with the current toward the dock, his shoulders bent, the hands that had twisted noses splayed on his flaccid thighs, his chest indented as though it had been stuck with a small cannonball.

I didn't like Billy Holtzner or the group he represented. But in truth some of my feelings had nothing to do with his or their behavior.

In the summer of 1946 my father was in the Lafayette Parish Prison for punching out a policeman who tried to cuff him in Antlers Pool Room. That was the same summer my mother met a corporal from Fort Polk named Hank Clausson.

'He was at Omaha Beach, Davy. That's when our people was fighting Hitler and run the Nazis out of Europe. He got all kind of medals he gonna show you,' she said.

Hank was lean and tall, his face sun-browned, his uniform always starched and pressed and his shoes and brass shined. I didn't know he was sleeping over until I walked in on him in the bathroom one morning and caught him shaving in his underwear. The back of his right shoulder was welted with a terrible red scar, as though someone had dug at the flesh with a spoon. He shook his safety razor in the stoppered lavatory water and drew another swath under his chin.

'You need to get in here?' he asked.

'No,' I said.

'That's where a German stuck a bayonet in me. That was so kids like you didn't end up in an oven,' he said, and crimped his lips together and scraped the razor under one nostril.

He put a single drop of hair tonic on his palms and rubbed them together, then rubbed the oil into his scalp and drew his comb back through his short-cropped hair, his knees bending slightly so he could see his face fully in the mirror.

Hank took my mother and me to the beer garden and bowling alley out on the end of East Main. We sat at a plank table in a grove of oak trees that were painted white around the trunks and hung with speakers that played recorded dance music. My mother wore a blue skirt that was too small for her and a white blouse and a pillbox hat with an organdy veil pinned up on top. She was heavy-breasted and thick-bodied, and her sexuality and her innocence about it seemed to burst from her clothes when she jitterbugged, or, even a moment later, slow-danced with Hank, her face hot and breathless, while his fingers slipped down the small of her back and kneaded her rump.

'Hank's in a union for stagehands in the movie business, Davy. Maybe we going out to Hollywood and start a new life there,' she said.

The loudspeakers in the trees were playing 'One O'Clock Jump,' and through the windows in the bar I could see couples jitterbugging, spinning, flinging each other back and forth. Hank tipped his bottle of Jax beer to his lips and took a light sip, his eyes focused on nothing. But when a blond woman in a flowered dress and purple hat walked across his gaze, I saw his eyes touch on her body like a feather, then go empty again.

'But maybe you gonna have to stay with your aunt just a little while,' my mother said. 'Then I'm gonna send for you. You gonna ride the Sunset Limited to Hollywood, you.'

My mother went inside the bowling alley to use the rest room. The trees were glowing with the white flood lamps mounted on the branches, the air roaring with the music of Benny Goodman's orchestra. The blond woman in the flowered dress and purple hat walked to our table, a small glass of beer in one hand. The butt of her cigarette was thick with lipstick.

'How's the war hero?' she said.

He took another sip from his bottle of Jax and picked up a package of Lucky Strikes from the table and removed a cigarette gingerly by the tip and placed it in his mouth, never looking at the woman.

'My phone number's the same as it was last week. I hope nothing's been hard in your life,' she said.

'Maybe I'll call you sometime,' he replied.

'No need to call. You can come whenever you want,' she said. When she grinned there was a red smear on her teeth.

'I'll keep it in mind,' he said.

She winked and walked away, the cleft in her buttocks visible through the thinness of her dress. Hank opened a penknife and began cleaning his nails.

'You got something to say?' he asked me.

'No, sir.'

'That woman there is a whore. You know what a whore is, Davy?'

'No.' There was a glaze of starch on his khaki thigh. I could smell an odor like heat and soap and sweat that came from inside his shirt.

'It means she's not fit to sit down with your mother,' he said. 'So I don't want you talking about what you just heard. If you do, you'd best be gone when I come over.'

Three days later my aunt and I stood on the platform at the train station and watched my mother and Hank climb aboard the Sunset Limited. They disappeared through the vestibule, then she came back and hugged me one more time.

'Davy, it ain't gonna be long. They got the ocean out there and movie stars and palm trees everywhere. You gonna love it, you,' she said. Then Hank pulled her hand, and the two of them went into the observation car, their faces opaque now, like people totally removed from anything recognizable in their lives. Behind my mother's head I could see mural paintings of mesas and flaming sunsets.

But she didn't send for me, nor did she write or call. Three months later a priest telephoned collect from Indio, California, and asked my father if he could wire money for my mother's bus ticket back to New Iberia.

For years I dreamed of moonscape and skeletal trees along a railroad bed where white wolves with red mouths lived among the branches. When the Sunset Limited screamed down the track, the wolves did not run. They ate their young. I never discussed the dream with anyone.

26

A psychologist would probably agree that unless a person is a sociopath, stuffed guilt can fill him with a level of neurotic anxiety that is like waiting for a headsman in a cloth hood to appear at the prison door.

I didn't know if Alex Guidry was a sociopath or not, but on Monday Helen and I began tightening a couple of dials on his head.

We parked the cruiser at the entrance to his home and watched him walk from his bunkerlike brick house to the garage and open the garage door, simultaneously looking in our direction. He drove down the long shell drive to the parish road and slowed by the cruiser, rolling down his window on its electric motor. But Helen and I continued talking to each other as though he were not there. Then we made a U-turn and followed him to the finance company his wife's family owned in town, his eyes watching us in the rearview mirror.

Decades back the wife's father had made his way through the plantation quarters every Saturday morning, collecting the half-dollar payments on burial policies that people of color would give up food, even prostitute themselves, in order to maintain. The caskets they were buried in were made out of plywood and cardboard and crepe paper, wrapped in dyed cheesecloth and draped with huge satin bows. The plots were in Jim Crow cemeteries and the headstones had all the dignity of Hallmark cards. But as gaudy and cheap and sad as it all was, the spaded hole in the ground and the plastic flowers and the satin ribbons that decorated the piled dirt did not mark the entrance to the next world but the only level of accomplishment the dead could achieve in this one.

The Negro burial insurance business had passed into history and the plantation quarters were deserted, but the same people came with regularity to the finance company owned by the wife's family and signed papers they could not read and made incremental loan payments for years without ever reducing the principal. A pawnshop stood next door, also owned by the wife's family. Unlike most businesspeople, Guidry and his in-laws prospered most during economic recession.

We parked behind his car and watched him pause on the sidewalk and stare at us, then go inside.

A moment later a brown Honda, driven by a tall man in a gray suit, pulled to the curb, on the wrong side of the street, and parked bumper to bumper in front of Guidry's car. The driver, who was a DEA agent named Minos Dautrieve, got out and met us on the sidewalk in front of the finance company's glass doors. His crew-cut blond hair was flecked with white threads now, but he still had the same tall, angular good looks that sports photographers had loved when he played forward for ISU and was nicknamed 'Dr. Dunkenstein' after he sailed through the air and slammed the ball so hard through the rim he shattered the backboard like hard candy.

'How's the fishing?' he said.

'They've got your name on every fin,' I said.

'I'll probably come out this evening. How you doin', Helen?'

'Just fine. Lovely day, isn't it?' she replied.

'Do we have our friend's attention?' he asked, his back to the glass doors.

'Yep,' I said.

He took a notebook out of his pocket and studied the first page on it.

'Well, I have to pick up a couple of things for my wife, then meet her and her mother in Lafayette. We'll see you-all,' he said. He put the notebook back in his pocket, then walked to the front doors of the finance company, cupped his hands around his eyes to shield them from the sun, and peered through the tinted glass.

After he had driven away, Alex Guidry came out on the sidewalk.

'What are you people doing?' he said.

'You're an ex-cop. Guess,' Helen said.

'That man's a federal agent of some kind,' Guidry said.

'The guy who just left? He's an ex-jock. He was all-American honorable mention at LSU. That's a fact,' I said.

'What is this?' he said.

'You're in the shithouse, Mr. Guidry. That's what it is,' Helen said.

'This is harassment and I won't put up with it,' he said.

'You're naïve, sir. You're the subject of a murder investigation. You're also tied in with Harpo Scruggs. Scruggs has asked for immunity. You know where that leaves his friends? I'd get a parachute,' I said.

'Fuck you,' he said, and went back inside.

But his shirtsleeve caught on the door handle. When he pulled at it he ripped the cloth and hit a matronly white woman between the shoulder blades with his elbow.

Two hours later Guidry called the office.

718

'Scruggs is getting immunity for what?' he asked.

'I didn't say he was "getting" anything.'

I could hear him breathing against the receiver.

'First guy in line doesn't do the Big Sleep,' I said.

'Same answer. Do your worst. At least I didn't flush my career down the bowl because I couldn't keep a bottle out of my mouth,' he said.

'Ida Broussard was carrying your baby when you killed her, Mr. Guidry.'

He slammed down the phone.

Three days later, in the cool of the evening, Lila Terrebonne and Geraldine Holtzner came down the dirt road in Clete Purcel's chartreuse Cadillac, the top down, and pulled into the drive. Alafair and I were raking leaves and burning them on the edge of the road. The leaves were damp and black, and the smoke from the fire twisted upward into the trees in thick yellow curds and smelled like marijuana burning in a wet field. Both Lila and Geraldine seemed delighted with the pink-gray loveliness of the evening, with our activity in the yard, with themselves, with the universe.

'What are you guys up to?' I said.

'We're going to a meeting. You want to tag along?' Geraldine said from behind the wheel.

'It's a thought. What are you doing with Clete's car?' I said.

'Mine broke down. He lent me his,' Geraldine said. 'I went back to Narcotics Anonymous, in case you're wondering. But I go to AA sometimes, too.'

Lila was smiling, a wistful, unfocused beam in her eye. 'Hop in, good-looking,' she said.

'Did y'all make a stop before you got here?' I asked.

'Dave, I bet you urinated on radiators in elementary school,' Lila said.

'I might see y'all up there later. Y'all be careful about Clete's tires. The air is starting to show through,' I said.

'This is a lovely car. You drive it and suddenly it's 1965. What a wonderful time that was, just before everything started to change,' she said.

'Who could argue, Lila?' I said.

Unless you were black or spent '65 in Vietnam, I thought as they drove away.

The AA meeting that evening was held in the upstairs rooms of an old brick church out on West Main. The Confederates had used the church for a hospital while they tried to hold back the Federals on the Teche south of town; then, after the town had been occupied and looted and the courthouse torched, the Federals inverted half the pews and filled them with hay for their horses. But most of the people in the upper rooms this evening cared little about the history of the building. The subject of the meeting was the Fifth Step of AA recovery, which amounts to owning up, or confessing, to one's past.

There are moments in Fifth Step meetings that cause the listeners to drop their eyes to the floor, to lose all expression in their faces, to clench their hands in their laps and wince inwardly at the knowledge that the barroom they had entered long ago had only one exit, and it opened on moral insanity.

Lila Terrebonne normally listened and did not speak at meetings. Tonight was different. She sat stiffly on a chair by the window, a tree silhouetted by a fiery sunset behind her head. The skin of her face had the polished, ceramic quality of someone who has just come out of a windstorm. Her hands were hooked together like those of an opera singer.

'I think I've had a breakthrough with my therapist,' she said. 'I've always had this peculiar sensation, this sense of guilt, I mean, a fixation I guess with crucifixes.' She laughed self-deprecatingly, her eyes lowered, her eyelashes as stiff as wire. 'It's because of something I saw as a child. But it didn't have anything to do with me, right? I mean, it's not part of the program to take somebody else's inventory. All I have to do is worry about what I've done. As people say, clean up my side of the street. Who am I to judge, particularly if I'm not in the historical context of others?'

No one had any idea of what she was talking about. She rambled on, alluding to her therapist, using terms most blue-collar people in the room had no understanding of.

'It's called psychoneurotic anxiety. It made me drink. Now I think most of that is behind me,' she said. 'Anyway, I didn't leave my panties anywhere today. That's all I have.'

After the meeting I caught her by Clete's car. The oak tree overhead was filled with fireflies, and there was a heavy, wet smell in the air like sewer gas.

'Lila, I've never spoken like this to another AA member before, but what you said in there was total bullshit,' I said.

She fixed her eyes on mine and blinked her eyelashes coyly and said nothing.

'I think you're stoned, too,' I said.

'I have a prescription. It makes me a little funny sometimes. Now stop beating up on me,' she said, and fixed my collar with one hand.

'You know who murdered Jack Flynn. You know who executed the two brothers in the swamp. You can't conceal knowledge like that from the law and expect to have any serenity.'

720

'Marry me in our next incarnation,' she said, and pinched my stomach. Then she made a sensual sound and said, 'Not bad, big stuff.'

She got in the passenger seat and looked at herself in her compact mirror and waited for Geraldine Holtzner to get behind the wheel. Then the two of them cruised down a brick-paved side street, laughing, the wind blowing their hair, like teenage girls who had escaped into a more innocent, uncomplicated time.

Two days passed, then I received another phone call from Alex Guidry, this time at the dock. His voice was dry, the receiver held close to his mouth.

'What kind of deal can I get?' he said.

'That depends on how far you can roll over.'

'I'm not doing time.'

'Don't bet on it.'

'You're not worried about a dead black woman or a couple of shit bags who got themselves killed out in the Basin. You want the people who nailed up Jack Flynn.'

'Give me a number. I'll call you back,' I said.

'Call me back?'

'Yeah, I'm busy right now. I've already reached my quotient for jerk-off behavior today.'

'I can give you Harpo Scruggs tied hand and foot on a barbecue spit,' he said.

I could hear him breathing through his nose, like a cat's whisker scraping across the perforations. Then I realized the source of his fear.

'You've talked to Scruggs, haven't you?' I said. 'You called him about his receiving immunity. Which means he knows you're in communication with us. You dropped the dime on yourself . . . Hello?'

'He's back. I saw him this morning,' he said.

'You're imagining things.'

'He's got an inoperable brain tumor. The guy's walking death. That's his edge.'

'Better come in, Mr. Guidry.'

'I don't give a deposition until he's in custody. I want the sheriff's guarantee on that.'

'You won't get it.'

'One day I'm going to make you suffer. I promise it.' He eased the phone down into the cradle.

On Monday, Adrien Glazier knocked on my office door. She was dressed in blue jeans and hiking shoes and a denim shirt, and she carried a brown cloth shoulder bag scrolled with Mexican embroidery.

721

The ends of her ash-blond hair looked like they had been brushed until they crawled with static electricity, then had been sprayed into place.

'We can't find Willie Broussard,' she said.

'Did you try his father's fish camp?'

'Why do you think I'm dressed like this?'

'Cool Breeze doesn't report in to me, Ms. Glazier.'

'Can I sit down?'

Her eyes met mine and lingered for a moment, and I realized her tone and manner had changed, like heat surrendering at the end of a burning day.

'An informant tells us some people in Hong Kong have sent two guys to Louisiana to clip off a troublesome hangnail or two,' she said. 'I don't know if the target is Willie Broussard or Ricky Scarlotti or a couple of movie producers. Maybe it's all of the above.'

'My first choice would be Scarlotti. He's the only person who has reason to give up some of their heroin connections.'

'If they kill Willie Broussard, they take the squeeze off Scarlotti. Anyway, I'm telling you what we know.'

I started to bring up the subject of Harpo Scruggs again and the possibility of his having worked for the government, but I let it go.

She dropped a folder on my desk. Clipped to two xeroxed Mexico City police memorandums was a grainy eight-by-ten photograph that had been taken in an open-air fruit market. The man in the photo stood at a stall, sucking a raw oyster out of its shell.

'His name is Rubén Esteban. He's one of the men we think Hong Kong has sent here.'

'He looks like a dwarf.'

'He is. He worked for the Argentine Junta. Supposedly he interrogated prisoners by chewing off their genitals.'

'What?'

'The Triads always ruled through terror. The people they hire create living studies in torture and mutilation. Call Amnesty International in Chicago and see what they have to say about Esteban.'

I picked up the photo and looked at it again. 'Where's the material on the other guy?' I asked.

'We don't know who he is. Mr. Robicheaux, I'm sorry for having given you a bad time in some of our earlier conversations.'

'I'll survive,' I said, and tried to smile.

'My father was killed in Korea while people like Jack Flynn were working for the Communist Party.'

'Flynn wasn't a Red. He was a Wobbly.'

'You could fool me. He was lucky a House committee didn't have him shipped to Russia.'

Then she realized she had said too much, that she had admitted looking at his file, that she was probably committed forever to being the advocate for people whose deeds were indefensible.

'You ever sit down and talk with Megan? Maybe y'all are on the same side,' I said.

'You're too personal, sir.'

I raised my hands by way of apology.

She smiled slightly, then hung her bag from her shoulder and walked out of the office, her eyes already assuming new purpose, as though she were burning away all the antithetical thoughts that were like a thumbtack in her brow.

At eight-thirty that night Bootsie and I were washing the dishes in the kitchen when the phone rang on the counter.

'This is what you've done, asshole. My reputation's ruined. My job is gone. My wife has left me. You want to hear more?' the voice said.

'Guidry?' I said.

'There's a rumor going around I'm the father of a halfwit mulatto I sold to a cathouse in Morgan City. The guy who told me that said he heard it from your buddy Clete Purcel.'

'Either you're in a bar or you've become irrational. Either way, don't call my home again.'

'Here it is. I'll give you the evidence on Flynn's murder. I said *evidence*, not just information. I'll give you the shooters who did the two brothers, I'll give you the guys who almost drowned Megan Flynn, I'll give you the guy who's been writing the checks. What's on your end of the table?'

'The Iberia prosecutor will go along with aiding and abetting. We'll work with St. Mary Parish. It's a good deal. You'd better grab it.'

He was quiet a long time. Outside, the heat lightning looked like silver plate through the trees.

'Are you there?' I said.

'Scruggs threatened to kill me. You got to bring this guy in.'

'Give us the handle to do it.'

'It was under your feet the whole time and you never saw it, you arrogant shithead.'

I waited silently. The receiver felt warm and moist in my hand.

'Go to the barn where Flynn died. I'll be there in forty-five minutes. Leave the muff diver at home,' he said.

'You don't make the rules, Guidry. Another thing, call her that again and I'm going to break your wagon.'

I hung up, then dialed Helen's home number.

'You don't want to check in with the St. Mary sheriff's office first?' she said.

'They'll get in the way. Are you cool on this?' I said.

'What do you mean?'

'We take Guidry down clean. No scratches on the freight.'

'The guy who said he'd dig up my grave and piss in my mouth? To tell you the truth, I wouldn't touch him with a baton. But maybe you'd better get somebody else for backup, bwana.'

'I'll meet you at the end of East Main in twenty minutes,' I said.

I went into the bedroom and took my holstered 1911 model U.S. Army .45 from the dresser drawer and clipped it onto my belt. I wiped my palms on my khakis unconsciously. Through the screen window the oak and pecan trees seemed to tremble in the heat lightning that leaped between the clouds.

'Streak?' Bootsie said.

'Yes?'

'I overheard your conversation. Don't worry about Helen. It's you that man despises,' she said.

Helen and I drove down the two-lane through Jeanerette, then turned off on an oak-lined service road that led past the barn with the cratered roof and sagging walls where Jack Flynn died. The moon had gone behind a bank of storm clouds, and the landscape was dark, the blackberry bushes in the pasture humped against the lights of a house across the bayou. The leaves of the oaks along the road flickered with lightning, and I could smell rain and dust in the air.

'Guidry's going to do time, isn't he?' Helen said.

'Some anyway.'

'I partnered with a New Orleans uniform who got sent up to Angola. First week down a Big Stripe cut his face. He had himself put in lockdown and every morning the black boys would spit on him when they went to breakfast.'

'Yeah?'

'I was just wondering how many graduates of the parish prison will be in Guidry's cell house.'

Helen turned the cruiser off the road and drove past the water oaks through the weeds and around the side of the barn. The wind was up now and the banana trees rattled and swayed against the barn. In the headlights we could see clusters of red flowers in the rain trees and dust swirling off the ground.

'Where is he?' Helen said. But before I could speak she pointed at two pale lines of crushed grass where a car had been driven out in the pasture. Then she said, 'I got a bad feeling, Streak.'

'Take it easy,' I said.

'What if Scruggs is behind this? He's been killing people for forty years. I don't plan to walk blindfolded into the Big Exit.' She cut the lights and unsnapped the strap on her nine-millimeter Beretta.

'Let's walk the field. You go to the left, I go to the right . . . Helen?'

'*What?*'

'Forget it. Scruggs and Guidry are both pieces of shit. If you feel in jeopardy, take them off at the neck.'

We got out of the cruiser and walked thirty yards apart through the field, our weapons drawn. Then the moon broke behind the edge of a cloud and we could see the bumper and front fender of an automobile that was parked close behind a blackberry thicket. I circled to the right of the thicket, toward the rear of the automobile, then I saw the tinted windows and buffed, soft-yellow exterior of Alex Guidry's Cadillac. The driver's door was partly open and a leg in gray pants and a laced black shoe was extended into the grass. I clicked on the flashlight in my left hand.

'Put both hands out the window and keep them there,' I said.

But there was no response.

'Mr. Guidry, you will put your hands out the window, or you will be in danger of being shot. Do you hear me?' I said.

Helen moved past a rain tree and was now at an angle to the front of the Cadillac, her Beretta pointed with two hands straight in front of her.

Guidry rose from the leather seat, pulling himself erect by hooking his arm over the open window. But in his right hand I saw the nickel-plated surfaces of a revolver.

'Throw it away!' I shouted. 'Now! Don't think about it! Guidry, throw the piece away!'

Then lightning cracked across the sky, and out of the corner of his vision he saw Helen take up a shooter's position against the trunk of the rain tree. Maybe he was trying to hold the revolver up in the air and step free of the car, beyond the open door, so she could see him fully, but he stumbled out into the field, his right arm pressed against the wound in his side and the white shirt that was sodden with blood.

But to Helen, looking into the glare of my flashlight, Guidry had become an armed silhouette.

I yelled or think I yelled, *He's already hit,* but it was too late. She fired twice, *pop, pop,* the barrel streaking the darkness. The first round hit him high in the chest, the second in the mouth.

But Guidry's night in Gethsemane was not over. He stumbled toward the barn, his lower face like a piece of burst fruit, and swung his pistol back in Helen's direction and let off one shot that whined away across the bayou and made a sound like a hammer striking wood.

She began firing as fast as her finger could pull the trigger, the ejected shells pinging off the trunk of the rain tree, until I came behind her and fitted my hands on both her muscular arms.

'He's down. It's over,' I said.

'No, he's still there. He let off another round. I saw the flash,' she said, her eyes wild, the tendons in her arms jumping as though she were cold.

'No, Helen.'

She swallowed, breathing hard through her mouth, and wiped the sweat off her nose with her shoulder, never releasing the two-handed grip on the Beretta. I shined the light out across the grass onto the north side of the barn.

'Oh, shit,' she said, almost like a plea.

'Call it in,' I said.

'Dave, he's lying in the same, I mean like, his arms are out like—'

'Get on the radio. That's all you have to do. Don't regret anything that happened here tonight. He dealt the play a long time ago.'

'Dave, he's on the left side of where Flynn died. I can't take this stuff. I didn't know the guy was hit. Why didn't you yell at me?'

'I did. I think I did. Maybe I didn't. He should have thrown away the piece.'

We stood there like that, in the blowing wind and dust and the raindrops that struck our faces like marbles, the vault of sky above us exploding with sound.

27

The Argentine dwarf who called himself Rubén Esteban could not have been more unfortunate in his choice of a hotel.

Years ago in Lafayette, twenty miles from New Iberia, a severely retarded, truncated man named Chatlin Ardoin had made his living as a newspaper carrier who delivered newspapers to downtown businesses or sold them to train passengers at the Southern Pacific depot. His voice was like clotted rust in a sewer pipe; his arms and legs were stubs on his torso; his face had the expression of baked corn bread under his formless hat. Street kids from the north side baited him; an adman, the nephew of the newspaper's publisher, delighted in calling him Castro, driving him into an emotional rage.

The two-story clapboard hotel around the corner from the newspaper contained a bar downstairs where newsmen drank after their deadline. It was also full of hookers who worked the trade through the late afternoon and evening, except on Fridays, when the owner, whose name was Norma Jean, served free boiled shrimp for family people in the neighborhood. Every afternoon Chatlin brought Norma Jean a free newspaper, and every afternoon she gave him a frosted schooner of draft beer and a hard-boiled egg. He sat at the end of the bar under the air-conditioning unit, his canvas bag of rolled newspapers piled on the stool next to him, and peeled and ate the egg and drank the beer and stared at the soap operas on the TV with an intensity that made some believe he comprehended far more of the world than his appearance indicated. Norma Jean was thoroughly corrupt and allowed her girls no latitude when it came to pleasing their customers, but like most uneducated and primitive people, she intuitively felt, without finding words for the idea, that the retarded and insane were placed on earth to be cared for by those whose souls might otherwise be forfeit.

A beer and a hard-boiled egg wasn't a bad price for holding on to a bit of your humanity.

Fifteen years ago, during a hurricane, Chatlin was run over by a truck on the highway. The newspaper office was moved; the Southern Pacific depot across from the hotel was demolished and replaced by a post office; and Norma Jean's quasi-brothel became an ordinary hotel with a dark, cheerless bar for late-night drinkers.

Ordinary until Rubén Esteban checked into the hotel, then came down to the bar at midnight, the hard surfaces of his face glowing like corn bread under the neon. Esteban climbed on top of a stool, his Panama hat wobbling on his head. Norma Jean took one look at him and began screaming that Chatlin Ardoin had escaped from the grave.

Early Wednesday morning Helen and I were at the Lafayette Parish Jail. It was raining hard outside and the corridors were streaked with wet footprints. The homicide detective named Daigle took us up in the elevator. His face was scarred indistinctly and had the rounded, puffed quality of a steroid user's, his black hair clipped short across the top of his forehead. His collar was too tight for him and he kept pulling at it with two fingers, as though he had a rash.

'You smoked a guy and you're not on the desk?' he said to Helen.

'The guy already had a hole in him,' I said. 'He also shot at a police officer. He also happened to put a round through someone's bedroom wall.'

'Convenient,' Daigle said.

Helen looked at me.

'What's Esteban charged with?' I asked.

'Disturbing the peace, resisting. Somebody accidentally knocked him off the barstool when Norma Jean started yelling about dead people. The dwarf got off the floor and went for the guy's crotch. The uniform would have cut him loose, except he remembered y'all's bulletin. He said getting cuffs on him was like trying to pick up a scorpion,' Daigle said. 'What's the deal on him, again?'

'He sexually mutilated political prisoners for the Argentine Junta. They were buds with the Gipper,' I said.

'The what?' he said.

Rubén Esteban sat on a wood bench by himself in the back of a holding cell, his Panama hat just touching the tops of his jug ears. His face was triangular in shape, dull yellow in hue, the eyes set at an oblique angle to his nose.

'What are you doing around here, podna?' I said.

'I'm a chef. I come here to study the food,' he answered. His voice sounded metallic, as though it came out of a resonator in his throat.

'You have three different passports,' I said.

'That's for my cousins. We're a – how you call it? – we're a team. We cook all over the world,' Esteban said.

'We know who you are. Stay out of Iberia Parish,' Helen said.

'Why?' he asked.

'We have an ordinance against people who are short and ugly,' she replied.

His face was wooden, impossible to read, the eyes hazing over under the brim of his hat. He touched an incisor tooth and looked at the saliva on the ball of his finger.

'Governments have protected you in the past. That won't happen here. Am I getting through to you, Mr. Esteban?' I said.

'*Me cago en la puta de tu madre,*' he answered, his eyes focused on the backs of his square, thick hands, his mouth curling back in neither a sneer nor a grimace but a disfigurement like the expression in a corpse's face when the lips wrinkle away from the teeth.

'What'd he say?' Daigle asked.

'He probably doesn't have a lot of sentiment about Mother's Day,' I said.

'That's not all he don't have. He's got a tube in his pants. No penis,' Daigle said, and started giggling.

Outside, it was still raining hard when Helen and I got in our cruiser.

'What'd Daigle do before he was a cop?' Helen asked.

'Bill collector and barroom bouncer, I think.'

'I would have never guessed,' she said.

Rubén Esteban paid his fine that afternoon and was released.

That night I sat in the small office that I had fashioned out of a storage room in the back of the bait shop. Spread on my desk were xeroxed copies of the investigator's report on the shooting and death of Alex Guidry, the coroner's report, and the crime scene photos taken in front of the barn. The coroner stated that Guidry had already been hit in the rib cage with a round from a .357 magnum before Helen had ever discharged her weapon. Also, the internal damage was massive and probably would have proved fatal even if Helen had not peppered him with her nine-millimeter.

One photo showed the bloody interior of Guidry's Cadillac and a bullet hole in the stereo system and another in the far door, including a blood splatter on the leather door panel, indicating the original shooter had fired at least twice and the fatal round had hit Guidry while he was seated in the car.

Another photo showed tire tracks in the grass that were not the Cadillac's.

Two rounds had been discharged from Guidry's .38, one at Helen, the other probably at the unknown assailant.

The photo of Guidry, like most crime scene photography, was stark in its black-and-white contrasts. His back lay propped against the barn wall, his spine curving against the wood and the earth. His hands and lower legs were sheathed in blood, his shattered mouth hanging open, narrowing his face like a tormented figure in a Goya painting.

The flood lamps were on outside the bait shop, and the rain was blowing in sheets on the bayou. The water had overflowed the banks, and the branches of the willows were trailing in the current. The body of a dead possum floated by under the window, its stomach yellow and swollen in the electric glare, the claws of feeding blue-point crabs affixed to its fur. I kept thinking of Guidry's words to me in our last telephone conversation: *It was under your feet the whole time and you never saw it.*

What was under my feet? Where? By the barn? Out in the field where Guidry was hit with the .357?

Then I saw Megan Flynn's automobile park by the boat ramp and Megan run down the dock toward the bait shop with an umbrella over her head.

She came inside, breathless, shaking water out of her hair. Unconsciously, I looked up the slope through the trees at the lighted gallery and living room of my house.

'Wet night to be out,' I said.

She sat down at the counter and blotted her face with a paper napkin.

'I got a call from Adrien Glazier. She told me about this guy Rubén Esteban,' she said.

Not bad, Adrien, I thought.

'This guy's record is for real, Dave. I heard about him when I covered the Falklands War,' she said.

'He was in custody on a misdemeanor in Lafayette this morning. He doesn't blend into the wallpaper easily.'

'We should feel better? Why do you think the Triads sent a walking horror show here?'

Megan wasn't one to whom you gave facile assurances.

'We don't know who his partner is. While we're watching Esteban, the other guy's peddling an ice-cream cart down Main Street,' I said.

'Thank you,' she said, and dried the back of her neck with another napkin. Her skin seemed paler, her mouth and her hair a darker shade of red under the overhead light. I glanced away from her eyes.

'You and Cisco want a cruiser to park by your house?' I asked.

'I have a bad feeling about Clete. I can't shake it,' she said.

'Clete?' I said.

'Geri Holtzner is driving his car all around town. Look, nobody is going to hurt Billy Holtzner. You don't kill the people who owe you money. You hurt the people around them. These guys put bombs in people's automobiles.'

730

'I'll talk to him about it.'

'I already have. He doesn't listen. I hate myself for involving him in this,' she said.

'I left my Roman collar up at the house, Meg.'

'I forgot. Swinging dicks talk in deep voices and never apologize for their mistakes.'

'Why do you turn every situation into an adversarial one?' I asked.

She raised her chin and tilted her head slightly. Her mouth reminded me of a red flower turning toward light.

Bootsie opened the screen door and came in holding a raincoat over her head.

'Oh, excuse me. I didn't mean to walk into the middle of something,' she said. She shook her raincoat and wiped the water off it with her hand. 'My, what a mess I'm making.'

The next afternoon we executed a search warrant on the property where Alex Guidry was shot. The sky was braided with thick gray and metallic-blue clouds, and the air smelled like rain and wood pulp and smoke from a trash fire.

Thurston Meaux, the St. Mary Parish plainclothes, came out of the barn with a rake in his hand.

'I found two used rubbers, four pop bottles, a horseshoe, and a dead snake. That any help to y'all?' he said.

'Pretty clever,' I said.

'Maybe Alex Guidry was just setting you up, podna. Maybe you're lucky somebody popped him first. Maybe there was never anything here,' Meaux said.

'Tell me, Thurston, why is it nobody wants to talk about the murder of Jack Flynn?'

'It was a different time. My grandfather did some things in the Klan, up in nort' Louisiana. He's an old man now. It's gonna change the past to punish him now?'

I started to reply but instead just walked away. It was easy for me to be righteous at the expense of another. The real problem was I didn't have any idea what we were looking for. The yellow crime scene tape formed a triangle from the barn to the spot where Guidry's Cadillac had been parked. Inside the triangle we found old shotgun and .22 shells, pig bones, a plowshare that groundwater had turned into rusty lace, the stone base of a mule-operated cane grinder overgrown with morning glory vine. A deputy sheriff swung his metal detector over a desiccated oak stump and got a hot reading. We splintered the stump apart and found a fan-shaped ax head, one that had been hand-forged, in the heart of the wood.

At four o'clock the uniformed deputies left. The sun came out and I watched Thurston Meaux sit down on a crate in the lee of the barn and eat a sandwich, let the wax paper blow away in the wind, then pull the tab on a soda can and drop it in the dirt.

'You're contaminating the crime scene,' I said.

'Wrong,' he replied.

'Oh?'

'Because we're not wasting any more time on this bullshit. You've got some kind of obsession, Robicheaux.' He brushed the crumbs off his clothes and walked to his automobile.

Helen didn't say anything for a long time. Then she lifted a strand of hair out of her eye and said, 'Dave, we've walked every inch of the field and raked all the ground inside and around the barn. You want to start over again, that's okay with me, but—'

'Guidry said, "It was under your feet, you arrogant shithead." Whatever he was talking about, it's physical, maybe something we walked over, something he could pick up and stick in my face.'

'We can bring in a Cat and move some serious dirt.'

'No, we might destroy whatever is here.'

She let out her breath, then began scraping a long divot with a mattock around the edges of the hardpan.

'You're a loyal friend, Helen,' I said.

'Bwana has the keys to the cruiser,' she said.

I stood in front of the barn wall and stared at the weathered wood, the strips of red paint that were flaking like fingernail polish, the dust-sealed nail holes where Jack Flynn's wrists had been impaled. Whatever evidence was here had been left by Harpo Scruggs, not Alex Guidry, I thought. It was something Scruggs knew about, had deliberately left in place, had even told Guidry about. But why?

To implicate someone else. Just as he had crucified Swede Boxleiter in this spot to tie Boxleiter's death to Flynn's.

'Helen, if there's anything here, it's right by where Jack Flynn died,' I said.

She rested the mattock by her foot and wiped a smear of mud off her face with her sleeve.

'If you say so,' she said.

'Long day, huh?'

'I had a dream last night. Like I was being pulled back into history, into stuff I don't want to have anything to do with.'

'You told me yourself, we're the good guys.'

'When I kept shooting at Guidry? He was already done. I just couldn't stop. I convinced myself I saw another flash from his weapon. But I knew better.'

'He got what he deserved.'

'Yeah? Well, why do I feel the way I do?'

'Because you still have your humanity. It's because you're the best.'

'I want to make this case and lock the file on it. I mean it, Dave.'

She put down her mattock and the two of us began piercing the hardpan with garden forks, working backward from the barn wall, turning up the dirt from six inches below the surface. The subsoil was black and shiny, oozing with water and white worms. Then I saw a coppery glint and a smooth glass surface wedge out of the mud while Helen was prizing her fork against a tangle of roots.

'Hold it,' I said.

'What is it?'

'A jar. Don't move the fork.'

I reached down and lifted a quart-size preserve jar out of the mud and water. The top was sealed with both rubber and a metal cap. I squatted down and dipped water out of the hole and rinsed the mud off the glass.

'An envelope and a newspaper clipping? What's Scruggs doing, burying a time capsule?' Helen said.

We walked to the cruiser and wiped the jar clean with paper towels, then set it on the hood and unscrewed the cap. I lifted the newspaper clipping out with two fingers and spread it on the hood. The person who had cut it out of the *Times-Picayune* had carefully included the strip at the top of the page which gave the date, August 8, 1956. The headline on the story read: 'Union Organizer Found Crucified'.

Helen turned the jar upside down and pulled the envelope out of the opening. The glue on the flap was still sealed. I slipped my pocketknife in the corner of the flap and sliced a neat line across the top of the envelope and shook three black-and-white photos out on the hood.

Jack Flynn was still alive in two of them. In one, he was on his hands and knees while men in black hoods with slits for eyes swung blurred chains on his back; in the other, a fist clutched his hair, pulling his head erect so the camera could photograph his destroyed face. But in the third photo his ordeal had come to an end. His head lay on his shoulder; his eyes were rolled into his head, his impaled arms stretched out on the wood of the barn wall. Three men in cloth hoods were looking back at the camera, one pointing at Flynn as though indicating a lesson to the viewer.

'This doesn't give us squat,' Helen said.

'The man in the middle. Look at the ring finger on his left hand. It's gone, cut off at the palm,' I said.

'You know him?'

'It's Archer Terrebonne. His family didn't just order the murder. He helped do it.'

'Dave, there's no face to go with the hand. It's not a felony to have a missing finger. Look at me. A step at a time and all that jazz, right? You listening, Streak?'

28

It was an hour later. Terrebonne had not been at his home, but a maid had told us where to find him. I parked the cruiser under the oaks in front of the restaurant up the highway and cut the engine. The water dripping out of the trees steamed on the hood.

'Dave, don't do this,' Helen said.

'He's in Iberia Parish now. I'm not going to have these pictures lost in a St. Mary Parish evidence locker.'

'We get them copied, then do it by the numbers.'

'He'll skate.'

'You know a lot of rich guys working soybeans in Angola? That's the way it is.'

'Not this time.'

I went inside the foyer, where people waited in leather chairs for an available table. I opened my badge on the maître d'.

'Archer Terrebonne is here with a party,' I said.

The maître d's eyes locked on mine, then shifted to Helen, who stood behind me.

'Is there a problem?' he asked.

'Not yet,' I said.

'I see. Follow me, please.'

We walked through the main dining room to a long table at the rear, where Terrebonne was seated with a dozen other people. The waiters had just taken away their shrimp cocktails and were now serving the gumbo off of a linen-covered cart.

Terrebonne wiped his mouth with a napkin, then waited for a woman in a robin's-egg-blue suit to stop talking before he shifted his eyes to me.

'What burning issue do you bring us tonight, Mr. Robicheaux?' he asked.

'Harpo Scruggs pissed in your shoe,' I said.

'Sir, would you not—' the maître d' began.

'You did your job. Beat it,' Helen said.

I lay the three photographs down on the tablecloth.

'That's you in the middle, Mr. Terrebonne. You chain-whipped Jack Flynn and hammered nails through his wrists and ankles, then let your daughter carry your guilt. You truly turn my stomach, sir,' I said.

'And you're way beyond anything I'll tolerate,' he said.

'Get up,' I said.

'What?'

'Better do what he says,' Helen said behind me.

Terrebonne turned to a silver-haired man on his right. 'John, would you call the mayor's home, please?' he said.

'You're under arrest, Mr. Terrebonne. The mayor's not going to help you,' I said.

'I'm not going anywhere with you, sir. You put your hand on my person again and I'll sue you for battery,' he said, then calmly began talking to the woman in a robin's-egg-blue suit on his left.

Maybe it was the long day, or the fact the photos had allowed me to actually see the ordeal of Jack Flynn, one that time had made an abstraction, or maybe I simply possessed a long-buried animus toward Archer Terrebonne and the imperious and self-satisfied arrogance that he and his kind represented. But long ago I had learned that anger, my old enemy, had many catalysts and they all led ultimately to one consequence, an eruption of torn red-and-black color behind the eyes, an alcoholic blackout without booze, then an adrenaline surge that left me trembling, out of control, and possessed of a destructive capability that later filled me with shame.

I grabbed him by the back of his belt and hoisted him out of the chair, pushed him facedown on the table, into his food, and cuffed his wrists behind him, hard, ratcheting the curved steel tongues deep into the locks, crimping the veins like green string. Then I walked him ahead of me, out the foyer, into the parking area, pushing past a group of people who stared at us openmouthed. Terrebonne tried to speak, but I got the back door of the cruiser open and shoved him inside, cutting his scalp on the jamb.

When I slammed the door I turned around and was looking into the face of the woman in the robin's-egg-blue suit.

'You manhandle a sixty-three-year-old man like that? My, you must be proud. I'm so pleased we have policemen of your stature protecting us from ourselves,' she said.

The sheriff called me into his office early the next morning. He rubbed the balls of his fingers back and forth on his forehead, as though the skin were burned, and looked at a spot six inches in front of his face.

'I don't know where to begin,' he said.

736

'Terrebonne was kicked loose?'

'Two hours after you put him in the cage. I've had calls from a judge, three state legislators, and a U.S. congressman. You locked him in the cage with a drag queen and a drunk with vomit all over his clothes?'

'I didn't notice.'

'I bet. He says he's going to sue.'

'Let him. He's obstructed and lied in the course of a murder investigation. He's dirty from the jump, skipper. Put that photo and his daughter in front of a grand jury and see what happens.'

'You're really out to burn his grits, aren't you?'

'You don't think he deserves it?' I said.

'The homicide was in St. Mary Parish. Dave, this guy had to have stitches in his head. Do you know what his lawyers are going to do with that?'

'We've been going after the wrong guys. Cut off the snake's head and the body dies,' I said.

'I called my insurance agent about an umbrella policy this morning, you know, the kind that protects you against losing your house and everything you own. I'll give you his number.'

'Terrebonne skates?'

The sheriff picked up a pink memo slip in the fingers of each hand and let it flutter back to his ink blotter.

'You've figured it out,' he said.

Late that afternoon, just as the sun dipped over the trees, Cisco Flynn walked down the dock where I was cleaning the barbecue pit, and sat on the railing and watched me work.

'Megan thinks she caused some trouble between you and your wife,' he said.

'She's right,' I said.

'She's sorry about it.'

'Look, Cisco, I'm kind of tired of y'all's explanations about various things. What's the expression, "Get a life"?'

'That guy who got thrown out the hotel window in San Antonio? Swede did it, but I helped set up the transportation and the alibi at the movie theater.'

'Why tell me?'

'He's dead, but he was a good guy. I'm not laying off something I did on a friend.'

'You got problems with your conscience about the hotel flyer, go to San Antone and turn yourself in.'

'What's with you, man?'

'Archer Terrebonne, the guy who has money in your picture, killed your father. Come down to the office and check out the photos. I made copies before I turned the originals over to St. Mary Parish. The downside of the story is I can't touch him.'

His face looked empty, insentient, as though he were winded, his lips moving without sound. He blinked and swallowed. 'Archer Terrebonne? No, there's something wrong. He's been a guest in my home. What are you saying?' he said.

I went inside the bait shop and didn't come back out until he was gone.

That night the moon was down and leaves were blowing in the darkness outside, rattling against the trunks of the oak and pecan trees. When I went into the bedroom the light was off and Bootsie was sitting in front of her dresser in her panties and a T-shirt, looking out the window into the darkness.

'You eighty-sixed Cisco?' she said.

'Not exactly. I just didn't feel like talking to him anymore.'

'Was this over Megan?'

'When she comes out here, we have trouble,' I said.

The breeze ginned the blades in the window fan and I could hear leaves blowing against the screen.

'It's not her fault, it's mine,' Bootsie said.

'Beg your pardon?'

'You take on other people's burdens, Dave. It's just the way you are. That's why you're the man I married.'

I put my hand on her shoulder. She looked at our reflection in the dresser mirror and stood up, still facing the mirror. I slipped my arms around her waist, under her breasts, and put my face in her hair. Her body felt muscular and hard against mine. I moved my hand down her stomach, and she arched her head back against mine and clasped the back of my neck. Her stiffening breasts, the smoothness of her stomach and the taper of her hips, the hardness of her thighs, the tendons in her back, the power in her upper arms, when I embraced all these things with touch and mind and eye, it was like watching myself become one with an alabaster figure who had been infused with the veined warmth of a new rose.

Then I was between her thighs on top of the sheet and I could hear a sound in my head like wind in a conch shell and feel her press me deeper inside, as though both of us were drawing deeper into a cave beneath the sea, and I knew that concerns over winged chariots and mutability and death should have no place among the quick, even when autumn thudded softly against the window screen.

*

738

In Vietnam I had anxieties about toe-poppers and booby-trapped 105 duds that made the skin tighten around my temples and the blood veins dilate in my brain, so that during my waking hours I constantly experienced an unrelieved pressure band along one side of my head, just as though I were wearing a hat. But the visitor who stayed on in my nightmares, long after the war, was a pajama-clad sapper by the name of Bedcheck Charlie.

Bedcheck Charlie could cross rice paddies without denting the water, cut crawl paths through concertina wire, or tunnel under claymores if he had to. He had beaten the French with resolve and a shovel rather than a gun. But there was no question about what he could do with a bolt-action rifle stripped off a dead German or Sudanese Legionnaire. He waited for the flare of a Zippo held to a cigarette or the tiny blue flame from a heat tab flattening on the bottom of a C-rat can, then he squeezed off from three hundred yards out and left a wound shaped like a keyhole in a man's face.

But I doubt if Ricky Scarlotti ever gave much thought to Vietnamese sappers. Certainly his mind was focused on other concerns Saturday morning when he sat outside the riding club where he played polo sometimes, sipping from a glass of burgundy, dipping bread in olive oil and eating it, punching his new girlfriend, Angela, in the ribs whenever he made a point. Things were going to work out. He'd gotten that hillbilly, Harpo Scruggs, back on the job. Scruggs would clip that snitch in New Iberia, the boon, what was his name, the one ripping off the Mob's own VCRs and selling them back to them, Broussard was his name, clip him once and for all and take the weight off Ricky so he could tell that female FBI agent to shove her Triad bullshit up her nose with chopsticks.

In fact, he and Angela and the two bodyguards had tickets for the early flight to Miami Sunday morning. Tomorrow he'd be sitting on the beach behind the Doral Hotel, with a tropical drink in his hand, maybe go out to the trotters or the dog track later, hey, take a deep-sea charter and catch a marlin and get it mounted. Then call up some guys in Hallandale who he'd pay for each minute they had that fat shit Purcel begging on videotape. Ricky licked his lips when he thought about it.

A sno'ball truck drove down the winding two-lane road through the park that bordered the riding club. Ricky took off his pilot's glasses and wiped them with a Kleenex, then put them back on again. What's a sno'ball truck doing in the park when no kids are around? he thought. The sno'ball truck pulled into the oak trees and the driver got out and watched the ducks on the pond, then disappeared around the far side of the truck.

'Go see what that guy's doing,' Ricky said to one of his bodyguards.

'He's lying in the shade, taking a nap,' the bodyguard replied.

'Tell him this ain't Wino Row, go take his naps somewhere else,' Ricky said.

The bodyguard walked across the road, into the trees, and spoke to the man on the ground. The man sat up and yawned, looked in Ricky's direction while the bodyguard talked, then started his truck and drove away.

'Who was he?' Ricky asked the bodyguard.

'A guy sells sno'balls.'

'Who *was* he?'

'He didn't give me his fucking name, Ricky. You want I should go after him?'

'Forget it. We're out of drinks here. Get the waiter back.'

An hour later Ricky's eyes were red with alcohol, his skin glazed with sweat from riding his horse hard in the sun. An ancient green milk truck, with magnetized letters on the side, drove down the two-lane road through the park, exited on the boulevard, then made a second pass through the park and stopped in the trees by the duck pond.

Benny Grogan, the other bodyguard, got up from Ricky's table. He wore a straw hat with a multicolored band on his platinum hair.

'Where you going?' Ricky said.

'To check the guy out.'

'He's a knife grinder. I seen that truck all over the neighborhood,' Ricky said.

'I thought you didn't want nobody hanging around, Ricky,' Benny said.

'He's a midget. How's he reach the pedals? Bring the car around. Angela, you up for a shower?' Ricky said.

The milk truck was parked deep in the shade of the live oaks. The rear doors opened, flapping back on their hinges, and revealed a prone man in a yellow T-shirt and dark-blue jeans. His long body was stretched out behind a sandbag, the sling of the scoped rifle twisted around his left forearm, the right side of his face notched into the rifle's stock.

When he squeezed off, the rifle recoiled hard against his shoulder and a flash leaped off the muzzle, like an electrical short, but there was no report.

The bullet tore through the center of Ricky's throat. A purple stream of burgundy flowed from both corners of his mouth, then he began to make coughing sounds, like a man who can neither swallow nor expel a chicken bone, while blood spigoted from his wound and spiderwebbed his chest and white polo pants. His eyes stared impotently into his new girlfriend's face. She pushed herself away from the table, her hands held

740

out in front of her, her knees close together, like someone who did not want to be splashed by a passing car.

The shooter slammed the back doors of the milk truck and the driver drove the truck through the trees and over the curb onto the boulevard. Benny Grogan ran down the street after it, his .38 held in the air, automobiles veering to each side of him, their horns blaring.

It was Monday when Adrien Glazier gave me all the details of Scarlotti's death over the phone.

'NOPD found the truck out by Lake Pontchartrain. It was clean,' she said.

'You got anything on the shooter?'

'Nothing. It looks like we've lost our biggest potential witness against the boys from Hong Kong,' she said.

'I'm afraid people in New Orleans won't mourn that fact,' I said.

'You can't tell. Greaseball wakes are quite an event. Anyway, we'll be there.'

'Tell the band to play "My Funny Valentine,"' I said.

29

That evening I drove down to Clete's cottage outside Jeanerette. He was washing his car in the side yard, rubbing a soapy sponge over the hood.

'I think I'm going to get it restored, drive it around like a classic instead of a junk heap,' he said. He wore a pair of rubber boots and oversized swimming trunks, and the hair on his stomach was wet and plastered to his skin.

'Megan thinks the guys who did Ricky Scar might try to hurt Holtzner by going through his daughter. She thinks you shouldn't let her drive your car around,' I said.

'When those guys want to pop somebody, they don't do it with car bombs. It's one on one, like Ricky Scar got it.'

'Have you ever listened to me once in your life about anything?'

'On the perfecta that time at Hialcah. I lost three hundred bucks.'

'Archer Terrebonne killed Cisco Flynn's father. I told Cisco that.'

'Yeah, I know. He says he doesn't believe you.' Clete moved the sponge slowly back and forth on the car hood, his thoughts sealed behind his face, the water from the garden hose sluicing down on his legs.

'What's bothering you?' I asked.

'Terrebonne's a major investor in Cisco's film. If Cisco walks out, his career's a skid mark on the bowl. I just thought he might have more guts. I bet a lot of wrong horses.'

He threw the bucket of soapy water into a drainage ditch. The sun looked like a smoldering fire through the pine trees.

'You want to tell me what's really bothering you?' I said.

'I thought Megan and me might put it back together. That's why I scrambled Ricky Scar's eggs, to look like big shit, that simple, mon. Megan's life is international, I mean, all this local stuff is an asterisk in her career.' He blew his breath out. 'I got to stop drinking. I've got a buzz like a bad neon sign in my head.'

'Let's put a line in the water,' I said.

'Dave, those pictures Harpo Scruggs buried in the ground? That dude's got backup material somewhere. Something that can put a thumb in Terrebonne's eye.'

'Yeah, but I can't find Scruggs. The guy's a master at going in and out of the woodwork,' I said.

'Remember what that retired Texas Ranger in El Paso told you? About looking for him in cathouses and at pigeon shoots and dogfights?'

His skin was pink in the fading light, the hair on his shoulders ruffling in the breeze.

'Dogfights? No, it was something else,' I said.

The cockfights were held in St. Landry Parish, in a huge, rambling wood-frame nightclub, painted bright yellow and set back against a stand of green hardwoods. The shell parking lot could accommodate hundreds of automobiles and pickup trucks, and the patrons (blue-collar people, college students, lawyers, professional gamblers) who came to watch the birds blind and kill each other with metal spurs and slashers did so with glad, seemingly innocent hearts.

The pit was railed, enclosed with chicken wire, the dirt hard-packed and sprinkled with sawdust. The rail, which afforded the best view, was always occupied by the gamblers, who passed thousands of dollars in wagers from hand to hand, with neither elation nor resentment, as though the matter of exchanging currency were impersonal and separate from the blood sport taking place below.

It was all legal. In Louisiana fighting cocks are classified as fowl and hence are not protected by the laws that govern the treatment of most animals. In the glow of the scrolled neon on the lacquered yellow pine walls, under the layers of floating cigarette smoke, in the roar of noise that rattled windows, you could smell the raw odor of blood and feces and testosterone and dried sweat and exhaled alcohol that I suspect was very close to the mix of odors that rose on a hot day from the Roman arena.

Clete and I sat at the end of the bar. The bartender, who was a Korean War veteran named Harold who wore black slacks and a short-sleeve white shirt and combed his few strands of black hair across his pate, served Clete a vodka collins and me a Dr. Pepper in a glass filled with cracked ice. Harold leaned down toward me and put a napkin under my glass.

'Maybe he's just late. He's always been in by seven-thirty,' he said.

'Don't worry about it, Harold,' I said.

'We gonna have a public situation here?' he said.

'Not a chance,' Clete said.

We didn't have long to wait. Harpo Scruggs came in the side door from the parking lot and walked to the rail around the cockpit. He wore navy-blue western-cut pants with his cowboy boots and hat, and a silver shirt that tucked into his Indian-bead belt as tightly as tin. He made a bet with a well-known cockfighter from Lafayette, a man who, when younger, was both a pimp and a famous barroom dancer.

The cocks rose into the air, their slashers tearing feathers and blood from each other's bodies, while the crowd's roar lifted to the ceiling. A few minutes later one of the cocks was dead and Scruggs gently pulled a sheaf of hundred-dollar bills from between the fingers of the ex-pimp he had made his wager with.

'I think I'm experiencing Delayed Stress Syndrome. There was a place just like this in Saigon. The bar girls were VC whores,' Clete said.

'Has he made us?' I asked.

'I think so. He doesn't rattle easy, does he? Oh-oh, here he comes.'

Scruggs put one hand on the bar, his foot on the brass rail, not three feet from us.

'Has that worm talked to you yet?' he said to Harold.

'He's waiting right here for you,' Harold said, and lifted a brown bottle of mescal from under the bar and set it before Scruggs, with a shot glass and a saucer of chicken wings and a bottle of Tabasco.

Scruggs took a twenty-dollar bill from a hand-tooled wallet and inserted it under the saucer, then poured into the glass and drank from it. His eyes never looked directly at us but registered our presence in the same flat, lidless fashion an iguana's might.

'You got a lot of brass,' I said to him.

'Not really. Since I don't think your bunch could drink piss out of a boot with the instructions printed on the heel,' he replied. He unscrewed the cork in the mescal bottle with a squeak and tipped another shot into his glass.

'Some out-of-town hitters popped Ricky Scar. That means you're out of the contract on Willie Broussard and you get to keep the front money,' I said.

'I'm an old man. I'm buying quarter horses to take back to Deming. Why don't y'all leave me be?' he said.

'You use vinegar?' Clete said.

This time Scruggs looked directly at him. 'Say again.'

'You must have got it on your clothes. When you scrubbed the gunpowder residue off after you smoked Alex Guidry. Those DE357s leave powder residue like you dipped your hand in pig shit,' Clete said.

Scruggs laughed to himself and lit a cigarette and smoked it, his back straight, his eyes focused on his reflection in the bar mirror. A man came up to him, made a bet, and walked away.

'We found the photos you buried in the jar. We want the rest of it,' I said.

'I got no need to trade. Not now.'

'We'll make the case on you eventually. I hear you've got a carrot growing in your brain. How'd you like to spend your last days in the jail ward at Charity?' I said.

He emptied the mescal bottle and shook the worm out of the bottom into the neck. It was thick, whitish green, its skin hard and leathery. He gathered it into his lips and sucked it into his mouth. 'Is it true the nurse's aides at Charity give blow jobs for five dollars?' he asked.

Clete and I walked out into the parking lot. The air was cool and smelled of the fields and rain, and across the road the sugarcane was bending in the wind. I nodded to Helen Soileau and a St. Landry Parish plainclothes who sat in an unmarked car.

An hour later Helen called me at the bait shop, where I was helping Batist clean up while Clete ate a piece of pie at the counter. Scruggs had rented a house in the little town of Broussard.

'Why's he still hanging around here?' I asked Clete.

'A greedy piece of shit like that? He's going to put a soda straw in Archer Terrebonne's jugular.'

On Wednesday afternoon I left the office early and worked in the yard with Alafair. The sun was gold in the trees, and red leaves drifted out of the branches onto the bayou. We turned on the soak hoses in the flower beds and spaded out the St. Augustine grass that had grown through the brick border, and the air, which was unseasonably cool, smelled of summer, like cut lawns and freshly turned soil and water from a garden hose, rather than autumn and shortening days.

Lila Terrebonne parked a black Oldsmobile with darkly tinted windows by the boat ramp and rolled down the driver's window and waved. Someone whom I couldn't see clearly sat next to her. The trunk was open and filled with cardboard boxes of chrysanthemums. She got out of the Oldsmobile and crossed the road and walked into the pecan trees, where Alafair and I were raking up pecan husks and leaves that had gone black with water.

Lila wore a pale blue dress and white pumps and a domed straw hat, one almost like Megan's. For the first time in years her eyes looked clear, untroubled, even happy.

'I'm having a party tomorrow night. Want to come?' she said.

'I'd better pass, Lila.'

'I did a Fifth Step, you know, cleaning house. With an ex-hooker, can you believe it? It took three hours. I think she wanted a drink when it was over.'

'That's great. I'm happy for you.'

Lila looked at Alafair and waited, as though an unstated expectation among us had not been met.

'Oh, excuse me. I think I'll go inside. Talk on the phone. Order some drugs,' Alafair said.

'You don't need to go, Alf,' I said.

'Bye-bye,' she said, jittering her fingers at us.

'I've made peace with my father, Dave,' Lila said, watching Alafair walk up the steps of the gallery. Then: 'Do you think your daughter should talk to adults like that?'

'If she feels like it.'

Her eyes wandered through the trees, her long lashes blinking like black wire. 'Well, anyway, my father's in the car. He'd like to shake hands,' she said.

'You've brought your—'

'Dave, I've forgiven him for the mistakes he made years ago. Jack Flynn was in the Communist Party. His friends were union terrorists. Didn't you do things in war you regretted?'

'*You've* forgiven him? Goodbye, Lila.'

'No, he's been good enough to come out here. You're going to be good enough to face him.'

I propped my rake against a tree trunk and picked up two vinyl bags of leaves and pecan husks and carried them out to the road. I hoped that somehow Lila would simply drive away with her father. Instead, he got out of the Oldsmobile and approached me, wearing white trousers and a blue sports coat with brass buttons.

'I'm willing to shake hands and start over again, Mr. Robicheaux. I do this out of gratitude for the help you've given my daughter. She has enormous respect for you,' he said.

He extended his hand. It was manicured and small, the candy-striped French cuff lying neatly across the wrist. It did not look like a hand that possessed the strength to whip a chain across a man's back and sunder his bones with nails.

'I'm offering you my hand, sir,' he said.

I dropped the two leaf bags on the roadside and wiped my palms on my khakis, then stepped back into the shade, away from Terrebonne.

'Scruggs is blackmailing you. You need me, or someone like me, to pop a cap on him and get him out of your life. That's not going to happen,' I said.

He tapped his right hand gingerly on his cheek, as though he had a toothache.

'I tried. Truly I have. Now, I'll leave you alone, sir,' he said.

'You and your family pretend to gentility, Mr. Terrebonne. But your ancestor murdered black soldiers under the bluffs at Fort Pillow and caused the deaths of his twin daughters. You and your father brought grief to black people like Willie Broussard and his wife and killed anyone who threatened your power. None of you are what you seem.'

He stood in the center of the road, not moving when a car passed, the dust swirling around him, his face looking at words that seemed to be marching by in front of his eyes.

'I congratulate you on your sobriety, Mr. Robicheaux. I suspect for a man such as yourself it was a very difficult accomplishment,' he said, and walked back to the Oldsmobile and got inside and waited for his daughter.

I turned around and almost collided into Lila.

'I can't believe what you just did. How dare you?' she said.

'Don't you understand what your father has participated in? He crucified a living human being. Wake up, Lila. He's the definition of evil.'

She struck me across the face.

I stood in the road, with the ashes of leaves blowing around me, and watched their car disappear down the long tunnel of oaks.

'I hate her,' Alafair said behind me.

'Don't give them power, Alf,' I replied.

But I felt a great sorrow. Inside all of Lila's alcoholic madness she had always seen the truth about her father's iniquity. Now, the restoration of light and the gift of sobriety in her life had somehow made her morally blind.

I put my arm on Alafair's shoulder, and the two of us walked into the house.

30

Cisco Flynn was in my office the next morning. He sat in a chair in front of my desk, his hands opening and closing on his thighs.

'Out at the dock, when I told you to look at the photos? I was angry,' I said, holding the duplicates of the three photographs from the buried jar.

'Just give them to me, would you?' he said.

I handed the photographs across the desk to him. He looked at them slowly, one by one, his face never changing expression. But I saw a twitch in his cheek under one eye. He lay the photos back on the desk and straightened himself in the chair.

His voice was dry when he spoke. 'You're sure that's Terrebonne, the dude with the missing finger?'

'Every road we take leads to his front door,' I said.

'This guy Scruggs was there, too?'

'Put it in the bank.'

He stared out the window at the fronds of a palm tree swelling in the wind.

'I understand he's back in the area,' Cisco said.

'Don't have the wrong kind of thoughts, partner.'

'I always thought the worst people I ever met were in Hollywood. But they're right here.'

'Evil doesn't have a zip code, Cisco.'

He picked up the photos and looked at them again. Then he set them down and propped his elbows on my desk and rested his forehead on his fingers. I thought he was going to speak, then I realized he was weeping.

At noon, when I was on my way to lunch, Helen caught up with me in the parking lot.

'Hang on, Streak. I just got a call from some woman named Jessie Rideau. She says she was in the hotel in Morgan City the night Jack Flynn was kidnapped,' she said.

'Why's she calling us now?'

We both got in my truck. I started the engine. Helen looked straight ahead, as though trying to rethink a problem she couldn't quite define.

'She says she and another woman were prostitutes who worked out of the bar downstairs. She says Harpo Scruggs made the other woman, someone named Lavern Viator, hide a lockbox for him.'

'A lockbox? Where's the Viator woman?'

'She joined a cult in Texas and asked Rideau to keep the lockbox. Rideau thinks Scruggs killed her. Now he wants the box.'

'Why doesn't she give it to him?'

'She's afraid he'll kill her after he gets it.'

'Tell her to come in.'

'She doesn't trust us either.'

I parked the truck in front of the cafeteria on Main Street. The drawbridge was up on Bayou Teche and a shrimp boat was passing through the pilings.

'Let's talk about it inside,' I said.

'I can't eat. Before Rideau got panicky and hung up on me, she said the killers were shooting craps in the room next to Jack Flynn. They waited till he was by himself, then dragged him down a back stairs and tied him to a post on a dock and whipped him with chains. She said that's all that was supposed to happen. Except Scruggs told the others the night was just beginning. He made the Viator woman come with them. She held Jack Flynn's head in a towel so the blood wouldn't get on the seat.'

Helen pressed at her temple with two fingers.

'What is it?' I said.

'Rideau said you can see Flynn's face on the towel. Isn't that some bullshit? She said there're chains and a hammer and handcuffs in the box, too. I got to boogie, boss man. The next time this broad calls, I'm transferring her to your extension,' she said.

I spent the rest of the day with the paperwork that my file drawer seemed to procreate from the time I closed it in the afternoon until I opened it in the morning. The paperwork all concerned the Pool, that comic Greek chorus of miscreants who are always in the wings, upstaging our most tragic moments, flatulent, burping, snickering, cat-calling at the audience. It has been my long-held belief as a police officer that Hamlet and Ophelia might command our respect and admiration, but Sir Toby Belch and his minions usually consume most of our energies.

Here are just a few random case-file entries in the lives of Pool members during a one-month period.

A pipehead tries to smoke Dràno crystals in a hookah. After he recovers from destroying several thousand brain cells in his head, he dials 911 and dimes his dealer for selling him bad dope.

A man steals a blank headstone from a funeral home, engraves his mother's name on it, and places it in his back yard. When confronted with the theft, he explains that his wife poured his mother's ashes down the sink and the man wished to put a marker over the septic tank where his mother now resides.

A woman who has fought with her common-law husband for ten years reports that her TV remote control triggered the electronically operated door on the garage and crushed his skull.

Two cousins break into the back of a liquor store, then can't start their car. They flee on foot, then report their car as stolen. It's a good plan. Except they don't bother to change their shoes. The liquor store's floor had been freshly painted and the cousins track the paint all over our floors when they file their stolen car report.

That evening Clete and I filled a bait bucket with shiners and took my outboard to Henderson Swamp and fished for sac-a-lait. The sun was dull red in the west, molten and misshaped as though it were dissolving in its own heat among the strips of lavender cloud that clung to the horizon. We crossed a wide bay, then let the boat drift in the lee of an island that was heavily wooded with willow and cypress trees. The mosquitoes were thick in the shadows of the trees, and you could see bream feeding among the lily pads and smell an odor like fish roe in the water.

I looked across the bay at the levee, where there was a paintless, tin-roofed house that had not been there three weeks ago.

'Where'd that come from?' I said.

'Billy Holtzner just built it. It's part of the movie,' Clete said.

'You're kidding. That guy's like a disease spreading itself across the state.'

'Check it out.'

I reached into the rucksack where I had packed our sandwiches and a thermos of coffee and my World War II Japanese field glasses. I adjusted the focus on the glasses and saw Billy Holtzner and his daughter talking with a half dozen people on the gallery of the house.

'Aren't you supposed to be out there with them?' I asked Clete.

'They work what they call a twelve-hour turnaround. Anyway, I go off the clock at five. Then he's got some other guys to boss around. They'll be out there to one or two in the morning. Dave, I'm going to do my job, but I think that guy's dead meat.'

'Why?'

'You remember guys in Nam you knew were going to get it? Walking fuckups who stunk of fear and were always trying to hang on to you? Holtzner's got that same stink on him. It's on his breath, in his clothes, I don't even like looking at him.'

A few drops of rain dimpled the water, then the sac-a-lait started biting. Unlike bream or bass, they would take the shiner straight down, pulling the bobber with a steady tension into the water's darkness. They would fight hard, pumping away from the boat, until they broke the surface, when they would turn on their side and give it up.

We layered them with crushed ice in the cooler, then I took our ham-and-onion sandwiches and coffee thermos out of the rucksack and lay them on the cooler's top. In the distance, by the newly constructed movie set, I saw two figures get on an airboat and roar across the bay toward us.

The noise of the engine and fan was deafening, the wake a long, flat depression that swirled with mud. The pilot cut the engine and let the airboat float into the lee of the island. Billy Holtzner sat next to him, a blue baseball cap on his head. He was smiling.

'You guys on the job?' he said.

'No. We're just fishing,' I said.

'Get out of here,' he said, still smiling.

'We fish this spot a lot, Billy. We're both off the clock,' Clete said.

'Oh,' Holtzner said, his smile dying.

'Everything copacetic?' Clete said.

'Sure,' Holtzner said. 'Want to come up and watch us shoot a couple of scenes?'

'We're heading back in a few minutes. Thanks just the same,' I said.

'Sure. My daughter's with me,' he said, as though there were a logical connection between her presence and his invitation. 'I mean, maybe we'll have a late-night dinner later.'

Neither Clete nor I responded. Holtzner touched the boat pilot on the arm, and the two of them roared back across the bay, their backdraft showering the water's surface with willow leaves.

'How do you read that?' I said.

'The guy's on his own, probably for the first time in his life. It must be rough to wake up one morning and realize you're a gutless shit who doesn't deserve his family,' Clete said, then bit into his sandwich.

The next day two uniformed city cops and I had to arrest a parolee from Alabama by the swimming pool at City Park. Even with cuffs on, he spit on one cop and kicked the other one in the groin. I pushed him against the side of the cruiser and tried to hold him until I could get the back door open, then the cop who had been spit on Maced him and sprayed me at the same time.

I spent the next ten minutes rinsing my face and hair in the lavatory inside the recreation building. When I came back outside, wiping the water off my neck with a paper towel, the parolee and the city cops were on their way to the jail and Adrien Glazier was standing by my pickup truck. Out on the drive, among the oak trees, I saw a dark-blue waxed car with two men in suits and shades standing by it. Leaves were swirling in eddies around their car.

'The sheriff told us you were here. How's that stuff feel?' she said.

'Like somebody holding a match to your skin.'

'We just got a report from Interpol on the dwarf. He's enjoying himself on the Italian Riviera.'

'Glad to hear it,' I said.

'So maybe the shooter who did Ricky Scar left with him.'

'You believe that?' I asked.

'No. Take a walk with me.'

She didn't wait for a reply. She turned and began walking slowly through the trees toward the bayou and the picnic tables that were set under tin sheds by the waterside.

'What's going on, Ms. Glazier?' I said.

'Call me Adrien.' She rested her rump against a picnic table and folded her arms across her chest. 'Did Cisco Flynn confess his involvement in a homicide to you?'

'Excuse me?'

'The guy who got chucked out a hotel window in San Antonio? I understand his head hit a fire hydrant. Did Cisco come seeking absolution at your bait shop?'

'My memory's not as good as it used to be. Y'all have a tap on his phone or a bug in his house?'

'We're giving you a free pass on this one. That's because I acted like a pisspot for a while,' she said.

'It's because you know Harpo Scruggs was a federal snitch when he helped crucify Jack Flynn.'

'You should come work for us. I never have any real laughs these days.'

She walked off through the trees toward the two male agents who waited for her, her hips undulating slightly. I caught up with her.

'What have you got on the dwarf's partner?' I asked.

'Nothing. Watch your ass, Mr. Robicheaux,' she replied.

'Call me Dave.'

'Not a chance,' she said. Then she grinned and made a clicking goodbye sound in her jaw.

That night I watched the ten o'clock news before going to bed. I looked disinterestedly at some footage about a State Police traffic check, taken outside Jeanerette, until I saw Clete Purcel on the screen, showing his license to a trooper, then being escorted to a cruiser.

Back in the stew pot, I thought, probably for violating the spirit of his restricted permit, which allowed him to drive only for business purposes.

But that was Clete, always in trouble, always out of sync with the rest of the world. I knew the trooper was doing his job and Clete had earned his night in the bag, but I had to pause and wonder at the illusionary cell glue that made us feel safe about the society we lived in.

Archer Terrebonne, who would murder in order to break unions, financed a movie about the travail and privation of plantation workers in the 1940s. The production company helped launder money from the sale of China white. The FBI protected sociopaths like Harpo Scruggs and let his victims pay the tab. Harpo Scruggs worked for the state of Louisiana and murdered prisoners in Angola. The vested interest of government and criminals and respectable people was often the same.

In my scrapbook I had an inscribed photograph that Clete had given me when we were both in uniform at NOPD. It had been taken by an Associated Press photographer at night on a Swift Boat in Vietnam, somewhere up the Mekong, in the middle of a firefight. Clete was behind a pair of twin fifties, wearing a steel pot and a flack vest with no shirt, his youthful face lighted by a flare, tracers floating away into the darkness like segmented neon.

I could almost hear him singing, 'I got a freaky old lady name of Cocaine Katie.'

I thought about calling the jail in Jeanerette, but I knew he would be back on the street in the morning, nothing learned, deeper in debt to a bondsman, trying to sweep the snakes and spiders back in their baskets with vodka and grapefruit juice.

He made me think of my father, Aldous, whom people in the oilfield always called Big Al Robicheaux, as though it were one name. It took seven Lafayette cops in Antlers Pool Room to put him in jail. The fight wrecked the pool room from one end to the other. They hit him with batons, broke chairs on his shoulders and back, and finally got his mother to talk him into submission so they didn't have to kill him.

But jails and poverty and baton-swinging cops never broke his spirit. It took my mother's infidelities to do that. The Amtrak still ran on the old Southern Pacific roadbed that had carried my mother out to Hollywood in 1946, made up of the same cars from the original Sunset Limited she had ridden in, perhaps with the same desert scenes painted on the walls. Sometimes when I would see the Amtrak crossing through winter fields of burned cane stubble, I would wonder what my mother felt when she stepped down on the platform at Union Station in Los Angeles, her pillbox hat slanted on her head, her purse clenched in her small hand. Did she believe the shining air and the orange trees and the blue outline of the San Gabriel Mountains had been created especially for her, to be discovered in exactly this moment, in a train station that echoed like a cathedral? Did she walk into the green roll of the Pacific and feel her dress swell out from her thighs and fill her with a sexual pleasure that no man ever gave her?

What's the point?

Hitler and George Orwell already said it. History books are written by and about the Terrebonnes of this world, not jarheads up the Mekong or people who die in oil-well blowouts or illiterate Cajun women who believe the locomotive whistle on the Sunset Limited calls for them.

31

Adrien Glazier called Monday morning from New Orleans.

'You remember a hooker by the name of Ruby Gravano?' she asked.

'She gave us the first solid lead on Harpo Scruggs. She had an autistic son named Nick,' I said.

'That's the one.'

'We put her on the train to Houston. She was getting out of the life.'

'Her career change must have been short-lived. She was selling out of her pants again Saturday night. We think she tricked the shooter in the Ricky Scar gig. Unlucky girl.'

'What happened?'

'Her pimp is a peckerwood named Beeler Grissum. Know him?'

'Yeah, he's a Murphy artist who works the Quarter and Airline Highway.'

'He worked the wrong dude this time. He and Ruby Gravano tried to set up the outraged-boyfriend skit. The john broke Grissum's neck with a karate kick. Ruby told NOPD she'd seen the john a week or so ago with a dwarf. So they thought maybe he was the shooter on the Scarlotti hit and they called us.'

'Who's the john?'

'All she could say was he has a Canadian passport, blond or gold hair, and a green-and-red scorpion tattooed on his left shoulder. We'll send the composite through, but it looks generic – egg-shaped head, elongated eyes, sideburns, fedora with a feather in it. I'm starting to think all these guys had the same mother.'

'Where's Ruby now?'

'At Charity.'

'What's he do to her?'

'You don't want to know.'

A few minutes later the composite came through the fax machine and I took it out to Cisco Flynn's place on the Loreauville road. When no one

755

answered the door, I walked around the side of the house toward the patio in back. I could hear the voices of both Cisco and Billy Holtzner, arguing furiously.

'You got a taste, then you put your whole face in the trough. Now you swim for the shore with the rats,' Holtzner said.

'You ripped them off, Billy. I'm not taking the fall,' Cisco said.

'This fine house, this fantasy you got about being a southern gentleman, where you think it all comes from? You made your money off of me.'

'So I'm supposed to give it back because you burned the wrong guys? That's the way they do business in the garment district?'

Then I heard their feet shuffling, a piece of iron furniture scrape on brick, a slap, like a hand hitting a body, and Cisco's voice saying, 'Don't embarrass yourself on top of it, Billy.'

A moment later Holtzner came around the back corner of the house, walking fast, his face heated, his stare twisted with his own thoughts. I held up the composite drawing in front of him.

'You know this guy?' I asked.

'No.'

'The FBI thinks he's a contract assassin.'

Holtzner's eyes were dilated, red along the rims, his skin filmed with an iridescent shine, a faint body odor emanating from his clothes, like a man who feels he's about to slide down a razor blade.

'So you bring it out to Cisco Flynn's house? Who you think is the target for these assholes?' he said.

'I see. You are.'

'You got me made for a coward. It doesn't bother me. I don't care what happens to me anymore. But my daughter never harmed anybody except herself. All pinhead back there has to do is mortgage his house and we can make a down payment on our debt. I'm talking about my daughter's life here. Am I getting through to you?'

'You have a very unpleasant way of talking to people, Mr. Holtzner,' I said.

'Go fuck yourself,' he said, and walked across the lawn to his automobile, which he had parked under a shade tree.

I followed him and propped both my hands on the edge of his open window just as he turned the ignition. He looked up abruptly into my face. His leaded eyelids made me think of a frog's.

'Your daughter's been threatened? Explicitly?' I said.

'*Explicitly?* I can always spot a thinker,' he said. He dropped the car into reverse and spun two black tracks across the grass to the driveway.

I went back up on the gallery and knocked again. But Megan came to the door instead of Cisco. She stepped outside without inviting me in, a brown paper bag in her hand.

'I'm returning your pistol,' she said.

'I think you should hang on to it for a while.'

'Why'd you show Cisco those photos of my father?'

'He came to my office. He asked to see them.'

'Take the gun. It's unloaded,' she said. She pushed the bag into my hands.

'You're worried he might go after Archer Terrebonne?'

'You shouldn't have shown him those photos. Sometimes you're unaware of the influence you have over others, Dave.'

'I tell you what. I'm going to get all the distance I can between me and you and Cisco. How's that?'

She stepped closer to me, her face tilted up into mine. I could feel her breath on my skin. For a moment I thought she was being flirtatious, deliberately confrontational. Then I saw the moisture in her eyes.

'You've never read the weather right with me. Not on anything. It's not Cisco who might do something to Archer Terrebonne,' she said. She continued to stare into my face. There were broken veins in the whites of her eyes, like pieces of red thread.

That evening I saw Clete's chartreuse convertible coming down the dirt road toward the dock, with Geraldine Holtzner behind the wheel, almost unrecognizable in a scarf and dark glasses, and Clete padding along behind the car, in scarlet trunks, rotted T-shirt, and tennis shoes that looked like pancakes on his feet.

Geraldine Holtzner braked to a stop by the boat ramp and Clete opened the passenger door and took a bottle of diet Pepsi out of the cooler and wiped the ice off with his palm. He breathed through his mouth, sweat streaming out of his hair and down his chest.

'You trying to have a heart attack?' I said.

'I haven't had a drink or a cigarette in two days. I feel great. You want some fried chicken?' he said.

'They pulled your license altogether?' I said.

'Big time,' he said.

'Clete—' I said.

'So beautiful women drive me around now. Right, Geri?'

She didn't respond. Instead, she stared at me from behind her dark glasses, her mouth pursed into a button. 'Why are you so hard on my father?' she said.

I looked at Clete, then down the road, in the shadows, where a man in a ribbed undershirt was taking a fishing rod and tackle box out of his car trunk.

'I'd better get back to work,' I said.

'I'll take a shower in the back of the bait shop and we'll go to a movie or something. How about it, Geri?' Clete said.

'Why not?' she said.

'I'd better pass,' I said.

'I've got a case of 12-Step PMS today, you know, piss, moan, and snivel. Don't be a sorehead,' Geraldine said.

'Come back later. We'll take a boat ride,' I said.

'I can't figure what Megan sees in you,' Geraldine said.

I went back down the dock to the bait shop, then turned and watched Clete padding along behind the convertible, like a trained bear, the dust puffing around his dirty tennis shoes.

A few minutes later I walked up to the house and ate supper in the kitchen with Alafair and Bootsie. The phone rang on the counter. I picked it up.

'Dave, this probably don't mean nothing, but a man was axing about Clete right after you went up to eat,' Batist said.

'Which man?'

'He was fishing on the bank, then he come in the shop and bought a candy bar and started talking French. Then he ax in English who own that convertible that was going down the road. I tole him the only convertible I seen out there was for Clete Purcel. Then he ax if the woman driving it wasn't in the movies.

'I tole him I couldn't see through walls, no, so I didn't have no idea who was driving it. He give me a dol'ar tip and gone back out and drove away in a blue car.'

'What kind of French did he speak?' I asked.

'I didn't t'ink about it. It didn't sound no different from us.'

'I'll mention it to Clete. But don't worry about it.'

'One other t'ing. He only had an undershirt on. He had a red-and-green tattoo on his shoulder. It look like a, what you call them t'ings, they got them down in Mexico, it ain't a crawfish, it's a—'

'Scorpion?' I said.

I called Clete at his cottage outside Jeanerette.

'The Scarlotti shooter may be following you. Watch for a blond guy, maybe a French Canadian—' I began.

'Guy with a tattoo on his shoulder, driving a blue Ford?' Clete said.

'That's the guy.'

'Geri and I stopped at a convenience store and I saw him do a U-turn down the street and park in some trees. I strolled on down toward a pay phone, but he knew I'd made him.'

'You get his tag number?' I asked.

'No, there was mud on it.'

'Can you get hold of Holtzner?'

'If I have to. The guy's wiring is starting to spark. I smelled crack in his trailer today.'

'Where's Geraldine?'

'Where's any hype? In her own universe. That broad's crazy, Dave. After I told her we were being followed by the guy with the tattoo, she accused me of setting her up. Every woman I meet is either unattainable or nuts . . . Anyway, I'll try to find Holtzner for you.'

An hour later he called me back.

'Holtzner just fired me,' he said.

'Why?'

'I got him on his cell phone and told him the Canadian dude was in town. He went into a rage. He asked me why I didn't take down this guy when I had the chance. I go, "Take down, like cap the guy?"'

'He goes, "*What*, an ex-cop kicked off the police force for killing a federal witness has got qualms?"'

'I say, "Yeah, as a matter of fact I do."'

'He goes, "Then sign your own paychecks, Rhino Boy."'

'*Rhino Boy?* How'd I ever get mixed up with these guys, Dave?'

'Lots of people ask themselves that question,' I said.

The ex-prostitute named Jessie Rideau, who claimed to have been present when Jack Flynn was kidnapped, called Helen Soileau's extension the next day. Helen had the call transferred to my office.

'Come talk to us, Ms. Rideau,' I said.

'You giving out free coffee in lockup?' she said.

'We want to put Harpo Scruggs away. You help us, we help you.'

'Gee, where I heard that before?' I could hear her breath flattening on the receiver, as though she were trying to blow the heat out of a burn. 'You ain't gonna say nothing?'

'I'll meet you somewhere else.'

'St. Peter's Cemetery in ten minutes.'

'How will I recognize you?' I asked.

'I'm the one that's not dead.'

I parked my truck behind the cathedral and walked over to the old cemetery, which was filled with brick-and-plaster crypts that had settled at broken angles into the earth. She sat on the seat of her paint-blistered gas-guzzler, the door open, her feet splayed on the curb, her head hanging out in the sunlight as I approached her. She had coppery hair that looked like it had been waved with an iron, and brown skin and freckles like a spray of dull pennies on her face and neck. Her shoulders were wide, her breasts like watermelons inside her blue cotton shirt, her turquoise eyes fastened on me, as though she had no means of defending herself against the world once it escaped her vision.

'Ms. Rideau?'

She didn't reply. A fire truck passed and she never took her eyes off my face.

'Give us a formal statement on Scruggs, enough to get a warrant for his arrest. That's when your problems start to end,' I said.

'I need money to go out West, somewhere he cain't find me,' she said.

'We don't run a flea market. If you conceal evidence in a criminal investigation, you become an accomplice after the fact. You ever do time?'

'You're a real charmer.'

I looked at my watch.

'Maybe I'd better go,' I said.

'Harpo Scruggs gonna kill me. I had that box hid all them years for him. Now he gonna kill me over it. That's what y'all ain't hearing.'

'Why does he want the lockbox now?' I asked.

'Him and me run a house toget'er. Fo' years ago I found out he killed Lavern Viator in Texas. Lavern was the other girl that was in Morgan City when they beat that man wit' chains. So I moved the box to a different place, one he ain't t'ought about.'

'Let's try to be honest here, Jessie. Did you move it because you knew he was blackmailing someone with it and you thought it was valuable?'

Raindrops were falling out of the sunlight. There were blue tattoos of heart and dice inside Jessie Rideau's forearms. She stared at the crypts in the cemetery, her eyes recessed, her face like that of a person who knows she will never have any value to anyone other than use.

'I gonna be wit' them dead people soon,' she said.

'Where'd you do time?'

'A year in St. John the Baptist. Two years in St. Gabriel.'

'Let us help you.'

'Too late.' She pulled the car door shut and started the engine. The exhaust pipe and muffler were rusted out, and smoke billowed from under the car frame.

'Why does he want the lockbox now?' I said.

She shot me the finger and gunned the car out into the street, the roar of her engine reverberating through the crypts.

There are days that are different. They may look the same to everyone else, but on certain mornings you wake and know with absolute

760

certainty you've been chosen as a participant in a historical script, for reasons unknown to you, and your best efforts will not change what has already been written.

On Wednesday the false dawn was bone-white, just like it had been the day Megan came back to New Iberia, the air brittle, the wood timbers in our house aching with cold. Then hailstones clattered on the tin roof and through the trees and rolled down the slope onto the dirt road. When the sun broke above the horizon the clouds in the eastern sky trembled with a glow like the reflection of a distant forest fire. When I walked down to the dock, the air was still cold, crisscrossed with the flight of robins, more than I had seen in years. I started cleaning the congealed ash from the barbecue pit, then rinsed my hands in an oaken bucket that had been filled with rainwater the night before. But Batist had cleaned a nutria in it for crab bait, and when I poured the water out it was red with blood.

At the office I called Adrien Glazier in New Orleans.

'Anything on the Scarlotti shooter?' I said.

'You figured out he's a French Canadian. You're ahead of us. What's the matter?' she said.

'Matter? He's going to kill somebody.'

'If it will make you feel better, I already contacted Billy Holtzner and offered him Witness Protection. He goes, "Where, on an ice floe at the South Pole?" and hangs up.'

'Send some agents over here, Adrien.'

'Holtzner's from Hollywood. He knows the rules. You get what you want when you come across. I told him the G's casting couch is nongender-specific. Try to have a few laughs with this stuff. You worry too much.'

It began to rain just after sunset. The light faded in the swamp and the air was freckled with birds, then the rain beat on the dock and the tin roof of the bait shop and filled the rental boats that were chained up by the boat ramp. Batist closed out the cash register and put on his canvas coat and hat.

'Megan's daddy, the one got nailed to the barn? You know how many black men been killed and nobody ever been brought to cou't for it?' he said.

'Doesn't make it right,' I said.

'Makes it the way it is,' he replied.

After he had gone I turned off the outside lights so no late customers would come by, then began mopping the floor. The rain on the roof was deafening and I didn't hear the door open behind me, but I felt the cold blow across my back.

'Put your mop up. I got other work for you,' the voice said.

I straightened up and looked into the seamed, rain-streaked face of Harpo Scruggs.

32

His face was bloodless, shriveled like a prune, glistening under the drenched brim of his hat. His raincoat dripped water in a circle on the floor. A blue-black .22 Ruger revolver, with ivory grips, on full cock, hung from his right hand.

'I got a magnum cylinder in it. The round will go through both sides of your skull,' he said.

'What do you want, Scruggs?'

'Fix me some coffee and milk in one of them big glasses yonder.' He pointed with one finger. 'Put about four spoons of honey in it.'

'Have you lost your mind?'

He propped the heel of his hand against the counter for support. The movement caused him to pucker his mouth and exhale his breath. It touched my face, like the raw odor from a broken drain line.

'You're listing,' I said.

'Fix the coffee like I told you.'

A moment later he picked up the glass with his left hand and drank from it steadily until it was almost empty. He set the glass on the counter and wiped his mouth with the back of his wrist. His whiskers made a scraping sound against his skin.

'We're going to Opelousas. You're gonna drive. You try to hurt me, I'll kill you. Then I'll come back and kill your wife and child. A man like me don't give it no thought,' he said.

'Why me, Scruggs?'

''Cause you got an obsession over the man we stretched out on that barn wall. You gonna do right, no matter who you got to mess up. It ain't a compliment.'

We took his pickup truck to the four-lane and headed north toward Lafayette and Opelousas. He didn't use the passenger seat belt but instead sat canted sideways with his right leg pushed out in front of him.

His raincoat was unbuttoned and I could see the folds of a dark towel that were tied with rope across his side.

'You leaking pretty bad?' I said.

'Hope that I ain't. I'll pop one into your brisket 'fore I go under.'

'I'm not your problem. We both know that.'

With his left hand he took a candy bar from the dashboard and tore the paper with his dentures and began to eat the candy, swallowing as though he hadn't eaten in days. He held the revolver with his other hand, the barrel and cylinder resting across his thigh, pointed at my kidney.

The rain swept in sheets against the windshield. We passed through north Lafayette, the small, wood, galleried houses on each side of us whipped by the rain. Outside the city the country was dark green and sodden and there were thick stands of hardwoods on both sides of the four-lane and by the exit to Grand Coteau I saw emergency flares burning on the road and the flashers of emergency vehicles. A state trooper stood by an overturned semi, waving the traffic on with his flashlight.

'Was you ever a street cop?' Scruggs said.

'NOPD,' I said.

'I was a gun bull at Angola, city cop, and road-gang hack, too. I done it all. I got no quarrel with you, Robicheaux.'

'You want me to bring down Archer Terrebonne, don't you?'

'When I was a gun bull at Angola? That was in the days of the Red Hat House. The lights would go down all over the system and ole Sparky would make fire jump off their tailbone. There was this white boy from Mississippi put a piece of glass in my food once. A year later he cut up two other convicts for stealing a deck of cards from his cell. Guess who got to walk him into the Red Hat House?

'Lightning was crawling all over the sky that night and the current didn't work right. That boy was jolting in the straps for two minutes. The smell made them reporters hold handkerchiefs to their mouths. They was falling over themselves to get outside. I laughed till I couldn't hardly stand up.'

'What's the point?'

'I'm gonna have my pound of flesh from Archer Terrebonne. You gonna be the man cut it out for me.'

He straightened his tall frame inside his raincoat, his face draining with the effort. He saw me watching him and raised the barrel of the Ruger slightly, so that it was aimed upward at my armpit. He put his hand on the towel tied across his side and looked at it, then wiped his hand on his pants.

'Terrebonne paid my partner to shoot my liver out. I didn't think my partner would turn on me. I'll be damned if you can trust anybody these days,' he said.

'The man who helped you kill the two brothers out in the Atchafalaya Basin?'

'That's him. Or was. I wouldn't eat no pigs that was butchered around here for a while . . . Take that exit yonder.'

We drove for three miles through farmland, then followed a dirt road through pine trees, past a pond that was green with algae and covered with dead hyacinths, to a two-story yellow frame house whose yard was filled with the litter of dead pecan trees. The windows had been nailed over with plywood, the gallery stacked with hay bales that had rotted.

'You recognize it?' he asked.

'It was a brothel,' I said.

'The governor of Lou'sana used to get laid there. Walk ahead of me.'

We crossed through the back yard, past a collapsed privy and a cistern, with a brick foundation, that had caved outward into disjointed slats. The barn still had its roof, and through the rain I could hear hogs snuffing inside it. A tree of lightning burst across the sky and Scruggs jerked his face toward the light as though loud doors had been thrown back on their hinges behind him.

He saw me watching him and pointed the revolver at my face.

'I told you to walk ahead of me!' he said.

We went through the rear door of the house into a gutted kitchen that was illuminated by the soft glow of a light at the bottom of a basement stairs.

'Where is Jessie Rideau?' I said.

Lightning crashed into a piney woods at the back of the property.

'Keep asking questions and I'll see you spend some time with her,' he said, and pointed at the basement stairs with the barrel of the gun.

I walked down the wood steps into the basement, where a recharge-able Coleman lantern burned on the cement floor. The air was damp and cool, like the air inside a cave, and smelled of water and stone and the nests of small animals. Behind an old wooden icebox, the kind with an insert at the top for a block of tonged ice, I saw a woman's shoe and the sole of a bare foot. I walked around the side of the icebox and knelt down by the woman's side and felt her throat.

'You sonofabitch,' I said to Scruggs.

'Her heart give out. She was old. It wasn't my fault,' Scruggs said. Then he sat down in a wood chair, as though all his strength had drained through the bottoms of his feet. He stared at me dully from under the brim of his hat and wet his lips and swallowed before he spoke again.

'Yonder's what you want,' he said.

In the corner, amidst a pile of bricks and broken mortar and plaster that had been prized from the wall with a crowbar, was a steel box that had probably been used to contain dynamite caps at one time. The lid was bradded and painted silver and heavy in my hand when I lifted it back on its hinges. Inside the box were a pair of handcuffs, two lengths of chain, a bath towel flattened inside a plastic bag, and a big hammer whose handle was almost black, as though stove soot and grease had been rubbed into the grain.

'Terrebonne's prints are gonna be on that hammer. The print will hold in blood just like in ink. Forensic man done told me that,' Scruggs said.

'You've had your hands all over it. So have the women,' I replied.

'The towel's got Flynn's blood all over it. So do them chains. You just got to get the right lab man to lift Terrebonne's prints.'

His voice was deep in his throat, full of phlegm, his tongue thick against his dentures. He kept straightening his shoulders, as though resisting an unseen weight that was pushing them forward.

I removed the towel from the plastic bag and unfolded it. It was stiff and crusted, the fibers as pointed and hard as young thorns. I looked at the image in the center of the cloth, the black lines and smears that could have been a brow, a chin, a set of jawbones, eye sockets, even hair that had been soaked with blood.

'Do you have any idea of what you've been part of? Don't any of you understand what you've done?' I said to him.

'Flynn stirred everybody up. I know what I done. I was doing a job. That's the way it was back then.'

'What do you see on the towel, Scruggs?'

'Dried blood. I done told you that. You carry all this to a lab. You gonna do that or not?'

He breathed through his mouth, his eyes seeming to focus on an insect an inch from the bridge of his nose. A terrible odor rose from his clothes.

'I'm going for the paramedics now,' I said.

'A .45 ball went all the way through my intestines. I ain't gonna live wired to machines. Tell Terrebonne I expect I'll see him. Tell him Hell don't have no lemonade springs.'

He fitted the Ruger's barrel under the top of his dentures and pulled the trigger. The round exited from the crown of his head and patterned the plaster on the brick wall with a single red streak. His head hung back on his wide shoulders, his eyes staring sightlessly at the ceiling. A puff of smoke, like a dirty feather, drifted out of his mouth.

33

Two days later the sky was blue outside my office, a balmy wind clattering the palm trees on the lawn. Clete stood at the window, his porkpie hat on his head, his hands on his hips, surveying the street and the perfection of the afternoon. He turned and propped his huge arms on my desk and stared down into my face.

'Blow it off. Prints or no prints, rich guys don't do time,' he said.

'I want to have that hammer sent to an FBI lab,' I said.

'Forget it. If the St. Landry Parish guys couldn't lift them, nobody else is going to either. You even told Scruggs he was firing in the well.'

'Look, Clete, you mean well, but—'

'The prints aren't what's bothering you. It's that damn towel.'

'I saw the face on it. Those cops in Opelousas acted like I was drunk. Even the skipper down the hall.'

'So fuck 'em,' Clete said.

'I've got to get back to work. Where's your car?'

'Dave, you saw that face on the towel because you believe. You expect guys with jock rash of the brain to understand what you're talking about?'

'Where's your car, Clete?'

'I'm selling it,' he said. He was sitting on the corner of my desk now, his upper arms scaling with dried sun blisters. I could smell salt water and sun lotion on his skin. 'Leave Terrebonne alone. The guy's got juice all the way to Washington. You'll never touch him.'

'He's going down.'

'Not because of anything we do.' He tapped his knuckles on the desk. 'There's my ride.'

Through the window I saw his convertible pull up to the curb. A woman in a scarf and dark glasses was behind the wheel.

'Who's driving?' I asked.

'Lila Terrebonne. I'll call you later.'

*

At noon I met Bootsie in City Park for lunch. We spread a checkered cloth on a table under a tin shed by the bayou and set out the silverware and salt and pepper shakers and a thermos of iced tea and a platter of cold cuts and stuffed eggs. The camellias were starting to bloom, and across the bayou we could see the bamboo and flowers and the live oaks in the yard of The Shadows.

I could almost forget about the events of the last few days.

Until I saw Megan Flynn park her car on the drive that wound through the park and stand by it, looking in our direction.

Bootsie saw her, too.

'I don't know why she's here,' I said.

'Invite her over and find out,' Bootsie said.

'That's what I have office hours for.'

'You want me to do it?'

I set down the stack of plastic cups I was unwrapping and walked across the grass to the spreading oak Megan stood under.

'I didn't know you were with anyone. I wanted to thank you for all you've done and say goodbye,' she said.

'Where are you going?'

'Paris. Rivages, my French publisher, wants me to do a collection on the Spaniards who fled into the Midi after the Spanish Civil War. By the way, I thought you'd like to know Cisco walked out on the film. It's probably going to bankrupt him.'

'Cisco's stand-up.'

'Billy Holtzner doesn't have the talent to finish it by himself. His backers are going to be very upset.'

'That composite I gave you of the Canadian hit man, you and Cisco have no idea who he is?'

'No, we'd tell you.'

We looked at each other in the silence. Leaves gusted from around the trunks of the trees onto the drive. Her gaze shifted briefly to Bootsie, who sat at the picnic table with her back to us.

'I'm flying out tomorrow afternoon with some friends. I don't guess I'll see you for some time,' she said, and extended her hand. It felt small and cool inside mine.

I watched her get in her car, drawing her long khaki-clad legs and sandaled feet in after her, her dull red hair thick on the back of her neck.

Is this the way it all ends? I thought. Megan goes back to Europe, Clete eats aspirins for his hangovers and labors through all the sweaty legal mechanisms of the court system to get his driver's license back, the parish buries Harpo Scruggs in a potter's field, and Archer Terrebonne fixes another drink and plays tennis at his club with his daughter.

I walked back to the tin shed and sat down next to Bootsie.

'She came to say goodbye,' I said.

'That's why she didn't come over to the table,' she replied.

That evening, which was Friday, the sky was purple, the clouds in the west stippled with the sun's last orange light. I raked stream trash out of the coulee and carried it in a washtub to the compost pile, then fed Tripod, our three-legged coon, and put fresh water in his bowl. My neighbor's cane was thick and green and waving in the field, and flights of ducks trailed in long V formations across the sun.

The phone rang inside, and Bootsie carried the portable out into the yard.

'We've got the Canadian identified. His name is Jacques Poitier, a real piece of shit,' Adrien Glazier said. 'Interpol says he's a suspect in at least a dozen assassinations. He's worked the Middle East, Europe, both sides in Latin America. He's gotten away with killing Israelis.'

'We're not up to dealing with guys like this. Send us some help,' I said.

'I'll see what I can do Monday,' she said.

'Contract killers don't keep regular hours.'

'Why do you think I'm making this call?' she said.

To feel better, I thought. But I didn't say it.

That evening I couldn't rest. But I didn't know what it was that bothered me.

Clete Purcel? His battered chartreuse convertible? Lila Terrebonne?

I called Clete's cottage.

'Where's your Caddy?' I asked.

'Lila's got it. I'm signing the title over to her Monday. Why?'

'Geraldine Holtzner's been driving it all over the area.'

'Streak, the Terrebonnes might hurt themselves, but they don't get hurt by others. What does it take to make you understand that?'

'The Canadian shooter is a guy named Jacques Poitier. Ever hear of him?'

'No. And if he gives me any grief, I'm going to stick a .38 down his pants and blow his Jolly Roger off. Now, let me get some sleep.'

'Megan told you she's going to France?'

The line was so quiet I thought it had gone dead. Then he said, 'She must have called while I was out. When's she going?'

Way to go, Robicheaux, I thought.

The set that had been constructed on the levee at Henderson Swamp was lighted with the haloed brilliance of a phosphorus flare when Lila Terrebonne drove Clete's convertible along the dirt road at the top of

769

the levee, above the long, wind-ruffled bays and islands of willow trees that were turning yellow with the season. The evening was cool, and she wore a sweater over her shoulders, a dark scarf with roses stitched on it tied around her head. She found her father with Billy Holtzner, and the three of them ate dinner on a cardboard table by the water's edge and drank a bottle of nonalcoholic champagne that had been chilled in a silver bucket.

When she left, she asked a grip to help her fasten down the top on her car. He was the only one to notice the blue Ford that pulled out of a fish camp down the levee and followed her toward the highway. He did not think it significant and did not mention the fact to anyone until later.

The man in the blue Ford followed her through St. Martinville and down the Loreauville road to Cisco Flynn's house. When she turned into Cisco's driveway, a lawn party was in progress and the man in the Ford parked on the swale and opened his hood and appeared to onlookers to be at work on his engine.

On the patio, behind the house, Lila Terrebonne called Cisco Flynn a lowborn, treacherous sycophant, picked up his own mint julep from the table, and flung it in his face.

But on the front lawn a jazz combo played atop an elevated platform, and the guests wandered among the citrus and oak trees and the drink tables and the music that seemed to charm the pink softness of the evening into their lives. Megan wore her funny straw hat with an evening dress that clung to her figure like ice water, and was talking to a group of friends, people from New York and overseas, when she noticed the man working on his car.

She stood between two myrtle bushes, on the edge of the swale, and waited until he seemed to feel her eyes on his back. He straightened up and smiled, but the smile came and went erratically, as though the man thought it into place.

He wore a form-fitting long-sleeve gold shirt and blue jeans that were so tight they looked painted on his skin. A short-brim fedora with a red feather in the band rested on the fender. His hair was the color of his shirt, waved, and cut long and parted on the side so it combed down over one ear.

'It's a battery cable. I'll have it started in a minute,' he said in a French accent.

She stared at him without speaking, a champagne glass resting in the fingers of both hands, her chest rising and falling.

'I am a big fan of American movies. I saw a lady turn in here. Isn't she the daughter of a famous Hollywood director?' he said.

'I'm not sure who you mean,' Megan said.

'She was driving a Cadillac, a convertible,' he said, and waited. Then he smiled, wiping his hands on a handkerchief. 'Ah, I'm right, aren't I? Her father is William Holtzner. I love all his films. He is wonderful,' the man said.

She stepped backward, once, twice, three times, the myrtle bushes brushing against her bare arms, then stood silently among her friends. She looked back at the man with gold hair only after he had restarted his car and driven down the road. Five minutes later Lila Terrebonne backed the Cadillac down the drive, hooking one wheel over the slab into a freshly watered flower bed, then shifted into low out on the road and floored the accelerator toward New Iberia. Her radio was blaring with rock 'n' roll from the 1960s, her face energized with vindication inside the black scarf, stitched with roses, that was tied tightly around her head.

The man named Jacques Poitier caught up with her on the two-lane road that paralleled Bayou Teche, only one mile from her home. Witnesses said she tried to outrun him, swerving back and forth across the highway, blowing her horn, waving desperately at a group of blacks on the side of the road. Others said he passed her and they heard a gunshot. But we found no evidence of the latter, only a thread-worn tire that had exploded on the rim before the Cadillac skidded sideways, showering sparks off the pavement, into an oncoming dump truck loaded with condemned asbestos.

34

If there was any drama at the crime scene later, it was not in our search for evidence or even in the removal of Lila's body from under the crushed roof of the Cadillac. Archer Terrebonne arrived at the scene twenty minutes after the crash, and was joined a few minutes later by Billy Holtzner. Terrebonne immediately took charge, as though his very presence and the slip-on half-top boots and red flannel shirt and quilted hunting vest and visor cap he wore gave him a level of authority that none of the firemen or paramedics or sheriff's deputies possessed.

They all did his bidding or sought sanction or at a minimum gave an explanation to him for whatever they did. It was extraordinary to behold. His attorney and family physician were there; also a U.S. congressman and a well-known movie actor. Terrebonne wore his grief like a patrician who had become a man of the people. A three-hundred-pound St. Mary Parish deputy, his mouth full of Red Man, stood next to me, his eyes fixed admiringly on Terrebonne.

'That ole boy is one brave sonofabuck, ain't he?' he said.

The paramedics covered Lila's body with a sheet and wheeled it on the gurney to the back of an ambulance, the strobe lights of TV cameras flowing with it, passing across Terrebonne's and Holtzner's stoic faces.

Helen Soileau and I walked through the crowd until we were a few feet from Terrebonne. Red flares burned along the shoulder of the road, and mist clung to the bayou and the oak trunks along the bank. The air was cold, but my face felt hot and moist with humidity. His eyes never registered our presence, as though we were moths outside a glass jar, looking in upon a pure white flame.

'Your daughter's death is on you, Terrebonne. You didn't intend for it to happen, but you helped bring the people here who killed her,' I said.

A woman gasped; the scattered conversation around us died.

'You hope this will destroy me, don't you?' he replied.

'Harpo Scruggs said to tell you he'd be expecting you soon. I think he knew what he was talking about,' I said.

'Don't you talk to him like that,' Holtzner said, rising on the balls of his feet, his face dilating with the opportunity that had presented itself. 'I'll tell you something else, too. Me and my new co-director are finishing our picture. And it's going to be dedicated to Lila Terrebonne. You can take your dirty mouth out of here.'

Helen stepped toward him, her finger lifted toward his face.

'He's a gentleman. I'm not. Smart off again and see what happens,' she said.

We walked to our cruiser, past the crushed, upside-down shell of Clete's Cadillac, the eyes of reporters and cops and passersby riveted on the sides of our faces.

I heard a voice behind me, one I didn't recognize, yell out, 'You're the bottom of the barrel, Robicheaux.'

Then others applauded him.

Early the next morning Helen and I began re-creating Lila Terrebonne's odyssey from the movie set on the levee, where she had dinner with her father and Billy Holtzner, to the moment she must have realized her peril and tried to outrun the contract assassin named Jacques Poitier. We interviewed the stage grip who saw the blue Ford pull out of the fish camp and follow her back down the levee; an attendant at a filling station in St. Martinville, where she stopped for gasoline; and everyone we could find from the Flynns' lawn party.

The New York and overseas friends of Megan and Cisco were cooperative and humble to a fault, in large part because they never sensed the implications of what they told us. But after talking with three guests from the lawn party, I had no doubt as to what transpired during the encounter between Megan and the French Canadian named Poitier.

Helen and I finished the last interview at a bed-and-breakfast across from The Shadows at three o'clock that afternoon. It was warm and the trees were speckled with sunlight, and a few raindrops were clicking on the bamboo in front of The Shadows and drying as soon as they struck the sidewalks.

'Megan's plane leaves at three-thirty from Acadiana Regional. See if you can get a hold of Judge Mouton at his club,' I said.

'A warrant? We might be on shaky ground. There has to be intent, right?'

'Megan never did anything in her life without intending to.'

Our small local airport had been built on the site of the old U.S. Navy air base outside of town. As I drove down the state road toward the hangars and maze of runways, under a partially blue sky that was starting to seal with rain clouds, my heart was beating in a way that it shouldn't, my hands sweating black prints on the steering wheel.

Then I saw her, with three other people, standing by a hangar, her luggage next to her, while a Learjet taxied around the far side of a parking area filled with helicopters. She wore her straw hat and a pink dress with straps and lace around the hem, and when the wind began gusting she held her hat to her head with one hand in a way that made me think of a 1920s flapper.

She saw me walking toward her, like someone she recognized from a dream, then her eyes fixed on mine and the smile went out of her face and she glanced briefly toward the horizon, as though the wind and the churning treetops held a message for her.

I looked at my watch. It was 3:25. The door to the Lear opened and a man in a white jacket and dark-blue pants lowered the steps to the tarmac. Her friends picked up their luggage and drifted toward the door, glancing discreetly in her direction, unsure of the situation.

'Jacques Poitier stopped his car on the swale in front of your party. Your guests heard you talking to him,' I said.

'He said his car was broken. He was working on it,' she replied.

'He asked you if the woman driving Clete's Cadillac was Holtzner's daughter.'

She was silent, her hair ruffling thickly on her neck. She looked at the open door of the plane and the attendant who waited for her.

'You let him think it was Geraldine Holtzner,' I said.

'I didn't tell him anything, Dave.'

'You knew who he was. I gave you the composite drawing.'

'They're waiting for me.'

'Why'd you do it, Meg?'

'I'm sorry for Lila Terrebonne. I'm not sorry for her father.'

'She didn't deserve what happened to her.'

'Neither did my father. I'm going now, unless you're arresting me. I don't think you can either. If I did anything wrong, it was a sin of omission. That's not a crime.'

'You've already talked to a lawyer,' I said, almost in amazement.

She leaned down and picked up her suitcase and shoulder bag. When she did, her hat blew off her head and bounced end over end across the tarmac. I ran after it, like a high school boy would, then walked back to her, brushing it off, and placed it in her hands.

'I won't let this rest. You've contributed to the death of an innocent person. Just like the black guy who died in your lens years ago. Somebody else has paid your tab. Don't come back to New Iberia, Meg,' I said.

Her eyes held on mine and I saw a great sadness sweep through her face, like that of a child watching a balloon break loose from its string and float away suddenly on the wind.

Epilogue

That afternoon the wind dropped and there was a red tint like dye in the clouds, and the water was high and brown in the bayou, the cypresses and willows thick with robins. It should have been a good afternoon for business at the bait shop and dock, but it wasn't. The parking area was empty; there was no whine of boat engines out on the water, and the sound of my footsteps on the planks in the dock echoed off the bayou as though I were walking under a glass dome.

A drunk who had given Batist trouble earlier that day had broken the guardrail on the dock and fallen to the ramp below. I got some lumber and hand tools and an electric saw from the tin shed behind the house to repair the gap in the rail, and Alafair clipped Tripod's chain on his collar and walked him down to the dock with me. I heard the front screen door bang behind us, and I turned and saw Bootsie on the gallery. She waved, then went down into the flower bed with a trowel and a plastic bucket and began working on her knees.

'Where is everybody?' Alafair said out on the dock.

'I think a lot of people went to the USL game today,' I replied.

'There's no sound. It makes my ears pop.'

'How about opening up a couple of cans of Dr. Pepper?' I said.

She went inside the bait shop, but did not come back out right away. I heard the cash register drawer open and knew the subterfuge that was at work, one that she used to mask her charity, as though somehow it were a vice. She would pay for the fried pie she took from the counter, then cradle Tripod in one arm and hand-feed it to him whether he wanted it or not, while his thick, ringed tail flipped in the air like a spring.

I tried to concentrate on repairing the rail on the dock and not see the thoughts that were as bright and jagged as shards of glass in the center of my mind. I kept touching my brow and temple with my arm, as though I were wiping off sweat, but that wasn't my trouble. I could feel a band of pressure tightening across the side of my head, just as I had felt it on night trails in Vietnam or when Bedcheck Charlie was cutting through our wire.

What was it that bothered me? The presence of men like Archer Terrebonne in our midst? But why should I worry about his kind? They had always been with us, scheming, buying our leaders, deceiving the masses. No, it was Megan, and Megan, and Megan, and her betrayal of everything I thought she represented: Joe Hill, the Wobblies, the strikers murdered at Ludlow, Colorado, Woody Guthrie, Dorothy Day, all those faceless working people whom historians and academics and liberals alike treat with indifference.

I ran .the electric saw through a two-by-four and ground the blade across a nail. The board seemed to explode, the saw leaping from my hand, splinters embedding in my skin like needles. I stepped backward from the saw, which continued to spin by my foot, then ripped the cord loose from the socket in the bait-shop wall.

'You all right, Dave?' Alafair said through the screen.

'Yeah, I'm fine,' I said, holding the back of my right hand.

Through the trees next to the bayou I saw a mud-splattered stake truck loaded with boxes of chrysanthemums coming down the road. The truck pulled at an angle across the boat ramp, and Mout' Broussard got out on the passenger's side and a tiny Hmong woman in a conical straw hat with a face like a withered apple got down from the other. Mout' put a long stick across his shoulders, and the woman loaded wire-bailed baskets of flowers on each end of it, then picked up a basket herself and followed him down the dock.

'You sell these for us, we gonna give you half, you,' Mout' said.

'I don't seem to have much business today, Mout',' I said.

'Season's almost over. I'm fixing to give them away,' he said.

'Put them under the eave. We'll give it a try,' I said.

He and the woman lay the flowers in yellow and brown and purple clumps against the bait-shop wall. Mout' wore a suit coat with his overalls and was sweating inside his clothes. He wiped his face with a red handkerchief.

'You doing all right?' he said to me.

'Sure,' I said.

'That's real good. Way it should be,' he said. He replaced the long stick across his shoulders and extended his arms on it and walked with the Hmong woman toward the truck, their bodies lit by the glow of the sun through the trees.

Why look for the fires that burn in western skies? I thought. The excoriated symbol of difference was always within our ken. You didn't have to see far to find it – an elderly black man who took pride in the fact he shined Huey Long's and Harry James's shoes or a misplaced and wizened Hmong woman who had fought the Communists in Laos for the French and the CIA and now grew flowers for Cajuns in Louisiana. The story was ongoing, the players changing only in name. I believe Jack Flynn understood that and probably forgave his children when they didn't.

I sat on a bench by the water faucet and tried to pick the wood splinters out of the backs of my hands. The wind came up and the robins filled the air with a sound that was almost deafening, their wings fluttering above my head, their breasts the color of dried blood.

'Are we still going to the show tonight?' Alafair said.

'You better believe it, you,' I said, and winked.

She flipped Tripod up on her shoulder like a sack of meal, and the three of us went up the slope to find Bootsie.